M9D9

This book is a work of fiction. Names, characters, businesses, organizations, government agencies, places, events, and incidents are products of the author's imagination or are used fictitiously. Any resemblance to actual events or locales or persons living or dead is entirely coincidental.

Copyright 2013 © by M. C. Miller

Published by M9D9 Enterprises, LLC
www.mcmillerbooks.com

ISBN: 0982930577   EAN-13: 978-0-9829305-7-1

First Edition

For the daring ones
who bring about liberating transformations
with their perseverance and inspired cleverness.

1

a novel by
m. c. miller

"We have one day.
It arrives and is taken away at midnight.
In between, we decide one moment at a time
whether or not to make a difference."
—1021

PREFACE

Journal Entry #1

What have I done?
In my frenzy to prove a point, have I given the Devil the keys to the kingdom?
Such power used in secret by one nation would be questionable enough, let
alone giving it to one group of shadows. They're nothing but a black box,
cloaked in security clearances and masked behind scientific facades. How will
I ever know who I've been working for? What if it's not the government?
Maybe it's the government—working for someone else.

Whoever they are, there's no way they'll let the truth be known. Not when they
have so much to gain by keeping it hidden. They'll use the national security
excuse, of course. Or maybe they won't need to. Anything above Top Secret
doesn't exist by definition. Anything's possible when national security and
competitive advantage are synonymous. They're beyond any accountability.
They're beyond everything now.

I can't help but imagine where it will lead. Commerce and communication
constitutes the very fabric of society. The final concentration of power will
occur when they know everything, they interdict competition before it has a
chance to start, and they manipulate and control finance and business on a
global scale. The only missing piece is now structural; they need the new
material perfected for the chipset. Without it, the holy grail of zettaFLOP
speed is out of reach. Once they get that piece in place, it's only a matter of
time before one final system is built interconnecting all advantages.

For my part, they gave me an award, a hollow token I can never show anyone.
Is that what my career, my life has become? All of this makes me doubt myself.
What am I left with—a unique vantage point or simple paranoia? I need to
know more. That's hard to say when even mentioning it is dangerous. At this
point, I don't care. I need answers for my own peace of mind. I can't escape
the fact: I'm responsible. What if I'm the only one with a chance to make it
right? Is such a thing even possible?

The old man gazed upon the written page then closed the finely-bound journal. It was curious. Someone so brilliant, who had just revolutionized mathematics and computer science, wrote their journal with pen and ink. But then, notation on paper was hard to hack. He left the book on the desk. Strolling from the office, he glanced at the awards and degrees framed nearby. He headed downstairs into the quiet, lost in thought. The house was empty. Outside, the sun was warm. But now the hope of spring felt deceiving.

1

0000 0000 0001

12:59 pm EST, Friday December 1st, 2017

Adam Perez was one minute away from a changed life. He slumped in his chair, lost in thought, and focused on work. His 24th birthday had come and gone a week before. The passage of time only made him more determined. This was the year he promised himself he'd branch out. That was the plan. It was still the plan but in the moment, business had to be done. He had to think.

The investment bank trading floor pulsed around him. Perched twenty-six stories high near Wall and Broad Streets, the billion-dollar firm enjoyed impressive views of Lower Manhattan. But no one looked out the windows. If they worked it right before another wanton weekend, some might even chase down a late bull rally and perform up to the hype of the company's prospectus.

Cramped in a low-wall cubicle, Adam's lean frame was a reservoir of fragile quiet and deceptive calm. Nothing distracted his calculating thoughts from the busy screens before him. He studied colorful displays of equities, bonds, derivatives, and currencies tracked and charted down to the single basis point and pip. Entrenched in the task at hand, he held back a confined hunger. There had to be a more challenging purpose to reward his talents and passions. To simply be busy was no guarantee of satisfaction.

Incoming text popped into a chat window at the right corner of one of Adam's three screens. It registered as a speck nuisance on the edge of sight.

"Hey AP—did u have a chance to chk that calc?"

Annoyed, Adam reread the text. Being the go-to guy to "put eyes on" other people's algorithms wasn't about merely double-checking the work of bed-wetting Wharton pukes and slack-jawed Stanford Business School posers. Over the past six months, more of Adam's workday had evolved into tutoring such ingrates on transaction fundamentals, if not basic algebra.

Too many grunts in the cubicles around him were in-the-moment bottom feeders, the kind of insect-like opportunists who had no qualms about burn-and-turn, bash-and-dash tactics if it meant a boost to their wallets. They were insatiably hot with big strategies, talking flashy trash about their next big score but when it came down to it, they had no time to sweat what they considered trivial, technical details—the things necessary to make it happen.

Many were like the MBA candidates he had run into at MIT. They all had big schemes for billion-dollar high-tech startups but none of them had the technical chops to realize any of it. Usually they'd co-opt someone in engineering or computer science to do the hard stuff while structuring the recognition and rewards for the big ideas to flow to them.

Seeing it on campus was bad enough but Adam never suspected how the same parasitical mentality permeated the workplace. He regretted the day he told his hiring manager that he was a full year into Quant school. No wonder the guy's eyes lit up. Some called it "scope creep." Management called it being a "team player." Others saw it for what it was.

The advertised job Adam had been hired for paid like a Financial Technologist but in fact his unofficial duties involved much more. He was paid to create infrastructure around financial models but he frequently wound up being the go-to design and code monkey on the models themselves.

It sucked in so many ways. Besides being shortchanged in the paycheck, it was just as bad that much of his real work existed above his job title. That meant he couldn't believably list it on a resume in hopes of getting future gigs more in line with his ambitions. The conceit was insidious in that it seemed designed to make it more likely he'd stay mired with the same firm that was overworking and underpaying him. More reasons to finish Quant school in a couple of weeks and get the hell out of this place.

Adam doubled down on his concentration. He rubbed a hand over his close-cropped hair before shooting off a reply to the chat. He typed even as his eyes darted to changing indices on another screen.

"y use vanilla P/E ratio? must use FORWARD P/E=current price/ forecasted yr-end earnings."

Just then, the digital display on the electronic tote board on a far wall switched to 1:00 pm. Adam looked up, attracted to the sound of disgruntled comments rising from other analysts and traders on the floor. In unison, a collective cry rose up laced with heaving expletives. Frazzled traders, stranded on calls with confused clients, had no choice but to hang up.

Adam looked right as the next guy threw up his hands. "What the fuck?"

Seeing universal frustration and disbelief directed at computer screens, Adam looked back to his own trio of dual-outputs arranged in a curving group in front of him. What he saw made no sense. He reached for mouse and keyboard and attempted to refresh the displays. It had no effect.

The mouse cursor no longer tracked. Numbers and shapes marched in wayward diagonals off their proper window boxes and down the screen. As they wandered they overwrote unrelated parts of the display. Graphs and charts melted and became impressionistic patterns that duplicated, then reverberated outward in chaotic feedback loops.

It wasn't one or two workstations affected. All screen displays were unresponsive. Garbage characters danced every which way across real-time stock futures and options. Ghost images of inverted numbers incremented over financial portals of intraday, historical, summary, and reference data. Forex price quotes morphed into odd geometric shapes and splintered into fractal color iterations converging on nothing. All at once across the wide open trading floor, hundreds of data screens were rendered useless.

Over the next sixty seconds, pandemonium replaced profit-taking. Talk of malware and system glitches circulated in the grumbles and rumors.

Then at 1:01 pm, as fast as it began, the aberration stopped.

All screens refreshed. With sudden clarity, displays reset to where they should have been, correct for that precise moment. Nothing was lost, no data changed, no windows had been permanently marred. The frantic hubbub of traders and analysts near riot was driven silent with stunned surprise. No one moved. Everyone watched their screens for the slightest signs of recurring trouble, for any indication that normal operations wouldn't last. As the next minute passed, many sat back down. Some laughed.

Adam could feel the tension in their laughter. It was relief, not humor.

A floor supervisor rushed by Adam on his way to the usual suspects.

"What kind of shit is this? Somebody's idea of a joke?"

Two aisles over, an analyst stood with headset held to one ear and his other hand raised. "Hey, I've got BATS on the line. It happened over there too."

Adam and the rest of the room raced to check social media and major newswires. Reports of similar troubles happening at other financial firms clogged social cyberspace. As time passed, a mélange of hearsay, guesswork, and horseplay slowly replaced concern about problems with Adam's firm.

The fact was, it wasn't only Adam's firm or BATS who got hit. It was Direct Edge. It was NYSE Euronext. It was anyone receiving data streams from the main financial datacenters in New York and New Jersey. So much for it being a prankster inside any one company—unless the firm in question was much larger in scope than any top trading house or hedge fund.

NYSE and NASDAQ assured the media and transacting public that the transient glitch was in none of their direct systems. They repeatedly pressed the point—while widespread, the anomaly wasn't malevolent since no actual data was lost or tampered with. In fact, the only thing affected was the way data appeared on computer screens. While this was bizarre, there had to be a technical explanation and the best and the brightest were looking into it.

Despite assurances there was no reason to overreact, nervousness and rampant speculation drained energy from the trading floor. After such unexpected excitement on a Friday afternoon, some found it hard to shift back into work mode. Mostly it went unsaid, but everyone resumed their duties with key questions in mind. What had happened and was it planned?

Adam preferred not to get sucked into side conversations exploring what-ifs. He went back to watching his screens and writing tight code to spec.

By 1:59 pm, all agitation across the floor had been steadily replaced by rote rhythms of global finance at work. Practical realities of chasing profits were too strong a lure and the room settled back into a lucrative status quo.

On the far wall, the digital tote board switched to 2:00 pm. Coaxed more by curiosity than by prescience, Adam looked up at the bright LED readout at the exact moment the new hour began. When he dropped his gaze back to his screens, what he saw raised hairs on the back of his neck.

In a perverse replay of an hour before, all display screens went haywire. The effect was morbid and playfully sinister. Once again, existing displays twisted in chaotic but systematically designed aberrant ways. The screen of a Financial Technologist normally is busy with lines and numbers and colors in motion. But the anomaly took the intricate and sensible and played with it in random-walk ways until it made no sense at all. Numbers and graphs melted then gyrated on the screen like dozens of Pac-Mans and Marios gone berserk.

Once again the room erupted in confusion but this time concern trumped curiosity. Another anomaly had hit market systems exactly on the hour. This was too precise, too obvious to be a transient glitch.

A minute went by and the glitch persisted. This was no longer annoying nor interesting; this was serious. Financial markets depended on system stability. To have business interrupted drove to the heart of what worried markets the most, especially if it went unexplained. As powerful as any bomb, uncertainty could shudder trading to a stop like a bear falling into hibernation.

Despite official assurances, it didn't matter if data wasn't being lost or if it were only screen displays being affected. Those screens held the bulk of the business on them. In effect, those screens *were* the business. Without those displays, financial business as usual would grind to a halt. In fact, it had.

After two minutes, as fast as it began, the aberration stopped once again. All screens refreshed and displays reset where they should have been. Nothing was lost, no data changed, and the riot of traders stood frozen and silently watched to see if their screens would continue to behave.

Nearly an hour later, as 2:59 pm approached, trading floors across the world waited and worried. Adam paused to consider the obvious and found it remarkable. In a matter of only three minutes—one minute at one o'clock and two minutes at two o'clock, the entire financial world had been conditioned to expect an aberrant pattern, a toxic disruption to hit precisely on the hour. Knee-jerk anxiety fed a rising expectancy; both had been easily set and drew a disquieting pause as the time neared. Would it happen again?

As 2:59 pm became 3:00 pm, everyone's worst fears were realized.

This time the unnerving hitch lasted three minutes, leaving everyone helpless. This time it was not about wonder or concern. It was pushing people to the edge of panic. Something had to be done to get to the bottom of it. Whoever or whatever was behind it had to be rooted out and brought to justice. If this was planned, it was far beyond an anomaly, a prank, a one-of-a-kind system error. Little doubt was left in shared gossip that the three events were calculated. After all, how could such a thing occur precisely on the hour and with 1-2-3 clockwork?

The newswires filled with conflicting accounts. Some sources claimed trouble in a fiber optic trunk line. Others talked of possible hacks or terrorism.

The trading day had one hour to go. More than once the top exchanges considered whether or not they should halt trading. In the time it took to waver and argue the point, the passage of time decided it for them. Closing early would send the wrong message heading into the weekend.

If at all possible, the markets needed to stay open. There wasn't much left to the trading day. If they could make it to the closing bell without resorting to drastic measures, the psychology of it would be infinitely better. Caving in to generalized fear and overreacting would only foster the very thing everyone hoped to avoid. No sense giving the 24/7 news-cycle pundits more fuel for what was sure to be a wildfire of conjecture leading to exaggeration.

No doubt everyone would be watching what happened in after-hours trading. Since no one financial sector or business had been targeted, the general state of alarm might be more diffused, especially if things quieted down after hours. If so, hopefully blowback from all of this could be more easily managed. It certainly wasn't going to be forgotten.

At 3:59 pm, the financial world waited to see what would happen next.

Nothing did. At the NYSE a minute later, the bell rang, the gavel was pounded. Nervous dignitaries behind the broad podium braved smiles and applauded at the close of trading. If nothing else, an uneventful closing was a reprieve. Regrettably, it was laced with dreaded anticipation. No forced smiles could disguise or dissipate the pall. For all concerned, this was one Friday they would like to do over. But that wasn't the root of the lingering worry.

Everyone knew the real test would come Monday when trading resumed.

Down the street, on the 26th floor, Adam Perez pushed back from his desk. An uneasy sense of relief could not counteract the concern around him. The guy to Adam's right had bolted from his seat and stood with a small group huddled around a news feed jabbering away on a neighbor's screen.

Adam stood and looked down at the guy's workstation. He was the one who had painted the number 4 keycap on his keyboard in bright metallic gold paint. He was proud of his art work. The day he did it, he had explained to Adam how it would be a constant reminder of why they were there.

Millions of people used a standard keyboard but probably few had noticed that the dollar sign was paired with the number four. For many, when read together, it was an obvious sign, a revelation that it was all *4$* or *4 money*.

Adam turned and stepped to the window. While others watched the news or chased the latest blog post, he took one minute to look outside. It was the first time in six months he had stopped to consider the view. Looking into it, he sensed the remoteness of those unseen souls scrambling with their cares on the sidewalks far below. He was one of them, of course, but from up here, steeped in calculations designed to consolidate wealth, it didn't seem that way.

The scenery falling away below him was bluish grey, a view made indistinct by an icy fog rolling in from the northeast. Soon it would be time to get to class. He thought he'd feel better now that the week was over.

But something had changed.

2

0000 0000 0010

1:59 pm MST, Friday December 1st

Nelson Geiss was one minute away from a changed life. He turned his pickup truck off the main road and afternoon sunlight caught his face, adding a glow to his graying hair. He squinted and shifted into four-wheel drive. The crunch of compacted snow signaled he was almost home.

His ranch was eighty acres in beautiful country. Some of Nelson's friends thought the place too big and isolated for someone living alone. Nelson liked the place because it was close and far enough away from Cheyenne. He could make it as isolated as he wanted.

He also loved the house for the memories it evoked of Madelyn, his wife of twenty-six years. He had lost her to cancer three years ago. His friends thought he needed to move on; it wasn't healthy being secluded after such a loss.

Such concerns were not unfounded. Madelyn's death had hit Nelson hard. Going it alone had driven him to soul-search, questioning everything about his life. His biggest regret was not doing a life review while she was alive. If he had, maybe he would have listened to her and spent more time at home. So many days past might have been filled up with more of her and his son Brian.

Instead, incessant work had pulled him to far-flung places. Even when he had managed to be home, the clandestine nature of his work had forced him into silent places inside himself. The darker aspects of his work were best kept out of mind. His family needed to be shielded from such things. And yet, too much shielding had gotten between himself and the ones he loved.

For three years since Madelyn's passing, retirement for Nelson had become an on-again, off-again affair. Making a clean break was not simple. He was too experienced not to be offered work, work sold to him as vital and necessary. Worse yet, the work was too ingrained not to be drawn to it.

A secluded retreat came in handy for a sense of slipping off the grid. In his line of work you couldn't escape your history nor hope to disappear but the illusion of being remote allowed for psychic space. In the last three years, Nelson had needed that space more than ever. If time healed wounds, then he hoped this was the space where he'd find the time.

After spending his twenties lost in the misnamed "adventures" of Special Forces, Nelson had entered government service where he worked for several intelligence agencies. After switching to a private intelligence firm, he'd opted to go one better and become an independent contractor, offering his services for both private and government NCS assignments.

With the advent of DHS, the Department of Homeland Security, it had become preferred policy to say you worked for the "Intelligence Community," the IC. A broader term, encompassing governmental and private intelligence, was "National Clandestine Service" or NCS. Since the government employed so many private intelligence services, both terms were interchangeable.

The vague IC moniker gave homage to the umbrella function of DHS but it also meant assets never had to specify their precise employer. Intelligence agencies were the prime beneficiaries of this vague titling since they were masked behind a single, generic facade. Best of all, new agencies could be added to the mix without overt efforts to conceal them.

The bright sun filled a wide blue sky but near to earth an icy wind buffeted the truck. Field snow kicked up and obscured the frosty Laramie Mountains to the west. Deeper, slushy snow squished beneath the tires. The sound mixed with engine noise and masked the chirp of Nelson's phone receiving a text message. He barely heard the notification but waited until he parked at the house to pluck his phone from a pocket to check.

On the chirp, the hour had switched to 2 pm in the Mountain Time Zone. Nelson read the message, stared at it, and read it again.

"3 pm Warren AFB to Andrews. ETC."

Nelson checked the sender; a blind number, a D.C. exchange. He sat perplexed. He knew what it meant; it still didn't make any sense. At least not in a normal world. ETC was a code for Emergency Tactics Corps, a select IC group called up only for dire national emergencies. Nelson had only seen an ETC once—on 9/11/2001.

Among field assets, the expression of pride regarding the acronym ETC was reflected in the group's motto: *Exubero, Teneo, Callidus,* Latin for *abound, persevere, and be cunning.* Then again, the unofficial version of the motto promised that *Every Thing is Classified.*

Nelson looked to his phone to scan current headlines. He gravitated to leading news of computer trouble on Wall Street. The expanding rumors spanned from technical problems to state terrorism. So far no one had taken responsibility for the three on-the-hour glitches. All speculation buzzed around official assurances that everything was under control.

Nelson stuffed his phone in pocket while hurrying out of the truck. The news about Wall Street didn't seem ETC-worthy; then again, nothing else in the headlines warranted such a text message—if the message was in fact genuine. The first item of business was to verify that the text wasn't a prank.

Nelson stamped his feet on the front doormat to shake off the snow then rushed into the house and headed for his desk in his upstairs office.

On a pad of paper he quickly jotted down the number 523.

Then he called back the D.C. number that texted him.

A pleasant but automated female voice answered with abrupt precision, "Four...Seven...One...Nine." And then the line disconnected to dead air.

Nelson transposed the numbers and wrote down 174. He calculated the number of days from December 1st to May 23rd. It verified as 174. Nine was the last number in Nelson's eleven-digit QID, the IC employee ID number. It was an added check digit that bound the automated message to him and him alone and was triggered by the D.C. exchange identifying the phone calling in.

The text message ended with "ETC." E was the 5th letter of the alphabet, T was the 20th letter, and C was the 3rd and so 5, 20, 3 became 5/23 or May 23rd. If the answering voice said the correct number of go-between days from today to May 23rd in reverse, it was tentative verification.

Depending on the kind of operation being called up, the text message would have ended in a different three-letter acronym. Each acronym translated to a different day of the year to calculate on today's date and deliver a gap interval in reverse.

Nelson checked the time. It was after 2 pm. He had less than an hour to get to Warren Air Force Base for a flight to Andrews. If no flight was waiting with his name on it, the ETC was a hoax or a mistake.

Nelson grabbed a backpack full of clothes and basic supplies. Pausing at the dresser, he glanced at a photo of Madelyn and him in happier times. Rare as they were, ETCs weren't regular assignments. There was no telling when or if he'd be back. Thoughts of happier days faded. He hurried downstairs and out the door. It was time to get on Highway 210, also known as Happy Jack Road. Nelson steered his pickup east. With time to reflect, his call-to-duty reflex met with doubt and a rising distaste.

This was the thing he'd said he was done with when he left government service for private work and when he retired. Here he was, rushing into it again. He knew the way D.C. worked. Why was he hurrying back without question? Was his sense of duty so ingrained that he'd serve even when he no longer respected the structure that had taken over the service?

Most agents were never called for an ETC. This was Nelson's second call-up. 9/11 had been obvious but this time felt different. Being included given his age and retirement status felt odd. Maybe specialized expertise was required; possibly human intelligence from Nelson's past experience came into play. There had to be a reason why he'd be included. During the ride east, Nelson couldn't imagine what that would be.

Top retiring agents were offered the option of making themselves available for ETC service. It was more an honorary designation to make old war birds feel still of service. Most retired agents did retain vitality and a wealth of experience. Many had retired to double-dip in private work. But vitality was commonplace among youthful recruits; no one had to tap retirees to find it. And experience had a shelf life. Yesterday's experience was a good history lesson but oftentimes meant little in a rapidly evolving operational theater.

So why this ETC, why now? Nelson rolled up to Warren's main gate. He gave his name and showed his ID. With a sense of urgency, the guard directed him onto base. So much for doubt. The ETC was real.

3
0000 0000 0011

6:46 pm EST, Friday December 1st

"ur missing all the fun."
Adam Perez glanced at the text message while standing at a network management console. The chill of computer room fans whipped around him. He palmed his phone as the door opened and raised his eyes to his work. On the sound of someone moving his way, he set his phone aside.

The floor supervisor jockeyed in between the racks of computer gear and network cabling and poked in for a look. "Find anything?"

Adam typed the next diagnostic command. "Did you expect me to?"

"No," the supervisor admitted. "But the feds want us to look anyway."

"Why? They said on the news everything's under control."

"Yeah, sure." The portly man laughed while taking a glance at the console. "It's more like...*OK, move along, there's nothing to see here; the show's over.*" Pulling away, he headed back for the door.

Adam's face was devoid of humor. "I'm taking off after this."

"Fine with me." The supervisor held the door open long enough to add, "Might as well slip out before they find some other crazy shit for us to do."

The door closed and Adam was alone again. He reached for his phone and pressed thumbs to the onscreen keyboard.

"on my way - hold a seat for me."
He pressed send then logged out of the management console. Bolting from the network closet, he jogged down the stairs to drop one floor below his work level. Waiting for an elevator on his own floor was not advisable. Chances were he'd run into someone intent on delaying him half the night.

As it was, he had already missed an hour of class.

He rode down from the twenty-fifth floor to the lobby in silence. Maddeningly, the elevator car stopped several times along the way to pick up more of the day's stragglers, all equally anxious to start their weekend.

Adam hit the street to the sound of traffic and the rush of people navigating slick sidewalks. Finding a break in the flow, he jaywalked on a quick diagonal across four lanes of traffic and lifted his collar against a headwind of frosty air. All around him towered buildings reaching for the sky only to find an icy fog.

After hurrying two blocks up and one block over, Adam arrived at class to discover the lecture stalled on a discussion about the day's unusual events. He spotted classmate and sometimes girlfriend Jiaying Xianzi in her regular seat. She always sat three-quarters of the way up the tiered rows near the back.

Jiaying was a petite dynamo with a pert body, sharp wit and piercing eyes.

Among this bunch of over-poached eggheads, she was hard to miss. The two of them originally met in class months ago. After one hello had led to sporadic conversation, they gravitated to each other, first to compare class notes, eventually to compare libidos.

Jiaying made a point to schedule time together outside class. She was new to the city, needed a tour guide and study coach, plus she wasn't shy about enjoying the company of a virile native. Adam neither encouraged nor shunned her advances. He'd accept quality female attention if it was offered to him but hadn't the time to go looking for it. As long as it lasted, he considered himself lucky to have company that came with sensual diversions.

He slid into the seat beside her and let out a sigh.

"Hi stranger," she smiled.

Adam considered the discussion topic and whispered to her. "I ran three blocks to hear about this shit again? Why didn't you warn me?"

"Everyone's distracted," she shrugged. "You know, unusual situations bring it out in people."

"Bring what out?"

"Aimless distraction." Flirting, she pulled at her hair. "I guess it's no worse than the calculated distraction we usually get about this time."

Adam slumped back. "Whatever." The weight of the day and the long hours already spent at the keyboard pressed him lower in his seat. He looked around and sized up how fellow students were acting. The excitement about Wall Street's glitch had rocked them from their steady tedium of study.

Quant class was usually a sober, heady affair in the best of times. After what happened on Wall Street earlier in the day, students wanted to speculate about what it all meant. Maybe they could impress their guru teacher or failing that, at least outshine each other. In return, a glib and underwhelmed professor was more than happy to analyze and pontificate away their premises.

Adam was in no mood for all the slickness and exhilarating sarcasm but was resigned to it. At least it was a place to rest, in from the cold. He understood all too well where he was. In this room, alternate realities of combative logic, calculation, and one-upmanship were to be expected.

With all the apps on his phone as entertainment, he could ignore most of it. As he did so often, he'd sit through it for another night if that's what it took to please the professor enough to get a Quant Certificate out of him.

Quant was a nickname used disparagingly by some but offered as a badge of mental elitism by others. It referred to one who used computers, statistics, mathematics, and quantitative techniques to model the value of financial securities to determine how to structure and hedge them for profit. In such a study group, it was no surprise to find probing a topic until paralyzed was a standard operating practice. That included trivia of the day.

The entire class term lasted a year and a half and included long hours of independent research in the library. Many on the outside wanted a seat in this room but only those who could beg, borrow, or profitably steal the $80k tuition were allowed in. After getting in, it got more difficult.

The brutal fact was, even if one could buy in, only those with a gift for advanced math and computer science stood a chance of slogging through it and coming out alive. Many dropped out. Some hung on only to find they didn't do well enough on the final to warrant a completion certificate.

Adam had no problem with the smarts needed. If anything, he found the pace of the work tedious and the lecture style dragging and indulgent. When it came to numbers and computers, his gifts were in the top one percent. His problem had been finding the money. He barely managed to borrow the full amount and succeeded based solely on his post-graduate grades at MIT and a solid employment record on the twenty-sixth floor down the street.

His five years at the "Institute" in Cambridge tallied up to a $250k debt. That was being handled thanks to scholarships, more loans, and a finagled but small early inheritance. How he was going to pay that back plus a newly-owed $80k was easily explained away by the once-upon-a-time reasonable answer. It had been said one only had to consider the fantastic salary levels a good quant could demand. Or so the theory went.

In reality, given the cyclical contractions of the markets as of late and peaking interest in the field, top quant positions were growing scarce as the field of experienced applicants widened. Being a quant was not the new thing on the block anymore. Enough qualified people had rushed into the field over time to make it a crowded contest. After Adam had committed himself to the $80k program, he learned how much the competition for quant jobs had changed over the year and was now trending towards fierce.

One of the reasons for the tight job market was the brain drain that had occurred from science and academia. Many top performers there had traded dowdy posts for the allure of quick riches on Wall Street. The stories one heard were legendary. One of the original quant pioneers, Emanuel Derman, also known as the *Einstein of Wall Street*, had left the world of theoretical physics for a job at Goldman Sachs. After making his mark there, he moved on to Columbia University to train the next generation of quants. To have multiple PhDs as a quant nowadays was a given, like a carpenter strapping on a tool belt or a new sous chef showing up with a proper set of knives.

Adam's class was only a couple blocks from Wall Street. As was typical, the make-up of quant students filling the seats was primarily male, mostly Asian, Indian, or Eastern European. Chinese nationals predominated. Americans were in the minority. Jiaying was Chinese but stood out for being female. The only other woman in class was a stern-looking Middle Eastern protégé wearing a hijab who spoke to no one.

The man who taught them was rail thin, in his forties, a relic of academia wars. He taught this class at night while suffering being a daytime serf to some hedge fund mogul whose minions were ensconced in an office park in

"Hedgistan," the hedge fund capital of the world located along the I-95 corridor between Manhattan and Westport, Connecticut.

Adam wondered what it was that drove such a man to take on so much when it was obvious he held such distain for his students. Was it a steep alimony payment? Maybe a gambling debt? Either way, the guy loved to snap off biting answers to undercut presumptive statements made by young and eager minds. He had a way of pursing his lips, allowing for a slight smile to signal an involuntary dismissal of a student's worth as a life form.

Leaning back on the lectern, he cut off a student mid-sentence. "…yes, yes, and more people are involved in trading commodity derivatives than are involved in the actual production of the commodity. We're dealing with human nature. If that sucks, oh well. The fact is, as a quant, if you talk to the press, you will be fired. You can't be wrong or important people will lose billions of dollars and I guarantee you, they will hold you accountable. The uncertainty we've seen today is a taste of the stress you'll face as a quant."

The topic of stress invariably drew questions about the job interview process. Any interview for a quant job was automatically considered the most challenging of high stress interviews. Quants had a reputation as being the brightest bulbs in the bunch so employers took fiendish delight concocting outrageous and rigorous mind games to test job applicants.

Many smart people had been annihilated by job panels primed with brain teasers and off-the-wall technical surprises. Preparing for an interview to be a quant was a whole other form of major preparation, one that this $80k class didn't even cover except anecdotally. And yet, it was the one essential task that a good percentage of qualified applicants with newly acquired quant certificates in hand would never fully master.

The teacher gave a few words of advice. "Don't prepare for specific questions you've already heard, no matter where you heard them. Chances are you'll never be asked that exact question and all the memorization will only make you look more hopelessly stilted than you obviously are."

"You're saying there's no way to prepare?" a student challenged.

"Sure there is," asserted the teacher. "Be all you say you are. If you can't manage that, survey every question you've heard about. Note the different types. What are they asking for? A quick calculation, heuristics, self-assessment, finance fundamentals? Test the premises and ask yourself—is it a trick question? Know your approach for each type. Above all, be brief."

Illustrating his point by showing off, the teacher rattled off a series of sample questions. After each one, he pointed to a different student and demanded an immediate answer. Of course they had none in the time allotted but it allowed for enough of an awkward pause to let him swiftly move on.

He pointed. "How many bricks are there in Shanghai? Consider only residential buildings."

He pointed again. "How many games would need to be played to determine a winner if you had 5,623 participants in a tournament?"

After a pause, another pointing finger. "Give me examples of vertical and horizontal analysis used correctly and incorrectly. Use the correct examples together to demonstrate a favorable margin trend."

The pattern continued. "In the context of the Black-Scholes formula, what variables do you need to derive the hedge ratio?"

"What are the key assumptions behind Ito's Lemma? How do you decide if you can apply the lemma or not?"

"How would you implement an efficient database that can hold 50 years of price/volume/dividend data for all the stocks in the world? Describe your general implementation strategy."

"If I call the dog's tail a leg, then how many legs does the dog have?"

"Demonstrate a whisper number used in a forecasting algorithm. Explain the rule of thumb for using such a number in calculations."

"The following equation is wrong: 101-102 = 1. Move one numeral to make it correct."

"If 1 bottle of beer costs 1 yuan, how much will 100 bottles cost?"

"Explain what's happened in the world in the last ten years."

"Discuss the validity of using malloc() or calloc() for memory allocation in C++. Why or why would you not use these functions?"

"If you were shrunk to the size of a pencil and put in a blender, how would you get out?"

"Explain global macroeconomics in two minutes, starting now."

Adam leaned into Jiaying. "I've had enough. Let's get out of here."

Jiaying gathered up her things and followed Adam up the aisle to the rear exit. He stuffed his hands in jacket pockets and headed through the lobby. For every step he took, Jiaying took one and a half steps.

"What's the hurry?" she asked.

Adam kept pace out the revolving door onto the street. "I need to be somewhere else." They headed down the sidewalk.

"Why? You got an appointment?"

"No—not that kind of somewhere else."

"Wanna get something to eat?"

Adam hailed a cab. "How about a drink?"

They shared the ride to Midtown where they both had flats. On the way, Jiaying convinced Adam to stop at a watering hole where people from her work hung out. He was in no mood for a deep one-on-one with her anyway so he relented. They walked in to find a wall of noise. Raucous conversations drowned out the thump of background music. Friday's happy hour was ending but the overflow energy from it had yet to max out.

Jiaying only spotted two of her coworkers and headed straightaway in their direction. "Hey, there. Where *is* everybody?" she asked.

The tall woman with the margarita gave a glance to the suited man with the high ball. She sipped at the rim of her glass and had the last bit of salt.

"We're all that's left."

The man asked, "Aren't you supposed to be in class?"

Jiaying shrugged and nudged closer into Adam. "We got bored."

"They're off topic tonight," added Adam. He had joined Jiaying in this same place several times in months past. He didn't remember the names of the man and woman but he recalled being introduced to them once. He had no reason to call them by name; besides, he was sure they had forgotten his.

"You're the financial technologist, aren't you?" noted the woman, looking Adam up and down. "I bet you had an interesting day."

Adam paused to join Jiaying in giving the waitress a drink order then turned back to the woman and answered her. "I'm not invested in the markets. I don't think my day was as interesting as it was for those who are."

"You have no investments?" The man's shock deflected Adam's point.

Adam's wry smile faded. "If you count tuition, I have quite a portfolio."

"Now there's a long-term but high-risk speculation," the woman smirked.

The man pulled at the open collar where his tie was loosened. "At least they haven't figured out a way to repossess an education—no doubt they're working on it."

"They don't have to repossess it," countered Adam. "All they have to do is consider it obsolete. In technical fields, that system is already in place."

"I'm not going to spend my life being a student," asserted Jiaying.

The man swirled the last bit of bourbon in his glass while watching the ass of another woman walk by. "Even more reason to get it while you can."

"Unfortunately, as we've seen today, the bad guys are saying the same thing." Finishing her margarita, the tall woman slid her empty glass to the center of the table to signal she had reached her limit.

"What the hell are you talking about?" the man laughed. "On the street, we *are* the bad guys."

"I don't care. Somebody better clarify what happened today. The longer it goes without explanation, the worse it's going to be for everyone."

Jiaying gave voice to her fears. "Maybe they already know but they won't say. Maybe they think the truth would scare everyone."

The man leaned in. "What do they think the fucking rumors are doing?"

"So how did it go over at CIG+XM?" asked Adam.

The tall woman answered first. "No different than anywhere else."

"Except for the paranoia," added Jiaying. "Those news reports wondering out loud about state-sponsored terrorism didn't brighten the mood."

Jiaying's employer, the *Chinese Investment Group + Extra Measure*, was one of the newer investment firms in the city. It was backed by Chinese interests but over half its employees in town were a mix of American, Indian, and European talent. Regardless, the management was in Beijing.

The man reached for his wallet and shoved money onto the waitress' tip tray. "It's gotten more interesting than that. Did you hear the latest?"

Jiaying shook her head while Adam waited, his interest drawn elsewhere.

"They're saying now there's a good chance the whole glitch thing was the work of some little known terrorist outfit. Apparently, the terrorists have found common ground with that anarchist bunch—you know the one, that vigilante hacktivist group…"

"—RAPIER," added the woman.

"Yeah, RAPIER. That's it—*revolution by another name.*"

Hearing the name and motto, Adam pulled his attention back to the man.

"Reporters cornered a senator at the Capitol. He's on some security sub-committee. Off-the-cuff, they asked him if he thought today was a terrorist attack or some denial-of-service prank staged in protest against Wall Street."

The woman finished the story. "The senator would only answer, 'What's the difference?' For some reason, he won't distinguish between the two. He says that and the FBI admits they have evidence that RAPIER members have been seen with go-betweens who represent terrorists."

"Interesting." Adam accepted his microbrew and took a swig. "But they still haven't answered the questions about the problems with the fiber optic trunk lines between New York and New Jersey."

"And they won't," declared the man. "That story doesn't make sense. Some stupid shit about improper air-gap impedance isn't going to cause what happened today." He straightened his tie. "Hey, I've got to go…"

The tall woman was discreet. "Want to be my subway bodyguard?"

The man was transparently coy. "I don't know—the way you're looking, you really think I can keep all of them off you?"

She ignored him and patted Jiaying's hand. "Try to have a fun weekend."

The man and woman dashed off leaving Adam and Jiaying to their drinks. The ongoing commotion around them wavered between celebration and panic. No doubt, much of the blending conversation was on the same topic that was foremost in financial districts across the globe. Too recent a matter to be settled, the whole question promised two fitful days for everyone. For many, the weekend was being robbed of its relaxing and restorative power.

Adam upended his bottle of beer and gulped a long draft.

Jiaying sensed his restlessness. "I guess you don't want to go out tonight."

"Maybe tomorrow." Adam's offer was unconvincing.

"Why don't we stay in at my place tonight." She drained her appletini.

Adam looked into her eyes, sensing arousal in her invitation.

She smiled and hooked her arm with his. "Come on. We have all night to forget about today."

4

0000 0000 0100

10:18 pm EST, Friday December 1st

Nelson Geiss stepped out of the Air Force jet and stretched tall in the frigid air. The flight in from Warren Air Base was direct and, from all outward appearances, uneventful. For Nelson, having spent most of the trip gathering questions and doubts over what was going on, the journey was far from relaxing. He was glad it was over. Maybe now he'd get some answers.

Jet engines powered down with a whine behind him as he headed down the stairs. Waiting at the bottom, a security agent on point in suit and tie withheld comment until Nelson was near enough to hear him.

"Right this way, Mr. Geiss."

Stepping on the tarmac at Andrews Air Force Base with backpack in hand, Nelson glanced around. The one palpable attraction nearby was the roar and rush of wind coming off the spinning blades of a black, AH-G Little Bird, light assault helicopter preparing for takeoff.

"Where to now?" asked Nelson.

Pivoting with military position, the agent ushered Nelson toward the chopper. "JBAB, sir. Joint Base Anacostia-Bolling. You're scheduled for a briefing at DIAC."

Nelson knew DIAC to be the Defense Intelligence Analysis Center, the headquarters of the Defense Intelligence Agency. Riding there from Andrews in a light attack helicopter was highly unusual unless a combat air patrol or CAP was in effect for the D.C. air corridor. Nelson hadn't heard of one; then again, maybe that was the point. During an ETC, CAPs wouldn't necessarily be broadcast to anyone but those charged with the duties of enforcing them.

Ducking into the prop wash, the agent opened the helicopter door. Following alongside, Nelson climbed in and stowed his backpack.

In full flight suit and head gear, the pilot watched Nelson get settled.

Nelson strapped in and pulled the door shut. "All secured."

"Very good, sir." The pilot turned his attention back to the controls.

Without hesitation, the bird lifted fifty feet, pivoted 180°, then took off to the northwest. Dramatic as it was, it would be a short flight. Bolling was only a few miles away along the banks of the Potomac.

Fishing for information, Nelson tried making conversation. Presuming a CAP was in effect was a start. "How many CAPs have you flown stateside?"

The pilot glanced towards Nelson briefly. "Can't really say."

Nelson ignored the evasion. "It's amazing, since 9/11, the FAA has called in over 400 domestic airline incidents. That's a lot of scrambling to do but I guess it has to be done. You never know when the threat's going to be real."

"That's for sure." The pilot was intent upon his job.

Nelson watched the lights of Washington D.C. come nearer. "Who would have thought it would come to this? Spending $60 million a week for combat air patrols over the United States."

"Whatever it takes."

"They keep you in the air a lot or do they have you on strip alert?"

The pilot paused, weighing his answer. "A little of everything—to keep it exciting." Unwilling to offer anything more, the pilot fell silent.

For combat aircraft across the country, strip alert meant being fully armed, fueled, and ready to go. It was considered easier duty than having to maintain 24/7 patrols aloft. Nelson hoped to catch the pilot admitting to something but no such luck. To pass the time, it was worth a try.

They set down on a helipad near the six-story DIAC building. Another security agent was there, ready to escort Nelson inside to a conference room. The attractive space was set off from the Defense Intelligence Operations Coordination Center's main situation room.

DIOCC was the part of the Department of Defense responsible for integrated intelligence operations and collection. From what Nelson could see, activity at the center appeared normal. But in such situations, it was everything one was never shown that often mattered the most.

The security man led him to the conference room without comment and left him there. It was empty except for a large oval table and surrounding chairs. Nelson had assumed the briefing would include a select group of ETC staff. The prospect that he'd have a personalized briefing without others seemed more ominous than distinctive.

The door opened and a man Nelson immediately recognized hurried in. It was Owen Raedalus, a much younger Agency man, a man Nelson could do without. Owen and Nelson had crossed paths years ago, shortly before Nelson left government service. At the time, Nelson thought Owen was a brash and egotistical upstart. Owen clearly thought Nelson was an old-timer who was cruising on his seniority. Nelson resented Owen's contempt and Owen couldn't abide the thought of having to fawn over Nelson simply because he was part of the know-it-all old guard.

If sitting down with Owen Raedalus was the extent of his briefing, Nelson was not only disappointed, he was on guard.

Owen started off uncharacteristically gracious. "Mr. Geiss, welcome."

Nelson dropped his backpack and sat down. "It's been a while, Owen. Are you still slumming it with the Agency?"

"Not quite. I'm matrixed with several groups. At command and control, there's a lot of overlap now."

"So I've heard." The reference to *command and control* wasn't lost on Nelson. In no uncertain terms, Owen was putting Nelson on notice where the two of them related to each other on the current chain of command.

Owen stood at the table and checked the time on the wall clock. Since he was rushed, his hesitation was obvious avoidance. "There's a lot to do and little time to do it. I'm sure you appreciate the seriousness of the situation."

"I wouldn't be here if I didn't."

"Fine. Then whatever history we have is history. I'm not asking you to let it go. But for right now, can we agree to concentrate on the task at hand?"

Nelson was calm and cool. "I was hoping you'd say that."

The bullet-proof impact cover on Owen's tablet computer was covered in fine leather. He sat down, opened it, then tapped the screen for access to briefing notes. "Thank you for responding to the call. I realize that resuming service for professionals of your status is optional and voluntary, even if the caliber of skill you bring to the mission is essential."

Nelson was frank. "I came because the message said ETC."

"Yes, that's right." Owen scanned his notes, leaving Nelson to stew.

"It's not typical to call up retirees," Nelson challenged. Some of the frustrating wonder he'd collected during the plane trip out from Warren bubbled over. "In fact, I had always heard that the ETC option for retirees was more of an honorary thing; you know, something to give old-timers a little false pride in the idea they'd still be of service in some sort of bastardized reserves. In fact, the option didn't mean much."

Owen confronted Nelson's reservations head-on. "There's another side of that cynical argument. It says it's just as likely retirees might actually come in handy on rare occasions. They have experience and some of them even retain their skills. More importantly, they know where the bodies are buried. Getting them to opt-in to a reserve service, as you call it, would be a way to secure legally-binding access to them just in case—simply on the off chance they should ever come in handy. It's good to keep all options on the table."

"So which is it? Stroking an old man's false pride or gaining leverage?"

"Usually it's both. But this time there are special circumstances."

"ETCs are for dire conditions. They're always special."

Owen leaned forward and locked eye contact with Nelson. "An ETC is a call to arms when there's concrete evidence that the continued existence of the nation is at stake. I imagine you've heard the news about Wall Street today."

"Unless there's a lot more behind those headlines, it's hard to believe that's the reason why I'm here."

"The NCSMC believes it. They're so sure, they've activated Site R."

"That seems an over-the-top response to a hiccup on Wall Street."

"It's the *potential* we're looking at," stressed Owen.

"To have to run the government from a bunker?"

"It's precautionary. They're spinning up just in case."

"In case what?" asked Nelson.

"That's why you're here."

Nelson absorbed the impact. NCSMC, the National Clandestine Service Managing Committee, was known only to ETC assets. As a secret-select group ranked above the Joint Chiefs of Staff and Homeland Security, such a committee was necessary because totally black operations required an equally black managing body. If the NCSMC had activated Site R, the national threat was imminent and if not stopped, possibly cataclysmic.

Site R was another name for the Emergency Operations Center at Raven Rock Mountain Complex in Pennsylvania. During major threats, the *underground Pentagon* coordinated defense communications and planning. Created during the Cold War, the site was rarely used except for drills. Its mission was to implement the Continuity of Operations Plan, a blueprint for relocating the federal government in the event of a major catastrophe.

Owen folded his hands over his tablet and raised determined eyes onto Nelson. "The financial data centers that were compromised today were in the New York and New Jersey areas exclusively. All of them were constructed and are being operated by one company. That company is based in Northern California but sixty percent of its stock is controlled by foreign investors."

Nelson butted in. "I heard the rumors about state-sponsored terrorism."

"Rumors…" Owen flipped his hand in distain. "Nothing but fragments of fact or outright fabrication. For us operationally, one is as good as the other. We need to know everything about this and time is against us."

"What's the timeframe?"

"Wall Street opens for business Monday morning. Unless global markets are reasonably certain they won't suffer a repeat of today, business is bound to be bad. And that's bad for everybody."

"You expect to have this nailed down by Monday?"

"All we need is the perception we're in control. We'll solve it as soon as we can. Until then, we can't be sure what story might be best. Until we know more about what we're facing, anything we create is shooting in the dark."

Nelson smirked. "The mask must fit the face…"

"Investor confidence is volatile; it all depends on the security and stability of systems that provide over-the-counter trading. The National Market System was unavailable for six minutes today. Eight major financial data centers were compromised. The company that runs them operates 106 data centers around the world, yet only the eight centers in New York and New Jersey were hit."

"That doesn't prove the company is involved."

"It doesn't prove anything—except we're the target."

"I still haven't heard anything that warrants an ETC," Nelson asserted.

"A threat to the global financial system is not enough for you?"

"I didn't realize there was a *global financial system*—not in that way. I thought ETCs were for *national* emergencies."

Owen grinned. "You're not stupid and I'm not naïve enough to be provoked by you. You can drop the interrogator tactics and talk to me straight or this meeting is over."

Nelson let down part of his guard. "So what's the situation?"

Owen sat back as if prepared to leave the room. "I've told you the situation. I have instructions not to tell you more unless you agree to participate fully and without questioning orders."

Nelson balked. "What gives you or anybody else the idea that I—"

Owen cut him off with a raised hand. "I'm not saying that. This is something I was told to cover with all independent contractors. Anyone whose recent work experience is in private intelligence has to be vetted."

"You don't trust us?"

"Let's just say independent contractors have gotten used to doing things their way. They may not be used to the appropriate structure ETCs demand."

"I have more years in government service than anywhere else. Nearly a decade in Special Forces taught me quite a bit about structure."

Owen rocked in his seat. "Are you agreeing to terms?"

After a calculated pause, Nelson nodded. "The ones I've heard."

"Very well." Owen returned to tapping on his tablet. "As you may know, years ago DHS classified this type of financial datacenter as *critical homeland security infrastructure*. That designation gives us special rights and responsibilities. Naturally, the FBI and other agencies are involved in an extensive investigation around the edges. They only form the outer layer of what needs to operate now."

Nelson was dubious. "I thought the financial sector was prepared for this. What about all the tests and drills they've run?"

Owen referred to his notes. "The last major drill that was coordinated with all parties was *Quantum Dawn 3* in 2016. Before that, *Quantum Dawn 2* in 2013 and *Quantum Dawn* in 2011. These were mostly role-playing games cooked up by the Financial Services Sector Coordinating Council and the Securities Industry and Financial Markets Association."

"You're saying the drills were *not* effective?"

"I'm saying they were limited exercises that only tested how to react to simulated cyber attacks. The assorted attacks were planned by an industry Exercise Controller. They tested how various players communicated and responded. Due to time restraints, the attacks themselves had to be the obvious ones they guessed would be thrown at them. Drills like that never covered this scenario. This wasn't your typical distributed denial-of-service attack."

"What about DHS? The government's been beefing up security. There was an Executive Order…"

"Yes," noted Owen. "February, 2013—*Improving Critical Infrastructure Cybersecurity*. The Executive Order made the case but it had no teeth. Government didn't get involved enough. It didn't make strict rules for business. The program was voluntary. Companies were given incentives to participate but you know how far that goes."

"So what's your role in this?" asked Nelson.

"I work for Homeland Security at the DOD as senior liaison between several agencies of the IC. I've been called in as a Focal Point Officer on special assignment to coordinate information."

"So after the three o'clock glitch, has anything else happened?"

"Yeah, the media latched onto the event right away. Now we need to make use of that. They're already calling it the *Friday the 1st Event* or F1E. Public interest isn't going away; it's growing. Curiosity about F1E could turn into panic real quick if we don't work this right."

"So what's been done?"

"We've floated the story about a problem in fiber optic trunk lines coming into metropolitan New York."

"No doubt you've ruled that out as a root cause…"

"Hours ago. We anticipated the fiber optic story would only hold for 12 to 24 hours anyway but it was the obvious telecom thing to do to buy us time."

"What about the terrorist and hacktivist angles?"

"People were going to go there anyway so we primed the pump. We have selected people directing a narrow band of targeted innuendo."

Nelson's brow furrowed with guesses. "It sounds like you're running a full-blown SIR—a Staged Information Release."

"It's pretty basic. We're trying to maintain the high ground while doing what's necessary to position ourselves on the battle-space."

Nelson was amazed at how quickly government teams had responded. The F1E event was only hours old. Normally when running a SIR, an opposition research team would need time to study and explore before shaping public opinion with official statements, leaks, and data plants.

Such a broad effort to manage information and opinion normally would take time coming up to speed and getting traction. What was being done here was rapid prototyping of tactical spin and strategic slant on a grand scale.

"I thought ETCs were about countering a threat, not staging global PR."

"Public opinion could turn into a serious threat. Whoever did this today wants to trigger a perception that commodity markets are not a safe place to keep one's money…"

Nelson chuckled. "Some would say Wall Street's past behavior has already created that perception. Without pranks or terrorists."

"The point is, the ETC has two goals: manage threat perceptions and neutralize the source of the threat. Given the type of infrastructure in danger, both goals are equally important."

Nelson rocked back. "What about the event itself? How close are you to finding out what happened?"

"We know exactly what happened." Owen took pleasure watching Nelson freeze with interest. "An hour after the market closed, we found what's left of the code responsible. For what it's worth, I'll give you a copy if you want."

"What do you mean, *for what it's worth?*"

"Well, at precisely 4:00 pm, the malware created a temporary script in RAM. That script then turned around and deleted the originating program, basically self-destructing to cover its tracks. All we have is the RAM script."

"Where did this happen?"

"Right in the heart of the data centers."

"Damn! How did someone get through their security? From what I've heard, those places have more protections than Langley."

"That's what we have to find out. More critically, we need to know why. Despite what you've been hearing in the news, we don't believe this thing is intended to be a one-time event."

"So what about the glitch; did it do anything, I mean, besides screwing up screen displays?"

"No," announced Owen flatly. "That's the interesting thing. The whole thing was designed to mimic errors from old video games."

"You mean the way screens look when video games go haywire?"

"Yeah, what gamers call the kill screen."

"But those are bugs in game software, things like buffer overflows or out-of-range variables."

Owen nodded, then stood and paced. "Yes, they're usually caused by simple programming errors. Only, in this case, there's no bug in the data. It's a middle-man attack, placing itself in between the data and the output. All the code does is make garbage out of what should appear on the screen."

"So the datacenter servers weren't affected."

"No. That's why it was so easy for the code to appear to reset everything after one minute, two minutes, three minutes. There was no reset; the code simply switched itself off and allowed proper data to display."

"What does it matter?" noted Nelson. "Traders still couldn't work."

"That's why DHS is classifying anything about this event as an ADT, Advanced Persistent Threat. To keep any hint of our work out of the news cycle, they have the FBI chasing their tails every which way. They even have them checking into kill screens from old video games for clues."

"No stone unturned, huh?"

"More like tying two rocks together to see if they float. It makes for good theater under the guise of being thorough. I get copied on everything. A lot of it is crap.'"

Owen turned his tablet around and slid it in front of Nelson.

Nelson scanned down the first few entries:

DONKEY KONG—at 22nd level of game, programming oversight with the timer creates too low of time to complete the level.

DUCK HUNT—at level 99, counter goes to 100 but program doesn't support counter of 100 so ducks appear randomly all over screen.

JR. PAC-MAN—at level 146, screen area for Pac-Man is not drawn out or is not visible so Jr. and Ghost freely move about in erratic way.

PAC-MAN—integer overflow at level 255; the routine that draws fruit attempts to draw 256 fruits on screen, then displays hex values.

"Granted, this shit is old," noted Nelson. "But it could be simulated to represent something else—as code. Each game glitch could signal the use of a different substitution key."

Owen watched Nelson have a look at the text. "Maybe they'll turn up something. I don't think so. I think they're wasting their fucking time. If this was done by pranksters, then I could see something juvenile like hidden messages or *Easter eggs* in the screen scramble."

"The malware may appear childish, but the scope of what was affected can only mean we're dealing with major players."

"The access alone tells us that."

Nelson looked up from the tablet. "The potential here is insidious."

"No shit." Owen nervously tapped the table.

"There might be a message in this. It's inferred but fairly obvious."

Owen straightened up, skeptical. "And *you* figured it out."

"Sure." Nelson leaned back. "They're telling everyone—*Look, we can scramble your screens; now imagine—just as easily, we could have modified them…but only slightly.*"

Owen nodded. "And if they had, would anyone have noticed?"

Nelson pushed the tablet away. "Probably not, until it was too late."

5

0000 0000 0101

8:28 pm EST, Friday December 1st

Jiaying Xianzi switched on a light and dropped her door key onto a small square of laminate that passed for a kitchen table. "Someday I'm going to live in a place where I don't have to cram into a subway then wait for an elevator before getting to my front door."

The twelfth-story flat would be a tiny studio apartment in most areas of the country. In Midtown, it was prime real estate commanding rent higher than most mortgage payments. For Adam Perez, her furnished flat was as good as home. His place was no bigger and he was a bit jealous how she'd lucked out with a partial view of city lights.

He cruised in behind her, trying to relax and get into the mood for what, on any other day, would be a steamy private party lasting half the night.

"So what kind of front door *would* you have?" he asked.

She kicked off shoes in front of a decorative fireplace and lit candles on the coffee table and mantle. "Oh, I don't know. Maybe something with beveled glass fronting a warm ocean beach would be nice."

Adam paused before a blank section of wall and held up both hands to frame an idea. "How about a mural right here? Tahiti...Bora Bora..."

She handed him a bottle of chilled Merlo and an opener. "Funny man."

Adam glanced over and noticed the pull-down bed, already down. Clothes and sofa pillows were scattered over it in disarray. He doubted she ever bothered to fold the bed into its mahogany box up against the wall. He wondered if she could even lift it. It made getting into the refrigerator a problem but mostly she ate out at trendy bistros anyway. For her lifestyle, it worked. Besides, she liked the artwork recessed over the headboard too much to have it disappear with the bed pulled up.

He popped the cork while she brought glasses for pouring. She lingered at his side and asked, "When was the last time you took a vacation?"

"A few days ago. Weekends are my getaways."

"Seriously. You could take a little time off after classes are done. We could go someplace. We only have a couple of weeks to go."

"Now who's being funny?" Adam poured the wine while holding two glasses with one hand.

"Come on, you've got to live a little." She took her glass and headed towards the bed talking and sipping. "After we pass the final, we should go somewhere and celebrate."

"You're *that* confident you're going to pass?" He smirked.

1

"Why not? I have a friggin' savant for a tutor."

"Bullshit." He sauntered away and got comfortable on the sofa.

"The decision to have some fun should be an easy calculation for you."

"I'll think about it."

"It's not something to *think* about." She unzipped her dress and let it fall to the floor by the bed. "It's beyond all that; you have to feel it."

He watched her strip down to bare skin and slip an oversized sweater overhead, then let it fall mid-thigh. He had no defenses against female beauty. "I have a feeling if I let you, you might convince me."

Chuckling, she strutted to the sofa and then quoted someone. *"The difficulty lies, not in the new ideas, but in escaping from the old ones."*

"I've heard that before. Who said that?"

"I said it." She settled down next to him. "But maybe John Maynard Keynes said it first."

Adam let out a laugh. "I can't believe you're quoting Keynes to me."

"Why not?"

"Dressed like that?" Her sweater had crept enticingly higher.

"How should I be dressed?"

He leaned over and kissed her. "Right now, there isn't one other guy in all of Manhattan having Keynes whispered to him by a half-naked woman."

She hooked a leg over his and placed his hand on her inner thigh. She held it there. "Wouldn't you agree that aggregate demand is determined by the overall level of activity?"

Adam watched her eyes, grinning all the while. "You're full of surprises."

"It's that kind of day." She pulled away and got up.

Her reference to the day jogged Adam's thoughts back to what had happened at work. A feeling of nagging curiosity and dread shot through him. He tried to ignore it. "What are you up to now?"

She gathered clothes from the bed. "What does it look like?"

Adam finished his wine and set his glass down. Watching her, he joined her bedside and helped toss sofa pillows back where they belonged. With unspoken excitement, in no time at all, the bed was cleared.

Jiaying shed her sweater and jumped under the covers. "Oooh, it's cold. Get in here and warm me up."

Adam left his shirt and pants in a pile on the floor and climbed in after her. They met in the middle, a tangle of expectancy, then rushed to enjoy the familiar surprise of their bodies becoming one. The encounter was playful, turning amorous and then intense. As much stress as passion was released. Afterwards, only blissful sighs and soft cuddling were left to be enjoyed.

Adam was dizzy with thoughts and feelings and a body shivering with delight. He rolled onto his back, stared at the ceiling, and held Jiaying close.

She clung to his side and petted his chest. "You don't seem relaxed."

Adam smoothed back her jet black hair. "Oh, no, that was great."

She grinned. "I didn't say it wasn't great. What's wrong?"

Adam groped for words to describe the lingering unease that had mired his day in anxious wonder. "I don't know. It's nothing."

"Is it about what happened today?"

"No. Well, maybe. I mean, how did they do that?"

"I know what's going on…" She played with one of his nipples and got him to squirm. "The little computer whiz inside of you won't let that go. You think you can figure it all out tonight."

He grabbed her hand and held it at bay. The horseplay was more intrusive than arousing. "Why not? It's not a mystery to whoever planned it."

She relaxed back. "So you're with the crowd who thinks it was planned."

"Don't you?"

"From what I heard, they don't know yet. I'm not sure."

Adam sat up and swung his feet onto the floor. "I saw it happen. You can't tell me that was some random error. Do you really believe some system clock went berserk three times, each hour on the hour and tweaked switching software in a substation in some strange way that shot garbage bits into a graphics subroutine and managed to corrupt encrypted data streams?"

Jiaying laughed at the explanation. "Who said that?"

Adam rubbed both hands back over his head. "Oh, some federal agents that stopped by the firm after hours."

"Whoa…what were they, Secret Service…FBI?"

"Does it matter?" Adam leaned forward and rested arms on legs.

"I don't get it. Did they tell you this for sure or was it their best guess?"

"They made it sound like they had inside sources. There's no debate there. The whole point was to check out our equipment. To do it properly, they had to let us in a little on what the hell they were looking for."

"Are you supposed to be telling me this? I mean, I don't need any trouble. This would be no time to have my visa pulled and get deported."

"Don't worry," Adam assured her. "They told us to keep it to ourselves but I don't know how much they cared. I mean, they sure weren't shy about telling everybody in the firm's technical group all about it."

"That group?" Jiaying laughed and pulled the covers up over her breasts. "Can you say *tweet*? You know *that's* on the news by now."

"Probably."

Jiaying propped an arm upon a pillow. "OK, but don't tell me anymore. I don't want to know."

"I'd like to know." Adam gazed across the room into nothing. "I want to know what they know when they finally figure it out."

"Not me. All I want is to pass my test and go on vacation. After that, a quant job would be nice. That's what you should concentrate on."

"Yeah, I know," answered Adam but the enthusiasm was lacking.

"What's the matter? You always said getting a certificate was your ticket off the twenty-sixth floor."

"Maybe."

"More than maybe. With your background and the way you code, finding something good should be a snap."

"I guess so." Adam stood and walked naked to the window. In the near darkness, the candlelight from the coffee table and mantle etched him in flickering gold.

Jiaying sat up. "What's wrong."

Adam paused and lost himself in the partial view of city lights. "I don't know if I want that anymore."

"You're kidding, right?" Jiaying was stunned.

"I'm not sure if that's the thing to do."

"Since when?"

Adam said nothing. Jiaying got up from the bed and stood behind him. Her hands held him by the waist and arm. He turned to look at her but then looked away, into the view, his thoughts escaping beyond it.

"You're not dropping out of class, are you? It's only two more weeks."

Adam shook his head. "No, I'll finish it."

"Then what's the matter?"

He turned and they stood touching. "I've been thinking."

"Maybe too much…"

"No wait, hear me out." Adam drew her over to the bed where they sat down. "A few weeks ago, I read something from a guy at Goldman Sachs. He said, 'Quants had to adapt, be more dynamic and event-driven.'"

"Meaning what?"

"He was making the point that computer-driven hedge funds were going to have to exploit something else to make money. Quantitative methods are over-crowded. Everybody's doing it. When that happens, it no longer gives the same competitive advantage. Just like colocation. Anyone who matters is already colocated near the main feeds, so everyone has the same edge."

"So what? Everyone has algorithms; that doesn't mean they're all equal."

"That's his point," declared Adam. "What makes those algorithms different? What besides a technical edge drives competitive advantage?"

"Well…doing it better, faster, before the next guy."

"What else?" prompted Adam.

Jiaying thought. "Market information networks, believable sources."

"Exactly. In other words, like he said, data that is not machine readable."

Jiaying took it in, considered it. "…not machine readable?"

"Yeah. Databases, linkages, data-exchange partners, inside tips and patterns in the data known only to real people working the front lines."

"People's opinions only go so far. You have to crunch numbers."

"Which numbers? In class tonight, one of the interview questions was about using whisper numbers in algorithms. That guy in front of us couldn't answer the question but it's so easy."

"Why?"

Adam chuckled. "Because it's a trick question. Whisper numbers are estimates of earnings but they're unofficial. Basically, they're crap. Why would you want to crunch that? Give me a good reason."

"Maybe I want to artificially inflate expectations."

"And why would you want to do that?"

"Maybe I could trick investors into driving a stock price down by making them think a company's earnings didn't live up to what was advertised."

"Precisely. A company CFO estimates the upcoming post of earnings at $0.34/share. Your calc gets a whisper number of $0.36/share. Even if the company ultimately does better than their forecasts and posts $0.35/share, judging by your calc, the popular wisdom on the street believes the company fell short. Crunching numbers isn't enough. You have to know where the numbers come from. You have to know things that aren't machine readable and most of those things aren't numbers; they're not quantitative."

"What are you saying? Quants are obsolete?"

"No," snapped Adam. "I'm saying being a quant isn't enough. It's certainly not enough for me."

"Why not? Quants do research all the time. There's no SEC regulation against quants doing whatever legal research they need."

"Sure, but what firm lets them do it, I mean the whole thing? You know how it works; the bigger the organization, the more highly specialized it is. No quant on a corporate org chart is going to be given free reign like that."

"OK, so they'll have another department do that part and funnel the research to you. They retain competitive edge."

"And where does that leave me? I don't want to be someone's specialized tool. I don't want to be limited like that."

Jiaying grimaced. "Hey, this isn't the 1900s. You're not inventing something in your garage. You can't expect to do the whole thing yourself."

"It's not about doing it all; it's about doing the interesting part, the part that gives the competitive advantage. That's the exciting part, where you make a difference."

"You worry too much. First become a quant. Try it out. You never know what kinds of research you'll be doing."

Sensing her opposition, Adam deflated into himself. He had hoped she'd champion his vision for the way it could be. "Yeah..." he said at last. "Anyway, you wanted to know what was wrong, so there it is."

"OK, but I'm still not sure what's wrong."

Adam took a breath. "That guy from Goldman Sachs I talked about..."

"The one who wants quants to be event-driven..."

"Yeah. The thing he said about non-machine-readable data..." Adam raised his voice, driving home the point, "You know when he said that? Over four years ago! Imagine what the field is *really* into by now."

"We know what it's into; we hear about it in class."

"No, we hear basic shit we need to prepare for that fucking test. That's all that sorry-ass PhD from Hedgistan bothers to tell us. You can't tell me that's what passes for real competitive advantage at the top levels. Not anymore."

Jiaying pulled back. "So what do you want?"

"I want the freedom to go after the exciting part, to try it all."

"What kind of freedom?"

"I want the flexibility to react to opportunities as I find them; go anywhere in the world, be an intern somewhere if I have to if that's what it takes to get in with the right group, a cutting edge team doing the real work."

"You'll have lots of time for that."

"It's not that easy."

"Why not? Just go do it."

"I have 200k in tuition loans to pay off. I've seen what happens. People walk into a cubicle expecting to tough it out for a while. Before they know it, twenty years are gone. I don't want to be one of those guys. But right now, I don't see any other way."

"You'll be making a good salary. There's no reason why you can't have all that paid off long before you atrophy in some cubicle."

"I don't see it. I guess it's crazy. I don't want to wait to do what I want."

Jiaying got up and put her sweater back on. "I don't know. It sounds like the only thing holding you back is money. You need to pay off those loans. If that happened, your problem would be solved?"

Adam reached down for his pants. "Well, yeah."

Jiaying padded across the room to fetch the wine bottle. "Then you're going to have to find a way to pay it off quicker." She refilled their glasses. "Have you thought about taking on a second job?"

Adam zipped up his pants. "That's not likely."

"Why not?"

"Waiting tables in Soho for tips won't cut it."

"OK sure, you need a night job that pays the same as the day job."

"At least. What night job is going to do that?"

Jiaying gave it some thought. "There has to be some kind of moonlighting that pays. Maybe time shift, you know, work at night for a company on the other side of the world. Our nighttime is their daytime."

Adam put on his shirt. "I don't know. When would I sleep?"

"With the proper stimulants, who needs sleep?"

"What good is not sleeping if I fry my brain? I tried that during finals week in college once. It didn't go well. I can't think if something has me artificially racing."

Jiaying drew Adam back to the sofa and smiled. "There's always Powerball. As a quant, you should be able to pick great numbers."

"Now there's a plan." He slumped, propping his legs on the coffee table.

She paused with her glass suspended mid-air. "Come to think of it, there's a research job at my place."

"CIG+XM?"

Jiaying nodded. "Last I heard, they hadn't filled it yet."

"What are they offering?"

"As far as I know, pay is variable. It depends on how quick they get what they want. It's heavy research. At least, that's what I heard."

"Research?" Adam's interest was piqued. "Can it be done at night?"

She shrugged. "It could be done anytime. It's not on-site. It's a one-shot contract. If it works out, other projects might come available."

"They must have an upper range…"

"I'll check." Jiaying sat down next to him. "I can only gauge by what they've paid for other things. I know they want this done as soon as possible. I suspect, if they were pleased with how you turned it around, you might be able to pay off those loans in a year or two."

Adam decided to test the waters. He went fishing. "And what if they were *very* pleased?"

She hesitated long enough to take a long a sip of wine. "Well, in that case, I imagine you could pay everything off in a few weeks."

"What the hell!" Adam stiffened. "How's that possible?"

"Two years would be a long grind, a lot of work. Only problem is, things change quite a bit in two years and the research they need is time-sensitive."

Adam caught the inference and leaned closer. "You didn't answer my question." He repeated, "How is that possible?"

She studied his expression then averted her eyes. "To manage what they want in a few weeks—it might involve some computer tricks."

Adam froze. "You mean hacking."

"I mean whatever it takes to get it done in a few weeks."

Adam recoiled. "Oh my God, you're not seriously suggesting…"

She leaned back into the cushions, defensive. "Hey, I never said you had to hack. You can do it any way that works for you. Who knows, maybe you can convince them to go for the two-year option."

"There's no such thing and you know it. What part of *time-sensitive* doesn't apply? Two years my ass."

"Like everything else, there's an easy and hard way to do things. All I know is, they're looking for someone to do it the smart and quick way."

"I know exactly what they want." He lifted his hands as if holding them away from the fire. "I don't need that kind of trouble again."

"Again?"

"Long story."

"Tell me."

"Not now."

1

"All right but if you want to stop chasing the future, this is no time to get hung up on the past. Whatever happened before, leave it there. You're better now. Now is not then."

"Doesn't matter. There's no way I'm vacationing at Club Fed."

"OK, forget it." She got up and headed for the bathroom. "You're the one desperate to have your freedom, not me. Sorry I brought it up."

Adam watched her strut away dismissive and annoyed before calling after her. "Why don't *you* take the job?"

She stopped in the bathroom doorway. "Why? Because, if I got it done at all, it would take me at least two years. For you, I suspect it would take you a few days. Like I said, my tutor is a friggin' savant."

She closed the door and left Adam with his swirling thoughts.

After making love, being offered forbidden fruit was trying his resolve. But how could he even entertain the idea of hacking for CIG+XM? Then again, how could he pass it up? To be free of debt in a matter of days, what would that do for his life? What was that worth?

He could wind up sitting in a 6x12 cell for ten years. Then again, it was possible he wasn't getting the full story from her. He shouldn't dismiss it out of hand. He could at least inquire, find out directly from CIG+XM what was involved. Maybe it was a little corporate espionage, no big deal. He didn't have to commit to anything to find out. The thing that attracted him more than anything else were the possibilities. Who knows, something might work out. Still buzzing from bed-play and all the wine, it was easy to believe it could.

Jiaying exited the bathroom, her mood dampened. She made busy work out of handling the candles and avoided engaging with Adam right away.

He pulled his feet from the coffee table. "Want to get something to eat?"

Jiaying perked up but held back, doubtful and curious. "I thought you were dead to the world tonight."

He stood and pulled her into an embrace. "I was but I feel better now."

She pushed away. "You should after everything we did."

He watched her getting dressed then stepped to the window. The rolling fog had moved closer. The city lights were now softened and blurred. Here and there, bright areas that had been obvious before were now obscured.

Entranced with the shimmers of night, he was buoyed by prospects.

"You never told me where you want to go on vacation."

Zipping into her dress, Jiaying drew near behind him. "Now you know what I always say. Don't tease me—unless you're going to please me."

6

0000 0000 0110

8:31 pm EST, Friday December 1st

Secured within a DIAC conference room, Nelson Geiss listened as Owen Raedalus laid out the facts. Despite not having much respect for the man, Nelson was developing a deeper respect for why an ETC had been called.

The prospect of professional teams of state-sponsored hackers gaining access to sensitive data networks and injecting changes in screen displays was beyond ominous. Especially given the demonstration of their capabilities presented on Wall Street earlier in the day. If they could do this with systems as secured as those, they'd have no problem with any one of the other eighteen DHS-defined critical infrastructure sectors responsible for utilities, public health and safety, and transportation.

Regardless of the broader implications, high frequency traders worldwide depended on split-second timing to seize opportunities, secure profits, and avoid devastating losses. Computerized setpoints and benchmarks put in place by HFTs were designed to react instantly to fractional changes in prices and trends. Computers programs, fed by carefully-planned algorithms, placed and canceled thousands of orders per second in a race to sniff out opportunities. Fortunes were won or lost in microseconds based on shifting instantaneous values that varied in slight increments.

If someone were able to selectively tamper with screen displays in isolated but key places, they could crash currencies, bankrupt companies, and cause automated runs on markets. If only one hundredth of one percent of financial data was tampered with, none of it could be trusted. There would be no way of knowing in the moment where a small change had been made.

As Owen reminded Nelson, the sheer volume of financial activity potentially affected was staggering. In 2006, 30% of all trades were completed by HFTs. By 2012 that number had jumped to 70%. Since then, the priority of completing ever-quicker automated transactions had only strengthened. As a trend, the practice now branched beyond stocks into credit, currency, commodities, and emerging markets.

As a grim but comparably miniscule example of what could happen, on May 6th, 2010, the DOW plunged 600 points when a mutual funds computer mistakenly dumped $4.1 billion in securities in twenty minutes and triggered HFTs in reflex to gobble them up. By the time it was over, the *flash crash* of May 2010 saw $1 trillion quickly evaporate from stock markets.

On October 5th, 2012, $60 billion was temporarily wiped from the stock market value of India's biggest companies due to a *flash crash* on the country's stock exchange. Mumbai's Nifty index plummeted 16% in value. Trading was halted for fifteen minutes until the error was corrected.

Less damaging but just as troubling, on March 26th, 2012, BATS Global Markets, with a datacenter in Weehawken, Kansas, pulled back its own initial public offering after a computer glitch sent the stock plummeting. Also affected that day were shares of Apple Computer. The problem was quickly corrected and the public was assured that the computerized financial exchange maintained a record of 99.9 percent reliability.

Nothing was said about the 1/10th of 1 percent that remained unreliable.

Nelson was shaken, imagining what a coordinated and pinpoint strategy of targeted glitches could do. If slight enough, most of these tweaks wouldn't be discovered, not at first. It might be hours or days before the deception was rooted out through painstaking research. By then, the baseless shifts in markets would have already taken place. Meanwhile, the aftermath of even normal HFT activity could cascade and move markets in milliseconds.

No wonder institutional traders had long since raced to colocate their computers as close to market servers as possible. The privilege of having one's servers racked in pods with guaranteed near-access to market data only milliseconds faster than competitors was worth the price.

That price was expensive but anyone who seriously intended to play the game in a viable way gladly paid it. It wasn't unusual for one such colocation datacenter to cost hundreds of millions to build. Once completed, such heavily guarded facilities could house a half million square feet of computer trading space. Despite the massive size of such enterprises, available space in the pods was scarce and where accessible, far too expensive for the average investor.

Massive data centers in places like Mahwah, New Jersey had all but replaced the traditional trading floor on Wall Street. The days of runners frantic with order slips held high, watching the big boards for the latest numbers, was anachronistic now, a vestige of another time.

Given the dwindling percentage of real activity going on there, some had even suggested that the original NYSE trading floor on Wall Street be closed to business and preserved as a historical site. It survived only as a comforting pageant to lure 401k investors into believing old-time principles and traditions remained intact despite the high-tech sleight-of-hand and complex instruments that comprised business-as-usual that now mattered.

On one point, Nelson disagreed with Owen. "Looking for hidden messages in the scrambled screens might not be a waste of time. Whoever did this could have been testing something and they hid the test in the confusion of the kill screen. Patterns within that gibberish might be clues to what they were testing. Too bad whatever showed up on those displays is gone."

Owen was ahead of him. "The FBI is taking care of that."

"How could they? The scramble lasted six minutes. Unless somebody screen-scraped or video recorded at exactly that time, those displays is gone."

"That's right." Owen chose his words carefully. "Fortunately, at least one ongoing investigation being conducted at a trading house. Their management suspected a hedge fund manager might be involved in fraudulent activities."

"They were recording his screen?"

Owen gave a nod. "They've been tracking everything on his workstation. A recording of his screen display exists. They've turned it over to the FBI."

"I'd be interested to see it."

"Yeah, well, there's more than enough for you to do. In fact, one of the reasons you're here is your background in conspiracy theories."

"You're kidding."

Owen's temperament shifted, briefly more amiable. "From what I've read, you have extensive knowledge of the conspiracy underworld."

Nelson grinned. "I wouldn't exactly call it an underworld."

"Subculture," Owen offered. "The point is, years ago you completed an assignment dealing with conspiracies. Afterwards, you kept up an interest."

Nelson wondered where this was going. "I find the topic fascinating. You could say it's been a hobby of mine."

"From what I've read in the record, you contributed to a few conspiracy theories of your own. You were the primary on a disinformation campaign."

Nelson showed his poker face. "I can't imagine where you read that."

"Exactly what I thought you'd say," smiled Owen. "It's OK. I realize you have to disavow your participation. I only bring it up because it seems you need proof why a retiree might actually come in handy on rare occasions."

"I don't follow."

"Over the years, you've developed an impressive network of contacts; those you've worked with in private intelligence and others feeding the field of conspiracy theories. We believe you're in a unique position to blend the two, root out things in plain sight, things we may be missing. You might be able to highlight someone or some group with a motive to stage an F1E event. DHS is looking in all the regular places. I need someone to look everywhere else."

Nelson laughed. "You flew me all the way here so I can submit a brief on conspiracy theories, something freely available on the internet?"

"Data is not information. Your discernment and analysis is key."

"I know at least three agencies with staff who track conspiracies; two of them interact with the public space, adding to it. Why not ask them?"

"They haven't tracked this as long or in the same way as you have."

"They're highly capable of analyzing the space. My God, they created a fair percentage of it!"

"But you've done it as a hobby of real interest, not a job. You don't just know *about* these people; you know them, the way they think."

"I thought time was critical with this. What about driving to an answer before Monday morning when markets open for trading? Asking me to go down the conspiracy theory rabbit hole seems out of line. Even if something of interest turned up, it would take longer than 48 hours to run it down."

"That's not the only thing we need you to do."

Nelson looked around the room. "I don't understand this. We're having a briefing but where's the team? ETCs work in cells. Where's the..."

Owen interrupted, "I told you before; these are special circumstances."

"Special enough *not* to follow protocol?"

"You're not in the position to judge that."

"As a trained asset, I'm *expected* to evaluate the entire situation. Robot compliance gets one killed. How else are false flag operations rooted out? "

"You know what you have to know—*that* is proper protocol. As far as your cell, I'll tell you about them if you're done with your questions."

Nelson forced himself to calm down.

Visibly annoyed, Owen straightened up and tapped his tablet. "You've been paired up with Zack Hollister and Mike Dystrom."

The names registered right away. Nelson had worked with both of them before. They were good men. He hid his reaction and waited for more details.

"The three of you won't be working together directly but will collaborate and share aspects of the same target."

"Which is?"

"CIG+XM. It stands for *Chinese Investment Group plus Extra Measure*. They're a financial firm, based in New York, new in town but coming on strong. From the outside they look like an investment bank. We have reason to believe they're a cut-out company with most of their backing funneled in from a Chinese sovereign wealth fund. We've been watching this fund. It's the same group that has financed false fronts for PLA spooks and insider manipulations in at least five countries."

"What's the name again?" asked Nelson.

"CIG+XM. Why?"

"It's interesting; even the name has a double meaning."

"What part?" Owen was taken off-balance.

"The lettering, CIG+XM. Didn't you take economics in college?"

"I vaguely remember one class."

"How about the formula for GDP? I'm surprised you guys didn't spot it. It's trivia, I know, but a lot of what some call trivia I call the details."

"So it's Gross Domestic Product."

"Yeah, C+I+G+(X-M)—consumption, investment, government spending, and net exports, which is exports minus imports."

"Impressive," sneered Owen. "I hope your uncanny powers of observation extend beyond acronyms. The concept of state capitalism is relatively new; it's still to be seen how strict central planning and world markets coexist. Suddenly, socialism wants to make a profit. The question is, are they going about it with old, hardliner tactics, or new ones."

Nelson was direct. "You think China's behind F1E?"

"It's up to your cell to find out. You'll work their New York office. Dystrom is covering their London branch. Hollister is here in D.C. He'll follow up on the lobbying firm that does their bidding on Capitol Hill."

Lost in thought, Nelson spoke what was on his mind. "China holds so much of our debt, why would they want to sabotage the economy? Wouldn't that be shooting themselves in the foot?"

"No one said sabotage. We're talking manipulation. How valuable would it be to have the power to adjust at will our financials and key indicators—to pick winners and losers? Transfer of wealth has always been the ultimate force multiplier."

"How much more leverage do they need? They can already buy bonds directly from the U.S. Treasury, bypassing middle-man fees and masking their movements. No other country in the world has that privilege."

"It's like asking how much power is enough. The Far East already believes it was the victim of financial warfare launched in 1997."

"You're talking about the currency manipulations that went on."

"Of course. They consider what happened asymmetrical warfare from the West. Since then, they see themselves as needing to come up to speed to remain competitive. I know you're into gray literature. You've accessed a lot of material from the Open Source Center. You must have read the paper put out in '99 by the two PLA colonels…"

"*Unrestricted Warfare.*"

"That's it. The whole thing talks about how China needs to wise up to real world conditions and re-evaluate the concept of warfare."

Nelson quoted the book from memory. "… *'the first rule of unrestricted warfare is that there are no rules, with nothing forbidden.'*"

"Exactly. They call nuclear weapons '*mantelpiece decorations that are losing real operational value.*'" Owen leaned forward to read from his tablet. "They call financial warfare a '*hyper-strategic weapon…easily manipulated …allowing for concealed actions, and is also highly destructive.*'"

"What links CIG+XM to F1E?"

"Opportunity, motive, and a track record that is suspect."

"All right," concluded Nelson. "What's the approach?"

"That's up to you. You might start with one of their analysts. Her name is Jiaying Xianzi. A few months ago she walked into a stake-out set up by Treasury agents. She did nothing wrong at the time but just being there was suspicious so they put her on a watch list. Some of her activities since then have raised a red flag in more ways than one."

"Is that it?"

Owen stood and shut the cover on his tablet. "That's a start. There's a flight at Andrews waiting to take you to New York. For the time being, we'd prefer it if you weren't booked on any commercial rosters."

Nelson stood and followed Owen to the door. "What's with the Little Bird that brought me here? Is there a CAP in effect?"

"I can't say either way."

"Compartments are that tight?"

Owen paused at the door and turned to face Nelson. "You're going to have to trust the process. Remember our discussion about structure."

Nelson bristled. "It was a simple question."

"And you got a direct answer. Do you have a problem with that?"

"I don't know. Why does command and control seem so adversarial?"

"That's your perception, coming from private intelligence."

"I forgot; perceptions are to be created—how did you say? '*By a narrow band of targeted innuendo.*' I must have missed my cue."

Owen seethed. "Listen, this is off the record. I didn't want you for this."

Nelson laughed, "What a surprise."

"The only thing worse than the concept of integrity in private intelligence is a mercenary independent contractor who is so undisciplined that he won't even align with a private intelligence company."

"You jealous?" grinned Nelson. "By the way, are there still fifteen grades and ten steps to the GS pay scale?"

Owen glanced at a black dome camera jutting from the ceiling and lowered his voice. "Care to explain the contracts you completed for Chimaera?"

Nelson thought back to gray areas from his past. Chimaera was a major private intelligence firm he had subcontracted with a few times. Their clients didn't always reveal themselves or their real motives in hiring the firm. Unfortunately, that was not uncommon, even if major corporations were funding the job. To gain a competitive advantage, business leaders were more than willing to approach market research as a covert affair.

Contractors who were assigned those tasks sometimes walked into compromising surprises. Whatever happened, Nelson had cleaned it up and extracted himself, doing the right thing. He had nothing to be ashamed of.

Nelson countered, "Nobody's innocent. Care to explain all the redacted things done in the name of government service?"

"Mercenaries don't belong in an ETC," declared Owen. "We're not here to please the highest bidder."

"Since when? Contractors get a lot of their work from the government. I guess you've forgotten about all of the *green badgers* in Baghdad and Islamabad. Your sanctimonious DHS hires them all the time for chrissakes!"

"I don't care how much experience or connections you have. In my book, you're not worth the risk."

"What's worse, a mercenary who is what he is and does the job he's paid for—or a man sworn to public service but really is a double-agent for the right price? With the low pay and bureaucracy that grunts like you face, I'd say you're the one that's suspect. You're ripe to be subverted."

"Be careful with that kind of accusation."

"Simple question. It's not like I haven't seen it before with others."

"Avoiding criminal and corrupting influences is a top priority of this ETC. If you get on that plane for New York, you better respect that."

"What are you talking about?"

Owen came in close with an intensity that rocked Nelson back. "I'm talking about *The Shadow Class*." Owen read Nelson's confusion but assured him, "You know what I mean."

"I'm not sure I do," prompted Nelson.

He was gratified that his efforts to get Owen worked up was yielding results. One way or another, Owen *was* susceptible to interrogator tactics. Then again, the direction this was going was puzzling if not disturbing.

Was Owen for real or was he playing a role, feeding into what he thought would be Nelson's penchant for conspiracy theories? Either way, in the moment, Nelson needed to play along.

"They don't have a name; they don't want a name," stressed Owen. "I once heard someone call them *NABs*, the *New Age Barbarians*."

Nelson was perplexed. "What about them?"

"You're well aware that NABs control the illicit trade in the world. There are lots of cartels and individual groups, it's not monolithic, but until recently, all of them were content working their side of the street."

"Are you saying they've crossed over?"

"They've reached a point where their net worth gives them global reach. That kind of influence spills over. We see more of them wanting to conduct business across all sectors now. They've begun to appreciate the power and prestige of appearing legit. Vegas went corporate; why shouldn't they?"

"Why? Because the profit margins aren't the same."

"It's not all about profit. They don't need money. Money's the easy part. Their annual take from drugs alone is about $400 billion. From gambling, $500 billion. When you add in racketeering and money-laundering, gun-running, pirated intellectual capital, the sex trade and all the rest, you're looking at $1 trillion in annual revenue."

Nelson sneered, "Tax free with no regulation—without having to buy Congress to get protection."

"There are 227 countries in the world but only 18 of them have GDPs over $1 trillion. These syndicates have a presence everywhere."

"You're saying they want a seat at the table."

"You're damned right. But they don't want to play by the rules."

"Whose rules?" asked Nelson.

Owen ignored the question. "Imagine if their way of doing business starts getting injected into regular business practices. To compete, others will need to follow suit or be out of business. Before long, everyone will have to be a barbarian to survive. No one wants that."

Nelson played with the concept. "According to some conspiracy theories, it's more like established elites don't like competition crashing their party."

"Don't you understand? State terrorists might not be responsible for what happened today. It might be a shot across the bow by crime syndicates who want to set up the granddaddy of extortion schemes."

"Extort from global bankers, billionaire traders, and investment firms?"

"Yes! Pay tribute or suffer more incidents like F1E. If that's the case, the global economy has a dangerous new enemy. You said it yourself—*'we can scramble your screens; now imagine, just as easily, we could have modified them but only slightly.'* Just like 1, 2, 3. The global economy can't function if it allows itself to be taken hostage, not under the threat of shakedowns at the whim of barbarians. There's no question they have the money and resources to hire and incentivize the talent they need to make such a move."

"You don't know this for sure."

"No," admitted Owen. "But we can read the signs. It's a distinct possibility, one we are determined to keep off the evening news."

"But pushing state terrorism on the news is OK, I guess. From what I've heard, you haven't ruled out the possibility that it was a hacktivist protest against Wall Street by some nerd revolutionary group like RAPIER."

"We have to consider all options. There are things about this ETC that present special circumstances, things we've never faced before. I can't go into all of it. We may not know who's behind this yet, but we damned well know to be careful. If the NABs are involved, they won't just clawback your bonus if you cross them; they'll cut your head off and throw it on the dance floor. That's how they conduct business—on both sides of the street."

Owen reached into his pocket and handed Nelson a slip of paper. "Here. It's a quote from that PLA paper, *Unrestricted Warfare*. Something to think about on your flight to New York."

Nelson took the paper as Owen opened the door and rushed out.

Standing with his back to the empty room, Nelson scanned the quote.

"I usually make surprising moves; the enemy expects surprising moves;
but I move in an unsurprising manner this time to attack the enemy.
I usually make unsurprising moves; the enemy expects unsurprising moves;
but I move in a surprising manner this time to attack the enemy."
—Li Shimin, Emperor, Tang Dynasty China, 626 to 649 CE

In the next corridor, Owen swiped his keycard in anger and entered an empty conference room. Punching a secure line active, he dialed a direct number to an extension at the Office of Director of National Intelligence.

"It's Owen," His tone was dutiful. "Briefing's done. Nelson's onboard."

The man's voice was aloof, distracted. "It's up to you to make this work."

"I know." Owen was resolute. "It's all about New Year's. Four weeks is not that far away. Don't worry. I've got this."

7

0000 0000 0111

9:49 pm EST, Friday December 1st

Nelson gazed out the window as the jet lifted into the night. Avoiding the spread of city lights falling below, he stared into darkness. This was a night that would be darker than most. It was a counterintuitive kind of dark, a deep and penetrating void that had things to reveal rather than hide.

Nelson wanted to trust his gut feeling but knew how selective and reserved such a rare and beguiling night could be in choosing those it favored.

The transfer from DIAC had been through frigid air. A touch of arthritis in Nelson's knuckles complained enough to ground him in practicalities. A wave of displacement coursed through him. During the transfer back through Andrews, a security agent had notified him of his hotel reservation in New York. The room was prepaid for a week.

Climbing aboard, Nelson had taken note: the jet had no identifying insignias. It was a plain white jet, the same one that brought him east from Cheyenne with only a required FAA registration number on its tail.

Operational concealment was normal but this time it left Nelson cold. Faced with doubts, he adjusted to the bare facts. He was alone on the flight. His task was open-ended with not much to go on. He was told he'd be part of a cell that would work together, only Hollister and Dystrom were scattered to other cities. He'd been reminded of the value of *structure* but the parameters of the engagement so far was nothing but moving walls and shifting floors.

The pilot and copilot were locked away on the flight deck. The unusual circumstances and isolation gave Nelson time to reflect. What was leaving him so cold? Was it something to do with the ETC assignment, or was it personal?

He had retired from the NCS when the changes he had seen became too much for him. Owen was definitely pulling his chain about distrusting the *mercenaries* of private intelligence. Nelson knew that DNI documents proved that Washington spent over $40 billion a year on private intelligence. That was 70% of the U.S. intelligence budget. Even the head of DNI once chaired the board of the Intelligence and National Security Alliance, the private intelligence industry's trade association.

Unlike the political appointees and bureaucrats who governed the field, having a career for life in a government agency was no longer typical for a professional intelligence asset. For many, government service was nothing more than a stopping point, a place to get CIA or NSA on your resume before going into the more lucrative private service.

Nelson had seen a lot of good people leave government service either on their own or because they were *cashiered* out for not evolving their principles and tactics to fit the times. Despite federal provisions like the Notification and Federal Employee Anti-Discrimination and Retaliation Act, better known as the "No FEAR Act," Nelson had known some who were pressured out and their whistle-blowing attempts within proper channels went nowhere. Reminded of their security oaths all the while threatened with insinuations, they were intimidated into not going to the press or risk prison time or worse.

Over time, a brain drain for higher salaries and rampant outsourcing had hit the government intelligence services. To try to stem the flow, some agencies dabbled in allowing agents to take private assignments on retainer. It wasn't unusual to find CIA *deception detection* experts sitting in on conference calls at Wall Street hedge fund consulting firms while senior managers of prospective investment partners went over quarterly reports.

One of the most troubling issues for governments everywhere was the fact that ex-veterans of NCS service were now working for private companies which had changed management more than once. These intel conglomerates were now owned or controlled by nested front companies incorporated in little known Swiss towns or on out-of-the-way tropical islands. Precisely who these front companies represented was anyone's guess.

Wealthy nation states no longer had exclusive access to the best intelligence. That went to the highest bidder regardless of purchasing motives. At first the highest bids went out to private intelligence firms but over time that changed and they went out to private contractors or the firms who used them. Soon they went to specialists within the private contractor community.

Forever chasing the money, the more experienced NCS assets had become independent contractors. Disenchanted with the overbearing structure and lack of mobility and variety in government service, Nelson had gone the same route. He held no illusions that private intelligence was any more principled than government work but at least by working privately he had more control over the assignments accepted or the repercussions if declined.

He had told himself he wouldn't be micro-managed by dense bureaucrats with suspect agendas. In truth it was mostly about the money. The hidden interests that paid for private work had their own secret agendas. No intelligence work was immune from duplicity. Nelson simply resented being under the thumb of people he disrespected. Now here he was, taking orders from the likes of Owen Raedalus.

The private intelligence industry had matured. Newbies no longer had to start in government service to develop credentials that mattered. To the contrary, government service to some was seen as a detriment. Many thought it was the mark of someone staid in their methods and unoriginal in finding ways to engage. What was needed was someone more dynamic than a *company man* who valued daily routines and easy duty.

Many now choosing government agencies to work for did so because they couldn't get accepted by the private companies. To plug away as a $50k per year analyst for the NSA with locked-in step-levels controlling one's advancement was seen as the consolation prize. Hot new assets in private work could double or triple that amount when salary, bonuses and perks were added up. Given a choice, no one preferred moving up through the GS pay scale.

It made Nelson wonder why someone like Owen Raedalus, who thought of himself so highly, would be content staying in harness in the government yoke. There had to be more in it for him than a high title and yet, stranger things had happened when ego gratification got involved.

Nelson was an independent contractor specialist, although his specialty was more of a character attribute. Nelson was tenacious about his analyses, persistently inquisitive and relentless in driving into a matter to find out where it led. When others were satisfied that the last rock had been overturned, Nelson got an itch to dig for more rocks.

In the past three years, Nelson kept in contact with a close group of buddy assets. Most of whom, like him, had gone from government service to private intelligence companies and had become independent specialists for both.

As Owen had said, one of Nelson's hobbies had been tracking conspiracy theories. Owen had tested Nelson in the briefing about it but Nelson hadn't taken the bait. Either way it was true: while still in the NCS, he had been called on a few times to create or enhance conspiracy theories and float them in key places. At the time, a little disinformation added to the public discourse was deemed necessary. Diffusing the truth hidden in plain sight had been critical in protecting ongoing operations.

Nelson knew from the inside-out how wrong, misguided, or inflated the vast majority of conspiracy theories truly were. But he also knew, when they were right, they wielded a clarifying power, the danger of unpredictability, and a kinetic potential on the grandest of scales. The real advantage was finding a way to discern the difference.

He had seen the unfiltered truth drive some people crazy when no one would believe it to be real. But just as often, he had seen convoluted lies set many free, even rescue a fragile sanity in the world at a time when nothing but lies would move people in the direction of their own best interests.

There was nothing more telling than lies, and many evils often hid behind what everyone accepted as truth. The field of intelligence, like conspiracy theories, was a gray area as ambivalent as the human heart. It would always be that way. There was no such thing as mastery over either one of them.

The suggestion that Owen was serious about assigning Nelson conspiracy theory study as an ETC task made him wonder. It seemed tacked on and thin. It sounded like something Owen had read about in Nelson's file and decided to include in his briefing as an inducement for Nelson to serve, nothing more.

City lights became dots on a miniature world canvas gliding by far below. The strange night flight played tricks with Nelson's moods, leaving him unsettled. His dislike for Owen and the curiosities swirling around the ETC were good enough reasons to take pause.

The feeling of losing himself by returning to government service invariably led back to thoughts about Madelyn and his own mortality. He wondered what life had amounted to. After all he had done in work and his private life, would anything be better because he'd been alive? Was having hope in contributing something enough reason to take this flight?

To fill the void of Madelyn's passing, was he about to risk his life on the one thing he swore he'd never do again? An assignment in private work would not affect him like returning to government IC. He needed to lift himself into a different energy and mindset, one more conducive to the challenges ahead.

Paralysis by doubt and confusion was unlike him. But so was re-immersing himself in the IC world. So was sensing the masking layers of conceit wrapped around Owen. Nelson was headed into a garden maze hidden in a house of mirrors. But his gut told him to wait and see; there might be important work to do, work that no one, least of all him, was in any position to be fully aware of yet. If he turned his back on this assignment now and went home, somehow home might never be the same. For whatever reason, he needed to be here.

The plane banked gently to the northeast. To pass the time, he needed something to get his mind off irksome doubts. An idea came to him, an ironic choice but maybe the thing to set the stage. He pulled out his phone and started browsing the internet. He figured, by the time he got to New York, he could browse the whole array of conspiracy theory portals, blogs, and websites.

Who knows what he'd find. Something might come in handy in the days ahead. Perhaps the truth about what was going on was hiding in plain sight— only designed to look like a lie.

8

0000 0000 1000

4:51 pm EST, Saturday December 2nd

Adam Perez entered the busy corner café with energy to spare but tamped it down as he glanced around at the throng of diners. At any other time this would be a go-to place to meet someone but right then, surrounded by people he didn't know, he felt uneasy, exposed and vulnerable.

He spotted Jiaying sitting by herself at a window and headed her way. She sat intent, texting with phone on lap, but finished up as he approached.

Looking up, her face lit up with anticipation. "How did it go?"

Adam took a seat on a stool opposite her. He spied nearby patrons with passing suspicion before answering, "I'm in."

"See, I told you! So what did they tell you?"

"I don't want to go into it now." He hunched forward in a field jacket with raised collar and adjusted a brimless knit cap back a bit on his head.

"You have to say *something*," complained Jiaying. "When do you start?"

"Now, whenever, it's up to me."

Adam reached across the narrow table and took a sip of her coffee.

"Did they ask you a lot of weird questions, you know, to trip you up?"

"Not really. It was pretty straightforward."

"So where'd they take you? Back to the big board room?"

"No, it was strange. They had this empty corner office with big windows, a killer view. It looked like a spare room. I don't know, it seemed bizarre."

"Why?"

"It's a primo space but it's basically unused. You know the room?"

"No. It must be on a different floor from where I work."

"How many floors are they on?"

Her nervous laugh was brief. "I don't know. So tell me, did you meet with the one guy I told you about?"

"Yeah, one guy but it wasn't the one you said; it was some other guy."

"Who?"

"I don't know; he never gave his name."

"Was he Chinese?"

"I guess but he spoke English like a first language. No accent."

Jiaying noted Adam's subdued manner. "You don't seem pumped up. What's wrong?"

"Nothing's wrong." He reached for her coffee again and kept it in hand, sipping between thoughts. "The whole thing's new to me…I'm getting used to the idea…it seems too good to be true."

"Don't talk like that," scolded Jiaying. "Of course it's true. Why not?"

Cynicism creased Adam's lips into a grin. "Lots of reasons."

"You worry too much."

"It's better than not worrying at all."

"They explained what they wanted, didn't they?"

"Well yeah, the one guy explained it."

"Whatever they want, you must think it's possible. You took the job."

"I know; that's not the point."

"I thought we had this conversation already."

"That was before I said yes."

"It makes no difference."

"Sure it does; I'm on the hook now."

"Wrong," snapped Jiaying. "You're only on the hook if you stay working on the twenty-sixth floor. This is your way out, remember?"

Adam nodded and dropped his gaze to the table. "Yeah, it could be. It could be lots of things. Some of them could bite me in the ass."

Jiaying reached over and took his hand. "You can't think that way. Do what's necessary and get beyond it. There's never any reward unless you risk something. That's the way it works with everything."

"Maybe," countered Adam. "But this would be a big reward. I have no problem with that part."

"Then concentrate on that." She squeezed his hand.

"And what about the big risk?"

"Keep your eye on the prize."

He said nothing but raised a more hopeful gaze her way.

"Besides," she added. "It's summer now in the South Pacific. We need to finalize vacation plans—or maybe reservations."

"Wait up—no celebrating until there's good reason."

"As far as I'm concerned, the hard part's over."

"Oh, really. How do you figure?"

She smiled. "You went in and did it. You got the job. CIG+XM is lucky to have a genius working for them. Finishing it up should be no big deal."

She got a smile in return. His smile didn't last as long as hers but then, she wasn't bearing any of the risk. He glanced out the window, avoiding her eyes, nervous about the days ahead. He could feel every muscle tighten. He was anxious to find out how difficult a task he had taken on.

"I'd better get going." He pulled his hand away and leaned back.

"What about the rest of the day? Are we doing anything?"

Adam stood and pushed in his stool. "You know the answer to that. I have work to do. This is not a regular Saturday."

She pulled her cup back and jiggled it to find it empty. "OK, but you better hurry up. I don't want to spend too many nights alone."

"Alone?" He cracked a grin. "I didn't say you had to stay away completely.

I *will* be taking food and recreation breaks."

"Oh no, nothing to interrupt your focus," she quipped. "I think it's best; until you're done, no bed play."

Adam leaned in near her. "You're holding out on me until I finish this?"

"That's right," she whispered. "None for you—until you're through!"

Adam took a moment to consider the new conditions then nodded, pretending that he took it in stride. He dug hands deep in his coat pockets and turned the tables on her. "Come to think of it, you have a final to study for. That's only two weeks away. You need your own time to focus."

Determined to have the last word on the matter, she raised the stakes. "I bet I'll have my quant certificate before you have me again."

"You don't think I can finish this job in two weeks?"

"The smart odds are against it," challenged Jiaying.

Adam pointed at her with renewed determination. "I'll take that bet."

She hesitated. "If I lose, you get me. What do I get if *you* lose?"

Adam called back as he headed out, "You get your certificate."

She jumped up. "Hey, wait up, I'll go with you."

He paused at the open door. "I'm going to walk home."

"OK, we'll walk."

Adam continued out onto the frosty sidewalk. "I need to work."

"I know. I'm going to my place, not yours. It *is* in the same direction."

Adam shuffled off with Jiaying keeping pace at his side. Saturday traffic on and off the sidewalk was typical for a late winter's afternoon. The sky was overcast but bright. The forecast for later predicted light snow.

Back at the corner, the café door opened again. Out stepped Nelson Geiss. He watched Jiaying and her friend stop a half block away. As they waited at a light to cross the street, Nelson bided his time.

Nelson had acquired Jiaying when she went out for a shopping trip and followed her all afternoon. Her habits appeared normal enough but her meeting at the café caught Nelson's interest. It was her first contact of substance that Nelson had witnessed. Restricted by noise in the café, Nelson had only heard a few words of Jiaying's conversation with the young man. From the give-and-take between them, Nelson got the impression their conversation wasn't all fun and games.

Nelson had already scoped out where Jiaying worked and lived. The main thing now was not letting her contacts get away without checking out what they meant to her. Chances were, whatever she was into had to be carried out both inside and outside of CIG+XM. Until Nelson got a handle on the basic players worth watching, everyone she took an interest in was suspect.

Right now, Nelson needed to take a walk. He followed them several blocks into Midtown. They led him back to the neighborhood where his hotel was located. A couple blocks past the hotel, Jiaying and the man stopped for a brief kiss then split off in different directions.

It looked like Jiaying was headed back to her place. Nelson followed the man to another apartment not far away. As the man entered the lobby, Nelson broke out in the run to catch up. He managed to slip inside in time to hear the man finish his climb up the stairs.

The man's flat turned out to be on the second floor, apartment 2C. Nelson went back downstairs and accessed a reverse lookup app. With address keyed in, the customized app sped through a remote data portal. Within seconds it returned the name of the current resident of apartment 2C.

Adam Perez. Good. Now Nelson had a lead.

He hurried back to his hotel to upload from phone to computer the photos taken at the café of Jiaying and especially those of Adam. After some crops and contrast enhancements, Nelson had a few mug shots of Adam.

Nelson set about leveraging a buddy contact. A name, an address, and these photos would be more than enough. Nelson sent everything off to his friend, a specialist in identities. Unless the subject was hiding behind multiple shell identities, it should be no problem to get a complete record on the man living under the name Adam Perez. Barring any snags, a bundled report should be minutes away.

While he waited, Nelson activated a connection to the bug he'd placed in Jiaying's apartment earlier in the day. He switched on record, turned up the volume, and adjusted filters. Earbuds in place, he listened to music and water running. No one was talking. It sounded like she was taking a shower. Luckily, the squat size of her place allowed one bug to pick up everything.

While Nelson waited, he had time to try calling Dystrom in London again. So far, he hadn't been able to contact Dystrom or Hollister. Dialing, Nelson stepped to the window with phone in hand and waited for someone to pick up.

"Hello?" The voice was deep and terse.

"Dystrom? Mike Dystrom?" Nelson brushed back the sheer curtains and looked down at the regular movement of cars and people on the street below.

"Yes, who is this?"

"Nelson Geiss."

"Finally. I thought you were avoiding me."

"What are you talking about? I've been trying to reach you."

"It might be things on my end," snapped Dystrom. "Some of my calls have been dropping out. I think this part of London has shitty reception."

"Have you talked to Hollister?" asked Nelson.

"Not yet. No reason to. I'm locked in on what has to be done here."

Nelson turned from the curtains. "What kind of briefing did you get?"

"It was quick. A lot of concerns; not many specifics."

"Same here."

"It's rough if they expect daylight on this before Monday."

"I know," agreed Nelson. "Did they give you anything to go on?"

"They gave me a name, a programmer at CIG+XM's office in The City."

"London..."

"Well, yeah, but I mean *The City*, what they call the financial district."

"That's right..."

"If you ask me, the weekend's a bad time to start this shit," declared Dystrom. "Business isn't happening; CIG+XM is closed down. The guy I'm suppose to be watching has only one kind of business on his mind. Watching him pound back Hefeweizen while trying to get laid isn't saving the world."

"I know but it can't be helped. This started on a Friday afternoon."

"So far it feels like I'm wasting my time. How about you?"

Nelson stepped back to his computer and checked his email. "Nothing yet but if anything raises its ugly head, I let you know. Coordination is key."

"I wish like hell I *had* something to coordinate."

"We've got a day and a half to go, plenty of time for something to pop up."

"If you say so but I'm used to having an action to complete, not babysitting duty. Maybe I need the patience of an analyst like you."

"Imagine this as sniper duty," answered Nelson. "Sit tight, wait a day or so. When the time is right, we'll squeeze the trigger on this together, OK?"

Dystrom laughed. "OK, but it'd better be a head shot."

"Talk to you later." Nelson hung up and checked email again. As if on command, a return message from his identity contact popped in unread.

"All right," he said to no one. "Here we go..."

Nelson read the bundled report generated off the name, address, and photos submitted for research. Scrolling through multiple pages, he was pleased.

Twenty-four-year-old Adam Perez had used one alias. It was the avatar or computer handle he'd chosen as a teenager at a time when his brilliance and sense of mischief collided and caused major trouble. That alias was MUTEX.

Nelson knew *mutex* as a computer programming term. Short for *mutual exclusion object*, mutex was a program object allowing multiple program threads to share the same resource, but not simultaneous access. The mutex unlocked when the resource was no longer needed or the routine finished.

The psychology of calling oneself MUTEX could be debated but was telling enough. Adam chose the nexus of action, a controlling point where all actions negotiated to gain access to resources. It was a power position.

According to school and university records, Mr. Perez had all the hallmarks of a phenomenon. His outstanding aptitude in math and computer science was recognized early on and rewarded with prizes and scholarships. His advanced degree with honors from MIT was recent, his job at an investment bank in Manhattan respectable, his enrollment in a class to become a Quantitative Analyst nearly complete. Surprisingly, even the NSA had approached him while in graduate school, trying to recruit him. He turned them down.

While Adam's life seemed normal, his potential to excel in any number of advanced technical positions was off the charts. In no way was he living up to his potential but youth sometimes took a while to find itself.

An episode from early days stood out for its boldness and appearing out of place. Was it youthful indiscretion or a sign of a possible double life to come? As a fourteen-year-old in 2006, Adam was arrested by federal agents after hacking into the inventory databases of the National Archives and Records Administration in Washington D.C. Not a typical teenage accomplishment.

In a sworn deposition, Adam said his interest in the archive began in March 2006 after he read the Archivist of the United States revealed in a public hearing that "*a memorandum of understanding between NARA and government agencies existed to reclassify, meaning withdraw from public access, certain documents in the name of national security and to do so in a manner such that researchers would not be likely to discover the process.*"

Adam said one concept struck him funny—"*in a manner such that researchers would not be likely to discover the process.*" That meant the archive didn't want researchers to know these documents were missing. The archive preferred that citizens didn't know these things ever existed. But why?

He discovered an audit indicating one third of the documents withdrawn since 1999 did not contain sensitive information. That *was* strange. Why hide things *not* sensitive? But Adam was more taken by the fact that the audit indicated that 2/3 of the documents *were* sensitive. Of course that depended on one's definition of *sensitive*. But the idea of there being *any* sensitive data at the National Archives intrigued Adam. He decided to check for himself.

He told agents he thought it'd be an adventure to stumble upon some document that revealed hidden facts about topics puzzling people for years. He could only imagine what gems he might find: eyewitness testimony about the grassy knoll in Dallas—lab reports on a liquid-metal material found at Roswell—descriptions of Lemurian shaman artifacts with magical properties discovered on the ocean floor—or maybe Air Force pay records for the crews of a secret squadron of UFOs that flew in outer space.

Nelson chuckled as he read the deposition. The whiz kid got his fingers burned and promised not to do it again. No doubt the feds didn't want a lot of publicity about the story; no sense highlighting their vulnerabilities or the fact that someone at the National Archive might be up to shenanigans. The Justice Department read Adam and his parents the riot act and threatened major danger if he ever transgressed again. Fly right or the dungeon for you.

According to records, Adam kept clean after that. One time he was pulled in again, two years later when someone using the handle MUTEX launched a denial-of-service attack on a federal drug-enforcement website. Adam denied involvement and evidence hinted that someone else used his avatar.

As Nelson read the report, one disturbing detail caught his eye. There were reports at the time that MUTEX had agreed to do the DOS attack at the request of a certain revolutionary hacktivist group—the one called RAPIER.

9

0000 0000 1001

6:19 pm EST, Sunday December 3rd

Nelson finished off a cold room-service sandwich with his mind on everything but food. He leaned back in his chair and considered Adam's identity report in light of how the day had gone so far.

So what did he have? A technical whiz kid with possible ties to RAPIER living in close with Jiaying Xianzi. It wasn't a smoking gun but as the hour got late, Nelson was desperate for any thread to pull before time ran out.

On the face of it, media rumors about a fringe group of hacktivists finding common ground with state terrorists seemed sensational, the kind of thing that opposition research specialists called *red meat*. It was sure to attract attention away from the hand that was doing the trick. But nothing could be ruled out, not with so little to go on; not this early in the game.

Nelson double-checked the thin dossier Owen had sent to him on the girl. It checked out with Adam's identity report; the two of them shared the same quant class. Maybe theirs was a relationship of lustful convenience or maybe they were study partners. Nelson couldn't wait to find out. It was Sunday evening and markets would open in fifteen hours. He had no choice but chase down what little he had. Why couldn't the truth be sensational?

He looked up Adam's cell phone number from the identity report and plugged it into a GPS tracker already programmed to alert on Jiaying. Whenever she stepped beyond a certain radius of any place she had been at for a while, Nelson got an alert she was on the move. With Adam's number in place, Nelson now had the same trace on both of them.

He grabbed a briefcase from his backpack and opened it on the bed. The case had a false bottom with insurance agent paraphernalia to use if he needed cover. He packed the false bottom with necessary supplies for a trip out. He needed to stop at a store for computer parts, but besides that, he was ready to go. He pulled on a jacket and set a tray of empty dishes on the floor outside his room. It was time to get into position.

Emerging from the hotel's revolving door, Nelson encountered the first few flakes of snow escaping from a brooding sky. His steps were quick and directed. The store was two blocks up and one over. Warm city lights were coming on and the mood of the city was on edge, expectant. Next time the city saw daylight, Wall Street would brave a new trading day.

Nelson navigated the store for computer parts then walked towards Adam's place. Along the way, a GPS movement alert buzzed in his pocket. He kept walking and checked it. It wasn't Adam; it was Jiaying. She was headed downtown in a taxi or had a ride that drove like one.

Nelson continued to a coffee shop near Adam's building. Now it was a waiting game. Chances were that Adam would head out to get something to eat or see friends. Nelson hoped the kid wasn't tucked in for the night. There was one critical piece of business Nelson needed to put into place. It didn't require much time but it had to go undetected.

Minutes passed and Nelson contented himself with sipping mochas and watching the trace on Jiaying's movements. Her ride had dropped her off in the financial district at the same address where CIG+XM had their main office. What she needed to do at the office on a Sunday night was a mystery. Chances were good she wasn't analyzing stocks. Confronted with the inscrutable, Nelson was buoyed; perhaps he was on the right track.

Two hours after settling in at the coffee shop, Nelson's patience was rewarded. Another motion alert buzzed only this time it was Adam on the move. Nelson stayed put until he saw Adam exit the building and head off alone towards Central Park. There was no way of knowing how long Adam planned to be out but Nelson couldn't be choosy. It was now or maybe never.

Nelson headed up to apartment 2C and knocked at the door before letting himself in. The motion tracker placed Adam three blocks up and slowing at an address near several restaurants. Hopefully, he was out for dinner.

Setting right to work, Nelson first placed a bug in a central location. The apartment was similar in size to Jiaying's; one device should be enough.

He double-checked the tracker; Adam's position was holding at the same place. There was a good chance he had gone out for food. Nelson had time.

He set to work on the main task at hand. He located Adam's laptop and sized it up. Flipping open his briefcase, Nelson grabbed a toolkit and necessary supplies and set to work flash-copying Adam's hard drive. As quick as the process was, it took time to cycle through disk sectors. Even waiting a couple of minutes to finish seemed too long.

Nelson was intent upon his work but froze when the GPS motion tracker buzzed again. He snatched phone in hand and had his suspicions verified. Adam was on the move. From the looks of it, he was headed home. What Nelson had hoped would be dinner out had become food-to-go.

Nelson couldn't stop now. He only needed a few minutes to finish up. If Adam returned at the same rate of speed, there should be enough time. Redoubling efforts, Nelson accessed the laptop's operating system and set about enabling remote desktop services. Then he copied over and activated an executable that allowed mirroring of disk read/writes as well as display output.

Nelson kept one eye on the tracker. By the time Adam reached the building, Nelson was done—but he wasn't out of the apartment. He rushed his tools into the false bottom of his case and headed for the door. Before exiting, he turned back and checked for anything left out of place. Things must be left as he found them. That's why he never wore cologne.

Opening the front door, he slipped into the hallway and heard footsteps in the lobby starting up the stairs. Nelson hurried to the staircase and climbed to the third floor. He stayed there until the footsteps reached the second floor. He listened as they found their way into the apartment. When the door to 2C clicked shut, Nelson made it to the lobby and escaped into the night.

Back in his hotel room, Nelson couldn't relax. He had to verify that what he had done actually worked. First he checked the bug and was pleased to be able to listen as Adam finished up his meal and cleaned up afterwards in the kitchen. The bug was helpful but the real test came when Nelson checked if the modifications to the Adam's laptop were working.

Sitting at his computer, Nelson typed commands and setup routines. Coupling the disk copy of Adam's hard disk into an external device tied into his own computer, Nelson was able to link his remote services routines with Adam's laptop. Within minutes, Nelson had a mirrored display of what was showing on Adam's screen within a window before him.

Nelson checked the status of the disk-copied drive. The read/write routine left behind in the BIOS of Adam's machine was functioning. Whatever changes Adam wrote to his hard disk would mirror to Nelson's disk copy. Not only could Nelson look over Adam's shoulder as he worked on his laptop, Nelson would also have a disk record of everything the whiz kid did.

That would be telling one way or another. It would either expose nefarious wizardry driven by evil motives, or disappoint with hours spent at some multiplayer online role-playing game like *World of Warcraft*. Whatever Adam was up to, Nelson hoped he was into it on Sunday nights.

Nelson's phone rang. The number was vaguely familiar. The area code was D.C. so he answered right away. "Hello...?"

"Geiss? Is that you?"

Nelson matched the voice with a friend from the past. "Hollister?"

"I bet you think I dropped off the face of the earth."

"You would if it got you somewhere. What'd you been up to, Zack?"

"Trying to chase down this lobbyist I'm supposed to shadow."

"No luck?"

"He's out of the frickin' country."

"What?"

"Yeah, and most of his staff have time off for good behavior."

"What's up with that?"

"Just what I expected. K Street knows that Congress isn't doing squat before year end, not with Santa coming to town. There's not much more I can do here. Anything happening your way?"

"Maybe. I should know more before midnight."

"Give me a call if you find anything. I'm sitting on my hands here."

"Will do. I have to go." Nelson hung up. First Dystrom, now Hollister. So far, it seemed this ETC was turning out to be a frustrating waste of time.

10

0000 0000 1010

9:38 pm EST, Sunday December 3rd

Adam Perez wasn't sure how to react after one day on task. Now too deep into CIG+XM's special project to deny involvement, he was not far enough along to know the full effort necessary to finish. Time for second thoughts had passed. And yet he was hesitating.

The prospect of moving beyond prep work usually was an exciting time but he didn't feel it. Part of him wanted to press on. Another part wondered if working on the twenty-six floor was not so bad after all.

The walk to get food had done him good. The fresh air and light snowfall had anchored him in something tangible and unambiguous. He felt he could work until midnight. Six hours sleep before work in the morning should be enough. Never having a second job, he wasn't sure how to adjust. Especially tomorrow—Monday, a day every news outlet had circled on its calendar.

Tomorrow, everyone would find out if the trouble returned to the computer screens on Wall Street. Either way, the morning would be a bumpy ride. This might be the worst time for Adam to take this on. Maybe he should have waited until this week was over. But *maybe* didn't cut it anymore.

Adam sat in front of his laptop and considered what had been asked of him. He had only prepared the area; the real work still lay before him. Key to what he was attempting was being proficient at setting up layers of routes and online identities to hide behind. A visit from law enforcement was guaranteed if he didn't do a good job hiding his online activity. Key to this was masking his network signature and the paths he took through routers and switching networks to get to the servers he co-opted as hosts to exploit.

So far the prep work was in place. All that remained was the hacking.

Adam's laughter was scant relief. Having found Goliath, all that was left was to slay him. Hacking was the fun part even if it was the bulk of the job. So far, it didn't feel like fun. Either timidity or a new maturity possessed him. He couldn't enjoy the adventure and not consider possible consequences. He was too aware what could be lost by being reckless, cavalier, or merely unlucky.

He had to push through it. Doubts wouldn't stop him. He was too invested in realizing a dream to turn back now. He scrunched forward, hands hovering over the keyboard. Everything he was told by the man at CIG+XM about the assignment came back to him. He could see him seated in the corner office, the room that wasn't an office at all. The man, sharp in his suit and tie, had feigned friendship but was calculated, professional, and coolly determined.

He told Adam, "The project sounds simple but don't underestimate it."

Adam did more listening than talking, more questioning than answering. It was unlike any job interview he had ever been through.

The man didn't blink for a long while. He warned Adam, "The simpler something is the more difficult it is to execute it flawlessly."

"What exactly do you want done?" Adam had asked.

"Find out everything about Project G at Extasis."

Adam waited for more of an explanation but none was offered.

That was the job. And that was everything Adam knew about the job.

Project G—at Extasis.

It was easy looking up Extasis. Checking out their corporate website netted Adam everything interesting that wasn't of much value to him.

Extasis was a research and engineering firm located in the heart of West Virginia's I-79 high technology corridor. Their website touted a broad range of technical specialties with vague but important-sounding names, names like *advanced concepts and materials*, whatever that meant. As he expected, nowhere on the site did they mention anything related to the fabled Project G.

Adam didn't like his curiosity thwarted. It annoyed him to be told there was something he couldn't know. If information was worth hiding, it was probably worth his interest. The fact that Extasis was hiding something as important as Project G struck a nerve in him. He didn't like being told no.

He set to work testing the firewalls and other defenses of the Extasis intranet and exploring weaknesses in how internal nodes met the extranet. Where the outside world met their inside world, he probed for a way in.

One would think hi-tech corporations would have top-notch systems, which was true, but it was also true that the more complicated systems got, the more ways they could go wrong. Technology made everyone more vulnerable, not only because we'd become dependent and be lost without it. There were many more ways of hacking a text message from a smart phone than hacking a scribbled note passed on a slip of folded paper.

Adam concentrated on the complicated system parts, those he knew were cutting edge and fresh from development. They probably hadn't been patched with the latest updates for such systems, which were many. Fortunately, even if systems had been patched at their latest rev-levels, no system was prepared to protect itself from new bugs in its code, bugs just discovered. All Adam needed was a wiggle room and he'd have daylight into their systems.

As he worked, he couldn't help but assume Project G was some sort of Project Gizmo. It made sense that CIG+XM was more interested in that gizmo than Extasis. Extasis wasn't some think tank or market research outfit spouting white papers or demographic charts. They actually made stuff, hi-tech stuff, the kind of stuff that found its way into new products.

It was a good bet they were developing some new Gizmo that investment bankers would be happy to have progress reports on. Knowing how feasible a new technology was before it went public would yield an advantage for those with money and companies to shift into place and leverage.

Just like an artillery drill, position and timing was everything.

Before 11 pm, Adam found a way in. He knew it was a matter of time but noted the milestone anyway when he slipped through a crack where outside field reps retrieved their internal emails. He thanked the rapid development of smart phones as all-purpose objects for adding complexity. On the downside, the robustness of the latest tunneling protocol over VPN connections was proven suspect.

Once in, he wasted no time getting familiar with the lay of the land—or, as he smiled to himself, the lay of the LAN. Like most corporate behemoths, the local area network and internal infrastructure configurations at Extasis were divided by silo, business group, application dependency, and practical realities of available datacenter space. All of it was ever-evolving and required constant restacks and adjustments to keep proper connections. That shifting landscape constituted another issue with complexity ripe for exploratory adventures.

Sensitive network areas had been cordoned off behind electronic gate-keepers charged with the duty of allowing two-way traffic on the inside but only one-way traffic on the outside. Chances were Project Gizmo was being kept safe within one of these loner inner sanctums. Approaching any of them was risking detonation of a security landmine. Adam didn't want to mount the effort to breach until he determined which one contained the right Gizmo. Which one concerned Project G?

How could he find that out? He had only one thing to go on—the letter G.

He already had the run of Extasis email servers as an Enterprise Admin, so why not search for Project G in company emails? For the hell of it, he ran a search and netted what he expected—nothing. No way was it going to be that easy. The possibility that Project G was named Project G asked too much.

Now that the exercise in futility was over, he confronted facts. The first answer was not always the wisest, especially if the first path was the easiest to travel but it led to quicksand. Searching email with nothing but a single letter of the alphabet to go on sounded like one of those stress questions from a quant interview. Either that or it was a perfect way to stump AI computers.

Tackling volumes of email with so little to go on would produce a cumber-some search space that even brute-force techniques wouldn't know how to handle. That's where algorithms came in. As quick as Adam could say Alan Turing, he gave himself a brain teaser. How could he whittle down the problem? The real trouble involved everything that needed to be excluded; so many words began with the letter G. Maybe he should try the most accurate heuristic of them all—human intuition. He could simply make an educated guess which G-words didn't matter and search on all the ones that were left.

He found a comprehensive online dictionary and copied every word beginning with "G" then put those words in a plain file. He scanned through the list, looking for any G-word that didn't conjure up something obvious and mundane. When he found one, he deleted it. In fifteen minutes he had reduced the assortment to a list of all G-words he guessed *wouldn't* be important.

Gabfest, *Gaia*, and *Gallbladder* stayed in.

Genome, *Geothermal*, and *Gyrostatics* were cut.

Now all he had to do was write a script that searched all emails for instances of G-words and return G-word passages from emails that contained G-words not on his revised list. To refine the search space, he coded to search emails flagged with high importance first. To trap new words the dictionary didn't know about, he had the script compare the complete and revise word lists against the emails and return on G-words missing from both.

As it turned out, it wasn't such a brain teaser after all. He ran the script and watched for output to begin posting in an active response window on his laptop. Where there were hits, the script returned G-words along with fifty characters found before and after the word. The excerpted passages gave the gist of the topic and from context he could infer why the email was sent.

It was nearly midnight when the script stopped running and Adam finished reviewing the output. The hardest part was deciding if anything was worth following up. A handful of words showed up that could be part of some hidden project. None of the excerpts gave anything away that sealed the deal one way or another. Once again, Adam was left with trusting his gut feelings. He read individual passages over and over trying to glean subtext and innuendo in the choice of language and the caginess with which it was being delivered.

It was late and the snowfall was a bit heavier now. Morning would come quickly. He didn't have to figure this all out before going to bed no matter how much it gnawed at him. Even so, he sat at his computer, unable to let it go. He felt he was so close. It would be such a major coup if he could at least end the night knowing what was meant by the letter G.

The quiet of nighttime gathered around him. He sat slouched in his chair and stared at the blinking cursor in the active results window. The insistence of the tireless blinking mocked him for freezing up, for being uncertain.

But he *was* certain. He'd been arguing with himself all around the point for half an hour but one excerpt did stand out. It struck him as being the one. Its confidential tone and furtive subtext was obvious. Its G-word had only returned once; perhaps it was an oversight that it even got through in unrestricted email. After searching all of it, he did have a word.

The word was *GRAPHENE*.

For the next half hour, he searched company fileservers for the word but it wasn't found. The context of the message made the absence irregular. That only left one place it could be—within one of the protected inner sanctums.

11

0000 0000 1011

12:13 am EST, Monday December 4th

One hotel room on the fifth floor still had its lights on. Seated at the desk with laptop open, Nelson Geiss squinted tired eyes and watched remote activity on Adam's screen. In a separate window, Adam's email search script was open for study. In a third window, an article from a science magazine described the history and nature of the substance called Graphene.

Nelson could tell that Adam was shutting down connections for the night. Keeping an eye on what Adam was doing, Nelson scanned the science article.

Graphene was a wonder material first identified in October of 2004. A form of carbon only one atom thick, Graphene was a two-dimensional honeycomb structure 100 times stronger than steel that conducted electricity better than copper. Only 1% of Graphene mixed into plastics turned them into electrical conductors. Resembling millions of unrolled nanotubes stuck together, Graphene had been heralded as a wonder material when also found to have a self-repairing process. Plenty of pure research was underway to discover the properties of Graphene. Many practical applications were expected from understanding the nature and behavior of the material.

Nelson finally had a line on criminal activity going on within the sphere of influence of his mark, Jiaying Xianzi but so far the crimes seemed to have nothing to do with F1E. If all Nelson was chasing down was a kid hacking into Extasis to snoop on Graphene R&D, then Owen had some explaining to do. Nelson could explain away the dead ends Dystrom and Hollister encountered in London and D.C. if what they were all after was in New York.

But how was Graphene applicable to the ETC?

Time was of the essence. The stock market would open in nine hours. Could it be that Owen wasn't sharing news from other cells? Given what Nelson had, there was no way to be certain that the disruptions of F1E wouldn't happen again. ETC priorities were untouched; negative public perceptions weren't mollified and the perpetrators were still at large, presumably capable of acting out again.

Owen's last contact had been early morning but there was no update for Nelson and Nelson had nothing new to offer him. Owen had asked about leads from reviewing conspiracy theories. Despite researching on the flight to New York, Nelson had found nothing. Conspiracy theories were too predictable most of the time. Owen's concern rang hollow anyway.

In the late hour, Nelson's unease had an edge. It felt like his cell was staged for something else with the actual operation due later. But that was ludicrous.

What could an uncoordinated cell like Nelson's ever be in position for? Yes, it was possible that Owen had to cast a broad net quickly and many of those leads would not pan out. Perhaps Nelson's cell was simply chasing leads that amounted to nothing. That wasn't all bad. Proving an ominous area was not a problem was valuable too.

Nelson fought back exhaustion and a tinge of healthy paranoia. It wasn't surprising to be suspicious of the competency or motives of government bosses but after the buildup of the briefing, Nelson expected more. Maybe he needed to dig deeper for more rocks. He reached for the phone. It was early on the west coast. Time to get a second opinion.

Geri Messare was a fair-weather friend and fellow contractor who had worked with him before. She was a sophisticated firebrand, a beautiful brunette avenger, a woman of means by inheritance who could have spent her life lounging on pink-sand beaches while cabana boys attended her every need. Instead, she had parlayed a globetrotting lifestyle into a refined private intelligence practice. She liked the adventure. She enjoyed being on the inside, knowing what others didn't. More than that, she loved the high-energy men it brought her in contact with.

Her resume included a stint in the Special Collections Service, a specialized group within the Central Security Service of the NSA. The existence of the SCS wasn't officially recognized by the agency although the group was chartered to find creative ways to combine spies with techies.

Nelson caught her on the second ring. "Geri, it's Nelson Geiss. Do you have a minute?"

There was sudden adjustment, then humor in her voice. "Nelson, now what could you be up to that's only going to take a minute?"

Nelson dodged the innuendo; she was famous for them. Despite years of flirting, she had never gotten Nelson in the sack. She knew he was faithful to Madelyn which made the game play between them all the richer for her. Nelson had never taken her advances as serious and she'd never let on whether or not they were. Nelson didn't see himself as her type. Then again, she was a mystery in many ways. There was one thing for certain: she took pleasure in playing that mystery for all it was worth.

"I'd like to get your take on something."

"Is that all? Well, I love giving my opinion. What is it?"

"A company called Extasis came up on my radar. Should I be interested?"

"That depends," she stalled. "What's the fascination?"

"Are they doing anything that China would be interested in?"

"China? They're interested in everything."

"Some things more than others."

"Yes…well…" It sounded like Geri was walking as she was talking. "I've heard of the company but nothing about it has been shaking of late."

"When *was* it shaking?"

"The end of last year, if I remember correctly."

Nelson sensed his minute was about up. "So what was the deal?"

"Who knows? It was a black hole; something massive was there even though no one claimed to see anything. Let's just say the event horizon around Extasis has been sharply defined."

"Explain," prompted Nelson. He knew what she meant but hoped to gain insights by hearing her clarify it. It was a long shot but he had to try.

"Maybe you should check with Chimaera. They did work for Extasis around that time. If anyone knows what's behind the curtain, they would."

With Geri's deflection, Nelson knew the conversation was over. Either she couldn't or wouldn't go into the subject. Some things were so sensitive that it wasn't wise to volunteer information even if only rumored, even to friends.

"Is the CEO still Aubrey Marks?"

"Yes, she works out of their main office in Alexandria."

Nelson knew enough not to overstay his welcome. "Thanks for the tip."

"No problem. It's good hearing from you, Nelson. It sounds like you're working again."

"Yes, something came up out the blue."

Their cell connection weakened. "Where are you?"

"New York."

"It must be important to get you off your ranch."

"That's to be seen. I'd better go; we're breaking up."

"Don't be a stranger."

The phone call ended. Nelson had whetted Geri's interest and her black hole comment was of interest to him. Something was going on at Extasis.

People in intel knew it not by what they saw but by all the places where nothing was seen. Contractors lived or died by knowing what was going on. One never knew when a tidbit of information about someone else's job would overlay theirs. For a wide-field perspective, contractors sometimes comped services to each other in exchange for data on the another's assignment. Networking was the lifeblood of a private asset but even friends had to be careful.

Geri's deflection was the best suggestion she could make and still keep her distance. Chimaera was a private intel firm with serious connections and global reach. Its headquarters in Alexandria, Virginia was sometimes referred to as "Langley South." It was closer to Andrews and the Defense Intelligence Analysis Center than Langley. Across the Woodrow Wilson Memorial Bridge and a short run along the Capital Beltway and a Chimaera CEO could be at DIOCC for in-person briefings in no time.

Nelson had worked only one job for Chimaera. That was years ago and as close to government work as one could get without collecting a pension. Chimaera's assets swung between corporate and government service so much that the lines between them no longer mattered.

Nelson had known Aubrey Marks long before she advanced through the ranks to capture the CEO position. Some falsely claimed that her husband had something to do with her meteoric rise. It was true Richard Marks left the CIA to assume special assignment work for the Office of the Director of National Intelligence, ODNI, but that was after she had been tapped to lead Chimaera.

They had been a formidable force before their divorce. Richard was near the top of the org chart for government intelligence and Aubrey commanded the top job at a premiere private firm. Their split was seen by some to coincide with a cooling of the relationship between corporate and government interests. Others thought that was reading too much into it; U.S.A. Inc. was intact. Either way, something had changed.

Nelson's phone rang. It was Hollister in D.C.

"Zack, what's up?"

"Checking in before I turn in for the night."

"I may have something," noted Nelson. "Check around and see if anyone's talking about a company called Extasis. Also, see what you can dig up about a new material called Graphene." Nelson spelled it out. "I know what it is; now I need what's being done with it. For some reason, Beijing is interested in both."

"All right," agreed Hollister. "It'll give me something to do. You know, lobbying money has to be reported; that's why $6 billion is spent in D.C. on 'consulting.' Legally, consulting isn't lobbying so me being assigned to follow a lobbyist around is a fucking waste of time. Whatever CIG+XM is doing on the Hill, you can be sure it's not going through the front door on K Street."

"Yeah, I thought about that too. It's strange. On this Extasis thing, be careful. We need to find out without spreading it around."

"That's always the trick, isn't it?"

"Whatever's happening, it might have been hot last year."

"This'll take time. What about markets opening in a few hours?"

"I don't know," confessed Nelson.

"It's one thing to go after an Advanced Persistent Threat but the way it was sold to me, I thought the threat was imminent."

"I don't think they know. They're assuming the worst just in case."

"It's a hell of a way to mobilize people. It's a fire drill in a cloud of smoke, if you ask me."

Nelson was tired. He'd already had this argument with himself earlier. Revisiting doubts was nonproductive at this point. He was in no mood for a pissing contest with Zack. "We'll find out what happens in a few hours."

"Another thing," Hollister persisted. "I checked into it and CIG+XM was incorporated in Delaware."

"What of it?"

"Well, corporations have the nationality of the nation in which they incorporate. If they incorporate in the U.S., they're a U.S. *person*, even if the corporate stock is foreign-owned."

"Yeah, I know," laughed Nelson. "That makes the Central Committee of the Communist Party of China a U.S. *person* with full rights. Bizarre, isn't it."

"Yeah, so technically we're spying on a U.S. person."

"But ETCs don't have limits. We're beyond Advanced Persistent Threat."

"You're right," agreed Hollister.

"Besides, if a corporation openly acknowledges it is directed and controlled by a foreign government, they're fair game."

"CIG+XM hasn't done that," shot back Hollister.

"You think technicalities like that matter with Site R activated?"

"Who said anything about Site R?"

"That's what I was told at my briefing."

Zack riled up. "Now wait; that doesn't make any fucking sense. I'm in D.C. and I don't see any evidence that the continuity of the federal government is being moved to a mountain in Pennsylvania."

"You see nothing; what does that prove?" groaned Nelson. "When I was in D.C., there must have been a CAP in effect but you wouldn't know it."

"A CAP? How does that fly? Air traffic out of National and Dulles is normal. Small private aircraft are flying with normal restrictions."

"Maybe, but I got a ride to DIAC in a fully-armed Little Bird."

For Zack, the image didn't register. "What the hell is going on?"

Nelson watched as Adam Perez's laptop screen went into hibernation mode. "I guess that's what they want us to find out."

"It doesn't add up. Do you think any of this makes sense?"

"You know how it goes; it has no logic at the beginning. They'll want us to connect the dots at the debriefing afterwards. Let's see what happens in a few hours. Meanwhile, see what you can find out about Extasis and Graphene. It's the one thing we've got to go on."

"All right." Zack hung up.

Nelson sat slumped in his chair. Geri Messare was right; Chimaera was be the key. Its CEO could drive to the heart of the matter. Aubrey Marks had to know about Extasis or at least know people who did. A simple phone call wouldn't impress what was at stake. He needed face-time with her.

Nelson returned to his laptop and searched the Amtrak schedule. A three o'clock train left Penn Station headed for D.C. He could be there at seven in the morning. That gave him two and a half hours before the stock market opened. It wasn't much time but at this point it was his only play.

He looked up Aubrey's cell phone number. It was private but that didn't mean he couldn't get it. Sending a message to her private line would leave the first impression. He needed to get her attention.

"Aubrey: Arrive DC 7 am. Need 1 minute. Critical. Nelson Geiss."

Nelson sent the message then checked the time. He had an hour and a half to get to Penn Station. There was time enough left to review the recording he started earlier in the day on the bug in Jiaying's apartment.

Morning wasn't far away. He'd sleep on the train.

12

0000 0000 1100

7:51 am EST, Monday December 4th

The taxi turned off of K Street onto 21st Street NW and headed south towards George Washington University's Foggy Bottom Campus. Crossing Pennsylvania Avenue, it wasn't immediately obvious that the university was all around. The neighborhood looked commercial, as if dotted with well-maintained office buildings. Regular city streets and sidewalks ran between them. On this day, the sidewalks were adorned with the bare trees of winter.

The taxi driver pulled to the left and double-parked in front of a newer red brick building set back from the street. "Here it is. 805 21st."

Nelson got out and paid. Across the street a trickle of foot traffic headed in and out of the Marvin Center, GWU's student union. Nelson turned back to the brick building behind him. A campus map said it was the Media and Public Affairs Building. Nelson went up the steps and headed for the main entrance. Before he could get there, a man in a suit exited the building and approached.

"Mr. Geiss?" Nelson nodded. "Right this way…"

Nelson was escorted inside and up to the sixth floor. There the two of them entered a door with no distinguishing marks. The door appeared to be a back door to a larger space with this side nearly vacant. Nelson followed the man to a multi-purpose office. It was functional, generic, austere. Nelson assumed it was time-shared by several, unrelated people. Behind the desk, deep in thought, sat Aubrey Marks. She read through something on her phone and flipped through pages with the swipe of a finger.

She looked up at Nelson but addressed his escort first. "Wait outside. See that we're not disturbed."

The suited man retreated with a dutiful nod and closed the door.

Aubrey slipped her phone in the pocket of her tailored coat.

"Nelson, it's been a long time. How are you?"

Nelson leaned forward to shake her hand. "I'm well. At the moment, pretty busy. How about yourself?"

She hesitated, giving the question due consideration. "I'm good."

Nelson sat down across from her and glanced around. He assumed he was being recorded but expected as much.

Aubrey crossed her legs and struck a thoughtful pose. "You said you needed one minute. Something was critical. What can I do for you in sixty seconds?" Unapologetically to the point, her abrupt statement put him on notice that she wasn't convinced their meeting was a good idea.

"I can tell you what it's about in sixty seconds. Based on that, you can decide how much time you'd like to spend."

"Fair enough." She waited. Her straight blonde hair hung to her shoulders. Her on-guard demeanor remained solidly in place. They'd worked together years ago as friends but there should be no mistaking friendship for gullibility.

Nelson gave his pitch. "I'm working on something with high priority. It's time-sensitive. I have reason to believe a world power is interested in Extasis Corporation. In particular, their interest may involve a substance called Graphene. I know that Chimaera has done work for Extasis in the past. You might even be working for them now. Either way, national security is involved. I need to find out why Extasis is so important all of a sudden."

Nelson stopped. He didn't want to exceed his sixty seconds.

"Is that it?" she asked.

"That's my sixty seconds. I came down from New York this morning to get your answer." He wasn't holding anything back—well, a couple of things, but that was savvy negotiation.

"My answer to what?"

"What do I need to know about this?"

"I can't answer a question like that," she shot back. "It's too general. Unfortunately, any other question would be too specific. I'm afraid I can't offer anything that would be of much help."

"I'm not asking you to cross lines of confidentiality."

She was graciously amused but coy. "I appreciate that."

"I know Extasis has a vested interest in keeping its research under wraps. I don't expect you to give away trade secrets."

"If you realize that, then you already know why someone would be interested in them. You don't need to know *what* to know *why*."

Nelson felt his opportunity slipping away. He had to press the point home otherwise he'd be shown the door. "If there's any chance their work involves F1E, I *do* have to know *what*. That's what it comes down to."

"F1E," repeated Aubrey as she froze. "The Friday the 1st Event?"

"Yes."

"What does F1E have to do with this?"

Nelson leaned forward. "You're asking *my* question."

"I don't see the connection."

"Neither do I; that's what's peculiar. Extasis may not be the main thing in this but somehow I think it's related."

"How? What makes you think so?" asked Aubrey.

"The timing of what's gone on and the location of the players."

Aubrey probed. "That's not enough."

"And that's why I came to see you."

"You're playing a hunch, nothing more."

"Let's just say it's critical that I play that hunch."

Aubrey stood. "I'm sorry. I can't help you."

Nelson was forced to play what he had held in reserve. He was gambling it would get her undivided attention.

He dropped it casually. "Even if it involves Project G?"

Caught off-guard, Aubrey's reaction told Nelson what he needed to know. If Project G wasn't significant, she wouldn't have stopped so suddenly and she knew it. For Aubrey, there was no point trying to pretend anything else.

She locked eyes with him. "Don't go fishing in troubled waters."

"I'll be careful." He didn't flinch.

"Care to share where you get your information?" She sat back down.

"We might be able to work something out."

She leaned back and folded her arms. "How invested are you in this?"

"I'm in for the duration."

She tried reading how much was acting and how much was sincere. "Are you working alone?"

He shook his head. "There are many more where I came from."

"Are you willing to work with me on this?"

Her offer seemed genuine even if her motive wasn't clear. "I'll work with anyone who doesn't present a conflict of interest."

"What specifically are you after?"

"No more F1Es."

"Is that it?"

"That's it."

"Well, there's no conflict of interest there. The problem is, I don't see any overlap either."

"Let me be the judge of that. This is time-sensitive. An hour from now, the markets open for trading. Anything new you have could make the difference."

Aubrey fought against her natural defensiveness. "Your urgency doesn't waive my responsibilities. There are many things I can't tell you."

"Then let's concentrate on the things you can tell me."

"All right." Aubrey considered her options. "I don't know if this is helpful, but any work Extasis has done that Chimaera knows about was the result of their In-Q-Tel contracts."

"Including Project G?"

She hesitated. "All of them."

Nelson took it in. In-Q-Tel was a private, non-profit spinoff of the CIA. It was a venture capital firm that invested in high-tech companies on projects with a single focus—keeping the Agency and other intelligence services equipped with the latest technology in support of the United States intelligence mission. The firm admitted to yearly above-board investments of around $40 million. No one except top insiders knew the actual amount.

Nelson pushed the issue. "So it's reasonable to conclude the government is developing Graphene into something they want kept under wraps."

Aubrey pressed for more. "Who exactly is interested in this?"

"Beijing." Nelson gauged her reaction. "Were you aware they even knew?"

Aubrey shook her head but her mind seemed somewhere else.

Nelson rushed to follow up. "You're surprised it wasn't someone else. Am I reading that correctly?"

Aubrey looked away and remained silent. Nelson could tell this was hard for her. She desperately wanted any information he had but wasn't sure how much she should give away in return. She looked back to him a long time before speaking.

"I've had my suspicions," confessed Aubrey.

"About whom?"

Aubrey held the name at the tip of her tongue before letting it go.

"Christina Parish."

"Who is that?"

"You don't know?"

Nelson returned a single shake of the head.

Aubrey was surprised. "You need to get better acquainted with your trade space. She's the Chief Operating Officer at Extasis."

"What kind of suspicions do you have?"

"The kind that aren't actionable. She's had a torrid romance that started the end of last year. He's a well-connected European."

"His name?"

"Liam Bargeau."

"What's wrong with romance? Is he the risk?"

"Probably not but I have my hunches too. I don't see them well-matched."

"How?"

"She's much older; he's too rich and available. If one were jaded, you'd have to conclude there has to be something else in play."

"You think he could get to Project G through her?"

"She's COO; why not?"

"What's in it for him?"

She shrugged. "Like I said, I've had suspicions, nothing more."

"What does he do?"

"His work?" Aubrey collected her thoughts. "He has many roles. I know he used to be a G20 sherpa representing the European Central Bank."

Nelson showed interest but inside he was wondering how this applied. He hoped Aubrey wasn't spinning a tale of unrelated but interesting-sounding facts so she could appear to be cooperating. A G20 sherpa was highly placed but seemed far afield of the topic at hand.

Sherpas were a specialized breed of technical expert in international finance who also needed to be diplomatic bureaucrats. They assisted heads of state before and during international conferences by handling much of the legwork and drafting the communiqués that followed each meeting.

Nelson knew he had overstayed his sixty seconds. He changed the subject.

"Does Chimaera have current contracts with Extasis?"

"With Extasis?" Aubrey considered the question a little too long.

Aubrey having to repeat the name seemed unnecessary to Nelson.

She continued, "No. They put together their own team to replace us. We haven't been able to get a line into the make-up of that group since it started earlier this year."

"Have you tried asking Richard?" The mention of Aubrey's ex-husband was sure to test her nerve but Nelson didn't care; he needed every rock overturned. Every reaction, all of her body language was telling him things.

Aubrey let out a slight laugh. "Richard? We're friendly for the sake of the children. I seriously doubt I could consider him a professional resource. He takes his title too seriously to ever jeopardize it by *colluding* with me." It was her turn to change the subject. "So what about China? What makes you so sure they're after Extasis?"

"They've recruited talent to do just that."

"You know this for a fact?"

"Yes."

"What's the conduit?"

"An investment firm in New York. CIG+XM."

"They're financing the operation out of investments?"

"Investments derived from a sovereign wealth fund."

Aubrey nodded her understanding.

Nelson asked, "Is it OK to contact you again?"

"Yes, but use my private line…" She gave him an amused and knowing look. "…like you did this time."

"I guess it's useless asking what Extasis is doing with Graphene."

"You've answered your own question. We're making progress."

"Who has the tighter lid on it, Extasis or In-Q-Tel?"

"Does it matter?" A moment of intensity came over her as if Nelson was missing the point she had offered between the lines. She stood and came around the desk to speak in hushed tones. Rushing hand into pocket, she accessed something. Nelson assumed she turned off the recording device.

"You need to understand, Project G is the tip of the iceberg. It was one small piece, farmed out at the last minute only to get things done. The rest never went out for bid; it was all in-house. Yes, they made it look like the money was In-Q-Tel's but they had to do that to be expedient. The Agency already had a system in place to award contracts to sanctioned companies. They piggybacked on the Agency's process. It was all about keeping to the timetable. No one knows who was behind Project G and, more importantly, no one wants to ask. You said you're going to be careful. You'd better be."

Her frankness stunned Nelson. She turned from him and started gathering up her things to leave. Her sudden actions inferred she had said too much.

"I consider you a friend. I don't want to see you get hurt."

Nelson could see her masking emotion. "I appreciate that."

She forced her demeanor back on business. "I have a meeting in a few minutes. We need to go."

Nelson stood. "You conduct business on a university campus?"

"Business is everywhere; you know that."

Nelson paused. "On the train down here, I was looking at the university website. One of the banners on the main page caught my eye."

She hesitated, relieved to hear lighter conversation. "Why is that?"

He watched for her reaction. "It said, '*Before you can run the world, you have to learn how the world runs.*'"

Tightening up, she opened the door. "Oh that, yes, I've seen that. It also says, '*For those who live for change, life will never be the same.*'" Her mood darkened. "Take care, Nelson. Remember, my private line only."

With that, she rushed away.

The suited man lagged behind to escort Nelson out of the building. Once Nelson was outside, the man turned and went back inside. Nelson stood a moment in the cold air, taking it all in. It was telling that neither the escort nor Aubrey had left the building.

Nelson started to walk. He strolled to the corner of 21st and H Streets. The newer brick building he had left sat at the corner and spanned down both streets. He decided to take a walk going east on H Street. It would take him past the other side of the building and a pair of non-descript rollup doors watched over by security cameras. He merely glanced at them as he passed.

805 21st Street NW was the Media and Public Affairs Building for GWU.

But 2035 H Street NW was the Office of Public Affairs, CIA.

Same building. Like Aubrey said, there was only one world for business.

13

0000 0000 1101

8:41 am EST, Monday December 4th

For Nelson, the plan was to go see Zack Hollister before hopping on a train back to New York. The International Monetary Fund was down the street at 19th and Pennsylvania Avenue. Nelson reached for his phone. It would take a few minutes for the cab to get there. Meanwhile, the brisk walk would do him good. He needed to burn off some unsettled energy.

He quickened his pace and dialed the cab company. His gaze shifted to the frosty grass of University Yard across the street. Before the number could connect, a black town car turned the corner at 20th Street NW and zoomed to a stop beside him. The passenger door opened and a security agent sporting a narrow black tie and trench coat got out.

"Get in the car, Mr. Geiss." The agent opened the back door as if Nelson's cooperation one way or another was a foregone conclusion.

Nelson canceled the call and stuffed phone in pocket. He stopped and turned but held his ground. "I have an appointment."

"You'll need to reschedule it."

Nelson reached again for his phone.

"Later," the agent ordered. He unbuttoned his trench coat.

Nelson relented and got in the car. The door was shut, the agent got in, and the driver kept at or below the speed limit on their way across town.

To Nelson's surprise, the town car took a direct route to Arlington National Cemetery. Entering cemetery grounds, the driver dropped their pace to a crawl. Rolling along winding roads, they stopped once at a guard checkpoint. The driver flashed credentials and the town car was let through. Nelson couldn't imagine where they were going. The mystery deepened as they turned down Roosevelt Drive and parked near the Tomb of the Unknown Soldier.

The security agent got out and opened the rear door for Nelson. He turned in the direction of the tomb and the Memorial Amphitheater beyond.

"Let's take a walk."

Nelson got out and followed along. The morning sun was bright as it filtered through the trees. The promise of possible warmth from the light was a stark contrast to the cold air hugging the ground.

Visitors willing to brave the winter weather were few at this time of day. The two of them appeared to be alone, surrounded by a peacefulness that belied the horrific events that had made such a place necessary. Nelson had friends buried here; any visit for him would always be personal.

After a minute of walking, Nelson caught sight of a man with his back to them. The security agent slowed his pace and let Nelson advance on his own. As the man turned, Nelson discovered it was Owen Raedalus. Measuring his next steps with annoyance and wonder, Nelson dug hands into coat pockets and slowed his pace. Saying nothing, he forced Owen to engage him.

Owen was as much concerned as disappointed. "You're a long way from CIG+XM, aren't you?"

"Just following leads," answered Nelson.

"Aubrey Marks?" Owen smiled away his distain and irritation then took a couple paces away. When Nelson didn't answer, Owen turned back to him. "Was she helpful?"

Nelson stood his ground. "It's yet to be seen."

Owen gave a nod and took a step nearer. "I appreciate your due diligence but suggest you narrow your focus back onto the assignment."

"Wherever it leads?" asked Nelson.

"Whatever that is, it doesn't require you leaving New York."

"Why the short leash?"

"I don't have time to explain."

"Even if it's imprudent not to? How do you expect your cells to operate under these conditions."

"I expect them to follow orders. If you have leads, you should clear them with me before sharing them with people like Aubrey."

"What makes you think I shared anything?"

"You have to ask that question?" Owen held his gaze on Nelson.

Nelson shook his head in disbelief. "Give *me* the assets you have watching me. I'll put them to work on the real task."

"What do you know about the *real* task?"

"Just what you told me. Are you holding back something?"

Owen said nothing. Nelson waited while Owen considered what to say but Nelson couldn't wait that long.

"I don't expect to know everything. But I need to know enough."

"You have enough to go on," answered Owen.

"Really? Dystrom is in London with nothing solid. No one told us the lobbyist Hollister is after would be out of town. The dossier on Jiaying is thin. I didn't get one on CIG+XM. I found out on my own they're incorporated in Delaware of all places."

"Doesn't matter. They're controlled by a foreign government."

"So, despite being a U.S. person, we're all OK. Is that it? There's always an exception to the rule. Fine, then tell me, what other exceptions are in play? I need to know before I take my cell forward into this."

Owen appeared disgusted. "The whole thing is an exception."

"What the hell is that supposed to mean?" Nelson looked around. "And what's the point of bringing me here of all places? Your sense of the dramatic is in bad taste but I doubt you have the capacity to recognize it."

"I thought it might drive home the seriousness of what we're doing."

"No," snapped Nelson. "I resent you using this place this way. Look around. Does this look like a conference room for one of your shady deals?"

Owen watched Nelson's temper flare and then subside. "They told me about you. I assumed they were exaggerating."

Nelson's breath became steam in the frigid air. "They? While we're at it, do you want me to tell you about *them*?"

"I'm sure we don't have that kind of time. Markets are going to open in less than thirty minutes and you won't be there. You're here. At the key time that CIG+XM may be making their moves, where are you? Hundreds of miles away chasing tangent leads to nowhere."

"Want to know what I think? I think, as far as you know, CIG+XM is a tangent lead. You don't have anything solid on them. If you did and time was of the essence, you would have turned it all over to my cell by now. Of course, if you did have something solid and held it back from us, that would be bad. Very bad. Mike and Zack and I would have to wonder why."

Owen turned and looked toward the Tomb of the Unknown. "You were already briefed about CIG+XM and China. They were the ones who called financial warfare a *hyper-strategic weapon.*"

"Yeah, in reaction to what they saw the West was doing."

"Like I said, the whole thing is an exception now."

"You say a lot of things you never explain." Nelson pulled out his phone. "I'm calling a cab."

Owen lurched to the side and grabbed Nelson by the arm to stop the call.

"You couldn't just do your assignment, could you? Guys like you blow operations. I said it before; you're not worth the risk."

To get information, Nelson allowed Owen's hand to remain on his arm. At any other time, he'd be on the ground. "What operation?"

Owen scanned the distance around them. "Let's walk."

Stepping away from the Memorial, Owen led them onto the grass. Eventually, they were among the ordered rows of white headstones. Only nature and honored resting places surrounded them.

Owen was grim but determined as he made his confession. "What happened last Friday was the trigger for the ETC—but it isn't the reason for it. Your instincts about that are correct."

"Then tell me what's going on," demanded Nelson.

Owen looked him in the eye. "NCS has been compromised. Some kind of cabal is operating on the inside. That's why the ETC operates under special circumstances. We've never had to conduct an internal affairs investigation of this scope before. As far as we know, it goes to the highest levels."

"What's the point? What are they after?"

"It's rumored they want to acquire something off-book."

Nelson knew *off-book* to refer to something so sensitive that it was not even acknowledged within the secrecy classification system.

"How does F1E fit in? How is that the trigger?"

"We aren't sure. It might be a diversion. They could be testing something —or it could be a shot across the bow by barbarians. All we know for sure is that the panic surrounding F1E has forced Congress to give DHS sweeping new powers to address the APT. It's possible the whole thing was staged to force the hand of Congress. For whatever reason, the cabal might need to go places and do things that are only allowed under emergency powers. We think F1E was the trigger for something larger."

Nelson reeled with the repercussions of what Owen was suggesting. "If that's true, then how is any ETC even possible? Who could you ever trust?"

Owen looked Nelson up and down and showed him a weak grin.

Nelson read into it. "Oh, now I get it. The briefing. *Retirees might actually come in handy on rare occasions.*"

Owen explained. "Retirees and private contractors on the fringe. The order that came down said it plainly—'*anyone who for whatever reason wouldn't be a good candidate to be selected for a cabal of this caliber.*'"

"That's what you think of us, huh? Has-beens and misfits?"

"No. Just people who aren't the types to be picked as cabal insiders."

"I don't buy it," challenged Nelson. "You're not going to collect together everyone you consider oddballs and old men and expect them to save you."

For once, Owen enjoyed being candid. "You're right. We don't expect you to save us, not directly. We expect you to draw them out."

"You're using us as decoys?" Nelson was incensed.

"Why denigrate it. We see it as the tip of the spear. You're entering a space no one else knows how to penetrate."

"Bullshit," sneered Nelson. "You're raising targets to draw their fire, that's all, and my cell's the target. You don't have any idea where to begin."

Owen didn't argue. "We're dealing with a black box. But there are certain advantages to knowing we're all inside it. The moves you make are crucial. Watching how things adjust around you might be the only way to sort the players and the motives. It's vitally important."

Nelson took it all in but found it hard to accept their real position. "It's nothing but fucking shadow boxing. You don't know players or motives."

"No idea," admitted Owen. "It could be a foreign state, it could be the NABs, it might even be financed by corporate interests outside the country. All we know is that the National Clandestine Service has an autonomous covert structure operating inside it. That structure answers to its own policies. It's driven by goals we believe are not aligned with those of the government of the United States."

"It doesn't make sense," declared Nelson. "If you don't know the players or motives, then how can you know any of this is going on?"

"Until F1E, it was all suspicion; things out of place, tracks left behind, rumors from third parties with unique perspectives. After all it took to pull off F1E, there's no other answer. Last Friday, all the ragged edges lined up."

Nelson stared at Owen, "You're admitting that the intelligence apparatus of the United States has been hijacked by outside interests. Probably by the highest bidder."

Owen didn't deny it. "They don't have to control much to move their plot forward. The right people in key places should give them everything they need. Whatever that may be, we believe F1E was a bold and public first step. In what direction they're headed, we need your movements to shed light."

"Why didn't you tell me this at the briefing?"

"Think about it. Your assignment remains the same regardless. There was no reason to add more complexity to your decision-making process. We need your cell to operate as assets, not decoys. Being too conscious of your role might give that away. The cabal has to see you as viable. We need them to react to you as if you are counter-intel on this. I suggest you keep our conversation to yourself. Dystrom and Hollister shouldn't know. Agreed?"

Nelson gave it some thought. "Agreed."

"Another thing," added Owen. "We let your meeting with Aubrey Marks go ahead because we want to see where it leads. But that's the exception. We prefer you don't go advertising what you're doing. Your regular assignment is designed to be draw enough. Follow the leads in your assignment space and the cabal will find you; we're certain of it. As long as you stay close to their areas of interest, they'll be interested in you."

Nelson said nothing. Owen pushed ahead assuming he had acceptance.

"One last thing," stressed Owen. "I've arranged to have a secure channel available any time you need to get leads to me directly. Just show ID at any one of the 72 Fusion Centers around the country. Ask for the Fusion Liaison Officer. They've been instructed to fast-track you to a secure line that connects directly to DIOCC. If anyone wants to know under what authority you make your request, tell them their cooperation is mandated by the SAR Initiative. DIOCC has been told to back you up."

Nelson knew SAR to be the Nationwide Suspicious Activity Reporting Initiative. Fusion Centers were located in every major urban area in the country. According to DHS, they were *"...focal points within the state and local environment for the receipt, analysis, gathering, and sharing of threat-related information between the federal government and state, local, tribal, territorial (SLTT) and private sector partners."*

Nelson wondered if Owen would appreciate some conspiracy theory input right about then. Many in the conspiracy theory world saw Fusion Centers as nothing but coordination points for ongoing spying operations conducted on citizens by their own government. Worst of all, the centers encouraged citizens to spy on fellow citizens in grand truth squad fashion.

At any time unrest against the established order was deemed to exist, these same centers could transform into collection points for undesirables to be herded off to internment camps. Each center would have its list of local people red-flagged by past behavior. Preemptive roundups could be expected. According to wildest theories, the infrastructure of the New World Order was taking shape under the guise of *protecting the country* and *securing the peace*.

Nelson decided Owen wasn't ready for such candor. Besides, it was nothing he didn't already know. Nelson pulled out his phone again.

"Anything else?"

Owen looked over Nelson's shoulder and signaled to the security agent waiting in the distance. "Yeah. If you go snooping around any computer systems, I suggest you beware of honeypots."

Before Nelson could answer, Owen walked off.

Nelson was left standing. The rising morning sun casted angular shadows off the blazing white headstones around him. Nelson gave it some thought.

Honeypots were used by computer security agents as traps for hackers. Honeypots were positioned to appear as integral parts of an important network but in fact were isolated and monitored. Their job was to deflect, detect, or otherwise counteract attempts to gain unauthorized access to the information technology. Anyone taking the honeypot bait would rapidly be traced, tracked, and then either monitored or apprehended.

Why was this Owen's parting statement?

Was he suggesting that Nelson's efforts to monitor Adam's work to penetrate Extasis might be leading to a trap set by the cabal? Owen's words were definitely a dose of cold water thrown on hot leads. But why would he give a warning to back off something that appeared so promising?

Maybe it was Owen's attempt to be clever, comparing Nelson to a honeypot. He and his cell members had been strategically placed as traps. But if any one of them fell prey to a similar device set out by the cabal, then all of Nelson's efforts and those of his teammates would be in vain.

Being a decoy that only triggered decoys set in place by the other side was a possibility Nelson had to consider. The goal of the ETC was to draw out real cabal members operating in their real space. Knowing the difference from now on would be a complicated guessing game.

Nelson called for a cab and started to stroll. Owen had already disappeared beyond the trees. As Nelson walked, the black town car came into view in the distance but it was driving away. Nelson knew his cab would take a few minutes to get there. It gave him time to pay his respects.

Walking closer to the Memorial, Nelson stood and solemnly watched as a sentinel of the 3rd U.S. Infantry Regiment walked the mat in front of the tomb. In a world turned upside-down by decoys and subterfuge, global agendas and loyalties for sale, the sentinel's unquestioning devotion and sense of duty to country suddenly seemed too pure for the city around him.

Nelson checked the time. It was 9:30 am. The markets were open.

14

0000 0000 1110

9:30 am EST, Monday December 4th

The rising sun chased away wisps of ground-hugging fog that clung to the earth around the gravesites. Even so, the biting cold numbed to the bone. Dressed in black, Katherine Stalt palmed her camera and held position among the foliage. Far enough away to avoid suspicion but close enough to capture photos, Katherine had gotten what she needed. If spotted, her story about a friend's resting place nearby would have invoked the rising sun as reminiscent of the resurrection and the utter quiet as a reminder of the sacrifice given.

Her mark was Owen Raedalus. She had been paid to track his meetings arranged away from his office. The assignment usually meant fancy restaurants or yacht moorages on the Potomac. Today when she left her house, she had no idea she'd be going to Arlington. But that wasn't the only surprise.

When the town car pulled up and the second man got out, she zoomed in and thought she was mistaken. Nelson Geiss, here with Owen? Of all people to cross paths with in the most unlikely of places, how was it that an old friend stepped out of that car? He was retired, comfortable on his ranch in Wyoming. If lured back into taking a job, he certainly wouldn't take Owen Raedalus as a team member. But then why else were they meeting?

Katherine's concerns for a friend lingered but she had to let it go. Her job was straightforward: collect evidence on Owen Raedalus' meetings outside the office. Whatever she collected was to be sent directly to her handler. It was a simple contract but the mark was high-level as was the pay. Whoever wanted this information placed great value on it. That's all she needed to know.

Katherine took one last photo of Nelson as he stood watching the sentinel march back and forth in front of the Tomb of the Unknown. She knew about the friends he had lost. One of those friends they had in common. Searing thoughts shot back to a rugged valley in Afghanistan. She owed her life to the heroism of that day. The pain was too deep to dwell on; she had to focus. It was time to leave but she wanted no harm to come to Nelson. Would her photos compromise him in any way? She couldn't imagine he was up to no good but many good people got caught up in things that took them down.

Her photos would go to her handler, a mystery man with a government address and deep pockets. It wasn't her job to question such things. As long as strangers were involved, it didn't matter. But now that a friend might be at stake, a heavy grayness pressed in on her. Should she warn Nelson? Such a breach of procedure would cross a line. She stuffed camera in pocket. She had to trust that Nelson knew what he was doing.

15

0000 0000 1111

9:59 am EST, Monday December 4th

The last half hour had been madness. Adam Perez sat at his desk on the twenty-sixth floor, dazed by lack of sleep. Around him, the frantic energy of techies and traders amped higher with the dread of the expected.

Markets had been open for half an hour with no glitches reported but no one believed the smooth opening proved anything. The DOW was down 2% and the big players were sitting it out with a wait-and-see attitude on the day. Adding to the skittishness was the fact that all of the F1E glitches had occurred precisely on the hour at one, two, and three o'clock. None had happened at any other time. For many, that meant that ten o'clock would be the first true test.

As seconds ticked away, Adam pressed back in his rocker chair and held a silent vigil on the digital board across the room. One second would be the difference between this hour and the next. If markets could make it through that one second without a repeat of last Friday afternoon, it would go a long way to calm the disruptive cries from the most vocal doomsayers.

Displayed in red light, the numbers flipped to 10:00. Nothing happened. Adam waited and looked around to see everyone else holding their breath. Nervous gazes at computer screens slowly gave way to expressions of relief. One or two guys made jokes or laughed and applauded but they were the exceptions and their frivolity was brief.

Everyone in that one moment knew what it felt like to dodge a bullet.

Of course, it was only one bullet. There were many more hours in the day. But when one was looking for any reprieve, no one questioned that this was a good sign. Certainly, the markets would have to plow through Monday one hour at a time. Most critical would be the hours 1, 2, and 3. It was possible that the glitch was exclusive to those hours, maybe as a message, perhaps for another reason no one understood. Either way, the financial world wouldn't be able to absorb any relief until the trading day had ended at 4:00 pm.

As ten o'clock became eleven and then noon, the uneasy relief started to sink in. When one o'clock came and went without interruption, the positive outlook seemed justified. The trading floor started to ease back into its old rhythm. Returning from the restroom, Adam saw CNBC's *heat map* in a window on someone's monitor: more of the red squares were turning green.

The loose activity and hyped-up distractions swirling around Adam began to subside, giving him time to think. By 2 pm he had gotten his second wind. He was still tired but he no longer felt drugged from lack of sleep. A quick lunch and walk outside had done wonders. He was ready to multi-task.

He couldn't get his mind off his new nighttime job. Both jobs were technical but worlds apart. One felt assembly line, the other like a nighttime zip-line adventure. The leading problem he faced with Extasis nagged at him. If the word he was looking for was Graphene, how did that help him decide which inner sanctum to break into? He was no closer to narrowing down the target and he damned well couldn't attack them all, one at a time, and expect success. The quandary kept him distracted all afternoon.

Several blocks away, uptown from Adam, Nelson Geiss sat at the desk of his fifth floor hotel room doing research. Open before him was a report on Jiaying from his identity contact. It detailed her past history, much of it missing from the brief that Nelson had gotten from Owen.

It was reported that Jiaying was in the U.S. a couple of years after living in British Columbia, Canada. She had emigrated there from Hong Kong. Her parents were from Guangzhou about 75 miles from Hong Kong. She had migrated to Hong Kong by herself in 2008, ten years after the Asian financial crisis. Very young, she had gone to work for a wholesale exporter although, based on its import activity, it was unclear why the company's official description stressed exporter. There wasn't much else to report on regarding Jiaying although her family's history was a bit more eventful.

Prior to 1997 when China resumed sovereignty over Hong Kong from the British, Jiaying's father was suspected of being involved in the grey channel, the name given to luxury commodity smuggling on the Pearl River between Hong Kong and Guangzhou. At least one acquaintance of her father was arrested and convicted after being found with a small amount of contraband but Jiaying's father was never charged and had never been convicted of anything. Shady activities around her seemed to go way back.

Nelson noted: Jiaying's rapid ascendancy from import clerk in Vancouver to quant candidate on Wall Street was surely suspect. If anything, her family's background pointed more to criminal underworld activity rather than being groomed as a PLA agent. Maybe something recorded by the bug in her apartment would shine more light.

Nelson brought up the playback analyzer and patched Jiaying's recording into it. The analyzer sampled at high speed and stopped where it interpreted possibly significant content. For half an hour, Nelson listened to samples and was unimpressed. Then Jiaying took a phone call and spoke Mandarin.

Nelson fed the sample through a translator and listened in. It didn't take long to realize the man she was speaking to was her boyfriend. He was in Hong Kong for a visit but expected to be back in New York shortly. He missed her and promised they'd be together soon. She assured him her work in New York was almost finished. She expected to have something to give him soon.

Nelson sat back. The private reality show was all too clear. From phone messages left between Adam and Jiaying, it was certain her intent was to make

Adam believe they were a happy couple about to enjoy a celebration trip to the South Pacific. Someone was being snookered and it wasn't the guy speaking Mandarin. That left Adam as a quite resourceful patsy.

Jiaying obviously had recruited him for the Extasis gig and kept her distance while he did the dirty deed. Once he succeeded in drilling down to secrets about Graphene, she would be long gone. If at any time the hacking was discovered, Adam would take the fall, not Jiaying, and not CIG+XM. Direct payment by them wasn't necessary as a motive; gaining insider knowledge about Graphene was enough to convict.

Nelson bolted from his seat and paced the floor. This was craziness. With all the talk of cabals, honeypots, and secret projects funneled through places like In-Q-Tel, for Nelson to sit by and watch Adam Perez blunder forward was ridiculous. Adam only wanted to make a quick score but he was ignorant of the game being played. He must have been one of many techies handpicked to go after, then recruit and groom. With his record of hacking into the National Archives at fourteen and having the infamous handle MUTEX associated with him, who in the Justice Department would suspect it went any deeper than him if the whole thing blew up in his face?

There was a vast difference between being a necessary decoy and setting oneself up as a clay pigeon. Adam was too brilliant to go to waste. He needed to be flipped, so his talents could be used on the right side of things. And Nelson was the one person in position to flip him.

Owen shouldn't mind. Adam wasn't a good candidate for the cabal. Whatever CIG+XM thought they were getting close to needed to be shifted away from them. Maybe that would get the cabal's attention.

Bringing Adam along for the ride would screw up somebody's day. F1E hadn't repeated on Wall Street so the cabal must be moving into its next phase. Nelson had to find a way to interject himself into that process and quickly. Aubrey Marks said Project G had a timetable. No doubt the cabal had one too.

Owen wanted Nelson to be a decoy but not act like one; his mission—act like he had a mission. Nelson liked operations with definable goals and a sense of urgency. Lacking the goals, he'd settle for stirring up some urgency.

Pacing to the desk, he looked down on a slip of paper tossed aside. For whatever reason, Owen had given him that paper. Whether Owen liked it or not, perhaps Nelson should make it a point to live by those words.

"I usually make surprising moves; the enemy expects surprising moves;
but I move in an unsurprising manner this time to attack the enemy.
I usually make unsurprising moves; the enemy expects unsurprising moves;
but I move in a surprising manner this time to attack the enemy."
—Li Shimin, emperor, Tang Dynasty China, 626 to 649 CE

16

0000 0001 0000

5:51 pm EST, Monday December 4th

Nelson sipped coffee and waited on a stool in the warmth of a small deli. Through the half-fogged window, the jostle of people and cars was a constant blur. Twenty-six floors above him, the downward rush of an elevator triggered a motion alert in Nelson's pocket. Sensing the vibration, he ditched the coffee, stepped outside, and hailed a taxi.

At first the driver balked when told to park and run the meter. Nelson slipped him an advance on the fare. The driver wasn't convinced but he was willing to wait until the meter ate up the advance.

One minute later, Adam Perez emptied onto the sidewalk with a group of other office workers leaving for the day. Nelson watched as they invited him to share some pub grub at a hangout down the street. Adam declined as Nelson suspected. Also expected, Adam failed to mention to them anything about the serious work waiting for him at home.

Following his regular pattern, Adam lifted his collar and walked in the direction of the subway entrance down the block. Between Adam and the entrance, Nelson waited next to the taxi as it puffed hot exhaust into cold air.

"Mr. Perez..." Nelson called out. "May I speak with you a minute?"

Adam slowed his steps and eyed Nelson and the idling car.

"It's very important," stressed Nelson. "It'll only take one minute."

Adam didn't stop walking but a rising curiosity dragged his steps.

Nelson stepped up and nudged him by the elbow, directing him out of the pedestrian flow. "You need to hear this. You're in great danger."

Startled off-guard by the warning, Adam accepted redirection to the taxi where wariness brought him to a halt. "Who are you?"

Nelson opened the door. "I'm the one friend you have. Come on. Get in."

Adam gave the confused taxi driver a glance before confronting the older man. "You're crazy. I'm not going anywhere with you."

Nelson flipped up a hand as if giving up. He reached for his phone and set one foot in the street next to the open door. "Have it your way. I wouldn't go back to apartment 2C—federal agents will be there before you get off the subway." Pressing phone to ear, Nelson got in the back seat.

"Hey, wait," Adam called out. He stepped closer "What is this?"

Nelson leaned out a bit. "It's your fucking life—for what it's worth." Nelson turned to the driver as if he was about to give a destination. As he did, he reached out and shut the taxi's door.

Adam stood rooted in place, wavering between disbelief and flight.

Nelson turned back to the window. He pointed at Adam. "Whatever you do, stay off those secure nodes you're looking at. They're honeypots."

Nelson gave the driver the name of a restaurant near his hotel.

Adam was shocked, his mind flooded with questions. How did this guy know so much? Who was he? Was he right about the federal agents and a trap at Extasis? Why did he want Adam in the cab? Where was he going? Adam had to choose: heed the warning or assume the guy was a crank.

How did a crank get so much private information?

Adam reached out for the door handle. "Hey, wait up!"

Nelson scooted over and Adam got in. The driver pulled away from the curb, merged into traffic, and headed for the restaurant.

Adam was all nerves. "Where are we going?"

Nelson relaxed back. "Dinner."

Adam suspected he had been had. "What about the agents?"

Nelson waved the suggestion off. "Oh, they'll wait. To wrap you up, they'll wait all night."

"There aren't any agents, are there…"

"Not yet, but I can call them quick enough."

Adam leaned towards the front seat. "Driver, let me out…"

"I wouldn't do that if I were you. I *will* call them."

"Hey, listen, I don't know what you think you know but—"

"Save it," Nelson butted in. "I've heard that speech. So have they. It's probably the same one you gave them when you broke into the Archives."

Adam was prepared to protest but mention of the National Archives took the wind out of him. And that was the point. Nelson needed to impress on him that this was serious and Nelson was the genuine article. How that played into Adam's future was the agonizing thing Adam needed to come to grips with.

Mention of the star item on Adam's rap sheet had muted him. Nelson proceeded to reel him in. "You're lucky I came along when I did. One more night of what you've been doing and it would have been all over."

Adam was stone-faced. "What makes you think you know anything?"

"People in the know have told me."

"And why would they tell you?"

"Because I'm in position to do something about it."

"What position is that?"

"I see without being seen. I know without being known. I can be your worst enemy or best friend. Tonight, I'm your friend. If that's reciprocated, tomorrow I'm your friend again. It's one day at a time, like everything else."

Suddenly, Adam was mad that he'd allowed himself to be jockeyed into the cab so easily. The anger projected. "Do you always talk in riddles?"

"What's the matter? You're supposed to be good with riddles. You're going to be a hot-shot fucking quant, aren't you?"

Another personal item divulged. Again, the shock of it knocked the fight

out of Adam. There seemed to be no limit to what this old guy knew about
him. If he wasn't the police or FBI, then who in the hell was he to have such
information? Had someone hired a private detective to watch him?

"You said I'm lucky you're here," noted Adam. "Why do I deserve all this
luck and friendship from you?"

"Like any friendship, it's a mutual thing."

"You want something," challenged Adam.

Nelson looked him in the eye. "Do you know anybody that doesn't?"

"So what is it?"

Nelson glanced away, feigning interest in traffic. "Dinner first."

"Why? Because all good seductions take time?"

Nelson laughed, then gave the kid a studied glare. "Listen, kid. You don't
have to love me—but you're damned well going to respect me in the
morning."

They rode the rest of the way in silence.

The small bistro was close enough to Nelson's hotel that he'd eaten there
more than once since getting into town. The vibe was noisy enough to make
close conversation private but contained enough to allow one to concentrate on
dinner partners and food. Nelson had reserved a booth in a corner across from
the bar area. They were seated and served drinks without fanfare.

Adam absorbed the improbability of the situation as he looked over the
menus and table setting. "You're serious. You're going to buy me dinner?"

"You can tell a lot about a person by the way they eat."

Adam unfolded his napkin. "Why bother? You act like you know everything already."

Nelson sipped his gin and tonic. "There's one thing, the most important
thing, I don't know yet."

"Yeah, what's that?"

"How you're going to react under the pressure of what's coming."

Adam's grin was brief. "Watching me eat isn't going to tell you that."

"No," Nelson shot back. "But you watching *me* eat will." Nelson brushed
the menu aside and leaned forward. "You have no idea the shit you've gotten
yourself into, do you? You thought you'd make a quick score then kick back
in the South Pacific. You think anything is that fucking simple? You're
running blind."

Dropping the bit about the South Pacific only added to Adam's unease. "If
you're such a friend, then enlighten me."

Nelson held two fingers a hair width apart. "You're this far from a charge
of espionage and you don't even know it. Do you have any idea who's behind
this *night job* you've taken?"

Adam was silent. The intensity of Nelson's approach was getting through.

Nelson continued. "Listen, if you've got bills to pay, you better do this
right. Extasis may be a private company but they have a lot of government

contracts. I don't care if you're looking for Graphene or G-strings, chances are you're going to step on a landmine that has nothing to do with your target. And you know what; it won't matter. No prosecutor is going to let you off because you claim what you stepped into wasn't what you were looking for."

Adam's brow furrowed. "I don't get this. Are you warning me not to do something or telling me the best way to go about it?"

"What does it sound like?"

The waitress approached and interrupted, "What can I get you two?"

"I'll take the special and a refill," answered Nelson right away.

Adam tried shifting gears onto the menu but gave up. "Ah, same for me."

The waitress scooped up the menus and hurried away. Adam returned to considering his answer but got distracted by the conclusions drawn from it.

"I get it," announced Adam, probing. "You must be a hacker, hired by a competitor of Extasis. You don't want anyone getting sloppy and setting off alarms in the space where you're working."

Nelson eased back and took a healthy swig of his drink. "That's what I like about you nerds; you're scheming little bastards. You don't miss a thing, except in this case, you're missing the obvious."

Adam considered it. "Yeah, like how would that work? What if we're going after the same thing?"

"Who said we are?"

"What are you after?" asked Adam.

"I'm interested in a money trail. I know people who are prepared to be generous if someone got them the financials of a few key projects."

"Someone," repeated Adam. "Are you trying to recruit me?"

"Hey, it worked for Jiaying."

Another bit of personal information dropped into place.

Adam bristled. "Keep her out of this."

Nelson laughed. "Ah yes, such a rare flower. I'm sorry. She was only trying to help. I understand."

"I don't think you do," snapped Adam.

"I know enough about love to be sure it's the only thing that can truly exist and still be too good to be true. Everything else you'd better mark as suspect any way you look at it."

"What's your point?"

"If you're going to risk going after Graphene, you might as well double down and follow the money trail too."

Adam sipped his beer. "I don't want to work for you."

Nelson hardened. "I don't remember offering you an option."

"You can't make me do anything,"

"I can prevent you from having a life. I *will* have federal agents at apartment 2C within the hour if we don't finish this dinner amicably."

Adam took a deep breath and nodded. "So you're not a recruiter, you're a blackmailer."

"Don't think so small." Nelson finished his drink. "You need a mentor and I've decided to accept the position. Your kind of brilliance will only get you so far; you must have realized that by now. If you want those loans paid off and avoid doing time, there's no other choice."

"I have no proof of what you're saying. I don't even know your name."

Nelson extended a hand across the table. "Nelson Geiss…" Nelson waited until Adam took his hand. "…good doing business with you. By the way, don't think of wiping any disks in your apartment. I've got a copy of all of it."

"Damn it, who the fuck *are* you!"

The waitress brought Nelson's drink. He shifted it in front of him but didn't touch it. Instead, he held a steady gaze on Adam as he answered.

"I told you. I'm your worst enemy or your best friend. Tonight, I'm your friend. Tomorrow, I hope to be a friend again."

"It's one day at a time…"

"…like everything else."

Adam lifted his napkin from his lap and set it on the table, preparing to leave. "Yeah, well, we'll see about that."

"You want more proof?" Nelson reached for his phone and brought up a map of Manhattan. On it he highlighted a single address.

Adam added, "I still have no idea who you are. Working with you might be the one sure way to get me that espionage charge. How do I know?"

Nelson turned his phone around and showed it to Adam. "You see this?"

"What of it?"

"Check it out. It's the closest Fusion Center to where we are."

"Fusion Center?"

"Yeah, Department of Homeland Security, Manhattan Emergency Operations Center, Suspicious Activity Reporting. You've heard of the Patriot Act, haven't you?"

Adam took Nelson's phone and checked the address then handed the phone back. "You're no fed."

"A second ago you didn't know who I was. Maybe I'm an informant. Maybe I'm undercover."

"Maybe I don't give a shit. Maybe I'll ignore you."

Nelson pressed the screen to dial the Fusion Center. "Yes, I'd like to speak to the on-duty Liaison Officer. My name is Nelson Geiss."

Adam stiffened. "What are you doing?"

Nelson shot Adam a cold stare. "You want proof I can fuck you up? I'll give you proof."

Nelson's attention was drawn back to the phone. "Hello…who am I speaking with? Special Agent Martinez? Yes, we spoke earlier today…" Nelson listened to the agent speak as he watched Adam's reaction. "That's good to know…as a matter of fact, I'm sitting with someone right now. I believe he has a question for you..." Nelson thrust the phone across the table.

Adam froze with Nelson's phone only inches away.

Nelson prompted, "Go on, ask him anything. They don't give tours but I guarantee you, you'll see the inside of it later."

Adam leaned back, refusing the phone.

Nelson waited as long as he could then returned the phone to his ear. "I'm sorry, I guess it's not a good time. Maybe later. Thanks for your help. OK. Good night."

Content he had made his point, Nelson settled back and looked around for their waitress. "I hope you like tripe..."

Adam was taken aback by the change of topic. "What?"

"Trippa alla Romana is the special tonight. That's roman-style tripe. You ordered it."

Adam avoided Nelson's gaze, unsure what to do.

Nelson shook his head. "You need to be more observant."

"It wasn't important."

"How do you know what's important? You have to be on your game at all times. No detail gets overlooked from now on."

"Yeah, sure."

"You better take this seriously," warned Nelson. "All it takes is one thing, one little thing to trip us up."

Adam remained silent and nursed his beer.

Nelson let down some of his harder attitude. "You're in way over your head; you have to know that by now. You're never going to find your way out of this alone. You need someone like me. If we both get something out of it, all the better. It doesn't have to be a zero-sum game."

Adam fired up. "What do you know about game theory?"

"I know the way things work in the real world."

"The real world? Have you ever heard of a zero determinant strategy?" Adam didn't wait for an answer. "What about the game called Prisoner's Dilemma? Ever heard of it?"

"I've heard of it," answered Nelson.

"I doubt you've ever studied it," countered Adam. "I mean, studied the *real-world* implications."

"And you have..."

Adam decided to put the old man in his place. "Game theorists have a thing called the Ultimate Game. The interesting thing is, when both players are aware of the zero determinant ruse, the Prisoner's Dilemma turns into a whole different game. It's important that one player be unaware they are being manipulated. But that's no longer the case with us, now is it?"

"Meaning what?" prompted Nelson.

Adam finished his beer and signaled the bar for another one. "Just to keep things real, I think both of us should know—it's hard to find a scenario where zero determinant strategies remain stable. I mean, they don't perform well against each other and they're not that resilient when strategies begin to evolve. They only have one chance of approximating stability and that condition can only be maintained temporarily."

Nelson played along. "So how do we do that?"

"We need additional information about our opponents. And we need some kind of camouflage to prevent being spotted and exploited."

Nelson grinned, "I could have told you that. No PhD required."

"Yeah, that's the part I thought you'd know. Like most people, that's as far as you take it."

Nelson could only follow along. "Where else is there to go?"

"You tell me. Where would you go with a strategy that's weakly dominant but evolutionarily unstable?" As Adam expected, Nelson had no answer; he sat appearing unimpressed but uninformed. With cleverness shifting into concern, Adam continued, "When you think about it, it's bizarre. Nobody's ever found an example of a zero determinant strategy occurring in nature. Imagine that. Do you know why?"

Curious enough, Nelson took the bait. "No, why?"

"That's the big question, isn't it? So far, no one knows."

Nelson glanced around at the nearby bar crowd. "Injecting human nature into the equation must make a hell of a difference," he reasoned.

"Are you saying the human element is somehow unnatural?"

Nelson's wry grin was faint. "Do you consider Manhattan a natural landscape?"

Adam paused, prepared to concede the point, but he wasn't consoled. "Doesn't it bother you that our fate may rely on strategies that don't occur in nature? I mean, ultimately, game theory implies only one thing about all of these zero determinant strategies."

"One thing?" noted Nelson. "And what's that?"

Adam waited until the waitress set a fresh beer in front of him. "It implies that winning isn't everything." Adam took a healthy swig. "At least what *we* call winning."

Nelson watched the steaming tripe arrive. "That's funny, since you seem to be enjoying your attempt to win points against me in a game of wits. Either way, I'll let you worry about it. My *job* is to win. And I'm good at it."

17

0000 0001 0001

11:38 am EST, Tuesday December 5th

Katherine Stalt sat in her parked car and uploaded photos taken that morning. Keeping a wary eye across the street, she selected the blind-drop email address of her handler and pressed send. If her mark exited the building, she'd be on the move again. A minute after the email was sent, her phone rang. She checked the number. It was her handler. He rarely called.

"This is Katherine." She kept her eye trained on a door across the street.

The voice was male, older, refined, obviously well-placed. His tone was edged with the interest of a scientist. "Where are you?"

"State Department. Parked across from the 23rd Street entrance."

"Are you any closer to finding a way in?"

"Even if I did, the place is too big, I'd have to go in when he did."

"Have you tried the guards?"

"I can't risk the exposure. I don't have their confidence."

With rare frustration, the handler's words quickened. "This is the only stop we have no idea who he meets with. We need coordination on the inside."

"I thought you wanted to avoid involving anyone else."

"They don't have to know they're involved."

"I'll see what I can do."

"There's one other thing. These pictures from Arlington—you've ID'd the other man as Nelson Geiss but you didn't say much about him."

Katherine had wondered if her handler would accept bare bones on Nelson.

"Like I said, Geiss is a semi-retired contractor from outside the Beltway. Besides not fitting your profile, there isn't much else to say about him."

"What do you mean—semi-retired?"

Katherine was defensive. "For the last three years, he's stayed mostly on his ranch. He has a network of friends; they call on occasion, asking for help."

"Would he consider Owen one of these friends?"

"No, I don't believe so. They shared some Agency work a while ago."

"How did it go?"

"I wouldn't know," lied Katherine. She held her silence and waited.

In time, the handler spoke. "Where is Geiss is now?"

"No idea."

"Very well." The handler was abrupt. "Keep me informed."

"I will." The call ended.

Katherine now knew the handler was interested in Geiss—but he might not go through her to get to him.

18

0000 0001 0010

3:39 pm EST, Tuesday December 5th

Backpack in hand, Nelson Geiss took a call while hustling down a midtown sidewalk. "This is Geiss."

"Hey, it's Hollister."

"What's up? Did you get a line on that guy?"

"It's like you said. He landed at JFK. Came in from Vancouver. The manifest had him in first class."

"I guess the girlfriend picked him up. I went over to CIG+XM to check on her and found out she'd left early."

"The way he talked to her on the phone, you know he's more than a boyfriend. I sent you a photo; got it from Hong Kong police."

Nelson was surprised. "What do *they* have on him?"

"Nothing solid. They suspect he's a courier or some kind of advance man. He manages to show up in places right before something happens."

"Like what?"

"Major drug deals, online IDs getting compromised, witnesses changing their stories, it goes on from there."

"A handy guy for someone to have around."

"Except he doesn't stay in one place that long," noted Hollister.

"More reason to push this forward. Did you find out anything new about Liam Bargeau?"

"I know he has no official business going on with Extasis."

"What he and their CEO agree to in the bedroom is another thing. Dystrom is in Europe; he's checking it out too. I suspect he'll be able to turn up more. Where's Christina Parish now?"

"She's keeping a regular schedule at the Extasis head office."

"And Bargeau?"

"He's in Europe but he visits D.C. on a regular basis. When he flies in, he always has a good reason besides Christina to be here."

"Good reason or good cover?"

"Probably both. When he's not being a sherpa, he works as Director of Research and Institutional Relations for a company incorporated in Zug, Switzerland—in other words, his headquarters is a P.O. box."

"That's a lot of help," growled Nelson.

He knew Zug as one of the premier corporate tax havens in the world, not only for global hedge funds and commodity traders but for many companies one might not suspect. Zug was a picturesque spot nestled between an Alpine lake and scenic mountains, but it was also the headquarters of record for tens of thousands of multinational corporations.

Although the city had only one shopping street, the Bahnhofstrasse, and the one item of note for those who stopped by was a cherry-liqueur torte, corporations didn't seem to mind. Not when foreign company tax could be deducted from Swiss federal tax, making business nearly tax-free. As a bonus, Zug was only a twenty-minute train ride from Zurich's discreet banks.

Hollister added, "For what it's worth, it's common knowledge that Christina joined Liam at the World Economic Forum last January."

"The Davos shindig?"

"That's right; the elite jewel of Graubünden. They were seen attending conferences and sampling the night life."

Nelson turned off the sidewalk and entered a hotel lobby not far from where Adam Perez lived. "What exactly does a Director of Research and Institutional Relations do?"

"Let's see..." Hollister checked his notes. "There's something here about Strategy and Mechanics of Economic and Market Research, if that helps."

"Yeah, I get the point." Nelson hesitated before stepping up to the reservations desk. "Keep on it. I'll let you know what happens here."

With the phone call done, Nelson booked a room in the hotel. He would stay checked in at the other hotel, the one Owen had reserved for the week, but Nelson wouldn't live there any longer. Too much was going on to trust one place. Now that he had flipped Adam to do work for him, flexibility was key.

Nelson checked out the new room, scanned for bugs, then set up a computer link to Adam's laptop. Adam was at work so Nelson was more interested in listening in on Jiaying. If she had picked up her boyfriend from the airport, maybe they had gone back to her place. As soon as he connected and donned earbuds, the sound of Mandarin being spoken came through loud and clear. This wasn't a phone call; they were together in Jiaying's apartment.

Nelson switched on the translator. They talked about arranging a meeting and needing to pick up new business cards. Nelson had to get over there before they left so he could follow them. He stuffed his tablet computer into a pocket in the inside lining of his jacket and hurried down to the street.

The city churned towards the end of another business day. Nelson gripped his phone, alert for a vibration that would signal Jiaying on the move. Blending in with pedestrians, Nelson stepped inside a pharmacy and browsed newspapers and magazines. When the motion signal finally came, Nelson stepped back on the sidewalk and waited until Jiaying and her man emerged. He followed them to an art supply store where they inspected the business cards and paid. Nelson kept phone to ear and took photos while pretending to be on a call. He captured shots of Jiaying and her man in and out of the store.

When they grabbed a taxi, Nelson had no way to follow. Traffic was heavy and by the time Nelson flagged down a ride, the driver wouldn't be able to follow. Nelson watched the motion tracker and noted the drop-off address. They had gone to the financial district but not to CIG+XM.

Nelson saved the address. He'd research it later.

He checked the time; Adam should be off work. Nelson had told him to be prepared to work together tonight. The next few hours were critical in forging the right dynamic between them. Either Nelson's gamble to flip Adam would pay off or he'd have to cut Adam loose. It was time to find out.

Nelson backtracked to Adam's neighborhood, entered his building, and knocked at apartment 2C. Adam left the door open without saying anything and walked back to the kitchen area.

Nelson stepped in and closed the door. "How did it go today?"

Adam plucked a beer from the fridge. "What do you mean?"

"At work? Any more glitches?"

Adam switched on the TV. "If you're going to ask me questions you already know the answers to, it's going to be a long night."

Nelson watched Adam sit down and flip stations on the remote until a cable news channel came on. Nelson took off his coat and sat down. He glanced at a news anchor talking away. "I know what they're saying in the press. I'm more interested in what really happened."

"You don't believe the news?" Adam's sarcasm was hollow and bitter.

"I believe it is what it is. Did your company get more visits from the feds?"

"If they did they didn't tell me."

"The worst of it must be over, except the markets are still down."

"Hell yeah, there's a lot of uncertainty out there," explained Adam.

Nelson nodded. "Nobody's sure who did it...or why."

"Or when they'll do it again," added Adam.

"Maybe they're done; they accomplished what they needed. Now they're onto something else."

"Don't start with that," complained Adam. "I heard that shit all day long."

"What?"

"Rumors about what it could be."

"No one knows, so what's wrong with guessing?"

"People have a warped sense of the dramatic. They need to be entertained so they make up shit. The truth is probably pretty simple."

"Even simple can be dramatic," asserted Nelson.

"Worrying about it won't do any good."

"So what would be simple to you?"

Adam shrugged. "Following the money is usually a good bet."

"How do you make a profit off F1E?"

"In my line of work, they make profit off everything."

"You don't think there could be a political reason?"

"What—terrorists? They don't have the brains or resources to pull off something like F1E."

1

"Really. Where did you get such a low opinion of terrorists? There are plenty of countries who would back the right group."

Adam returned his attention to the TV and changed the subject. "What exactly are we doing tonight?"

Nelson remained relaxed, deferential. "You just got off work. Don't you want to go eat first or something?"

"No. Let's get into it. I want to find out what you have in mind."

Nelson kept seated. "Even if I have a warped sense of the dramatic?"

"This whole thing is warped," shouted Adam. "I need to plow through this and get it done. OK?"

Nelson paused, unflustered. "You need to understand; I'm here to help."

"This whole thing blows. That's what I understand."

"Just as I thought. You spent your whole day arguing with yourself. How could you get in that taxi with that guy? How does he know so much? What is this really about? You don't have answers so you want out—quick. There's only one problem with wanting nothing more than the quickest way out—it can get you put in jail or killed."

Adam took a swig of beer. "Once again, how dramatic."

"I don't think we can begin anything." Nelson got up and fetched his tablet computer from his jacket. "Not until your perspective gets an adjustment."

In defiance, Adam propped his feet up on the coffee table. "And you think you can do that?"

Nelson sat back down. He tapped and swiped away at his tablet computer. "I knew you'd be having second thoughts, so I came prepared." Nelson glanced at the TV. "Mute that thing."

Adam complied, curiosity tempering his anger.

Nelson was ready. With a final tap of the screen, he looked up as another voice filled the room. It was Jiaying's voice, speaking on the phone with a man. Nelson could tell right away that Adam recognized her voice. But it would do him no good. She was speaking in Mandarin.

"What is that?" demanded Adam.

"What does it sound like?"

Unsure of what Nelson was up to, Adam didn't answer.

"I recorded this the other day," explained Nelson. "Jiaying on the phone in her apartment. Luckily for me, she was busy that day and put the call on speakerphone." Nelson watched Adam's face. "I imagine you'd like to know what she's saying. Maybe you'd even like to know who she's talking to."

"What a surprise; you speak Mandarin." Adam's distrust was obvious.

"I know a little," admitted Nelson, "but I'm not fluent enough to follow this. Thankfully, someone programmed an app that does." Nelson stopped the playback and navigated to the translator program. "Let's hear that again."

Nelson played the call and let the sound of the translation dominate. He watched as the expressions on Adam's face changed. Jiaying and her boyfriend were heard lamenting how they missed each other. Jiaying talked dispassionately about how her work in Manhattan was almost done. The boyfriend gave details about his plans for a return trip to New York. They both were happy they'd be together again soon. Important work remained for both of them to do but Jiaying was sure the breakthrough she had had with Adam was the key to their success and getting out of New York for good.

As Nelson expected, Adam processed what he heard through shock, then anger and denial and hurt until all he had left to cling to was a suspicion propped up by hope that the translation was nothing but a fabrication orchestrated by Nelson.

"What does that prove?" challenged Adam.

"I'll give you a copy of the original recording. Go have it translated any way you'd like. You'll see it checks out."

"So you had her voice synthesized. Of course it would sound like her."

Nelson took out his phone and brought up the photos taken of Jiaying and her boyfriend walking together in front of her apartment, inside the art supply store, and getting into a taxi. He handed Adam his phone for a look.

"I guess I rigged these too."

Adam took the phone reluctantly. He looked down, expecting something else that would seem plausible but he could easily question. As he cycled through the photos, they hit him hard but the effect was mostly confusion.

"I took those an hour ago," explained Nelson. "This is the man on the phone with Jiaying. He flew in from Hong Kong earlier today after stopping off in Vancouver, B.C."

As Adam got to the last photo, he could only stare at it.

Nelson expected a certain amount of surprise, but Adam's reaction was more disbelief than anything. "What do you see?"

Adam handed the phone back. "He didn't just get in from Hong Kong."

"What?" Adam's rebuff took Nelson by surprise.

"He's the one who interviewed me for the night job."

"The job for CIG+XM?"

Adam nodded. "I met with him Saturday afternoon."

Nelson scooted to the edge of his seat. "This is important. Are you sure this is the man who interviewed you?"

Adam nodded. "Yeah, that's him."

"This man isn't on the payroll of CIG+XM. Not officially, not in any office they have worldwide, not even in Hong Kong."

"Of course not. They have him recruiting hackers for chrissakes."

"And you're sure about that?" asked Nelson.

"Yeah. He took me to the corner office—it wasn't really an office."

"What do you mean?"

"No one was using it." The strangeness of the interview returned and deepened Adam's confusion.

"Where did the interview take place?"

"CIG+XM."

"Where was that?"

"You don't know?" challenged Adam.

"I know the building. What floor?"

Adam thought back. "18th floor."

"CIG+XM is on the 19th floor."

"Yeah, so?"

"Did you ever go to the 19th floor?"

"No."

"That didn't bother you?"

"No. I wasn't there for regular business."

"Yeah, no need to check in with Human Resources, huh?"

"That's what I expected."

"Did he tell you his name?"

"No."

"Did Jiaying ever mentioned him?"

"Not by name."

"So when you get what he wants, what are you supposed to do with it?"

"Put it on a clean drive and go sit by the window in the coffee shop across the street."

"They'll see you and make contact. Is that it?"

"Yeah, I guess so. It seems simple enough."

"Do you know how you'll be contacted?"

Adam thought a moment. "No, I imagined they'd come get it or call me with more instructions."

Nelson sat back and thought a second. "You don't know who you're working for. It could be CIG+XM but just as likely it's someone else."

Adam gave a laugh. "Hey, if I'm in the dark, you're there with me. You've got it all wrong; that guy didn't fly in from Hong Kong today. Wherever you're getting your information from is messed up."

Nelson took the criticism to heart. He reached into a pocket. "You're right, something is messed up. We need to verify this ourselves."

"What are you talking about?"

Nelson handed Adam a thumb drive. "Here. I want you to turn this in. Tell them it's what you've been able to hack so far."

Adam hesitated. "What is it?"

"Go ahead. It's some research about Graphene."

"Where did you get it?" Adam took the drive.

"A friend of mine poked around."

"I can't turn in this shit. It's not Project G."

"Wise up. They don't know what Project G is, that's why they hired you."

"What if they want to know where I got it—the site location, the source?"

"Tell them you don't disclose sources in the middle of a job; it's too risky. Tell them you thought they were all about results so don't question your methods."

Adam made a fist around the drive. "What is this going to prove?"

"Just do it. It contains a router-activated beacon. We need to trace where it goes."

"They'll sweep the drive; they'll find it."

"Trust me. They won't find this."

"Should I trust your flight information from Hong Kong too?"

"Listen, there'll always be more going on than either of us know about. In that regard, it's a level playing field. Believe it or not, the other side has the same problem. If they didn't, they wouldn't have hired you."

Adam stared at the mute image on the TV. Nelson could see him retreat inside himself, lost in rising emotion. It was easy to guess what it was about. Nelson got up and helped himself to a beer from the fridge. After opening it, he took a swig and turned back to face Adam.

"For what it's worth—you can't lose what you never had."

The vagueness of the change of subject attracted Adam's attention. He glanced over at Nelson for a moment but remained quiet.

Nelson sat back down. "Face it. You were recruited. She never loved you. Come on, we have work to do."

Adam stared at the TV image a long while and then with a twist of his hand, pressed down on the remote control. Just like that, the image faded.

19

0000 0001 0011

6:41 pm EST, Tuesday December 5th

Nelson took his time eating a double slice of pizza. Cattycorner across the street, Adam sat at the window of the coffee shop, sipping a latte, and waiting. His cooperation hadn't been automatic. Nelson had stood by while Adam reviewed the Graphene research on the thumb drive.

This was Adam's first data drop. Knowing that Nelson backed him up was scant assurance things would go right. Adam had no more trust in Nelson than in CIG+XM. At least he hoped Nelson's self-interest overlapped his own.

Nelson scoped out the coffee shop in advance. It was small with no public back door or restroom. Adam's contact would have to enter through the front door. They must have plugged into a live feed from the coffee shop's security cameras. Either that or they put a camera with a view of the shop's window.

Twenty minutes after Adam sat down, a taxi pulled to the curb and a teenager, a gangbanger type got out. Jumpy and hunched in his oversized coat, the kid entered the store and went right up to Adam.

"Adam? You got something for me?"

Taken off-guard, Adam asked before thinking, "What do you want?"

"You sittin' here for a reason, aren't you? Come on, give it up. I ain't got no fucking time to waste."

Adam glanced outside; the taxi waited with its rear door open and the medallion number on the top unlit, an indication the taxi was not available.

Adam felt his heart race. The kid knew his name and he'd entered the store on a mission. Adam reached into his pocket and handed over the thumb drive.

The kid looked down on the drive in his hand and acted offended then his anger flared, "This all you got?"

Adam was caught off-guard.

The kid watched him stammer over a moment of indecision, then laughed. "You all worried and shit, aren't you? That's OK; I'll catch you later."

With that, the kid bolted from the store and jumped back into the taxi. The driver wasted no time accelerating away into traffic. At the next corner he turned. He was obviously paid in advance to expedite matters.

Adam crossed the street and met Nelson in his apartment lobby.

Nelson handed him pizza to go. "You did good; the package is on its way."

Adam took the food but was preoccupied. "I'm not hungry."

Nelson led him to the stairs. "You will be. It's going to be a long night."

Adam paused. "That can't be right."

"What?"

"That kid. How does he work for CIG+XM?"

"What did you expect—a limo and butler service? That kid was given a c-note and told to do one thing. He's got no idea what's going on."

"This isn't what I signed up for."

"You should have thought of that before crossing the street—and I don't mean the street outside." Nelson led the way to the second floor.

Nelson's phone rang. He stopped to check the number while Adam opened the apartment door. Adam stepped in with Nelson on his heels.

It was Dystrom in London. Nelson had been waiting for his call.

"Hey there, what do you have for me?"

Dystrom was rushed. "We got somebody's attention."

"How?"

"Must be checking into Mr. B."

"You sure?"

"None of this shit was happening until you told me to check him out."

"What's going on?"

"The usual—rental car stolen, my hotel room ransacked. After that, I spent the last six hours with BMP getting interrogated."

"BMP? What for?"

"They wanted to know what someone with my illustrious background was doing in their fair city."

"They're fishing…"

"More like trying to intimidate. They knew that lake was dry."

"What did you tell them?"

Dystrom laughed. "I confessed to my fondness for East End wenches."

"And they weren't surprised."

"I told them the scrubbers remind me of royalty. They got pissed."

"So, in the hotel room, the car…was anything compromised?"

"Nothing was kept there. Maybe that's why they pulled me in. They wanted to pick my pockets."

"So where's the goods on Mr. B?"

"I put it in a safe place."

"All right. Keep low for a while. Enjoy the East End."

Dystrom groaned. "Yeah, I think I'll find a pub in Whitechapel. Maybe a frank discussion of football with the regulars will keep me busy."

"Later." Nelson ended the call.

Adam was listening and wondered aloud, "Who's Mr. B?"

Nelson paused. Part of flipping Adam would necessitate trusting him with certain information. Nelson's resolve to be partners was being tested.

"Liam Bargeau," Nelson answered bluntly.

"Who's he?"

"Someone of interest."

Adam pushed further. "And BMP?"

"British Metropolitan Police, otherwise known as Scotland Yard."

Adam bit into a slice of pizza. "You don't trust your cell phone?"

Nelson smiled. "Do you?"

"You think that simplistic code is going to protect you?"

"You have to learn what works and what's necessary if it doesn't work."

"That must mean you talk in code on the phone all the time."

"Unlike what you do, my work is not a precise science."

Adam sat down at his computer and checked his email. "Billions of calls get made every day. No one can listen in on all of them."

"What's OK to say one day may not be OK the next."

"Most people don't care if they're being listened to. Who cares about all the boring shit people talk about?"

"You may think you have nothing to fear because you have done nothing wrong, but you're not the one who determines what's considered wrong. What will people say when simply disagreeing with some bureaucrat gets them flagged as an enemy of the state?"

"Whatever. I still don't believe secret agents are listening to everything."

"They don't have to. Certain words are put on watch lists. Computers use *deep packet inspection* to hear those words and flag the calls for more thorough analysis by deeper algorithms."

"Every private call? Give me a break…"

"Yeah. And if your name is on a watch list, it doesn't matter what words you use. In that case, everything gets looked at. The Terrorist Watch List alone has over a million names on it. Anyone talking to them gets included."

"Nothing is big enough to do that."

"The NSA is four times the size of the CIA. Some of their top jobs are in *Computational Linguistics*. Ever hear of their Stellar Wind Program?"

Adam shook his head.

Nelson pulled up a chair. "I guess you also never heard of the Signals Intelligence Automation Research Center—or the Community Comprehensive National Cybersecurity Initiative Data Center at Camp Williams."

"Why should I?"

"When it came out that Stellar Wind was illegally monitoring domestic phone calls and email, Congress wasted no time—in 2008 they passed the FISA Amendments Act. Except, that law didn't stop the practice; it legalized it. Why am I not surprised you don't know what's going on?"

"That's impossible," asserted Adam. "They can't collect everything. A lot of that is encrypted; it wouldn't do them any good anyway. There are limits."

"Yeah, they have limits and they spend billions of dollars finding ways around them. Did you know that collecting isn't the same thing as listening or reading? Under the law, an item isn't considered an official *intercept* until they listen to it or read it."

"So what are you saying? They can collect as much private stuff as they want as long as they don't look at it? What good is that?" scoffed Adam.

"Think about it. They have everything for a future date when they know they'll be able to look at it. The future happens any day you make it onto one of their watch lists. If the criteria for that is loose, they can go after anyone."

"Why are you telling me this?" asked Adam.

"You need to know the scope of what you've gotten yourself into."

"What are you talking about? I'm not into any of that."

"You don't know what you're into. What is Project G?"

Adam hesitated. "Probably a cutting edge product some company is developing using Graphene."

"Maybe, but you don't know. Most people know more about conspiracy theories than you do about your own assignment."

"There's more to go on with conspiracy theories than what I've been told."

"And yet, despite common sense and logic, people still miss the point."

"What point?"

Nelson scooted his chair nearer. "All right, for example: when the NSA was making plans to install tapping gear so they could intercept international and foreign communications, the logical place was at cable landing stations, about 24 U.S. sites where fiber-optic cables come ashore. Sounds reasonable, doesn't it? That was the logical place to do the installations. So tell me, why instead did they choose to install their gear at key junction points around the country, dozens of windowless telecom buildings simply known as switches? Form follows function. It's not a conspiracy theory to follow simple logic."

"How does that help us?" asked Adam.

"Is there any conspiracy you believe in?"

Adam thought a moment. "Yeah, I guess so."

"Which one?"

Unsure of what he should divulge, he wavered. "It's called USEUCO."

"I've heard of that," Nelson answered right away.

"You have?" Adam rocked back in surprise.

"Sure. It's gone by various names over the years. USEUCO is only the latest version. It was popularized by the group RAPIER. They came up with the name. It stands for *U.S./European Ultra Class Oligarchy,* the small group of moneymen who supposedly run the world. It's also part of an online role-playing game—*New World DisOrder*, but the game is pretty simplistic compared to the conspiracy theory. You might say the game sucks."

"Damn. How do you know all that?"

"What? You think I'm too old to track video games?"

"It's not something I'd expect you to give a shit about."

"For someone who believes in conspiracy theories, why not?"

"You're going to try to tell me there's no such thing as USEUCO?"

Nelson baited Adam. "I've followed those theories a long time, in ways you wouldn't believe. I guarantee you, only 1/100th of 1% are ever true."

Nelson's calculated denial raised Adam's ire, as Nelson wanted.

"For someone who tries to come off like they're on top of everything, that's naïve. How can you look at the concentration of wealth in the world and the way it's trending and not see what's going on?"

Nelson shrugged. "I think if anything is in control, it's blind greed that runs through the motivations of people everywhere, nothing more."

"You don't think blind greed can self-organize and merge in upon itself until it becomes global and centrally planned?"

Nelson disagreed. "It's never black and white. Most conspiracy theories oversimplify; they need to fit preconceived assumptions. Reality is not so simple or clean. If anything, given the complexity of society, I'm more afraid that it's all racing forward with no one, nothing in control. Maybe we'd all be better off if there really was a monolithic power managing things."

Adam slumped in his chair. "Don't discount the effect that 1/100th of 1% can have. In finance, one basis point or beep is the smallest measure used in quoting yields on bills, notes and bonds. But just because it's the smallest measure doesn't mean it's insignificant."

"How is that?" asked Nelson, leading Adam on.

"One basis point is .01%, or one one-hundredth of a percent of yield. That means 100 basis points equal 1%. It's common practice to use basis points to denote a rate change in a financial instrument, or the spread between two interest rates, including the yields of fixed-income securities."

"That quant stuff loses me..." grinned Nelson; he started to turn away.

"No, wait. In hedge funds and high frequency trading, fortunes are won or lost on a change of one basis point—1/100th of 1 percent. Take, for example, the waiver of lock extension and renegotiations in mortgages and roll costs for a current coupon. It can cost a company that's hedging and selling on a mandatory basis about 1.04 basis points per day. Round to 1 basis point and extend for 15 days, it costs the firm 15 basis points. Each day adds another beep of loss."

"Meaning what?"

"Even 1/100th of 1% can be significant. Someone once said, '*A little of a lot over time can be much more than a lot of a little right now.*' To me, it's plain: the consolidation of money and power in USEUCO is just as incremental but steady."

Nelson stared at Adam. "When's the last time you worked for RAPIER?"

Adam was caught off-guard. Suckered by the diversion, Adam's reaction told Nelson most of what he needed to know. But he pushed it further.

"I guess you don't work under the name MUTEX anymore."

The revelation of Adam's old avatar dropped another bit of personal information into place. Adam turned back to his computer.

"You assume a lot. In your line of work, isn't that dangerous?"

"I'm about facts, not assumptions. People follow their passions one way or another. There's nothing wrong with that unless it gets in the way with what we need to do."

"You still haven't told me what that is," deferred Adam.

"You haven't been up front with me. Why did CIG+XM recruit you? Why did they think you'd be their type? And don't give me that quant crap. They wanted MUTEX, not a Poindexter, admit it."

"They wanted someone they knew could hack."

"And you're not rusty at it, are you?"

"If I was doing that, then why am I still in debt?"

"Why? Because you don't do it for money; you do it for a cause—*revolution by another name*, isn't that what they call it?" RAPIER's motto was evident between them. Nelson waited.

Adam stared ahead at his computer. "Believe what you want."

"I don't care if you think you can fight the system or how you go about it—just don't fucking lie to me, ever. I *will* find out and I'll make things right between us."

"What about you?" asked Adam, turning to Nelson. "Are you up front with me? You're not saying who you are or why you're doing this. You won't admit the truth; you force my cooperation with threats. Don't lecture me about being up front."

Nelson returned to topic. "Have you been hacking for RAPIER?"

Adam steamed at the question but thought it through. Maybe by giving away something he didn't care about, he could get something from Nelson that would shine more light on what was going on. "Not recently."

"More recent than the anti-drug website when you were sixteen?"

By now, Adam was not surprised to hear more of his personal details coming out of Nelson's mouth. "A couple of things in college. That's it."

Nelson watched Adam's body language. "So you still have contacts."

Adam showed reluctance but then gave in. "Yeah."

"All right," concluded Nelson. "That's good to know."

Adam looked back to his computer. "Let's get on with it. What do you want me to do?"

Nelson shifted his chair alongside Adam. "First we need to go to our *safe place*."

Adam leaned back from the keyboard as Nelson typed a website location into a browser on Adam's screen. "If you ever talk about this site, it only has one name—*safe place*. Nothing else. Got it?"

"Yeah, sure…" Adam watched a website for a life coach and motivational speaker fill the window. Sunbursts and flowers provided the backdrop to inspirational quotes and personal testimonies. All of it was surrounded by links encouraging readers to buy audio-lectures and a variety of conference materials guaranteed to improve their lives.

"Memorize the URL," ordered Nelson. "This site has a special subpage.

There are no links to it. The only way to get there is to type it in directly." Nelson typed the revised URL, including a secure "https" connection, then added a *dassergill* subpage reference. He paused so Adam could take it in.

A prompt for login came up. Nelson typed in *sirdassergill* as the login name. "The password is strong but easy to remember. Here…look…" Nelson directed Adam's attention to the keyboard. "Just remember to alternate between opposite ends…top and bottom starting with z…"

From the bottom left of the letter keys, Nelson went next to top right, then from top left to bottom right. He repeated the pattern twice, moving inwards one letter each time and dividing each pass with the numbers 6 and 1.

The full password was typed—*zpqm6xown1cieb*.

"Got it?" asked Nelson.

"No problem."

Nelson pressed enter and a black page appeared with file name references in white ordered alphabetically down the left side. "For the work we're doing, we'll use this temporarily as a place to transfer material."

Adam noted the contents. "Why is stuff in here already?"

"I never said I was working alone."

"Are you going to introduce me?"

"Only if it becomes necessary."

Adam shook his head. "You realize, this isn't that secure."

"Right, but anything can be gotten into."

"I mean it would be nothing to hack this."

"That's not where you put your efforts. Some of the best spies used blind drops in public places for years and were never detected."

"Maybe…"

"No maybe about it. Leaving a paper bag behind a park bench doesn't sound secure either, does it? It's not the method but the knowledge of the method that secures or makes something vulnerable. As it turned out, the secrets transferred in those paper bags were more secure, even in transit, than atomic bomb secrets kept under heavy guard in locked-down installations."

"So what do we do with this stuff?" asked Adam.

One by one, Nelson began opening the documents provided by Dystrom. "We need two things. First, follow up on leads about Liam Bargeau and find out where they take us. We also need to dive into the financials of Extasis."

"Looking for what?"

"Anything out of place, something that stands out from the rest. Project G was unlike any project Extasis ever had. Something in the financials might be the best way to pick up the trail, especially if any reference is made to an organization called In-Q-Tel."

"Where have I heard that before?" Adam asked himself.

"It's the CIA as venture capitalist, making grants for private research."

Adam took note. "So you *are* after Project G…"

"I'm after whatever is going on."

"You told me you wanted the money trail on a few key projects."

"Yeah, and Project G is one of them. All you have to worry about is cracking into Extasis financials without setting off any alarms."

"While I'm doing that, what are you going to do?"

Nelson grabbed his tablet computer out of his coat. "I'll look into Liam Bargeau. By the time you finish with the financials, I should have some other places where you can do your magic."

"This Bargeau guy, who is he?"

"You'll find out soon enough. Get going on Extasis."

Adam opened several of Dystrom's documents and read down the list of phone calls and credit card charges made by Liam Bargeau. Seeing a trend right away, Adam gave a laugh. "This Bargeau guy really likes Jersey. What's up with that? Does he have some racket going on in Atlantic City?"

Nelson grinned. "You're thinking of the wrong Jersey."

"How many are there?"

"That's not *New* Jersey," explained Nelson. "It's the *Bailiwick* of Jersey."

"*Bailiwick*? Where the hell is that?" asked Adam.

"It's an island off the coast of Normandy, France—a self-governing democracy but also a member of the British Commonwealth. It has its own financial and legal systems. It's a special arrangement that makes it the world's number one offshore financial center; you know, a tax haven."

"Whoa, never heard of it."

"Some fucking quant you're going to be if you don't know about Jersey."

Adam ignored the remark. "You expect this financial thing done tonight?"

"Aren't you that good?"

Adam couldn't back down from the challenge. "…yeah."

Nelson went to work. "All right, then show me."

20

0000 0001 0100

6:18 am EST, Wednesday December 6th

A light dusting of snow had fallen overnight on Silver Spring, Maryland. The townhouse was quiet, blankets warm, and the alarm was not set to go off for twelve minutes. On the nightstand nearby, the ringing of a phone rousted Katherine Stalt from her dreams. She reached beyond her pillow. "Yes?"

An unidentified male voice came to the point. "I got what you wanted but be done before noon. Use the C Street Entrance. Sign in as yourself. When asked, you're part of the advance team for the Patterson delegation. You'll be taken to a conference room. Use the workstation at the facilitator console; the section you're interested in will be queued up. If anyone asks, tell them you're a private contractor in for one day on a targeted task. After you're done, walk through Edward Kelly Park so I know you're out of the building. Got it?"

The flurry of details buzzed through Katherine's head. Calling in favors the day before with a connection to the security archivist for the State Department buildings had netted her a major opportunity. "Will anyone else be there?"

"No. They have an afternoon session. It's customary for the advance team to prep but today's docket is light; the main team won't be in until noon."

The vestige of sleepiness cleared. Katherine thought it through. "I'm not comfortable signing in as myself."

"There's no other way," the voice assured her. "A friend advised Patterson that extra security precautions are in order. He suggested it'd be prudent to review traffic from yesterday. You're there to do the ID-sweep. Don't worry. They're expecting you as part of today's advance team."

"Patterson's group agreed to an outsider on this?"

"With recommendation plus, as a favor repaid, you'll comp your services."

"All right, that'll work but what about security at State? They have no issue with outside security on premises?"

"Every delegation is allowed certain latitude when taking precautions. State security is still in control; allowing you in is the diplomatic thing to do. Don't worry, they have the place tight. You have a small window. Stay in it."

"All right," sighed Katherine. "Thanks."

The line went dead and Katherine threw back the covers. She never expected to get the access she had asked for so quickly. This was promising.

Identifying who Owen Raedalus met with ad hoc at the State Department was a nagging gap she needed to fill in. Now that she knew Nelson Geiss might also be involved, her motivation to be included went deeper. She took an abbreviated shower and dressed then took off in her car.

Parking down the street from the State Department, she entered the C Street entrance. After processing by the guards, she was escorted to a conference room and facilitator's station. She had to review the security camera footage from the C Street and 21st Street entrances. Both were queued up but her hunch was on 21st Street so she started there.

For the next two and a half hours, she fast-forwarded and paused, rewound and watched people come and go from the two entrances. Between 10:45 am and 11:15 am, her target window, a number of cars and pedestrians were suspect. The process of elimination was tedious but narrowed down to three possibles. At 10:52 am, a suited man with an attaché case entered from 21st Street. At 10:56 am, a sharply dressed woman entered from 21st Street. Katherine captured still shots of their faces and copied them onto a flash drive.

Returning to footage from 11:01 am, Katherine watched a black SUV drive up to the C Street entrance. A suited man got out. The vehicle drove on and the man made his way inside. He carried airs of being the kind of D.C. insider expected to meet with Owen. Apparently aware of the security camera, he turned his head at the right time and no clear photo of his face was possible.

Katherine rewound the footage. She drew a bounding box around the rear of the SUV, zoomed in, and captured an image of the car's license number and saved it. With that, she had her three possibles.

Shutting down the workstation, she buzzed security for an escort out. Only one thing was left to do. She headed down C Street and turned north on 21st. Crossing the street, she completed the requested stroll through Edward Kelly Park. When her phone buzzed, she read a text message, its intention plain.

"CLEAR."

The time was before 10 am. She needed to get into position.

Owen Raedalus might be on the move at any time.

21

0000 0001 0101

7:51 am EST, Wednesday December 6th

It was a rare day when Adam Perez called in sick to work but after going nonstop through the night with Nelson, Adam knew he wouldn't have the energy or focus to survive the demands of the 26th floor. Not today. With so much riding on their marathon, the all-nighter had drained concentration and vitality from them both. Regardless, the work had remained intense.

Adam sipped at cold coffee and double-checked his work.

Nelson was beat but determined to see it through. The two of them had survived the night and made progress, but the time had come to take stock of where they were and to consider getting some sleep.

Adam pushed back from his computer, locked in thought.

"How's it going?" asked Nelson.

"You tell me."

Nelson was ready to cut Adam some slack. Extasis financials had been a tougher nut to crack than either expected. Half the night was spent finding out where the important data was kept and breaking into it. The other half had been taken up with devising ways to analyze any sense out of it.

Nothing was obvious in the figures. Whoever kept books for Extasis did so in a way that assumed it *would* be seen by prying eyes. Projects and clients were not readily discernable without a key to interpret internal acronyms. Company income had been laundered until it was virtually anonymous. Project expenditures were diffused using a number classification system that defied comprehension unless one knew a particular project's variations.

Nelson checked the time; it was an hour and a half later than he'd thought. He stretched. "Come on, let's get breakfast. I need some fresh air."

"One minute," deferred Adam. "I may have something."

Nelson dragged his chair closer.

Adam tapped a spot on his computer screen. "This cost code appears across all silos, in all projects—but I don't think it belongs to any of them."

"What would be the point of that?" asked Nelson.

"I don't know," admitted Adam. "But I've been thinking. If I wanted to hide a project but still account for it…"

"Don't define it as a project."

"Exactly. Bury it as a cost code. Then you could spread the reporting through *all* projects. Project numbers would become its cost codes."

"OK, that's possible but why *this* cost code?"

"I've been running a routine for the last hour. It's looked at every code, one by one, using Benford's Law. So far, the only wonky code is this one."

Nelson took note; the cost code was ZYN1.

"What's Benford's Law?" asked Nelson.

"Frank Benford. You never heard of him?"

Nelson shook his head.

"He was an engineer who accidentally discovered a handy mathematical law. The IRS uses it to catch tax cheats."

"What law?"

"A law of the universe; one of those quirky things about numbers. Benford found out, no matter what numbers you're dealing with, some numbers will always be more popular than other numbers."

"Popular?" quizzed Nelson.

"It's called the first-digit law. As it turns out, the number 1 is the most popular number. It randomly appears more often than any other number. In fact, 30% of the time it appears first."

"First where?"

"As the 1st digit in any list from real-life sources of data. Study any list of numbers and you'll find the same distribution of leading digits. Numbers 1 through 9 always appear in a non-uniform way; the larger the digit, the less it appears first. Number 9 shows up only 4% of the time. It works for all numbers—mountain heights, populations, lengths of rivers, and tax returns."

"I guess that would come in handy," mused Nelson.

"It's admissible in court. Some say it proved that the 2009 Iranian elections were a fraud. Others used it to study the macroeconomic data the Greek government used to justify why it should be admitted to the Euro Zone. In both cases, the first-digit number distributions weren't right."

Nelson drew Adam's attention back to the computer screen. "So how does it apply to Extasis?"

Adam shrugged. "I'm not sure. It looks like ZYN1 is more related laterally across silos than it is to the individual projects that claim it. It's related by containing the only numbers that disobey Benford's Law."

"If the numbers aren't right, how does that help us?"

"It must be the one place where they cook their books using somebody else's recipe. Something else is weird. Here, look..." Adam opened a spreadsheet. "I extracted values of ZYN1 for every project across the board and listed them together. I matched each extracted value with the original project number it corresponded with to keep a reference to the point of origin."

"Yeah...so?"

Adam selected the full range of ZYN1 numbers, right-clicked his mouse, then fed the list into his Benford routine. A small results window opened.

"Look at the distribution of first digits. Numbers 1 and 6 have reversed places. For values of ZYN1, the number 6 is the leading digit most of the time—30% of the time, exactly the percentage the number 1 should be."

Fighting exhaustion, Nelson refocused. "...the number six."

"Yes, there's something that's key about the number 6. I think we need to pull out all projects that have a leading digit of 6 in their ZYN1 cost code. For some reason, those projects have the swapped leading digit."

"All right. Get me the tax ID numbers, in fact, any number associated with accounts receivable for those projects."

Adam shifted forward and set to work.

"Another thing..." Nelson shifted mental gears. "How long would it take to run variations of ZYN1 against the Extasis email database?"

"Not long. I can reuse the routine I wrote to search for Graphene."

"Do it," ordered Nelson.

As Adam worked, he watched Nelson turn back on his tablet computer. "What are you thinking?" asked Adam.

"I saw something last night while researching Bargeau. It may be nothing but I want to find it again. Give me a minute."

Reinvigorated, they worked away for the next half hour. Using material that Mike Dystrom had supplied from London, Nelson scanned through every line item that detailed sources where Liam Bargeau had been mentioned. That included newspaper articles, economic journals, G20 press announcements, and European Central Bank whitepapers to name a few. There was much more to go through than one would imagine. Finally, one item caught Nelson's eye.

"Here it is," he remarked. He selected the reference and did an internet search on the name.

Adam rolled his chair over to see. "What've you got?"

Nelson scrolled through the search results. "I'm not sure. You tell me."

Adam read the name out loud. "Z/Yen...as in ZYN1, is that it?"

"Maybe; it's a hunch." Nelson clicked on a link and the two of them scanned the page. "Z/Yen...London's leading commercial think tank," read Nelson. "Z/Yen was founded in 1994 to promote societal advance through better finance and technology..."

"What's the connection between Bargeau and Z/Yen?"

Nelson went back to Dystrom's original material and looked up the reference. "Liam Bargeau was listed as someone who did work for the Bank of International Settlements." Nelson drilled deeper for detail. "Here it is...Bargeau was a BIS consultant in their paper on the External Position of Central Banks. That paper was used by Z/Yen in their GFCI report."

"What's GFCI?" asked Adam.

"The *Global Financial Centres Index*—twice a year it rates and ranks 77 global financial centers."

"What does that have to do with Graphene?"

Nelson deflated. "Probably nothing."

Adam rolled back to his computer and typed away. "Bargeau to BIS to Z/Yen—two degrees of separation. I'll run the smart-agent and see what else comes up two degrees from Z/Yen."

Nelson leaned over to watch the outcome on Adam's screen. Adam had downloaded all of Dystrom's data from the *dassergill* subpage and loaded it into a unique relational database, one accessed by software agents Adam had programmed to search out webs of connectivity among discrete components.

Adam scanned the results screen. "There's only one other connection two-degrees deep. It goes from Bargeau to QinetiQ to Z/Yen."

The new name rang a bell with Nelson. "QinetiQ?"

"Yeah," confirmed Adam. "What's that?"

"It's a British defense contractor."

Adam linked to more detail. "Bargeau was listed as an associate expert on a project at QinetiQ. That project commissioned a study by Z/Yen."

"A study on what?" asked Nelson.

"Projecting the stability of global financial markets out to 2025."

"Interesting topic for a defense contractor. Does the project at QinetiQ have a name?"

Adam searched. "No, I don't see anything…no, wait, here's something." Adam scanned the text. "In the project name field they've got the number 1 with square brackets around it."

Nelson slid over to have a look at [1]. "Maybe it's a footnote reference."

Adam scrolled down. "Yeah, you're right. It says '*see Dstl.*'"

Nelson thought a moment. "Fascinating; the name *Dstl* is usually branded officially with square brackets around it—[Dstl]."

Adam slumped back. "OK, but what the fuck is it?"

Nelson tensed. "The *Defence Science and Technology Laboratory* in Britain, that's my bet. Their Porton Down location southwest of London is one of the most sensitive and experimental sites in the UK."

Adam read from search results. "[Dstl]'s stated purpose is '*to maximize the impact of science and technology for the defense and security of the UK.*'"

"Yeah," confirmed Nelson. "In 2001, Britain's *Defence Evaluation and Research Agency*, known as DERA, split in two parts—[Dstl] and QinetiQ. Dstl was chartered to carry out science and technology work that had to be done by the government. Related private sector work went to QinetiQ."

Adam's fingers hovered over the keyboard. "So [Dstl] in Britain is like DARPA in the U.S., is that it?"

"That's exactly it." Adam's reference to the *Defense Advanced Research Projects Agency* animated Nelson. Impressed by Adam's insight, Nelson was quick to add, "And QinetiQ in Britain is like In-Q-Tel here."

Nelson's thoughts raced back to his meeting with Aubrey Marks in D.C. and talk of Christina Parish's relationship with Bargeau. Aubrey had assured Nelson that any work Extasis had done that Chimaera knew about was the result of In-Q-Tel contracts given to Extasis—that included Project G.

"OK," sighed Adam. "I've heard of DARPA but what's In-Q-Tel again?"

"The American version of QinetiQ; it's technology R&D by the federal government, leveraging the best of the private sector. In-Q-Tel is the CIA as venture capitalist. It awards contracts to private firms to develop advance technology for the military and intelligence services."

"Are these British and U.S. agencies related?" asked Adam.

"In some ways. They overlap in places but they're not identical. The CIA created In-Q-Tel in '99. At one time, In-Q-Tel owned $2 million of Google shares. The CIA sold the stock in 2005 because Google bought Keyhole."

Adam recognized the name Keyhole. "The satellite mapping software..."

"Developed by the CIA. It's now called *Google Earth*."

Adam brought to the foreground the Extasis cost code screen. "Maybe this ZYN1 cost code is a mix between Z/Yen and footnote #1 from the project name field in the QinetiQ document."

"A footnote pointing to [Dstl]." Nelson considered it. "But what project is [Dstl] doing? And what is Bargeau's part in it?"

"How are we going to find that out?"

Nelson paused in thought. "[Dstl] has another site at Harwell, Oxford, their science and innovation campus. Let's look for any reference that ties Bargeau to work going on at Porton Down or Harwell. Whatever work that is, we need to drill into it."

Adam rocked back. "Getting into Extasis is one thing. You said Porton Down was some kind of secret site. Who runs it?"

"Britain's Ministry of Defence."

Adam bolted from his seat and paced to the window. "No way! You said if I help you, you wouldn't call the feds but this is getting into shit that *guarantees* I'll get caught. Going any farther with this is stupid."

Nelson sat, unresponsive. He knew they were too tired to argue. A lot had happened overnight. There was much to process. For now, it was best not to push things too far. Nelson stuffed his tablet into his jacket's inside pocket.

"Let's get some breakfast."

Adam remained at the window. "I'd rather get some sleep."

Nelson stood a moment, holding back what he wanted to say. "All right, but don't sweat this, OK? We're doing fine." Turning to go, Nelson pulled on his jacket and zipped it up. "I'll give you a call later."

Adam said nothing. Nelson left the apartment and made his way downstairs to the lobby with a swirl of revelations busying his mind. Maybe Adam had a point; it was time to regroup instead of rushing forward. Owen wanted the ETC to be a decoy to draw out cabal members within NCS. Such provocations should be done in stages. Waiting a few hours might serve them well.

Nelson pulled out his phone to call Aubrey Marks. Bouncing some new information off her might yield more without having to risk more hacking. Nelson dialed Aubrey's private number.

"*...the number you have reached is no longer in service...*"

22

0000 0001 0110

9:17 am EST, Wednesday December 6th

Bright sun and cold air swept the Midtown sidewalk. Nelson wavered between stopping for breakfast and heading to his hotel room. Struck by winter's chill, he tried rubbing the ache from his hands. Lack of sleep made it hard to concentrate even as he wondered about the way forward.

The darkness surrounding the ETC was designed to hide things, but why? Finding a way through such an engineered dark challenged all he thought was true. Without better reference points, few ways measured progress. He'd never faced a task so undefined yet presented as if so much hung in the balance on making it work. He changed direction toward his hotel and his phone rang.

It was Hollister in D.C. "Zack, what's going on?"

"I've connected the dots on the beacon trace."

Nelson slowed his steps. Adam's drop of the Graphene research harvested by Dystrom had been processed by handlers at CIG+XM. Plotting its path through network routers might be the break Nelson was waiting for.

"Where did it go?"

"Not where we expected."

"The Mainland?"

"Briefly. It went through Hong Kong, but no CIG+XM servers were touched along the way."

"What about the sending node?" asked Nelson.

"No, not even that. If they're running this, they're going to a lot of trouble to keep it completely separate from CIG+XM."

"Their Manhattan location is high profile. It might make sense to stay insulated in case the whole thing gets busted."

"Maybe," commented Hollister. "But then it gets strange. If Beijing is behind this, why would it route something to Hong Kong just to bounce it back across the Pacific and into the Caribbean?"

"Where to?"

"Curacao."

Nelson stopped on the sidewalk. "Curacao? That's the end of the trace?"

"Yeah. I checked it every which way. The drop zigzagged the world, winding up on a mobile device in Curacao, its final destination. I know exactly where it landed when it made delivery. I'll text you the coordinates."

For a moment, Nelson was stymied. Exhaustion mixed with surprise and left him standing in the cold, waiting for a street light to change.

"The Caribbean…what is that all about?" he asked rhetorically.

"I'm about to find out," answered Hollister. "I'm at the airport. In seven hours I'll be there. I'm going to check it out."

"Wait up! I was told we weren't supposed to get on public carriers."

"No one told me that. We have to follow up on this. The connection is in Curacao. It could be the Chinese but it might be someone else."

"It doesn't make sense," concluded Nelson.

"All the more reason to run it down."

The light changed but Nelson stayed rooted in place. "There's no other way we can track this?"

"Not if we need a fast turnaround. I'm not doing anything in D.C. anyway; my lobbyist is still on holiday break."

Nelson struggled to understand. "Why an island off the coast of Venezuela? Does CIG+XM have anything located around there?"

"Nada. Nothing I can find."

"How are you getting there?"

"A flight to Aruba. From there it's a short hop by local carrier."

"All right," agreed Nelson, reluctantly. "Call me when you get in. We need to go over what I got into last night; it has a European connection. I'll put it in a *safe place* in case you get time to check it out."

"All right, wish me luck."

"To hell with luck." Nelson stepped across the street. "Watch yourself."

The call ended. By the time Nelson reached the other side of the street, his phone buzzed again. It was Zack's text message with the trace coordinates.

23

0000 0001 0111

2:13 pm EST, Wednesday December 6th

News of an incoming message glowed in the middle of the dashboard. Katherine Stalt recognized the sender and steered through traffic.

Two of three possibilities from her State Department sweep already had been eliminated by facial recognition cross-indexed to biographical data. It was unlikely that either of them met Owen Raedalus in the maze of corridors and offices at State. The only unanswered question concerned the license plate on the SUV that delivered the mystery man to the C Street entrance.

Tapping the middle console, she raced through the text, her eyes catching sight of a telling acronym: ODNI—*Office of the Director of National Intelligence*. There was no way the mystery man she'd seen at the State Department was the Director, so who was he? Her scrolling stopped as the message ended on a name.

The SUV was assigned to a pool of vehicles used by staff members of the ODNI, but that particular car was being used by an agency man on Special Assignment to the ODNI from DHS. His name was Richard Marks.

Katherine sat with the flow of traffic rushing past her and absorbed the news. Richard was a good match for the profile expected. He was highly placed in the Intelligence Community like Owen. Both were matrixed between agencies, Owen as Senior Liaison and Focal Point Officer at DOD for DHS and Richard on Special Assignment at ODNI for DHS. Neither man had a core function, as defined by job descriptions, rooted in State Department business.

The fact that two high-placed IC officials had arrived at separate entrances at State near the same time was circumstantial. Linking them meant follow-up confirmation. Either way, her handler needed to know. It was possible what he knew might make further validation unnecessary. She dialed and waited.

"Katherine, I hope you have something for me. Where are you?"

"Not far from Andrews."

"You lost Raedalus, didn't you." The revelation was matter-of-fact.

Katherine stammered, "He went on base; I couldn't follow him."

"It doesn't matter now; his plane is already gone."

"His plane?" Katherine was blindsided. "He didn't have a trip scheduled."

"A salient point that proves why you were following him."

"Do you have someone else on him besides me?"

"I can pinpoint locations but not who he's meeting with. That's your job."

"Do you know where he's going?"

"A vector is not confirmation, but I'll have it soon."

"Should I follow him?"

"There isn't time. He'll be done before you get there. Now, did you call to tell me you lost him or is there something else? You have more about State?"

"Yes," confirmed Katherine. "I ran the license plate on the SUV. It's listed in a pool assigned to ODNI. Lately, it's been used by Richard Marks." Katherine waited but heard only silence. "You still there?"

"Yes, I'm here." The voice was deeper and subdued. "I need this verified some other way," he ordered, his voice graveled with concern. "I suggest you follow Mr. Marks from now on. Leave Owen to me."

"You're changing the assignment?"

"The assignment stays the same. All that changes is the method to accomplish it. That method is now focused on Richard Marks."

"Same parameters? Who he meets with outside his regular schedule?"

"Yes. If he should return to the State Department, I'll pinpoint Owen's location when he does. It'll be another way we can verify your information."

Katherine hesitated, unsure if she should accept the new terms.

The handler asked, "Do you have a problem with that?"

"We're talking about the ODNI..." started Katherine.

"You follow Raedalus; why should Richard Marks be different?"

"He's not different; it's a matter of scale. Besides, Richard is on Agency special assignment. How do we know what constitutes his regular schedule?"

"On special assignment doesn't mean going rogue. I don't understand your objection. I've been providing you with Owen's schedule..."

"Yes, but only the one he publishes on his calendar. We both know that calendar by necessity doesn't cover everything of substance."

"If you're uncomfortable with the assignment, I'll find someone else. I'm not asking you to provide classified content from these meetings."

"No but monitoring movements and collecting names of contacts might be seen as advance work abetting serious crimes against classified materials."

"Everywhere you've gone has been public space. You've done nothing more than what paparazzi do to famous people everyday around the world. If you are ill at ease with it, I'll find a replacement. But I need to know now."

Katherine thought of time already invested. She thought of Nelson Geiss. If she quit, she might never know his involvement. And quitting now would not forego her culpability; she had done too much already to claim no part in this.

She asked, "I'll have schedules for Marks, the same way as Raedalus?"

"I would imagine; I'll have to see. All I can tell you is, this work is vitally important. We have little time to understand what's going on. You can't imagine the possible repercussions if we let this go. So few are in the position to know the truth. Turning away now is not an option for me. Are you in?"

Katherine was startled. Her handler had never said so much with such gravitas. Was it genuine? She could only be sure how she felt.

"I'm in."

24

0000 0001 1000

5:43 pm EST, Wednesday December 6th

The alarm in Nelson's dreams grew louder until it became a ringing phone. He awoke with a start in the fading light of day of his hotel room and tossed back the blanket. Sitting up on the side of the bed, he grabbed his phone from the nightstand and heaved into it, "Yeah…who's this?"

"Dystrom. It sounds like I caught you sleeping."

Nelson rubbed his face. "I needed to get up. What's going on?"

"I checked into Aubrey Marks like you wanted."

"Did you find out why her phone is out of service?"

"No."

"Were those people you know at Chimaera any help?"

"They confirmed what I suspected; she's not onsite. They said Aubrey's on a medical leave of absence."

The news woke Nelson up. "Medical leave? What's wrong with her?"

"No one knows. That's the story the main office is giving out."

"That makes no sense. I met with her a couple days ago; she was fine."

"Rumor has it she kept something private until the last minute."

"No one saw it coming?"

"No one I talked to."

"So where is she now? At home?"

"Nobody's sure. Her kids have gone to stay with her ex-husband."

"Richard—is he still in D.C.?"

"Are far as I know. I heard he has a nanny looking after the kids."

"So what happened to Aubrey's phone? She might be on medical leave, but that doesn't cancel phone service."

"No one I talked to has ever heard of the number you had for her."

"Bullshit."

"They all gave me the number to her office at Chimaera. It still works but you get a recording. If you go through the main switchboard, you can get to Aubrey's personal assistant but all he'll say is that she's not available."

"So there's no way to contact Aubrey, even through Chimaera?"

"Apparently not. Not until after the first of the year."

"What's magical about then?"

"That's when she's scheduled to come off leave."

"Her return date's already been set?"

"Tuesday the 2nd of January. Until then, she's incommunicado; that's the official word. No one at Chimaera will say anything more."

"That's damn weird," concluded Nelson.

"Do you think your talk with her had something to do with this?"

"If I was the paranoid type, I might think so."

"I'm *not* paranoid and I think so," asserted Dystrom.

Nelson thought back to Monday's meeting with Aubrey. Her parting words to him had come from a place wrapped in ambiguity and danger. At the time, he could tell she was out on a limb even broaching the subject.

"You need to understand," she had impressed upon him. "Project G is the tip of the iceberg. It was one small piece, farmed out at the last minute only to get things done…they made it look like the money was In-Q-Tel's but they had to do that to be expedient…It was all about keeping to the timetable. No one knows who was behind Project G…and no one wants to ask."

Nelson wondered if Owen had something to do with Aubrey's leave of absence. As Owen divulged at Arlington, he knew about Nelson's meeting with her. It seemed Aubrey's willingness to divulge anything to Nelson had earned her a month of house arrest out of reach of Nelson and his crew.

Nelson shared his thoughts. "Aubrey told me that no one knew who was behind this—but the thing that struck me is when she said that no one wanted to ask."

"Sounds like, in a roundabout way, everyone got the word. We've all been there. You know what that means."

"She also said there's a timetable; timing is all important."

Dystrom added, "You wanted to know what was magical about the 2nd of January? Maybe there's your answer."

"You mean New Year's. You think that plays into this?"

"That'd be my guess. How do they know already she'll be well enough to return to work."

"It could be elective surgery; they might know the recup-time."

"You believe that?" chuckled Dystrom.

Nelson let his pause answer for him. "If that's the timing, then they've got three weeks. Whatever scams they're running to conceal what they're doing have to be kept going for the next three weeks."

Dystrom's cynicism flared, "Does that include running us in circles?"

"Are you suggesting we're part of the scam?"

"I'm just saying—something is seriously wrong with what we're doing. For chrissakes, it's a joke what they told me to go after. There's nothing to discover at CIG+XM in London. Give me a break. Ever since the police hauled me in, I've been followed by somebody, probably not the police—but they're bloody obvious about it. Now why would they want me to know I'm being watched? What kind of operation is this? If the whole point is to get noticed while accomplishing nothing, then I'm doing a bang-up job."

Nelson hesitated. Owen had told him not to divulge the decoy aspects to the ETC and yet, Dystrom was making sense. Nelson could see how what they had him doing in London wasn't being effective as a decoy or anything else. Nelson decided to bide his time before agreeing with Dystrom.

"If what you say about New Year's is true," reasoned Nelson, "we've got three weeks to shake something loose. Let's give it a little more time."

Dystrom pushed back. "I don't see what good that'll do. More of nothing isn't going to get us anywhere."

"For now, let's assume we're part of a larger effort. Our piece alone might not make sense. If you need something to do, check out the safe place. Let me know what you think about the new material."

Dystrom was not convinced. "All right, but I want you to know—I don't feel comfortable like this. This isn't what I'm trained to do."

"Hang in there," concluded Nelson. "I'll get back to you."

The call ended. Nelson dropped the phone on the bed and went into the bathroom to splash water on his face. He sighed into a towel then looked into the mirror and his disbelieving eyes. He hadn't convinced Dystrom and he certainly hadn't convinced himself. If anything, it was the other way around.

Back on the bed, his phone buzzed with an incoming message. He returned to it and punched up the text display. It was Zack, now in Curacao.

"Just arrived. On my way to the coordinates."

25

0000 0001 1001

8:41 pm EST, Wednesday December 6th

The room of quant students had nineteen minutes to finish the sample test question posted on the board. Adam stood; he was done. He gathered his things and dropped off his paper at the lectern. Catching the wary eye of the professor behind his laptop, Adam turned and headed up the aisle to the exit.

Along the way, he noticed Jiaying stuffing paperwork into a binder and heading for the exit without bothering to turn in the assignment. She had obviously abandoned the sample question for a chance to leave when Adam did. Adam was noncommittal about her tagging along.

Jiaying approached as her normal, friendly self. "You blew through that question like you worked on it all night."

Mention of working through the night hit Adam uncomfortably. He shot back, "And you bailed." Anticipating the cold, he raised his coat collar.

Jiaying took the rebuke in stride. "I could've finished, given more time, but I wanted to catch you on your way out."

"What for?"

"I thought we could have dinner."

Adam remained neutral. "Fraternizing before I finish my assignment?"

"It's just dinner. Besides, there's something we should talk about."

Adam exited onto the sidewalk and shuffled to a curious stop. "Fine with me. Where do you want to go?"

Jiaying hailed a taxi. "I don't know; maybe someplace new."

They got in the cab and Jiaying told the driver an address. The car took off and she settled back. "Tell me the secret; how do you finish a question like that so fast? We had thirty minutes; you were done in what, eleven?"

"You weren't timing me or anything, were you?" grinned Adam.

"I just noticed. So what's the trick?"

Adam tried to relax between thoughts of her phone call in Mandarin and the photos Nelson had taken of her with her man-friend. "What makes you think it's a trick? It's calculation."

"Who calculates like that in ten minutes?"

"You're right," confessed Adam. "It would be a hard thing to calculate off the top of your head—if you didn't have some things memorized."

"Like what?" asked Jiaying.

"A question like that assumes you won't have key information. Without that data, a lot of prep-calc is required before going after the core issue."

"OK, so what did you memorize?"

Adam decided to play with her. "What do I get if I tell you?"

Jiaying thought. "I'll buy dinner."

"Fair enough," he agreed casually then let her in on the secret. "I happen to know the top five countries with the highest Per Capita GDP."

Jiaying thought about it. "Oh, I see. Knowing the correct order..."

"Not just the order," interrupted Adam. "The order plus the per capita amounts. The amounts are key."

"OK," challenged Jiaying, looking up the GDP list on her phone's browser. "So tell me, what are they again?"

Adam saw she had them and wanted to test him. He recited the top five from memory. "#1 Liechtenstein at $141,100. #2 Qatar at $102,700. #3 Luxembourg, $84,700. #4 Bermuda, $69,900. And #5 Singapore at $59,900."

Jiaying chuckled. "Whoa, check out the big brain on Adam. So where is the U.S. on the list, any idea?"

Adam guessed. "It's several places down; I don't know exactly."

"It's #12 at $48,100."

"Yeah." Adam reached for her phone. "Let me see."

She handed it over. "So what other kinds of things have you memorized?"

Adam didn't answer. As he checked the GDP list, he noticed #6 on the list—*Jersey* at $57,000. Thoughts jumped to the night before researching Liam Bargeau and the mix-up with New Jersey. If he had memorized the top ten, he would have known that Bargeau's Jersey was not the home of Atlantic City.

"What's wrong?" asked Jiaying.

Adam's reverie faded. "Nothing. It's interesting how many little, out-of-the-way places are at the top. When most people think of the world's richest countries, Liechtenstein, Luxembourg, and Jersey don't come to mind."

"They must be doing something right." She accepted her phone back.

"It's not their large industrial base or natural resources," mused Adam

"Financial services is the number one profit center in the world, not industry," announced Jiaying confidently. "Every quant knows that."

"Most people would be surprised at that," noted Adam. "It's curious: betting on transactions is more profitable than making them, especially if the instrument guarantees profit if you win and big insurance payouts if you lose."

Jiaying smiled. "I like win-win situations. Financial services makes a lot of amazing things possible. New instruments can be created at any time and the transactions moved around in creative ways. It's wide-open territory designed for global players. In America, you'd call it the Wild West."

"The problem is, the Wild West wasn't stable. Which is strange, because I didn't think China liked instability."

"China?" Mention of her home country was taken as a non sequitur.

"Yeah, Chinese Investment Group—you know, the place where you work."

Jiaying grinned. "Capital is not a philosophy; it's a tool, like anything else. Not having proper tools for global work, *that's* instability. Debt is instability."

The taxi pulled to the curb at a Mexican restaurant.

Adam paid the fare and joined Jiaying on the sidewalk. "I didn't think Latin food was one of your favorites."

She took his hand. "Oh, I don't know; I've been developing a taste for it."

They headed inside and were seated. After ordering food and margaritas, they turned their attention to the chips and salsa and each other.

Adam observed, "You've kept your promise and stayed away from me."

"I know what a distraction I can be," she confessed with noticeable pride. "No sense interfering with your work."

"Is that from self-control or self-interest?"

"One begets the other, don't you think?"

"Which comes first?"

"Self-interest, always; you know that."

"So what are you interested in?" asked Adam.

"Your success, of course. It's been a few days; I thought it would be good to check in and see how you're doing."

"Don't you know already?" challenged Adam.

"Why would I know?"

"I assume someone at your work might let you in on developments."

Jiaying waited until the waiter left drinks. "I'm told some things, but that doesn't tell me what you think."

"Is that why you're here? To gather my thoughts for your report?"

She acted hurt. "You make it sound so cold. Why say that? We have plans, you know that. I'm interested in this working—for both of us."

"What have you been told?" Adam waited; if she truly wanted to make him believe they were a couple, she should have no problem answering.

As it was, she paused. "I wasn't told much, only that they received something from you—but they weren't satisfied with it."

Adam deflected the news. "Not satisfied. That's helpful."

She reached over and took his hand. "It's just that they expected more."

"It's early. They'll get more."

"I know, but they're worried about time slipping away."

Adam pulled his hand from hers and lifted his drink for a sip. "They have to understand the complexity of what they've asked for."

"They know it's big; that's why they're willing to pay so much."

"It's more complicated than they let on. Do they realize what's involved?"

"They know more than you think," Jiaying assured him. "They know you're working with someone else. What is that all about?"

Adam was stunned. "Is someone spying on me? They don't trust me?"

"They're risking a lot; they need to know these things."

"How I decide to work is my business."

"And theirs," asserted Jiaying. "It reflects back on them."

Adam answered in a rushed whisper. "What they want is hidden behind layers put in place by top people. What I gave them was the first layer. To get that far went beyond their job description. Certain methods require specialists. If I need to subcontract to crack this, that's what I'll do. I was given no instructions. They left it up to me to figure this out so that's what I'm doing."

"How much does this subcontractor know about the assignment?"

"Only what he needs to know." Adam pointed across the table at her. "You go back and tell them I'm going to use whatever I need to see this through. They'll get what they want." Adam looked away. "If I had any sense, I'd walk away. They weren't upfront about what this was all about."

"That's not the way they see it."

"No? Well, they don't see very much."

"When they hire someone to go into the unknown, they don't expect to hear complaints about the indefinite," charged Jiaying.

"They said what they wanted was at Extasis. It's not. It may be in a dozen places in pieces. As far as I'm concerned, they pointed to the tip of an iceberg and said lift it. Now, either they didn't see the whole thing or they suckered me into thinking this could be handled by one person."

"Why shouldn't they think that? You're the best."

"Even if that's true, some things can't be done by one person. No one believes stealthy cyber tools like STUXNET or GAUSS, FLAME or DUQU were the work of one person. A secret laboratory of top people worked for years to make them functional. If these people you talk to think anyone can do something like that alone, then they aren't as sophisticated as they pretend."

"So what are you saying? You can't do this?" asked Jiaying.

"Is that what you heard?" challenged Adam.

She hesitated. "I'm not sure…"

"I said I'm handling it. If they want something else, they need to step up and supply the means to do it." Adam leaned back as the food arrived.

Jiaying stared with frosty resolve and paused. "I would rather have a positive message for them."

Adam reached for the hot sauce. "Then say nothing."

26

0000 0001 1010

8:46 pm EST, Wednesday December 6th

The financial district of lower Manhattan was a ghost town compared to the crush of activity that occupied its skyscrapers during the day. Nelson Geiss stood in a building's lobby and read the directory board. CIG+XM was not on the list. He hoped another name listed would jog his memory.

Jiaying and her Hong Kong mystery man had come to this building the evening before. Nelson hadn't been able to follow them but he needed to know the layout inside the building in case they returned. Knowing if stairs were accessible or if check-in was required might be the difference between following them or getting stranded in the lobby.

His phone rang. It was fellow contractor Geri Messare. On their last call, she had suggested checking into Chimaera and Aubrey Marks. Maybe her take on recent developments would shine a light on areas gone dark.

"Geri, thanks for returning my call."

As usual, the brunette firebrand was on her game. "Nelson, you're a hard man to get a hold of, in so many ways."

"How so?" Nelson ducked into a lobby alcove away from the windows.

"Only that I've been trying to reach you since Monday afternoon."

"I've had no messages."

"I couldn't leave any," Geri explained. "Has your phone been down?"

"No, I've been making and receiving calls."

"We shouldn't even be talking on the phone," warned Geri.

"How many times did you try to call?" asked Nelson.

"I don't know; I lost count. After I heard you went to D.C. to meet with Aubrey, I tried calling right away."

"How did you hear about that?"

"I'm the one who suggested Chimaera, remember? I suspect you called me in the first place because you know I keep lines of communication open."

"Why were you trying to reach me?"

"Now that I hear the trouble you're having with your phone, I'm not sure I want to go into it."

"If someone is listening to us, you can bet they already know what we're about to say. They only want confirmation."

"So why give it to them?" asked Geri, flippantly.

"I need to know. Why did you try to call after I met with Aubrey?"

Geri became evasive. "Why did you call me today?"

"Because Aubrey's dropped out of sight. They say she's on a medical leave until January 2nd. We both know that isn't true but I want to hear it from you."

Geri was steamed. "I suggested Aubrey to you as a resource. I didn't propose you storm into D.C. to meet with her in person, not the way you did."

"Why does that makes a difference."

"Are you trying to be obvious? Is that the point? Because if it's not, then you've had a serious breach of logic as well as protocol."

"I see no reason why contact would be that sensitive."

"You know better," Geri admonished. "I can't believe this is all your own doing. Someone must be giving you bad advice."

"In critical times, desperate measures *are* logical."

"Are we in critical times?"

"You tell me. Last time we talked, you said there was a black hole around Extasis. The event horizon around it was clearly defined. That doesn't sound like business as usual."

"And tell me, what would that look like in our business?"

"That's why I met with Aubrey—to find out."

"And now she's disappeared behind that event horizon. How is that working out for you?"

"What are you afraid of?" challenged Nelson.

"Afraid?"

"I never knew you to look away just because you were told to do so."

There was a pause. When Geri spoke again, her tone was subdued. "You'd rather be blinded by the light, huh?"

"What are we talking about here?" prompted Nelson.

"If I had known your intentions, I would have told you to walk away."

Nelson gripped the phone. "You're not going to tell me why, are you?"

"You know why; I shouldn't have to say it."

Nelson's frustrations boiled over; he pressed her for more cooperation. "Whatever you think you know, it's not the whole story. Something is about to happen. You can't trust what you've heard officially."

Geri chuckled. "Did we *ever* trust anything official?"

"Where are you? We need to meet?"

"No, we don't. You need to give it a rest; you're tilting at windmills."

The rebuke, coming from a friend, was bitter for Nelson. "You told me there was something massive around Extasis, something you couldn't see; those were your words."

"Yes, well…words are up to interpretation, now aren't they?"

"You didn't try to call me, did you."

"What?"

"Those calls you made, the ones you said never got through. They never happened, did they? Someone got to you."

She laughed. "Oh, my dear, you have a talent for concocting conspiracies, now don't you."

Nelson was matter-of-fact. "If you change your mind, you know where to reach me. But do it quick; I think the timetable only has three more weeks."

Nelson didn't wait for an answer. He ended the call and stuffed phone in pocket. Through the windows, he could see the nighttime traffic cruising by; its motion took him back to what Mike Dystrom in London had said. *"Something is seriously wrong with what we're doing... the whole point is to get noticed while accomplishing nothing."*

Nelson grappled to find a clearer focus. Had someone gotten to Geri, ordered her silent, or was she simply too frightened to say more? Her reaction was evidence enough that Nelson was onto something big and seriously real.

If there was a cabal within IC trying to enact a time-sensitive plan, one would expect them to shut down avenues of inquiry. Secrets by themselves weren't dangerous; it was their relative value and the efforts legitimatized to keep them hidden that made activity around them treacherous.

Geri knew more now about Extasis' true sensitivity. Perhaps being the curious type, she'd looked into it after the first call and got burned. Nelson had hoped to find a way to contact Aubrey. Instead, this reaffirmed how sensitive was the path he was on. If nothing else, that was proof it was the right path.

Nelson checked the time. Adam should be done with quant class. Heading back midtown was the thing to do. Nelson exited through the large revolving glass doors and stepped out on the sidewalk, ready to hail a taxi. As he did, two suited men approached. An unmarked car accelerated to a stop.

One of the men opened the car's rear door as the other one flashed FBI credentials. "Mr. Geiss, you need to come with us."

"What is this about?" asked Nelson.

"Your questions will be answered, but not here. Get in the car."

Nelson compiled. One agent got in the back with him; the other agent hurried around and got in the front passenger seat.

As they drove off, Nelson looked to the agent beside him. "It takes three of you to pick me up?"

The agent gave him a furtive glance but said nothing.

27

0000 0001 1011

9:39 pm EST, Wednesday December 6th

The unmarked car entered underground parking at 26 Federal Plaza and navigated narrow turns leading to a guarded elevator. Nelson was rushed to the 23rd floor where a waiting agent manned an identification kiosk.

"Place your right hand on the glass," ordered the agent.

Nelson asked, "Why am I being fingerprinted?"

The agent's simmering annoyance was held in check. "Standard procedure to be sure you are who you say you are."

A swipe of green light passed beneath Nelson's fingers. The guard checked a monitor then ushered Nelson to a room with one table and two chairs.

"Wait here" was the curt instruction.

Nelson recognized an interrogation room. In the hall of mirrors his ETC assignment had put him in, he had no guidance how to respond. Had his decoy work gone awry or was it working? He had to disavow knowledge of the ETC and yet the special circumstances of that assignment had authorized him to act.

These agents were ignorant of the cabal and the ETC or were aligned with one of them. The truth that could save Nelson was the last thing he was in the position to offer. The door opened and an agent strolled in. To emphasize they were being recorded, the agent glanced at the one-way glass opposite Nelson.

"Mr. Geiss, would you like some coffee? Something to drink?"

"No, thanks." Nelson watched the man take a seat.

"Sorry for the inconvenience; this shouldn't take long."

"What shouldn't take long?" prompted Nelson.

"I have a few questions. We need to document your answers. If everything checks out, we can wrap this up tonight."

"Are you with the FBI?" asked Nelson.

The agent flipped open credentials then returned them to pocket. "You're retired from government service, aren't you?"

"Yes," answered Nelson.

"Before retirement, you were in Special Forces; you've done intelligence work, publicly and privately, isn't that right?"

"You have my record. That's already established."

"Just the same, for sake of clarity, it's good to know." The agent settled back unsatisfied. "Are you still retired? Have you taken assignments lately?"

Nelson knew any hesitation would be detected by the tactical behavioral assessment being conducted on the other side of the camera lens. He answered without diverting his eyes from the agent's face. "I'm still retired. The last private work I did was completed over two years ago."

"That was private work…" The agent nodded. "You have a ranch near Cheyenne…Wyoming, isn't that right?"

"Just west of Cheyenne."

"Beautiful county," the agent deferred. "Have you lived there long?"

"My wife and I bought the place years ago as a refuge, our hideaway."

"Your wife, is she in town with you or back home?"

A pang of sadness and anger through Nelson. Knowing interrogator tactics didn't make one immune from them. The man knew very well where Madelyn was. Nelson was stoic in response, "Madelyn passed away a few years ago."

"Oh, I'm sorry." The agent's false remorse showed hollow. "I experienced a loss like that myself. It was quite an adjustment. How has it been for you?"

Nelson remained even tempered. "I miss her but I manage. Friends help."

The agent nodded. "Are you staying with friends while in town?"

Nelson knew where this was going. A foundation was being laid, a baseline of conditions and motivations to make reasonable whatever conclusions they had in mind. Nelson had no choice but to explain away inconsistencies while maintaining the assignment that had caused them didn't exist.

"No," answered Nelson. "I'm in town alone."

"Staying in a hotel, I suppose?"

"That's right."

The agent paused and let the next question carry more weight. "Have you changed hotels since arriving?"

"Yes," admitted Nelson. "I moved once. I didn't like the first place."

"Was there something bad about it?"

"It was a variety of things?"

"Did you mention your concerns to management; ask for another room?"

"No, I didn't bother."

"I see…so you checked out and went somewhere else."

"I got another place."

"Just to clarify, did you check out or not?"

Nelson knew he'd been had but there was nowhere to go to make clear the intensions he couldn't be upfront about. "No, I meant to but I got busy."

"Got busy. Interesting. You disliked the place enough to leave, but you're still checked in. Still paying for the room you dislike? Why is that?"

"I wasn't in the mood for hassles, you know what I mean?"

"I'm not sure I would let that go. Paying for something I don't like and I'm not using wouldn't set right with me."

"Everyone picks their battles."

"Interesting choice of words. I'm curious; why are you so busy? What exactly brings you to town?"

Nelson took a breath. "It's been a long time since I've been here during the holidays. Madelyn and I had a some good times here at this time of year. I thought it would be good to stay through the holidays, recapture some of that."

"So you're busy visiting places, remembering good times from the past."

"Yes. It puts me in a nice frame of mind; helps me through the holidays. I don't want hassles; I want to enjoy myself."

"You and your wife must have had favorite places in town? Rockefeller Center? Time Square? Central Park?"

"Oh yeah. Restaurants too, although many of those are long gone."

"Was Midtown significant to the two of you?"

"Not particularly," answered Nelson.

"But that's where you're staying."

"It's a central location; easier to shoot up or downtown from there."

"What day did you get here?"

Nelson thought back. A few days seemed an eternity. "Last Saturday."

"Saturday. You've had several days to be busy about town, revisiting those good times. So where have you gotten out to?"

"A few places here and there, not as many as I wanted."

"Oh, why is that?"

"I didn't feel well on Sunday. I'm fighting off something. Most of the day today I slept."

"That's tough. It would be a shame to let this time go to waste."

Nelson forced a smile. "That's one of the luxuries of being retired. I have all the time in the world."

A weak smile passed over the agent's face. "Did you and your wife share any special times around the financial district?"

"We were all over. It's hard to remember. New York has a lot to offer."

"Is that why you were in the financial district tonight?"

"It's not so busy at night. I thought I might recognize something."

"And did you?"

"No, when Madelyn and I were here before, I guess we weren't thinking much about finances."

"At this time of night, there's not much to see in the area where you were. Any reason for going inside the building where you were picked up?"

"Spur of the moment curiosity. I read the directory to see which companies have offices there. It's a distinctive building; I've seen it in pictures."

"Did you recognize any companies?"

"A few, only by name. Nothing noteworthy."

"So, how long are you planning on being in town?"

"I'm not sure," answered Nelson. "It depends how I feel once I get out, visiting the old places. I might stay through the holidays. I might not."

"Any plans to visit other cities? Philadelphia, Boston—D.C.?"

The agent's eye contact set up Nelson to lie. "No…no plans."

The agent sat, his silence impressing on Nelson that the FBI knew about his train trip to see Aubrey Marks. Why the agent didn't press the point was more ominous than a relief. "Very well. I think that's all the questions I have." He took a breath, "You don't have plans to move to a third hotel, do you?"

"No, I'm pretty well settled in."

The agent stood. "Fine. For now, you're free to go. Sorry we can't drive you back to Midtown but the official business ends here."

Following the agent's lead, Nelson stood and turned towards the door. "No problem. It'll give me a chance to do more exploring."

The agent reached for the doorknob then paused. "One other thing. Do you happen to know a Financial Technologist by the name of Adam Perez?"

The gotcha question was meant to blindside. Nelson had to think fast. He rolled with it. "Financial Technologist? I'm not sure what that is. I know a student who's studying quantitative analysis. His name is Adam Perez."

"How do you know Mr. Perez?"

"I bumped into him the other day; struck up a conversation."

"A passing conversation?"

"No, actually we got something to eat and talked a while. I'm fascinated with what he wants to do. I've heard of these guys called quants but never had an opportunity to talk with one before. It's fascinating stuff."

"Have you seen him around much since then?"

"We've talked once or twice; he lives close to my hotel. He's a good resource. There's nothing like asking a native New Yorker if you want to know the best places in town for anything you need."

The meeting was over. The agent nodded, unconvinced but willing to let Nelson go. Nelson wondered why he was being let off so easy; the agent left obvious questions unasked, even as he let Nelson know by inference they were known to both of them.

Nelson wasted no time getting into the elevator and pressing the down button. Exiting into the lobby, an incoming text message from Owen Raedalus drew his attention. He read it as he walked.

"Pre-paid taxi is waiting outside, the driver knows where to go."

28

0000 0001 1100

10:44 pm EST, Wednesday December 6th

As the message had promised, the taxi waited, parked at the curb. Nelson got in and said nothing. If the text was right, the driver knew the destination. Content that the meter was running, the driver gave a glance back and sized up his mystery passenger before driving off and turning north. Nelson sat back, a bit anxious. At least one of them knew where they were going.

The ride lasted a few minutes. On the way, another text message was received. Nelson checked it. Again, it was from Owen.

"Walk 1 bk N—201 Varick—US-DLA"

The taxi driver made two right turns, then headed south and stopped double-parked. He announced their arrival as Nelson put his phone away.

"Here we are—Courtyard Marriott, 181 Varick."

Nelson got out and the cab sped away. Turning around, Nelson gave the hotel entrance a cursory glance. The hotel as destination was an obvious dodge, something innocuous for official taxi records, should they ever be checked into. Owen was taking normal precautions and muddling the trail.

Nelson walked north and crossed King Street. It became evident that the building in the next block was another federal building. It was not as large as the one he had come from but obviously it served multiple purposes.

Nelson passed signs for the post office, passport services, and Department of Veteran Affairs. Finally, he came to an entrance that was labeled only by its address: *201 Varick Street*. The text message had directed him to *US-DLA*. In this context, that meant only one thing—the *U.S. Defense Logistics Agency*.

The DLA was chartered to provide any and all consumables to agencies that came under the umbrella of defense. From food and fuel, to construction equipment and spare parts. In the context of the ETC, Nelson could see no link between DLA and his assignment. The location must simply be an unexpected place under federal control where Owen could meet with him after office hours. By morning, all traces they had been there would be gone.

Nelson stood in winter darkness and considered his options. He noticed a man standing back, across the street, against a red door. The man wore a dark windbreaker and a plain baseball cap. As soon as Nelson looked his way, the man headed in Nelson's direction. Nelson assumed it was his escort. As this time of night, federal offices in the building would be closed, locked, and guarded. Entry to the building would be by invitation only.

The man approached Nelson and asked, "Are you meeting someone?"

"201 Varick," answered Nelson. "*US-DLA*."

The man held his phone up, close to Nelson's face. "Don't blink."

The camera lens angled close to Nelson's eye. There was a soft, red flash. The man pulled his camera back to check. It only took a moment to send and receive verification of the retinal scan. Turning towards the doors of 201 Varick, the man led the way. "Follow me."

Neither man said a word on the way up. The offices of the US Defense Logistics Agency normally would have been locked. On this night, another man wearing a dark windbreaker stood guard at the door. He let Nelson pass, directing him back to a windowless conference room. Nelson was told it would be easy to find; it was the only area in the office space with lights on.

Nelson opened the conference room door to find Owen sitting behind a large, horseshoe-shaped table. He was on his phone, deep in thought. He looked up and waved Nelson in with one hand. Nelson closed the door behind him and took a seat. It only took a minute for Owen to wrap up his call with a scattering of words, all of which were non-telling.

Owen set phone on table and leaned back. "You've had quite a day."

Nelson maintained watch-and-see mode. He would let Owen talk. Hopefully, there'd be revelations of what the day's events were all about.

Owen sucked in a breath, his frustration epitomized with a sigh. "Somehow I don't think interrogation by the FBI was part of your schedule."

Nelson worked to steady his nerves. "Maybe you can explain it."

"What good would it do? You seem intent on having things your way regardless what I say."

"You can contact me anytime you like. I don't hear from you."

"Maybe I *have* been distracted," offered Owen. "I wrongly presumed I wouldn't have to micro-manage this."

"You're over-reaching. What part of C4ISR have you provided me or my crew? If anything, acting as your decoys means fending for ourselves."

"Obvious logistic lines between us might be easily detected. If they were, that would defeat the point of placing decoys in the field. You know that."

"Just how disposable are your decoys?"

Owen stood and slowly circled the horseshoe. "I didn't come here to argue. I'm not supposed to be here at all. Thanks to this unfortunate episode tonight, I now see how much this visit is overdue."

Nelson followed Owen with his eyes. "Why was I picked up?"

"Why? Because you went into that building in the financial center after hours. I told you; that's exactly how Jiaying Xianzi first appeared on the radar. She walked into a stakeout and got herself on a watch list. Now you've gotten yourself on one. That's the last thing we needed."

"That doesn't make sense," railed Nelson. "They've been watching me since I got here. They knew my movements from days ago, not just tonight."

Owen stopped and stared. "Then it was something else, days ago, that got you on the watch list. Maybe it was taking up with that Perez kid; you did *that* without consultation. Perez is in bed with Jiaying; what do you expect? For someone bitching about lines of communications, you have a piss-poor track record. When have you have cleared any of this through DIOCC?"

"Adam has talents we need," explained Nelson.

"An arguable point. What's not contestable are the facts: he's connected to her; now you're connected to him. Christ Almighty! A junior achiever could connect the dots."

"You told me to act like I had a purpose. That's what I did."

"A purpose, not a crusade! It doesn't matter now. You're no good to me as decoys if the cabal thinks you've been made by feds not in on the game."

"There's no proof of that," declared Nelson. "As far as we know, that interrogator tonight might be part of the cabal."

"For what reason would the cabal bring you in?"

"Intimidation. See what they can find. Record my answers for blackmail or evidence to use later. Or maybe to give you a warped impression of their motives, like the one you may already have."

Owen raised his voice. "You were given one assignment: use Jiaying to find out what CIG+XM is up to. You weren't told to hack for them! My God, you spent an entire night going farther into it than even *they* asked for."

"Nothing of importance was turned over to them."

"You think that's all there is to it? The hacking *itself* has gotten noticed. Look at London. Your man Dystrom has made himself into a pariah in Europe on account of the snooping you told him to do."

Nelson shouted back. "Since when are we only interested in *who* is snooping and not *what* the hell they're after? Knowing the kinds of secrets they're trying to steal might be more important in figuring this out than catching a few cyber criminals on your *10 Most Wanted List*."

"That's not your assignment," Owen reaffirmed.

"My assignment is find out what CIG+XM is up to. That includes why they're so interested in the things they're going after. For some reason, they know full well that something strategic is going on. It's obvious to me. It's warping lines of communication all throughout the IC community. That isn't natural and is the clearest indication that this needs to be rooted out. Look at what happened to Aubrey Marks."

"Nothing happened to Aubrey; she's on medical leave."

"And unreachable."

"She's out of the loop for her own reasons. We have to respect that."

"You believe that?"

"And you don't. I know you have a high opinion of yourself but people don't disappear simply because they talk to you. The one thing we don't need going forward are operations driven by narcissism and magical thinking. I don't have to explain anything to you but I want this to work."

"Then hear this: waiting for someone to react to decoys isn't going to cut it.

We may only have three weeks left before something happens, something we might not be able to take back."

"I realize you're an expert in conspiracy theories," Owen started. "But this is no time to get lost in them."

"That's so convenient, isn't it?"

"OK, how's this: I can't pivot a worldwide intelligence apparatus on the whims of conjecture—and that's all you've got."

"All leads are conjecture at first; if they were anything else, we wouldn't have to run them down, now would we?

"We don't have time to chase every pattern in the data. Stay focused."

"It's leading somewhere, I know it."

Owen shook his head in disbelief. "Everything leads somewhere. Meanwhile, you still haven't answered the original question. While you're busy hacking away at phantoms, CIG+XM operates with impunity. Jiaying is probably running six or seven patsies like Adam under your nose but you don't know about them because you're doing *her* assignment instead of mine."

"Six or seven patsies?"

"What do you think the business cards were for, the ones she and her Hong Kong friend delivered to the financial district? You were in the same building tonight—did you find out? No, instead, you've been spending your time investigating the purchasing habits of European financiers."

"Liam Bargeau is connected to this in some way," declared Nelson.

"Don't start with that. Besides the fact that CIG+XM hired Adam Perez, we know nothing more of substance than when you got here."

"We know about the Curacao connection."

"That's another thing," roared Owen. "Hollister leaves the country without backup, without a plan. How smart was that?"

"It's more productive than waiting around D.C. for lobbyists to return from vacation. What was that? Where's the criticality?"

"The lobbyist Hollister was assigned to is part of a firm. It's the firm that represents CIG+XM. They aren't *all* out of town."

"Even the ones in town aren't doing anything until after the 1st."

Owen walked back around the horseshoe and picked up his phone. "I need to get back to D.C. There are certain things I have to put in place while I'm here. I don't have time to debate this. There's a matter we need to talk about; it's too important to handle over the phone. It concerns Curacao."

Nelson reengaged. "I don't get why CIG+XM would send the information that Adam gave them to a mobile device in South America."

Owen sat down. "I agree. As a matter of fact, it's the one thing you've discovered that the ETC finds promising."

"The route trace on the Graphene material went through Hong Kong but it never touched CIG+XM servers."

"We can't conclude anything from that. China and Venezuela have been increasing their partnership deals. China's biggest investments in Latin America are in Venezuela. And China is Venezuela's second-largest trading partner. They've made billion-dollar deals for oil, railroads, and cell phone factories. Together, they put up a communications satellite. The fact that Curacao is off the coast is incidental. The fact that your Graphene data didn't go to Beijing doesn't rule out the Chinese."

"So what do we need to talk about?"

"It concerns Hollister."

"What about him?"

"We intercepted a message from him—it was meant for you."

Nelson was stunned. "You blocked the call?"

"We had to process it through Site R."

Nelson flew to his feet and paced the open space of the horseshoe. He thought of Geri Messare, Dystrom at the start of the ETC, and Aubrey Marks. If the ETC was screening agent calls with the NSA on a check-delay, how would he ever be sure if Aubrey or anyone else had tried to reach him?

"What other calls have you intercepted?"

"We're talking about Curacao."

"What the hell is going on?" demanded Nelson.

"Once Hollister left the country, we had to intervene."

"How many layers of insulation do you need?"

"We couldn't let something like this run wild; you know how it works."

"When did Hollister send the message?"

"Earlier this evening, about 6:30 eastern time."

"Was it text or voice?"

"Voice."

"What did he say?"

"He indicated that he had made a significant find. He wouldn't talk about it in detail on the phone. He sounded rushed. He said it was imperative that you and Adam get down there right away."

"Go down there?"

"He said there's a window of opportunity but it's closing. If the three of you work it right, you might be able crack what's behind this."

"You're telling me this now so why couldn't you have let the message go through when he sent it? It's been hours and he hasn't heard back from me."

"We sent confirmation back for you."

Nelson was livid. "You sent a message to Hollister, impersonating me?"

"This is too important to go rogue on. We have to coordinate and we need DIOCC involved. This has priority status in the Site R situation room. We have a Defense Intelligence Operations Coordination Center for a reason. I didn't want you to run off and do something until we had a chance to talk. The text we sent told Hollister to hold tight; that you'd get back to him."

Nelson sat silent, his thoughts pulled in several directions. Anger at having

1

his phone calls intercepted was tempered by the possibilities suggested by Hollister's call. Nelson asked, "When can I hear his call?"

"I don't have it with me…it can be arranged."

"So what are you suggesting I do?"

Owen took a breath. He looked down at the table and then up at Nelson. "I want you to follow up with Hollister; go to Curacao—but the whole thing gets coordinated out of Site R. No moves are made without clearance."

"What moves?"

"Exactly what Hollister suggested."

"That's open-ended, way beyond decoy work."

"That's right."

"You're prepared to authorize unrestricted OCONUS operations?"

"If it gets to the bottom of this, we'll do whatever it takes."

Nelson found the shift in strategy unnerving. Going from decoys on a leash to unhindered operatives operating outside the continental U.S. was a sea change in responsibility hardly justified by one rushed call from Hollister.

"There's a lot more to this you're not telling," challenged Nelson.

"There always is; that's the way it works with command and control."

"Why does my cell rate the upgrade? I thought we were just retirees and private contractors on the fringe. If you don't think we're good candidates to be selected for the caliber of cabal we're facing, why have we suddenly become qualified to lead an effort like this offshore?"

"Any answer I give, you'll question," quipped Owen. "Maybe if I said you're expendable, you'd believe it. You know as well as I do, precise battle plans are only good until the battle begins. It's an unfortunate fact that Hollister got injected into Curacao this way—but now that he's there, we have to roll with it. You know him better than me so you get to go."

"What about Adam? You said Hollister asked for him too."

Owen stood and prepared to leave. "He's your problem. You flipped him, you can saddle him up."

"He's not an asset, he's a civilian," reminded Nelson.

"A fine point to be recognizing now," snapped Owen.

"When I get down there, do I reach you the same way?"

"No, Site R will have an encrypted satellite number for you to contact. I'll be copied on everything. They'll have more details on the trip by morning."

"Why can't I have them now?"

Owen checked the clock on the wall. "Because I've got to get to the downtown Manhattan heliport. You're not my only business."

With that, Owen left the room. In time, so did Nelson. He stepped back out on Varick Street. By now, it was close to midnight and a light snow was dusting the street. One day had changed everything—and tomorrow was another day.

29

0000 0001 1101

11:56 pm EST, Wednesday December 6th

Nelson walked a block east then headed north on 6th Avenue. At the corner of 6th and W. Houston St., he flagged down a taxi to take him north to his hotel. Along the way, a darkened city passed by the half-frosted window. Trapped by the ride, his thoughts couldn't escape the changing landscape. Dismissing he was part of that landscape was out of the question and yet, as he watched it pass by, crucial details defining his place within it were blurring.

He had to accept the fact; it was no longer only the terrain around him that moved in dark and disorientating ways. Despite the ETC or jarring orders from Owen, now he had his own interest in going forward. Finding the one answer to explain it all seemed like asking too much and yet he had a strong instinct to pursue it. He wasn't sure of it but he was sure of himself.

If he decided to move ahead, he had to speak with Adam Perez right away. What to say was far from certain. Accepting the ETC had been a leap of faith born on a call to duty even if it meant relinquishing much of the control over his life. Now that he was days into it, he had to ask: how much would he invest in something so ill-conceived and dangerously expansive? How deep would rising interest in what was going on drive him into the unknown?

To accept the assignment change from Owen, Nelson would be swept into deeper waters where tidal forces could be too strong to move against. Once he left the country and joined Hollister, there would be no chance to second-guess or decide to turn back unilaterally. He'd have to see it through. Was curiosity enough to overrule lingering doubts? If not, he had better turn back now.

The taxi pulled up in front of Nelson's hotel with its windshield wipers slapping flecks of wet snow into oblivion. Nelson paid his fare and stepped out onto the sidewalk. After the relative warmth of the taxi's back seat, the after-midnight chill was both invigorating and discordant. Nelson presumed he would go upstairs to his room and give his decision more time to settle.

As it was, the cold air reminded him of his ranch. If he went back there now, he'd never have answers. Who knew what would happen to Hollister. In three weeks, if something horrendous greeted the new year, what would he tell himself about what might have been? Knowing the answer, he turned and started walking. He didn't stop until he was knocking on Apartment 2C.

Adam Perez answered the door in a somber daze. "It's after midnight. You're showing up now?"

Nelson stepped in and closed the door behind him. "It couldn't be helped."

"I expected you hours ago."

Nelson could see that Adam had been on his computer. "You've been working on cost codes?"

Adam gave his workstation an irritated glance. "Yeah. Opening doors to find more doors."

"They've hidden it well for a reason. It's a good sign."

Adam finished off a beer and dropped the empty bottle in the trash. "I still think they have it behind one of those nodes you call honeypots."

"The places you call inner sanctums."

"Financials have to be derived from something. So where are the project documents, test cases, the prototype designs? They have to be somewhere."

Nelson sat down. "If you're so certain of that, then we need to use the financials and email to identify which one is *not* a honeypot."

"Easier said than done." Adam steered away from his workstation and slumped down on the couch.

"What about the traffic monitors we put on them? Any patterns?"

"You can always find patterns but what good are they?" complained Adam. "Should we go after the one with more or less traffic? You said someone told you the project was hot at the end of last year; does that mean less traffic now? Wouldn't honeypots have less traffic too? Maybe not. How can we know? If I set a trap, I'd mimic the real thing—or would I?"

"There's no way to use a sniffer and catch patterns in the data stream?"

Adam shook his head. "It's all encrypted so why go there? Besides, all we could sniff would be traffic from the inside coming out; traffic that stays inside is blind to us but that's the real project traffic."

"There has to be another way to get at it."

"There is," Adam was quick to add. "Have someone on the inside give us a hint. You know people; why don't you arrange it?"

Adam thought back to his dinner with Jiaying and word her bosses were impatient with him. Adam needed to catch a break if he was ever going to have a payday. As long as he had to work with Nelson, he might as well leverage the old man's connections. For Adam, CIG+XM's little project could become an ever-widening sinkhole if some help didn't step in to rescue him.

Nelson hunched forward. He needed to convince the kid to go to Curacao with him. How to do that was a worry since leaving Owen. Adam couldn't be told the true mission with Hollister. Adam was not apt to agree to investigate his bosses at CIG+XM. To get him to go along with the plan, Nelson would have to lie. How much would Adam believe and how far could Nelson push it?

He looked over and caught Adam's eye. He would start with something true and take it from there. "No one inside Extasis is going to help us. But I do know people. Some have been working with me since the beginning of this."

"Doing what?" asked Adam.

"Approaching it from other angles. Whatever CIG+XM is after must be important otherwise they wouldn't be willing to pay you so much to get at it."

"Don't waste my time with the obvious."

Nelson nodded. "And it must be obvious to others. Whatever you're after, you can be sure you're not alone; you're got competition."

"You're sure of that?"

"From what I've seen, it's a crowded field. You're competing not only with others like you that CIG+XM has working on spec; you're also working against competitors of CIG+XM."

Adam took it in. "They have others going after this?"

"Five or six as far as I can tell. One of them is down in the financial district, close to where you work. That's where I was tonight, checking it out."

Adam tensed. "You're sure they're going after the same thing?"

"Whoever gets to it first gets paid; that's the way it goes. These guys are serious about the timeframe, so they're multi-tasking. With only three weeks left, they want parallel effort. They know competitors are doing the same."

Adam stared at the floor. "Shit!"

Nelson pressed the point. "This game isn't over in a matter of weeks; it's sudden death right now. If we don't find what they want within a few days, there will be no payday. Someone else will have it by then, guaranteed."

"How can you be so certain?"

"I know people. I have one of them in Curacao checking things out."

Adam was interested, but defensive. "Why there?"

Nelson lied. "Hold on; it's not what you think. Your Graphene data got intercepted in transit. The first stop on its way to Beijing was Hong Kong. But someone copied it and sent the copy to Curacao, to a competitor."

"That mobile trace went to another company, not CIG+XM?"

"We don't even know if it's a company. All we know is that it's people representing someone else. The guy working with me, his name is Hollister. He checked it out. He's down there now."

"How close can he get?"

"He's on it but there's only so much he can do. He says the competitor has leads it can't work because it needs inroads at some key places. They're places we have leverage with but we need the leads before we can approach them."

"Where are these leads?"

"On the competitor system, on the island. There's a window of opportunity in the next couple of days but Hollister says it'll take a team to go through it."

Adam stood and paced. "You're not suggesting we go, are you?"

"You know the lay of the land at Extasis already. I know Hollister."

"That's way more than what I signed up for," complained Adam.

"It's quick in, quick out. Hack the competitor systems and secure copies of their leads. Once we're back, I'll work the leads and give you what turns up."

"Why not hack the systems from here?"

"They're not reachable from here. It's a local network, that's why they had to use a mobile device as an end node for the Hong Kong copy. It looks like they limited themselves on purpose as extra security. If you're not connected to the internet, you have the ultimate firewall."

Adam rubbed a hand through his close-cropped hair. "It wouldn't work anyway. I don't have a passport."

"We can get around that."

"How are you going to get me out of the country without a passport?"

"Let it go. It's a detail I can handle."

Adam stopped his pacing to look at Nelson. "So what, now you're going to tell me you work for the feds?"

Nelson confronted him. "Would you believe it? What if I told you I was a government agent, undercover in a private intelligence firm that was secretly hired by a competitor of Extasis to test their security? If Extasis doesn't pass the test, not only will the competitor take advantage of what they discover, Extasis won't get any more government contracts. Does that satisfy you?"

Adam stood a moment, trying to read Nelson's face. "No," he answered.

"See what I mean? Answering those questions is a waste of time. All you need to know is what will happen to you if you don't cooperate." Nelson was adamant. "I said the passport isn't a problem. You don't need to know how."

Adam laughed and restarted his pacing. "Oh, man, this is so fucked!"

"You want a payday by Monday? Then do this. If anything, CIG+XM will bonus you for ripping off their competitor and denying them the prize."

"I don't know," declared Adam. "I can't see how I'm going to get through this without some kind of blowback from somebody."

"That's a risk no matter what you do. It's certainly a risk I take."

"You're not a civilian, are you? You're protected."

"Like shit I am," snapped Nelson. "Every agency has a memorial wall. On those walls are nameless stars. But they're not nameless. Ask their families about blowback." Nelson stepped closer. "We go down, we hack the local network and get the leads and then get our asses back here. Once we have those leads, we won't have to worry about cost codes or honeypots."

"If you don't know the leads you can't be confident we can use them."

Nelson stared Adam down. "I've been networking with people in intelligence longer than you've been on the fucking planet. Don't tell me what I can't do. Everyone is reachable, by degrees."

Despite Adam's apprehension, Nelson could see that the kid was caving. The prospect of wrapping this up by the end of the weekend had revived his dream of paying off loans with money to spare.

Adam thought back to the excuses he had told Jiaying at dinner. He had tried to explain to her, "*Certain methods require specialized experts. If I need to subcontract to crack this, that's what I have to do.*" Adam had to admit, from the outside, it might be hard to tell who was using whom.

If Nelson and Hollister and whoever else aided Adam in getting to a payday, then all the better. After days of hacking himself into a bottomless pit,

Adam couldn't help but worry he wasn't going to succeed any other way. No wonder CIG+XM had several hackers working independently on the same task. Even they knew no one alone was going to crack this in time.

"If I go with you, when do we leave?" asked Adam.

"I don't have an exact time but within hours. You'll need to call in sick at work; tell them you won't be back until Monday."

"What's the chance I'll be back by then?"

"That gives us four days. If we can't do it by then, it's not possible. That's the way we approach it. No shit, no fooling around, no doubts. We go in, take what we want, then get the hell out of there. Are you up for that?"

Adam paused. He wanted to say yes but at the same time it seemed impossible he would commit to such a wild-hair thing.

Nelson straightened up and stuffed hands in pockets, preparing to go. He asked, "Where's your sense of adventure? What would MUTEX do?"

Invoking the more radicalized side of Adam's character struck to the heart of one side of his nature, a side he repressed but couldn't deny.

Nelson added, "Where's the guy who toured the National Archives—the kid who wanted to find the grassy knoll testimony or the reports about liquid-metal at Roswell, the Lemurian artifacts, the bad-ass who wanted to see what the insignia patch looks like for that squadron of Air Force UFO's?"

Taken with the details that Nelson knew, Adam couldn't help but feel transparent. "That was a time without consequence," offered Adam.

"You're right," agreed Nelson. "Now it's more complicated—there's consequences if you do, and also if you don't. Now you realize there's consequences either way. The only question is, which one to choose."

Adam stood in place, unable to answer.

Nelson had seen enough. Adam was tipping; he would fall Nelson's way without any more pushing. Given the hour, it was best to go.

Nelson zipped up his coat and headed to the door. "Get some sleep; we're both going to need it. Keep your phone nearby. I'll call when it's time."

Using the assumptive close, Nelson presupposed Adam's concurrence. All Adam had to do to agree to terms was stand there without protesting.

Adam watched Nelson open the front door to leave. He knew he had little room to maneuver. It made no sense to complain about being forced to have other people help him to his goal. It was clearly what he needed.

Nelson stepped out and started to pull the door shut. "Don't share what we talked about with anybody. That includes Jiaying. Remember, you're sick; you want to be left alone—until Monday."

With that, Nelson closed the door and headed downstairs. The walk back to the hotel was not direct. Nelson couldn't help but take precautions about being followed; it was beyond habit now, it was part of his nature. The fact was, if anyone else but the FBI had their places staked out, they already knew the two of them had been in a late-night meeting. Given the events of the night, he could only hope, if that were the case, they'd think the meeting was more about the FBI interrogation than anything else.

As soon as Nelson got to his hotel room, he sent Owen a message requesting a passport waiver to get Adam out of the country. There was no messages from Owen or Site R as of yet, no instructions or itinerary for their trip. Nelson assumed he would have all that by the time he woke up.

He started to undress for bed then remembered the coordinates from Hollister. He said they pinpointed the location on Curacao where the mobile phone received the Graphene data copy from Hong Kong.

Nelson hadn't tracked the coordinates to see where on the island they were located. Now that he and Adam would be traveling there, Nelson's curiosity couldn't wait. He opened his laptop and searched on the coordinates. Drilling into the results, he sat back, entertained as much as confused.

The coordinates corresponded to a place on the island known as Campo Alegre or *Happy Camp*. Others knew the establishment as *Le Mirage*, the largest state-controlled legal brothel in the former Netherland Antilles.

It was one o'clock in the morning. Nelson was tired. He could only imagine why the drop for hacked secrets should wind up in a Caribbean whorehouse. Whoever had that mobile phone obviously enjoyed being on the move.

30

0000 0001 1110

7:28 am EST, Thursday December 7th

Katherine Stalt leaned towards the bathroom mirror to touch up her makeup before putting on a blouse. Between thoughts of herself and what the day would bring, details of work intervened.

Richard Marks wasn't scheduled at the Pentagon until lunchtime. Given the unsteady way she felt, the wait was a reprieve. She brushed through her hair. From the mirror, a reflection looked back. What it saw was a woman, forty-six years smart at the top of her game, capable of whatever she went after. Maybe she was too focused, too adept at one thing to the exclusion of others.

Turning away, she stepped into a skirt. Traces of introspection lingered. She had good friends, a full life. After a brief, misguided marriage when young, she had found love twice in her travels. It had been love as intense as it was ephemeral, but it was love nonetheless.

Maybe the strangeness of her assignment was unnerving. Such things usually weren't a bother. If anything, she craved the adventure and volatility of her work; it made her feel alive. Perhaps working within the Beltway was grating. Most assignments were beyond the Capitol's concentrated intrigue.

Stepping into shoes, she plucked a coat from the closet and considered the holiday season. She never liked this time of year. It always felt better when January 1st was over. She strode towards the kitchen, determined to perk up.

Crossing the living room, the phone rang. It was her handler, energized and to the point. "Katherine, are you free this morning?"

"Yes…"

"I thought so. Marks is busy at DOD, isn't he?"

"Until noon."

"Perfect," the handler stressed. "I need you to move something for me."

"Move what?"

"A pair of sunglasses and sunglass case. They're waiting in the lost and found of Belle Haven's Pro Shop."

"The Country Club?"

"Yes, south of Alexandria. I need them picked up and put in a post office box across town. It should take an hour at most."

"This is not about sunglasses," noted Katherine, directly.

"Of course it isn't but it's all you need to know." The handler's impatience was tempered by his need to get cooperation.

Katherine slowed her steps as she entered the kitchen. "You expect me to be a courier for a black box—no explanations?"

"It's a simple pickup and delivery. I told you what it is."

"No," Katherine corrected. "You told me what it appears to be."

"What it appears to be is all you need to be concerned with."

"Really? If moving it is so simple, why don't you do it?"

"Don't be absurd. I'm not in D.C., you are. This needs to be done now."

Katherine resisted. "Somebody put those sunglasses in the lost and found. Why didn't *they* go to the post office instead of stranding them at the club?"

The handler paused. "They had done enough already."

"You mean they wouldn't go that far?"

"No, they had done more than enough. That last step would have been beyond their routine, impossible to explain."

"But I'll be able to explain it? I'm not a member of Belle Haven. I've only been there as a guest."

"Then, as my guest, you can go there again."

Katherine laughed, astounded at what he was asking. "You expect this with no details, no cover, no backup position? I have no way to knowing how hot this is. It's important to you; that tells me something."

"Everything in your line of work is hot."

"But not blind. The line gets drawn somewhere," declared Katherine. "I don't go out on a limb unless I know the objective, the true objective. It's the way I work; it's the only way to be effective. I can't put that aside any longer."

"I told you the objective," the handler countered.

"Yeah, the sunglasses. I don't know your background, but people in my profession don't risk all on trust alone. The game is enough of a masquerade without expecting a win by stumbling on success. I need to know more."

The handler was unflustered. "I'm prepared to do more. I'm making you an official member of staff."

"Whose staff?"

"Mine. You won't have to hide the fact that you work for me."

"Why the change?"

"You must have heard about the blanket order for security checks throughout all agencies. Every department has to double-check their staffs and recertify security statuses before month's end. Sound familiar?"

Katherine deferred without confirming. "Go on…"

"There's no way of knowing how thorough these checks will be, given the short timeframe, but I can't take the chance. If our connection is discovered, we'll both need a reason for interacting."

"It sounds like a fishing expedition. They're looking for something."

"Or someone. The best thing to do is make you official, at least on the surface. Your real work stays as is."

"I'll need more than my real work to appear official."

"You'll spend an hour on Thursdays at the National Defense University until month's end. I've gotten you a 12:30 pm research clearance. Material is reserved in your name at the library's Classified Documents Center. Library staff will sign you in. An escort will lead you to and from your workspace."

"Does this research have a purpose or is it just cover?" asked Katherine.

"It's your official reason for being on staff, nothing more."

"What if I'm asked about the research...officially?"

"Invoke classification protocols. Any inquiries, no matter who they're from, get directed to your boss, R.Z. Barnett."

For Katherine, hearing a name was a revelation. She had nicknamed the man on the phone her *handler* only because up to now she knew nothing else. Going official with him was a signal of trust on his part; nevertheless, given the black box nature of the request, she hesitated to commit.

"I'll get back to you," she concluded. "I need time to think this over."

"If we're in luck, you're a quick thinker," quipped the handler. "The morning is slipping away. Don't be long. I need this transferred today."

She dropped the connection and leaned back on the kitchen counter. What he was asking went way beyond her original mandate. It was hard to tell if she'd be going out on a limb or moving up in ranking.

She hurried to her computer. It was after 8 am, just in time to catch a friend in an online chat as he arrived at his office. She asked a favor—search government employees for the name R.Z. Barnett. It took a few minutes to get back to her but when he did, a chat window filled with details.

"R.Z. Barnett / research scientist at the Nanomaterials Theory Institute, Center for Nanophase Materials Sciences at Oak Ridge National Laboratory"

Katherine noted Barnett's office phone number had the same area code as the number the handler used. Oak Ridge—no wonder he had kept his identity under wraps. She thanked her friend and called the National Defense University Library. The reference desk verified that materials reserved by Dr. Barnett were waiting for her. Both items verified, she called the handler back.

Barnett explained, "The box key is in the sunglass case."

"What if I get stopped, heading for the post office?"

The handler didn't hesitate. "If it comes to that, identify yourself as a staff researcher for R.Z. Barnett at the Department of Energy."

"How do I explain the sunglasses or the key?"

"I'm a scientist, not a spy. Say what you'd like. Make up something about Belle Haven. Better yet, don't get caught. I'd rather you toss the sunglasses away than risk exposure." He gave her the post office address. "So, are you in? Can I count on you?"

Katherine wavered. Was R.Z. Barnett a scientist or an intelligence agent posing as one? He didn't approach covert work as a seasoned agent. Trusting someone with little experience to lead a covert effort could mean things would turn out badly. But was that reason enough to walk away?

Despite apprehensions, Katherine couldn't resist. Something about all she had seen so far pulled her in line. "I'm in. I'll have it done before lunch."

"Good. We'll talk later. Remember your library appointment today."

"I will."

"And keep your distance from Marks. He's savvier than Owen."

With that, the call ended. Katherine left the house and hit the road.

It took nearly two hours to complete the task. Before entering the post office, she inspected the sunglass case. Under the felt inside the case she found a 2 gigabyte microSD memory card, 15mm × 11mm × 1mm in size, one of the smallest memory cards available.

She fetched a card reader from a travel kit. Before putting the sunglass case in the post office box, she copied the data card. There was no way she was going to let it get away from her without finding out what it contained.

It would be an hour before Richard Marks got out of his Pentagon meeting. She drove to a nearby park and loaded the card copy onto a mini-tablet that traveled with her. She watched as a video playback filled the screen. The camera's angle was static. It pointed obliquely at the ceiling of a car and part of the car's tinted side window. Sounds of rustling were heard but little else. The awkward picture and unintelligible audio tested her patience.

This couldn't be what her handler was so interested in.

On the recording, a phone connection cycled through on speakerphone. A man began to speak. The audio of him and the woman he spoke with was muffled, barely clear enough to be understood. As Katherine listened, it became evident what she was listening to—and why it was important.

"Hello?" the woman answered.

"This is Richard Marks, checking back. How did it go?"

The woman was anxious, guarded. "I did what you said."

"You talked quite a while for saying nothing," chided Marks.

The woman's discontent flared. "Why is this necessary? No doubt you listened in on the call. There's no reason to ask me how it went."

"I need you to understand why this is necessary," stressed Marks.

"As if I couldn't guess." Her sarcasm was bare.

"National security is not an excuse. There are real threats to avoid and real secrets to keep. It won't help to dismiss it all as spin."

"I did what you asked. What else do you want from me?"

"You've known Nelson Geiss a long time. Is there anyone else he might reach out to?"

"You can't expect me to name names like that, not when I know what you'll do with them."

"It's merely a vetting process; don't paint it as being so Machiavellian. Let me remind you that your cooperation will be remembered by the DHS."

"Oh, yeah," chuckled the woman. "And those who don't cooperate will also be remembered."

"And why not?" Marks was adamant. "In times of critical need, it's

important to clearly define who is reliable and accountable and who is not."

"You're either for us or against us, is that it?"

"Just give me the names and you can go back to your life."

The woman tried putting him off. *"I don't know why you come to me. You people have files on everything. You already know his associations."*

"And you know that data is not information. A list of names won't tell us which people Nelson most likely will trust. Only someone in his network might know that kind of soft intelligence."

"I worked with Nelson only a couple of times, years ago. That doesn't mean he bared his soul to me."

Marks added with some relish, *"No matter how much you tried?"*

The innuendo of past advances towards Geiss disturbed her. It was one thing to know a personal fact, quite another to have it served up so blatantly by a representative of the Office of the Director of National Intelligence.

"If I give you names, will you leave me alone?" her voice wavered.

Marks was businesslike with a tinge of menace. *"If you don't give them, it's a certainty I won't."*

She took a breath, struggled with her decision, then spoke with a weakened voice, *"When Nelson was in Special Forces, he fought alongside a British unit of the UKSF. He was close with a British Officer named Gilford Nash."*

"Do you know where Nash is now?"

"Last I heard he had been selected for the Special Reconnaissance Regiment based out of Hereford, but that was a while ago."

Pushing for more, Marks persisted. *"There has to be something else, something that wouldn't be in the files."*

The woman thought a moment. *"Well, I don't know…"*

"Whatever comes to mind," pressed Marks. *"Something you think trivial."*

The woman gave it a moment's thought. *"I once heard Nelson refer to Gilford by a nickname, one he had given him—it was DASSERGILL."*

"Anybody else use that name?"

"No. Even Nelson stopped using it. From what I heard, Gilford hated it."

"I need another name," prompted Marks. *"Someone he trusted."*

There was a moment of silence and then the woman spoke. *"Geiss had such a long career…he knows so many people."*

"Someone he worked with on a covert project, in the field. That kind of environment forces people to bond. I'm looking for someone he might reach out to, someone he would confide in."

Based on the prompting, the woman narrowed the field. *"Only one person comes to mind—that's Katherine Stalt."*

"Why her?"

"She worked with Nelson on a DARPA Forward Cell Security Team in Afghanistan. From what I heard, it was DARPA's first forward presence in a combat zone since Vietnam."

1

"Do you know what DARPA was testing?"

"Certainly not. That lid was tight. I know their chain of command went up through the Adaptive Execution Office; that's all."

"How long did they work together?"

"Must have been...close to a year."

"Where is she now?"

"I think she works out of D.C. on assignment. She's independent."

"All right. I think we're done." Marks struck a conciliatory note. *"I can't always explain why I need to be a hard ass; I hope you realize that."*

The woman was not persuaded. *"I know. You can't help yourself."*

Marks was terse. *"Don't share this call with anyone."*

There was a satirical smile in the woman's voice. *"That's the last thing I would want to do and you know it."*

The call ended. The next sounds were of Richard Marks opening the car door and calling back his driver. Once the driver returned, the video ended.

Katherine sat transfixed. Whoever this woman was, she had given Katherine's name to the person Katherine was tailing. Katherine's handler had to know this if he had listened to the recording and yet he had said nothing. How could Marks be followed if he was now having her watched?

Katherine used her mini-tablet and reached out to a contact she knew could do voice-print identification. It took a while but the woman on the phone was identified as Geri Messare. Katherine knew her by reputation as a topflight IC asset based out of Northern California. For some reason, Nelson Geiss had contacted her, needing information.

Marks seemed convinced that Nelson would pursue other trusted sources. But Katherine had seen Nelson with Owen Raedalus at Arlington. Did Marks know about that? Was Owen a source for Nelson or the other way around? She had no choice; she'd have to tell her handler about making a copy and listening in. She needed to confront him about her situation with Marks.

With voice-print ID in mind, she got an idea. Ever since she had become wary of her assignment, she had recorded her calls with the handler. That included her last call with him, the call in which he identified himself as R.Z. Barnett. She accessed her contact again and requested another ID scan.

"db match negative"

She slumped back. It was logical to think the more notable and strategic government employees had been catalogued. The absence of R.Z. Barnett's voice from the database wasn't conclusive proof of anything.

But it was odd. A high ranking scientist within National Laboratories like Oak Ridge, Los Alamos, Sandia or Lawrence Livermore warranted a complete biometric profile. There was no way to know what the negative results meant. Frustrated, her aimless gaze searched the park around her for answers. Maybe something Barnett had left for her at NDU would be more revealing.

31

0000 0001 1111

12:26 pm EST, Thursday December 7th

The phone rang without an answer from R.Z. Barnett. It was Katherine's third attempt to reach him during the drive to the National Defense University. She approached Ft. McNair and parked her car near the library entrance, then sat in silence and considered her options.

She dare not trail Richard Marks from the Pentagon or anywhere else until she talked with Barnett. As he had warned, Marks was savvier than Owen and Marks wouldn't hesitate to react promptly to tips from Geri Messare. There was no way to know when the phone call between them was recorded. If Katherine was to be followed, let it be pursuing her cover research at NDU.

The NDU Library was an information fortress reserved for active duty military or DOD civilians. For anyone else, access was limited to special cases of alumni or select scholars with specific requests. Every request was processed through strict security protocols and access was limited, monitored, and restricted to an exact date, time, and purpose.

The fact that the handler had gotten Katherine one hour a week in the Classified Documents Center was evidence of the man's influence. To make her cover research appear legitimate, he had to reserve materials for Katherine to pretend to work on—but what were they? Walking between the tall columns of the building's entrance portico, her rising curiosity pushed away worrying thoughts on why she needed to be there.

She passed through security scan and ID check before being signed in, given a visitor badge, and escorted to a work area in the Library's Classified Documents Center. Her phone was taken away and she was instructed not to leave her designated area without an escort. Soon after, a librarian arrived with the materials reserved for her by R.Z. Barnett. Unlocking them from a cart, she reminded Katherine her appointment was over in fifty minutes.

All around was quiet but not calm. A heavy atmosphere of study pervaded occupied cubicles nearby. Katherine looked down on the metal case on the table before her. It was ledger size, 11"x17" and identifiable only by a laminated barcode clipped to its upper right corner.

She slid the locking side-clasp down and pulled open the cover. Inside she found a stack of documents, many on Oak Ridge National Laboratory letterhead. Some were memorandums; others were abstracts from scientific papers. A few were complex diagrams of things Katherine couldn't recognize and didn't understand even when she read the annotated captions. The material appeared to be samples randomly clutched from a catch-all drawer, fragmented research and scientific ingredients without a coherent blueprint.

Despite initial confusion, she was hit with the potential and importance offered by the opportunity to view what lay before her. Given the vagaries of IC work, it was possible she would never gain admittance to this material again. She had to scan as much as she could while she had it in her sights. Barnett had a reason why he wanted her to see this. She had precious few minutes to absorb what she could.

Leaning forward, she was immediately engrossed by the first document. It was a position paper, strategizing on the viability of using a new kind of particle in a quest for a faster computer chip. The particle, 1/100th the diameter of a human hair, was crafted by scientists by altering the architecture of colloids, which were tiny particles suspended in liquids.

By discovering a way to affect directional bonds, amazingly these new particles could be engineered to self-assemble like atoms. The result was a whole new construction set of particles, similar to the periodic table of atoms, with which scientists could design larger-scale molecules and crystals. The crystals in particular were of interest. Using single strands of DNA to create *sticky ends*, the scientists found they could manipulate the number of bonds to create colloids with specific electrical conductivity characteristics. These were distinct enough to make possible the required design parameters of a supercomputer of phenomenal speed and power.

Katherine flipped the page.

The next document was a classified study and comparative review detailing the operational specs and design limitations of the DOE's supercomputer known as Titan. Publicly announced by the Oak Ridge National Laboratory on October 29th, 2012, Titan was heralded in the press as having ten times the power of ORNL's last world-leading system, a computer called Jaguar.

Titan was described as being capable of 20 petaflops—20,000 trillion calculations per second. Of special note was how it creatively employed graphic processing units or GPUs in a powerful new way within its central processor. The public announcement heralded Titan as ushering in a new era in scientific supercomputing. It was publicly touted as an unprecedented breakthrough in computing power for research into energy, climate change, and efficient engines, clearing the way for a wide range of future achievements in science and technology to benefit society.

As Katherine read on it became obvious that, despite the glowing press releases tailored for the public, the classified study report was unimpressed with the Titan achievement. The report noted how Titan's *research-grade speeds* were insufficient for the required analysis of cryptosystems, especially the Rijndael Cipher, the basis for AES Encryption.

The paper then related how the NSA was still under pressure to change policies that were seen as hindering U.S. industries that wanted to use or sell strong cryptographic tools, especially after the development and spread of commercially available public-key tools. It was noted that those policies, by necessity, could not change until the NSA held in private reserve a new benchmark system that would render existing standards obsolete.

The paper ended with the acknowledgement that all modalities, platforms, and meta-logic routines associated with the classified, *crypto-grade* system under development would, by necessity, have to be kept out of Capstone. A footnote described Capstone as the U.S. government's long-term project to develop a set of standards for publicly available cryptography. The primary agencies responsible for Capstone were listed as NIST, the National Institute of Standards and Technology, and the National Security Agency.

Katherine checked the time. She had twenty-five minutes left. Feeling rushed, she turned the page but what she saw, for the most part, was unintelligible. Under a title of *Riemann Zeta-Function Generalities*, a mass of complex math equations filled the page. The next page was the same. Finally, on the third page, a heady discussion of prime numbers, factoring schemes, and known algorithms interrupted the flow of math symbols.

Unable to comprehend the advanced mathematics, Katherine was relegated to skimming. Passing over the pages, her eyes caught keywords and glimpses of the intent behind the topic. There was talk of "*factoring public modulus into two primes then combining the output with the public exponent to crack the private exponent.*" It was noted that hardware improvements would only increase the security of the cryptosystem.

The abstract ended by reminding the reader that Euclid had proved over two thousand years ago that there are infinitely many prime numbers. However, because crypto-algorithms were generally implemented with a fixed key length, the number of primes available to any user of such algorithms was effectively finite. Even so, this still left researchers with a daunting problem.

The Prime Number Theorem stated that the number of prime numbers of length 512 bits or less was roughly 10 to the 150th power—that was greater than the number of atoms in the known universe. It would take more than a paradigm shift in supercomputing to overcome such a calculation problem. It would take a herculean effort with a high-risk/high-payoff strategy to ultimately achieve what was once, most assuredly, the unimaginable—the combined math and computing resources to defeat strong AES encryption.

Startled by the subject matter but with only ten minutes left to her research appointment, Katherine hurried to the next document. It was a whitepaper summarizing recent advances made from spin-offs of DARPA's *Information in a Photon* program started years ago. The breakthrough succeeded in using beams of twisted light for wireless, inter-modular links between super-computer subcomponents. The initial throughput was 85,000 times faster than broadband internet speeds, effectively transmitting 2.56 terabits per second—roughly the equivalent of beaming 70 DVDs every second through free space.

Using the orbital angular momentum of light, researchers had leveraged earlier work that was able to bundle together eight 300Gbps visible light data streams. One bundle of four was transmitted as a thin stream, like a screw thread, while the other four were transmitted around the outside like a sheath. Experimenting with advanced helical shapes not unlike the complexity of DNA, scientists demonstrated that the throughput of the eight bundles of twisted light could be increased in exponential degrees, making possible extremely fast parallel processing units of unlimited size without the need of fiber optic cabling to connect them.

Katherine turned the page and discovered a different fabrication report, one that detailed plans for a prototype process to produce integrated-chip substrate material made from a substance called Graphene.

Efforts to solve the problems of perfecting Graphene as a semiconductor material had been explored. The results of experiments detailed how Graphene was cooked from material called silicon carbide. These new, one-atom-thick sheets of carbon had contacts attached to them and were exposed to a specialized field where room-temperature superconductivity was tested.

The results were promising and demonstrated how the new material could exhibit extraordinary properties that guaranteed transistor-like operations well beyond the terahertz frequency range. The newly-synthesized Graphene composite was deemed ready for use in a proposed *System-On-A-Chip* (SOC) design to be prototyped as a submodule of a new, classified supercomputer. The new composite was called EKAGRAPHENE.

Katherine sat back and stared at the pages. With five minutes left in her appointment, she was too engrossed to accept that her time was about to expire. The material before her was obviously chosen to outline the scope of a classified effort underway. How far along it was one could only guess.

Supercomputers, new material research, higher mathematics, and cryptography—advances in any of it would be game-changing but only one thing would require all of them to succeed. Only one thing could redefine the need to play the game at all. If the intent was to secure a way to defeat AES encryption, then all bets were off. AES encryption was used worldwide by governments, financial institutions, corporations, data networks universally. Having the keys to AES would allow access to all information everywhere.

Katherine paused. But who would gain the access? If AES encryption should ever be cracked and such an awesome ability was kept secret—someone would be granted an incredible advantage over all systems and processes worldwide. The old adage proclaimed that information was power. Being the only one with the ability to open AES meant nothing less than possessing the universal tool of the ultimate insider.

Katherine startled with a more fundamental realization—the documents before her were far from busy work. Being at NDU and having permission to see all of this was not pointless cover activity to provide an excuse for following Richard Marks. If anything, the material was explanation for her assignment. She was being shown puzzle pieces to a secret so valuable, so well protected that even her handler dare not speak of it. Perhaps this was his way of showing suggestive traces in hopes she would deduce its implications. No doubt whatever she was shown was a fraction of what was involved.

She glanced around, her resolve tested. She had rebuked her handler for keeping her in the dark. Was this enough to lift the veil? The material was tantalizing, but was it telling? How could she be sure it was accurate or genuine? As compelling as it was, it had no context. The disturbing fact was, no matter how much she was shown, moving forward would be a leap of faith.

She turned the pages back, one by one, restoring the order of the original pile. As the pages turned, she noticed the stamp of *TOP SECRET* prominent on top corners. Then she noticed another mark. Overlooked before, it was a smaller mark but it appeared in the lower right corner of every page.

Inscrutably, it was one number—*5300*.

It wasn't a page number; it never changed. It couldn't be a section number since the documents were from a grab bag of disparate sources.

The librarian approached. "Your time is up."

Katherine startled at the intrusion. She nodded her acknowledgment then slid the locking clasp closed. As she placed the case on the locking security cart, her escort approached to lead her to the exit.

Stepping outside, Katherine paused between the grand columns of the portico. Knowing secrets had always made her feel disjointed at first. She never knew a secret that wasn't demanding of the one who held onto it. Secrets were expensive personally in ways one could never predict. Privileged knowledge had a way of setting one apart. It wasn't always an elevated position. Those who knew secrets often saw them more as burden than privilege. One had to wonder who was being protected by so much secrecy.

She walked to her car, the weight of her expanding role upon her. She looked west. Across Ft. McNair's parade grounds, beyond the fairways of the East Potomac Golf Course, the Pentagon was a short drive along I-395. Richard Marks would be getting out of his meeting about now. But she wouldn't take that drive. Her destination was now indefinite.

Even so, her purpose felt more assured.

And that was the most inexplicable thing of all.

32

0000 0010 0000

6:34 pm AST, Thursday December 7th

The commercial flight from Aruba touched down at Hato International Airport on the island of Curacao then taxied onto the apron near the terminal. For Nelson Geiss and Adam Perez, it had been a short half-hour trip after a brief layover from their nonstop flight from JFK in New York. They hadn't spoken much. The proximity of other passengers wouldn't allow it.

After a walk to the terminal, they filled in the necessary paperwork for customs and had their passports summarily stamped. For Adam, it was only the second mark made in his new booklet; the first was received in Aruba.

He inspected the stamp and then pocketed the passport with a mumble. "Imagine that. It still works."

Nelson led the way past baggage claim with a carry-on backpack slung over one shoulder. He glanced back. "I hope you realize what a black swan it is for anyone to get one of those in less than twelve hours."

With a shrug, the marvel of an instant passport was dispensed with. "I assume it'll be revoked just as fast, once this is over."

Adam's sarcasm sent Nelson back into himself with a studied reflection. He steered their path through a mélange of passengers and headed for the taxi stand. Dodging errant pedestrians and scampering children, he let his cynicism simmer away. After the long flight with little to do but second-guess his options, there was enough to wonder about.

For starters, the ETC had begun for Nelson with a directive to keep off commercial carriers. All of a sudden, that order had been reversed with no explanation. If it had been important enough before not to leave a paper trail regarding his travels, then why had Owen directed them to charge their own flights and get reimbursed later? It made no sense.

Up until now, Nelson's stateside travel was provided by unmarked DOD jets, like the one that flew him from Warren AFB to Andrews and then on to New York. Why would leaving the U.S. dictate anything less? Being visible now kept only one thing in the dark—the connection between the U.S. government and the two of them arriving in Curacao. It was obvious; they were onto something that must be disavowed. The reason for the change must be as simple at that. If it was, then simplicity only complicated matters.

Waiting in queue for a taxi, Adam grew restless. "When are you going to tell me where we're going?"

Nelson didn't look up. He texted a confirmation of their arrival to the encrypted satellite phone number that Owen had said was patched into Site R.

"We're going to a Gentleman's Club," announced Nelson, matter-of-factly.

"Yeah, that makes sense." Adam squinted at the setting tropical sun.

"I'm not kidding." Nelson sent a second text message, this one to Zack Hollister, notifying him that they were on their way to the rendezvous point.

"A Gentleman's Club. That's the endpoint?" asked Adam.

"That's where the mobile phone took delivery." A taxi pulled up and Nelson got in first. "It all started there."

Adam slid into the back seat next to Nelson. "OK, maybe, but where is the phone now?"

Nelson turned to the taxi driver and gave directions. "Campo Alegre."

The driver gave the two men the once-over. He nodded agreement with a snide smile then lurched the car forward.

Nelson eased back and hung his arm on the open window before turning to answer Adam's question. "We don't know where it is. It's not turned on. But it doesn't matter. From what I've heard, we're beyond that now."

Nelson gave a wary glance at the back of the driver's head and then looked back to Adam. Adam got the message: no talking business in front of anyone, especially the locals.

Adam probed what he could. "So what is this club we're going to?"

"It's called Happy Camp," explained Nelson. "It's been operating near the airport since the 1940s."

"Doing what? Giving lap dances?"

Nelson was expressionless. "Happy Camp is a state-run brothel."

Adam shook his head and looked out the window. "Geez, what the hell are we getting into?"

Nelson looked in Adam's direction. "We're not getting into anything."

"Hey, whatever. We have to do what it takes, don't we?"

Nelson ignored the insinuation and returned his gaze to the tropical scenery. Dense, humid air buffeted his graying hair. It would be a quick drive to the compound east of the airport. The trip didn't amount to much of a fare for the driver. Most tourists wanted to be taken to the capital, Willemstad. Upon arrival, Nelson gave a generous tip.

The taxi took off, leaving them in a parking area near the club's entrance. There weren't a lot of customer cars but it was early. The club wouldn't be rocking until later, which was just as well. Nelson didn't want the complications of a crowd.

Across from the entrance, a large sign jutted high on twin red poles. A huge neon leaf, emblazoned in green, provided an airborne canvas for *Campo Alegre* in glowing purple. It wasn't dark enough yet for the neon to cast its shroud of electric colors over the parking area but Nelson could see how the elevated sign would soon dominate the area.

Nelson and Adam headed to the bar area and roamed around. Along the way they passed a hand-painted notice that proclaimed Campo Alegre was *for*

1

pleasure only. The welcome sign also summarized the rules: *18 years and up, no food, no drinks, no weapons, and parking at your own risk.*

"What does this Hollister guy look like," asked Adam.

"We're not meeting Hollister." Nelson quickly scanned the room.

"Any reason for keeping me in the dark?"

Nelson's irritation wore through. "We're both in the dark."

"Since when?"

"Since we arrived in the shit."

"You lost me."

Nelson sat at a table and ordered a drink, then answered Adam. "Haven't you seen enough movies to know; an operation is nothing like its plan?"

"Action flicks, is that where you guys get your training?"

"It's how people like you think you know what the shit is like."

"I know enough. I know agents go into *the shit* and soldiers go into *the suck*. I guess if you hear someone say *this shit sucks*, that means intelligence operatives have gone to war." Adam laughed.

"Some call that *wet-work*," added Nelson, humorless.

"I take it you guys like to avoid that."

"If an operation goes as planned, no one should even know it went down. Even the responsible assets forget about it—officially. As we will."

"So where does that leave us?" asked Adam.

"Once the shit starts, you have to assume that no one knows any more than anyone else. Someone may think they do but that's impossible."

"How can that be? Someone always has the advantage, don't they?"

"Every position holds a unique view. Every view has advantages. You might know more about where you are—but you can't be everywhere. As far as what's going to happen to us, I don't know any more than you do."

"Then we're in trouble," muttered Adam. He watched the drinks arrive.

Nelson took in the vibe of the room and mixed it with rising hunches. "Maybe that's the point."

"To find trouble?"

"Yeah." Nelson considered all the ways he had put the past week together during the long flight from New York. "Why else would we be cut loose?"

Nelson's momentary honesty raised Adam's concern. "Cut loose?"

"It doesn't matter now," recanted Nelson. "Just remember, no matter what happens, keep your mouth shut. We have to keep it together."

"What are you talking about? You're acting like you expect something to go wrong. I thought you said this was a quick in-and-out."

Nelson threw back half of his gin and tonic and swallowed. "Never mind. It was a long flight; I had too much time to think."

"We should have done more of that before getting on the plane."

"We knew enough," countered Nelson. "No one ever knows how it will turn out. And that's the only thing that matters."

Around a corner, two men entered the room. One man was obviously the wingman for the other. Both were casually dressed but well appointed. They strutted in with an air of confidence and entitlement. Exuding a smarmy but charming mix of sophistication and macho arrogance, they knew the street but didn't have to live there.

Silently, unapologetically, they put everyone on notice that being both offensive and smooth would be no effort for them. In fact, they'd relish an opportunity to demonstrate some bad-ass prowess.

Nelson noticed the bartender direct the men with a dutiful swivel of the head and a directed gaze. The lead man didn't acknowledge the tip-off but nonetheless followed it towards the table where Nelson and Adam sat.

"Pardon me," the lead man began, his etiquette marginally out of place. "Is one of you Nelson Geiss?" The man stared at Nelson and broadcasted he knew the answer to his own question.

Nelson returned the favor. "Carlos?" It was the name Hollister had sent as the contact for them to meet. Nelson purposely used only the given name.

"Carlos Guerro." The muscled Latin tipped his head towards them slightly as introduction. "Did you just arrive?"

"Direct from the airport," answered Nelson.

"Too bad we won't have time to enjoy the amenities of the club, at least not now. First business, then pleasure, don't you agree?"

Nelson finished his drink. "Let's do it."

Out of habit, Carlos worked a gold ring round and round the middle finger on his right hand. He shifted his gaze to Adam. "I'm glad to see that Mr. Perez could join us."

Adam said nothing but stood when Nelson did. The two of them followed the men out of the bar. In the parking lot, a slate-colored Hummer H3 Moab waited for them.

Carlos ushered them towards the vehicle's rear door. "After you."

Nelson and Adam got in as Carlos made his way to the front passenger seat. His wingman was quick behind the wheel and drove.

"How far do we have to go?" asked Nelson.

"Not far," offered Carlos. "Nothing is far on the island. While we're there, you can get something to eat if you like. Have you been to Curacao before?"

"No," answered Nelson as Adam shook his head.

Carlos noted both answers with a glance. "If you want to be an insider on Curacao, there's one secret you must learn. Some of the best places to eat at are hard to find. Sometimes I think that's on purpose." Carlos chuckled and waved his hand toward a small wooden structure amidst the passing vegetation. "The locals call these places *snacks*. Many of them feature Chinese food. Most snacks are out of the way and out of sight. You have to know where they are to find them. Most tourists are too intimidated to seek them out, which is just as well."

"What are they?" asked Adam. "Small restaurants?"

Hearing from Adam for the first time, Carlos looked into the back seat with renewed interest. As he spoke, he sized up the young man. "They're much more than that. Some have bars, others have strip shows. After a show, some have little shacks around back where you can get to know the strippers. Every snack is different."

"Which one are we headed to?" asked Nelson.

"One of my favorites," admitted Carlos, facing front again. "A friend of mine owns it. It's hard to find if you haven't been there before. Funny, but it's also hard to get away from once you find it. It's that kind of place."

Nelson thought it was time to raise some business. "Is Hollister there?"

Carlos stared at the road ahead. "Zack Hollister. Yes, he's there, waiting for us. I thought it best he stay out of sight. You never know who's watching."

Nelson pressed the issue. "And no one's watching us?"

Carlos' admission was cagey. "A calculated risk—to bring you in."

Nelson kept his thoughts to himself. Four men in a new H3 Moab on an island like this was anything but a calculated risk; it was more like a calling card, a parade float celebrating a wanton kind of dominance.

The wingman turned off the main road and shifted into four-wheel drive. The dirt road was rough but not impassible. Carlos was right about one thing; the snack they were headed to was off the beaten path. The more the road wound its way up through the vegetation, the more likely the place they were headed to was a private club, a club that didn't want to be found. It even made club members work to get there.

On the way up, Nelson spotted two motion sensors and coaxial cabling on a tree that probably supported a monitoring camera to watch the road. Whatever was at the top of the hill had a need for an early warning system.

After a few minutes of bumping along, the Hummer leveled out on a verdant plateau that overlooked the ocean. Up ahead, tucked back in the trees, a series of one-story, garishly painted wood structures were grouped together in a colorful enclave of bright and pastels shades.

The wingman parked the Hummer in a small clearing among small pickup trucks, tricked-out jeeps, and mud-splattered motorcycles and ATVs. Carlos led Nelson and Adam away from the main building.

The wingman reached for Nelson's backpack as Carlos spoke. "You'll need to check your things in while you're here. House rules. A precaution. We don't permit guests with weapons."

After a flinch of hesitation, Nelson complied and then Adam.

Carlos held out his hand with a cordial smile. "And your phones." Sensing resistance, he added, "They don't work up here anyway."

Nelson wasn't about to admit that his phone used satellites, not repeating towers to relay signals. Carlos had framed the request so anything but compliance would expose capabilities. They had no choice but to comply.

Carlos led them around back where a series of small shacks lined a cobbled walkway. On a small porch, two shapely women, one wearing a bikini top and turquoise Capris and the other one in a tank top and shorts sat, smoked, and watched with guarded interest as the men passed. As the walkway curved, the last shack came into view. Standing in front of its porch was two men. Nelson recognized one of the men as Zack Hollister.

Shuffling to a stop several shacks away from the men, Carlos called out to one of them. "Rodolfo!" When the man looked, Carlos jerked his head, gesturing him to come away with him. Then Carlos stopped and turned to Nelson. "I'll be up at the snack if you want to eat. But first, you and Hollister have things to catch up on. I'll give you a minute."

Rodolfo joined Carlos and the two of them strolled back to the main buildings. Nelson restarted his walk forward but Zack waited where he was. Nelson could tell he was in no hurry to converse with anyone.

Nelson approached him. "Zack, what's going on?"

Hollister was a hulk of a man, bald and Germanic in appearance. His answer wavered between humor and annoyance. "Hey, buddy. I'd like to say welcome but I'm sure it doesn't apply."

Nelson glanced back towards the snack. "This isn't what it seems, is it?"

Zack shook his head. "They told me as long as I stay here I'd stay alive. They've never had a guard on me. I don't think they need one. There's no way off this rock without someone noticing. You can't be sure who's on their team. It's a sure thing they have a knack for recruiting mercenaries on the fly. After payoffs and intimidation, anywhere they go is pretty well covered."

"What about the messages you sent me?" asked Nelson.

"Bullshit. They want you here. They told me to say whatever it took to motivate you. I had three days to get it done or they'd kill me."

Adam tensed with fright. "Holy shit! You mean we're prisoners?"

"I'm not sure what you are but we're about to find out."

Nelson did the introductions. "Zack, this is Adam Perez."

"Yeah." Zack held his ground with hands in pockets. "He's the hacker you told me about. That's probably why you're here."

"Can't they get their own?" raged Adam, almost humored by their predicament. "They have to kidnap people?"

Nelson addressed Zack but held out a steadying hand to calm down Adam. "What were you told?"

"Not much," admitted Zack. "I know chasing the mobile phone was bait. They moved it around the island and watched whoever came to follow it. Once they had me up here, I guess they shut the thing off."

"Yeah," agreed Nelson. "It's nowhere."

"*We're* fucking nowhere," snapped Adam. "Damn it, why did I let you talk me into this?"

Nelson got in his face but spoke softly. "Because you're a greedy bastard who wanted a payday, that's why. Let it go. If we start fighting amongst ourselves, we'll never get out of here."

"You think these assholes are going to let us go?"

"Hold it together or we'll drop you."

Adam got himself under control but the fright returned. "All they want is something done and then they'll get rid of us."

Zack scratched his second-day beard. "The kid has a point."

Nelson turned to Zack. "We have options. Don't limit them, especially the ones we don't know about yet. We haven't heard what Carlos wants."

"That's not my problem with this. I want to know what stateside wants."

"Stateside?" asked Adam.

Zack noted the kid's ignorance. "The kid doesn't know?"

"Know what?" Adam demanded.

Nelson was curt. "You have a job to do. That's all you need to know."

"We need to know what they expect," declared Zack.

"Maybe they expected your messages about leads not to be bullshit. Maybe, like us, they want to know why the drop was sent down here?"

"Are you guessing or did they tell you that?"

Nelson noticed Rodolfo returning. "This is no place to discuss it." On being seen, Rodolfo waved them towards the main building.

Nelson started to walk. "Come on, let's do this."

Without comment, they were led through the main snack. They found it to be a hodgepodge of outdoor and indoor alcoves decked out with wide umbrellas and plants and unusual wall-hangings, many of them antiques from the 18th century slave trade. In the middle of the floor, a scattering of wooden tables and chairs surrounded a horseshoe-shaped bar that was decorated with strings of colored lights.

A smattering of men relaxed at the bar or ate at the tables and conversed in Papiamentu, the native Creole language. They all gave the pass-through group a steady but benign stare before turning back to their diversions.

In an adjoining, more private space, Carlos and his wingman dined on a spread of food served family-style in small dishes. Carlos invited them to join him and had a waiter bring them beer.

"The best conversations are over food, don't you agree?" Carlos was deceptively cordial. "Have whatever you like. If you don't see it, ask for it."

Having had little lunch, Nelson and the others were glad to comply.

Carlos eased back but sharpened his resolve. "You can always count on this place to serve you well. In business, one should demand nothing less."

As Nelson sampled the food, he noted Carlos' change in tone.

"Given the late hour, I'm afraid our business must be handled right away."

"I was hoping you'd say that," answered Nelson.

"Good," smiled Carlos. "Then I'll be direct. I need to know why you're spying on Extasis Corporation—and don't tell me you're not. I have no patience for those who are not candid with me."

"Which one of us are you talking to?" asked Nelson.

Carlos shot a glance at each of them. "Whoever needs to answer."

The three men were silent.

Carlos stopped eating. "We don't have time for this." He flipped a hand at Nelson. "You, Nelson Geiss. You're a retired intelligence agent, another way of saying you've gone independent. Why are you working with Mr. Perez? And don't lie to me. I've had you followed as soon as the two of you hooked up in New York. I know about your all-night parties on the computer."

"What's the matter?" asked Nelson. "Didn't you like what you got?"

"Answer the question," snapped Carlos.

Nelson complied. "I was helping him with his assignment."

"What assignment?"

"I thought you said you didn't want to waste time. You know very well what assignment. You gave it to him."

"I gave it to him?" smiled Carlos. He turned to Adam. "Have you ever seen me before?"

Nelson butted in. "That proves nothing and you know it."

Carlos continued eating. "I'm glad you see the futility of prolonging this with nonsense. Why aren't you sending me everything you're finding?" Carlos watched the reaction. "That's right. My people went into your apartment when you weren't there." Carlos pointed at Adam. "You. Answer me."

Adam hesitated and glanced at Nelson.

"Don't look at him!" roared Carlos. "You know the answer. Why are you collecting information but not sending it?"

After glances at Carlos' stern wingman, Adam answered. "I don't send something until I'm sure it's good."

Carlos pointed to Nelson. "You have no problem sharing it with this man. Did you not know he had a partner?" Carlos pointed at Zack.

"Not right away," admitted Adam.

"What about his other partner in London? The man named Dystrom." Carlos looked to Nelson. "Isn't that right?"

Nelson could only imagine what else Carlos knew but had to ask, "How do you know this?"

"How does anyone know anything? You either have access, you buy it, or you take it. Obtaining phone records is not a problem. The three of you are obviously working as a team. A team to do what? CIG+XM is not your target, is it? It can't be; not the way you've been working." Carlos' assertion was said as a fact, not a question.

Given all that Carlos knew, Nelson could only hope to steer the discussion away from the wider aspects involved with Project G. "I was looking into Jiaying Xianzi. Adam got in the way."

"Who told you to follow Jiaying?"

"I don't know. I was paid anonymously."

"Of course," laughed Carlos. "That explains your trip to Washington and your peculiar interest in visiting federal buildings late at night." Carlos turned back to Adam. "Why was information about the Commonwealth of Jersey found in your apartment? What does that have to do with Project G?"

"I don't know yet," stammered Adam.

"For someone so brilliant, you're ignorant of an awful lot."

"Your assignment is ignorant," barked Nelson. "You don't even know what you're after."

Carlos jerked to his feet. "Enough of this. Take them away."

The wingman responded. Behind them, Rodolfo and another man appeared from the other room sporting KRISS Super V submachine guns.

Nelson took his time standing up. "You didn't lure us all the way down here to interrogate us. I'm sure you have resources in New York to do that."

"If you want to presume what you don't know," countered Carlos. "Then I'll do the same." He stepped around the table and met Nelson eye to eye. "You didn't have to pair up with Adam to follow Jiaying. I'm sure you're after something much more attractive." Carlos relaxed into a vulgar grin. "Given what I know about Jiaying, that has to be something worth pursuing."

"So what now?" asked Nelson.

"Now?" Carlos read the expressions on his henchmen's faces. "I've done all I can do here. It's what I expected, not what I hoped for."

"You don't want to get rid of us," warned Nelson. "You don't need that kind of trouble."

Carlos brushed by them. "Oh, it's no trouble—but it would be a lost opportunity."

33

0000 0010 0001

7:22 pm EST, Thursday December 7th

By 7:05 pm, the "dry cleaning" was done. For Katherine Stalt, making sure she wasn't being tailed was crucial if her meeting was to be successful. She had managed to enlist friends to check if she was being followed. It was a favor all of them reciprocated for each other when asked.

At a designated time, she walked a specific route designed to contain choke points. Those points were impossible to pass through without being noticed. By the time she had run the maze and cleared each point, she was confident, as much as possible, that her travels would not be observed. After the walk, she ducked into a taxi. Now it was time to get to the meeting.

So important was this meeting that her handler had instructed her to leave her phone at home. The prospect of being tracked by it was too risky. In its place, she carried a new, disposable phone loaded with minutes.

It was a known fact that many government buildings in the Washington D.C. area were connected by tunnels. Some of those passageways made it easy for workers to pass between related agencies without the need to brave traffic or the weather. Other tunnels were off-limits and reserved for first responders, emergency evacuation, or special-purpose transport of items or people needing enhanced protection.

What was not so well known was that some residences and diplomatic missions in and near the Beltway also had service tunnels, some dating back to the turn of the previous century.

Just off R Street in the Georgetown section near Embassy Row, Katherine exited the taxi, scurried up a walkway onto a front porch and after a knock, was admitted to a house. Little was said; there wasn't time and explanations were unnecessary. She made her way to the basement and then a subbasement landing where an unlit service tunnel diverged in opposite directions. The owner of the house wouldn't be told which way Katherine would go.

Being unaware was as much desired as it was expected.

Katherine set out, mini-flashlight in hand, hunched over since the ceiling was a smidge shorter than she was. As she walked, the old walls showed character but kept fast to their secrets. This particular tunnel had been dug before fortunes changed, property values increased, and ground-level sub-divisions made economic sense.

The previous manor that had stretched above ground had been as elaborate as it had been stately. As time passed and newer construction prevailed, most offshoots from the original service tunnel had long since been blocked off.

Most, but not all. One access point in particular had been reopened when like-minded owners agreed such a feature came in handy.

Katherine found the passageway exit and climbed narrow stairs. In the beam of her flashlight, the steps appeared to end at a ceiling. That ceiling was a tiled plate that slid horizontal to open. The opening let Katherine out in a rear-yard single-car garage. The garage abutted a carport that was fed by a cobbled driveway leading to the street.

In the garage, a car awaited. The keys were in it. Limited use of the car, with prior arrangement, was shared by those with tunnel access privileges.

Heading out past Dumbarton Oaks Gardens, Katherine navigated the quickest way to Massachusetts Avenue, past Dupont Circle, then northeast on Rhode Island Avenue NW. Her path would take her up Highway 1 to the University of Maryland district.

It was unknown why her handler wanted to rendezvous at the College Park Airport Museum. It didn't matter. She hadn't questioned it. To finally meet face-to-face was enough. Any location where he felt comfortable would do. The offer to meet had come as a surprise. In her line of work, surprises were usually not a good thing. This time, she determined to prove that worry wrong.

She drove with anxious glances diverted into the rearview mirrors. No matter how many precautions one took, being safely incognito was never assured. Between pattern recognition on the traffic in the mirrors and thoughts of the material she had seen at the NDU Library, the ride to College Park took an eternity that was over too soon. She needed more time to consider what this meeting meant, even as she couldn't wait to get into it.

Her handler, also known as R.Z. Barnett, refused to speak to her on the phone. When she finally had gotten a call through to him and started with the questions, he had grown distant and threatened to shut down the conversation. He didn't seem surprised when she refused to follow Richard Marks any longer, at least until the two of them had a chance to talk it out. He admitted, without going into detail, that the time had come to level with her. As good as it was to hear such an offer, nevertheless it was infuriating to consider how long she had worked without a net to prove herself to him.

The College Park Airport Museum had been closed for three hours by the time she got there. The small parking lot was next to empty. She parked and waited, having been given no other instructions. The lot was lit only by the nightlights left on around the museum building. Seconds later, she watched in her side mirror as a dark form exited a car in another part of the lot. He was an older man, tall and stooped, moving with a vigor induced by a sense of purpose rather than physical stamina. As he approached in the dim light, she could see he wore a tweed sports coat over black jeans.

He knocked on her window with a knuckle. "Katherine, open the door."

She pressed a button and all four doors unlocked. The rear door opened on the driver's side and the man slid into the back seat behind her.

Katherine turned, uncomfortable with his placement. "Why don't you sit up front?"

The man closed the door. "Why don't we talk and not worry about it."

"You know my name. What's yours?"

"Unless you're expecting someone else, I must be Dr. Barnett."

Katherine turned, facing forward again. "Doctor of what?"

The man settled back. "My advanced degrees are not germane, suffice to say they're not medical."

Katherine's gaze trained on the rear mirror. Leaning slightly to her right, she saw enough of her visitor to engage him. "You said you weren't in town."

"I wasn't," came the reply. "Something came up."

"So why here? Why this parking lot?"

"No reason, really. I do have a fondness for the museum. It's energizing to be near places of great accomplishment, technical or scientific in particular."

"Such as?" Katherine baited him. The more he lost himself in sharing his opinions meant extra time to study him in the mirror. His features were gaunt, deepened by character and a concentration that made the intensity in his face magnetic. Regardless of age, this was a man with a sharp mind, a depth of experience, and uncommonly broad view of the world.

Reacting to Katherine's nonchalance about the museum, Barnett was incredulous. "You live in the area and don't know about this place?"

Katherine was droll. "I'm still trying to get through the Smithsonian."

Her handler was unfazed. "College Park Airport may be small but it's had remarkable firsts: the first mile-high flight by a powered military aircraft, the first IFR cross-country flight, the first controlled helicopter flight in 1924. Right here in 1909, Wilbur Wright trained two military officers to fly the government's first airplane. Such things sound tame today but back then they were advanced R&D."

"Your forte, I presume?" prompted Katherine.

"Other people would call it that, yes. I used to lay claim to being a *left-brain romantic* until someone discovered that the whole left-brain right-brain theory was an oversimplifying myth. Now I prefer to think I'm merely emotionally persistent about being inquisitive."

Katherine went right to the point. "The material you had me review at the library—how much of *that* is myth?"

"I'm afraid a new mythology is being formulated around such things. But don't be fooled, the things themselves are not myth."

"Who's doing the formulation?"

"Anyone with an inkling of what I'm talking about wouldn't ask that question."

"So they're anonymous?"

"I'm saying it doesn't matter."

"It would seem the one, logical place to start," countered Katherine.

"First moves are often in error. Those in power know this quite well."

"Even *they* have to make first moves."

"Or send someone in their place. Maintaining a proper distance from such things has been refined to a science, although most have neglected an appreciation for the art."

"You lost me," admitted Katherine.

"Put it this way," offered Barnett. "The Amaranth hedge fund once gave out chess sets as gifts with the words of grandmaster Alexander Kotov inscribed on them. The inscription read, *'It often happens that a player carries out a deep and complicated calculation, but fails to spot something elementary right at the first move.'*"

"Why do I need to know this?" asked Katherine.

"A first-move miscalculation is the reason why we're here. It's why you have your assignment."

"I take it you're not the one who messed up."

"No one messed up. It's simply impossible to consider everything at all times. Being devious and keeping secrets is a delicate and difficult business."

"Are you referring to Owen Raedalus?"

"And Richard Marks."

"You weren't surprised when I told you I wouldn't follow him."

"No more surprised than finding out that you copied the recording picked up at the pro shop. I expected it; in fact, I was counting on it."

"If that's so, then why didn't you just tell me what's going on?"

"There's something about direct evidence that's more compelling, more persuasive, especially when it involves something personal. I wanted you to hear it for yourself. But more than that, I wanted to see if you had it in you."

"What? To disobey you?"

"To be smart about it. I don't need blind obedience. I need a qualified asset, someone with the smarts and force of will to do what it takes. If the only moves you make are direct orders from an official command structure, you'll be no good to me."

Katherine was direct. "Who collects from that post office box?"

"A congressional staffer. A friend of a friend. He works for a senator who's on the Senate Select Committee on Intelligence."

"The oversight committee."

"For what it's worth, yes. I was trying to get the senator to back an effort to look into what's going on. So far, with little success."

"You're certain this needs that level of attention?"

"I've seen enough to know something's not right."

"What makes you think you're in a position to know?"

Barnett spoke with pride. "Without me, there *is* no mythology. My work is primary, center to the core; it's fundamental to everything."

"I take it you can't tell me what that work is."

"The more you know, the more danger you're in. I prefer to shield you within *an enlightened darkness*."

Katherine laughed. "Spoken like a government representative. You might as well say we're in a *limited kinetic action* instead of calling it a war."

"I work for them," flared Barnett. "I'm not one of them. Besides, double-speak is human; governments have no monopoly on it. To a derivatives trader, *regulatory arbitrage* simply means finding a way around the law. For many, saying Happy Valentine's Day is another way of saying I've done my duty. I don't dislike them for what they say. It's more about what they value."

"If you despise them so much, why work for them?"

There was a pause, then bitterness. "It's the way of the world. To do what we're passionate about, we're forced to become whores."

"That's defeatist. It makes it sound like there's no other way."

"The fact is, some questions have billion-dollar answers. Most people are content to ask the questions and keep wondering but they leave it at that. Those who have a passion for the answers, like me, we have to know."

"You can't split loyalties forever," noted Katherine. "You'll have to commit to their project or devote yourself to exposing them. No one gets to have it both ways."

"That's why verification is critical, as soon as possible."

"Verification of what?"

"Misappropriation, collusion, conspiracy, espionage, who knows, probably rendition and murder. They won't let anyone stand in their way; the stakes are too high."

"What stakes? What are they after?"

"Open up a history book to any page, you'll find it."

"You mean power...control?"

"The one commodity that commands all the others."

"So, why me?" demanded Katherine. "You didn't pick me at random, did you?"

"No," admitted Barnett. "You came up in my research."

"On what?"

"Nelson Geiss."

Katherine jerked around to look into the backseat directly. "Nelson! But you didn't know about Nelson until I took those pictures at Arlington."

"Wrong." Barnett was even-tempered, subdued. "I didn't know *your* name until I looked into Geiss. I tripped upon your DARPA assignment, the same one that Geri Messare was coerced into talking about with Richard Marks."

"So why investigate Nelson? What has he got to do with this?"

"The first thing that came my way—the one thing that told me something wasn't right, was about Geiss."

"What was it?" demanded Katherine.

"Another recording." Barnett paused and let the inference sink in. "The disk you copied today is not the first recording to come to my attention."

Katherine reeled with the potential. "You mean Nelson's been involved in this all along?"

"No. Only when they found it necessary."

"For what?"

"I wonder if it would be as clear to you as it is to me?"

"When can I hear the recording?"

Barnett plucked his phone out of a coat pocket. He explained as he navigated to an audio file. "This was captured by accident, the details of which we needn't go into now. Luckily, it fell into friendly hands, someone who thought I should listen to it."

"Who's on it?" prompted Katherine.

"Owen and Richard, two weeks ago, over the Thanksgiving holiday. Their conversation was rushed; maybe that's why they had to be so candid." Barnett played the file and set the phone down on the top of the car's front seat so Katherine could listen.

The recording started at the end of a meeting between the two men.

Richard Marks was in the middle of wrapping up. "...have their own security. We'll get a recap of everything we need by next Thursday."

"That's the best they can do?" asked Owen Raedalus.

"One day is enough. Don't worry about it. Our role in this is reactive; we don't need that level of detail. If something should come up post-op, they'll make whatever we need available. What time is it?"

"12:30."

"I've got to get across town." Richard was heard packing up in preparation to leave.

Owen was concerned. "I don't like this exposure. Large pieces of our responsibility are out of our direct control."

"It's no different than coordinating between agencies."

"But they're on our soil. There can't be any fuck-ups."

"I share your concern but we're all motivated. They have just as much invested in seeing this through. Unless you can think of something we've overlooked or you have a plan guaranteed with no exposure, I say let it go."

"What about a fall-back position, in case something goes wrong?"

"Fall back where?" asked Richard.

"Deniability. Shift blame. Be ready with another reason for whatever."

"What would that look like?"

Owen thought a moment. "Maybe it could be something we detected as part of the Threat Detection Program."

"You mean Homeland Security Intelligence?"

"Yeah, internal affairs, counterintelligence. Every agency head has to coordinate information on insider threats with ODNI. It would make sense that

such a thing would come to your attention. It's the law."

"Something tells me this idea of yours isn't spontaneous."

"Insider Threat Detection was Section 509 of Senate Bill 3454, originating with the 112th Congress. I didn't want to bring it up until I checked into it."

"It's dicey. There's not enough time to plant background and spin up."

"We don't need background if it's a sudden call-up, like an ETC."

Richard headed for the door. *"Get real. We can't call an ETC for this."*

"Who said we would?"

"You'd run it as a false flag?"

"No one but the setup cell has to know they're in play. It's not like they can ask around. Protocols will keep them tight."

"But what the hell would they do for a month?"

"Nothing," answered Owen. *"We wouldn't use them unless something went wrong."*

"You'd string them along until after New Year's?"

"Yeah."

"Then what?"

"If everything went off as planned, we'd call off the ETC, hang out the 'Mission Accomplished' sign. They'd have no idea how many cells we were running. If their part of the world didn't see action, oh well. We'd send them home with patriotic thanks and remind them not to talk about it."

"And if something goes wrong and we have to use them?" asked Richard.

"Then we work it as we need it, depending on circumstances. Either we say they screwed up working for us or we make them out to be a cabal competing with us. Which way it goes would depend on what goes wrong."

"I don't know," hesitated Richard. *"They'd still be out there, live wires. Even if they did nothing, it could turn into an unwanted dangle. I don't like unintended consequences. Someone might notice."*

"Notice what? Assets in play? After the Friday event, that's to be expected. We can't lose. If the main op works, no harm no foul, they never existed. We dismiss them and they melt away. If the main op goes south, we tag them as bad guys and they give us the plausible excuse to ask for more leverage to do even better threat detection work."

"Who would you recruit for this?"

"Independents, retirees still available; you know the type."

"You already have someone in mind." It was a statement, not a question.

"I've got a short list. Nelson Geiss, Zack Hollister, a few others. If we had to fall back and use them, it would give DNI reason to ask Congress for more regulation of the private intel sector, greater oversight of contractors."

"I don't know," Richard wavered.

"A big percentage of what's happening in the next month is domestic. What our national security looks like going forward depends on this. This has to work or the world might look very different next year. You know the risk. This

1

is big. With so much on the line, we need this."

Going out the door, Richard gave in. "All right, but you run it. You're responsible. Keep me informed but don't expect me to dig you out."

"No problem."

The recording ended with silence. Katherine sat stunned.

Her first thought was for her friend. "We have to warn Nelson!"

"Wishing for something is not a plan." The handler casually pocketed his phone.

"But they're setting him up!"

"You're talking about the fall guy. I'm interested in what the fall guy is covering for. We must keep focused on the reason for the operation."

"I can't believe they're faking an ETC to do this."

"ETC. I've been meaning to ask you about that," prompted Barnett.

"Emergency Tactics Corps. It's a call-up of covert forces in a severe emergency. It's only used for something that threatens the entire country."

Barnett brooded. "On that part, they may be right."

Katherine raced through details from the call. "This was two weeks ago. They talked about running it for a month."

The handler leaned forward and rested a hand on the seat back next to Katherine. "They were talking this way before F1E happened; if that isn't telling, I don't know what is."

The reference jogged Katherine's memory. "My God, on the recording, they even called it *the Friday event.*"

"Yes, *F1E* as a nickname was not a spontaneous invention of the press."

"They're not working alone," noted Katherine.

"So it would appear. Much of the reason why Owen is determined to have fall guys in place, just in case, is due to his nervousness over having a large, domestic operation executed by foreigners. As he puts it, *they're on our soil.*"

"Marks didn't seem concerned," noted Katherine.

"Marks is on a different level than Owen, a higher level. His comfort with this is telling, and unsettling. It says something when a broader view sees nothing to worry about. You might say he lacks nationalistic fervor."

Katherine's due diligence shifted onto Barnett. "How did you get this? Who are you, really?"

"A scientist, nothing more."

"That makes no sense. Why would this fall into your hands?"

"Let's just say whatever they're up to, it wouldn't exist if it wasn't for me."

"That doesn't explain why you would be given a recording like this."

"For a long time now I've felt something was wrong. The work I do mandates I have security clearances that are given to very few. In my position, I was able to see things, become aware of irregularities as they happened."

"Like what?"

"Things out of place, materials shared, patterns of suspicion that would go unnoticed by anyone without a privileged view, a view like mine. Make no mistake, what they are doing is being executed adroitly, with precision. Even at my security level, finding traces is circumstantial at best."

"So what's the difference this time?"

"I've worked in classified research a long time. I know how it works. I also know many people, some I trust enough to share my doubts with. Apparently, those doubts got passed around; I'll never know to whom. All I know is, the result was this recording."

"What did you think when you got it?"

"I wasn't sure. I thought what I wanted was confirmation. When it finally came, it seemed more like someone was brazenly throwing it in my face, daring me to do something about it. To tell the truth, at first, I took it more as a warning than a call to action."

"They would show you evidence like this as a warning?"

"I may be a valuable tool, but tools that dare to question the blueprints often get thrown away. In one way or another, they are made to disappear."

"You could have acquiesced. What changed your mind?"

Barnett didn't hesitate. "F1E. Of course, by then, I already had you following Owen. I had to do something. The thought of what they might try with what I created—well, let's just say I had my Oppenheimer moment."

As the father of the atomic bomb had done, Katherine quoted the Bhagavad-Gita. *"Now, I am become Death, the destroyer of worlds."*

In the near darkness, Barnett's grizzled jaw was firm. "Not so dramatic, but you get the point."

"So what do you think they're doing?" Katherine knew the question was bold but she threw it out in light of Barnett's confessional approach. If she was ever going to get details out of her handler, this would be the time.

Barnett turned it around, using it as an opportunity to test her. "You were at the library. You tell me."

"If I had to guess..." Katherine paused. "I'd say they're trying to crack strong AES encryption. Some new supercomputer is about to go online."

"A reasonable guess, if we lived in reasonable times." Barnett grew more serious; his tone deepened with gravitas. "Remember, finding the magic lamp wasn't Aladdin's true windfall or his real problem. The difficult puzzle was figuring out what to do with the three wishes. That is our problem now."

"They've already cracked it." The words gushed from Katherine as much a harbinger of things to come as it was a revelation.

"Correction," snapped Barnett. *"They* don't do anything but exploit what others create."

"So you know everything except—what's going to happen?" The question had to be rhetorical but it escaped from Katherine nonetheless.

"The future can always be gauged by a simple test. Where morality is present, laws are unnecessary; without morality, laws are unenforceable. It all depends on what kind of world you're living in."

"We can't let Nelson be used like this," demanded Katherine.

"You heard the recording. His part is insignificant, anecdotal."

"But it may be our only way in."

"Shadowing Oswald will never lead us to the grassy knoll."

"OK, then what do you hope to accomplish?"

"I have no parameters around it yet, except that the solution be positive."

"You think you can set things right all by yourself?"

"What did Andrew Jackson say? '*One man with courage makes a majority.*'"

"Ben Franklin was more pragmatic. '*One man may be more cunning than another, but not more cunning than everybody else.*' You know the odds of going up against them. Do you want to be the tool that disappears?"

"I'm old enough to think it might be worth it."

"This isn't your line of work. You're out of your depth."

"I'm a quick learner. And my security level blows away anything you can deliver."

"Doesn't matter. You're never going to get at them directly. You need a back door, a side show, a fringe way of inserting instability, something they didn't expect."

"Such as?" Barnett sounded interested.

Katherine's thoughts flew back to Nelson and the team required by the ETC. If she could convince Barnett to shift her assignment onto Nelson and his cell, it might be a way to leverage all Barnett knew to help her friend.

"The ETC thing. It's not part of the original plan. It's tacked on. Richard Marks clearly doesn't care about it; he only agreed to let Owen run it to pacify him; that was obvious."

"How would that help us?"

"You heard Owen. The cell that Nelson is embedded with, by design, has nothing meaningful to do. We could change that."

"You want us to use them?"

"Hell yes."

"What makes you think they'd go for it?"

"I'm betting they'd have a grudge against being hung out as patsies."

"Even so, they're out of alignment."

"No. Nelson is a good asset. They're close enough to Owen to get our foot in the door. We have three weeks. It's the only chance we might reach inside the plan in time."

"Someplace vulnerable?" asked Barnett.

"It depends. What's your endgame?"

"I'm not even sure what they're doing. I only know what they have."

"If you know what kind of people they are, deciding what to do might be simple."

"Believe me, complicated is easy, simple is hard. As a mathematician, I should know." Barnett eased back. "Even if we wanted to, we can't use your connection with Nelson; it's been made. There's no way to let him know what's going on or coordinate any action going forward."

Katherine thought. "That may not be true."

"You know another way?"

"We would have to go through somebody else, but yes."

"I don't want this expanding too far; it only risks our exposure."

"Don't worry. Nelson and I have a history. It's not in any file. Besides, exposure, like everything else, can be a tool."

Barnett hesitated. "All right. I'm in town until Saturday morning. Meet me back here at 9 pm tomorrow with a plan. Don't write it down. You'll have five minutes to pitch it to me. If I like what I hear, we'll move forward."

Without waiting for an answer, Barnett opened the car door and got out.

The door shut abruptly. Katherine watched as he walked back to his car slightly hunched over. Satisfied with her marching orders, she started her own car and drove away.

In a dark corner of the parking lot, R.Z. Barnett sat behind the wheel and watched as the taillights from Katherine's car faded in the distance. Turning back to face the steering column, he started his car but let it idle as thoughts raced. Their meeting had gone more smoothly than he had expected. He had played his part well. Katherine drove away convinced that the idea of flipping the ETC cell into their service was her own idea.

And that's the way it should be.

34

0000 0010 0010

8:17 pm AST, Thursday December 7th

The Hummer Moab raced through darkness along narrow roads. Despite a partial view out the side window, Nelson Geiss had studied the island of Curacao well enough before leaving New York to know where they might be headed. Dorp Sint Michiel was an area about ten kilometers northwest of Willemstad. Villas and private neighborhoods lined the dark inlet.

Down a side street near a private dock, the driver parked the Moab. Right behind them, a pickup truck with submachine-gun toting guards pulled up. There was no need for discussion. Adam, Nelson, and Hollister were being transferred somewhere. Only when they were led across a path onto the dock did it become plain that a boat, a small cabin cruiser, was waiting for them.

Before leaving the hilltop snack, all three had been forced to change clothes and submit to a body search. Now they had no IDs, no phones, nothing they brought to the island. Wherever they were being taken, Carlos Guerro didn't want their movements tracked.

Adam looked out to sea at the amber lights of a yacht anchored offshore. He whispered, "Who do you think is out there?"

Hollister grunted. "Who needs this kind of firepower on vacation?"

Before Nelson could answer, one of the guards barked, "No talking!"

The trip out to the fantail of the yacht was a quick, straight shot. As Nelson stepped aboard, he glanced up at the railing of the upper deck. There, a trophy woman, too refined for the company she was keeping, stood in silk pants and halter top and watched their arrival with dispassionate interest.

A well-dressed onboard guard waited under the upper deck overhang. He directed them to keep moving forward into the aft drawing room. Upon entering, they were surrounded by opulence, which wasn't surprising. But then they were joined by someone immediately recognizable. His presence onboard ship stunned both Adam and Nelson.

Upon seeing his interviewer from CIG+XM, Adam tried starting a conversation with humor. He assumed there would be little chance for levity as the night wore on. "Don't tell me this is part of my interview."

The interviewer's smile was brief and acerbic. "Follow me."

He led them near the bow to a staircase rising to the upper deck. There they found a man seated and attended to by a wait staff. He was obviously the master of the vessel. He was South American, middle-aged, bearing none of the outward roughness or incivility of Carlos and his crew. He wore dress pants and sandals with a casual but tailored shirt open at the collar.

The CIG+XM interviewer made his approach with due respect. "Here they are, sir." Job done, he retreated back into the cabin.

The master of the ship smirked and nursed a thin cigar. "Yes, I see. It looks like Carlos has terrorized them enough to get their attention." The man waved a hand towards empty deck chairs. "Go ahead, have a seat. I refuse to look up to anyone when I talk."

Nelson, Adam, and Hollister did as he suggested. The waitstaff brought drinks for all as the man of the boat watched with keen interest. When he was satisfied they were all settled in, he raised his own glass and took a sip.

"Most people in my position would not introduce themselves but in this case I see no reason, in the short term, why we shouldn't get to know one another." He relaxed his arms on the sides of the chair as if possessing his throne. "My name is Alonzo Elijah Lutane. People who don't know me call me Alonzo. Friends call me Elijah. You can call me Mr. Lutane." He puffed on his cigar and silently guessed among the three of them, "Which one of you is Nelson Geiss?"

Nelson spoke up right away. "I am."

Elijah nodded, as if confirming his suspicions. "You have an unnatural interest in the work of the man next to you. Why is that?"

Nelson suspected that this meeting might be deceptively cordial but brief if progress to the topic was not swift. This was a man who would not be made to wait for what he wanted. Nelson spoke forcefully.

"Adam matters because CIG+XM hired him. My job is to find out why Jiaying recruited him."

Elijah leaned his head back and blew smoke but didn't break eye contact. "Your job sounds confusing." He shook his head in dismay. "Who gave you such a perplexing assignment?"

Nelson didn't hesitate. "I'm an independent contractor. I'll work when I'm paid. The people who hire me appreciate the fact that I don't mind not knowing who they are."

Elijah held one hand to his forehead and lurched the other hand out in a stop motion. "Enough! This is so sad. I expected so much more from you. We can go back and forth like this but the end result will be the same. Luckily for you, I am entertaining friends tonight. I don't have time for not-so-clever conversation."

Nelson engaged him. "What exactly do you have a problem with?"

Elijah acted hurt and angered. "You come to this island for God knows what reason, you interfere and you plot and then you think you can lie your way out of here. This is madness. Is this what people like you do when you're caught in a hopeless place?"

Nelson looked around. "This boat looks far from hopeless."

"For me, yes. For you, all three of you know it's the end of the line."

"If that's true," asked Nelson. "Then why bother meeting with us? Your boy Carlos didn't have to bring us here."

"Again, you're wrong," Elijah retorted. "You don't know what's going on here any more than you knew what was going on in New York. Adam was never recruited to work at CIG+XM." Elijah raised his voice and tapped on his chest. "Adam works for me!"

Adam chimed in, "How did the guy who interviewed me get here?"

"He also works for me," explained Elijah. "As does his twin brother. Their shared likeness comes in handy in many ways, in many places."

Adam took it in. "What about the corner office on the 18th floor?"

"In New York?" asked Elijah. "An empty space. Convenient. It has nothing to do with CIG+XM except its proximity is useful."

Hollister said it plainly. "So you recruit Adam to hack for you and if something goes wrong, you hope the blame lands on the Chinese."

"Think what you like." Elijah settled back and crossed his legs. "Why should it matter to me? Your government has hung you out to dry. How do I know this? Because they sent you here. Did you really think you were going to walk through my front door and do as you please? It's obvious they want you dead but, as always, they would prefer I do their dirty work"

"I don't work for the government," Adam protested in his defense.

Elijah grinned. "Many people work for them who do not realize it. Governments comes in many disguises, as do corporations. It's the same everywhere you go. Don't be so unoriginal."

"Why are you so interested in Extasis?" asked Nelson. "What do you know about Project G?"

Elijah was wide-eyed. "Now *you're* asking the questions? Oh, I see, you think we can talk to each other as equals."

"What's the point of this?" demanded Nelson.

"Nothing but curiosity, believe me. You took the bait and now you're here. For the life of me, I can't figure this out. They made you part of it but then they treat you like you don't exist. They can't be using you as a way to get at me; they wouldn't be so naive. You say you were told to watch Jiaying but you spend all your time going after Project G."

Hollister was annoyed. "What's so hard to understand?"

Elijah laughed. "Project G is a delusion. From what I hear, the G stands for *gullible*. Your bosses created Project G to lure people like me away from the real work being done. Now, I can see why they would want *me* chasing such a thing..." Elijah turned to Nelson. "But why are *you* chasing it if you work for them?"

Nelson challenged him, "You're the one who hired Adam to go after it."

Elijah smiled. "More importantly, why has your chase bothered them so much? These are questions worth pursuing."

Nelson needed clarity. "You're not making sense."

"That's sad because I'm only explaining your situation," laughed Elijah.

"You're too blind to explain it to me, I guess."

"They've got you thinking Project G is an empty shell, a diversion?"

"I don't think it, I know it," confirmed Elijah.

Adam spoke up. "They why tell me to hack at it?"

"It was the safest way to test your skills and draw out people like Nelson who think they're clever. His bosses pretend to be concerned about the project; it's part of the game they must play until New Year's Eve is over."

"What's magic about New Year's Eve?" asked Nelson.

"That's the question, the reason why you're here. It's why Project G was invented to confuse the issue. And why people like you were put into motion." Elijah pointed at Nelson. "But you wouldn't color inside the lines, would you? You took your assignment to places it wasn't supposed to go. You touched a nerve with all the digging you did with Adam. Something got to them. What was it? The Bailiwick of Jersey or QinetiQ? Maybe Z/Yen or [Dstl] or looking into Liam Bargeau set them off. I think they never expected anyone to be able to get that close, especially by accident doing nothing more than busy work."

"Close to what?" asked Adam.

"Once again, that's the question, the reason why you're here."

Nelson was unconvinced. "Why should we believe you over anything else we've been told?"

Elijah lit another cigar. Puffing away, he squinted and locked eyes with Nelson. "I'll tell you what you were told. Other people have heard it too. You were told there's a cabal festering inside the intelligence community. Isn't that right? They told you some evil group was hijacking the covert powers of the western world. This group has a wicked plan that must be stopped. Isn't that what you were told?"

Stunned that Elijah knew such detail, Nelson said nothing. His memory shot back to the original briefing with Owen at DIOCC. Owen had warned him that *New Age Barbarians,* the NABs might be trying their hand at global extortion. If anyone fit that description, Alonzo Elijah Lutane certainly did.

Elijah spat a piece of tobacco and watched Nelson's reaction. "The tricky thing is, what they told you is true, except they left out one thing. Interestingly enough, it's the most critical thing." Elijah's eyes narrowed in wisps of cigar smoke. "They neglected to tell you that *they* are the cabal."

Nelson showed a wry grin. "Is that your big secret?"

Elijah eased back. He checked his emotions and regained an air of affability. "I'm not surprised you don't believe it."

"It's a matter of opinion, that's all," explained Nelson. "To you, they're a cabal. If you ask them, you're an international criminal. The labels switch around, depending on one's perspective."

Elijah was stern. "You appear to me as one too shrewd for his own good. You're working for the cabal and don't know it."

"Interesting theory," admitted Nelson.

1

"You're jaded by your line of work. You can't even see the conspiracy around you."

"Funny you should say that," remarked Nelson. "Conspiracy theories are a hobby of mine. You know they have theories about crime syndicates too. Some say you have the money and global reach to threaten civilized life on the planet. You are called *New Age Barbarians*, warlords of a new and terrifying kind of business ethic."

Elijah laughed and flicked ashes on the deck. "I'm far from being a warlord. You can call me a *more*-lord; more of this, more of that, more of everything. It's our nature, all of us. Like my competitors, I only want more."

"Except, your way of doing business is different."

"Wrong!" roared Elijah. "There's *never* been a difference. What they wouldn't do for themselves, they hired people like me to do for them. To say anything else is hypocritical. I don't *pretend* to play nice; they do. The real liars are the politicians and CEOs and the slimy wunch of bankers who conspire to grab the same money and power everyone is after."

"They believe their way is more civilized."

Elijah chuckled. "Mix favored status with ego and one gets some unique delusions. They're easy to manage when you're two-faced. Come to think of it, there *is* a difference between them and me. Everyone knows about the *war on drugs* but no one hears about a *war on corrupt bankers*. That's because, no matter what they do, they are too big to fail. Meanwhile, I get CIA militias sent after me—and for what reason? To stamp out drugs? No! They do this so they can pick the winners. It's the same game they play everywhere. At least I supply products and services in demand, so much in demand people risk going to jail to get them. Tell me what product or service the moneymen provide for the people? Can you think of one? How about a credit default swap or leveraged buyout under the holiday tree?"

The three captives said nothing. Mr. Lutane was clearly on a rant. It was best to let him vent without provocation.

Elijah shifted forward in his chair. "People in your cabal see nothing wrong with making money by gambling away other people's profits or flipping companies and robbing pension funds. If *I* changed my name and used thirty aliases to get lucrative government contracts, *I* would go to jail for fraud, conspiracy, and false personation. They do the same thing using dozens of cutout companies and offshore partnerships and get rewarded. Why shouldn't *I* be able to play that game?"

Elijah stood and paced to the railing, his eyes attracted to a jetliner overhead. "Your Air Force was told they could have 132 B-2 bombers if the people gave them $22 billion. Eight years later, the $22 billion was gone. Only one B-2 was built. And they have the cajones to say *I'm* the crook? *I'm* the barbarian? *One* fucking bomber is worth three times its weight in gold! Did anyone investigate? Was anyone indicted? No! Instead, they get rewarded by doing the same thing with the F-35 Joint Strike Fighter. It's the unwritten rule: industry can't afford to be ethical and stay in business."

Nelson knew he had to stay engaged with Lutane somehow, at least enough to channel the discussion to information that might be valuable. Nelson downed the rest of his drink. "What about drugs, gambling and the sex trade?" began Nelson. "Along with everything else, they bring in trillions of dollars. Why do you care if taxpayers become servants of a money class?"

Elijah turned, his gaze sweeping the three captives. "If you're not a master, you are a servant, no matter who you are."

"I think they're willing to let you have the dirty money," offered Nelson. "They just don't want you going after the legit money."

"Money is not dirty or legit. There is only money. On the news, you see crime and you see business. But in reality, there is no difference. Business has become a criminal enterprise and crime has always been a business. There's only one thing left to decide, one thing to do—pick the winner."

"No one does that," countered Nelson. "It happens by default."

"When you're put in a place where you can no longer move, it's checkmate. While people like you chase after Project G, they are moving their pieces into place."

"Is that what you're worried about?"

Elijah took steps closer. "You should worry too. There will come a time when power concentrates and aligns with technology in an absolute way."

"Why would I want you controlling that any more than them?"

"It will happen," asserted Elijah. "Someone will win."

Nelson played along. "You know something about what they're doing?"

"Who knows? They are masters of mixing cold truths with hot lies. The warm gruel that results satisfies no one. From the way they react to me, I believe I know enough to be dangerous."

"You think you can stop them? They have advantages."

Elijah shrugged. "They have armies, I have mercenaries. They make laws, I buy judges. They have secret FISA courts, I have private councils. They feed the people propaganda with their media machines; I feed the basic desires of our animal nature. They have one disadvantage I don't have. They must pretend, on the surface, to want to do the right thing. Their public face must never show what they really have in mind."

"Exposing them won't do any good," bantered Nelson. "That's been tried."

"It's not about that. I must know what their plan is," declared Elijah. "I can't fight the man hidden behind the curtain."

Nelson challenged, "What do you think you know?"

Elijah breathed heavily and stared down at them. "Your Congress has given them emergency powers. It's the kind of access to all the private financial networks they've been after for years but couldn't get. The men behind those networks are not as gullible as most people. It took real fear to get to them. By making them afraid of me, they've gained all the access they need to put their final plan in place."

"A plan to do what?" prompted Adam.

"Anyone could see it was bound to happen. Moneymen are always after the next advantage, the next score. Once you have all the machines and technicians you need, what's next? The intelligence services became their guilty pleasure, an anonymous way to grab insider information but now, even that isn't enough for them."

Adam made the connection to something he had read and told Jiaying about days ago. "...non-machine readable data..."

Elijah smirked, "Spoken like one of them."

"Corporate espionage is not new," asserted Nelson.

"Nothing is new except the ways in which old things get done. Global financial power is about to merge with Western intelligence in a way we can't imagine. They'll have capabilities that will network the world into their coffers. The game will be over."

Nelson restrained a smile. "Some might say you're going off the deep end."

Elijah bristled at the insinuation. "They started the clock on December 1st at 1 pm. That was their operation. They caused it and now your government puts them in charge of protecting everyone from it happening again."

"They say F1E was the way you tried extorting protection money from Wall Street. So what happened? Did they call your bluff?"

Elijah lunged close to Nelson's face. "Think for once! Think! They now have the power to activate their Clipper Chips, their Law Enforcement Access Fields, and all of their system trapdoors! They have unprecedented access to datacenters that control world markets! I don't have that power!"

"They claim they need that access to prevent people like you from playing by your own rules."

"Rules!" roared Elijah. "They pay others to make rules that sound noble but are only designed to limit their competition. When people wanted banking regulation, what happened? Their rules forced smaller banks out of business. The banking business consolidated into fewer hands. Those hands are too big to be accountable for what they do, which was the plan all along."

Nelson held his ground. "All of that might be true, but as far as we know, you are a Chinese agent pretending to be a member of a crime syndicate. You want government and corporate secrets. Should you get caught, you've set it up so the Chinese can blame New Age Barbarians. Now that would be much simpler to believe than the mash-up of paranoia you're spinning."

Elijah laughed and sat back down. "I don't need to convince you of anything. The cabal in your own government let you come down here because they want me to get rid of you. Either that or they want you to be seen publicly associating with me; it might be useful to them later. Getting rid of you would only do them a favor. You ask too many questions. You're too gung-ho to understand; as long as the clock is ticking, no one is allowed to do that."

"You're doing it," asserted Hollister.

Elijah reached for his drink. "That's right. And you're going to help me."

"How?" asked Nelson.

"By doing the same thing you've been doing for them—only now you'll do it for me."

Adam glanced at Nelson to read his reaction, then turned back to Elijah. "You want us to hack for you?"

Elijah settled back. "I'm not asking you. You will do it or you will die right now. You might be onto something; you might not. But something about what you were doing bothered your bosses. That intrigues me. At least that much is clear. And that's an opportunity. One I can't let go to waste."

Nelson asked, "Where do you expect us to do this and not be immediately shut down?"

"You'll be taken to a secure site. I expect you to leverage your network of intelligence contacts. Of course, should you try to give away your situation or location to anyone, all of you will be killed right away. That shouldn't come as a surprise."

"It won't work," challenged Nelson. "My bosses know where I am. A strip search isn't going to prevent them from coming after us."

"Oh, I would expect them to," began Elijah. "Unless, of course, they're members of the cabal. I see no reason why *they* would want you rescued. To them, you're either a liability or a throw-away excuse to grab more power. On the other hand, if your bosses are against the cabal, I should have no concern. In that case, we're on the same side, aren't we?"

"If we do this," asked Nelson. "What are your expectations?"

"I'm a reasonable man. I'll give you three days to justify your existence. I want to know their plan. I want to know the timetable. I don't want rumor or bullshit. As long as you give me details, you can live. Don't squander the time trying to escape. You should be dead already so think of this as a gift."

Elijah gestured with a flip of his hand. Out of the shadows stepped his guards to take the three of them away.

As Adam passed his interviewer, he asked, "Where are they taking us?"

The interviewer was expressionless. "The belly of the beast."

35

0000 0010 0011

9:29 pm EST, Thursday December 7th

Katherine sat in her parked car with engine and lights off. The residential side street was chosen at random, a quick escape off the main highway. All that mattered was watching next moves. Looking down, she tensed at what she saw. A mini-tablet rested in her lap. A sweater, pulled over the steering wheel as a shield, confined the glow. On the tablet screen, the trace of Barnett's movements inched along a display of the area.

She watched as a pulsing dot left the College Park Airport parking lot. To the west was the University of Maryland. To the east, Annapolis. Fort Meade and the National Security Agency was north. Washington, D.C., a short drive south. She'd have her answer soon enough.

The plan to lock onto Barnett's phone during their meeting couldn't have gone better. The way he'd played the recording by setting the phone out on the seat only assured that her wireless coupling gadget could train on his antenna. As she expected, he exited the airport onto Paint Branch Parkway, but his car didn't head toward well-traveled arterials. Instead, the pulsing dot turned onto River Road heading south then turned again onto a smaller access road that serviced an industrial park. His car slowed as it entered a parking lot no more than a mile from the airport.

At the far end of the industrial park, a dense tree line surrounded a plain rectangle of a building on two sides. By the looks of it, Katherine estimated the building to be 120,000 square feet in size. Punching the display with a finger, she switched on a descriptive overlay to show the names of places. The screen peppered with pinpoint icons. Clicking on a few, she read pop-ups for the NOAA and USDA buildings nearby.

Oddly enough, the structure where Barnett's car had stopped had no descriptive label. Switching to 3D building mode, she saw that the building was recent construction; vegetation around its pad had yet to mature. She drew a bounding box around the area with her finger, then tapped an analyze function and waited for mapping software to return site descriptions.

As she waited, she had the feeling this was something she should remember. Before fragmented memories could coalesce, the mapping program returned with a pop-up answer on the screen—M-SQUARE.

The connection flashed through Katherine. M-Square was the University of Maryland's newest Research Park. It was now obvious where Barnett had gone. If he truly was who he said he was, it all fit. No wonder he wanted to meet where he did; it was next door to his temporary office while in town.

The building had to be the headquarters of the IARPA—the *Intelligence Advanced Research Projects Activity*. IARPA was like DARPA, only specialized for the intelligence community. It existed as an independent activity of the ODNI. It was relatively new, created in 2006 from the NSA's Disruptive Technology Office, the National Geospatial-Intelligence Agency's National Technology Alliance and the CIA's Intelligence Technology Innovation Center. Its mission was to invest in high-risk/high-payoff research programs that cut across multiple IC agencies. Its goal was generating revolutionary capabilities to surprise adversaries and avoid being surprised.

As she scanned the pop-up on her screen, her phone buzzed with an incoming text message. The message was from Barnett, but how could he be calling her? Her phone was a new disposable. She raced to read the text.

"Very good Katherine, but keep in mind, while the eagle faces right, he carries his arrows on the left"

Katherine sank back. Barnett was more clever than she had surmised. He knew she'd try to track him and used the opportunity to prove a point. No matter how much experience one had, technology went beyond being the great leveler. The *eagle* he described was on the Great Seal of the United States. No doubt the R&D trolls at IARPA and DARPA had all sorts of witticisms about their methods of operation and code of conduct. When it came to technical superiority, she had better forget trying to match wits with one of the government's top scientists. Katherine reminded herself: the eagle faces right on the NSA emblem too. Barnett would expect a response. She sat a moment, undecided on what was appropriate. Finally, her thumbs punched in a reply.

"Annuit Coeptis"

Taken from the same Great Seal, the translation would confirm what she assumed: *He approves of what we have begun.*

She started her car and refocused on the task at hand. She had twenty-four hours to finalize her plan to contact Nelson, warn him about being set up, then enlist his help to get to the truth. To do so wouldn't be easy. Richard Marks was augmenting his files with personal information about the two of them. To leverage something he wouldn't already know about meant accessing places Nelson and she had held in reserve for only the most critical of times.

The drive home was a blur. A nagging doubt crept in. Was she being thorough or masking the danger of this new exposure? The friendship angle was ripe for exploitation. Her need to warn Nelson could be used to blind her to the better angels of discretion. What she *did* know was certain enough. Nelson was being set up. And he was her friend.

Arriving home, she parked the car and headed to her unit. At her front door, she turned a key in the lock then caught herself mid-motion and froze. Looking down, she stared at the word WELCOME on the mat under her feet. There was only one problem. She didn't have a welcome mat—until now.

She stepped back to survey the area. The only thing different was the unexpected mat, placed there while she was away. She pulled the mat back to reveal a blank, sealed envelope. She picked it up and hurried inside her townhouse. With back to the door, she held the envelope next to the light bulb of a nearby lamp. On cursory inspection, it was hard to distinguish anything except that the envelope was light enough to be empty. She took it to the kitchen sink and soaked it in water. Donning rubber gloves, she opened it.

Inside, she found a typed message on a torn scrap of paper.

"We need each other. Midnight, Jesup Blair House. Come alone."

Katherine stared at the words in her sink. Jesup Blair Park was a wedge of land on the south side of Silver Spring next to the Metro train tracks. The old house on park grounds had been built in the 1850s and was now owned and preserved by the state of Maryland. It was surrounded by a greenbelt with tress and walking paths and scattered picnic tables. A few parking spaces lined the entrance of an extended driveway. It wasn't the first place one would pick for a stroll by themselves late at night. Someone was being overly dramatic or sincerely desperate about being careful.

Katherine checked the time. She had over an hour to comply. Whether or not she'd accept the invitation didn't take long to decide. Someone knew where she lived and was asking for a get-together. If the intention was to harm her, they could have done so outside when she got home and parked her car. The fact that they went to the trouble of arranging a welcome mat as a signal told her the dynamics of the situation were complicated. Complications implied details, something she had an intense interest in uncovering.

Flipping on the garbage disposal, she ground the note and envelope down the drain. From force of habit, she turned and checked messages on her ground line. One voicemail was waiting. She recognized the voice. It was her contact who had looked up Barnett's name for her in the government registry. His words were unexpectedly rushed, pressured, disturbing.

"I hope you get this, Katherine. Something is up. I don't know if you had any business over at State, but it's triggered the shit. The guy who got security access through the archivist is dead. Bystanders near Connecticut and K said he looked in a daze when he walked into traffic. The archivist at State is on administrative leave. From what I hear, the Patterson delegation is being pressured for information. Luckily, they're pissed at the rude way they've been approached. They're invoking diplomatic privilege. No telling how long that'll hold. If any of this rings a bell, I'd find a hole. Whatever this is about, this is no time to be close to it. Anyway, I hope you get this. Don't call me. I don't want to know."

The message ended, leaving Katherine flushed and on edge. If her contact had gone down, was she next to be targeted? If viewing exterior security footage from State was enough to approve wet-work on assets, the delta-sweepers in play wouldn't be satisfied until their search space was clean. Life and death now hinged on whether Patterson would be able to resist with only diplomatic immunity and a grudge to keep the DOJ at bay. Was that enough? Could Richard Marks ID her some other way? What about the text message— *CLEAR*—sent as she walked through Edward Kelly Park? The phone she had used was disposable but was that enough?

She hurried into the bedroom closet and chose a Glock 36 from her arsenal. The clip of the G36 held six .45 caliber rounds. Other models held seventeen but she pocketed the G36 anyway.

An exchange between professionals would be over after one or two rounds got squeezed off. Spraying an area with ordnance was for amateurs and film-makers. Steady nerves and a true aim would always outmatch a banana clip. The Glock 36's subcompact size made for easy concealment and its one-inch width assured easy control of recoil, improving accuracy.

On second thought, she reached back into her duffle bag and grabbed an extra clip, just in case any professional she encountered had friends.

With an hour to spare, it was time to stake out the meeting site. If a welcoming party was being set up for her, she might as well sneak a peek at where the balloons and noisemakers were being staged for her arrival.

Shedding her clothes, she changed into dark apparel that included a Kevlar vest and extra layer of microfleece to give more warmth. It was a frosty December night. The last thing she wanted was to turn up cold.

36

0000 0010 0100

11:54 pm AST, Thursday December 7th

Nelson, Adam, and Hollister had settled in but were far from comfortable. The only indication that they were still airborne was the incessant drone of the airplane's engines and the slight tilt of course corrections along the way.

With no windows in the aft section of the cargo jet, they had no reference points. As Carlos reminded them, they were lucky enough that the space was pressurized and heated, let alone offering a modicum of light. As best as Nelson could tell from runway turns and takeoff, they were headed northeast. That put them over the ocean with nothing to see anyway.

Having been taken directly from Mr. Lutane's yacht to the Curacao airport, the three captives had escaped being accounted for by customs. With rapid efficiency but casually, Rodolfo and company had loaded them with the rest of the cargo, most of which was packaged on shrink-wrapped pallets or in metal cabinets, the contents unknown. Undoubtedly contraband was included but key airport personnel must have been given incentives to process them through and look the other way. Everyone treated the journey as a routine flight.

Even after they took to the air, their destination was never mentioned. Not knowing how long the journey would be proved unnerving. Carlos and crew spent their time in another section of the plane. Two guards rotated shifts to watch the captives in the back. As night wore on, Carlos and friends began to enjoy the flight. They passed the time laughing and drinking and carrying on.

Slumped against a bulkhead, Adam glanced over at Hollister and marveled at him sleeping. "He's dead to the world. How does he do that?"

Nelson's legs stretched out; his head rested back against a cargo container. Lost in thought, he rarely blinked. "He's a grunt. He grabs sleep when and where he can. We could bounce around with wind shear; it wouldn't matter."

Adam murmured, "Who wants to sleep with three days to live?"

Nelson glanced over at the kid. "Don't think that way; it'll eat you up."

"What should I do? Plan our escape?"

The sarcasm was weak. Nelson decided to match it. "I don't know. I would think you'd have a lot in common with Mr. Alonzo Elijah Lutane."

The accusation prompted a glare. "What's that supposed to mean?"

"You've worked for RAPIER. They share Lutane's distain for the rich 1% and their New World Order. You and he should have common enemies."

Adam looked away. "The enemy of my enemy is not always my friend."

"True, but you might be able to parlay a reprieve out of these guys if they thought it would net them some RAPIER help."

"They don't need me for that. They have far better connections."

"Really," grinned Nelson. "I thought that was just a conspiracy theory."

"Living in the underground, you get to know your neighbors. So what?"

"Nothing, except it might work to our advantage if we play it right. Instead of worrying about three days to live, I'd be scheming a way to work it into the equation, you know, the way a good quant would."

Adam's desperation showed. "You're full of great ideas."

Nelson was firm. "You wanted *non-machine readable data*? Now you've got it in spades. So what's the matter? It doesn't compute for you?"

"Fuck off."

"The easy answer when you have none." Nelson settled back into a trance.

Adam wouldn't let it go. "You're the know-it-all. Why put it on me?"

Nelson stared and let the late hour and critical nature of their situation evoke a haunt of memories. "Never mind. I was talking to somebody else."

Adam's confusion evoked curiosity and humor. "Anybody I know?"

"It doesn't matter."

Baffled, Adam pressed the point. "An easy answer when you're crazy."

Nelson blurted, "My son, Brian. OK?

"I didn't know you had a son."

"Huh…" laughed Nelson. "He'd probably he'd say that too. You're about his age. I have to remind myself not to talk to you the way I'd talk to him."

Adam savored the admission. "Can't get out of parental mode, huh?"

Nelson was vulnerable but circumspect. "I was hardly a parent. Being a friend was difficult enough."

"Was?"

"My job took me away a lot. When I *was* around, I couldn't talk about it. He wanted to be like me. So now he is."

Adam shook his head. "It's weird the way it goes. He can talk to you anytime he wants and he doesn't. I would like to talk to my Dad and can't."

"He's gone?" asked Nelson.

"No. He doesn't recognize me—he's got some kind of dementia."

"They say out of sight, out of mind. What do they know? Some say being a parent comes naturally. If that were true, why would so much go wrong?"

"It's backwards. Hard things easy, easy things hard. Is that why you like this kind of work?"

Nelson closed his eyes for a moment. "Who said I like it?"

"Then why do it?"

Nelson hesitated. "Should I say it's the only thing I know?"

"And what's the reason for that? Maybe because you love it."

"When you've spent a lifetime doing something, it's part of you. Who knows why we get stuck doing the things we do. Did you think as a kid you'd want to spend your whole life doing math so other people could get rich?"

Adam's grin faded. "Put that way, the whole thing blows, doesn't it?"

1

Nelson chuckled. "Yeah. So how do you explain that to RAPIER?"

Adam grew serious. "What, you mean me working for the 1%?"

"I don't have a problem with it. The thing is, to most of the world, even *we're* rich. That's the funny thing about railing against the 1%. Compared to most of the world, *anyone* living in one of the top countries is rich. It's a matter of perspective."

"RAPIER has to be practical to survive. It needs technicians, especially those who know the game. The best of those are still playing."

"I see," smiled Nelson. "It's kinda like what governments do, making deals with dictators and crime syndicates. The ends justifies the means."

"You know all about that, don't you, in this *work* you do?" Adam didn't wait for a confession that wasn't coming. "You heard Lutane. The lines have been blurred for a long time."

"Now you're quoting Elijah. He'll be pleased."

"You know what I mean," pressed Adam. "Global governance is a rigged game. They've made news entertainment and entertainment the news. They hide behind patriotism to protect a system they've hijacked and perverted."

Nelson raised a hand to preempt a lecture. "Believe me, I've heard it all."

"With all the shit you've seen, you still don't believe it?"

"I didn't say that," remarked Nelson. "I don't think it's that simple."

"There's nothing simple about it. It's a self-organizing structure, the same way flocks of birds somehow move as one and decide where to go."

Nelson sighed. "Next you're going to tell me you've posted a YouTube video exposing the whole thing."

Adam shook his head. "I don't get you. You see what's happening and yet you doubt it."

"Believe me, the more you see, the less you're willing to believe *anything*. It gets to the point where you become agnostic about all of it."

"How convenient. Right where they want you."

"If the game is so rigged, why do you think you have any chance against it? As long as you're an acceptable risk, they'll leave you alone."

"And that's enough? That's slave mentality."

"Yeah, well, what do you expect from a wage-slave?"

"The difference between you and me? You've given up."

"I see the way it ends. It's closer for me than for you."

"Wrong," countered Adam. "It's three days for both of us." Coming full circle, back to his fear of dying, Adam sunk within himself and was quiet.

Nelson sensed the anguish of the young man and wanted to distract him from it. "Did you know, it is said during the American Civil War, J.P. Morgan agreed to finance the purchase of guns for the Union Army. The profits he made helped him start his banking empire."

Adam didn't look up. "Yeah...so?"

Nelson watched the kid's reaction. "When the guns were delivered, many of them turned out to be defective. Lots of them were old, re-machined rifles that had seen better days. But by then, the profits were already in the bank."

Adam said nothing. Before Nelson could comment, a commotion was heard farther forward in the plane. They could hear Carlos shouting at their guards, laying into them for falling asleep. A minute later, Carlos appeared aft, carrying a laptop computer. He sized up the captive group with a glance and then shoved the laptop in Adam's direction.

"Here you go. Something to do. You might as well be useful on the trip."

Adam accepted the computer. "What's this for?"

"Your government has confiscated all recordings of the F1E event."

"What kind of recordings?"

"The screens—the way the screens looked."

"During the six minutes of glitch?"

Carlos nodded. "They say it's garbage and yet they don't want anyone to look at it. Mr. Lutane wants to know why."

Nelson's thoughts raced back to his briefing and talk of the *kill screen*. Owen had mentioned that the FBI had taken possession of such a recording. Nelson asked, "How did you get a hold of that?"

"Why ask stupid questions?" Carlos was half-drunk. He picked at his teeth and turned to Adam. "Maybe by the time we get where we're going, you'll find something. If you find something big, it might buy you an extra day."

Nelson pressed his luck; he had no way of knowing how Carlos would act after drinking half the night, but if his judgment was impaired, perhaps he would share more than he intended. "Where is this plane going?"

Carlos was caught off-guard by the directness of the question. "It doesn't matter; it's not where *you're* going."

"How does that work?"

"When we get to France, you will be put on another plane."

Hearing an answer with information spurred Nelson on. "Another one! Why? We can hack anywhere. Why waste time flying us around?"

Carlos pulled a pint bottle of tequila out of his pants pocket and took a swig. "You can piss anywhere too, but it's not advised. Understand?"

Adam spoke up. "Back on the ship, I was told we were going to the *belly of the beast*. Where the hell is that?"

Hearing the phrase, Carlos' resentment simmered into anger. "Any time we do business with the cabal, it's the *belly of the beast*."

"The two of you work together?"

"There are times even enemies find ways to profit from each other."

Nelson pushed the inference. "So, this place where we're going, it's operated by them, not you?"

"It's not so hard to understand. You'll be there soon enough. It's a data-center." Carlos turned to Adam. "It's full of computers; you'll love it."

"You're lying," asserted Nelson, hoping to provoke Carlos to talk.

Carlos spun around, humored. "You think so?"

"I know so. You want us to hack into the cabal's secrets. You wouldn't take us to one of their datacenters to do it. How would you get in, and if you did, how would you explain it to them?"

"You don't know the arrangement we have." Carlos stared Nelson down then started to walk away.

"Why not tell us?" asked Nelson. "We're going to die in a couple of days anyway; it doesn't matter what we know."

Carlos paused. "Exactly, so why waste my time."

"Because they could be using your arrangement against you. If we don't know about it, we won't know what to look for when we're hacking."

The point was weak but in the late hour, given Carlos' condition, it was enough to make him waver. "If anything, it would be the other way around."

"Maybe," conceded Nelson. "Mutual profit, mutual exposure, but who has more of what? You think you know and that's the way they want it. The problem is, how can you be sure?"

Carlos turned back to them. "What did Lenin say: '*Trust but verify.*'"

"Didn't Reagan say that?" asked Adam.

"He stole it from a Russian proverb," corrected Carlos. "Don't you know by now, nothing is as it seems."

"Even more reason to tell us," pressed Nelson.

Carlos stepped back to him. "It's simple. They let us keep our servers in their datacenter and they have a place to wash their money when they need it. It's there as a fail-safe for them, nothing more. For us, it's profit."

"Why do you need servers?" asked Adam.

"For online gambling."

"You're into e-gambling?"

"Gambling is bigger than drugs, bigger than sex. Americans spend more on slot machine gambling than on movies, baseball, and theme parks combined. Imagine how much is spent on gambling worldwide. When you gamble online, you can do it anywhere, anytime." He laughed, "You can do it in your underwear."

Nelson prodded Carlos to divulge more. "You wouldn't put those servers just anywhere. You'd want them out of the reach of the taxman."

Adam joined in. "You'd have to place it offshore somewhere."

Nelson added, "But where? The GFCI compiles data on all international financial centers."

"GFCI?" Carlos asked.

"The *Global Financial Centres Index*. According to the index, the top five offshore centers are Jersey, Guernsey, the Isle of Man, Bermuda, and the Cayman Islands."

"Those are all British sovereign territories," noted Adam.

Carlos laughed, "Sounds like a cabal to me!"

"So which one are we headed to?" asked Nelson.

Carlos was proper. "They call it the *Bailiwick* of Guernsey."

"Oddly enough," noted Nelson. "Guernsey issues its own coinage and banknotes. It's fiat money, not tied-in to any fractional banking system. In fact, most of the top offshore locations do the same."

"Of course!" roared Carlos. "They don't want the governments of their friends impoverished with debt and interest payments. They create places in the world where the rules they impose on the rest of us don't apply to them."

"How do you know so much about finance?" Adam asked Nelson.

Nelson glanced at Adam but looked to Carlos. "My hobby is conspiracy theories, remember? What do they say? *'Follow the money.'*"

"Money is their domain," asserted Carlos. "They make it, they loan it out, they decide how and where it flows. Money exists only by their rules."

"And you're bitter about it," prompted Nelson.

"It's been coming a long time. They don't like competition. Thirty years ago, in the '80s, you could see it then. They made an example of BCCI."

"What's that?" asked Adam.

Nelson was stunned. "You want to be a quant and you don't know the dark side of financial history?"

"Algorithms are now. History is what happened last week."

"No wonder the moneymen operate with impunity." Nelson shook his head and then recalled, "BCCI was the *Bank of Credit and Commerce International.* The scandal was all over the news..."

Carlos butted in, "They made sure of it."

Nelson explained, "It was an international bank set up by a Pakistani financier who registered the bank in Luxembourg. Investigators claimed it was set up to avoid regulatory review."

"Code words for not playing by the rules," Carlos commented.

"The officers were sophisticated international bankers but they were accused of keeping secrets, committing fraud on a massive scale, and manipulating whatever they could to avoid detection."

"And now it's thirty years later," observed Carlos. "And we have the same thing; but now only those who make rules can act that way. They get to play the game by different rules and pick the winners too."

"I suppose going after BCCI was never about doing the right thing," concluded Nelson. "They had a system and power structure to maintain, nothing more."

"You don't have to believe me," chuckled Carlos. "But maybe you can explain why the same authorities that took down BCCI let Nicaraguan drug traffickers sell and distribute crack cocaine in the United States. The profits were used to finance the Contras, a CIA operation. You see, when it suits their purposes, there are no rules for them. But tell me, I'd like to know—how do you get to be one of them? Do you know? Is there a form I fill out or do I go someplace and pay a fee, and after that, the rules don't apply to me?"

Nelson waited for eye contact with Carlos. "Some say the two of you are merging. It's not about who's going to win. It's more about what the final org chart is going to look like."

"You think it's a merger of only two?"

"There's somebody else?"

"My world is not as structured as yours."

"What do you mean? Mr. Lutane has a competitor?"

"Oh, yes. Why do you think some cartels are taken down and others are left alone? Military force is the biggest protection racket in the world."

Nelson grinned. "What's the matter? Is the cabal playing one cartel against the other?"

"Why should that be any surprise? Even Walmart does the same thing with its overseas suppliers. Every year they go in and say, produce more for less or I'll go to your neighbor and squeeze them too. These tactics are not new."

Adam concluded, "They've got you in a bind. To beat out the competition, you have to give away the store. But if you do that, the cabal will own you."

Carlos' anger flared. "They'll never own me! We'll take them down before that happens!"

"And what about your competitor?"

"They've made their choice."

Nelson read Carlos. "They're merging with the cabal, not with you."

"What do you think? Look at Afghanistan; 90% of opiates for the world market come from there. In 2000, the U.N. made a deal with the Taliban to get rid of heroin production. Growing poppies was declared un-Islamic. As a result, in one year, opium production dropped 90%. Then, conveniently, the war came and what happened? The Taliban chief championing the restriction on poppies was assassinated. Since 9/11, opium production in Afghanistan has soared to its highest levels, twice the production of before, a new record."

"So what?" asked Adam.

"Why do they keep opium illegal when three-fourths of all legal opiate supplies are used by only six countries? Many kinds of medicines are made from opiates. The pharmaceutical companies know this. Controlling the price of those medicines around the world means huge profits."

"As your boss said, crime is a business. And business is criminal."

"The world is a business."

"It always has been." Nelson couldn't help referencing history. "It reminds me of the Opium Wars between Britain and China in the 1800s. The British East India Company mixed tobacco with opium and flooded China with it. The addiction rate soared and China was drained of silver. When China moved to stop the opium trade, the British went to war to keep it going."

"The cabal is not new." Carlos' glare shifted between them. "They want people like me around, but they want me to know my place. '*You can carry out the trash for me but you can't marry my daughter. "'*

"And people like Mr. Lutane aren't going to accept that anymore."

Carlos took a long draft from the pint bottle of tequila, then smiled. "Elijah says—if he can't marry their daughter, at least he's going to have her—and make her like it." Laughing, Carlos turned and walked away.

Adam waited until he was certain Carlos was gone before asking Nelson, "You believe any of that?"

Nelson sat as before, his legs outstretched, his back against the bulkhead. He glanced in the distance, to where Carlos stood kibitzing with the guards, then he looked back and answered, "Should I?"

"Not even the part about Guernsey?"

"I don't disbelieve it," noted Nelson. "I'm just not in the habit of believing anything until I see it."

Across the way, Hollister re-crossed his arms across his chest and shifted into a better sleeping position. "I believe it, every goddamn word."

"You're awake?" asked Adam.

"No," barked Hollister. "But I'm not sleeping either."

Nelson grinned and turned to Adam to explain. "He's pulled too many guard-duty shifts in his life. He can't help himself."

Hollister's eyes were still closed. "Don't go talking shit about me over there. You know damned well no one ever got by me."

Nelson wadded up a strip of packing material into a pillow and slumped to one side. "Keep up the good work. Don't let anybody through here."

With both of them snoozing, Adam was left alone with the laptop. He opened it and orientated himself to what it contained. On the desktop, he found a video file and played it. The image had no sound but what he saw took him back to the 26th floor, to December 1st at 1 pm.

Garbage characters danced every which way across real-time stock futures and options. Ghost images of inverted numbers incremented over financial portals of intraday, historical, summary, and reference data. Forex price quotes morphed into odd geometric shapes and splintered into fractal color iterations converging on nothing. For Adam, the feeling of surprise was no longer there. Now he was gripped by a sense of subterfuge and urgency.

He set the video in an infinite loop and stared into it. Looking for patterns, he ran the loop in slow motion. Mesmerized, he surrendered to a math meditation that transcended numbers. As his fear of death subsided, he was overwhelmed by a sense of recognition that something intelligible might emerge from the glitch screen chaos. He could only assume how difficult it would be to solve. Perhaps as difficult as their ongoing puzzle of staying alive.

37

0000 0010 0101

11:31 pm EST, Thursday December 7th

Katherine Stalt parked her car on the north side of Jesup Blair Park, next to a sign that read, *'No Parking Any Time'*. To her right was the back side of the Montgomery College Campus. To the left, darkness and park vegetation hid the footpaths to Blair House. She checked the Glock pistol, holstered under her left arm, then zipped up her jacket halfway.

Outside, it appeared no one was around. She could sit and watch for movement or get out and explore. Waiting in the car was being a sitting duck. She'd rather be out, moving through the darkness. It made for a harder target and was the only way she'd discover more about her surroundings. The time had come to find out if arriving early paid off.

She got out of the car and headed across the street, aimed for the park. Immediately from behind, a figure approached. The person must have come from the walkways leading into the college campus, closed for the night.

Katherine tensed and turned to find a woman intent upon her.

"You're early," observed the woman.

Katherine looked her over. "How would you know?" The woman was her same height, slender, with blonde hair pulled back into a chignon. Blending with the night, she too wore black, a short Burberry trench coat over pants.

"There's no time to waste." The woman caught her by the arm; the contact was directive, not insistent. "Katherine, let's walk."

"Why should I go with you?" asked Katherine, ignoring the familiarity.

"Like I said in the note: *'we need each other.'*"

Quoting the note under the welcome mat proved little. The meeting time was still half an hour away. If this woman was not Katherine's appointment, it still might be good to get a second opinion about what was going on.

Katherine didn't resist; she paused. "Where are we going?"

"The pedestrian walkway." The woman turned towards the east end of the street where it dead-ended. "Over there."

Katherine knew about the enclosed, elevated walkway that connected one part of the campus with the Student Services Center across the Metro tracks. The raised walkway was a confined space, away from vulnerable places in the park. But it also led to Fenton Street, where another car and backup support for the woman might be waiting to whisk them away.

"First, tell me who you are," demanded Katherine.

"You don't recognize me?" The woman seemed surprised.

"Should I?"

"It was years ago," reasoned the woman. "I was in uniform, a brunette." She took a step closer through darkness. "I'm Aubrey Marks."

"Aubrey?" Katherine was taken aback. They had met in passing at the Pentagon, years ago. Aubrey had been with the Air Force's Air Intelligence Agency, now the AFISRA.

Although they had never worked together, they shared enough social events at the time to believe they had. In D.C., attending any event meant conducting business, no matter how casual, social, or diplomatic. Diplomacy was a strategic euphemism for so many things. To be social was diplomatic.

The woman motioned for her to follow. "Please, we must hurry."

Katherine followed along but only because the woman's face began to register with her. It *was* Aubrey, albeit older, civilian, and under stress.

"Why didn't you meet me at my place?" asked Katherine, catching up.

Aubrey kept a brisk pace. "I have to assume your place is compromised. I couldn't take the chance so I paid a messenger to leave the mat."

On the northeast side of the park, a zigzag ramp led up to the enclosed pedestrian bridge. Aubrey led the way up then out to a spot over the train tracks. There she checked the bridge for foot traffic. Finding none, she drew close to Katherine. With sudden urgency, she confided in her.

"There's little time to explain. I can't stay in one place for long. If I do, I'll be dead."

"What's going on?" Katherine's concern, genuine but not gullible, was immediate.

"I think it's Richard...I *know* it's Richard."

"Your husband..." Katherine corrected herself, "...ex-husband."

"I think he's been up to something for a long time."

"Something to kill you over?"

"It's not up to him. It's the people he works for."

Katherine was alarmed. "The DNI?"

Aubrey rolled her eyes. "Hardly. Richard split loyalties long ago."

"How do you know?"

"It was long before the divorce. At first I thought he was having an affair. He started keeping secrets, missing appointments. I was certain he was keeping something from me. It got to the point I was desperate to know one way or another."

Katherine was well aware of Aubrey's position. At the time Aubrey spoke of, Richard worked at Homeland Security and Aubrey was a rising star at Chimaera, one of the premiere private intelligence firms. "You didn't!"

Aubrey nodded. "I knew better than to use Chimaera assets to check it out but I thought it'd be quick, I could contain it."

"So you found something?"

"Enough to know it wasn't sex he was after."

"What was it?"

"Foreign accounts were opened, money deposited. He met with people that didn't make sense. There had to be a shadow agenda but he never would admit to it. The problem was, while I was having him followed, someone else had him under surveillance."

"The foreign accounts…"

"Of course," confirmed Aubrey. "Whoever opened those accounts were watching their protégé, making sure he was on their team. In due time, they discovered assets from Chimaera were onto him too. Of course, my operation wasn't official. It was personal, but they didn't know that."

"Is that why they're after you?"

Aubrey chuckled, as if to cry. "No! Whoever was vetting Richard didn't know I was worried about an affair. When they checked, Chimaera knew nothing about the surveillance on him. How could they? I kept it off-book."

"Did they confront him?"

"Privately. They wanted to know what kind of shenanigans he and his wife were into." Aubrey let out a painful laugh at the absurdity. "Because we were married, they assumed the agents I had around him were there to *assist* him. When they asked him what we had in play, naturally, he couldn't answer."

"Not good for building trust," noted Katherine.

"To stay with them, the bar was raised on demonstrations of loyalty."

"The divorce?" Katherine was shocked.

"Even that wasn't enough. He's been proving himself ever since. As long as he jumps through hoops, they keep making deposits in foreign accounts."

"What else has he done?"

"Chimaera's contract with Extasis was canceled with no explanation. To keep me busy, he started a fight over the custody of the kids." She sighed. "He didn't care about them; he just wanted me occupied and off-balance."

"How could you be any threat?"

"I got the job as COO. Chimaera was providing security for Extasis. But something big had happened. A breakthrough of some kind. Those at the top didn't want to take any chances with players outside their circle discovering what it was. Last-minute arrangements with In-Q-Tel were dissolved. Extasis had to go. Naturally, they wanted insurance against any backchannel links. As COO of Chimaera and wife of Richard Marks, I became a double liability. They gave him an ultimatum. Lose me or lose his membership in the inner circle."

"Why are you coming to me with this?" asked Katherine.

"I know your background with Nelson Geiss."

"Nelson?"

"I figured, if something had motivated Nelson to come out of retirement, you might be with him, working with a larger team. I thought, maybe I could find a place with your group. In exchange, I could help."

"Working together?"

"Why not? It's push-come-to-shove time."

"Over what?"

"You don't know?"

Katherine wouldn't tip her hand. "And you do?"

Aubrey rushed to speak. "Look, last week I met with Nelson. He asked me for a meeting. He seemed to be in the middle of something he didn't understand and couldn't control. I tried to warn him the best I could. As a result, I was ordered to stand down for a month."

"By whom?"

"Chimaera's board of directors."

"Why would they be upset you talked to Nelson?"

"Honestly, I don't think even they know. Ideas like that are heard in the wind; they certainly don't originate with them. They simply understood they had better comply. Without questioning it, they sent their COO away for a month. When that happened, I knew whatever was going on had gone critical."

"Do you still have Chimaera assets loyal to you?"

"One or two, but we're scattered, cut off."

"Are they the same ones you had on Richard?"

"Yes, without them, I wouldn't know what I know. They shadowed him and made recordings when they could."

"Recordings?" Aubrey was eager to wrap up but Katherine needed to engage even more. "Were they audio recordings?"

"I was after audio," admitted Aubrey. "But some came with video."

"How many recordings are there?"

"A dozen, maybe, made over the last year."

"You kept recording him after the divorce?"

"Well, yeah, if it wasn't an affair, I still wanted to find out what was going on. You have to understand, this is a man who flipped 180 degrees into a black hole. Something that big can't hide completely, not from people like us, not in a town like D.C. To go solid black, it has to be something major. Who would have the resources and clout to seal up something that tight?"

"You've listened to all of these recordings?"

"All the ones I know of."

"Why would there be others?"

"I've had to take precautions; that creates delay. It might take days or weeks for an asset to get me their latest recording. It's been a problem."

"So when you met with Nelson, there could have been other recordings out there, ones you hadn't heard?"

"More than likely. Like I said, I've been cut off."

"Sending you away is one thing but you said somebody wants you dead."

"A recent development."

"Why, all of a sudden?"

"I made the mistake of sharing the recordings with someone."

"Why do that?"

"I wasn't getting any traction; time was slipping away. I wanted answers, raise awareness, get somebody else on my side. I had heard enough to know I wasn't going to pry this open by myself. This isn't something you go public with on your own. They'll make you into a joke or you'll disappear."

"So what happened? You shared it with the wrong person?"

"No. *He* shared it with the wrong people."

Katherine's heart raced. "What would be wrong?"

"The Senate Intelligence Committee." Aubrey shook her head, exasperated. "How incredibly stupid!"

The reason was now absurdly clear but Katherine had to hear it from Aubrey anyway. "Why?"

"The committee was the *first* thing to be compromised! They're oversight! To run something this dark, this huge, you have to know what they know. Beyond that, you have to *control* what they know. At the very least, anything passing through them has to be pulled into the black hole to be studied."

"But how does that link the recordings to you?"

"Digital signatures. Forensics. They have classified tools. Once they got more than one of the recordings for comparison, tracing it back to Chimaera was only a matter of time. From there, simple deduction pointed to me. With my history with them...well, it went over the line."

Katherine felt exposed. If this was true, then she was partly responsible for the threats on Aubrey's life. Without her visit to drop off the sunglass case at the post office, final forensic confirmation might never have been made.

Katherine thought of Barnett. "What about your contact, the man you shared it with? There's no blowback on him?"

"Why should there be? The recordings went to a blind drop. A staffer picked him up. If anyone was detected, it would have been the courier he used. It all depends on whether or not the drop site was being watched."

Katherine's blood ran cold. "How did you get the recordings to him?"

"One of my Chimaera assets left a copy at a country club."

Katherine had heard enough. It was possible that Aubrey's whole speech was an act, an elaborate ruse to entrap Katherine into admitting her connection with Barnett. But it didn't add up, not emotionally. She knew Aubrey well enough; this was a woman fearful for her life. And yet, no matter how certain Katherine felt, she'd be out on a limb to trust that the situation was real. All she had was gut instinct and a desire to go deeper.

"Belle Haven..." Katherine spoke and the words hung between them, waiting to either bond the two woman together or blow them apart.

Aubrey froze. She studied Katherine's face. "How do you know about that?"

Pushed to the edge, Katherine hedged. "I know the courier."

"How?"

"Overlapping operations." Admitting to being the courier might be too much information. Katherine hoped some frankness would prevent Aubrey from pursuing the topic. "I was paid to follow Owen Raedalus."

"Owen..." The name registered with Aubrey. "One of Richard's field commanders."

"There's no official org chart with that relationship on it. You make it sound like a military operation."

"That's the way they're running it." Aubrey went to the heart of the matter. "Who hired you to watch Owen?"

Katherine watched for a reaction. "R.Z. Barnett."

A hand flew up to Aubrey's mouth. "My God!"

Katherine tried to explain. "After Barnett heard the recordings, he must have come to the same conclusions you did. There was much to know and little time left." The explanation was as much for herself as for Aubrey. "Richard and Owen aren't enough. Barnett wants to find who's behind them."

"That's crazy! He's a scientist! He's not qualified to run ops, certainly not of this magnitude!" Aubrey turned to the glass enclosing the pedestrian walkway and stared down at the darkness. Somewhere out there was an unseen vanishing point where train tracks disappeared south, headed for D.C.

Katherine glanced at the darkness but couldn't stay on it. "You wanted to raise awareness, get somebody concerned, and you did. Once you had Barnett's attention, what did you think he was going to do?"

"I don't know," cried Aubrey. "He's the center of gravity in this; I thought he'd have more sense!"

"Could it be, he's worried for his life just like you?" asked Katherine.

"He should be immune. He's too important to them."

"Unless they have everything they need from him. Is that possible?"

"You know the answer to that. Is Nelson working with you?"

"Nelson is being set up. He's part of a false flag ETC."

Aubrey swung around with the news. "That's impossible."

"Apparently not. Not if it comes from this black hole you talk about."

"There's too much involved in an ETC. They'd never be able to hide it."

"All they have to do is hide from the ones who think they're in it."

"Nelson's cell..."

Katherine nodded. "Owen sold Richard on the idea of having scapegoats, in case whatever they're working on blows up."

"Does Nelson know?"

"No."

"So you're not working with him?"

"Not yet, but that's the plan."

"Whose plan? Barnett's?"

Katherine considered the option. "I'm the one who suggested it to him."

Aubrey turned back to the glass. "The fool! How can someone that brilliant be so clueless? He's going to get us all killed."

"More reason why I have to warn Nelson."

"You haven't told him yet? What's the problem?"

"Richard's group may be after me too."

Aubrey reengaged. "Why are you on their radar?"

"Geri Messare gave me up. He called her, wanting to know details about people Nelson might trust. Richard already suspected me; he's read our files."

"You know a lot to be working this alone. Where'd you get all this info?"

Katherine prepared for Aubrey's reaction. "I heard a recording."

"What recording?"

Katherine confessed. "I've heard two recordings. In one, Richard spoke with Geri. In the other, he was talking with Owen about the ETC."

"You've been listening to the recordings from my agents?"

"Only those Barnett shared with me."

Aubrey realized, "Those two are recordings I haven't heard."

"It's like you said; your agents are still out there. They're active. But that means copies of any new recordings are still going to Barnett."

"Can it get any worse?" fretted Aubrey. "He's getting information I don't have. Who knows what he'll do with it next. I have no way of anticipating it."

"We need resources. We need to team up with Nelson."

"How can we do that? Do you even know where he is?"

"No," admitted Katherine.

"When was the last time you saw him?"

"On Monday, at Arlington, talking to Owen."

Aubrey paced to the other side of the walkway and back. She shook her head and stared at the floor. "This is not going to work."

"We haven't tried."

"Tried what? Joining with you is the same as working for Barnett. Excuse me, I don't see a future in that."

"We don't know what Nelson's been able to find out."

"You have no idea where Nelson is, and even if you did, according to you he's wrapped up tight. You know they've positioned his cell to get caught with their hands in the cookie jar. You want to join them?"

"Do we have a choice? If so, I'd like to hear the options."

Aubrey stopped her pacing. "If I'm so wrong, then give me a plan."

"There might be a way to get to Nelson."

"How?"

"A go-between."

"Someone that Richard's HUMINT won't know about?"

"I can't give you guarantees. All I'm saying is, it's our best shot."

"What would it take?"

"We have to get out of town."

Aubrey laughed. "That's brilliantly obvious. I have to do that anyway."

"Then come with me," implored Katherine. "We'll have a better chance of surviving if we work together."

"There's no logic to that," countered Aubrey. "It's just as likely we'd be concentrating our liabilities."

Katherine made her last pitch. "My go-between might have a way to reestablish contact with your agents. How much is that worth to you?"

Aubrey thought it over. "We'd have to leave the city right away, tonight."

"OK, but it's not something I planned for."

"Doesn't matter. I have a way."

"Adding me to it is no problem?"

"No problem if we go now. But you can't contact anyone. We simply disappear. It's the only way."

Katherine considered what she would be agreeing to. She promised Barnett she'd have a plan for him. They had arranged to meet back at the College Park Airport tomorrow night. How would he react if she didn't show up and gave no explanation? "I need to make a clean break."

"Is leaving word the right thing to do if it gets us killed? Your message could be the one thing that leads them to us."

"OK." Katherine relented but made a demand. "I pick the destination."

"It's your go-between."

Katherine nodded. "All right. Let's go."

"In your car. I don't have one."

Aubrey led the way back down the pedestrian ramp to Jesup Blair Park. As they walked across the grass, Katherine checked the time. It was one minute after midnight. The Glock pistol hung ready at her side. She reached out and touched Aubrey's arm and changed their direction. "This way…"

Aubrey stopped, curious at what Katherine was up to.

Eyes adjusting to the dark, Katherine didn't blink. "I need to go by Blair House." She let the insinuation sink in. "I always keep my appointments."

Aubrey drew what she needed from the moment. Katherine was with her but wouldn't accept anything on face value. If Aubrey really was her midnight appointment, a slight detour wouldn't matter. If she wasn't, they were about to have company—and the detour might lead to the end of the road for one of them, or maybe both.

38

0000 0010 0110

10:21 am GMT, Friday December 8th

Nelson Geiss stared out the window as the G550 banked on approach for a landing. A ways out and far below, the island of Guernsey appeared through the clouds as a ragged patch of green in a restless indigo sea.

Glancing left, Nelson could see how the tiny Bailiwick made a matched set with another emerald jewel, the nearby island of Jersey. Both defied the cold, encroaching waters of the English Channel off the coast of France.

As the jet leveled out through brief turbulence, Nelson caught a glimpse of anchored boats and the historic Castle Cornet at St. Peter Port, the capital city. The plan had been for their flight from Paris to take off as soon as they arrived from Curacao, but Guernsey airport had to shut down for an hour to reposition equipment and complete aircraft deicing.

After enduring a long flight and a night of drinking, Carlos was in no mood for delays. The guards had convinced him that breakfast would be a good way to pass the time. Once everyone was fed, word had come that the flight was given clearance from their offshore destination.

Nelson shook the shoulder next to him. "Adam, we're landing."

Slumped to one side, Adam raised his head but his eyes remained closed.

A corner of Hollister mouth tugged up into a grin. "Damn, that kid can sleep through anything."

"He's not asleep," joked Nelson. "He's dazed, maybe hypnotized. He stared at that friggin' laptop half the night."

Hollister turned to the view out his window. "Better him than me."

"I just wonder if he found anything."

Hollister's attention refocused on the laptop. "If he did, what should we do about it?" He leaned to one side and glanced into the forward section where Carlos sat. "Do we give it to them?"

Nelson took a moment. Hollister raised a good point; what were their rules of engagement? If they spent the next three days hacking, should they turn over everything they found? Was there a reason to hold back key items? Did they really think there would be a reprieve from death if they did a good job for Lutane? If they were going to die anyway, why use up what time they had left helping these murderers? Three days might be enough time to plan an escape or contact help. The problem was, they had to stay alive for three days to have that chance. Only by showing cooperation with Carlos were they going to live from day to day. Carlos wasn't going to wait three days for results. He was shrewd enough not to be strung along.

"Let's give them this one thing," answered Nelson. "Show them we're working together. After we see the datacenter, we can make adjustments."

Adam opened his eyes but squinted at the brightness off the clouds. He caught the tail end of the conversation. "What about the datacenter?"

"It's our next stop," answered Hollister.

Nelson leaned closer. "Fill me in. Did you find out anything last night?"

Adam took a breath and yawned. He gazed down at the closed laptop on the seat next to him. "That shit's bizarre."

"But is it gibberish?"

"Hell yes, but it's not random."

"What does that prove? Aren't all kill screens like that?" Nelson drew upon his research on video game error screens. "A game's strange behavior comes from programming errors. Different errors get generated from distinct code. Each snippet of code has its own way of making nonsense."

Adam looked to Hollister and grinned. "Check out the big brain on Nelson."

Nelson wanted an answer before they landed. "Come on, I need to know. Finding out it's not random doesn't tell us anything."

"That's right," answered Adam. "The cool thing is finding the order in the chaos; the unique way it's random."

"Enigma patterns," offered Hollister, nodding his concurrence.

"What the hell is that?" asked Nelson, startled at Hollister's input.

"I don't know. I just made it up."

"I like it." Adam looked at his left palm. "It's as good a name as any."

"What's on your hand?" asked Nelson.

Adam showed him ink scribbles. "My notes from last night."

"Where'd you get the pen?" asked Hollister.

"I bummed one from a guard; he was half asleep, bored out of his mind."

"OK, so tell us," prompted Nelson.

Adam studied his hand. "Well, I found some graphics tools on the laptop so I started playing around. I watched the glitch in slow-mo a long time. I put it on a loop. I wanted to get into the rhythm."

Hollister grimaced. "The rhythm of chaos?"

"Wait. Then I speeded it up, ten times faster. I watched the one-minute glitch, then I compared it to the two- and three-minute versions speeded up. That's when I saw it."

"It? You mean some kind of pattern?"

Adam nodded. "It has cadence and progression. It's not something you'd see in a minute or three minutes, not at regular speed."

"So what is it?" asked Hollister.

"It's wild. As far as I can tell, the screen divides into six areas of randomness. Each area has its own thing to do but, as time goes on, each area does more things that connect with the other areas next to it."

Hollister asked Nelson, "Are you buying this?"

Nelson reserved judgment; he turned back to Adam and waited.

"There's more," assured Adam. "Inside each area, the randomness gets 1/6 of the allotted time to cycle. At the end of each cycle, it resolves to a letter."

"Letter? You mean alphabet?" asked Nelson.

"Yeah. During the glitch, the six areas are using all the letters and numbers but the cycle end-state favors only one letter per area. When read left-to-right, top-to-bottom, the end-state letters from all six areas spell out SAFE MU—S, A, F, E, M, U. I'm assuming that's the way to read it since it's in English."

Hollister's brow furrowed. "You stayed up all night for this?"

Nelson butted in over Hollister's attitude to ask Adam, "What do you think it means?"

The G550 made its final approach but Adam was oblivious to the fact they were about to land. "There are six areas, each completing six cycles of randomness in the allotted time: one minute, two minutes, three minutes."

Nelson worked it out. "OK. So, six times six, thirty-six cycles—at one o'clock, two o'clock, three o'clock. Three times thirty-six, that's 108 cycles completed on F1E."

"Right, and each time it got to the last cycle, only one thing had changed. The six separate areas were communicating more with each other. By 3:03 pm, activity in the six areas was primarily on communication among them; they weren't doing so much their own thing anymore."

Hollister grunted, "You think that means something?"

"Yeah," snapped Adam. "They're learning."

"Bullshit."

Nelson gave Hollister a look to stand down on the attitude, then turned back to Adam. "Who's learning?"

The jet touched down on the runway at Guernsey. The brakes were applied and the engines whined. Adam braced himself. "If I had to guess, and I guess I do, I'd say it's an artificial neural net. You can call her ANN; the eggheads do."

Hollister checked out the window. "Yeah, that's where I was going…"

Adam talked over him. "The Greek Letter MU is used to signify the learning rate for neural networks. It's a control parameter for algorithms that control the step size when weights are iteratively adjusted."

The explanation went over Nelson's head. "So why SAFE MU?"

Adam shrugged. "It's probably arbitrary, a cooperative signal confirming when all six areas reach a state of mutual coherence. With each iteration, a higher state of coherence is achieved in the same allotted slice of time."

"But I was told the code that did this was uploaded in borrowed RAM, right in the datacenters. When it was all over, all that was left was a file it generated to delete itself."

"No way," laughed Adam. "To get these results in six minutes, you'd need some sort of tricky back-propagation I've never seen. Just to interact with that volume of data in real-time, there had to be a gazillion Threshold Logic Units firing away like mad someplace."

"Why did it need to be so beefy? I thought it only scrambled the data," noted Hollister.

"The rearrangement looked scrambled, but the pattern shows a method to the madness. I'm not sure what it was doing, I didn't have time last night to get into it, but I know damned well it was being smart about something. To me, the whole thing looks like a pilot test—under real world conditions."

Hollister was slightly more interested. "All we hear on the news is how the F1E glitch screens are meaningless."

Nelson countered, "If they're so worthless, why has the government quarantined any recording of the ones they find? If they're doing that, you know they're going after private collectors." He turned back to Adam. "So what's the bottom line?"

"F1E was used to train pieces of a neural net to talk to one another."

Nelson added, "By jacking into Wall Street's datacenters to do it."

"A good neural net has to be able to generalize, apply and adapt rules, and cope well with noise. Wall Street data would be the acid test for that."

"How many datacenters does Wall Street have?" asked Hollister.

"Several," answered Adam. "Spread out over New York and New Jersey."

"Homeland Security considers them critical infrastructure," noted Nelson. "The places are fortresses."

The jet slowed and began to taxi. No longer was Nelson certain he wanted to give up such information to Carlos. Adam might have stumbled on key items more valuable than any of them knew. They had to give Carlos something but choosing what wasn't likely before he pressed the point.

Nelson focused on the one thing that stood out. "Is there anything special in neural nets with the number six? Six random areas…six cycles?"

Adam answered, "Not that I know of. Why?"

"Back at your place, when we worked on Extasis financials, you told me you found something out of the ordinary about the number six."

Hollister asked, "Are you two keeping secrets?"

"Nelson and I have a history with the number six."

"We found something at Extasis," explained Nelson. "In their financials, they have one cost code that doesn't obey the rules."

"What rules?"

"A mathematical rule called Benford's Law." Nelson looked to Adam for confirmation. "Is that right?"

"It's the first-digit law," confirmed Adam. "It governs the probable distribution of first digits. We found a wonky cost code where the number six acts like the number 1. It appears first more than any other number."

"The code is ZYN1. It appears across all projects at Extasis, regardless of silo, but the numbers it tracks in the financials don't add up. Adam says it proves they're cooking their books." Nelson shifted back to Adam. "Six was a key number with that, now it pops up again."

"It's interesting," conceded Adam. "But I don't see a connection. We're not even sure how they're using ZYN1. Is it a cost code or a project number hidden across all projects *as* a cost code? There's no way to tell. If it's a project number, then the dollar values held by code may, in fact, be the true codes linking somewhere else. The possibilities are endless. Whoever hid the financials on this definitely knew something about cryptography."

Hollister groused, "What a mind fuck. We're surrounded by fascinating things that don't help us. I hate this computer shit: they might be able to win at chess, but they don't know when to come in from the rain."

"That's right," agreed Adam. "Easy things are hard. We're least aware of what our minds do best. I didn't know you read Minsky."

"Who's he?" Hollister unbuckled his seat belt and gave Nelson a knowing glance. The jet rolled to a stop and the engines powered down.

Nelson checked out the window and then turned to Adam and whispered, "Give Carlos something on this, but not all of it, OK?"

A moment later, Carlos and a guard came down the aisle.

"All right, all right, vacation's over." Carlos handed out especially wide sunglasses meant to blind them. "Here, when you get in the car put these on. I'll tell you when you can take them off."

Nelson and Hollister stood up, ready to go. Carlos turned to Adam.

"And you—you have something for me?" He pointed at the laptop.

Adam returned the computer to Carlos and then unbuckled his seatbelt.

Ready to be disagreeable, Carlos passed the laptop off to a guard and confronted Adam. "Is that all? You're supposed to be so fucking smart; didn't you find anything?"

Nelson could see that Adam was pissed and barely holding it together. Nelson had already seen how surly the young man could get when he got overtired. The one thing they didn't need was a confrontation right away before they got to the datacenter.

Nelson stepped between them, wanting to head on out, and confronted Carlos. "We just got here. Do you need a report right this minute?"

"Maybe I do." Carlos got in Nelson's face. "You want to make a complaint?"

Adam eased back to break the tension and spoke to Nelson, "Hey, if the man wants a report, he's the man, he can have his report." Then Adam turned to Carlos and stood eye to eye. "As a matter of fact, I *did* find something."

"I don't like to wait," sniped Carlos. "And I don't like to ask for things you know you need to give me."

"Sorry," Adam placated. "I'm sure Mr. Lutane wants an update on this right away, so you tell him this—the crap on those screens is mostly random, but not all of it." Adam paraphrased what Nelson had told him minutes before, "It's like a kill screen in a video game; the strange behavior is a product of the program that produces it. Each snippet of code has its own way of making nonsense. F1E contains hints of the Monte Carlo method."

"Monte Carlo?" Carlos tried to follow.

"Not the city, the *method*," Adam corrected; he assumed Carlos had the wrong idea. Then Adam rattled off his own embellishment, "I think the screen glitch is doing what's called *importance sampling*; it's simulating Monte Carlo paths using a probability distribution. It's trying to solve a problem by simulating an underlying process and then calculating the average result. Coupled with the Wall Street data at one, two, and three o'clock, it uses a black-box technique to calculate the delta from an analysis of sources of uncertainty. It uses bumps in the input parameters that quickly graduated down to fractions of a second. That generates a huge number of sample paths, which come in handy for filtering out noise. Of course, as you know, the advantage of using Monte Carlo methods over other techniques steadily increases as the dimensions of ambiguity grow. During F1E, I think we all agree the panic on Wall Street certainly did that."

Overwhelmed, Carlos zipped up his jacket. "What the hell does all that mean? You think this is a joke?"

"You want me to explain the explanation? I described it as plainly as I can," offered Adam.

Carlos turned away. "Good. When we get to the datacenter, you can explain it to Elijah."

Nelson fought back a grin.

Hollister whispered to Adam, "What kind of bullshit was that?"

Adam was deadpan. "Hey, I gave him a valid answer."

Perplexed, Nelson leaned in, "You mean all that was for real?"

"The whole thing."

"You said nothing about that before?"

"I didn't have time."

Hollister brushed by them on his way out. "Damn! This is going to be three days of ever-living hell. Where do I sign up?"

In deference to Hollister, Nelson offered Adam an excuse. "Never mind him. He's not good with mathematics...or people."

Adam rubbed his face awake. "That qualifies him for something?"

"Yeah..." Nelson had his fill of everyone's edginess. He answered while heading out. "He doesn't waste time with a body count."

39

0000 0010 0111

11:27 am CST, Friday December 8th

Aubrey Marks stared ahead at an endless road. Despite traveling all night, she had yet to adjust to the feel of the rental car. In the seat beside her, Katherine Stalt settled into her sitting-up sleeping position. The sound of the road and warm air gushing through the heater vents promised to make sleep easy. Regrettably, that was true no matter where one sat.

Both of them had given up on playing the radio to try to stay awake. Neither had the patience to search for something to listen to. When they had found something tolerable, intervening thoughts about what they might be rushing into had distracted them. Only a steady silence assuaged the nerves.

For nearly twelve hours they had endured the nonstop trip by switching off in shifts between driving and catching sleep. With their marathon ride past its halfway point, it was Aubrey's turn to drive.

They had made good time through the night but with the rising sun came heavier traffic. Toughing it out, they now left Tuscaloosa, Alabama. After stopping for gas and paying in cash, they headed south on I-59. The next leg of their race would take them to the Gulf of Mexico.

Katherine shut her eyes and tried to drift off but couldn't. Her second wind had kicked in near the end of her last two hour turn behind the wheel. Noontime was no time to sleep, anyway. With eyes still closed, she let her thoughts drift to concerns and the details of how they got away from D.C.

Katherine had driven the first leg of the trip out of Washington thanks to Aubrey sharing her emergency way to get out of town without leaving a trace. The method wasn't foolproof; nothing was, but it was adequate enough to keep anyone who wanted to locate them guessing for a while.

After leaving Jesup Blair Park at midnight in Katherine's car, Aubrey had Katherine drive to National Airport in D.C. They parked in long-term parking then, oddly enough, took a taxi to Dulles Airport. Aubrey directed the driver to take them to a rental car drop-off lot near Dulles. Aubrey showed the attendant on duty a special business card and they were given an undocumented car.

As Aubrey had explained, it was an arrangement between the rental car company and top executives at Chimaera. The agreement was profitable to both but, by necessity, neither side publicized it. The lot attendant, ignorant of the true nature of the deal, simply followed procedures that specified certain cars to be released when presented with certain business cards.

Anyone finding Katherine's car at National's long-term parking might think she had taken a flight from there; that was the idea. Meanwhile, there was no record of them being at Dulles or that the car they now drove ever left the storage lot. Should anyone suspect anything, by the time they managed to sort it out, Aubrey and Katherine would be long gone.

One fact nagged at Katherine. It was something she had done on the spur of the moment, hedging her bets that teaming with Aubrey was the right thing to do. Aubrey didn't know it, but Katherine had kept the disposable phone she had taken to the meeting at the College Park Airport Museum. It was the same phone that Barnett had called her on after she had tracked him.

No doubt he still had a way to track that phone. Keeping it was her way of reporting in to him even though she wouldn't be calling him or making their follow-up meeting tonight. It was also a hedge against Aubrey's presence being a snare.

Katherine knew Aubrey wouldn't approve of keeping such a device with them. But Katherine wasn't willing to cut all ties with Barnett yet. The only question was, what would she do if Barnett decided to call her directly? Would she dare answer it in front of Aubrey?

Anxious at being indecisive, Katherine gave up trying to sleep and sat up.

Aubrey noticed the movement. "Want to try the back seat?"

Katherine turned the car's heat down a notch. "No, I'm all right."

"As long as you're awake, you want to talk?"

"You're wondering about where we're going," assumed Katherine.

"You told me where. I want to know more about why." Aubrey took her eyes off the road briefly to watch her passenger. "Who's this go-between? And what are they doing in a place called *Cut and Shoot*, Texas?"

"You have a problem with the name of the town?"

"No, but I might have a problem if I drive twenty-two hours only to wind up going nowhere. What's the deal between the two of you?"

Katherine was surprised she had held off discussing this as long as she had but Aubrey was fearing for her life and needed to believe Katherine and Nelson could insulate her from the threat. The night before, all she'd told Aubrey was that their destination was a small town about forty miles north of Houston. There they'd find the go-between they needed to get in touch with Nelson Geiss. When they were driving near Harrisonburg, Virginia, during the night, Katherine had mentioned the town was called Cut and Shoot.

"There's no deal," admitted Katherine. "But he's our best way to Nelson."

"No deal? How does that work? Who is this guy?"

"You know him," asserted Katherine. "Lots of people do."

"Why would I know him?"

Katherine looked out the side window. "He has a popular radio show; plus, his webpage has a large following."

"And he's *our* go-between. I can't imagine who that would be."

Mentioning a name without an explanation would get a rise out of Aubrey but it couldn't be helped. "It's Max Engle."

Aubrey balked. "The talk radio guy? Conspiracy nut? You're kidding…" Aubrey knew Max Engle as a showman, exploiter of fringe groups and panderer to bottom feeders. He hosted a catch-all radio talk show which reportedly originated at midnight from the nameless boondocks of Texas.

On any given night, the irrepressible Max Engle would explore topics such as the Bilderberg Group's complicity with the Trilateral Commission, the latest plans of Monsanto Corporation to rule the world's food supply, or the real reasons behind cattle mutilations near UFO sightings.

Katherine explained, "Nelson has always made it known that following conspiracy theories is a hobby of his so it's perfect cover for him to be part of sites like this. Max's webpage is number one in popularity with the conspiracy crowd, so it's a great go-between. If Nelson posts something there, it should be no surprise to anyone."

"A webpage as go-between? What are you talking about?"

"It's something Nelson came up with in Afghanistan."

"Why there?"

"You know how it is on security patrols: 99% boredom and 1% carnage. Nelson and I had lots of downtime to talk about things; conspiracy theories were an endless source of entertainment."

"OK but talking about Max Engle isn't the same as enlisting his help."

"No, but we agreed, once we got out of there, if one of us ever needed help, we'd watch for word on Max's website."

"How does that work?" asked Aubrey.

"Simple. Max hosts a forum where listeners of his program discuss conspiracies and post comments. The forum is divided by topic. Once a day, Nelson and I check the forum for messages. If we find any, we know the other one needs help but can't risk the exposure of making direct contact."

"Which forum topic are you supposed to use?"

"The Club of Rome or The Committee of 300. Either one."

"And how do you signal it's you?"

Katherine wasn't prepared to tell all. "We have appropriate names…"

"I must be missing something," concluded Aubrey. "If that's your idea of a go-between, then why drive halfway across the country? You could post on that website from anywhere."

"True, but passing messages isn't enough anymore, not with all that's going on." Katherine fell silent. She had had all night to think things over and redouble her determination. Hours spent in the dark, behind the wheel while Aubrey slept, had given Katherine time to go even deeper into her fears.

After Barnett had managed to track her disposable phone so quickly, it was the last straw. Her sense of comfort about what was going on had vanished. Right then and there she had resolved she'd find a way to provide cover for herself. Her original plan was to take this drive after her second meeting with Barnett, after telling him about passing messages to Nelson via Max's webpage, but Aubrey's appearance had pressed the issue.

"What do you have in mind?" asked Aubrey.

It was time to come clean with the full reason for their drive. Katherine was blunt, "I don't know anyone's real agenda; so far, that includes Nelson. Barnett's motives are unknown. I don't know who is behind Richard and Owen or what they're trying to do. I'm not even sure why you're here."

"I told you why."

"Do *you* have confidence in what people say? The fact is, I'm in the middle of something unlike anything I've ever been a part of before. I'm out on a limb. The only thing clear is that that solid ground is falling farther away. I'm not on a mission. How can you call this an assignment? I've been pushed into the middle of something and I don't know why."

"You were hired to follow people; your role is minimal."

"No," Katherine interrupted. "Maybe that's how it started, but I've seen things. Barnett showed them to me."

"Showed you what?" Aubrey tensed with curiosity.

"I'm not going into it now. The point is, everyone has a story. Now I want an alibi. I want some kind of insurance in case this whole thing blows up."

"What kind of alibi can you get with Max Engle?"

"The same kind the people behind all of this would manufacture—disinformation, something not to be believed, something for the media to ridicule and most people to forget. It's the only way left to hide in plain sight and possibly wiggle out of this unscathed."

Aubrey was lost. "What are you talking about?"

Katherine unloaded, "I'm talking about getting Max Engle involved, telling him what's going on, letting him run with the whole thing on his show."

"That's crazy! You can't go public with this?"

"Why not? Who will believe me?"

"You don't know the repercussions."

"People still believe a plane hit the Pentagon on 9/11, don't they?"

"Don't you?" asked Aubrey.

"Exactly my point. The official story never gets debunked. Anything else is ridiculed or diffused with wilder stories that get planted alongside the truth. Nelson told me how it works. Why shouldn't I play that game too?"

"You can't expect that to help," insisted Aubrey.

"Whatever happens, whatever they come after me with, I can say it was all a conspiracy theory. I was duped into falling for it but now I see the light. The worst I can be found guilty of is being gullible."

"If you do this, there's no way to predict what will happen."

"It's better than staying under the radar, an easy target to eliminate."

"They can get to anyone at anytime, doing this won't matter."

"Then why are you here—if they can get to anyone at any time?"

"I have no choice," admitted Aubrey.

"Neither do I. If I publicly recant everything as a joke, a half-baked conspiracy, that should make me an asset instead of a liability. With any luck, the people behind F1E might even put me on their PR tour."

"It's just as likely going public will put people in danger."

"They're already in danger. What do they say, light is a disinfectant?"

"What about Nelson?" asked Aubrey. "How does this help him? You don't even know his situation. Shouldn't you ask him first?"

"I won't include his part, not at first," reasoned Katherine. "There's enough to talk about without mentioning him. Besides, this may be my only way to reach him, to let him know what's going on."

"And what about the go-between?"

"The webpage?"

"Yeah. You still intend on calling Nelson for help, don't you?"

"Of course. There's strength in numbers."

"Really? Even if all you're doing is looking out for number one?"

Katherine slumped into her sitting-up sleeping position. "Everyone has their own way to CYA—some, like you, join up with others, diffusing the responsibility. Neither of us have to apologize. We're in a business without a moral high ground."

Aubrey stared at the road ahead. "God help us all."

Katherine closed her eyes. "Let's hope, some more than others."

40

0000 0010 1000

11:41 am GMT, Friday December 8th

It was a quick drive from Guernsey Airport. Carlos let them take off their blinding sunglasses after being guided inside the datacenter. Despite being prodded on by Carlos' guards, Nelson, Adam, and Hollister took a moment to discover the scope of the place as one passageway led to the next.

The datacenter was a monument to high-tech function and redundancies. Every inch of space maximized equipment and efficiency. With raised floors, intersecting cable trays, and endless racks of servers and routing gear protected by halon systems, the floor plan mimicked a scaled-up integrated circuit board.

There would be no tour. Instead, they were hustled down a flight of stairs to a windowless room. The room wasn't large and the computer equipment, sleeping cots, and supplies stacked to one side made it appear even smaller.

Carlos pointed to cameras at the corners of the ceiling. "We can see and hear everything you do in here." He turned their attention to one side of the room. "There's food and water and a bathroom over there. This is your home for the next three days. More importantly, this is your work area."

Nelson stepped to the tables holding the computer gear. "How does this work? You want us to hack. So, we go at it anyway we want?"

"The computers have already been set up to mask their location. Anything else you want to make them more secure is fine with me but don't be foolish. We have key loggers and other ways of knowing everything you do. There will be no second chances. Whoever tries to call for help or give this position away will be executed. Anyone who tries to leave this room will die; the guards outside have orders to ask no questions."

Adam approached the computers; he couldn't help but be interested. "What else do you have on these things besides key loggers?"

Carlos smiled. "Maybe then you could plan a way around it?"

"Just curious," Adam backed down.

Carlos motioned to the computers. "These systems are mirrored by identical systems elsewhere. The mirror systems stand between you and the outside world. Everything you do here is on a fifteen-second delay. So you see, there's no point in any one of you sacrificing himself by typing something stupid. Try it and it will never leave this room."

"What about making internet calls? I take it we're not getting our phones."

"No calls," ordered Carlos. "But you can text message and chat."

"Am I allowed to contact other members of my group?"

"As long as pertinent information flow is one way, towards you." He turned to go. "This room is sealed except for what I allow in and out. The floors and walls have EMSEC measures installed to prevent eavesdropping from the outside. Your time is limited; don't waste it being stupid. If you find something valuable, you will be granted more time. It's as simple as that."

"How much time can we earn?" asked Hollister.

Carlos shrugged. "Depends on how valuable it is."

"Where you do want us to start?" asked Adam.

Carlos motioned to the guards that it was time to leave. "Start where you left off—and check the leads my group has turned up—they're on the computers. You have three days. I expect daily progress or one of you will be gone."

"How do we contact you?" asked Nelson.

"Call out my name," smiled Carlos. "Someone will hear you."

Carlos left and the room's one door closed and locked behind him.

Nelson stood with little recourse. "OK, let's check things out."

Adam sat down at a computer. Hollister rummaged through their food and water supplies. For what it was worth, Nelson inspected the bathroom. Besides the obvious, he found the bathroom's utility negligible.

"Hey, Nelson, look at this…" Adam tapped a computer monitor.

Nelson pulled up a chair. "Are you into their leads?"

"If you trust any of this, I guess so…"

Hollister joined them. "Why would they feed us phony leads? Wouldn't that defeat their purpose?"

Nelson gave Adam a glance, acknowledging his suspicions. "It would, if we could be sure anything they told us aligned with their real purpose." Nelson glanced up at a camera in one of the corners.

Adam scrolled down the page. "This document claims someone is sitting on a new kind of supercomputer. They call the thing Z."

"Z—as in the last word in computing?" remarked Hollister.

"More like Z as in zettaflops," countered Adam.

"Meaning what?"

"FLOPS are floating-point operations per second—it's a measure of how fast the thing can think."

"Or how much…"

"Same thing. Zetta is a number; it represents a sextillion—a 10 with 21 zeroes after it."

"That's not possible, is it?" asked Nelson.

"What's possible is philosophical. I'm more interested if it's probable."

"What would that take?"

Adam sat back. "A whole hell of a lot of what we've never had before. The fastest computers are in the 100 petaflop range, the Cray XC30, China's Tianhe-2. A petaflop is a quadrillion calculations per second. A quadrillion is a thousand trillion, the number 10 followed by 15 zeroes."

Hollister pulled up a chair. "Good old Z would blow that away."

"Along with everything else."

Nelson leaned in. "You thinking what I'm thinking?"

Adam gave it a moment's thought but his mind shot in several directions.

"Cost codes," explained Nelson. "Z as in ZYN1."

Adam thought back to their Extasis research. ZYN1 was the cost code that disobeyed Bedford's Law. "It's a stretch, but maybe."

Nelson eyed the monitor. "What other kind of leads do they have?"

Adam returned to the keyboard. "They've got this email. Not much to it, it's unsigned, the header's garbled, but one word stands out. It's all in caps."

Adam opened the document containing the email. Nelson stared at it a while before turning to Hollister. "That makes no sense."

Hollister craned his neck to see the word.

HUSIGINT

Hollister shook his head. "I've heard of HUMINT and SIGINT…"

"What are you talking about?" asked Adam.

Nelson explained. "Abbreviations. HUMINT stands for *Human Intelligence*, SIGINT for *Signal Intelligence*." Nelson pointed at the email. "What *Human Signal Intelligence* means, I don't know."

"Somebody's confused," concluded Hollister.

"What else have you got?" asked Nelson.

Adam hurried to the next item. "You'll like this…"

Nelson was unconvinced. "*Like* is a strong word around here."

"This'll change your mind." Adam shifted between open windows. "It's about our old friend, Liam Bargeau."

"You mean we might have been onto something all along?"

"Check this out." Adam summarized as he scrolled the document. "It seems Carlos had someone tail Bargeau when he was in Davos, Switzerland, attending The World Economic Forum…"

Nelson added, "Attending with the Chief Operating Officer of Extasis, Christina Parish."

"No doubt." Adam pointed to a photo enlargement on the document. "Here's what they found in the fireplace of his suite."

"They had somebody comb through the ashes?"

"Looks like it," concluded Adam.

Nelson read the letters from the scorched fragment of paper. "*UKQ…*"

"Yeah," confirmed Adam. "UKQ. Mean anything to you?"

Nelson shook his head.

Hollister guessed, "United Kingdom…something?"

"There's not enough to go on." Nelson eased back.

Adam was not so sure. "Maybe, but why would he need to burn documents in his fireplace. That's strange, don't you think?"

"It's interesting, but we need more."

Adam sat back. "So where do you want to start?"

"Are there more leads?"

Adam yawned and rubbed the sleepiness from his eyes. "There's a whole directory of crap; I just started going through it."

Nelson turned. "Hollister, why don't you sort through this? Adam needs to concentrate on hacking."

"What are you going to do?" asked Adam.

Nelson accessed the next computer. "I'll try to set up a chat with Dystrom."

"Where's he?"

"He might still be in London, I don't know. It doesn't matter. The main thing is getting more resources to bear on the problem."

"Let me in there." Hollister took Adam's seat at the computer with leads.

Adam switched to a third computer. There he could check on hacking defenses set up to hide the fact that a major datacenter was right above them.

As morning became afternoon, Nelson made text messages with Dystrom.

Nelson typed, "Do you still have a contact within GCHQ?"

Adam, taking a break, looked over Nelson's shoulder. "What's GCHQ?"

"The British version of the NSA," answered Nelson.

"Never heard of it."

"Most things in my business you haven't heard of." Nelson waited until Dystrom's text message answered back, *"Yes—with limits."*

Nelson mumbled, "There's always limits." He typed back, *"I need to/from phone calls by Liam Bargeau in Davos or Bailiwick of Jersey. Within limits?"*

Adam asked, "What do you expect to get, metadata or transcripts?"

"At this point, I'd take either."

"Let's hope it's transcripts."

Dystrom's answer came back. *"Might be possible."*

"All right," said Nelson. "Just one more thing." He typed away at another text message, *"Hope you can connect the dots. Here's the inter-agency authorization code: G566-2566-3566-5566-6566-8566-9565-CG."*

Moments after sending the message, a voice was heard through a speaker in the room. "Your last message was not sent. Explain those last numbers."

Nelson spoke to the voice, "The message explains it. It's the authorization code. If you expect me to do this, don't tie my hands."

The voice hesitated. "Can you prove the number is what you say it is?"

Nelson stood and flailed his arms at one of the cameras. "How am I supposed to do that? Do you want Bargeau's phone calls or not?"

Another minute went by before the answer came. "OK. Send it again."

41

0000 0010 1001

11:18 pm CST, Friday December 8th

Katherine and Aubrey endured the drive north out of Houston in silence. After a full day of driving along Interstates, an exit ramp finally emptied them onto a quiet frontage road in a sleepy little town.

"How much farther?" asked Aubrey.

Katherine turned the wheel onto Texas State Route 105 east out of Conroe.

"A couple more miles."

Aubrey switched the dashboard GPS from map to satellite display. "From it way it looks, Cut and Shoot is not much more than a post office."

"The turnoff for Max Engle's place is after the post office but before Austin Elementary School."

Aubrey explored the neighborhood from orbit. "That school's in the middle of nowhere."

"Do you see Max's place?"

"Yeah. It's set back from the road. Looks like he's cleared out a few acres among the trees. There's a main house and one outbuilding behind a separate fence. The outbuilding looks half the size of the house."

"That must be where he does the radio show," added Katherine.

"You said you haven't talked to him before. Are you sure he'll see us?"

"No," admitted Katherine.

"So how do you know he's going to go for this?"

Katherine stared at the road, her answer fading into the darkness beyond the headlights. "How do we know anything?"

After a few miles of watching and waiting, the GPS navigation line on the center console jutted right. Katherine pulled the car onto the dirt shoulder and slowed to a stop. In front of them, a lone mailbox perched on a weathered 2x4 driven into the ground. To their right, a ranch-style fence ran parallel to the road; its gate was shut closed across the driveway entrance.

Aubrey searched the woods beyond the gate. "I don't see a welcome sign."

Katherine had come too far to have doubts. She accelerated the car and turned down the dirt driveway. Their headlights flashed on the closed gate. Preempting further discussion, she got out of the car and walked up to the wide planks blocking their path.

Standing in the beams of the car's headlights, she made an easy target. Being so visible, she also showed anyone watching that she wasn't afraid for her identity to be known. If Max was watching, which she suspected, he could see his visitor wasn't trying to sneak in.

Katherine stepped to the securing latch holding the gate in place. She inspected the anchor post and noticed an electrical junction box on the inside. The gate was rigged with sensors; she expected it. A man like Max couldn't be too careful. Opening his gate would do more than ring his doorbell.

According to the sat-map, his place was situated a good two thousand yards down the driveway beyond a buffer zone of trees and scrub brush. Depending on how paranoid he might be, it was anyone's guess what other security measures he had in place between the street and his front door.

Katherine swung the gate wide and returned to the car. She asked Aubrey, "How long has it been since you've done field work—instead of managing it?"

"It's been a while."

Katherine put the car in gear. "You know what they say…"

Aubrey unclipped her seatbelt. "Expect anything."

The car rolled forward. The dirt path was barely wide enough to make passage through the wooded zone. Halfway down the twisting path, a pair of headlights switched on behind them. As soon as the twin lights pierced the darkness, the following driver toggled the beams up into highway brights.

Katherine checked the rearview mirror. "He sure came out of nowhere."

Aubrey checked her side mirror. "An escort is supposed to lead the way."

"I guess they don't want us leaving until they find out who we are."

"So much for a hasty retreat."

Not long after, they entered a large clearing. A fallow farm field stretched to the tree line on their left. A ranch house and garage sprawled with several custom additions on their right. Directly ahead, behind another fence, the porch of the outbuilding was lit.

Katherine slowed the car to a stop as three large dogs surrounded them and barked disapproval of the late-night intrusion. She watched in the mirror as, behind them, the doors on a king cab pickup truck opened up. Two men got out and the driver approached. The truck's passenger took up position behind an open door of the truck with a semi-automatic rifle pointed at the car.

Katherine looked out the driver-side window. The man outside gave a loud whistle to settle down the dogs. Knocking on the window, he shouted the order, "Out of the car."

Opening her door, Katherine confronted a stocky man with a Sig Sauer pistol gripped at his side. Beneath a black baseball cap, he peered past Katherine at Aubrey still seated inside.

"Everybody out." His free hand pointed, then waved at Aubrey.

As Aubrey complied, the man dipped down to inspect the rear seat before stepping closer to Katherine. "It's a little late for Girl Scout Cookies."

Katherine glanced at the man with the semi-automatic rifle. "It's too dark for target practice."

The man wasn't humored. "I'll cut you some slack and assume you got lost. Why else would you be opening other people's gates?"

"I had no choice," countered Katherine. "I couldn't find the doorbell."

"Who do you think you're looking for?"

"Max Engle."

"If he had business with you, I would know."

"If you knew everything, you wouldn't have to ask me these questions."

A shout came from behind. "Who are they?"

The stocky man called back to his partner with the rifle. "A couple of wise-ass bitches on their way back out."

Aubrey stepped around the front of the car and joined them. "You might want to double check. That's easier than explaining why you sent us away."

"I don't waste my time." The man signaled to his partner. "Check the car. Get their IDs." The partner lowered the rifle and set to work. After rummaging through the rental car's backseat, he found their IDs in the front seat and glove compartment and took pictures of them with his cell phone.

Katherine was blunt. "If you send us away, the secrets we have die with us." Her seriousness registered with the man but he wasn't convinced.

"Sounds dramatic," he scoffed. "Where'd you get that line? CSI, Miami?"

Katherine grew impatient. "I'm guessing you're not stupid, so I assume you're just rude. I understand; we woke you up. Sorry about that."

"Hey, if this was important, we'd already know about it."

"That's pretty arrogant, coming from someone who should respect the fact that many things are kept from all of us."

"Who are you to know?"

"That information is for Mr. Engle."

The stocky man asked his partner, "Do we know them?"

The partner checked the IDs on his phone and reported back, "Aubrey Marks and Katherine Stalt. Virginia and Maryland driver's licenses."

The man shook his head and feigned a leer. "I thought for a minute maybe we met at the junior prom but you're way out of your neighborhood."

Aubrey bristled at his attitude. "You trying to be clever is a waste of time. I thought you didn't waste time."

Katherine talked over Aubrey's provocation, "I have sensitive information others are willing to kill for. Exposing them may be the only way left to stop whatever they're planning. I'll tell no one but Max Engle."

The man chuckled. "You think that bullshit works around here?"

Aubrey presented a united front. "We couldn't give advance notice. People are looking for us, people with global reach. I'm sure you wouldn't want a trail of breadcrumbs leading to your door. Who are *you*, anyway?"

"I'm the last person you'll see on this property. And if you don't cooperate, I'll be the last person you'll ever see. Trespassing is a serious crime—especially when you come packing."

The stocky man lunged forward and twisted Katherine around, slamming her body face-first against the car. With knee pressed between her legs to prevent her from moving, he groped up her side until he found the Glock 36 and stripped it from its shoulder holster underneath her jacket.

"What's this for?" he asked, releasing her.

She turned around and recovered. "What the fuck do you think it's for?" She'd expected to surrender the weapon to get in to see Max but had hoped to simply be asked for it. She straightened her clothes and glared back at the man.

The man stuffed her gun in his pants. "*Now* who's being rude?"

Before Katherine could answer, the man held an index finger up to his ear. In the dark, his earbud communicator had gone unnoticed. He listened for a moment and then looked dismayed. He waved his pistol at Aubrey and gave his partner an order. "Check her for weapons. We're taking them up."

Surprised, the partner balked. "He wants to see them?"

Perturbed, the stocky man led Katherine back to the king cab by grabbing her by the arm. "Just do as I say."

Directed to the backseat with the gun-wielding partner guarding them, Katherine and Aubrey were driven across the clearing to the gate of the outbuilding. The stocky man led the way onto the porch where he punched in numbers unlocking an odd front door security system. The partner stayed in the foyer as the stocky man led them back to a set of interlocking rooms that doubled as a radio recording studio and elaborate man cave.

With a raised arm, the stocky man ordered them to halt. Beyond a nearby pane of glass that took up the top half of a divider wall, they watched as a thin, middle-aged man nursed the last puffs from a cigarette and occupied himself with computers and broadcast equipment.

The stocky man rapped three times on the glass to get the man's attention. The reaction was delayed, but when the man behind the glass finally did move, his motion came in fits and starts, like a small animal foraging then freezing to watch for predator and prey. He attended to some final work then stabbed his cigarette dead and joined them in the anteroom.

Katherine had only heard Nelson Geiss talk about Max Engle; she had never seen a picture of him. He wasn't one that enjoyed having his picture taken. Photos that did circulate were at least twenty years old and rumored to be either faked or woefully unlike his present day appearance. It was rumored that he purposely leaked bogus pictures of himself in order to confound any pursuers or deranged fans. If this was him, to be allowed to see him close up had to be an honor that belied his level of interest in them.

"Visitors in the night," he began, quixotically. "How exotically trite. Do either one of you believe in fate?"

Katherine started to answer but he interrupted her.

"Doesn't matter. What we believe makes a prison of our mind. The universe doesn't care either way, now does it?" He waved them forward. "Come on, it's lucky you intruded on a rare night when most of the midnight show is prerecorded. On any other night, I would have been too busy and you would have been treated to a very impolite exit from the property."

Absent an introduction, Katherine held her ground. "We've come to see Max Engle."

"And you were brought to me." The man's pasty skin and wispy hair were no match for the quickness of his smile and the mesmerizing penetration of his gaze. "The question is: am I Maximilien Engle?"

The man gave a nod at the stocky man standing guard behind them. "He's not saying and I won't tell. You are free to presume all you like. Presuming and assuming is what the masses of people do so well. With the barest of outlines, they can be made to see any picture. It's better than CGI." He turned and led the way to a sitting area in back of the radio production area.

Katherine and Aubrey followed him and settled into plush seats. It seemed an infantile evasion, given the circumstances, but not acknowledging who he was somehow had to figure into his logic or showbiz persona. Perhaps never going on record identifying himself ensured that he'd never be secretly recorded as having said so.

In his line of work, such levels of paranoia were as much stagecraft as they were psychic necessity. Just how much he believed his own act was hard to tell. Despite him skirting the issue of identity, Katherine was willing to take for granted that the man sitting across from her was the man she had come to see. Such an assumption betrayed Katherine's own tradecraft but couldn't be helped since they were on his playing field now.

He stared across the dim space at Aubrey as if a rare bird had flown in through his dungeon's window. "Of all the improbable events; Aubrey Marks, snared in the woods at midnight. I was ignoring your little disturbance until I heard the name. It's not every day the CEO of Chimaera comes calling." He ignored her blank expression. "Yes, your reputation precedes you. You're either in some grave trouble, which I doubt, or you want to pretend you are so you can use my show to plant some ridiculous story among my audience and hope they run with it. I can tell you now: that's not going to happen."

Aubrey didn't blink. "You already doubt the truth—but assume what's going on. How quickly you become everything you say you despise."

"So you are in grave trouble." The inference was not a surprise. "Are we talking about you personally or your organization?"

"Me personally." Aubrey hadn't planned on being the focus of attention. This was Katherine's means to a go-between; it was her cover. Aubrey was not convinced divulging her story to this sideshow barker would be wise.

"And why would that be?" asked the man.

Aubrey glanced at Katherine. "My friend here is closer to the details."

"Your friend?" He was obviously suspicious of the handoff. "Are you also an employee of Chimaera's Board of Governors?"

"No," answered Katherine. "But we're in the same line of work."

"Private intelligence—yes, mercenaries without a soul or a savior. Too bad, since those who have lost their souls need to be saved the most."

Aubrey tired of his erudite indulgences. "There's a huge difference between losing a soul and never having one, so there's no need to go there."

Katherine fed into his instincts. "Our craft was created by a government that wanted a way around regulation, oversight, and budgetary constraints on clandestine services. Of course, we are also contracted by corporations and individuals who see competitive advantage as a matter of intelligence."

"Or a paramilitary objective. Convenient for the power brokers." He glared at her. "How does it feel to be a tool of your oppressor?"

"You tell me. You have to know your program is used by them on occasion but you can't be sure when or how, can you? But not knowing doesn't stop you from broadcasting, does it? Why is that?"

"It's the same with freedom of speech. To ensure everyone's rights, you have to let the absurd be said."

"Even if what they interject poisons the well for everyone else? It's hard to recognize a truth surrounded by so many earnest and engineered lies."

Aubrey added, "It's even harder to be taken seriously when the platform you're standing on is made into a joke. If you need to yell *fire*, it doesn't help to dress up as a clown to do it."

The man smiled. "Sounds like you two have great reasons why coming here would be the dumbest thing imaginable."

Katherine was direct. "Everything has unintended utility. You put something out there, people will use it in ways you didn't imagine."

He was more interested. "Such as?"

"Your webpage as a signaling device."

He rocked in his chair. "I'm listening."

"It's hardly high-tech. It's merely coded posts to your listener forum."

He added his own explanation. "You post and anywhere in the world it can be read. OK, not very original and it doesn't explain tonight's intrusion."

"I want to post something from here."

"Why would I want the people after you suspecting me of something? If it comes from here, they might."

Katherine chuckled. "Pardon me, but with all the wild things you say night after night, my one post should be the least of your worries."

"What I worry about is my own business. I take it your post is not a conspiracy theory. Your one post might be specific in a critical way, something no one but the people after you or their enemies would know."

Aubrey challenged him. "How much are you into conspiracies? You talk a lot about them. Do you turn real ones away when they come knocking?"

"You believe you're in the middle of some conspiracy?"

Katherine confessed, "It's big enough to drive us here in desperation."

The man nervously lit a cigarette. "I have no interest in being used as a shield. *Collateral Damage* is not something I want on my tombstone."

"What have you got to fear?" asked Katherine. "Do you believe any of the conspiracies you talk about on the air?"

"Damned right I do," he answered.

"But you talk about them anyway. Aren't you afraid?"

"Talking about conspiracies and being a direct part of one are two different things. I've been left alone because I'm an acceptable level of risk—and, as you said, I'm useful at times since I allow a certain amount of disinformation through even though I suspect the official skunkworks where it's coming from. You two showing up around here could change that equation."

"Then talk about me on your show; spin it anyway you like. If you make my story out to be ridiculous, how can they fault you for that?"

"You don't mind if I make you out to look ridiculous?"

"I'd prefer it." Katherine didn't blink.

The man flicked cigarette ashes and watched them fall to the floor. "The better answer is to send you back out on the road where you came from."

"You don't believe that," countered Aubrey. "We're already here. You know the kind of technology *they* have. It's only a matter of time until they track us." Aubrey glanced at the stocky man waiting on the other side of the glass. "It was all over once your guards brought us in here."

Katherine added, "If you send us away, we might be gone, but you'll still have questions to answer. Saying you don't know won't cut it."

The man paused. He had imagined so many ploys and reversals in his line of work that deciding which one was facing him was impossible. He had to know more to make a decision.

"What exactly do you want to post?"

"It'll be short, generic, meaningless to anyone but my contact."

"What's so urgent?"

"I have to warn him. He's being used, along with his whole group."

"Used how?"

Katherine needed him to identify with their cause, if only subliminally. Instead of specifics, she offered an analogy. "Let's just say he's been asked to wait in the 2nd floor break room of the School Book Depository Building until it's time to meet his contact at the movie theater."

The reference to Lee Harvey Oswald was clear. "How do you know this?"

Aubrey answered, "Chimaera agents captured audio of the plan."

The man dug deeper. "What would be the point?"

Katherine leaned forward, resting elbows on knees. "A government scientist showed me evidence; apparently, he's distressed at what they're doing with his work. Strong AES encryption has been cracked. Some unknown agency used a new kind of supercomputer to do it. Somehow, it all ties into the *Friday the 1st Event*."

The man reacted. "F1E? What's the connection?"

"We're not sure but it's in the same pipeline with a covert operation. They have a timetable. All indications point to its completion in weeks if not days."

"Completion of what?"

Katherine paused. "I've asked myself the same thing for last twenty-two hours. F1E was precise; it struck on the hour for three hours and lasted one minute longer each time—exactly six minutes. It's hard to believe something that precise was a random error. The covert op may be its greater purpose."

The man was inclined to agree. "F1E is a hot topic. There's a thousand different theories about the who, what, and why. Why should I believe yours?"

"I don't care if you believe it," answered Katherine. "All I'm asking is that you let us put our theory on the air. You'll be reporting another theory, nothing more. Spin it as you like. Even if it's true, it'll hide among all the others."

Aubrey offered a snide mumble, "*We* are Spartacus."

Sensing him waver, Katherine added, "The world's financial transactions are secured by AES encryption. More importantly, the private strategies and forecasts of insiders are secured the same way. Having the keys to AES would mean ultimate insider information. Imagine what could be done globally."

The man asked, "You suspect a government agency has this?"

"Who else has the resources for a project of this scope and still keep it secret? This is on par with the Manhattan Project to create the A-Bomb."

The man thought it through. "Of all the places to go with this news, you come here?"

"It's the only place where truth like this can hide in plain sight," offered Katherine.

In an effort to read Katherine, he tried provoking her, "You want to hide the truth?"

"The Senate Intelligence Committee has been compromised," noted Aubrey. "You know what happens when stuff like this is taken to the media."

"Right now," stressed Katherine. "I'm not trying to convince anybody. I'm trying to *warn* somebody. Finding a way to communicate and link up together may be the only chance we have to get to the bottom of this. If you don't want to tell our story, fine but at least let me post to the forum."

The man checked a clock on the wall. "I have to check the show." He hesitated then waved Katherine forward as he stood up. "Come with me."

Katherine and Aubrey were led into the radio production room. The man offered them seats before a computer while he worked on the radio show gear. While handling his tasks, he spoke to Katherine without looking her way.

"Use the open browser. Bring up the forum. Tell me when you're ready."

Katherine navigated to the Max Engle conspiracy website and through the subpages to The Committee of 300 forum. "All set."

The man squinted through cigarette smoke and rolled in his chair to her side. "The Committee of 300? Why not. All right, let me at the keyboard. You tell me what you want to say. I'll type it in."

He was going to screen the content of her message. She didn't mind. It didn't matter who typed it as long as it went out. But there was one issue.

"I have to log into my account."

The man relinquished the keyboard. "Go ahead."

He looked away as she typed her username—*deeRooz*.

Quickly, she entered her password and offered the keyboard back to him. "Type this message," she announced, glancing at Aubrey.

"*300 minus 1-a-day. In less than one year, no Rhodes scholars left at The Round Table. I would annex the planets if I could.*"

The man's fingers wavered over the keyboard. "Is that it?"

"That's everything. It has to be in that order."

He had her repeat it as he typed. After she inspected it onscreen, he entered the post. He asked, "Care to tell me how that's a warning?"

She scooted her chair back. "I'd rather hear what your program is about tonight." She pointed at the screen. "Could you log me out?'

He complied. "It's playback of an interview I did last week with a man who claims he works for the US Defense Logistics Agency."

"They provide consumables to any agency connected to defense."

"That's right. We haven't been able to verify his employment but his story is compelling. He knows an awful lot; some of it we've tracked down."

"Such as?"

"He claims a splinter group within the DLA is secretly gathering large stocks of weapons, ammunition, and the latest security devices and shipping them to several sites—but only one of those sites is in the U.S."

"What's unusual about that?"

"It's odd for something so large to be passing under the radar. Also, the cities involved with the other five shipments don't align with any current theater of operation that would warrant such items."

"Where are the shipments going?" asked Aubrey.

"You name it. Europe, Africa, the Middle-East, South America, Asia."

"Hasn't he dealt with classified deployments before?"

"He has, but not with a scope like this. This spreads out everywhere, going to places where we don't have huge military bases or operational presence."

Katherine asked, "Is that all he's got?"

"There's more to it. Listen to it sometime. He thinks it's peculiar how some of the same people involved also organized the rapid deployment of arms and ammunition that went out to federal agencies in 2012."

"I remember that." Aubrey explained, "Homeland Security said it was prepping for possible counterterrorism activities."

"Bullshit," answered the man. "They bought 750 million rounds of ammo, much of it special caliber, the kind that can blow a basketball-sized hole in a human body. What kind of counterterrorism battle are they expecting?"

"It was odd," commented Katherine. "The armies of many countries would be jealous of a stockpile like that."

"It wasn't just about counterterrorism," asserted the man. "That year they used the excuse of the presidential conventions and the inauguration to stock up on surveillance drones. The DHS Secretary said it was done to '*conduct domestic surveillance for the sake of public safety*.' For chrissakes, NOAA got ammunition and shooting targets. Even the Social Security Administration got 200,000 rounds of hollow points. The whole thing is way out of proportion."

"What do you think is behind it?" asked Katherine.

The man stabbed his cigarette out in an overfull ashtray. "Some conspiracy theories say we'll never know until it's too late. To me, it looks like they worry something major might come unhinged. When and if it does, they want the firepower to stay in control."

"What about *public safety*?" asked Katherine, leading him on.

The man laughed. "You don't need a billion rounds of .50 caliber and hollow point ammo to stop a terrorist cell. Public safety means *their* safety—from the rest of us. It all comes down to a definition of terms. A terrorist is anyone who disagrees with them, foreign…or *domestic*."

Katherine was direct, "Will you tell my story on your show?"

He gave Aubrey a quick look and then stared back at Katherine. "If I do, no second thoughts; you need to be all in. That means you go on the air with me. That's the only way I'll do it. Are you up for that?"

Katherine gazed at the radio gear. "If we do it like this, prerecorded—I want the chance to edit and I need to stay anonymous."

"You want your voice masked?"

"Yes."

He rolled his chair back to the controls. "All right. Let's do this."

She was taken aback by his sudden willingness. "Right now?"

Lighting another cigarette, he exhaled smoke with his answer. "Now is the only time we have."

42

0000 0010 1010

8:08 am GMT, Saturday, December 9th

Nelson Geiss twisted his face away from his wadded-up jacket and stretched awake on the folding cot. The sleeping arrangements in their basement prison were bare bones but after a marathon night of hacking and follow-up research, all of them could have fallen asleep anywhere.

By 5 am, Nelson had been ready to give up the ghost. Adam, who'd stayed awake the night before on the plane from Curacao to analyze the glitch screens, only made it to 3 am before succumbing to exhaustion. Hollister, not a hacker and so relegated to support tasks, had run down everything he had been asked to do and drifted off an hour earlier.

Why Nelson jerked awake after only three hours of sleep must have been an unwelcomed startle reflex in reaction to his dreams. In many ways in recent days, real life and the dream world equally evoked the peculiar and horrific.

The three of them had been at it for nearly a day. In less than three hours Carlos would want an accounting of their progress. No one wanted to test Carlos on his promise to get rid of one of them if they hadn't turned up valuable new information.

The harsh fact was, so far there was precious little to report.

Nelson sat up and gazed into a corner of the ceiling where one of the security cameras monitored their every move. A gnawing restlessness drove him to stand and return to the computer workspace. There he scanned the monitor windows set up overnight. They cluttered the computer screens.

Adam had a handful of proprietary web bots trolling networks at Extasis and Chimaera and a couple new places found on Carlos' list of leads. All bots were snooping for patterns to alert on. Verbose readouts of white text on black scrolled endlessly in pop-up windows, punctuated by interested pauses where spinning cursors measured potential progress.

If the bots ever found something worthwhile, the spinning cursors would lock in place and send out an audible alarm. Overnight, there was only spinning and silence as the digital foraging continued without success.

Nelson had already reviewed everything in Carlos' directory of leads and didn't expect to hear back from Dystrom so soon on the GCHQ phone records. To start the morning, there was little left to do except follow habit and instinct.

After checking email, Nelson cycled through the top conspiracy websites, noting their headlines. Given the confluence of events since the 1st of the month, the content was predictable. He ended up at the user forum maintained by Max Engle. A quick perusal led him to the subdirectory labeled *Committee of 300* where he executed an avatar search for *deeRooz*. Out of habit, he quickly prepared to move on. Instead, one entry returned.

Any entry demanded his undivided attention.

The entry read: "*300 minus 1-a-day. In less than one year, no Rhodes scholars left at The Round Table. I would annex the planets if I could.*"

Over the years, Nelson had stopped by the forum and searched on *deeRooz* countless times without finding anything posted. Not finding something was a good thing. No message from *deeRooz* meant everything was all right. Receipt of anything else was serious and the *"annex the planets"* message signaled the most serious state of all.

Already tensed by the message, Nelson felt a presence at his shoulder and jerked to find Adam partially awake and eavesdropping.

"What? Are we going after King Arthur, now?" asked Adam.

"Hardly." Nelson wondered how the kid managed to sneak up on him but discounted it, given the shock of finding the post from *deeRooz*.

"Don't tell me. It's another kind of shit code." Adam pulled up a seat and straddled it. Making an ordeal out of rubbing his face awake, he eyed the spinning cursors of his busy bots with annoyance, then leaned in and squinted. "Who's *deeRooz*?"

Nelson was well aware they might be overheard, along with their keystrokes monitored, but it couldn't be helped; Adam needed to know what was going on. Told just enough, Nelson was confident the kid was smart enough to grasp the importance. "A friend…from the past."

Adam leaned back. "The past is catching up with you. What does it mean or can't you tell me?"

Nelson stared into the message. "It's a warning. I'm in danger."

Adam laughed. "No shit! Your friend's late to the party."

Nelson stared at Adam. "She doesn't know anything about where we are."

"She?" smirked Adam. "Now we're getting somewhere."

Nelson ignored the innuendo. "It has to be something else."

"You've got somebody else who wants to kill you?"

"Something like that."

"Oh well, for you, a daily occupational hazard, huh? No big deal."

Nelson unmuted a radio station set up on the computer to make eavesdropping harder. He turned to Adam with words hushed and rushed. "This is no fucking joke. In ten years I've never received a message this way."

Adam switched serious. "All right. So, who's annexing the planets?"

"That's not the point! It's just a quote from Cecil Rhodes…"

Still groggy with sleep, Adam stumbled over the logic. "OK, sure. Cecil. Namesake for the Rhodes Scholarship. Made a bundle of money by ripping off resources from the southern part of Africa. Got Rhodesia named after him. So what? What's he got to do with The Round Table?"

Nelson couldn't help exasperation at Adam insisting on being so literal.

"For someone who hates the 1%, you know so little about them. The Round Table today has nothing to do with King Arthur. In fact, there are many round tables—the Bilderberg Group, the Royal Institute of International Affairs, the Club of Rome, the Trilateral Commission, the Council on Foreign Relations."

Adam sneered, "Oh, I see, basically the whole fucking Illuminati."

"But there's one Round Table that's arguably superior to the rest."

Adam glanced back at the screen, taking his cue from the online forum. "The Committee of 300."

"Very good," commented Nelson, distracted.

Adam was confused. "They want you dead?"

"I wouldn't be surprised." Nelson suffered the annoyance. "Like you said, it's a shit code, nothing more."

"A code posting quotes? Where's the code?"

"Each fragment of a quote means something else."

"A code signifying what?"

"This one's a distress signal."

"With the danger coming at you."

"And others."

"It's not coming from Carlos or Lutane?" Adam quizzed.

"No." Nelson turned back to the computer.

"So now what?"

Nelson's fingers hovered over the keys. "The message has another warning: nothing is as it seems."

Adam gave a laugh. "That's restating the ground rules."

"I need to send an answer."

Adam reached for a bottle of water. "*More* shit code."

"Whatever works."

Adam noted Nelson's hesitation. "You said it's been ten years. Do you even remember what you need to send back?"

"I remember. I'm trying to decide how much is appropriate."

"What's the difference?"

"The more we post, the greater the warning. Like I said, each part of the quote means something else."

"How much did *they* post?

"All of it."

Adam glanced at the corner of the ceiling. "Considering where we're at, you better answer with everything."

Nelson wavered, aware of the camera. "Will they let it through?"

"What is it?"

"Another quote from Cecil Rhodes."

"Seems harmless. It's certainly explainable. Rhodes was a British fat cat during the time of Empire. This forum is about the Committee of 300. It fits."

"That's the idea, except you never know how they might react."

"Try it." Adam drained a plastic water bottle. "What have we got to lose?"

Nelson glanced at Adam long enough to catch the sarcasm then turned back to the keyboard. He logged into the forum using the avatar "*seeyah.*"

Adam took note. "*See yah.* That's cute."

Nelson was deadly serious as he corrected Adam. "It's a Farsi word, meaning *black.*"

"As in black ops," noted Adam. "Cool. What about *deeRooz*?"

Nelson explained as he typed. "DeeRooz is *yesterday* in the Dari version of Farsi, the kind spoken in Afghanistan."

"Why would someone pick *yesterday* as a handle?"

"It was a running joke. Everything on the Afghan mission was needed *yesterday.* It was one of my friend's famous complaints."

Adam watched the screen as the return quote was typed. "So that's where you two were friends…"

"That's where it started." As Nelson typed, the two of them fell silent and let the music from the background radio dominate.

Adam read the return quote to himself as it appeared on the screen. "To and for the establishment, promotion and development of a Secret Society, the true aim and object whereof shall be for the extension of British rule throughout the world…and, finally, the foundation of so great a Power as to render wars impossible, and promote the best interests of humanity.—1905."

Nelson clicked the post button, sat back, and waited.

"Another Cecil Rhodes quote?" asked Adam.

"From 1902," answered Nelson, then added an explanation without prompting, "The difference in dates is a measure of the days we have left, best-case scenario."

"What else does all of that tell your friend?"

Nelson sat back. "Among other things, I said, even if I wanted to answer plainly, without code, I couldn't. Things are that bad. And we've got three days to rectify it."

One full minute passed without objection from Carlos' watchdogs. It appeared that the message would be let through.

Nelson logged out from Max Engle's forum then pointed at one of the spinning cursors in a status window. "How do you know those bots aren't stuck on doing nothing?"

"I know." Adam relaxed. "Those look like ancient command window interfaces but they're not. I don't like wasting cycles on graphics. Don't worry; it's working."

Nelson surveyed the handful of small windows filled with blackness. Except for the sparse command abbreviations entered the night before, there was nothing else to see but spinning white cursors cycling clockwise at consistent speed. Nelson noted the repeated command: "*exec nomask 9x –vfa.*"

"Execute *nomask*?" asked Nelson. "What is that?"

"My own version of a searchbot director doping zombie net crawlers."

Nelson let it go over his head. "I should have known. So how do you tell one from the other?"

"Command syntax."

"Which one is working on Carlos' Euro lead?"

"The one in the middle."

Just then, Hollister raised up from his cot and walked over. "OK. Somebody is fucking rude playing the radio this early in the morning."

Nelson swiveled his chair but Adam answered, "We're working, Grumpy."

"You know Zack," interrupted Nelson. "He'd sleep if he wanted to."

Hollister pulled up a chair then abandoned it for a walk to the bathroom. "It's obvious nothing's going on here. If you need me, I'll be in conference."

Adam got up and crossed to their food stores to rummage for breakfast.

Nelson sat, his thoughts pulled back to the Cecil Rhodes quote and what it meant. He hadn't seen Katherine Stalt in person for a couple years but they had emailed once or twice in passing. To get the warning from her now was that much more ominous, especially since she had added the final section to her post. *"I would annex the planets if I could."* How telling, especially the part: *"if I could."* Adding that part let him know she was in grave danger too.

Nelson sat, submerged within his concern, and stared at the computer screens. He hardly noticed the activity. Instinctually, his sight gravitated to small changes. Soon, his gaze locked in on one spinning cursor—as it slowed. He startled alert, rolled his chair closer, and called out.

"Adam, what does it mean when a cursor really slows down?"

Adam rushed back with a half-opened container of food in his hands. He followed Nelson's line of sight to a cursor in the middle status window. Indeed, the spin of the cursor was slowing. As they watched, the cursor's movements became jerky, enticingly hesitant before continuing around.

Adam tossed the food pack onto a nearby table and rushed to take a seat. "I think we've got something," he said, excitedly.

"What's that window tracking?"

"The lead Carlos gave us on QinetiQ."

"What delimiter did you give the web bot?"

"I gave it a few things. Basically, the number six," answered Adam. He opened up another window and began typing as he talked. "Six aligns with the weirdness we saw at Extasis."

Nelson followed along. "Benford's Law…"

"Right. The law of leading digits. Number one usually appears the most; nine the least. Except at Extasis. For cost code values of ZYN1, number 6 leads the digits most of the time—30% of the time, the exact percentage the number 1 should lead." The cursor's audible alert sounded.

Nelson followed along with the speed of Adam's typing. "What are you going to do?"

"Try to pinpoint where this is coming from."

"You said QinetiQ."

"That's where I set it loose. It's a bot—it goes wherever the logic takes it, based upon what it finds along the way." Adam's brow furrowed with doubt. "You said QinetiQ is the British version of In-Q-Tel, didn't you?"

"Yeah, why?"

"It's more corporate, not governmental."

"Sure but it works on government contracts…"

"I know, I know," rushed Adam. "I mean, if we're still in QinetiQ, we shouldn't be inside some government site."

"Right."

Worried, Adam double-checked the references. "Does QinetiQ have a location southwest of London?"

"Not that I know of," shot back Nelson.

"The IPv6 I'm getting resolves outside of QinetiQ. Whatever the bot found there took it someplace else. I think it's now at a government site."

"British?"

"Of course!" snapped Adam. "Like it or not, I think we're somewhere in the Defence Science and Technology Laboratory."

"[Dstl]," Nelson confirmed. "That must be their Porton Down location."

Adam kept typing, drilling deeper. "Didn't you say they're like DARPA?"

"Yes. QinetiQ must be doing work for them, the least classified parts of some project. But how could the web bot jump across one to the other?"

"One thing leads to another. One degree of separation." Adam's excitement was palpable. "Once it found a way into QinetiQ, it rooted out a trusted source to piggyback into [Dstl]. It looks like it wasn't challenged because it came from a trusted place, knew what to ask, and used the right digital certificate."

"Wherever it wound up inside QinetiQ was good enough."

"Yeah. It drilled deep into their CMS. Using ZYN1 and the number six as a parameter paid off."

"What do you mean, CMS?"

"Their content management system. QinetiQ must use a content repository for all written material and images. Once we found our way in, the web bot found a link to shared material at Dstl. The link shouldn't exist. It's an obvious security flaw. Someone probably forgot to scrub one of the QinetiQ documents before checking it back into the repository."

Nelson's hopes were buoyed. "All we need is one oversight."

Adam scanned the field headers before him. "Yeah…here it is. Actually, it looks like the document was checked out by someone for use at [Dstl] but they never checked it back in. The [Dstl] credentials still have a shared hold on it." Adam bore down on the task at hand. "It's a lot of grunt work to impersonate credentials but in this case, we don't have to. Luckily, the QinetiQ document contained a link to a [Dstl] resource."

"How long do we have inside?" asked Nelson.

Adam worked feverishly. "A minute, at most."

"Even with credentials?"

"Eventually they'll spot the fact that the credentials originate outside the trusted internal domain."

"Didn't you say the credentials were trusted?'

Adam worked away. "Yeah, but it's like a party hat everyone knows you're only supposed to wear inside the party. If there's a knock at the door and you look through the peephole to see some guy standing outside already wearing the hat, you know something's wrong. Besides, I'm certain the servers at [Dstl], at the level we're at, are not dual-homed. My bet is an ACL rule on one of their core access routers will raise an alert soon enough."

"ACL?"

"Access Control List—the rule base for routers. I seriously doubt they normally allow this level of server access at Porton Down from QinetiQ."

"How are you going to direct things, now that we're in?" asked Nelson.

"Don't have to. The bot zeroes in on the one thing that satisfies the parameter the most. Something at the end of the line has a strong component that resolves to the number six in the mix I gave it."

Nelson checked the time. "By the time it finds it, we won't have time left for anything else."

"Most likely, not." Adam eased back, waited and watched. "We should cut the connection before the ACL rule gets tripped. Once the alarm is raised, it'll be harder to make a clean break without tracking protocols sniffing to the source. That source may lead them beyond QinetiQ, to a place closer to us."

"There's no way of knowing when that might be. It could be any time."

"It sucks. Even more reason to stay out and let the bot do the work. Two-way messaging with the bot at this point would raise a red flag. If we ever want back in using this same document, it's better not to raise an alert."

"So when do we get out?"

Adam thought a second. "As soon as the bot answers back through QinetiQ. We have to be satisfied with what it returns on first contact. We won't have time to scavenge for more."

Nelson watched the cursor crawl to a stop and the audible alert sounded again. "This is it."

Adam worked to clear back channels and secure a spot for the web bot to return its prize. As the two of them watched, an empty directory created by Adam in the QinetiQ CMS populated with a single flat file. Adam checked file properties; it was barely one kilobyte in size.

Adam hurried to shut down the bot's connection at [Dstl] and backtrack out of QinetiQ with a copy of the flat file safely mirrored to their basement computer. As he left QinetiQ, he cleared the file and temp CMS directory, as well as the CMS and Linux-OS activity logs.

Nelson edged closer. "What did we get?"

Adam opened the retrieved flat file from local storage.

The two of them stared at the file's enigmatic list:

> *U.S.—UKQ*
> *Europe—EKQ*
> *Asia—AKQ*
> *Africa—FKQ*
> *Middle-East—MKQ*
> *South America—SKQ*
> *MCDC/DD/ZYN1*
> *cc: Beef Hollow*

Nelson took a count. "Six locations…some kind of site code."

"The number six." Adam spotted it right away, "And there's UKQ."

"Just like on the fragment from Bargeau's fireplace in Davos…"

"But it's *not* the United Kingdom. The first letter represents region. That means UKQ is a *KQ in the U.S.*"

"Whatever KQ is," remarked Nelson.

Adam pointed. "And there's the cost code—ZYN1"

"This ties Extasis, Bargeau, QinetiQ, and [Dstl] all together."

"Along with Chimaera." Adam's finger slid over to point at MCDC. "What about this? Roman numerals? M is 1000. C is 100. D is 500. That doesn't make sense."

Nelson scanned his memory of acronyms. "It's not Roman numerals."

Adam hurried to add, "I don't think this is from a document. We never got into a document. I bet this is nothing but a routing slip using a lower encryption level. The bot stopped at the last thing it could make sense out of."

"Like reading the outside of an envelope of snail mail." Nelson leaned in. "One fucking important routing slip…"

Adam read Nelson's increased intensity. "What do you see?"

"Beef Hollow." Nelson let the words hang, unexplained.

"Yeah, so?" prompted Adam. "Some place called Beef Hollow got cc'd on the document. It's either a seventh location…or someone's nickname."

"Oh…it's a location, *and* a nickname."

"How do you know?" Nelson's level of certainty drew Adam's interest. "What is it?"

"Look it up. Beef Hollow is a road—in Utah." Rubbing the scruff of his beard, Nelson drew upon what he knew and the rest partially remembered. "Beef Hollow is not only a road, it's one of the nicknames for a $2 billion datacenter run by the National Security Agency."

"Holy shit!" exclaimed Adam.

"It's their new pride and joy, five times the size of the U.S. Capitol—

located on Beef Hollow Road in Bluffdale, Utah. The place is part of Camp Williams, an old National Guard training site. The electricity bill alone at the datacenter costs $40 million a year."

"OK, but how does the NSA tie into this?"

Nelson pointed at the screen. "MCDC has that slash-DD after it. Combining the cost code and the leads we got about a Z computer with the Beef Hollow reference—I think MCDC could only mean one thing."

Adam reeled with the NSA implication. "This can't get any spookier..."

"Some conspiracy theories claim the shadow government leverages a hidden research bureau, something like a DARPA, some call it DEEP DARPA. It has no official name. Those who need to know about it don't need a name; it's understood. DEEP DARPA works on all the secret shit you wouldn't believe and they'd never admit to."

Adam decoded the file fragment. "slash-DD..."

"A shiny new Z supercomputer would be a DEEP DARPA type of project. I don't think it means Department of Defense; that's *DOD*."

"But what about MCDC?"

"On the East Campus of Oak Ridge National Laboratory in Tennessee, the NSA has a five-story building with brick walls and green-tinted windows. Over 300 scientists and computer engineers work in secret on cryptanalytic applications, high-speed computing, and other classified projects. In recent years, they've added two new buildings; those are about 260,000 square feet. People who snoop around there say the buildings are unmarked but that doesn't matter. They go by many names. The one reasonably official name is the *Multi-program Computational Data Center*."

"MCDC," confirmed Adam. "Whatever they're into, it's global. Those site codes cover every place but Antarctica."

Hollister exited the bathroom and returned to his empty seat. Before sitting down, he offered his usual brand of sarcasm. "Did I miss anything?"

Nelson and Adam shared a look. Nelson preserved his deadpan stare but Adam couldn't help a fading grin as he pointed to the screen.

Hollister leaned in and took a look. Right away, he zeroed in on the site code list for KQs. "Weird," he said after a moment of reflection. "A list of six. Didn't you said the F1E glitch screens divided into six areas of randomness?"

Adam and Nelson jerked with the realization and looked at each other.

Confused, Hollister tried to interpret their surprised reaction. "You did say that, didn't you?"

Adam nodded, his mind reeling away with the implications. "Yeah..."

Nelson smiled, "We were just about to get into that."

Hollister settled back. "OK, good."

Adam looked down to the faded notes, written in ink, smeared on the palm of his hand. Another bit of logic fell into place. "Bedford's Law...leading digits...and now leading letters."

1

Nelson read Adam's intensity. "Letters?"

Adam looked up at the site code list onscreen and decoded the pattern, seemingly out of order. "South America, Asia, Africa, Europe, the Middle East, and the U.S."

Catching on, Nelson filled in the blanks. "SAFE MU! You said MU was the learning rate for neural networks. A coincidence?"

"Or someone, designing a system, trying to be clever." asked Adam. "Who loves to use acronyms—the government, the military?"

"Economists…scientists…corporations," added Nelson.

"But why this one? A control parameter for algorithms that control the step size when weights are iteratively adjusted." Adam showed Hollister a sheepish grin. "You're a genius."

Satisfied that whatever had happened was good, Hollister rocked back and accepted the accolade without fully understanding why. "It comes naturally."

"Yeah," Nelson added with some relish. "Without even thinking about it."

43

0000 0010 1011

3:09 am CST, Saturday, December 9th

Katherine slept in her clothes, a sure sign she was not confident in her surroundings. Being always at the ready was a habit ingrained by hard-duty forward deployments in Afghanistan.

The room that Max let her and Aubrey spend the night in was adequate. The spare room down the hallway from his recording studio featured twin beds, nightstands and lamps, and little else. No doubt he'd had other late night guests that preferred not to leave the studio in the dark of night.

By the time Max had finished recording his interview with Katherine, the prospect of heading back on the road was not a serious option. The two women had made no plans beyond Max's place; they would need a little time to agree what came next. Max was inclined to have them stay the night for his own reasons. Extra time spent with the two of them might yield more information, hopefully the kind that was meant to be kept off the record.

Across the room, in the other twin bed, Aubrey had no problem sleeping. The long road trip and late night in the studio had done her in.

Katherine's disposable cell phone was set to vibrate. When it went off after 3 am, she startled out of a shallow dose. She hadn't allowed herself to sleep and real relaxation was out of the question; not with everything on her mind.

Katherine used a pillow to smother the vibration noise, even as she peeked at the display. Caller ID displayed a useless *unknown* but only one person should know the number. And only one person had a burning reason to call her. She had missed the 9 pm appointment with him the night before.

No doubt he had used his technical tricks to locate her. But that wasn't the real issue. Katherine would have to explain her impulse to go public with Max. How Barnett would receive the news was anyone's guess. She suspected he might not be pleased. It was her job to sell it to him as a productive strategy rather than worried impulses.

She turned on her side, away from Aubrey, and cushioned her head by the pillow, answering the vibration with a whisper. "Hello?"

Barnett was direct, reserved, but forceful. "I saw your post."

"How long have you been tracking me?"

"Since Jesup Blair Park."

"You know who I'm with?"

"Aubrey Marks." Barnett was matter-of-fact.

"How did you find out?"

"Surveillance cameras at service stations along your route."

"She confirms your suspicions about Richard Marks."

Barnett stressed the point, "You missed our appointment."

"It couldn't be helped. Aubrey said her life was in danger. I had reason to believe I might also be targeted."

"What reason?" Barnett's concern was evident.

"My contact at State walked into traffic; he's dead. For now, I'm shielded by Patterson's diplomatic immunity but I was warned that might not hold."

"This is a terrible turn of events but we have work to do. You were supposed to pitch your idea to me."

"There wasn't time. I had to go with it. Besides, you said you wanted someone who could think for themselves."

"You're certain Nelson will read your innocuous post?"

Katherine startled at how much Barnett knew but kept the conversation moving at pace. "If he doesn't read it, then we'll know he's not alive."

"Someone's alive..." prompted Barnett.

"What do you mean?"

"Someone responded."

"To my post?"

"Not long ago. I thought you should know as soon as possible."

Katherine excitedly propped up on one elbow. "What does it say?"

"It's another gem from Cecil Rhodes, a fragment of the original."

"Tell me exactly; it's very important."

Barnett read out loud, "*To and for the establishment, promotion and development of a Secret Society, the true aim and object whereof shall be for the extension of British rule throughout the world...and, finally, the foundation of so great a Power as to render wars impossible, and promote the best interests of humanity.—1905.*"

"You're sure it says 1905?"

"I'm sure. Now what does it mean, besides the fucking New World Order implications so obviously intended by our dearly departed Cecil?"

Katherine thought it through then translated the quote into declarative facts. "Nelson's in Europe, somewhere. He's compromised. Unless something drastic happens, he has three days."

"Three days for what?" asked Barnett.

"Three days to live."

Hearing the true meaning of the traded posts was the real reason for the call but now that Barnett had what he wanted, what it amounted to was unsatisfactory. "And *this* is the man you were going to get to help us?"

Katherine shot back, "Does he sound like an insignificant decoy now?"

"The fact that he's in trouble doesn't prove he's important."

"He must be onto something."

"Pure conjecture," declared Barnett.

"If someone has him and wants him dead, why wait three days?"

"Any number of reasons—as a lure for people like you. You assume he's a captive."

"The message is clear. A captive who's been given an ultimatum."

"To do what?"

"I don't know," snapped Katherine.

"It doesn't matter," concluded Barnett. "He's out of the picture. He can't help us and there's no way *you're* going to get to him."

Katherine raised her voice. "You don't know that! There might be a way to help him from where I am."

In the other bed, Aubrey stirred, twisting alert. "What's going on?"

Katherine shifted around and held out a calming hand then muffled the phone to her chest. "It's all right. I'm on the phone."

"Who is it?" asked Aubrey, sitting up.

Katherine ignored the question and returned to the conversation. "He's still able to post online. That gives us something."

"What does it give us?" Barnett became sarcastic. "Don't tell me you and he have codes for every possible thing you might want to say to one another. If your code was adequate, he could tell you where he's being kept."

"What if he doesn't know? How many people snagged for rendition ever knew where they were being taken?"

"Is that Barnett?" asked Aubrey.

Katherine nodded. "Don't discount what Nelson can do. He may be closer to what's going on than you are. That's probably why he's in trouble."

"You have no plan," Barnett alleged. "How are you going to align with him in the next three days without bringing trouble onto us? We have our own fires to put out. And hooking up with Aubrey doesn't help. Whoever's after her will find you if they find her. You work for me. I can't have those associations."

"She still has Chimaera agents loyal to her we might be able to use. I can't continue what I was doing; Owen's call to Messare took care of that."

"Is Aubrey with you now?"

"Yes."

"Put her on the phone," demanded Barnett.

Katherine handed the phone over. Aubrey hesitated before taking it.

"Who am I talking to?" asked Aubrey.

"Who do you think you're talking to?"

"Someone who goes by the name of Barnett." Aubrey held the phone so Katherine could hear both sides of the conversation.

"I don't expect you to trust me," he admitted.

"Maybe you're not evil, simply in over your head."

"Early on, we were both in the learning stages."

"Your learning curve included the basics. I don't trust amateurs."

"Then trust this: one of those agents still loyal to you, a certain courier of surveillance recordings, he's dead. I thought you should know."

"What's his name?" Aubrey's concerned was tempered with skepticism. She needed some kind of verification.

"You don't trust my name but I should trust his? As far as I know, he went by many names. The fact is, he made certain deliveries to the Belle Haven Country Club. A sunglass case, as I remember, was one of them."

"How do you about his death?" demanded Aubrey.

"How would you know it's raining outside?"

"If you want to continue this conversation, explain yourself."

"As you know, not long ago I became curious if anyone else thought the actions of Richard Marks seemed odd. With my security clearance, I was able to search the available clues. That's when I discovered you and some of your most loyal agents were running your own investigation of him."

"You shadowed my agents," declared Aubrey.

"We were both following Marks; you might say I bumped into them. When the Chimera Board sent you to your room and ordered you to stay there for a month, I kept your communications with the agents going."

Aubrey's temper flared. "You've been directing them in my name?"

"Well, one of them; the one that's dead, unfortunately. I figured, good work should not end before its time. I knew you were being monitored; you couldn't contact him. I simply kept your operation going the best I could."

"And collecting the results. For what purpose?"

"Same as before; for my own education." Barnett wavered, "At first, I thought some evidence of wrongdoing, shown to the right people, might be the catalyst for a proper investigation. Admittedly, on that point, I was naïve. I still believed that going through channels might work."

"What right people?" worried Aubrey.

"A senator on the Intelligence Oversight Committee."

Aubrey shot back in anger, "That's the *last* place to take such a recording! You should have never shared my recordings with the committee."

"I know that now," offered Barnett. "I've changed my ways."

"And a good agent lost his life!"

Barnett ignored Aubrey's rage. "As I said, unfortunate, to be sure, but I suspect others will die before this is over."

"For you it's easy to be cavalier about the murder of good people..."

"Some games require pieces to be lost if you ever expect to win. In chess, when one expert plays another expert, they both expect 80% attrition before checkmate. I assume we're all experts at this game."

"I can't be that calculating about life and death," countered Aubrey.

"Excuse me if I don't believe you, especially in your line of work. For me, as a scientist, calculation is necessary. In this case, it's terribly practical. We simply don't have time for eulogies. You should appreciate the fact that stopping the game to reflect and weep might cause others to fall."

"How did it happen?"

"His death, yesterday, is officially an accident, of course. He leaves behind a widow and two children in Falls Church, Virginia. Ring any bells?"

The added details struck home; it was enough to identify the agent for her. She held back emotion. "Go on…"

"They say he slipped in the shower at the Hyatt; collapsed his windpipe."

"Showering at the Hyatt? That doesn't make sense."

"Apparently, he was cleaning up after a rendezvous with his mistress; at least that's the story being floated. He registered under another name."

"Salacious," snapped Aubrey. "More reason for people to believe it."

"How many trusted agents do you have, as they say, out in the cold?"

Aubrey was somber. "You know I can't answer that."

"You could…but you won't," sniped Barnett. "Meanwhile, you're telling Katherine we're all one big team, isn't that right?"

"I went to see her to find out if we could help each other."

"Correction. You went to her because you're worried you're next."

"There's a reason why this is happening." Aubrey raised her voice. "We're all going to fail if we don't stay together."

"Together? Since when? We've *never* been together."

"That needs to change."

"A lot of things *should* happen, but we're not likely to trust each other enough to make them materialize, now are we? You started off this conversation by suggesting I'm not who I say I am."

"You don't seem eager to convince me," countered Aubrey.

"Why should I? I can't convince you of something you don't want to believe. As far as your utility, what do you add to the game?"

"I know Richard. I know the kind of people he's dealing with."

"All you've done is stir up the hive," declared Barnett. "I don't need your kind of help, except if you deliver to me the services of the other field agents loyal to you. It may be too late, but it's worth a try. Unless you can do that, I suggest you and Katherine part ways as soon as possible."

"I think that's up to her, don't you?"

"Be realistic. Between the two of us, what's her safer bet?"

Aubrey hesitated, her options narrowing.

Barnett added, "After the Hyatt accident yesterday, any remaining agents you have in the field will be hard to find and harder to make productive. They have good reason to believe they're next. Being out in the cold gets colder."

"They work independently. Losing one doesn't light up the others."

"Process of elimination. They're Chimaera agents; how long do you think it'll take? Even if you could guarantee me their services, it's hard to imagine any will be in a position to be effective anymore. Without them, you have no leverage. Face it: you alone are a liability. Put Katherine back on the phone."

Aubrey wouldn't argue with him. She handed the phone to Katherine.

"This is Katherine…"

Barnett was terse. "Don't tell me this was the plan you were going to pitch to me. Spare me the disappointment."

"You only know part of it."

"I'm listening."

Katherine tried to remember her lines as rehearsed but couldn't. The fact was, there was no easy way to explain or sell it. Finding a clever way to make her own CYA maneuver look like a continuation of his plan wasn't easy. "First off, I've established communication with Nelson. It's crude, to be sure, but even Morse code has saved lives."

"A throwaway point. Go on," ordered Barnett.

"I've learned his situation and once he read my post, he now knows mine. He knows I'm in trouble too and it may be related to what he's working on."

"So now what?"

"I'll post again, he'll be looking for it, but this time my post will have a link to a radio show he needs to listen to."

"Presumably, something from Max Engle."

"Yes…" Then Katherine admitted, "Something I recorded last night."

There was silence on the line as implications surfaced. Finally, Barnett spoke. "Max Engle deals in sideshow schemes and the conspiratorial fringe. Why would you talk to him?"

"You're right," began Katherine. "The codes Nelson and I set up long ago are limited. I'm can only say so much by posting on the user's forum."

Barnett hurried to add, "And you can only say so much on a radio show."

"Not this show," asserted Katherine. "Max will talk about any conspiracy theory, no matter how wild. The wilder the better."

"I don't follow," lied Barnett.

Katherine paused. "What's wilder than the truth?"

"What's wilder? Any suggestion that you'd confess all to Max Engle and have him broadcast it to the world. That's wilder. You can't do that."

"Why not? Who's going to believe me?"

"The people involved in this will believe you. They know the truth too."

"I'm not telling them anything they don't already know. For the rest of the world, it's a wild conspiracy theory; it's entertainment. Meanwhile, Nelson will know it too—and that's the point! Connected to my post, he'll realize it isn't a wild theory. It's true. He'll know what we know."

"What exactly did you tell Max Engle?" demanded Barnett.

"I told him F1E was just the beginning. I told him that secret government research had cracked hard AES encryption. But that kind of power was too tempting to be held by government bureaucrats for long. A global consortium bought its way into play and now they're about to highjack the new capability for their own purposes. They have a timetable and are desperate to keep to it."

"You know none of that for sure," challenged Barnett.

"I've seen and heard enough. What difference does it make? It's a reasonable deduction. It's a conspiracy theory. Call it what you will."

"What else?" commanded Barnett.

"I said, the fact that F1E affected Wall Street is an ominous sign of what the *people in the shadows* have in mind. Something is going to happen before the year is over, something that will consolidate their power. Once that happens, this consortium will have unlimited, global insider knowledge that reaches into everything. They'll be able to read every correspondence, every secured financial file, every record, database and account profile. Anything they want to know will be theirs. What they do with this knowledge can swing markets, currencies, and elections."

Katherine could tell Barnett was livid but he needed details and couldn't afford to lose his temper. His tone was flat but studded with extra gravitas. "What about the material you saw at the National Defense University? Did you talk about that in this interview?"

"I never said how or where I came across the information…"

"Did you go into any of it specifically?" demanded Barnett.

"I said there's a new kind of supercomputer. It uses new materials and processes never seen before."

"Such as?" roared Barnett.

Flustered at his anger, Katherine stumbled, "I don't know, basic things… something about twisted light communication and Graphene."

In his rage, Barnett was blunt. "How could you do such a stupid thing!"

"My name is not on the radio show," Katherine challenged. "There's no way to trace me so no way to align me with you."

"When is Max planning to put this on the air?"

"He scheduled it for tonight."

"That can't happen," Barnett asserted. "That *won't* happen!"

"I know this will work," Katherine insisted. "Nelson will listen to the show and find out everything we know. Somewhere in there may be the one missing piece of information he needs to free himself. As far as Max's show, the regular listeners will take it as just another conspiracy theory about F1E, nothing more. He's had much wilder things on and no one panicked."

"I don't care," snapped Barnett. "You can't get to Nelson this way."

"There's no other way in the time we have."

"No one explodes a nuke to light their garden party. That's what you're doing."

"You're wrong!"

"Don't tell me this is your elaborate scheme to get at them indirectly. You said we need a back door, a side show, a fringe way of inserting instability, something they didn't expect. But this is not the way."

"Why not? Exposure, like everything else, can be a tool."

"You think because you withheld your name they won't track this back to me? Even if Max disguises your voice, voiceprint analysis might be able to filter that shit out and have you ID'd in minutes. Once that happens, tracing you to NDU and me is a foregone conclusion. I can't believe you wouldn't know this! What are you really up to?"

"I told you!"

"You can't be that irresponsible! Nelson isn't the only reason you're doing this. What else is going on?"

"That's my question for you! You've maneuvered me deep into this without me fully knowing my role. Whatever it is, it's changing and it's not what you've been telling me. Between the two of us, you're the one hiding."

"I don't have to explain myself. I hired you to do a job. That doesn't require you to know everything about my business."

"You said it yourself; I work for you. That makes *your* business *my* business."

"Is that what this is about?" reasoned Barnett, groping for motives. "You think going on record like this is going to provide you with some kind of insurance, no matter which way this goes?"

"I have no other explanation for what I've been doing," confessed Katherine. "To the law, being gullible is no excuse."

"And if it should ever become an issue, you know what they'll say? They'll claim if you had been serious about exposing what was going on, you would have gone to the legitimate media or proper government agencies."

"And be ignored or branded a wacko like some 9/11 Truther?"

"I'm confused. Isn't that what's going to happen by talking to Max?"

"At least this way, Nelson will know different."

Barnett mixed practical logic with rich sarcasm. "Doesn't matter. The media are the arbiters of truth. Only the *real* conspiracies are exposed by them. Their world view is the correct one. You can't avoid them. If you thought you had the truth, you would have gone to them. Any other way of getting information out is specious and must be self-serving. What they don't condone will be tacitly ridiculed into oblivion by their stooges and minions."

"If the worst that happens to me is being laughed at, that's all the insurance I need. I'm not worried about the media," admitted Katherine.

"I hope you've thought it through. If I were the people behind F1E and come January 1st I was successful in whatever I was planning, the next order of business would be cleaning up any loose ends that might unravel in the future. People like them are antiseptically vigilant."

"It's like you said, if I was serious about exposing the truth, I'd take it to the media. I'll tell them it was my job to go to Max Engle as a simple case of disinformation. By making the truth ludicrous, I shielded F1E from further scrutiny. How can the powers behind F1E fault me for that?"

"Simple: they know who's on their team and who isn't. Anyone with foreknowledge of what was going on who acted on that knowledge in any way will find a spot on their cleanup list. It's the safest way to proceed. It won't matter if you claim you took the truth on a UFO to an alien reptilian base buried below Dulce, New Mexico where an army of zombies are being bred using cloned DNA from Elvis. The fact remains; you're not on their team and you had the truth at a time when you had no business knowing it."

Katherine took a moment to let it sink in. "I can see only one benefit in doing it my way." Barnett waited until she added, "I know exactly, good and bad, what might happen if I go my way. Going your way tells me nothing."

"What do you need to know?" demanded Barnett. "In your line of work, do you always know everything about the people paying for your services?"

Katherine completed her line of thought. "I don't know who or what you represent. I know nothing about your agenda. But I do know I've been to Belle Haven. I can be placed at that post office at a certain day and time. I've signed into NDU and looked at secret documents. I've operated a mil-spec GPS tracker within a mile of IARPA headquarters. I've reviewed privileged State Department security footage under false pretenses. I've let myself fall too deep into this. Any deeper, and I'm afraid there's no safe way back."

Barnett sighed. His tone calmed but turned cold. "There's no point in discussing this further," he concluded. "You always said I was out of my depth delving into this spy thing. I guess you're right. I have no experience with your line of work. No wonder I hired someone not up to the task."

The slam only hardened Katherine's resolve. "I don't envy you," she shot back. "As far as I can see, you don't have a clue what you're after. No wonder you don't know how to lead an operation."

"You know my wishes," Barnett concluded. "The interview must not air."

Katherine considered the risk of exposing Barnett and caved to it. "I'll tell Max not to air it. I can't guarantee he'll listen to me. Now that he has it recorded, he can do what he wants. I signed no contract with him."

"Impress on him it would be unwise," warned Barnett.

"I think he's used to threats but I'll tell him, for what it's worth."

"I need to go," Barnett announced, his tone conciliatory. "Whether or not you want to work together going forward is up to you. Maybe Aubrey's right; we stand a better chance sharing information than going our separate ways."

Katherine met him halfway. "I have no problem sharing information."

"All right. Take care."

Barnett hung up. Katherine was left sitting in the dark on the edge of the bed. Next to her, listening all the while, sat Aubrey.

Aubrey's voice was slight. "We're on our own."

"No different than before," answered Katherine. "Only now we know it."

Aubrey watched as Katherine dropped the disposable cell phone to the floor. With one stomp of her shoe, the crunch of plastic and delicate, metal components confirmed the phone's demise.

"We'd better go," announced Katherine, standing up.

Aubrey kept her spot on the side of the bed. "Where to?"

"Anywhere but here."

"We'll have to wake Max…"

"Don't worry. He's awake," surmised Katherine. She made short work out of finding Max and telling him the bad news he'd probably listened in on. Whether it was the early hour or the fact that he was used to such reversals, he took the news about not airing the interview in stride. He explained his easy-going attitude by reminding them he had no shortage of strange tales to tell. If he didn't tell theirs, oh well. He had heard far stranger explanations for F1E.

It was after 4 am when Katherine drove the car west on SR 105 and away from Cut and Shoot, Texas. At Conroe, they headed north towards Austin.

"Why Austin?" asked Aubrey.

Katherine checked the rearview mirror and gave it some thought before settling on the truth. "I don't know if it's better heading east or west. Until we know, north will do. South will only lead us to the Gulf."

Aubrey settled back, "In Austin, we need to get another phone."

"Being practical or something else?" asked Katherine.

"Barnett gave me an idea how we might contact one of my agents."

"What idea?"

"The agent that was killed at the Hyatt," started Aubrey. "I know his widow. She has to know his death wasn't an accident. She might help us."

"She'll know how to contact the other agents?"

Aubrey stared into the darkness of the road ahead. "She might. I know her husband was suspected of sharing details of his operations with her."

"That kind of pillow talk isn't allowed…"

"No, but this time, I hope they broke the rules."

44

0000 0010 1100

10:22 am GMT, Saturday, December 9th

Finished with his explanation, Adam slumped back. His gaze focused on the surveillance camera in the corner of the ceiling. Out of weariness, his studied contemplation faded. In its place, a vacant, thousand-yard stare set in, as much catatonic as fatalistic.

Nelson sat not far away. He avoided eye contact with the camera lens, having already said his piece. Somewhere behind the prying camera, Carlos and crew listened without comment. Both Nelson and Adam had spent the last twenty minutes going over all they'd discovered after their first day and night of hacking. They hadn't found much and they knew it.

But that wasn't the real question. The important question was about to be answered. Would the little they had managed to produce prove significant enough to appease their captors? Would quality trump quantity?

A voice crackled through the surveillance speaker. "Is that all?"

Adam nodded and Nelson let the motion answer for both of them.

The voice didn't belong to Carlos. It certainly wasn't Elijah Lutane. Obviously, the job of dealing with the three of them had been left for others to complete. Carlos and Lutane were leaders, managers who made decisions. As such, they could be swayed. Talking to them would have been preferable.

But their foot soldiers knew only to obey. Grunts had their marching orders. There'd be no reasoning, no negotiating with faceless button men. They would do what was necessary with dispassionate precision. They had no latitude, even for reason.

The results of one day's hacking efforts either met the assigned quota or it didn't. Never having been told what that quota was, the three captives could only wait in silence. That silence was broken with the opening of a door.

Abruptly unlocked and swung wide, the basement's open door revealed two armed guards. They wore casual clothes, resembling tourists except for the MP5K tactical machine pistols clutched in hand.

One of the men waved the snub-nose barrel and gave Hollister a head tilt. It was his direction to get up and follow them outside. Hollister gave Nelson and Adam a stoic, parting glance, then stood and followed the men.

As quick as the door had opened, it closed and the dead bolt slammed into place. Hollister was gone with no explanation given.

In a futile act of defiance, Nelson tried opening the door. Sensing the lock firmly engaged, he turned and marched towards the corner of the room where the surveillance camera peered down on them.

"What was that about? Where did you take him?" Nelson demanded.

The faceless voice was heard once more through speakers. "Each day you disappoint us, another one will disappear."

"We were told we had *three* days!" roared Nelson.

The voice remained calm. "That's right. At the end of three days, if we don't have what we want, none of you will be left. Now get to work."

Nelson swung around and struck the wall with his fist. "Damn it!"

Adam's stare sunk to the floor. The rules were now clear. No doubt, Hollister was the first to go since his forte wasn't hacking. With that criteria, one would expect Nelson to be the next one taken away if progress wasn't made by the end of the second day. Adam would survive the longest; he would be slated for elimination on the third day if the disappointment persisted.

Nelson returned to his chair and sat down. There was no point arguing with faceless barbarians. It was far from consolation, but at least they wanted the same thing. Nelson wanted to uncover the same information they wanted.

The only problem was, common sense guaranteed, even if Adam and he gave them what they wanted, there was no way the button men were going to let them live. The only reason for Nelson and Adam to do anything they were ordered to do rested in the fleeting hope that somehow, someway, a timely black swan event would change their fate.

Adam swiveled his chair until he faced the locked door. Hollister's departure drove home the point: that door was the way out if they lived or died. The overriding perspective was utterly binary. The resolution would either be starkly triumphant as a *"Hello World"* from a student programmer's fledging output or as final as a bullet in the head.

Dwelling on either alternative made no sense.

Adam let his field of vision widen. When it did, he noticed a new object on the table by the door. It was a laptop. It had to be left there by one of the guards when they came in for Hollister. Adam went over and picked it up.

"Did they leave this?" he asked, turning back to Nelson.

The diversion from other thoughts appeared to be a welcomed relief for the older man. Nelson recollected, "They must have. It wasn't there before."

"Why didn't they say anything?" wondered Adam.

Nelson ignored the question as rhetorical. If anything, a perverse kind of logic drove these barbarians. He was in no mood to second-guess his captors' motives. Given what must be boredom of their assignment, chances were their actions reflected more pernicious pleasure than meaningful intent.

Adam brought the laptop back to his work area. With a new series of bot cursors already twirling away and the directory of leads supplied by Carlos already exhausted, having the laptop to work on was a good thing.

Adam powered it up. "Looks like the same one I had on the plane."

"The one with the glitch screen recording," confirmed Nelson.

"Yeah." Adam began navigating the directory structure.

"You already drilled into that," noted Nelson. "Is there more to find?"

"Only one way to find out." Adam glanced toward Nelson as the older man swung around to his own keyboard. "What about you?"

Nelson began to type. "I'll ping Dystrom. We need those phone records from GCHQ."

"No more Cecil Rhodes?"

Concern for Katherine Stalt flooded back into Nelson. "I checked the forum earlier. There was nothing new."

"Don't wait for her; post something. We need a break."

"I don't know about using those quotes…" Nelson shook his head. "It's too limited for this. It's only an alarm. It was never meant to be an alphabet."

Adam's anger at their situation flared. "Then post something else."

"Like what?"

Facing his own mortality, Adam felt emboldened. He glanced up at the surveillance camera. "Fuck it. Post the routing slip."

Nelson considered it. "These barbarians won't want that to get out."

"Why should they care? Go for it. It only exposes the other guy, not them. If they expect results, they can't *regulate* every fucking thing we try!"

Nelson brought up Max Engle's website. He logged in as *seeyah*. After posting the [Dstl] routing slip, an idea occurred to him. He added one line.

"Can you find out where this originated from? Maybe GG can help you."

He pressed the enter key and waited for a reaction from his captors.

None came. His hopeful mumble was tentative, "They let it through."

Adam hunched over the laptop and worked away. "Regulatory arbitrage."

45

0000 0010 1101

11:41 am CST, Saturday, December 9th

Katherine and Aubrey parked their car near the southwest corner of Speedway & 21st Street. They sized up foot traffic in the neighborhood then walked to a brick planter and bicycle rack set back from the street. Behind them sprawled the flat-gray facade of the Perry-Castañeda Library at the University of Texas at Austin.

Aubrey stood with her back to the planter. "I'll make the call from here."

Katherine turned to look at the library entrance. "You said the computers are on the second floor?"

"That's what the online campus map shows."

"All right. I'll meet you here. I shouldn't be long."

Katherine hurried away. Aubrey pulled a new, disposable cell phone out of her pocket. This would be a relatively expensive call since she intended to talk on this phone only once. She dialed the number and waited.

A woman's voice answered. "Hello?"

"Cassandra?"

"Yes?"

"It's Aubrey Marks. I need to talk to you; it's important."

Cassandra was surprised, then defensive, concerned, and halting. "Aubrey? This isn't a good time."

"I know. I'm sorry about your loss. This can't be helped. It's critical we talk."

"There's nothing to talk about."

"You don't know that."

"I know my husband is dead." Cassandra's emotions couldn't be held back. "I know he worked for you. What else do I need to know?"

"You're at home; you understand I can't tell you anything there."

"Whatever you're into, I don't want any part of it."

"All I want is follow through, so Dylan's sacrifice is not in vain."

Cassandra cried though her anger. "Dylan was reliable to a fault. He did as he was told and didn't question it. He obeyed orders. He trusted whoever was giving him those orders knew what they were doing and were honorable."

"You know as well as anyone, the official story is rarely the truth. At least, not the full truth. Knowing details makes all the difference."

"And you want me to believe *you* have the full truth?"

"No one has it. That's the problem. Dylan knew that. He accepted it. It's why he was willing to risk his life. It's the nature of the work we do."

"The work got him killed. And for what? I dare you to explain that."

Aubrey needed to end the call soon. The longer they stayed on the line, the more material they offered up to NSA pattern scanners that monitored phone traffic for intercepts to red-flag for storage or analysis.

Aubrey rushed her words. "The last time the three of us were together, I told you this was not about me. Dylan was there; he agreed."

"And why not? He only knew what you told him."

"I'm calling that same location tonight, at the same time we were there. If you want answers, take the call." Abruptly, Aubrey ended the conversation.

Noontime activity around the corner of Speedway & 21st Street appeared normal. Cars came and went and people waited at a bus stop not far away.

Aubrey lowered the flip phone and in one easy movement, broke it in half. Stepping to a trash can not for away, she snapped the phone in pieces, removed the battery, then dropped all of it into the trash.

Within minutes, Katherine exited the library and returned to the planter.

"All done?" asked Aubrey.

Katherine nodded. "I'll tell you later. So how did it go?"

Aubrey shrugged. "We'll see what happens tonight when I make the call."

Katherine gazed west. "Ready to check in or do we need anything else?"

"I'm not convinced the conference center hotel is the right move."

"They'll expect us to dodge off the beaten path. If I were them, motels, cabins, hostels, RV parks, and rooms for rent would top the search list."

Aubrey retorted, "There's off the beaten path...and there's the obvious."

"Cash transaction, different names, and we're only staying two days."

"Why two days?"

Katherine glanced at the library. "That's all the time my friend has left."

Aubrey self-reflected. "Which friend are you talking about?"

Katherine was about to answer when she noticed a man crossing the street glancing at her. She hooked Aubrey's arm in hers and walked them to their car. "Remember, when we get there, we're celebrating our anniversary."

46

0000 0010 1110

5:56 pm GMT, Saturday, December 9th

If it wasn't for the digital readout at the corner of the screen, the time of day wouldn't exist in their basement lockup. Nelson shifted his gaze from web research and glanced at the spinning cursors of web bot monitors before settling on an instant message received from Mike Dystrom.

Dystrom was still somewhere outside London pretending to chase the phantoms of CIG+XM. Nelson had him finishing up the last, pinpointed investigations into the few remaining leads given to them by Carlos. The message exchange with Dystrom had ended over an hour ago. Nelson was anxious for an update. Dystrom's last line summed it up.

"Nothing yet from GCHQ. My contact agreed to work the request but his inside man is busy offsite and may be hard to reach."

Nelson had responded: *"No news is not good news. The fuse is burning."*

With a turn of the head, he checked in on Adam. The kid was hunched over in a lotus position on a cot in the corner. Leaning against the wall and surrounded by empty water bottles and granola bar wrappers, he had done nothing all day but pour over the glitch-screen laptop and mumble to himself.

They had barely said two words in the last six hours. It was best to give the kid a block of private time to keep on task. Absurd as it was, making sense out of six minutes of video chaos might be the last option they had to bargain for another day of life.

Nelson noted the time: 6 pm. On every half hour, Nelson had checked Max Engle's forum for another post from Katherine. So far there was nothing. It was time to check again. This time when he scrolled down the entries for *The Committee of 300*, one perplexing post popped up. It was new from *deeRooz* and spoke about the [Dstl] routing slip he had left for her.

"Re: Your Post
We both know where it originated from—
From Inside Out:
The Round Table
The Committee of 300
Society of the Elect
General of the Society
Junta of Three
Circle of Initiates
Association of Helpers

The Masses of Amnesia
Muster now or the swirl of conspiracies will consume us."

For Nelson, this much made sense. Katherine had answered his earlier post by concluding that the [Dstl] routing slip originated from some secret society. To fit in with the forum's stated topic, she used the secret society rumored to have been created by Cecil Rhodes and Alfred Milner in 1891. She didn't propose it as a possibility; she stated it as an established fact.

Her inside-out listing of the stepped levels within that society was accurate except for one thing. *The Masses of Amnesia* was never part of Rhodes' and Milner's organizational hierarchy. She added that undoubtedly to represent the general public, oftentimes ignorant of the deeper lessons of history and ever unaware of the true forces at work around them.

Even so, *The Round Table* was a placeholder for any controlling force that wielded global power in secret. To *muster now* was an obvious call to join forces. That much was clear. What was confusing was the odd advertisement that someone, presumably she, had posted below that.

"Married but looking? Tempting diversions galore!
Discreet, anonymous meet-ups! Don't be shy; come inside!
Recommended by TigerLily"

Nelson hovered the cursor over the name *TigerLily* and found it was a link. He also knew it as the unflattering nickname his associates had long ago given to Geri Messare. Why such a name should appear in such an ad in a post by Katherine was bizarre but intriguing. Obviously she meant for Nelson to follow the link. When he did, as promised, it took him to the log-in page for a discreet cheater's website. The ad didn't lie.

Nelson registered as a user, selecting *seeyah* as his profile handle. Once established, finding *TigerLily* was a matter of a quick search. Her profile was scant. Her hometown was listed as *Washington D.C.* Her occupation: *myth busting*. Her main passion: *racy online chat*. Nelson was interested but skeptical. For one thing, the hometown was out of place for Geri Messare; she lived on the west coast. It fit for Katherine, but why would she be using Geri's old nickname? It had to be the association to the site—a place where people went to break their vows.

Obviously, *TigerLily* wanted to hook up. Nelson could see the advantages right away. The site provided its members with instant message capability that was guaranteed discreet and private. He doubted that but having a new way to communicate with Katherine opened up possibilities. The only problem was, at the moment, she wasn't logged in.

If one liked a profile, you could *poke* the other user with a canned message expressing interest. Nelson selected one at random and sent it.

"Feeling frisky?"

Settling back, he decided to stay logged in to see what happened.

Curious about Adam's ongoing intensity, Nelson got up, stretched, and strolled to the cot in the corner. Adam was too absorbed in thought to notice.

"You're either onto something or confused as hell. Which is it?"

Adam raised a finger to request quiet. He searched the screen then his thoughts for something out of reach. Letting it go in frustration, he looked up. "You say something?"

"Did you find something?"

"You're kidding, right?" Adam's look bordered on annoyance.

Nelson pulled up a chair. "I hope this is good."

Adam glanced at the ceiling camera in the opposite corner. "What good is it? We'll tell them and these dumb fucks won't know what they've got?"

"If they have to be quants to be impressed, we're dead."

"What do they want us to do? We've exhausted everything else."

"They don't want equations. They want names. They want plans."

"Oh, yeah, like we're going to get that in the next twelve hours."

"We don't need twelve hours. If we knew what they wanted, we could tell them in one minute."

"Sure, that's the trick, isn't it?" Adam shook his head and laughed.

"We need them to extend our time."

"I know. I don't have to search for that brainstorm."

"It has to be something they want—but for us, it has to be something they need more of. We need them to keep us around." Nelson motioned to the laptop. "Anything like that in there?"

Adam set the laptop aside. "I don't know. The more I look into it, the more I see. But what good is that going to do? You see the way they act."

"Don't concentrate on that," countered Nelson. "The guards are one thing but we don't know who's listening to us behind that camera. They're the ones who make the decisions, not the guards."

"It's like you said; it's too complicated."

Nelson turned the laptop around so he could see the screen. "But it adds up to something. What you've found might be OK. Don't stress the mechanics. They want to know how it's going to be used."

"All that's conjecture. There's no way to be sure."

"Let them make the conclusions. We need to draw them a detailed picture that leads them somewhere. Is there enough to do that?"

"We don't have time to take it all apart." Adam thought a moment and returned his gaze to the laptop screen.

"Maybe we don't have to go that far," stressed Nelson. He sat and drove home the urgency of the question, "Can you draw the picture or not?"

"F1E drew the picture." Adam was obviously impressed with what he had found. "It's all there. But man, it's freaky."

"What's freaky?"

Adam leaned his head back against the wall. "To think, I sat there on Friday with everyone else and watched this shit happen." He gave a laugh, "We didn't know what we were looking at." He dropped his gaze to the laptop screen. "Right in front of us—we looked at it and couldn't see."

"You mean the neural net thing you talked about?" asked Nelson.

"Yeah," confirmed Adam. "But it's more than that; it's the way they went about it." He shook his head with wonder and admiration. "Whoever's behind this—they're not Wall Street, and they're not some tight-ass government bureaucrat. I mean, this thing is out there."

"Out there, how? You mean complicated?"

"I mean genius...elegant...almost fractal, but engineered, like...layered in a way that each subroutine, going deeper, gets more intricate."

"All right, so it's intricate, but it has to be doing something."

Adam laughed, "Fucking-A, yeah, it's doing something..."

"Well, that's what we need."

"Maybe," hedged Adam. "But like you said, who cares what impresses a quant?"

"Explain it to me. Impress *me*," Nelson challenged fervently.

Adam stared up at Nelson and saw the old man's interest. It seemed genuine, motivated by something beyond the need to save their lives. It struck Adam at a moment of weakness, of doubt. It was this honest curiosity and concern that made a connection. Few people had ever engaged with him that way. Those that had were far out of reach and had been so for too long. As a sense memory of social interactions truly personal, Nelson's authenticity was enough to loosen Adam's defenses, allowing him to talk freely.

"OK, you know the thing about the artificial neural net," started Adam.

"SAFE MU," Nelson rejoined. "That training thing."

Adam hurried through the preamble of all he had to tell. "MU...just MU. It signifies the neural net learning rate. When weights are iteratively adjusted, it's one of the control parameters algorithms use to control the step size. In this case, it also functions as a cooperative signal; it confirms when all six areas of the glitch screen reach a state of coherence. With every cycle, a higher state of coherence is reached in the same allotted slice of time."

Nelson tried to follow. Now that Adam was talking, he didn't want to squelch it by appearing lost. "One minute at one o'clock, two minutes at two, three at three..."

"Precisely." Adam was into it. "A total of six minutes with six divisions to the glitch screen. Six times six—thirty-six cycles on the hour. Three hours times thirty-six cycles, that's 108 cycles overall."

"Cycles of learning," Nelson prompted as best he could.

"Not just learning—adjusting, coordinating, *reacting*. Like I said on the plane, it's a riff on the Monte Carlo method."

Nelson jumped in with an assumption. "Which has nothing to do with gambling…"

"No, it does," corrected Adam. "In a sense because it involves probable distributions. In training trials, you can use Monte Carlo paths to do what's called importance sampling. Only in this case, the input they used was live data from Wall Street. The mechanism was there to compare simulations with instantaneous values. It's a black-box technique that calculates the delta of the two from an analysis of probable uncertainties."

For Nelson, it was making more sense than he expected. "They're trying to predict outcomes…"

"Precisely, but given the hyper-velocity of data flow, they need an insane rate of coherence between the six divisions of the screen to achieve it."

"Six screen divisions…six site codes," added Nelson.

"It's a distributed system," concluded Adam. "They're building a brain. One brain comprised of six pieces, located in six different places."

"Sounds like a pilot test."

Adam nodded. "The kill screen chaos everyone saw was the output from the six locations. Coherence was key. So was speed. Each part of the screen had a set time to reach coherence."

Nelson was puzzled, "But didn't they have more time from hour to hour?"

"No," corrected Adam. "More cycles of the same time, with the cycle window decreasing logarithmically. Bumps in the input parameters graduated down to fractions of a second. That created a huge number of sample paths."

"Samples of what?" asked Nelson.

"Predictive paths. Alternate realities. Possible outcomes. They used sample paths to filter out noise."

"What kind of noise?"

"My guess? Noise is a bad guess. Remember, the system is learning."

"So what was the final threshold for success? You said coherence was reached when all parts of the screen spelled out SAFE MU. How long did that take?"

"You mean how long did it take for flagged cycles to be successful?"

"Yeah?"

Adam paused for effect. "Under one second."

"One second…" Nelson tried to fathom it.

"SAFE MU couldn't appear until all six sites reached coherence with each other in under one second."

"I guess that's amazing but I'm not sure why."

Adam leaned forward; he pointed at separate areas of the cot. "Six locations around the globe, each inundated with data, all parsing through 108 cycles of learned coherence with each other—in under *one second*."

Nelson jumped on the chance to show Adam a little of his financial knowledge. "OK, impressive, but I thought high frequency traders sliced and diced data in microseconds. Isn't one second *slow*?"

"For HFTs, yeah, but remember, this is just to reach coherence. Once the system has unity, there's no telling how fast it can think. It's like taking one calculation to open your eyes but after you're awake and coherent, the sky's the limit."

Nelson thought back to their conversation. "Wait a second. When I told you on the plane that the feds believe the F1E code was loaded into borrowed RAM, you said no way—and that's when you thought it took *six minutes* to get to SAFE MU."

"Amazing, huh," agreed Adam. "Not only that, but I also said there had to be a gazillion threshold logic units firing away like mad someplace to manage it. The F1E code they loaded into RAM in the New York and New Jersey datacenters was just a stub, nothing but pointers to the real code."

"Code kept where?" asked Nelson.

"Where else—at the six sites."

"Hold on. Wouldn't that take an unreal transfer rate to sync those up? Those places are spread out on six continents."

Adam nodded. "Unreal and unbelievable, isn't it? We're talking mega-terabits per second, at least. Digesting 2-1/2 terabits per second is the same as reading the data on 70 DVDs in a blink of an eye."

"How did you lock in on this?" asked Nelson.

Adam pulled the laptop toward him. "It's all there but not on the surface. Like I said, it's fractal. The closer you get, the more detail you can drive down through. For a while, I studied one section of the screen to death. I assumed that all sections shared a similar architecture, and they do, up to a point."

"Like what?"

"Well, each screen section hones in on coherence using a different fundamental math function. The functions by themselves are nothing special but like everything in math, achieving them takes a certain level of precision. Not only that, these functions are sometimes plotted and colored in as a demonstration of how one can graphically see a math relationship on a complex plane. Conveniently enough, plotting the real or imaginary part of some functions in the complex plane results in fractal-like structures that fit in quite well with the motion of the glitch chaos."

Adam turned around the laptop to show Nelson. "Here are the six functions, one for each section of the glitch screen."

function KleinInvariantJ[z] (= g_2^3 / \Delta) in the complex plane
function ModularLambda[z] in the complex plane
function RiemannSiegelTheta[z] in the complex plane.
function RiemannSiegelZ[z] in the complex plane
function Complex_theta_minus0point1times_e_i_pi_0point1
function Complex_Reciprocal_Gamma

Nelson took a look. "I'll trust you on that one."

"Like I said, the whole thing's designed to look like a kill screen from a video game. Each snippet of code has its own way of making nonsense, but that nonsense steps towards a graphical expression of these six complex functions, but all six must be mediated over the six sections of the screen. When that happens, SAFE MU is declared. The trick is, SAFE MU is not recognized unless the six sites do this in under one second."

For a moment, Nelson sunk into himself. What Adam was able to uncover was impressive. The implications, while still being in the realm of conjecture, seemed to be clear. And yet, the nagging doubt lingered: would it be enough for Carlos and Lutane? Would it buy them another day to find out more?

"How much more do you think you can find before tomorrow morning?" asked Nelson.

Adam's energy level had pumped up while he was lost in the subject. Having to face more grim realities, away from the pure interest he enjoyed in deciphering the puzzle, left him deflated. "It doesn't look good," he admitted.

Nelson was concerned with the certainty with which Adam had answered. "Why? Did you find something else? A block somewhere?"

Adam pushed the laptop away. "It's like dark matter. You know it's there but you can't see it, can't measure it. It exists solely because of the way everything else acts around it."

"What are you talking about?"

"I'm at a level where anything deeper is protected from hacking."

"Encrypted?"

"Something like that. Like I said, it's dark matter. I only know the general shape of it by the way everything else gets out of its way."

"What do you think it is?"

"A protection scheme. If I had to guess, I'd say it's an exotic new kind of something called *Unbalanced Oil and Vinegar*."

"OK, you lost me," admitted Nelson.

"It's a digital signature scheme, a part of multivariate cryptography."

"How much do you know about that?"

"From math class. UOV is based on an NP-hard mathematical problem."

Nelson chuckled at himself. "That helps."

Adam remained serious. "To get into these signatures, you have to solve quadratic equations."

"And quants can do that…" Nelson added, more sarcastic than hopeful.

Adam shrugged as he shook his head. "Solving m-equations with n-variables is an NP-hard problem, even if you used a quantum computer. That's why digital signatures based on systems of multivariate equations are considered *quantum resistant*. In other words, in a billion years, no fucking way. Give me a trillion years…maybe. Except, in this case, like I said, this thing is new. It's dark matter."

"If it's so dark, how can you tell?"

"UOV is tough but it's predictable. This thing ain't. It's the motherfucker of clever."

Nelson settled back. "So what are we left with?"

Adam was detached, embracing his cynicism. "What did Hollister call them? *Enigma patterns*?"

Mention of their missing teammate hit Nelson as a sour note. He quickly changed the topic. "There's one thing I *really* don't get."

"What's that?"

"What's magical about 108 cycles? Why not 110? Why not 100? If one second is the success threshold and they were dealing with minutes, why not keep it simple and stick to 60 cycles—60 seconds in a minute."

Adam thought for a second. "Good question. I wondered the same; in fact, I spent some time looking into it."

"And...?"

"There's no mathematical reason, at least none I could find."

"So then, it's arbitrary, an artifact of having six areas of randomness."

"Makes sense. Inside each area, six randomness cycles. Six screen sections perform six cycles three times. It's about 6, not about 108."

"It's just math. We accept it for what it is, nothing more."

"Seems logical," answered Adam. "Inputs and outputs, except you know how I like those analytical advantages only realized by going beyond machine-readable data."

Nelson was surprised. "Spoken like a heretic quant..."

"Not necessarily."

"So what does your gut say?"

Adam thought a moment and couldn't help but smile. "It's easy to conjure up conspiracies, isn't it? You're the expert on that."

"It's all right," Nelson assured him. "You can tell me. Something struck a nerve."

"Do nerves have intuition?"

Nelson was curious and didn't want to shoot him down. "A lot of tradecraft is following hunches. There's no reason to ignore instincts. But remember, they're not the same as facts."

"When are facts just facts? And when do they become a pattern?"

"Facts are never just facts," countered Nelson. "They always form patterns. That leaves one critical question: which pattern is meaningful?"

Adam nodded in deference to the point made, then offered, "F1E happened at 1:00, 2:00, 3:00. So let's take the powers of 1, 2, 3—1 to the 1st power is 1; 2 to the 2nd power is 4; 3 to the 3rd power is 27. 1 times 4 times 27 is 108."

Nelson showed interest. "Go on..."

Adam announced another fact. "The diameter of the Sun is 108 times the diameter of the Earth. The distance from the Sun to the Earth is 108 times the diameter of the Sun."

While perplexed, Nelson couldn't help but grin. "OK…"

Adam added, "The average distance of the Moon from the Earth is 108 times the diameter of the Moon."

Not sure where this was going, Nelson let his curiosity overrule the impulse to interrupt.

Adam recalled another. "There are 12 constellations and 9 arc segments, 12 astrological houses and 9 planets. 12 times 9 is 108."

Then another. "Or how about this? The volume expansion of freezing water is roughly 108%."

Sure that Adam had at least one more, Nelson waited.

Adam didn't disappoint. "The human body's vital organs begin to fail from overheating at the internal temperature of 108 degrees Fahrenheit."

"These are all facts?" asked Nelson, giving up on finding connections.

Adam nodded then added, "Here's the one I really like: the angle formed by two adjacent lines in a pentagon equals 108 degrees."

"A *pentagon*…" mused Nelson. It was easy to bypass geometry and think of a building by the same name. No doubt that's why Adam liked it.

"Yeah…" Adam left it up to Nelson, "So which pattern is meaningful?"

Nelson didn't hesitate. The choice was obvious. He got up from the cot, prepared to walk away. Neither conspiracy theories nor hi-tech mysticism mattered in the moment. But one thing did.

He asked Adam back, "Which one buys us another day?"

Adam watched Nelson walk away.

Nothing more was said until Nelson sat down and swiveled around. He eyed Adam with amused interest. "By the way, in case you didn't know, the toll-free emergency telephone number in India is…108."

47

0000 0010 1111

4:41 pm CST, Monday, December 11th

With brisk steps, Katherine braved the chilly air and busy streets of the University of Texas before turning south on Guadalupe Street. This was the last of several walks taken this afternoon. Erring on the side of safety, Aubrey and Katherine had parked their car, intent on not using it until the time came to leave Austin. If they could get what they needed within walking distance, no sense taking the chance of being spotted driving around.

One complication was the use of library computers, either at the university or the city's public branches. Ideally, while in town, Katherine didn't want to use the same computer more than once. At worst, someone could track them to Austin. At best, they could harden themselves as targets by not forming habits of visiting the same places when they went out.

Another difficulty was user IDs needed to access computers, even those meant for the general public. Gone were the days of anonymous web browsing, even on most public computers at libraries. To qualify for a user ID at public and university libraries, one needed to register with a valid government-issued photo ID. It was ironic: more ID was needed to surf the net via public computers than was required to vote.

Katherine had brought two fake IDs on the trip in her travel pack. In a perfect world, such valuable resources would only be used for critical escape points, such as emergency getaways at airports or tense searches at border checkpoints. To have to use them to browse the internet at the local public library was a costly burn of resources. But one that couldn't be helped.

Earlier in the day, at Perry-Castañeda, Katherine had created an EID and enabled it at the library's courtesy borrower desk. The ID would work anywhere on campus, yet on weekends, access options were limited.

Originally, she intended on going to the University's Mallet Chemistry Library but it was closed on Saturdays. Faulk Central, one of the city's public libraries, had 52 workstations but closed its doors at 6 pm and the computers, while plenty, could be crowded since patrons were allowed to hold timeslots in advance using the Pharos reservation system.

As Katherine feared, when she arrived at Faulk she found the computers booked up. With an hour left before the library closed, the librarian gave her limited hope that someone might leave. If so, she could squeeze in 15 or 20 minutes before closing. Most locations restricted customers to 30 minutes but at Faulk Central, that limit was an hour. No wonder there was a crowd.

At 5:39, a workstation had opened up. By the time she settled in and logged on, ten minutes remained. For Nelson, the time must be somewhere around midnight, depending on where in Europe he was being kept. Katherine could only hope, wherever he was, he'd be working late.

She accessed the cheater's website and logged in as *TigerLily*. As a new user, she was bound to get a hefty measure of emails and online pokes by experienced users trolling fresh waters with old bait. Filtering through them by username proved effective for narrowing the field. When she saw a poke from *seeyah*, she knew she had a match. She read, *"Feeling frisky?"*

Right away she returned the poke, even before checking if such a user had a completed profile or if he was currently online.

"Like to stay up...late?" Her poke was canned but appropriate.

The system showed *seeyah* logged in but inactive. She waited for an answer and reviewed his profile. His hometown was listed as: *Cheyenne*. His occupation was simply: *tool*. His main passion: *living one day at a time*.

With precious minutes passing by, she watched as other online users sent her provocative come-ons via instant message. She ignored them and occupied herself by wondering how things were going for Aubrey. She had taken a new cell phone to a public location for her follow-up call. That excursion would be brief if no one showed up on the other end to talk.

In the background, Katherine could hear the librarians reminding patrons that 6 pm was closing time. Some people near Katherine were gathering up their things and logging off.

Finally, with three minutes left, an instant message from *seeyah* popped in. *"Hey there, I'll be up all night."*

Katherine hurried to respond. *"I'd like to join you."*

The text exchange followed, fast and furious.

"Not a good time. Cat can't play until the dog's away."

"I know what you mean. For me, every day is cat and mouse."

"You sound familiar. I wonder if we know each other."

Katherine responded, *"Nothing is as it seems. TigerLily is neither animal nor flower, but she's looking for a true partner. Aren't you tired of users who pretend to make you a priority, a confidant, a life's partner, ETC.?"*

Nelson paused before replying. *"You speak from wild-field experience?"*

"I stand on tall shoulders."

"Maybe, but do you have goals?"

"Yes, but it makes me sad to see them so clear and yet so far."

"Don't worry. Remember that you are a beautiful, smart woman, and have consequently won first prize in the lottery of life."

"No winner yet. The wheel keeps spinning the rest of this month."

"No doubt put into motion on the first Friday."

"No doubt." Katherine had one minute. *"Someone is here. I'm running out of time but I'd like to meet you. We'd be good for each other."*

"Agreed but first things first. Tomorrow is another day. Beyond that, no."

Katherine saw the final signal from the librarian, reminding her to log off.

"Tomorrow is already here," she typed. *"Tomorrow is Farda."*

The response came, *"One way or another, there's only one way out."*

"Sounds like you need a third option. May you find the way."

The hour was up. Katherine stared into the chat screen awhile before logging out and closing the browser.

The walk back to the hotel seemed colder and longer than the journey out. The torment wouldn't relent. The message exchange with Nelson turned over in her mind. Their dance had been frustratingly tentative, too cryptic, and worst of all, abysmally abbreviated. She had hoped for more. She knew she was out of position to help him and yet she'd hoped an opportunity would materialize if she put herself in contact with him.

She could have predicted that such a limited chat would be strained. Both of their circumstances left little room to be candid. Trying to couch the truth in innuendo and metaphor had proved woefully inadequate. And yet, being too direct was not a risk to be taken on a first exchange.

Maybe some of her intent had gotten through. There was no way to tell. Hopefully, she'd find another way of contacting him before morning.

She entered the hotel room to find Aubrey already back.

"How did it go?" asked Aubrey. "Did you reach Nelson?"

Katherine's nod was reserved. "We had a few minutes. The library was closing; I couldn't say much. How about you?"

Aubrey sipped at a wine glass. "She's going to help us."

"How?"

"She's putting me in contact with the remaining agent."

"There's only one? You confirmed that with her?"

Aubrey's nod was slowed by the disappointment she saw in Katherine.

"With the other agents down, how much help is he going to be?"

"I don't know. I'll find out. He might be compromised."

"That would rule out any new operations."

Aubrey hung onto hope, "But he might know something—something from what's already gone on."

"How many more phones do you have?"

"Two." Aubrey changed subjects. "When do we find out about Nelson?"

Katherine reached for the wine. "Tomorrow. If I can't reach him, most likely he's gone."

Aubrey studied Katherine's reaction. "Don't beat yourself up over it. It was a long shot we'd be any help."

Katherine sat on the bed and stared into the carpet. "I needed more time."

"Time for what?"

"I couldn't even answer his question from last time."

"What question? You mean that list he posted?"

"Yeah."

"Where were you supposed to begin? It made no sense. How could *you* find out where that originated from? He gave you nothing to go on."

Katherine considered the criticism. Aubrey was right—*if* that was Nelson's intent. If it wasn't, what else might his question mean? She recited it again in a whisper, desperate to glean another vantage point.

"*Can you find out where this originated from? Maybe GG can help you.*"

"And who is GG?" asked Aubrey. "You said you didn't know."

Katherine explored a different viewpoint. "...*find out where this originated.*" She looked up at Aubrey. "What if *this* doesn't refer to the list; maybe he's talking about his own post—find out where *this post* came from."

"Perhaps, but why GG? We went through everybody. The initials don't line up with anyone we know."

A flash of insight hit Katherine. "What if it's not a person?"

"What else could it be?"

Katherine jumped up and called the hotel's concierge. "...Yes, the country code GG, top level domain. Could you look it up for me?"

The concierge complied. "Here it is. The Bailiwick of Guernsey."

"In the English Channel off the coast of Normandy. Thank you." Katherine turned to Aubrey. "That's it! Nelson was telling us where he is."

Aubrey was subdued. "Guernsey. Great—now what do we do with that?"

48

0000 0011 0000

12:26 am GMT, Tuesday, December 12th

Looking over Nelson's shoulder, Adam sipped lukewarm coffee and muttered so Nelson would hear. "Well, that's a bust."

Nelson couldn't disagree but didn't have it in him to admit anything else. He sat and reread the online exchange as if it contained more.

Adam plopped down in a nearby chair. "Probably just as well. We don't know who this *TigerLily* is anyway."

"I know who it is," Nelson asserted. He rubbed exhaustion from his face. "I'm sure of it." Before Adam could speak, he added, "Sure as I can be."

"Why, because you got a few key words, a couple lines with double meanings? Anybody that profiled you could have clued in on that."

"It's more than that." Nelson didn't have the energy to explain. How does one explain a familiar give-and-take that added up to recognition? It was like dancing at a masquerade ball and knowing exactly who was behind the mask.

Adam pursued it anyway. "Like what?"

Nelson sorted through the reasons, like the fact that *TigerLily* had capitalized ETC in a line that describes intimate betrayal. Nelson's ingrained training held him back from divulging anything about the Emergency Tactics Corp to Adam. Even so, *TigerLily*'s ominous heads-up was obvious.

Instead, Nelson returned to something that would be familiar to Adam. "We managed to work in more quotes, just like on Max Engle's forum."

"Cecil again? Where?" asked Adam. Nelson highlighted the lines.

"Yes, but it makes me sad to see them so clear and yet so far. Don't worry. Remember that you are a beautiful, smart woman, and have consequently won first prize in the lottery of life."

Nelson quoted the original, *"I would annex the planets if I could; I often think of that. It makes me sad to see them so clear and yet so far."*

"And the other one?" asked Adam.

From memory, Nelson recited, *"Remember that you are an Englishman, and have consequently won first prize in the lottery of life."*

Adam eased back, visibly unconvinced. "That proves nothing. Anyone who read your forum posts could have picked up on that."

Nelson sighed. "It doesn't matter." He stood and walked over to the food stores for a bottle of water. Needing a break, he sat down on a cot and leaned back against the wall. He might not be able to see the darkness outside but all too well he could feel the lateness of the hour.

Adam swiveled around in his chair, then carried his coffee over by Nelson.

Sliding down the wall, Adam sat on a box of unopened water bottles.

Nelson admitted their predicament. "Any other night, we'd be crashing by now, getting some sleep."

"Too much left to do," countered Adam, staring across the room.

"We've done everything we can. I don't know where else to look."

They shared a moment of silence. Adam added, "We've got the rest of the night. We'll go over what we've done. Maybe we missed something."

Nelson appreciated the effort, but Adam's attempt to make their situation sound better than it was only underscored how stumped they were. If they really had so much to do, they'd be busy at the computers, not sitting with their backs literally against the wall.

Facing what might be his last night alive, Nelson felt no pressure to withhold questions that came to mind. To satisfy a nagging curiosity he'd carried with him from New York, he asked, "So tell me, is MUTEX really on the shelf? You have no connections with the hacktivist underground?"

Adam gave Nelson a glance. To tell him the full truth at this point seemed inconsequential. "MUTEX is on the shelf—but within reach."

With the tacit admission, Nelson sported a hint of a grin. "If I didn't know better, I'd say Adam the Quant is the avatar and MUTEX is the real person."

Adam looked away. "How does anyone know who the real person is?"

"Maybe MUTEX is the one you think you should be. Adam is the compromise you made to fit in, to match some image of success."

"People do what they have to do."

"Not what they want to do."

"Like it matters."

Nelson's memories sped through a life review. "I've come to the conclusion that those who help you put off living the life you want are either risk-adverse or they have something to gain by keeping you in your place."

"Sounds like the 1%: they're the epitome of risk-adverse while always having something to gain."

As Nelson thought back, he entered the confessional. "I guess every generation is sold the same load of crap."

"Like what?"

"Like it all adds up to something—if you work hard, if you wait, if you're patient and you conform, your life will amount to something. That's what I thought growing up; we all did."

Adam was in no mood for a lecture from one of his wise elders. "Things have changed since your generation."

Nelson found the distinction amusing. "Nothing changes except the way the same things get done. Kings in the Middle Ages used the fear of hell to keep peasants outside the royal gates. OK, so now there is no hell. Now, contending with a world of hedonists, they have to go the other way."

"The glitter of success at million-to-one odds and pleasure distractions

24/7. What's wrong with that?"

"The cynical, the jaded say it keeps the majority looking the other way. Psychology says it's more effective to condition and control by pleasure than by pain. Plus, the limits of what success looks like are already defined. You're free to run wild—as long as you stay within the garden maze."

Adam chuckled. "You don't believe everybody has an equal chance to be the capstone of the great success pyramid? Like *that* makes common sense."

"It would if wealth and power didn't concentrate and corrupt so naturally."

"Everyone knows, in a game of chance, the house ultimately wins."

"Maybe, but it shouldn't be a rigged game. It was supposed to be about opportunity," stressed Nelson.

"There's a big difference between the opportunity to play the game and the opportunity to define it."

Nelson paused, "The things I've done for them for a paycheck."

"If you didn't think you had options, what else could you do?"

"Oh, I don't know, maybe spend less time overseas, *making the world safe for shareholders*. Maybe stay closer to home."

"It's no different at home. Home is where it all concentrates."

"Yeah, one way or another." Nelson admitted, "I've let a lot of moments slip away without being who I should have been."

"How's that?" Adam looked over and studied Nelson. How the condemned man would face his last night became more than a curiosity.

"Madelyn's gone. My son Brian is somewhere…he won't talk to me."

"Why, what happened?"

"It's old news. Anything I say now will sound like excuses."

"Whatever. Tell me."

Nelson paused. "You know how it goes; you've heard it before. Work took me away, a lot. When I was home, I wasn't. Coming down off operations, I kept to myself. When I *was* around, I couldn't talk about what I had done."

"Well, yeah, you don't unload all that shit on a kid."

Nelson looked Adam in the eye. "Except that shit…was me."

"You had to do something for a paycheck."

"Is that my excuse?" Nelson shook his head. "The fact is, I liked what I was doing. It's seems crazy now, but I thought I was making a difference."

"You probably did, just not the difference you thought it was going to be. Either way, some things are better left behind us."

"It didn't matter; I was sworn to secrecy. I couldn't share anything at home even if I wanted to."

"Your family must have known that," noted Adam.

"Yeah, they knew. I know that now. But there's a difference between sharing classified information…and sharing yourself."

"So where's your son now?"

"California. He has a motorcycle repair shop out there."

"Motorcycles, huh."

"Yeah, he was big into that; used to race them. That's how he lost a leg."

"Jesus!" declared Adam. "Must have been one nasty crash."

"So they say. I didn't see the race. I was away. Madelyn stayed at the hospital with him. Later, she insisted he get professional help."

"Why? Rough adjustment?"

"His counselor concluded he'd been living his life at the red line for years, maxing out everything he did...motorcycles, X-Games, ultimate fighting, you name it. Naturally, they told him he was doing it all to impress me."

"He bought into that?"

A nod came from Nelson. "They convinced him everything he loved to do was nothing but a way to get attention from me."

"Whoa, what a mind fuck."

Nelson dug deeper. "Who knows, maybe they were right. Maybe it was all about me. Maybe, if we examine it honestly, everything we love to do is born out of something we lack."

"Sprinkle shit on the ground and up comes flowers."

"Something like that. Except after the accident, he physically couldn't do those things anymore, at least not at the level he was used to."

"Then everything changed, huh?"

"He started coming around the house only when I was away. That tore up his mom. She didn't want to be in the middle. I can't blame her. She wasn't about to take sides."

"But Brian got his repair shop; sounds like he got better," offered Adam.

"You tell me. Only the doctors are sure what's *better*. As far as I'm concerned, what they told him sealed the deal between him and me. What was worse, it alienated him from everything he loved to do."

"Well, yeah, if they define it that way," agreed Adam. "That could screw with your whole identity; you could wind up hating yourself."

"The counselors got into that. They went round and round with him but it only went so far. He ended up on medication, as you might expect."

"*Change your thinking and change your emotions*," recited Adam. "That's the mantra I heard. And if you have to do it chemically, oh well. Some nice pharmaceutical company will be your friend for life."

Nelson picked up on Adam's intensity. "Sounds like you've been there."

"They tried to take me there."

"When was that?"

"After I hacked the National Archives. At first they threatened jail time but I was young so they cut me some slack by forcing me into counseling instead."

Nelson commiserated, "There had to be something wrong with you, right? Somewhere you developed a problem with authority and you *acted out*."

"Yeah, they weren't sure what I had: ADD, ADHD, or a fucking Ph.D."

Nelson laughed. "The curse of being precocious."

"Something like that. Later, I figured out what they wanted was the whole thing to go away ASAP."

"How'd you find that out?"

"Years later, in college, when the NSA tried to recruit me. Among other things, they told me they had this thing called CRT-CEH."

"That's a job code," interjected Nelson.

"Yeah, for a *Certified Ethical Hacker*. The oxymoron overtones of that struck me funny. But they're not comical people. They were dismayed I didn't jump at the chance to be a cyber weapon for what's right."

"That can't be all," reasoned Nelson.

"No, they wanted more," confessed Adam. "They hoped, once I was in, I'd convince some buddies from RAPIER to join up too."

"And if they wouldn't?"

"It wasn't said but it was obvious: the expected thing was to be a team player and turn over their names and numbers."

"What a deal," declared Nelson. "A job for giving up your friends."

"At the time, the government had a lot of catch-up to do in some areas. They needed to brain-drain the underground to keep current. That's why they went after *Anonymous* so aggressively. They got some smart people to flip due to their out-of-proportion sentencing at some of the trials."

"If hacking is what you love to do, why not take them up on their offer?"

"It's not the hacking…"

"Is being a quant any more pure?"

"There's lots of ways to be a tool of the system," struggled Adam. "Passively going along with them is the best tool they have."

"So we're all tools, is that it? Silence is acquiescence."

"Rationalize it any way you like," explained Adam. "Working for them would be all about power. The quant stuff is all about greed. Somehow greed seems one step removed."

"One step is far enough away?"

Adam thought about it. "Greed can be a means to power, but power and control is always about itself and nothing more. I know that doesn't make sense, but like I said, I rationalized it. I guess I always fantasized about being my own boss when it came to that."

Nelson went deeper. "So, if everything we love to do is born out of something we lack, what's lacking in you that makes you hack?"

Adam bristled, "You're gonna try to fucking psychoanalyze me now?"

"You must be drawn to it for a reason."

"Yeah, because I like to know. I don't like people telling me there's limits on what I can know. Who are they to decide what or how much I can handle? They're never going to convince me it's all about keeping me safe."

"So what is it? A way to keep you in your place?"

"Indirectly. It's more about hiding the ways they're rigging the system. A rigged system keeps me in place. Knowing helps level out the playing field."

"How much of that system do you think is rigged?"

"Put it this way. I know a guy in RAPIER; he goes by the handle DPS."

"Which stands for…?" asked Nelson.

"*Damage Per Second*."

"Thinks a lot of himself, doesn't he."

"He specializes in tearing down sites, you know…*Tango Down*."

Nelson gave a nod.

Adam continued, "He explains it this way: the world is divided into three parts—the cocktail party, the mansion, and the woods."

"I take it you won't find a martini in the woods," mused Nelson.

"He says the cocktail party is the heart of the oligarchy, the inner circle. The mansion is where the relatively well-to-do middle class live—some as family, some as guests, others as house servants. The woods are everywhere else, the 3rd world or people who pull no influence so they might as well be off the fucking grid; you know, the *useless eaters*."

"I take it there's not a lot of movement in between the three areas. The conspiracy theories I've read say we're born into our destiny and that changes only if the cocktail party agrees. I don't get how any of that motivates you?"

"It's all about knowing," answered Adam. "There was a lot I wasn't told as a kid. I wound up spending most of my time believing in a world that didn't exist. You could say growing up was a huge disappointment."

"You blame that on the system or on being a teenager?"

"It wasn't a phase I was going through; it was the indoctrination of becoming an adult. Well-adjusted people are expected to have a certain world view. Think anything else about how things work and you get excluded."

"Hacking was a way of not turning into your parents."

"Hacking made up for lost time. In a rigged game, it opened up possibilities of being the great leveler. Tools like hacking made it possible that both sides could have an advantage. The internet was a new thing, the Wild West, something they didn't fully control yet."

"You think they control it now?"

"Not yet, not completely. But they will; they'll nail it down. They have endless resources and time to do it."

"MUTEX would never be so cynical," challenged Nelson.

"When MUTEX started, the idea of both sides having an advantage seemed real. With a bit of code and a proxy server, suddenly it was possible that not all of the benefits had to funnel into the cocktail party."

"Is that how you explained it to your counselors?"

"What do you think?" grinned Adam. "I told them what they wanted to hear. You know the drill; parrot back what they want you to believe. That's all any authority figure wants, anyway."

"You include your parents in that?"

Adam took a moment. "My mom is all right, except she won't take sides, she doesn't voice her opinion. With her, it's all about not making waves."

"What about your father?"

Adam looked down. "I never understood my old man but I respected him; I respected the way he worked, if nothing else. I mean, he was reliable as hell if nothing else. If he had something to do, it got done."

"You weren't close?"

"We lived in the same house. He did the father thing, I did the son thing. He was all about tradition and the value of experience. I had no connection to the past. For me, things were changing too fast to believe experience held any value. I figured as change accelerates, experience becomes a handicap."

Nelson smiled. "That means change is the only thing we can hold onto."

"Adaptation is the thing."

"You don't believe history repeats itself?" asked Nelson.

"Only in a *general* sense. You can say people go to war or betray each other over and over again, but how it happens makes all the difference. *How* is always changing. The details change and that's what will trips people up."

"Did you ever explain it to your Dad like that?"

"Back then, I didn't think it would do any good."

"Back then? What about now?" Nelson could see Adam's torment.

"Now it wouldn't get through." Adam hesitated, then blurted out, "He's sitting in a care facility in Brooklyn."

"Oh, that's right...dementia. You told me. I'm sorry."

"Nothing to be sorry about. That's the way it happens."

"How far along is he?"

"I don't know. I stopped visiting a year ago. He didn't recognize me. I didn't see the point after that."

"What about your mother?"

"She still goes. She knows not to bring it up to me."

"If he *could* recognize you now...would you go?"

Adam wouldn't look at Nelson; his voice trailed off. "Maybe...why not? Then again, what does it all mean anyway?"

Nelson considered his own life. "I ask myself the same thing."

"We get stuck on questions we can't answer."

"I've come to the conclusion there's only one way out of that—and it's not about waiting for a brighter future. You have to stay in integrity with the present moment. Right now is the only thing you have any chance of changing. If everyone put that into motion, we'd have a different world."

"And what do you call that? Your *Utopian Conspiracy*?"

Nelson leaned forward, restless. Looking over at Adam, he smiled. "Of course, that's my *experience*—in a *general* sort of way. Everyone has to figure out the *details* for themselves."

Adam's grin was interrupted as they were distracted by an alarm on one of the computers. It was the sound of an incoming message. Reacting together, they jumped up and rushed to their consoles.

The message was for Nelson. "It's Dystrom. He's come through."

Adam rolled his chair over. "The phone list?"

"Looks like it. He got us names and numbers, dates and times." Then Nelson was let down. "He couldn't get any transcripts."

Adam deflated back in his chair. "Shit!"

"Hold on…" Nelson read through Dystrom's attachment. "It may not be that bad. What he got goes beyond Bargeau. This takes it a layer deeper."

"You mean we have the same data on everyone who talked to Liam?"

"Yeah, we've got everyone *they* talked to. Two degrees of separation."

"Geez," complained Adam. "Nothing like being puzzle-fucked! That's a couple hundred names to go through."

"At least, but he broke them down for us."

Adam's sarcasm came through, "Don't tell me, alphabetical order?"

Nelson pointed at the screen. "No, look, the GCHQ computers managed to categorize them: family, work, personal business, outside business, unknown."

Adam rolled back to his console. "All right, send me a copy."

"Let's start with the direct contacts to Liam. One degree of separation."

"You start at the top of the list; I'll work up from the bottom." Adam sat, dissecting the task at hand while awaiting the file transfer. "Before I start, you have any idea what's the best way to go about this?"

Nelson kept working. "What do you mean?"

"What exactly are we looking for with these people?"

"You're asking that *now*, after two days of this shit?"

"Yeah, you know nothing's going to come up from a basic search. Whatever they're into is hidden well. A regular bio isn't going to flag them. How do we tell which one leads to anything?"

"It's not about the bio. It's about connections, patterns, something out of place. It could even be something perfectly *in* place, but too conveniently."

Adam leaned forward, fingers on the keyboard, accessing the attachment. He shook his head with exhausted frustration. "Sounds like guessing people's astrology signs by reading their name in the phone book."

Nelson glanced over. "You've got it."

Adam laughed, "That's stupid ass shit."

"You know what you should call it?" countered Nelson.

Adam looked up the first name and took the bait. "What?"

Nelson worked away as he answered. "Non-machine readable data."

49

0000 0011 0001

2:41 am CMT, Wednesday, December 13th

Katherine raised the protective plastic and took her laundered blouse off the hotel hangar. It was the last item to fold and pack away. She turned to her backpack as the door opened and Aubrey hurried in.

Their cheap cell phones didn't operate well in the room. Aubrey had gone outside to make her call. From the looks of it, she had news to tell.

"Did you get through?" asked Katherine.

"Yeah, but we had to rush." Aubrey shed her sweater.

"Where did Cassandra call from?"

"A convenience store, just long enough to give me his number."

Blouse packed away, Katherine zipped up her bag. "And the agent?"

"We had a few minutes."

"Was that enough?"

"It's a start. He's on the move."

"Does he have reason to think they're after him too?"

"No, not yet. He's on a regular Chimaera assignment. He needs to keep current with that work. It's the only cover he has."

"What did he say about the agent that got killed?"

"He managed to copy surveillance footage from the Hyatt before it got scrubbed. The coroner estimated the time of death so he did facial recognition on people coming and going around that time."

"Did he find anything?"

"Maybe. One face matches up with a German national who once was a member of the Korps Commandotroepen, the KCT—the elite special forces of the Royal Netherlands Army."

"Sounds like the beginning of an odd resume."

"An unusual pairing, that's for sure."

"I take it this German wasn't checked in at the Hyatt."

"No," confirmed Aubrey.

"Coincidence?" challenged Katherine.

"It may be a telling one, if it is."

"Why?"

Aubrey sat down. "About a year ago I was at a meeting at Chimaera. It was on a day when we hosted what were called *offsite observers*. At one point, a German security firm was mentioned in connection with Project G."

"Why would that be discussed at Chimaera? Wouldn't another firm be a competitor?"

"I think it slipped out during a break from one of the meetings. One of the observers, brought in for the day, spoke too freely. His associates glossed over it but I could tell they weren't pleased with him."

"Was that the end of it?" asked Katherine.

"Not quite. The next day I asked around and was told it was nothing. I pushed back by going higher. I explained I was rightfully concerned that this other security firm might be working on a deal with Extasis to take the Project G contract away from Chimaera."

"When you say higher, who did you go to?"

"Let's just say, a board member who should know."

"And that put the matter to rest?"

"Until tonight, when I heard about the Hyatt footage. The board member had assured me, with some humor, there was nothing to be concerned about. He said it was no secret; the security company in question was Steigbriar."

"Steigbriar," repeated Katherine, her interest piqued. "They're private paramilitaries based out of Frankfurt."

Aubrey nodded. "At least they've kept the same name, unlike Academi, formerly called Xe Services, better known as Blackwater."

"Why would Extasis need them? Are they going to war or something?"

"I thought it was strange too, but the board member explained it away, saying Steigbriar was onboard only as security consultants for GETTIS, the European construction company. I was assured our two paths didn't cross. GETTIS built things and Steigbriar helped out designing facilities with physical security for people, buildings, and transports in mind. Since Chimaera's role was protecting intellectual capital, I was told there was high confidence that Chimaera's contracts with Extasis were not in jeopardy."

"But you *did* lose the contract..." noted Katherine.

"Yes," admitted Aubrey. "Some time later. Again, we were assured that Steigbriar had nothing to do with it."

"You accepted that."

"There was nothing I could do. There were rumors, of course, but there are always rumors."

"What do you think happened?"

"I always thought Chimaera got the contract with Extasis as a fluke. No one behind Project G was ever comfortable about having such a high profile private firm involved. I could tell they were nervous; they felt exposed."

"Exposed by the very people contracted to shield them? Strange."

"I think we were useful at a desperate time, but eventually, the whole thing was taken back in-house, somewhere behind In-Q-Tel."

"And you think engaging Steigbriar was part of that."

A nod. "And now we may have proof with Steigbriar being at the Hyatt."

"If so, their operations extend far beyond GETTIS."

"And that's another thing," noted Aubrey. "What were they building for

Project G that needed paramilitary consultants? It's a European company but they're like Bechtel or Halliburton; their contracts could be anywhere."

Katherine stood. "Nelson is in Europe. I should warn him."

"Would it make any difference now? It's mid-morning over there. We need to check out and get on the road. We've been here long enough."

Katherine shouldered her backpack. "Check us out and get the car. I'm going to use a computer in the media room."

"I thought you didn't want to use them; that's why you used the library."

"If I'm going to pass this along, I have to do it now. Which computer doesn't matter anymore if we're checking out."

"All right," Aubrey relented. "But hurry up."

Katherine rushed down to the lobby towards the conference center. Along the way there were a couple of breakout rooms. In between them was a media room and lounge with copiers and computers for business travelers.

Katherine found the first workstation offline. She hurried to the next and found it operable but slowed down by an anti-virus scan. She managed to log in as *TigerLily* and post one message for *seeyah*. The system showed *seeyah* logged in but inactive. Logged in was no guarantee he was still alive.

She logged out and was about to leave but thought to check Max Engle's forum, in case Nelson had left something for her. He hadn't, but something else caught her eye. It was a new discussion thread that was getting a lot of activity. Katherine was drawn in by it.

A few minutes later, Aubrey started the car as Katherine rushed to get in. Before Aubrey could speak, Katherine shut the door and ordered, "Let's get out of here. Just drive."

Aubrey accelerated the car. "Did you leave a message?"

"Yeah."

"Then what's wrong?" Aubrey felt the rising tension.

Katherine tossed her backpack into the back seat. "Max aired my program anyway."

"After you told him not to? Even after Barnett warned him?"

"That's just it. Max didn't get very far into it."

"What happened?"

"Power to his studio went out a few minutes into the broadcast."

"It shut down right in the middle of the program?"

Katherine nodded. "The discussion boards are hot with talk about it."

"How widespread was the power outage?"

"That's the thing—the blackout only hit facilities that had anything to do with broadcasting Max's show. That includes a mirror site his syndicator uses in Atlanta. You can imagine the conspiracy they're making out of that."

"How easy would it be for Max to stage his own power outage?"

"The equipment that got fried in Atlanta was out of his reach."

"I don't understand. That plays right into Max's hand."

"It's the kind of publicity you can't buy."

"Why would Barnett do that? He may have stopped the show but he also launched a conspiracy. Barnett had to know what would happen."

Katherine watched the darkened scenery rush by. "He had to."

Aubrey read into Katherine's change of tone. "You think Barnett planned it this way?"

"Maybe not planned it, at least not from the start. But once I told him it was going to happen, I guess he figured out a way to use it."

Aubrey struggled to understand. "You mean hype the conspiracy angle."

"It certainly shines light on what I was saying on the program."

"Barnett must think he's clever."

Katherine thought back to her one meeting with him in the airport museum parking lot. "I have no doubt."

"But he didn't know you were going to Max's place until after the show was already recorded. Going to Max was your idea, not his."

"The way I was being pushed, I was bound to do something. All he had to do was sit back and find a way to use whatever I did."

Aubrey stared at the road ahead. "The same way he used my agents once he found out they were shadowing Richard?"

"Probably. He'll use whatever he can to find out what's going on."

Aubrey shot Katherine a glance. "Are you comfortable with that? Are you even sure that's all he wants?"

The two drove for a while without Katherine answering.

In time, the sound of the road had a sameness about it. Nothing was said.

50

0000 0011 0010

9:11 am GMT, Wednesday, December 13th

There was no way to prevent it. Morning had come.

Nelson and Adam stared into their consoles, numb from a grueling night of work. The basement's buried silence gave no hint of their feverish activity. Neither one had raised up from the task in hours. Slumped in their seats, they dreaded what the morning might bring.

Researching the phone list provided by GCHQ had proved tedious and confusing, the kind of thing top intelligence analysts earned their money doing in other windowless rooms and under even heavier, albeit friendlier guard. Any anticipation of a significant find was waning.

Their attention turned to the clock.

At any moment, their captors would want an accounting of their progress. The truth was, after hours of data mining, they wouldn't have enough. In fact, they had less than what got Hollister taken away the day before. As clear as their predicament was, it remained unspoken. Alluding to it somehow meant giving in to what the situation augured for one of them.

Nelson's dual monitors glowed with a half dozen different displays, each one a prospect, a possibility of a connection made. Each one was interesting, but none of them had aligned in an arrangement that revealed any secrets.

In the corner of one screen, a small window drew Nelson's repeated attention. It contained the latest post from *TigerLily*.

The post was a cryptic tidbit, so far significant only for its uncharacteristic starkness. No pretense was folded into it, no attempt to couch the intended meaning in an inappropriate quip between two would-be lovers wishing to hook up. This was a post made as direct and pointed as possible, a post probably made in haste, thereby eliciting Nelson's concern. Rereading it, he grasped for something beyond the words.

"Steigbriar—security for GETTIS"

Nelson knew of both Steigbriar and GETTIS, but why they should matter in the moment was lost on him. The fact that the post was so terse was either a sign that *TigerLily* thought its meaning evident or else the clue was enigmatic for her too. If only she'd added another line of detail, something else to go on.

Nelson let it go; there was no time for what-ifs. He looked over at Adam. "How are you doing on the second list?"

Adam froze in position, intent upon his work. "Ask me in an hour."

"I don't have an hour."

The finality of it shook Adam out of his trance. He raised up and glanced at the security camera in the corner of the ceiling. "They know we're close; that's why they're going to give us extra time this morning."

Nelson ignored the false hope. "I've gone back to the primary list, Liam's list. There's some on there that I want a closer look at."

Adam stretched the stiffness from his neck. "What's special about them?"

"One or two flags might turn red."

"Like what?"

"The number of calls, where they came from, the timing of events."

"OK," agreed Adam. "Compare notes. Who have you got?"

Nelson checked the list. "First off…Niles Davenport."

Adam frowned. "Investment banker. Lives in London."

"Yeah, he called Bargeau several times during the Davos trip. Some calls were after midnight."

"I'd let that go for now."

"Why?"

"The timing of events," guessed Adam. "All those calls align with bumps in the Forex market at that time."

"Niles doesn't work in Forex."

"He used to; apparently he's still well connected. Liam was moving cash between currencies, that's all. I see nothing there. Check out his portfolio."

Nelson rechecked his list. "All right. What about Bridgette Hayes?"

Adam checked his notes. "Daddy works out of Brussels, is into high tech; known for trading influences around the Pudong District, one of China's Special Economic Zones near Shanghai."

"Possible ties with CIG+XM?"

Adam frowned. "Don't bet on it. He's old money, has established partners that go back before CIG+XM existed. I don't think he'd jump ship."

"So what's Bridgette calling Liam about?"

"My guess?" offered Adam. "A little insider trading. Check it out. The day after her call, Liam put in a buy order for 10,000 shares of a shipping company that services Pudong."

For the next half hour, the two of them went at it. Each presented what they had found and the other held it up to scrutiny. Desperate to show their captors they were in the middle of something important, they vetted every detail they could. There were plenty of connections to make. The only problem was finding which pattern applied to what they were after.

Any second, a voice through the speaker on the wall might demand a reckoning. Any minute, armed guards might unlock the door and take one of them away. This was their last chance to show Carlos and his button men it was worthwhile to keep them around.

Nelson was nearing the end of the names he had flagged to take a closer look at. "OK, how about Greyson Talmadge?"

"Another officer of another multi-national. Works out of several places but seems to be based in the Dutch High Tech Campus in Eindhoven."

Nelson added, "He shows up on the boards of interesting companies."

"He was appointed to the FSA—Financial Stability Authority in Britain."

"I'm more interested in the association he has with a certain construction company based in Northern California."

"I saw that. It's the one that constructs and operates large datacenters."

"Exactly. All datacenters hit on F1E were either operated or constructed by them."

"But Greyson's a minor board member," noted Adam. "It looks like his participation is all about giving the company better access to the European market." He checked his research. "The secondary phone list doesn't show one call between Greyson and anyone at that company."

Nelson was back at the keyboard. "Who else did Greyson call?"

Adam was groggy with the swirl of details. "Ah...it looks like the usual spread of business and family contacts."

Nelson perused the list. "Yeah...I looked at this hours ago."

"We can drill into it but you said you wanted to concentrate on the primary list, the people Liam spoke to directly."

"I know but we've done that, twice." Nelson read the list of Greyson contacts again. "I thought the datacenter connection might be something."

"For Greyson, it's indirect, basically like holding stock."

Nelson returned to the list. "What about Soren Vincente? The name sounds familiar. He and Greyson had a couple calls. Do you have anything on him?"

"Haven't got that far on the secondary list."

"Check it out."

Both of them reengaged the search. Minutes later, Adam linked to a profile that raised his eyebrows. "Here's something you'll find interesting."

Nelson rolled his chair over to see.

Adam rested an elbow on the table and his weary head on his clenched fist. "Soren Vincente, blah, blah, blah, consultant and advisor..."

"I see it," snapped Nelson.

Adam played with him. "See what?"

Nelson read from the profile. "Consultant—to Steigbriar."

"Matches up with the post from *TigerLily*."

"I knew that name was familiar."

"It's a small world among paramilitaries, huh?"

Nelson's mind raced. "Too bad we don't have a third list..."

"You mean all of the people Soren Vincente talked with?"

"Precisely."

Burned out from the two-day marathon, Adam unloaded, "We don't need to go that far. We know Vicente talked with Greyson and Greyson talked with Bargeau, who's in a relationship with Christina Parish, the COO of Extasis, a company that contracted with In-Q-Tel to do some kind of Graphene work for black research called Project G. Did I miss anything?"

Nelson stared back at Adam. "Impressive, except you forgot to mention that Christina Parish contracted with Chimaera to handle Project G security and Chimaera's CEO was Aubrey Marks, the ex-wife of Richard Marks, who just so happens to be on special assignment for the Office of the Director of National Intelligence."

Adam pouted, "You done?"

"No. Whatever's going on, Richard Marks has partnered up with Owen Raedalous, a first-class prick who works for Homeland Security at the DOD as senior liaison. He was loaned out as Focal Point Officer on special assignment to coordinate information."

"What information?"

"What the fuck do you think we've been looking for?"

The men fell silent, exhaustion exposing the raw edge of exasperation. They were done with the situation but only had each other to take it out on.

Adam closed his eyes and rubbed his hands back over his hair. "Vicente talked with Greyson and Greyson talked with Bargeau."

Nelson dropped his gaze to the floor. "But the timing doesn't line up. It's not like one triggered the other."

"OK," reasoned Adam. "Then add in the other element."

"GETTIS."

"Your love note says Steigbriar is doing security for them."

Nelson struggled against fatigue to think it through. "And Greyson Talmadge talked with Soren Vicente."

Adam leaned back. "So what is GETTIS?"

"A European construction company, based out of London."

Adam leaned into his hacker hunch. "All right. Let's see what they're into."

Nelson rolled back to his workstation. "I'll check the news while you're getting inside."

Adam typed away. "You say that like you have no doubt I'll do it."

"If you can get into [Dstl], you can crack GETTIS."

It only took a few minutes for Nelson to turn up something in the British press. "I think we're onto something."

Adam hacked away. "What?"

"Here's an article from last year. It says GETTIS won a contract to build a datacenter in Manchester."

"Curious," observed Adam, layering on a stilted English accent. "Why Manchester of all places?"

"Manchester has the second highest number of colocation datacenter sites in Britain. London has the most with 62. It says here there are *194 colocation data centers in 54 areas of the United Kingdom*."

"And they need another one?"

"Apparently. And get this: the new Manchester D-C is going to have a sister site on the Isle of Man."

"Why not?" mused Adam. "Zero corporation tax, no capital gains tax, no wealth tax, no inheritance tax—and offshore banking is the primary economic sector. Does the article mention extra security for either site?"

"No, in fact, it doesn't say much."

Adam announced, "OK, I'm in."

Nelson rolled his chair over. "GETTIS?"

"Yeah, and guess who helped broker the financing for the Manchester project through *The City*."

Nelson's answer was indirect. "A board member of a certain Northern California company?"

"Greyson Talmadge," confirmed Adam.

"That's odd; that would mean the California construction company must have lost out on the deal."

"It's hard to tell. A whole consortium was involved in putting together the Manchester site; they mention its name, not the members."

"What about Vincente?"

"I don't see him yet but there's talk of Steigbriar."

"Doing what?"

"Subject matter experts on advanced security designs."

"Where does it mention that?"

"It's a line item on the proposal."

Nelson pointed to the screen. "The other items have links."

"It looks like the full architecture of the security design was kept secret, even from the construction contractor. How does that work?"

Nelson scanned the material. "Steigbriar tells GETTIS: *build me a room; I need it this size and here's the power and environmental requirements*. That's all GETTIS needs to know. Steigbriar fills in the room later. It's the same way the NSA kept the Camp Williams construction site compartmentalized."

"Camp Williams?"

"Beef Hollow, same thing."

Adam dug deeper through the directory structure. "The [Dstl] routing slip had six locations. You think this could be one of them?"

"Maybe this is EKQ—the European KQ. Is the Manchester site completed?"

"Should be. Occupancy was scheduled a couple months ago."

"Then Manchester should have been operational on the 1st. Is there any way to tell if any section of the F1E glitch screen contacted the Manchester site?"

Adam shook his head. "For that, we'd need more than a picture of what was happening."

"Wait," ordered Nelson. "Go back. What are those documents?"

Adam brought them up one by one into a previewer. "Looks like building permits, site surveys, inspection reports."

"Open up the permits."

Adam complied and the two of them studied several documents.

"You see what I see?" asked Nelson.

Adam was already on it. "One name appears on all permits."

"Douglas Kennigus."

"If he's so important, I'm surprised his name didn't show up on the GCHQ list. He's deeply involved but nobody called him?"

A quick search in another window yielded an overview. As Adam scanned the material, Nelson read snippets aloud. "Kennigus is a consulting advisor to many highly placed financial organizations...he's principally involved with a private equity investment fund headquartered in Basel, Switzerland."

From the text, Adam added, "He's also an advisor to the board of directors of BIS, The Bank for International Settlements..."

"The power behind the throne," commented Nelson.

"What do you mean?"

"Some claim global governance is being orchestrated through BIS. Every time the G20 meets, they have to report to BIS on progress in conforming to rules decided in Basel; a nation's lawmakers have no part in it."

"It says here BIS is '*an intergovernmental organization of central banks which fosters international monetary and financial cooperation and serves as a bank for central banks.*'"

"Don't you find it amazing that a private organization that answers to no national authority and allows no oversight, regulation, or transparency—such a private club should set the rules for all of the world's central banks? Especially since the central banks control a nation's monetary policy."

"The world's a smaller place," explained Adam. "With so much inter-national trade, you need standards and rules that cross borders."

"Yeah, it sounds important, perhaps important enough to at least coordinate and put it to a vote in the U.N. or Congress, not leave it up to closed-door committees in Switzerland. Some claim BIS has the first global currency."

"You're talking about SDRs, Special Drawing Rights," noted Adam.

"Exactly. BIS won't even use the Swiss Franc anymore; it has its own unit of account that all central banks and other organizations have to accept."

"There are exchange equity reasons why you wouldn't want to favor one nation's currency over another when central banks settle up with each other."

Nelson laughed in disbelief. "You talk about central banks like they're so systemic and necessary, like a law of nature or something. Did you ever think there may be better ways of organizing finance?"

"What?" huffed Adam. "You want everyone to trade gold and silver for everything?"

"Believe it or not, it's actually possible for governments to issue their own money without borrowing it from private cartels."

"Fiat money?" interjected Adam. "You want politics and government bureaucrats swinging the markets?"

"You mean our elected representatives? Why not? We give them the power to police us, tax us, send us to war, but issuing money would be dangerous?"

Adam balked. "You seriously believe fiat money works."

"Yeah. It worked for the Continental Army until the British got terrified of it and counterfeited it into oblivion. It worked for Lincoln to finance the Civil War when European bankers demanded obscene interest rates."

"Those were desperate situations."

"Oh, so desperate times call for *bad* solutions? The CBO estimates that by 2020, the U.S. will spend $1 trillion a year on interest on the debt. That sounds desperate. No wonder interest rates were forced so low for so long. Imagine what kind of desperation will happen if rates hit 20% like during the Carter Administration."

Adam reiterated, "Fiat money is not the way out."

"Then tell me, for some strange reason it works today for these offshore islands like the Isle of Man and Guernsey. If it's such a bad idea, why are the offshore tax havens of the powerful based on such a system?"

"Those island economies are not typical, that's why."

Nelson's head shook. "For someone who rails against the abuses of the 1% and hacks for people like RAPIER, you sure accept a lot of the cover story put out by the elites."

Adam tensed. "And for someone who claims to have seen the world and done so much, you sure are a sucker for conspiracies."

Nelson smiled. "'*Give me control of a nation's money and I care not who makes her laws.*'"

"I guess some dead guy said that."

"Yeah, one of the most famous bankers of all time said it 150 years ago, Amschel Rothschild."

"150 years?" Adam chuckled, "A different world. I have a quote too: '*The world is flat.*'"

"Oh, I forgot; the past is dead. Only the present is relevant."

Adam turned back to the keyboard. "Something like that."

"Martin Luther King is dead too; does that invalidate everything he said?"

"Let's get back to GETTIS."

Nelson paused then let it go. He turned and studied the document on the screen. "I find it interesting that a Swiss banker would be one of the names attached to every building permit issued by an official agency of the British government for the Manchester site."

"Kennigus must serve in another capacity. His bio says that he's an adviser in a lot of places."

Adam's guess fell flat with Nelson. "This permit looks nonstandard, something cooked up between GETTIS and some inside official."

"Maybe we don't normally see this kind of permit because of the classified sections."

"What's classified about a financial datacenter?" asked Nelson.

"Even you said Homeland Security considers them critical infrastructure. You told me DHS has Protective Security Advisors, PSAs, to support private sector partners in homeland security efforts."

"Yeah, but food and banking, dams and post offices are also critical infrastructure sectors; that doesn't mean building plans for a new post office or grocery store get classified."

"People don't try to hack grocery stores."

"And Swiss investment bankers have nothing to do with approving British secrets."

Adam's finger drummed a side of the keyboard. "So, what have we got?"

"We need to pursue Kennigus."

Adam hesitated. Neither of them knew where the tip might lead but there was one unknown that bothered him. "Agreed...but do we have time?"

Nelson checked the clock. It was an hour past the time he expected the button men to come for him. There was no telling why Carlos was holding off on contacting them this morning. All they could do was continue on and hope that their efforts would produce results before their time was up.

"Never mind the time," concluded Nelson. "Let's keep going."

Adam refocused what little energy he had left on the workstation before him. "All right. Kennigus. What's first? Business locations?"

Nelson went with his gut. "No. You said he's an adviser to many organizations but doesn't seem to be based anywhere. If I was going to break in somewhere to find out more, first I'd burglarize his home office."

"OK, we go where he lives. Problem is, a guy like that probably has estates on four continents plus a getaway on an island someplace. Many home computers get turned off or slip into hibernation."

Nelson kept his edge. "Then let's hope the boxes are on or they're configured for wake-on-demand."

Nelson pushed off and rolled back to his workstation. It didn't take long to find out about the properties owned by Douglas Kennigus. But it did take another hour to narrow them down. Of the three properties identified, only one had computer network activity. Hacking through the wireless router that serviced the estate, Adam was able to collect cached network signatures from Kennigus' other two sites; neither one was currently active.

Nelson sat and watched. The operation was fully in Adam's hands. The level of hacking ability required for what was being attempted went far beyond anything Nelson was capable of. Nelson observed as Adam used signal boosters and WiFi hotspots in the area, then searched the hard drives of two home computers at the active site in vain.

"Nothing," Adam concluded. "He's definitely not using these for business." Adam shifted to another screen. "There's only one thing left."

"Wake-on-demand?" guessed Nelson.

"Right," confirmed Adam. "Let's hope the other sites are hibernating."

"He has the house outside Paris…"

"And the Lake Maggiore vacation place on the Italian/Swiss border."

"I'd hazard a guess there's no hotspots around the vacation house."

"Don't need it. I'll use one of the boxes in the first house; he's got them networked together." Adam tried both of the remaining locations. To their surprise, a computer at the vacation house woke up when asked to.

Adam got his second wind. "If nothing's there, this is going to be quick." Adam secured remote access then executed his custom disk analyzer.

A minute later, the analyzer stopped with zero results.

It looked as if the Kennigus lead had hit a dead end.

"Is that it?" asked Nelson.

"That's everything the tool can do. Now we browse the directory structure manually. The tool looks for specifics. Now's the time to be non-specific."

Nelson rolled in closer and studied the contents of the vacation home's computer one directory at a time. Once again, it didn't appear to be a work computer; the directory structure showed no signs of business organization.

For a few more minutes they searched. Then Adam paused over an image file. "What's that mean?"

"What?"

"The name of that JPEG."

Nelson followed Adam finger to the file; it was an image file called *buonanno.jpg*. "*Buon Anno*. That's Italian for *Happy New Year*."

Curious, Adam clicked on it. "Party time at the lake, huh?"

The image opened but the contents were confusing, not at all what they expected. The picture looked to have been taken with a cell phone. It was a quick capture of writing on a whiteboard. The writing appeared to be ad hoc notes meant to facilitate discussion at a meeting.

"What the hell? What kind of *Happy New Year* is that?"

Adam echoed the puzzlement. "It isn't *Auld Lang Syne* in Italian, is it?"

"Looks more like a recipe for alphabet stew."

"I recognize some of this." Adam grew excited.

Nelson leaned in and saw it too. "Oh wow, I think we hit pay dirt."

Adam copied the file and shuttled it through proxy servers to his local drive. There he processed the image to enhance and gamma-correct for clarity.

Once done, he displayed a blowup of the image.

Crudely sketched out with a blue marker, a dozen or more circles and squares, connected by lines, formed what resembled an organizational chart. Inside the circles and squares were abbreviations and words.

Nelson grabbed a tablet of paper and wrote them down.

Adam studied an enhanced corner of the photo closer. "There's a patio or terrace in the background. I don't think this was taken in an office."

Nelson noted the corner enlargement then returned to the abbreviations. "He probably had the meeting right there at the vacation house."

"I see mountains in the background," added Adam, punchy from hours at the keyboard. "It must have been a *summit* meeting."

Nelson ignored the humor. "What better place to keep things private."

"The white board is a mess," noted Adam.

"It looks more like a strategy session than a presentation."

"OK, but why take a photo of the board?"

"Maybe in case it got accidentally erased, Kennigus didn't want to lose what they had come up with."

"Whatever *that* is." Adam gazed at the list on Nelson's tablet of paper.

Nelson read down the symbols again. Some items were obvious and others could be guessed at—but the ones most intriguing were total enigmas. One thing was now sure: Kennigus was a valuable find.

They were onto something. Now, if they could only decipher it, maybe it would buy more time from Carlos. Nothing yet was sure. If the list didn't make sense to them, it also might not make sense to their captors.

GFSA
F1E
LSEC
HUSIGINT
SIFIs
G-SIBs
KEYSERV
QDE
ADAPT
NAMAGIRI
PARABRAH
SWEBOT
MIN-Z
STUBS

"Any way to check when the photo was taken?" asked Nelson

"Yeah…" Adam checked. "Last September."

Nelson took a pen and circled F1E on the list. "They had F1E on the board three months before it happened. Too bad there's no group photo."

Adam pointed, "And there's HUSIGINT, the same thing that was in the garbled email we found in the Davos lead from Carlos."

Nelson set the writing tablet on the table. "What else do we know?"

"We can assume G-SIB stands for Global Systemically Important Banks."

"Then SIFIs must be Systemically Important Financial Institutions." Nelson wrote it down. "OK, and some of these others we can guess at. If we assume there's such a thing as a Z supercomputer..."

"MIN-Z could be a component of Z, a process; somehow it relates."

Nelson pointed out SWEBOT. "And this? You should know that."

"I know about web bots. I don't know what a SWEBOT is."

"Let's assume it's some special variant of a bot."

"I hardly think the S stands for special."

"Me neither," agreed Nelson. "I meant it's different, it's enhanced."

As Nelson wrote, Adam considered another item and searched the internet. "This is strange—NAMAGIRI is the name of a Hindu goddess."

"That's odd," remarked Nelson. "What the hell has *that* got to do with F1E and supercomputers?"

Adam typed away at a feverish clip. "PARABRAH doesn't mean much stuck together like that but if you break it up, Para Brahman is also part of Hindu philosophy. It means the Highest Brahman, the Supreme Lord beyond Brahman."

"I'll take the bet it doesn't mean that here," concluded Nelson. "It must be a code word or a name of a subproject."

"Or one hell of an acronym. You see anything else?"

Nelson entertained a hunch. "We've got that routing slip with six locations. We're pretty sure the first letter is a site code..."

Adam was ahead of him. "That leaves KQ. If KEYSERV and QDE are related, that would mean each location has one K and one Q."

"KEYSERV could simply be the Key Server at the site."

"And QDE some kind of module attached to it." Adam was anxious to discover more but was drawing a blank. "I don't know about the rest. ADAPT seems too obvious, but that one probably *is* an acronym."

Thoughts of his tour of duty in Afghanistan returned to Nelson. "I've heard of ADAPT before—but it couldn't be what I'm thinking."

"Why not? What it is?"

Nelson considered his security oath. His assignment in Afghanistan had exposed him to classified materials. It made no difference if a decade had passed and the technology involved in the mission had gone mainstream or was at least publicly known. Operation participants were sworn never to admit what was worked on or when such work had been done.

If it ever got out how early the government had advanced capabilities, the public would realize with certainty that, as a matter of ongoing policy, whatever technology was allowed for general use was generations and orders of magnitude behind what was available for official black ops. But with his life on the line and messages of ETC betrayal coming from *TigerLily*, Nelson felt no qualms about sharing what he knew.

"The ADAPT I know about was a program sponsored by DARPA," began

Nelson. "I worked security for it out of Bagram Air Base."

"I didn't think DARPA did field research in a war zone."

"They hadn't since Vietnam. But this became a priority for some reason. The remote battlefields were perfect for what they needed to test."

"What was it?" asked Adam.

"An Adaptable Sensor System for active control arrays. At first they tried it out managing multiple UAVs doing ISR."

"You mean drones."

"Yeah, intelligence, surveillance, and reconnaissance for unmanned aerial vehicles flying different sectors at the same time."

"You said *at first*. What else were they using it on?"

"Perimeter security; sensors hidden at airfields or underground at key intersections of the base, built into the roads. Sensors on security vehicles."

"What exactly were they sensing?"

"That wasn't important," admitted Nelson. "You can make sensors go after whatever you want. The cool part was how the sensors communicated."

"How they took commands and sent back data?"

"No. How they communicated with *each other*."

"They had sensors arrays set up as a distributed network?"

"It went way beyond that. They recruited the top software developers for smartphones to work on the project. They wanted these guys to strip out the user interface from their smartphone apps. The concentration was on pushing the limits of collecting, organizing, storing, and sharing information."

"Sensor apps," concluded Adam.

"Yeah, but the same app that allowed for autonomous operation in one sensor also had to manage concurrent hive communication."

"Hive communication?"

"They wanted an unlimited number of sensors to act as individuals in some respects but be synchronized as a swarm, controlled as a single unit with mission parameters shared but distributed among them dynamically."

Adam thought a second then reached for Nelson's pen and circled one item on the writing tablet's list.

"SWEBOT," announced Adam. "What if the S stands for *swarm*?"

"Apply ADAPT to web bots," added Nelson. "*Swarm* web bots."

Just then, a heavy thump came from behind them.

Startled, they turned to hear the dead bolt lock disengage from the door.

No one had spoken to them through the speakers and yet, the time of reckoning had come. A commotion outside the door did not bode well.

Sensing the worst, Adam swung back to his keyboard and tapped one key.

51

0000 0011 0011

11:18 am GMT, Wednesday, December 13th

The door swung wide and muzzles of automatic rifles breached the threshold with deadly aim. Behind infrared laser scopes stood commandos of indistinct origin, their trigger-fingers on high alert. The men rushed the room and within moments secured it and the adjoining bathroom.

Nelson and Adam remained seated, their backs to the computer consoles. This didn't look like a visit from Carlos' button men but they couldn't be sure. From the way the men had rushed the basement, whatever was about to happen would soon be over.

The squad's point man barked, "Which one of you is Nelson Geiss?"

Nelson stood but kept silent.

The point man glanced at Adam then read a signal from a trooper exiting the bathroom after checking it. "I was told there would be three of you."

Nelson volunteered, "Zack Hollister was taken away yesterday. Who are you?"

The point man lowered his rifle. "Your travel agent. Let's go."

Adam stood and walked to the cot to retrieve the laptop.

The point man noticed the movement and snapped, "Everything stays. You two follow me."

"Where's Carlos?" asked Nelson, standing his ground.

"Who?" The point man had no patience.

"Carlos Guerro."

"I don't know anyone by that name. If you're talking about the people who kept you here, they're long gone."

"Gone?" Adam glanced up at the security camera near the ceiling.

The point man waved them out the door. "From what we've heard, everybody cleared out of here yesterday morning. They've had you on remote control from offshore for 24 hours at least, maybe longer."

"Do you know why they left?" asked Nelson.

"They were probably tipped off we were coming."

Adam revisited Nelson's earlier inquiry, "And who are you again?"

The point man tailed them out the door. "Your tour guide off this rock."

52

0000 0011 0100

8:32 pm CMT, Wednesday, December 13th

The feeder road was east of downtown San Marcos. The motel was set back off the main road. They decided to park around back so the motel would block a view of the car from I-35. The rental car was a liability; driving it, especially on Interstates, was an increasing risk. For now, they would stay put.

Aubrey sat on the bed and configured a newly bought tablet computer, The door opened and Katherine rushed in. Her trip to the San Marcos library had been brief; the library had a limited number of computers for short-term use by patrons without library cards. On the return trip, she told the taxi driver to let her out at the fast food restaurant down the street from the motel in case pick-ups and drop-offs were being tracked.

Aubrey looked up from her work. "Any news for *TigerLily*?"

Katherine paced with excitement. "Nelson's alive. He was rescued a few hours ago."

"By whom?"

"Unknown. They weren't in uniform and the plane that flew him out of Guernsey was unmarked."

"Any idea where they're taking him?"

"He was told Fort Meade—for debriefing."

Aubrey tensed. "Well, there's your answer. Richard and his crew found him somehow. It's fascinating they would take him there, isn't it?"

"Home of the U.S. Cyber Command..."

"Along with NSA Headquarters," added Aubrey.

"I know it's walking into the fire but it's better than being dead."

"You believe the threat of death was real?"

"One of his group is missing. He's presumed dead."

"How did he manage to get you the update?"

"They gave him a phone so he could link up with what's left of his crew."

"But you're not part of them. Won't they get suspicious?"

"ETCs allow extended contacts to draw in specialties he may need. Contacting someone else wouldn't look out of order if it's not direct. In this case, it's through *TigerLily*." Katherine took interest in the tablet computer. "Any problem using the fake ID?"

"No. I picked out the tablet and data plan; the whole thing went smooth."

Katherine shed her sweater. "Great. We have backup. If we get creative enough, maybe we can cut out some cell phones and library trips." Katherine noticed how grave Aubrey's demeanor had become. "What's wrong?"

Aubrey stared down at the tablet's screen. "Something's happened."

"What?" Concern rising, Katherine sat down.

"I was checking news sources for the D.C. area and found this…" Aubrey handed the tablet to Katherine.

At first, the headline was obscure. The article was no more than a paragraph, one of many obliged to be posted as a matter of course. Then Katherine realized what they were—the obituaries for the week.

Research Scientist Celebrated at Tribute

Ralston Z. Barnett, research scientist at the Nanomaterials Theory Institute, Center for Nanophase Materials Sciences at Oak Ridge National Laboratory, was remembered today at a tribute celebrating his years of service. The memorial was held at the Laboratory's Visitor Center and attended by Barnett's family, friends, and coworkers. Barnett passed away at home yesterday in his sleep. His passing is all the more difficult for those who knew him since he was not known to suffer from any chronic disorder. He will be laid to rest Monday at Creekside Memorial Park in a private ceremony.

Aubrey waited until Katherine absorbed the news.

"What do you think happened?"

Katherine handed the tablet back. "What good is it to guess?"

"We *have* to guess. We may be *next*."

A spinning web of connections drove Katherine towards guilt. "Isn't it obvious? It's right after the power outage."

"You think shutting down Max Engle was overreaching?"

"Only if he miscalculated how to cover his tracks."

"You're not blaming yourself, are you?" asked Aubrey.

"If I hadn't recorded that show…"

"Don't go there. He knew what kind of exposure he was risking."

"Did he? He was a scientist; this wasn't his field."

"What about my agent at the Hyatt and the recordings Barnett intercepted at Belle Haven? Any of those transfers could have been traced back to him. You're not to blame. This means they're getting closer to us. We need a plan."

Katherine sat. "How do we plan if we don't know what we're up against?"

"We know enough. We know how high it goes. We know they'll stop at nothing and they have resources we can't imagine."

Katherine jerked to her feet and paced to the window. "What's the end game? What do we hope to accomplish? We weren't a target until we started poking into their hive. It's clear, isn't it? Mind your own business and you won't get stung."

"It's too late to put the honey back. You know that. We have to try to make contact with Nelson, real contact. We need to know what he knows."

"He's back under their control; he can only divulge that in person."

"Then you need to arrange it."

"How? We can't go to him and his movements are under watch."

"Ask him. He may have a way we're not aware of."

Katherine bolstered her resolve. "All right, but you need to do something too. You have a field agent near D.C. We need another recording."

"You think that's possible anymore?"

Katherine stepped back to the bed. "If Richard and Owen are following their same pattern, then they're meeting in non-official places. They were recorded before; it can be done again. We need an update on what's going on."

Aubrey shook her head. "It's different now. The agent who got those recordings is dead. He was targeted because they know what he did."

"We don't know that. Did they find out how the recordings were done? Maybe they only discovered that information was being passed through the post office to the Senate Select Committee and he was involved."

"Either way, they're on their guard now. Even if he got close enough to record them once, it might be suicide to risk doing it again."

"We'll take whatever we can get. At least ask him."

Aubrey reached for the tablet. "All right. But it's probably going to be a one-shot thing."

Katherine looked down at the tablet and the obituary. Thoughts of the man she had worked for distressed her into near-silence. She could only add, "Then let's hope one is enough."

53

0000 0011 0101

2:48 pm EST, Saturday, December 16th

A slate gray sky hung over DIA Headquarters on Joint Base Anacostia-Bolling. Owen Raedalus exited the town car's rear door without speaking to his driver. At entrance security, he slowed for a badge check and biometric scan before striding down a side corridor that led to the John T. Hughes Library at the National Intelligence University.

The attendant expected his arrival and directed him inside the library to one of the specialty rooms, the map room. Once there, Owen found the space reserved for the hour. Upon entry, he discovered Richard Marks in suit and tie, browsing a computerized catalog while checking incoming phone messages.

Owen expressed surprise. "I thought we were meeting tomorrow, offsite."

Marks looked up and abandoned the catalog. "I changed my mind."

"Has something come up?"

"What we're dealing with is quite enough, don't you think?"

It was obvious but Owen confirmed, "You read the brief..."

"As much as I could stand," snapped Marks with no time or inclination to be delicate. "This ETC, this fallback position, was *your* plan. I thought the whole idea was to *insulate* us in case something went wrong. Explain to me how it now turns out to be the one thing that *has* gone wrong!"

"We didn't expect any of them to be leveraged like this."

"What *did* you expect? Once Nelson went rogue, did you think the NABs were going to get rid of your problem for you? Is that it? What kind of reactive clusterfuck are you presiding over?"

Marks' eruption merely fortified Owen's defenses. "The ETC, by design, was out of scope, therefore expendable. With only one cell involved, there was no reason not to see where it went."

"The problem is, they were designed not to go *anyplace*. I was assured they'd be inert unless we needed them *later*. If we didn't need them, you said there'd be no problem making them fade away with a job well done, one only *they* would ever know about."

"Their capture proved the worth of the dangle. As decoys, they did their job attracting interest. Even if compromised, they know nothing."

Marks fought to keep his anger contained. "You can't be sure of that, not after Guernsey. You weren't able to get CEIs on either one of them."

"The British and French were aware of the rescue. We couldn't risk deviating from the protocol NATO expected. The evacuation had to go to an official site. Fort Meade gave us the most latitude, but once there, normal procedures took over and supplanted ours."

"How much is known by non-sanctioned personnel?"

"Very little but non-project people got involved. What they know has been kept outside-the-box but some may be aware of its existence."

"And how, exactly, did *that* happen?"

"Nelson used Dystrom to transmit a personalized distress signal, the kind selected by every ETC member and registered at the start of operations. The signal meant nothing to the Brits looking into phone records so they sent it up the chain of command. Eventually, they asked us about it. That's how they verified it was Geiss who was communicating with Dystrom."

"You think someone in the British chain of command got suspicious?"

"As you know, by design, Nelson's signal followed no standard protocol. For ETCs, we don't share that with anyone. Once we acted on it, the Brits knew it was code but a variety they'd never seen before. Once we received it, we had to put all resources into bringing them back as soon as possible."

"But why to a base? We have enough private locations."

"The code was out there. We couldn't raise more suspicion. I had to bring them back by the book. Chemically-Enhanced Interrogations require a less-than-official debrief. That wasn't possible with nonsanctioned elements within GCHQ and who knows who else watching the recovery."

"Complications like this should have never happened. You assured me you'd manage it. Was I wrong assuming you could?"

Owen had no intention of being made out to be incompetent. Any insinuation that his plan was worse than flawed, that it was shallow, made him bristle. "Granted, at first, the ETC had no active mission other than to be held in reserve in case we needed cover. But that changed."

"Why?" demanded Marks.

"The opportunity arose."

"That's one way to tell it. The other way would be to admit that Nelson Geiss turned this hacker kid into a loose cannon you couldn't control."

"We wanted a true threat assessment. Nelson and Adam gave us that."

Marks growled a laugh. "Is that what you call it? A threat assessment?

"It wasn't planned but that's how it turned out. We know more now about who is after project plans and how they're going about it."

"You know shit!" snapped Marks. "I saw the forensics. The Guernsey computers were wiped clean before you got anything useful off them. Worse yet, you don't know *who* wiped them—the captors or the captives."

"I see no reason why Nelson or Adam would provide cover for people who killed Hollister and threatened them with the same."

"Maybe it's not about cover. It could be about denying you what you want. You and Nelson have never been friends; isn't that why you chose him for this in the first place?"

Owen ignored the reference. "We believe the wipe was laid in from the beginning by the captors to clean the site in case a rescue was attempted."

"Indulgent speculation. All you know is what Nelson and Adam told you at Fort Meade—*without* the benefit of properly extracted answers."

"So far, what they said checks out. We have flights. We have a stopover in Paris. We have surveillance footage both at the datacenter and Hato International Airport. No one makes moves like that without leaving a trail. I have people reconstructing it."

Marks paced in frustration. "Yeah, like the team you had visit that hilltop snack on Curacao. They found squat. The yacht, you couldn't ID, and the one Hummer Moab on the island is a rental and oddly enough, records claim it hasn't been rented recently. We know Carlos Guerro is not his real name and as far as your big fish—this *Alonzo Elijah Lutane*, are you kidding me? What a joke. As far as you know, these really could be actors hired by Beijing to divert our attention. At least we *know* China's been suspicious."

"It's only a matter of time and we'll crack through," insisted Owen.

"It's time you don't have."

Marks gathered up his phone and attaché case, preparing to leave. "We have two weeks. The project's final window has opened. Everything must be buttoned down. We need this to go away."

"We can't shut it down now. We have leads to follow up on."

"What good are leads at this point? Did you uncover anything with that lead Messare gave you, the one about *dassergill*?"

"Not yet, but we're working it…"

"Like everything else. You need more than leads; you need the kind of HUMINT you're not going to get before the end of the month."

"What about the recordings of our conversations that got sent to The Hill? What if those get through to someone else, some reporter? We don't know if that was done by the same people who were running the show in Guernsey or not. We *do* know it involved an agent from Chimaera."

"We took care of that."

"What's the chance he acted alone?"

"Anyone seriously after us won't go to the media. They don't want to join the circus. They need more. They need to get on the inside. Leaking our conversations as *proof* would go nowhere. Everything we've said can be explained away; it can't be divulged because it's classified. A leak now would be like yelling *UFO* in a crowded movie theatre—it would be worse than annoying and counterproductive; it'd be stupid."

"Maybe, but as far as we know, whoever's behind Lutane bought themselves a mole—someone *close*." Owen made sure to emphasize *close*.

Marks paused, the logic rattling him with second thoughts. Couched in Owen's assertion was an intimation all too clear, one that pointed to Aubrey Marks. Ever since her fishing expedition looking for evidence of infidelity, his ex-wife had inadvertently brought them nothing but trouble.

Although implied, her name was being thrown up at him again. If Owen thought raising her as an issue would weaken him to give into more hare-brained schemes, he was wrong. Marks would address the issue of Aubrey directly, with practical and dispassionate precision.

Marks was frank. "No one at Chimaera is inside-the-box so if there is a mole, it's not from there. As far as Aubrey, she's always been a problem."

"At this point, is she acting out of curiosity or malice?"

"We have to assume both. It wasn't my decision to send her on medical leave. That only gave her an excuse to drop out of sight, as I expected."

"She hasn't made following after her easy, despite our tools. At her post at Chimaera, at least we could have watched her more closely in one place."

Marks switched subjects from his ex-wife to something that would raise the heat on Owen. "Which only proves you don't have the resources to watch over active ETCs. If you did, we wouldn't have had that radio fiasco. You still can't explain how someone got information like that or who orchestrated the power outage that elevated the show to crazy cult status."

"The crazy part only helps us." Owen's defense turned it around, "Besides, the show was thin on specifics. Much was speculation, the kind anyone doing security for Extasis might have access to."

"You're back on Chimaera," sighed Marks.

"It was their agent that recorded us! How many more agents and recordings are out there? If there is a mole, we have to close it down!"

"What do you expect? A tiger team? Delta Force? No, wait, how about we see if the Agency's Special Activities Division can spare a few cycles. Face it. It's too late in the game. We can't involve anyone new."

"We don't have to," countered Owen.

Marks shook his head. "Steigbriar is purposed for project security; it's not a private force to clean up your messes. Each time we engage them, we have more explaining to do at the top. Our task is to keep the project as transparent as possible. Each of these episodes weakens our stealth."

"But we *have* to go after it," stressed Owen. "A mole could be biding his time, waiting for the right moment to interfere. Yeah, Nelson created a mess, but it might be the mess we were missing and needed to see."

Churning with thoughts of his ex-wife, Marks bolstered his composure and headed for the door. "Chase whatever you want but the ETC has to terminate. We can't afford more surprises."

Owen spun around, his mind full of options but even more questions. "You want both cells shut down? They're insulated; they don't know about each other. That was the whole point—a backup position."

"It won't do any good to shut down only Nelson's. You can't send him home with a pat on the back and a job well done. I don't trust your insulation. The other cell is bound to find out and wonder why they're still active."

Owen saw his plan unraveling. If both ETC cells were told to disband, that would leave him with no insurance. Without fall guys in place in case the master plan went wrong, Owen felt exposed. He had risked much by joining forces with Marks despite strong reservations about the global players involved. He'd worked hard to put the ETC cells in place. Despite the promise of a big payoff in the New Year, he needed more. He needed to know there was a way out if the project's final window closed on them. Presented with no other protection, he faced the one suitable resolution that remained.

"What if Nelson's cell was taken out?"

Marks halted, his expression grim. "You're suggesting…"

"Hollister is already a casualty. Suffering a couple more would solve your question about how much they know. Plus, the other cell would still be operational. We could lock them down for the remaining two weeks by using the casualties as an excuse to order them to shelter-in-place. That would solve the problem and leave our original fallback position still viable."

"How would you explain it outside the ETC?" asked Marks.

"Accidents and natural causes don't need to be explained. We already crossed that line at the Hyatt in D.C. This would be the same."

"And what about the quant? You'd have to include him."

"Of course. Given his ability and background, he'd be the most dangerous one if left unattended."

Marks gave it thought. "I already told you, Steigbriar is not here to clean up our messes. How are we supposed to justify asking them to step in again?"

Owen thought quickly. "We don't need a new justification. We'll say it's a continuation of what was started at the Hyatt."

"If we do this, it has to be the last time we use Steigbriar. I know for a fact they will not engage outside their global charter past the 31st."

"Fine. It won't take that long."

"All right but close the loop. I don't want this coming back on us."

Owen watched Marks open the door and take strides into the library. Mind racing, Owen stayed behind to collect himself. There was much to do. He needed to contact project security to arrange for three prejudicial terminations.

Dystrom in London would be the obvious first target. With Nelson and Adam about to be discharged from Fort Meade, an accident happening immediately to both of them might raise suspicion. Owen would have to give them a couple days to blend back into a routine before scheduling anything.

He needed a story to occupy their last days. Project plants at Fort Meade could brief them and say they had helped uncover an international criminal group based in Hong Kong that was attempting to set up an advanced system for hacking into the central banks of several nations. This group had infiltrated CIG+XM in order to position themselves close to Wall Street and had recruited operatives in Latin America to provide regional cover should their activities be detected. This should shift Nelson's focus off the project.

Nelson and Adam would be instructed to concentrate their attention on discovering the base of operations for the Hong Kong group, with the grand prize being the discovery of what entities were sponsoring it. That should keep them busy until Steigbriar supplied the final solution.

Turning his head with restless energy, Owen surveyed the map room. His gaze came to rest on the catalog console that Marks had been looking at. One entry in Marks' search results caught Owen's eye. Interested, he touched the screen to bring the item up. Another window opened.

A map of Atlas missile sites appeared.

Owen recognized the site numbers: 566-2, 566-3, 566-5, 566-6, 566-8, and 566-9. Parsed a slightly different way, the same numbers comprised the distress code Nelson had used. Connecting the dots with his eyes, Owen saw the distinctive loop that formed around Francis E. Warren Air Force Base, the city of Cheyenne, Wyoming, and the ranch of Nelson Geiss.

In Owen's eye, the loop appeared as one half of a bull's-eye. Now the other half needed to be drawn. One call would set that process in motion.

54

0000 0011 0110

6:43 pm EST, Monday, December 18th

The afterglow of sunset faded in a stormy Western sky. Outside Hangar 85 at Tipton Airport, an unmarked helicopter waited on the pad. Nelson Geiss sat in the back seat and watched a black SUV approach. It meant his wait was over. Minutes before, the pilot had gotten word the SUV was inbound and spun up rotors in preparation for takeoff.

Tipton was formerly a U.S. Army airfield, one of the military locations designated for privatization by the 1988 Base Realignment & Closure Act. Repurposed for general aviation use, Tipton had no scheduled airline, commuter, or cargo service and yet it seemed officially busy nonetheless. No doubt the location had something to do with its popularity. A short drive down the Patuxent Freeway MD 32 was NSA Headquarters.

The SUV completed the quick trip through Fort Meade to Tipton's Hangar 85. Adam Perez was led from the rear seat by a dark-suited agent and escorted to a seat next to Geiss. A second agent stood guard at the pad's perimeter. After a quick buckle-in, Adam watched the helicopter's door shut. A moment later, the bird lifted with sudden purpose and jetted forward.

Nelson nodded a hello to Adam and Adam returned the same. The noise of jet-powered flight gave them an excuse not to talk. In fact, they had much to say but both knew none of it should be overheard. The flight to New York would take over an hour. Whatever they needed to share would wait until then.

Compared to commercial aircraft flying out of BWI Marshall Airport, their flight altitude was low. The unusual vantage point hypnotized with a rush of city lights and traffic arterials that glowed in snaking stripes of red and white.

For Nelson, the time was spent in reflection on haunting old business and disturbing new news. Sense memories of stealth helicopter night-rides in Afghanistan added to the mix. The only relief was the fact that the tedium of four days in debrief blurred to insignificance with the motion outside the window. The next thing was either rushing towards them or they were rushing towards it. The distinction was paramount. Staying focused was imperative. They were beyond failsafe now. For Nelson, the only way out was through.

Reaching new coordinates, the helicopter banked on a more northeast vector along its plotted course. As level as the ride was, for Adam it was a rollercoaster. He'd been overwhelmed by events of the past week. Everything he thought he knew or wanted was in question. To dwell on the rising chaos of what might come next held a morbid fascination and yet, the more he gravitated towards it, the more its allure merged with the perilous.

He never could have predicted that a second job to pay off student loans would set him off on such a turbulent path. But the immediate turmoil wasn't his main concern. He worried where all of this was headed. The possibilities that came to mind gave no comfort. Their arrival in New York couldn't come soon enough. Then again, there was every reason to want the ride to never end.

Ready or not, they sat as the helicopter made a beeline approach to Lower Manhattan by flying up the Hudson River's Upper Bay, threading the needle between the Statue of Liberty and Governors Island. A few minutes later, the two of them shared a taxi from the Downtown Manhattan Heliport.

The driver asked, "Where to?"

Nelson gave him Adam's address. Their ride uptown provided no decompression from the tension. For both, the cold city streets were as much wistful as foreboding, the bundled pedestrians otherworldly. Their ignorance of the real machinations that silently operated around them appeared deeper now; the scope of influence such schemes had on them more obvious. For Nelson and Adam, the beauty of knowing was offset by the horror of the emerging truth. Any perspective beyond ignorance offered a tacit hope that one would find a way to overcome or rise above it.

Such a feeling had possessed Nelson only a few times in his long career. He recognized it as a state of shock that masked itself as a sixth sense, a sense that made one believe it was possible to see the plans behind the design. Now Nelson recognized it as a false sense, fated to be delusional.

Adam collected a week's worth of mail from the lobby before leading Nelson up to the second floor. Once inside, Nelson kept his coat on.

Adam dropped the clutch of mail and settled in.

"Let's take a walk," suggested Nelson; his nonchalance belied insistence.

Adam stopped mid-motion, prepared to complain, then looked around. Their time away provided opportunities for bugs to be planted in places they'd never find. Adam pulled his coat back on and followed Nelson outside. They headed towards Central Park along frosty sidewalks disturbed by only the occasional passerby.

"How do I clean my place?" asked Adam.

Nelson was blunt. "You don't."

"Can't you do a sweep or something?"

"Wouldn't do any good. If they want to listen in, they'll find a way."

Agitation added energy to Adam's steps. "Then I'll move."

"They'll know that too."

"It doesn't fucking matter. I'm out of it anyway."

Nelson ignored the announcement. "What did you tell them?"

Adam gave a laugh. "You want everything that went on all four days?"

"They debriefed us separately for a reason. I need to know."

"I told them what happened. That's all."

"What did you say about the computers?"

"What about them?"

"They were all wiped. They didn't find a remote trigger. Was that you?"

"They'll never know." Adam's statement of fact was read as a confession.

"It *was* you. When did you have the time?"

"It only took one keystroke," admitted Adam, showing some pride.

"One key to do what?"

"Overwrite storage with random ones and zeroes. It's malware I wrote in college. I was going to hand it over to RAPIER but never got around to it." Adam added with relish, "I call it *SUCBAR*. It's gives you a *FUBAR*, *Fucked Up Beyond All Recognition*, and leaves nothing in storage or memory. It is *Success Beyond All Recognition*."

"How is *that* success? We don't have any of the data."

"Sure we do." Adam's gaze was telling. "I put everything in a safe place."

"A safe place..." Nelson's repetition became a question.

"Yeah, you know—our *safe place*. One keystroke can do a lot."

Adam's emphasis confirmed it. Nelson thought of the *dassergill* subpage hidden beneath the life coach's webpage that he had trained Adam to use early on. On the site, sunbursts and flowers were the backdrop to inspiration. And now so much more. Nelson was impressed that Adam had remembered.

"Why didn't you tell me?" asked Nelson.

"Couldn't take the chance of being overheard."

"You transferred everything?"

"Yeah, for what it's worth."

"What do you mean?"

"On the last day of the debrief, they told me all that Guernsey crap was planted to throw us off track. Carlos and Lutane, whoever they were, they wanted us to look in the wrong direction, away from them."

Nelson dug hands in his pockets. "They told me that too. They said we're supposed to be looking in Hong Kong."

"Yeah, some scheme to rip off the central banks. You believe that?"

"Even if it's true, it doesn't mean we weren't onto something."

"How so?"

"Maybe some hacker really *is* trying to siphon off funds from the central banks. Does that make the meeting in Lake Maggiore any less real?"

"That leaves you with a problem."

"Me?"

"You have to decide what's the real diversion, Guernsey or the debrief."

"That's *our* problem."

"Oh no, I told you, I'm out of it."

"Why, because you say so?"

"I'm done with this. I missed my quant test. I don't know what the fuck is going on. The only thing certain is, if I stick around, it's not going to get any better. It's guaranteed, I'm not going to pay off any student loans this way."

"After all you've seen, that's all this is about for you?"

"As far as I know, it's the only thing that's real."

"You want what's real? First day of debrief, I got word from Dystrom that Greyson Talmadge was kidnapped off the Isle of Man. Intel checked out airplane and boat traffic within a time window after the kidnapping. There were three escape possibilities. A ferry option was least likely and too conspicuous; the private plane had made similar trips before. That left a private boat to Carrickfergus, a one-off private excursion and most suspect."

"So? What does that prove?" asked Adam.

"Someone is already acting on the information we found."

"OK, but you said, just because it's real doesn't mean it *isn't* a diversion."

Nelson pressed on. "On the second day of debrief, I got word that a country house near Woodburn Forest had been locked down with lots of activity around it. Police weren't letting anyone near; government agencies brought in a special forensics team. Dystrom said he got confirmation Greyson Talmadge was tortured in that house and killed. Woodburn is near Carrickfergus."

Adam walked on. "Shit happens. OK, so what?"

Nelson grabbed Adam's arm to stop him. "The third day of debrief, I tried to contact Dystrom. He wasn't available. No call back. The last day of debrief, I was told Dystrom was in a car accident. He didn't make it."

"You think that's suspicious."

"It wasn't an accident," declared Nelson.

"Even if you're right, you don't know who did it. It could be Lutane or who knows, maybe it's your friends at Fort Meade. Is there someone else?"

Nelson gave it thought. "I don't know."

"Even more reason to leave this shit alone."

"Not now. We're onto something."

"Yeah, and whatever it is, we're not supposed to go there."

"I thought this kind of thing was *juice* for you."

"Suicide is not an adventure. You want to walk into the minefield at night? Go ahead."

"They're not going to let you turn your back on this."

"I'm nobody," Adam asserted. "You're the agent, the operative, the asset, whatever the fuck you call it."

"This month isn't over and you've seen too much. You can hurt them."

"Really? And what do you expect me to do?"

"Stay together. It's our only chance."

"A chance at what? This isn't about getting the truth anymore. The way you talk, the best we can hope for is surviving."

"Would that be so bad?"

Adam said nothing.

Nelson added, "New Year's is two weeks away. From what I've heard, whatever's supposed to happen will be over by then."

"Whatever it is, we have no part in it. It can end now. We walk away."

"We can't. We need to hang on, as least until January 1st. It's the only way they'll keep us in the picture. If we do what they say, even if we're a potential threat, we're manageable. Otherwise we become an unacceptable unknown. I know them. Risk protocols demand they assume any unknowns are liabilities."

"And after New Year's, then what? Will we know *any less* by then?"

"No, but it may not matter what we know by then."

"Meaning what?"

Nelson raised his collar to protect against the icy breeze. "You figure it out. You're the quant."

"No. Thanks to this shit, I'm not."

"You can always take the test later if that's what you want. I don't think it is. You want something more than being some billionaire's slave-brain."

"If it pays well, why not? Aren't *those* the correct values to have?" Adam drew in closer. "Besides, what *should* I be doing? Saving the world like *you*? Is that what you think *you're* doing? You don't have a clue what's going on."

"Like you when you hacked into the Archives. But that didn't matter, did it? All you needed to know was that they were keeping something from you, something that could be important. It's no different now."

"*Now* people are dying," Adam shot back.

"That's only an indication how important the thing is they're hiding."

"Maybe they hide it with good reason. What if we don't need to know?"

"You can try to convince me of that. You'll never convince MUTEX."

"Don't start with that. I told you, I'm out of it."

Adam turned to walk away, heading back towards his apartment.

Nelson caught him by the arm. Nelson's hand slid up into Adam's right armpit where it grabbed flesh. Adam winced in pain.

"Is that sore?" asked Nelson.

Adam stopped. "What the hell are you doing?"

"Do you have a sore spot in your right armpit? That's all I want to know."

Adam hadn't fully realized it until then. "Yeah, I guess so."

Nelson let go. "So do I."

Adam stood in place, his impulse to leave suddenly gone.

Nelson stepped closer. "It's where they implanted the RFID chip."

"A tracking chip?" Adam's concern raced into anxiety.

"They must have done it while we slept. It might do more than track us. It could be monitors, time-release substances—termination capsules."

"They can kill us by remote control?"

Nelson let go of Adam's arm. "You still want to walk away?"

55

0000 0011 0111

7:43 pm CST, Monday, December 18th

Katherine steered the car into the motel parking lot and pulled into an empty space. She shut off the engine and a stark silence surrounded her. The certainty and peace of the quiet gave her pause. She took a moment, sat and simply enjoyed a modicum of relief.

Renting the car with her fake ID had gone off without a hitch. There was always a chance that such a resource would be compromised. Unfortunately, the only one way to tell was to use it and find out. The result might spring a trap. Regardless, they had to take the risk. Aubrey's car from D.C. had outlived its usefulness. Chances that it might be tracked were too high to travel in it anymore. And yet, they needed to move on.

Thanks to the fake ID, they now had new wheels to take them away.

Katherine took one more deep breath then exited the car and entered the motel room. She expected to find Aubrey but the room was empty.

Stepping through it, Katherine revisited their plan. She would go rent another car while Aubrey ditched the old one. They had decided on a spot behind the public storage units nearby. The location was out-of-the-way and a place where a car might stay parked for days without raising concern.

Katherine checked the time. There was no sense waiting around; giving Aubrey more time might give someone more opportunity to compound their problems. It would be prudent to see if the other car was parked where they'd planned to leave it. If it was there, then she would look for Aubrey.

Reaching behind a nightstand to her duct-taped hiding place, Katherine grabbed her Glock 36. She stuffed it in her waistband beneath her coat and hurried into the night. She took the shortcut behind the fast food place and avoided the sidewalks of the feeder road.

Minutes later, she rounded a corner of a storage unit to find Aubrey's rental car parked in the distance. It appeared undisturbed but in the half-light from the fast food restaurant's road sign it was hard to tell.

Katherine made her approach with one hand poised near her Glock. Checking her surroundings, she inched closer. It appeared no one was in the car. Unhurried but determined, she approached the driver's side door.

Looking through the window, she could see Aubrey slumped to her right, away from the steering wheel, in a motionless heap, stretched across the seats. A maroon spatter of blood streaked the glass. In the dark it was hard to tell but it looked like a pistol was loosely entwined in the fingers of her right hand.

Katherine drew her gun and pressed it down to her side with forefinger primed outside the trigger guard. Adrenaline kicking in, she darted a defensive glance to prime spots in the surrounding area. No one was in the area. Nothing else was out of place. Whoever had done this was long gone.

Katherine tried the driver side door. It was locked. Aubrey was obviously dead. Or was she? To call the police or ambulance now might be futile, or it might save her life. Either way, the authorities would want to know more. Going on the record with their identities and location would only make them sitting ducks for the unseen forces behind this. Their deaths would only be delayed, not defeated.

Katherine wiped the door handle clean and then remembered she had shared this car with Aubrey for days. If anyone dusted the vehicle, it was a certainty that both their prints were all over it, inside and out. If Katherine left the scene, it might implicate her if forensics or the autopsy proved it wasn't a suicide. But what choice did she have?

She repositioned herself for another perspective through the front window. From that vantage point, Aubrey's wound appeared to be dead-center in the chest. Her head was intact but a chest wound was bad enough.

Katherine wavered but a quick calculation left her no recourse. Given the fact that Aubrey was most likely dead, and going to the authorities was out of the question, and whoever had engineered the hit had made it look like a suicide, there was only one thing to do.

Katherine backed away. She needed to make saving herself a priority. If she left now, before being spotted, the authorities would probably conclude it was a suicide. Given Aubrey's recent troubles, the tragic back story as motivation was already in place. Besides, whoever did this wanted it to be a suicide—and they had their ways of making the authorities see it their way. The same cover they'd provide themselves would shelter Katherine.

Retracing her steps, Katherine returned to the motel, gathered up everything, and took off in the new rental car. Approaching the highway, she hesitated over which way to go. The onramp south was convenient so she took it. Accelerating to cruising speed, she let the road signs tell her where she was going. San Antonio was not that far away.

For ten minutes she drove with a constant watch on the rearview mirrors. As fast as the scenery sped by, her mind raced to understand. How had Aubrey been found? What was it that had given her away? Was it the car? Had they kept it a day too long? Had she turned down the wrong street at the wrong time and been discovered?

Aubrey was supposed to ditch the car by the storage units; had she erred by first making an unplanned trip somewhere else? If so, where could she have gone, and why? Aubrey had also bought the tablet computer. Did something in that transaction trip her up?

After all the precautions both of them had taken, to be found like this was testament to what they were up against. Even using professional avoidance tools and techniques, they had been located and one of them dealt with.

Looking ahead, what would become of Aubrey's agent now that she was gone? Should he be told what had happened—or perhaps he was already compromised. Maybe contact with *him* was the catalytic connection that had sealed Aubrey's fate.

Regardless, what did the turn of events mean for Katherine's safety? Were the hit men aware they were traveling together? Did they even care? Was their job completed or only half-done? Were they only targeting Aubrey or were they also the ones who had taken out Barnett? Would they follow her now, patient enough to see where she would go before they finished the job?

Katherine hated being so creative at guessing all that could go wrong when it was not as obvious how to make things right. She stayed at the speed limit and used the sameness of the road to level her emotions. It did no good. On her right, a sign signaled drivers that the exit to a rest area was one mile ahead. Following a gut feeling, she took the next exit and parked at the far end of a row of empty parking places.

The rest area was empty of travelers. The isolation weighed on Katherine. As much as it was desirable to be alone, being remote from others carried with it an undeniable vulnerability. Aubrey had been in a secluded spot too.

Katherine parked perpendicular to the parking space lines and left the engine running. If anyone approached, she'd take off and see if they followed. Turning to the back seat, she rummaged through things from the motel room. Along with her backpack were Aubrey's things including the tablet computer.

Playing a hunch, Katherine tapped the system out of hibernation and checked for messages. Aubrey had one. It was from her agent in D.C.

> *"Recording complete. Subject's side of phone conversation.*
> *3:28 pm, December 16th. Audio attached. Transcript as follows:*
> *'This is Owen...yeah. There's another part to the same job.*
> *We have a rogue cell to shut down—project safety priority.*
> *The point man is Nelson Geiss.*
> *I need you to start with his man in London.*
> *Give the rest a few days to settle in, then finish it like before...*
> *OK. Good.'"*

Katherine reread the message, not for meaning but for emphasis. The meaning for her was clear enough—she needed to contact Nelson right away. But in the moment, she had to pause.

The silence surrounding her in the empty car no longer conveyed something peaceful and comforting. Now it was the silence of a future fate, hiding but drawing nearer. Recurring thoughts of Aubrey brought tears to her eyes. To avoid breaking down, she turned her glance to the roadway and the indifferent cars rushing by. It was time to join them.

56

0000 0011 1000

6:58 am EST, Tuesday, December 19th

Adam navigated through a frosty sidewalk bustle. Surreal as it was, another business day was lurching to life in wintertime Manhattan. The prospect of being followed sharpened his senses but left him numb with anxiety and foreboding. Like it or not, more primal considerations than those offered by the workaday world were now in focus as his new normalcy.

Ducking into the lobby of Nelson's hotel, Adam stepped into an elevator and found respite in the ride to Nelson's floor. The day ahead would be hectic. He welcomed any brief calm and seclusion. Besides returning to a job he wasn't sure he still had or even wanted, he was left with only one certainty—his day would be preoccupied with self-preservation.

Nelson answered the door, prepared to leave. "You look like shit."

Adam winced. "Where the hell are you going? I have to get to work."

Nelson brushed by him, headed down the hall. "Something's come up."

Energy already flagging, Adam turned, desperate for any excuse not to follow. "Fucking-A, what now?" His mumbles went unanswered.

Nelson led him to another floor and into the hotel's gym. The place was vacant. Nelson made strides past the equipment and entered a sauna room.

Adam followed, more curious than obedient, less encouraged than defiant. Nelson closed the door, shutting them inside with the sauna turned off. Saturated with dread and disgust, Adam sunk into a snide appraisal.

"You're going to start rumors about us."

Nelson sat down on the wooden bench. "Don't get your hopes up."

Huffing out a laugh, Adam shook his head in resignation and took a seat opposite the older man. "You crack me up with this spy shit."

"Having an attitude problem today?" Nelson was humorless.

Adam read the intensity coming his way. Nelson was stone-cold serious. Adam dropped the cocky facade and stared back. "I get that way when someone sticks a suicide chip in me after a four-day interrogation."

"It's not a suicide chip," Nelson corrected.

"Oh, OK, a *homicide* chip, like it makes a big frickin' difference."

Intent on his sense of urgency, Nelson produced a UPS letter envelope from his coat's inner lining. "Two things happened last night after we split. I got a message from *TigerLily*—and I got this."

Adam took hold of the envelope and looked inside. "What is it?"

"Take it out," ordered Nelson, anxious to get on with it.

Adam inspected an object sandwiched between ultra-smooth sheets of cellophane. He saw an intricate design, a moiré pattern of curved black lines forming an oval the size of an egg. Shaking the object into his open hand, he made a guess but remained puzzled. "A temporary tattoo?"

Nelson tapped his upper arm by the bicep. "It goes here, on the same side as the armpit that hurts."

Adam gave the tattoo's design a closer look. It resembled a hi-tech industrial logo reinterpreted as Tā moko, the permanent body and face marking of the Māori peoples of New Zealand.

"Are you wearing one?" asked Adam.

"Yeah, but like yours, it won't be turned on for a couple of days."

Adam leaned back. "What are you talking about—*turned on*?"

Nelson hunched forward, driving home the point. "This was waiting for me when I got back to the hotel. The note inside said to wait for an explanation. An hour later, some guy claiming to be from a courier service delivered a small package to my room. Inside was this…"

Nelson shoved his coat's sleeve up from his dominant hand, exposing a wrist bracelet. Its unmarked design was two inches wide, paper thin, and composed of an intricate lattice weave of various metals.

Adam looked closely. It was coated in a deep burgundy resin-like layer flecked with flat, sand-sized, iridescent particles. The particle distribution was random but the orientation for all particles had the same slope.

Nelson moved his hand and watched Adam's reaction. As the wrist turned, the tiny particles thought to be embedded in the resin reoriented en masse.

Adam gaped, "How is it doing that…I mean, *what* is it doing?"

"It aligns itself to magnetic north when I move."

"Why?"

"It's a comm-device. North gives it a vector to establish coordinates."

"So what is it? Some new military smart phone?"

"I don't know. I was told it doesn't link with satellites. It uses low frequencies and the ionosphere to reach over the horizon—no satellites or cell towers needed. Normal surveillance intercepts won't see it."

"No way. That shit doesn't work, does it? Didn't the Navy have trouble using ELF to talk with their submarines?"

"I know. Extremely Low Frequencies require humongous antennas."

"Yeah, the things have to be thousands of miles long, like from here to L.A. To make something like that work, the antenna would have to match the length of the frequency. We both know that's not going to happen."

"Exactly what *I* said last night, right before I was warned not to start claiming that anything is impossible. I was also reminded that one way or another, there'll always be technological equivalents that approximate magic. As it turns out, this thing finds the necessary equivalent by using the nervous system of the human body as the antenna."

"No way." Adam checked Nelson's expression to be sure he was serious.

"The nerves of the human body, all combined, are long enough to stretch around the Earth two and a half times. That's at least twenty-four times the antenna length needed to do the job."

"Maybe, but how is that possible?"

"Bioelectronics. I was also told, the more a body is grounded to the Earth, the better it works. Grounding isn't necessary to make it operational but it can use the Earth to boost the signal before completing a circuit with the antenna. Oh, and this thing uses the human body for its power source."

Adam touched it, glancing his fingers over the highly-buffed sheen. "You really used this to talk to somebody?"

Nelson nodded. "Last night."

"Where's the microphone and speaker?"

"It doesn't need a speaker. It uses microwaves and voice-to-skull technology. I'm wearing it so I'm the only one who can hear it."

"You're saying it broadcasts the call right into your head?"

"Look up the patent, granted in 1989. They've improved on it since then."

"What about the transmission rate? I thought ELF messages could only manage a few characters per minute. How can you talk like that?"

"The conversation was normal. I don't know how it's done," admitted Nelson. "Something about ELF being the carrier wave but the data are modulated onto the carrier using something else."

"Who told you all this?"

"The same guy who sent the tattoos."

"A *guy*? You don't know who he is?"

Nelson paused, "He wouldn't give his name, only a number—1021."

"No name, just a number?" Adam rocked back, his face igniting with a grin. "What the fuck? You're kidding, right? And you believe this shit?"

Nelson lowered his sleeve over the wristband. "I don't have to believe it. I'm all about viable options, no matter where they come from."

"And you have confidence in that?"

"It's not hard to understand. He wants to help but he needs to remain anonymous. He says he's in the position to know things. A practical demonstration speaks for itself. The fact is, the damned thing works."

"OK, so he can access some classified toys. That doesn't make him believable or trustworthy."

"I trust *TigerLily*. They're on the same page. Too many things line up."

"So why 1021; why *that* number? What the hell does it mean?"

"You're the quant. I thought you'd know."

"Yeah, sure. And what about the tattoo? What magic does that do?"

"He said it'll cancel out the responder signal sent from the RFID chip, kind of like noise-canceling headphones. When he activates it in a couple of days, we'll be free to leave the city. If we use the tattoos, we'll drop off the *shadow-grid,* a general name used by the *Dark Eye Network.*"

"*Dark Eye?*"

"Shadow surveillance in all of its forms, done off-book by private contractors so it can't be traced to a government agency. The DEN doesn't bother with closed-door FISA courts. They do what it takes."

Adam examined the tattoo. "Won't this piss them off? What about those *risk protocols* you talked about? You know, *unknowns are liabilities?*"

"This buys us time. If they come after us, they'll be swinging in the dark."

"Maybe, but if 1021 is so helpful, why doesn't he turn it on now?"

"He didn't say. Perhaps we have a few days before they come after us."

"Who's coming?"

"The same people who debriefed us. That's the main thing he and *TigerLily* both stressed. The tracking chips are not our biggest problem."

Adam turned pale. "They're going to kill us?"

Nelson's nod was shallow and brief. "They have orders to shut us down. Until then, everything must run smoothly, according to their plan. If anything deviates from what they expect, they'll accelerate the schedule."

"Why let us go if they're going to kill us?"

"It has to look like an accident—like Dystrom. First they needed to pump us for information. They were hoping to find out more about what went on with Carlos on Guernsey. After Fort Meade, we're fair game."

Adam looked down at the tattoo in his hand. "So some guy, out of the blue, wants to help us. He says we're OK once this thing is turned on. I mean, they won't be able to activate the suicide chip."

"I told you, the chip's not like that. It can't kill us. He said it's only for tracking. The crazy thing is—he said they didn't chip us at the debriefing."

Adam felt his armpit. "What about the soreness? Then why the tattoo?"

Nelson paused, anticipating Adam's reaction. "They want us to be aware of the chip—the one *already* inside of us; the one that's been there for a while."

"When did *that* happen?"

"The way I heard it, most people are already tagged with *smartdust.*"

"What the hell is *smartdust?*"

"It goes by many names. It's a tiny RFID chip, the size of finely ground pepper. It's tiny enough to sprinkle around like glitter."

"So what's with the soreness?"

"We were dusted quite a while ago. But no one is supposed to know. Except now, they *want* us to know we're being tracked. They figure it'll make us less likely to do anything out of line in the last few days before they shut us down. The soreness was done to raise our suspicion of being tracked."

"I don't know," remarked Adam, his head spinning with revelations. "This is too bizarre. It feels like we're being punk'd or something."

"It gets stranger. The guy on the phone said every human body has a unique electromagnetic signal, like a fingerprint. The smartdust encodes our natural signal and registers it internally on the chip. Transponder signals can be targeted from orbit and relayed by satellite."

Adam shook his head. "Maybe they're researching this stuff, but they couldn't have rolled something like this out over the whole population."

"Would it be so hard to do?"

"According to 1021, you said nearly everyone in the country has one of these dust particles inside of them, is that it?"

"That's what he said. It's easy enough to include a speck of smartdust inside the immunization shots for children. Tag them while they're young. For anyone who missed their shots as a kid, yearly flu shots are pumped out."

Adam countered, "They're trying to avoid a pandemic."

"Maybe, and while you're at it, get yourself tagged. What you don't know won't hurt you. Why do you think there's a marketing blitz to convince people to get flu shots each year? The CDC knows those shots are a shot in the dark. They don't match the strain of influenza going around. The way it works, they can't. Viruses mutate too quickly. It takes too long to isolate the strain and manufacture enough vaccine. Dark Eye won't pass up an opportunity. Flu shots are more about dispensing smartdust upgrades and rewarding cooperating corporations with pharmaceutical profits than it is about influenza."

"That's some wild paranoia," countered Adam. "They don't barcode and tag every dose of vaccine and cross-index it with someone's identity."

"They don't have to. Smartdust uses a passive registration system. The chip that winds up inside of you gets associated to you easily enough after-the-fact, through commerce. Every time you use an ATM or go through an airport scanner, take an eye test to get your driver's license or drive on a toll road, the chip and your ID are reverified and the master database updated."

Adam grinned. "You see what they're doing, don't you?"

"What?" Nelson was thrown off by the reaction.

"They know how you follow conspiracy theories so they're playing to it. You don't know what's going on and we're not likely to figure it out spinning our wheels on wacko bullshit. Somebody wants you dazed and confused."

Nelson tapped the arm wearing the wristband. "Is this bullshit? This works. I used it last night."

"And that's another thing. Why would somebody send you a super secret advanced prototype just so they could relay a warning message?"

"He thinks we're onto something and wants us protected."

"Protected? Somebody's going ape-shit when they find that missing."

"He said it was the only way to communicate and keep the transmission private. You're assuming it's only a prototype."

"ELF is no more private than any other RF medium."

"That's right. The privacy is in the encryption key."

"You don't need a fancy wristband to encrypt a message."

"Unless old-style encryption isn't good anymore."

"Here we go; another conspiracy theory."

Nelson grabbed Adam by the wrist. "Listen to me. It's not just this guy, 1021 or whatever the fuck he calls himself. I told you; I also got a message from *TigerLily*. She confirmed everything. She's risking her life to warn us. They *are* coming after us. We have at most a couple days to live unless we figure this out. Now we can sit here and blow all this off and wait and see what happens, or we can evaluate what they're telling us and decide how to use what they're giving us to take cover."

"I'm not spinning my wheels on stupid shit." Adam got up to leave.

Nelson held Adam's arm. "You know what happened to Hollister and Dystrom. You want to be a goddamn know-it-all? You'll be dead by the end of the week. What's it going to hurt to put on the stupid tattoo?"

"You haven't convinced me what good it would do."

"They won't be able to use the smartdust particles to track us."

"We'd still have to run and there's no place to go."

"You're sure of that?" Nelson stood and looked Adam eye-to-eye. "You have friends in RAPIER. I've heard rumors they have safe houses."

"Even if they do, why would they help us?"

"Why help MUTEX? Because the 1% is after him, that's why. Besides, aren't you the least bit curious to survive and find out where this goes?"

"Where *what* goes?"

"All the crap we've found so far. You know we're onto something. It's why we're a threat to them."

"If they want us shut down, as you say, we can't stop them. We're one cell against the whole apparatus."

"Spoken like someone educated to be powerless. Don't start thinking like another product of their system."

"No, that's right, I should charge up the hill with you. Honor and glory, is that it? You want to be a nameless star on a memorial wall? Count me out."

"And then what? If right now they said all's forgiven, you can go back to the life you had before, we'll leave you alone. Would that satisfy you?"

"I'd be alive."

"In a fantasy. They're not going to forgive and forget; you know too much and you have skills that can hurt them. You really can't wait to rush out of here and get back to humping it on the twenty-sixth floor? You're content slaving away in a rigged system making someone else the big money?"

"It's always been the same—crumbs at the table or out in the cold."

Reading Adam's hesitation as ambivalence, Nelson pressed a slip of folded paper into Adam's hand. "Go to this site and listen, listen to *all* of it."

Nelson let go of Adam's arm but Adam stayed in place. "What is it?"

"A dose of self-preservation. Something to inform your perspective."

"I won't have time for this today," objected Adam.

"Make time. I'll meet you after work. One way or the other, I need to know by the end of today—are you with me or not?"

57

0000 0011 1001

4:59 pm EST, Tuesday, December 19th

On a far wall, the digital tote board switched to 5 pm.

Adam looked up at the bright LED readout then back at the cluttered displays on his desk. His compulsion to repeat the same fleeting look at the lighted board had returned on the hour throughout the work day. The significance of his glance, slight as it was, was not lost on him. It reenacted the moment the glitch pattern had taken over computer screens.

By catching the change in time, he tried recapturing the feeling of that seminal moment. The actual moment was locked away, in the past, a place many thought would never change. But like everything else, he was learning how such things would forever recede and be reinterpreted.

Spending a day back at work, he saw it firsthand.

Since that day, business had returned to normal. Attention spans had contracted around the next big thing. For the bulk of the populace, even for those in positions of higher finance, the ones initially so disturbed by the glitch, nothing had been deduced, nothing was inferred, nothing was learned. The immediate game of taking-and-getting returned quickly enough to seduce the players back to the table with little regard to what had happened or how they might be affected.

Profits and pleasurable diversions ruled the day.

Adam swept his gaze across his desk in frustration. To one side of the keyboard, there was a pair of ear buds. He had placed an audio file on pause. This was the recording Nelson had told him to listen to. Throughout the day, Adam had managed to listen to it when he could. The effect was disturbing. Going back and forth between the ragged pace of work and what he heard on the audio file only heightened the disassociation he felt with his surroundings.

Listening to the file only steeped him further in the shadow world he had fallen into with Nelson. All the while throughout the day, his eyes beheld the frenzied world of short-term gain made possible by unbridled greed and a willing state of denial. Neither world was his now. If anything, he was a ghost moving between them, condemned to an unwanted fate no matter which world he decided to rejoin.

He marveled at how easy it had become to hide so much in plain sight. No wonder shadowy forces could pull off such a blatant pilot project across live markets in real time and get away with it. It reminded him of the advertised glitch in the Universal Trading Platform's Security Information Processor that presumably took down NASDAQ for three hours in 2013's *Flash Crash*.

Popular perception was a manufactured construct disseminated top-down, not a bottom-up consensus. The more one saw from the inside, the more such a concept was validated.

Minutes after F1E glitch events, the message had gone out via newswires, bloggers, and television talking heads reading prepared teleprompters— *Nothing to see here, everything is OK, go on with your lives, continue those routines narrowly defined for you so you don't interfere with grander designs you wouldn't understand anyway.* Media framed the reality. Anything outside of their frame should be discounted, marginalized, ignored, or ridiculed.

Every hour, every time Adam glanced up, he faced the same thing. He knew now; reliving such a moment was impossible, at least reliving it the way it had been. Now he had more on his mind. Any déjà vu he expected was incomplete. This time the glitch hadn't happened. This time so much more was at stake personally. Now he needed another decisive moment, one that was not so much a surprise as it was a revelation.

December 1st at 1 pm had marked the juncture, a narrow space in time that had momentarily lifted the veil between the method and the madness. Since then, Adam's world had been governed by a strange attractor, spinning it onward in ways he had not decided, couldn't control nor predict.

The glitch screens, clever as they were, only proved obvious clichés. One's eyes could be deceived. Very little was as it seemed. Then as now, one minute replaced another, a new hour began, and with it a calculated web of things continued to move in front of and behind the curtain. But this time the crazy pattern wasn't on the screen. This time he was living it.

Adam dropped his gaze to his desk to distract himself. The fact that the investment firm had taken him back after the unscheduled absence was a mixed blessing. Their leniency was more about them needing his skills than being indulgent with him. If today was any indication, no doubt they intended to work him sufficiently raw to make up for inconveniencing them.

If only quant school was as accommodating. When he contacted them, they said his failure to take the final exam was not their problem. Make-up exams were outside standard policy. Adam could petition the instructor directly but it was unlikely an exception would be given. Each test was specific. There was no guarantee that Adam wouldn't talk with someone who had taken the test. They couldn't take a chance and they wouldn't create a new test just for him.

Adam's gaze returned to the ear buds. He placed them in his ears and toggled back to the audio file placed on pause. He only had a couple minutes left to finish it. He clicked on play and returned to the interview by radio host Max Engle of an anonymous source with synthesized voice and secrets to tell.

"...so, over the last half hour, you haven't given your name and you wanted me to mask your voice. You must have reason to believe you'd be in danger for coming forward with this information."

The altered voice of the guest appeared to be female. She answered without hesitation. "Isn't that obvious?"

"Would you care to share how you know this?"

"That isn't important," stressed the woman. "What's important is that people realize the kind of technology that's being wielded behind the scenes by silos of power answerable to no one."

"It's obviously the kind of technology that's easy enough to hide under the guise of national security..."

"It's gone beyond that," snapped the woman's voice. "The technologies of true advantage are out of reach of such labels. When no one's watching, there's no reason to have to make up alibis."

Max Engle chuckled in cynical agreement with her point. "Even when we watch, we are told repeatedly we're not seeing what we see."

"I'm afraid that's happening again. Something vitally important is due to complete by the end of this month. What it is is being kept from us. It's a secret guarded by forces that extend beyond our borders and yet elements within our own intelligence services are cooperating with them."

"And yet you say command and control extends high up."

"Yes."

"It's hard to believe something run from the top, with such a broad scope, could simply be the unauthorized shenanigans of a few rogue agents."

"Hardly. I know for a fact that even the House Permanent Select Committee on Intelligence has been either blinded to this or compromised in other ways, effectively nullifying the committee's function."

Max Engle could be heard taking a puff off his cigarette. "Some might say your evidence of wrongdoing is thin. How would you answer your critics?"

"I'm not here to debate people who lack common sense or deductive imagination. F1E has never been adequately explained, even though emergency measures have been enacted behind the scenes. Psy-Ops and paramilitary contractors have been deployed and yet no one will say what for. Good people have been threatened. I don't have to know the whole plan to understand something is very wrong."

Max was still playing the devil's advocate. "Which is more to the point. Much of what you've presented is advanced research into things like computer systems, new materials, and encryption systems. There's no surprise there; everyone knows that kind of development goes on. Even studies into Graphene, synthetic crystals, or twisted light propagation of data streams are no surprise. That's not why I invited you on the show."

"I know. I mention the technology only to get people thinking about the capabilities behind it. I believe the opportunities for abuse are about to be exploited in ways that pose a danger to our fundamental institutions."

"You say you were told that strong AES encryption, in effect, the Rijndael Cipher, has been cracked. Just like when AES replaced DES, the Data

Encryption Standard that was cracked, this implies that AES has now been supplanted by something else. Do you agree? You haven't mentioned what if anything they've developed to take its place."

"Whenever systems and algorithms get fast and smart enough, it's logical to assume that eventually a new standard will take AES's place."

"And that's my question. Are you saying that AES has been cracked with nothing to replace it? What's the situation? Has strong encryption been defeated but a whole new way of encrypting is now being held in secret, presumably to be used by the privileged few?"

"The material I saw didn't say either way."

"Well, I can't fathom there not being a replacement standard if AES were no good anymore. If that were the case, secrecy would not be possible. There would be no way of securing data, at least not from those who had the AES decryption key."

"Maybe that is why this is such a tightly guarded secret."

"I should say so," Max emphasized. "As long as they were the only ones holding the key, all information would be open to them. But they would be vulnerable. If the key ever got out, all bets would be off."

"You know as well as anyone how well they keep secrets."

Max blew smoke, then added, "Some better than others. By design, no doubt. The trouble is, even with information like yours, so many people feel remote from the playing field. The powers that be have them convinced there's nothing they can do with the truth once they find it."

"Awareness has to be the first step," stressed the woman. "They will never be held responsible if we stay unaware of the designs unfolding around us."

"How true. And if this key, this decryption ability, should fall into the wrong hands, there's no telling what kind of world could be made from it."

"That's why I'm here," reiterated the woman. "Just think of the institutions that depend on AES. Governments, financial institutions, corporations, data networks universally rely on the security of private data. Being in the position to tap into that at will would grant someone an incredible advantage over all systems and processes worldwide. Gaining possession of such a tool would mean nothing less than anointing oneself as the ultimate insider."

"Exactly," commented Max with typical gravitas. "And on that note, we should wrap up for now. Will you come back when you have a follow up?"

"Certainly."

"Maybe after the 1st would be a good time. We can compare notes and see what if anything we can detect that's changed."

The woman paused. "By then, I'm not sure if it will matter, but yeah."

"If nothing else, you can stop by and say I told you so." Max laughed.

Adam pulled the buds from his ears and shut down the audio file. He had nervously doodled all the while as the program played, his hand scribbling lines, designs, and numbers on a pad of paper next to the keyboard.

He pushed back from the desk, spun around, and stood to take in the view out the window. Behind him, he could hear people leaving for the night. Others were busy on phone calls with clients. The din of the regular workday was winding down even as the audio file had wound him up.

So much of what the woman on the program had said fell in line with what he and Nelson had discovered in the past few days. No doubt this woman was the *TigerLily* Nelson was so connected with from operations worked together long ago in Afghanistan and other places.

She had seen the dark outlines of something ominous and imminent, just as they had, only she had seen it from another perspective. Putting the two views together made the urgency expressed by Nelson that much more compelling. It made Adam's decision to determine what to do more difficult.

No longer was it so easy to simply walk away from what they'd uncovered so far, especially after a day spent back on the twenty-sixth floor. The juxtaposition of hearing her warning while sitting at his work desk had only drawn the distinctions clearer.

Adam stared down at the lights on the streets below. Some of them moved, and with them, the lives of the *PIPS*, the *post-industrial peasants*. A part of him could no longer see himself doing what he did. The problem was, the rest of him had no conception what might be possible to put in its place.

He turned back to his desk and stood staring down at it. His wandering glance gravitated back to his doodles. All at once, something spun out of the gibberish and swirls left there in ink. An idea sprung to mind. He scribbled it down and circled it, then grabbed his coat and headed for the elevators.

Emptying out on the sidewalk with others a short time later, Adam stood in place and looked uptown, in the direction of the subway entrance he normally aimed for. Not far away, he could see Nelson standing next to a waiting taxi. History was repeating itself, but the spiral of its motion was never quite the same. This time, he wouldn't need any coaxing to join Nelson in the back seat.

Nelson stood surprised when Adam walked right up and got in. Nelson ducked his head down to check Adam out. "Are you sure you don't want to argue with me about something first?"

Adam gave Nelson a smoldering glance. "Fuck off."

Nelson filled the other rear seat, shut the door, then barked directions to the driver. Settling back, he made sure he didn't look at Adam. The taxi pulled out into traffic and accelerated.

"I guess you heard the program," started Nelson.

"Yeah, I heard it."

"So what convinced you?"

"Convinced me of what?"

"You're here. You're not on the subway."

Adam watched the city lights blur by. "It wasn't any one thing."

"That's hard to believe. There's always one thing that makes the difference —the one drop that makes the cup overflow."

"Spare me your instant analysis."

"OK, so how was work?" Nelson knew the change of subject would grant no relief to Adam.

"Just leave it alone," snapped Adam.

"Don't want to talk about work? That's telling."

"You should have stayed back in your hotel room and jacked off."

"Too late. I hit my daily quota talking with you this morning."

"I knew something was wrong with you."

"So how am I to take this nasty mood? Are you with me or not?"

"I got in the car, didn't I?"

"You did that because maybe you think you're getting a free dinner."

"Bullshit. Your idea of dinner is tripe as the chef's special."

"OK, this time, you pick the place. It's been a while since I've had a Happy Meal." Nelson gave Adam a glance and got little reaction.

Adam reached into his coat pocket and produced a slip of folded paper. He took his time unfolding it.

Nelson could tell there was hesitation to share it with him.

"What's that?" asked Nelson. "Your list of demands?"

Adam jerked his hand over and gave Nelson the slip of paper. "You want one thing. This'll have to do."

Nelson held the paper up near the window so he could read it by street lights. Amidst a jumble of doodles, one item at the bottom was circled. Nelson's gaze was drawn to it. It was a number, expressed in power notation.

10^{21}

"What's this?" asked Nelson, truly surprised.

Adam looked over. "I thought you should know, ten to the twenty-first power might refer to zettaFLOP."

Adam paused and let Nelson fill in the blank. For Nelson, that blank could only mean one thing, the basis for the Z computer. He left it unsaid. Intent on needling Adam, he handed the paper back as if unimpressed.

"Nice try but I looked it up already: 1021 is a labor union. SEIU Local 1021 is based in Northern California." Nelson held his serious face as long as he could, then let the corners of his mouth creep up with satisfaction.

Seeing Nelson's grin, Adam gave a nod and glanced at the back of the driver's head. He was fully aware Nelson wouldn't say much with a third party within earshot. But the grin told him, he got the point.

Adam stuffed the doodle paper back into his coat pocket. "Yeah, you're right. And I guess you're going to remind me—I haven't paid my dues."

All humor dropped from Nelson's face. He turned away and took in the ordered chaos of the city streets. "Don't worry. By the end of the month, you'll be a journeyman."

58

0000 0011 1010

7:02 pm CST, Friday, December 22nd

The commuter bus pulled into a dimly lit parking lot on Whitis Avenue between West 20th Street and West 21st. Ninety minutes of motion and confinement with nothing to do but sit and think left Katherine sick to her stomach and unsettled. Outside the window, a lighted sign for the Dobie Center announced their arrival in Austin. Passengers gathered up their things and filed along the aisle, down the steps, and scattered into the night.

Katherine followed them, exited the bus, and took up position with her back against a plastered wall. The evening was already a blur. She had turned in her rental car in San Antonio two hours before. Now she was waiting, out in the open. She needed only one more sign to give her the confidence that the way forward was secure enough to proceed.

If everything had gone as planned, her shadow escort would appear at any moment, first as a drive-by and then as an idling car that would guard from a distance as she walked the few blocks to the safe house.

Her escort guard was another independent contractor like her. She had recruited him, along with several others while in San Antonio, by letting it be known throughout the intelligence contractor network that their members were being set up as fall guys, targeted as expendable cover. News of the subterfuge against Nelson's cell had spread like wildfire throughout their alliance of private assets. Katherine had added context to what had happened to Dystrom and Hollister. In response, many operatives answered her call to help.

The escort drive-by soon arrived and circled the block. The second time the car appeared, it idled across the street. That was Katherine's signal to begin walking. Pushing off from the wall, she cut through the chill in the air, bolstered more by anticipation than the ample adrenaline coursing through her. At the end of her walk, Nelson Geiss should be waiting. For her, their reunion was as much personal as professional, as much fated as planned. She expected it would go unspoken but hoped their reunion would mean the same to him.

A convenience store called *Purple* occupied a corner location a few blocks away. She entered the store as her guard rolled by and found a place to park. Following the plan as instructed, she strolled to the cold case where the beer and soft drinks were kept. She stood there until approached by the store clerk.

He studied her face, obviously matching her to a picture he had seen. From what she had heard, he was sympathetic to RAPIER's cause and used his position in the store to help them when he could.

"If you're not finding what you want, we have more varieties in the back."

He played his part well, sounding bored and disinterested, even as he made sure to direct her to a small, cluttered hallway that led to the backroom.

"Thanks," she offered. "I'll check it out."

Passing through the hallway, she entered a back stock area lit by a single fluorescent tube. She paused until Nelson stepped out of the shadows.

There were no words between them. They hurried into each other's arms and hugged as if holding on could prevent either of them from slipping away.

Nelson whispered, "It's good to see you." Pulling back, he noticed her eyes flooded with joy.

"Has it been so long?" she asked, smiling away the tears.

He reassured her, "It never seems to matter."

She caught her breath. "We can do this…"

Nelson nodded. "Come on, we have to go." He led her outside through a rear door to a parked old car, noting as he got in, "It's not your Humvee."

Katherine hurried to the passenger side. "Then I'll let you drive."

As he pulled out through the alley, she handed him a slip of paper. "Here's your contact if you need a way out of Austin."

"Thanks." Nelson stuffed the paper in his coat pocket. "You did a great job getting the word out."

"I got six who say they're all in, whatever we need. Several more will do what they can. Even Geri has come around, in her own way."

"Messare?" Nelson was startled.

"She's gotten bitchy about the pressure Marks put on her."

"Grudges and profit have always been her stock in trade."

"She said the more she thought about it, the more she got steamed."

"Sounds like her," noted Nelson. He gave Katherine a long, studied glance. "You realize, of course, what you've done."

"What?"

"You've managed to put together a *real* ETC. Quite an accomplishment."

Katherine downplayed it. "We'll see. Now if we only had access to Site R or some other resources, huh?"

"Carry light, run lean. We're a smaller target."

"Up against precision weapons," countered Katherine.

"Don't give Steigbriar too much credit."

"I'm not talking about Steigbriar," Katherine corrected, looking forward. "I'm worried about the weapons we *don't* know about."

Nelson drove into an alley, parked the car, and switched off the headlights. Looming before them in the dark was the back end of a three-story brick building that had seen better days.

"This is it?" asked Katherine, checking the structure out the side window.

"Yeah. Art gallery is on the first floor. The second floor is work space and artist storage area. The third floor is makeshift living quarters. From the looks of it, whoever shows up crashes and hooks up. It's their safe house."

"How tight is Adam with these RAPIER pukes?"

Nelson took note of her attitude. "You're not *down* with the revolution?"

"Some radical change might be good. Just never could see the point of being a part-time anarchist. So what about Adam?"

Nelson hesitated. "A marriage of convenience, I suspect. They both talk about *revolution by another name*, only like the rest of the Western world, they don't know how much comfort they're willing to give up to get it."

"More Montessori Marxists."

Nelson opened his door. "Marx is history. They don't know history."

He led the way inside. Katherine caught a glimpse of the gallery before being shuttled upstairs. The second floor was dark but from light filtering in through the windows, she could tell it was a cluttered and disorganized space.

On the third floor, Nelson headed for the corner lit by a single desk lamp. It was the only light in a large and open area capped off with high ceilings.

He motioned to computers on folding tables and mattresses on the floor. "This is it. Adam is out with DPS getting supplies." Sitting at one of the computers, he typed away.

Katherine pulled up a chair. "How much to you know about DPS?"

Nelson navigated a webpage. "He calls himself *Damage Per Second...*"

"In other words, you'd like to know more."

"It couldn't hurt." Nelson pointed to the screen. "Here's what I wanted to show you."

Katherine scooted closer. "The stuff from Guernsey?"

"Along with everything else we've compiled." Nelson opened the whiteboard photo from the Lake Maggiore. "*Buon Anno.* Douglas Kennigus had a good reason to name this file *Happy New Year* while enjoying his summer vacation. Have a look at the rest. It matches what you saw at NDU."

Nelson let Katherine browse. It didn't take long for her to see complexity. "There's so much to it. How are you going to crack it on the run?"

"Hard to say. I never thought we'd get this far," admitted Nelson.

"You find encouragement in that?"

"Hell, yeah. I'm surprised, and I thought we were good."

"Oh, I see, so that makes you better than good."

"I'm all about options. We still have a few. I'll take it as far as it can go."

"Dragging Adam along for the ride?"

"Adam doesn't know how much he wants this."

"What do you mean?"

"He's young. This is no time for him to get stuck in a cubicle. He needs to try out a few things, push himself, you know, get dirty."

"The way you did?"

Nelson wavered. "No, but you get the point."

"I don't know...the more you uncover, the larger it becomes. You're going up against power. You know they claim the highest ground."

"They opened the door when they drafted me for the ETC. Access is the critical thing and they gambled it away. That makes them vulnerable."

"Maybe, but one mistake and they'll shut you down."

"Something tells me, after the 1st, they'll be out of reach. In the new year, they'll leave us alone simply because none of us will matter." Nelson tried to gauge Katherine's silence. "You said you hadn't decided what to do."

"Not until I got here," she declared.

Nelson pretended he didn't hear the inference. "You wouldn't go back to D.C.?"

"Perhaps. I still have a line on Aubrey's contact…"

"You mean that last agent, the one under her control?"

"Yes, he could be useful. He might know others who would join us."

"Don't do it," suggested Nelson. "He orbits too close to the fire." Nelson phrased it carefully, "Is there any other reason for you to go back?"

It was generic enough, but the way he asked told Katherine he wondered about connections in her personal life. "No," she assured him as openly as she could with her expression, then she changed the subject. "If Barnett were still alive, maybe. Maybe there would be something more to discover."

"You're sure he wasn't working with anyone else?"

"I doubt it. He was too much a loner, brilliant, but in his own world." Katherine grasped for anything that could help. "He did arrange the NDU appointment for me. In fact, I was supposed to go back every Thursday during the month. Now, there's an idea; there should be one appointment left. I could try to keep it. Who knows what else he put in the secret files before he died."

Nelson paced into the shadows by the window. "You can't risk that. Besides, he's dead. Appointments like that would've expired with him." Looking down on the street below, Nelson was unsure what to suggest.

"I could stay here with you," offered Katherine.

Nelson took off his coat and dropped it on a coffee table. "That might make things easier, but not safer. It's hard to coordinate cover from the inside. All of us shouldn't be sitting on the bull's eye."

"There's others with us now. They'll report from the perimeter." She stood and went to him. Waiting for a response, she noticed the metal wristband. She reached out and slid his shirt sleeve up to see the tattoo.

"So these are the toys."

Nelson was still thinking it through. He let silence be his confirmation.

She ran her fingers lightly over the design hugging the side of his bicep. "Why did 1021 wait to turn these on? Did you ever find out?"

"He's spoofing the DEN satellite trackers."

"How?"

"He told me bare bones. Somehow he used a modified GNSS…"

"Global Navigation Satellite Simulator. What's he simulating?"

"He recorded movements of Adam and me during the last two days in New

York. He's using the recording to feed the smartdust tracker."

"He's playing it back?"

"Yeah, the satellites think we're still in New York. At least, that's where our smartdust signal will come from if they check."

"Genius," noted Katherine. "But that'll last two days before it repeats."

"No. He segmented and randomized paths in predictable chunks so no day is like another. As long as we keep the tattoos on, the only signal they'll get from us is from his machine located somewhere in Midtown Manhattan."

Out of a backpack, Nelson produced the UPS envelope from 1021. Katherine found the note inside, handwritten on a slip of paper from a memo pad: *Wait for an explanation.*

Her eyes shifted to the paper's lower right corner. A fine watermark could be seen, so light it was almost unnoticeable. The mark was a number.

"Did you see this?" She handed it back. "The watermark. It says *5300.*"

Nelson brought the paper close. "It's news to me. What about it?"

"That number was stamped on every document I saw at NDU."

"You're sure? 5300?" Nelson turned the paper over to check it out.

"Barnett and 1021 must have access to the same things."

"They work at the same place," surmised Nelson.

"On the same team?" She stopped cold. "What if they're the same person?"

"What about the obituary?"

"What about it? Deaths have been faked before."

Stunned, Nelson sat down. "I'm glad *you* said that. Coming from me, the whole idea would be labeled wild speculation."

"Only because you've cried wolf too many times. That's the problem with you conspiracy nuts." Katherine sat and held Nelson's hand and wristband. "Why don't you call him? Let's see who answers."

"How will we know?"

"The guy you talk to on this—what does he sound like?"

"Just a guy," stalled Nelson. "An older guy, intelligent, determined."

"Sounds like Barnett to me," declared Katherine.

"It could sound like a lot of guys," countered Nelson.

"Let's find out. If he won't tell us, at least he'll know we're onto him."

"And that's a good thing?"

"He respects smarts. He told me once he didn't want to do business with someone who blindly followed orders. I wouldn't put it past him to test you."

"How much did you know about Barnett when you took the job?"

"He's listed as a research scientist at the Nanomaterials Theory Institute, Center for Nanophase Materials Sciences at Oak Ridge National Laboratory."

"Oak Ridge...wait a minute." Nelson rushed to a computer console and typed in a search. As soon as he entered *OAK RIDGE 5300*, the search engine suggested *OAK RIDGE BUILDING 5300*. Nelson took the suggestion and immediately found a government website that noted the address:

Cyberspace Sciences and Information Intelligence Research (CSIIR) Group
/Information Operations Center (IOC)
/Center for Quantum Information Science (CQIS)
P.O. Box 2008
One Bethel Valley Road
Building 5300, MS-6418

Returning to search results, Nelson found articles on the *High Productivity Computing Systems Program* and the *Multiprogram Research Facility*, or Building 5300 located on the East Campus of Oak Ridge National Laboratory.

The Program was an undertaking like the Manhattan Project, tasked with the goal of advancing computer speed a thousand-fold. The Research Facility had been occupied since 2006 with experts working in secret on cryptanalytic applications of high-speed computing and other classified projects under the watchful eyes of the DOE and NSA.

Nelson murmured, "The *Program*…the *Facility*…the *Project*. Project G."

Katherine read over his shoulder then insisted, "You have to call him."

Nelson spun around. "OK, but the way it works, you have to be wearing the wristband to hear the call. I'll make the connection, then you put it on."

She sat down beside him. "All right, let's do it."

Clasping the wristband with forefinger and thumb from his opposite hand, Nelson initiated the link. "Call 1021."

An anxious wait followed. Nelson was about to give up when he heard a response. "We agreed to keep calls to a minimum. This better be important."

As Nelson answered 1021, he watched Katherine's reaction. "It's a matter of life and death. Is *that* important enough?"

"Not if you're going to tell me you're in danger. That's redundant."

"It's not about me. It's about you."

"If you're going to be esoteric, I'm hanging up."

"No, it's simple. Someone here wants to talk to you."

"Adam already knows what to do…"

As Nelson removed the wristband, the sound disappeared from his head.

Katherine pressed the band into place on her wrist and immediately picked up the continuing signal. "…enough to anticipate and react appropriately."

Katherine listened for a while and then interrupted. "You sound the same…except you're more on edge. Why so testy?"

"Katherine?" 1021's question was more about shock than inquiry.

"Yes, surprised? Or maybe I should be."

"A matter of life and death, huh?"

"Yes, yours. I don't know what to call you anymore. First a name, then a number. What's next, a symbol, a question mark? I thought you were dead."

"What has Nelson put you up to?"

"You shouldn't talk about him if he can't hear what you're saying."

"All right, then. I'll include him."

"You can do that?"

"When will people stop asking if I can do that?" 1021 did his technical magic and switched on a conference call among the three of them. "What are you trying to prove by this, Nelson?"

"A demonstration of our curiosity, nothing more."

"Wrong," snapped 1021. "You want answers, whether or not it matters."

Katherine reiterated, "I warned you that IC assets don't work blind."

"What's the problem? You both know the objective," asserted 1021. "Get to the bottom of this, hopefully with enough time left before New Year's so something can be done about it."

"You know damn well that's not why we called you."

"Is it so hard to understand?" pressed 1021. "R.Z. Barnett was a terrific friend, a great scientist, and he died of natural causes much too soon. A year ago we both saw signs of what might be happening. When I moved on, he allowed me to use his mailbox to mask my movements. He didn't want to go as deep as I did but he agreed to help."

"So you impersonated him..." charged Katherine.

Nelson added, "And if anything went down, he'd take the fall."

"Don't be melodramatic. He knew what I was doing. We made sure he had his own evidence that proved his accounts had been hacked. At worst, he would have been consoled as another victim of cybercrime."

"You worked with him at Building 5300?" asked Katherine.

"We worked together at several places. Over time, we saw how new technology was cherry-picked away and classified, intended for use by a privileged few. We started to suspect the reason wasn't so noble as protecting the motherland—or should we say, the *fatherland*?"

"So why hide behind him?"

"It was the only way we could devise to disappear behind each other. We wanted to know where the technology went and why but that wasn't allowed. We had to use the advantages of our security clearances to cover our tracks. We both agreed, I'd do the digging and he'd provide the cover. If the snooping was discovered, he'd be the victim and I'd be long gone and nameless."

"Nameless, even to us?"

"*Especially* to you. And after your fiasco on the radio, Katherine, I should think you'd understand why."

"All that did was provide cover for *me*," rejoined Katherine. "The show created no uproar. Most people ignored it, as I expected they would. It's nothing but another conspiracy theory."

"I don't worry about *most* people," 1021 replied angrily. "Most people bleat nonsense and wait to be sheared. I worry about the shadows that move in the light without being seen. You alerted them to how much we know. You warned them that somebody in a position to hurt them wants to know more."

"They already suspect that with Alonso Lutane," said Nelson.

"Lutane is not inside the circle. I'm talking about a mole, something they fear the most. I may not be a certified spook but I damn well know, when it comes to being a mole, it's better if they don't know about the game they're in rather than getting a heads-up that the game's in play."

"Is that why you cut the power to the radio show? You think they didn't notice that?"

"Max Engle is suspected of that as much as anyone."

"So why do it?"

"To feed the conspiracy angle and to send you a message. Haven't you noticed? The more something appears to be a true conspiracy, the less people believe it. Instead, by repetition, it becomes folklore, nothing but tribal knowledge, an entertaining myth that gets repeated like some family ghost story about the grassy knoll. It's uncanny. They have trained us well."

"And the message for me?" asked Katherine.

"Simply to get back in line and do your job or bow out quietly."

"As far as being a mole, I suspect you tipped your hand earlier," accused Nelson. "They were onto you some time ago, weren't they? Maybe you needed a way to spread the blame around."

"Ridiculous," laughed 1021.

"Maybe you want to make it look like we *came to you*. You're the innocent scientist, caught up in the subterfuge of private contractors who said they were protecting secrets but were really after them."

"Is this what you called me for?"

"We're not sure who you are," concluded Nelson.

"Or what you really want," added Katherine.

"I'll tell you what I want," snapped 1021. "Greyson Talmadge talked before he died. While being tortured, he answered questions, some of those questions were on a cell phone call from Curacao. His kidnappers didn't try to hide what they were asking. In fact, GCHQ got a recording. I heard it. As a result, I have new leads key in getting to the heart of the matter we should be focusing on. Now, you can blather on with this nonsense about who I am and what my motives are—or take my actions as proof of my intentions. I'm prepared to turn over the leads and do whatever else I can to expose what's going on. New Year's Eve is only days away. I don't want to wake up on the 1st of January with terrible regrets about lost opportunities to do what's right."

Nelson and Katherine looked to each other in thought.

Nelson saw room to bargain. "I'll take the leads on one condition."

"Only one?" 1021 asked, sarcastically.

"You need to send Katherine a tattoo and wristband."

"Out of the question," came the reply.

"She's vital to the effort. She's coordinating our support team."

"Even if I wanted to, it's too risky. Too much stock, missing for too long, gets noticed."

Nelson held firm. "That's the deal. You want Adam and me to work these leads, find a way."

There was a pause. "A wristband might be possible but there's no way I can get another tattoo by the end of the month."

Nelson pushed past frustration. "All right. Have your courier bring the wristband to the Purple convenience store tomorrow at noon."

"What about the leads?" asked 1021.

Nelson reached for the band on Katherine's wrist. "Send them over. I'll put them in a *safe place*." With that, Nelson squeezed forefinger and thumb to the sides of the band and ended the call.

Katherine handed back the band and stepped away to look out the window.

Nelson could tell she was trying to hide her emotions. With so much in play, he had to ask to be sure. "What's wrong?"

Arms folded, Katherine held a steady gaze down upon the street below. "Why did you ask him for a tattoo for me?"

Nelson went to the truth. "He told me the rumors about smartdust are true."

Katherine spun around. "Then I can't stay here. I shouldn't even be here."

"You were in Austin with Aubrey, now you've returned. There's no red flag in your pattern so far."

"But what about tomorrow and the next day? I can't stay with you. I'd mark your position no matter where you went." She spun around and paced. "Jesus! No wonder they got to Aubrey despite all we did."

Nelson couldn't answer. She was right. He was going to ask 1021 for another tattoo when the time came, when he knew she intended on staying.

She turned back to the window. "I don't know if I'm being targeted or not. How could they hit Aubrey and miss me?"

Nelson came to her side. "I don't think they're after you."

"Why, because I'm still alive or because of Richard?"

"From what you said, he had motive. You weren't part of their dynamic."

"But what if Patterson caves to the DOJ? What about the radio show?"

"Who knows *you* did that? Your voice was masked."

"In Richard's position, he could have forensic voiceprint tools."

"Those tools can only do so much. Did Max add filters or did he run it through transforms and synthesizer?"

"It had to be more than filters. He had a shitload of gear."

"All right then. Plus Max Engle is now playing Aubrey's *suicide* for all it's worth. He says she was silenced because of the show."

Katherine spun around. "He's making it look like *she* did the show?"

Nelson nodded. "Assassinations are good for ratings. So you see, unless Owen and Richard are gullible enough to believe some wild conspiracy theory, they'll probably come to the conclusion that Aubrey did the show off secrets she discovered while Chimaera ran security for Extasis."

"That still leaves me with smartdust and no tattoo. I can't take the chance of giving you away."

"We'll think of something," offered Nelson, unable to decide what to do.

The thought of separation after arriving tore at Katherine. "I don't understand. If you knew this, why did you have me come here?"

Nelson was laid bare. "I needed to see you."

Katherine caught his eye. In it was everything personal and nothing about the work to be done. The unspoken admission was huge for both of them.

They had been on many missions together, life and death situations that had bonded them in ways only combat veterans would understand. She had long ago fallen in love with him, yet he was married and her feelings, while evident at times, had to be stowed away. Nelson had been faithful to Madelyn, his wife of twenty-six years, although far-flung operations had demanded he spend much of his time away from her and their son.

For Nelson, Katherine was a confidant and soul mate of a different order, forged through time and trials. Their respect and trust in one another had survived the tests of a profession that saw very little respect or truth survive the expediency of ends justifying means.

The chemistry between them went beyond a natural attraction that had always been sublimated away, even if jokes, horseplay and innuendo by others had sometimes alluded to it. Seeing her again in the familiar context of a mission made him realize how much they both missed each other.

For both of them, there was nothing else to say. They embraced, only this time it wasn't a hug of welcome, but of love.

Katherine asked the fates, "What are we going to do?"

Nelson fought through a fog of rising impulses to find an answer. "You'll have the wristband…"

"But where to go?"

Nelson broke from the embrace and jotted down a series of numbers. He handed the paper to her. "I have a survival shelter on my ranch. Underground. This is the combination to get in. You'll have food, provisions, weapons, the computer and comm gear you need to run the ETC."

She took the slip of paper and considered it but said nothing.

"We're nine days away," reminded Nelson. "You can make it your base as long as you need it."

Just then, there was noise on the stairs. From the sound of it, Adam and DPS had returned. Katherine hurried the slip of paper into her pocket.

DPS was first to the landing with Adam right behind. DPS was a rail gun of intensity and attitude, hungry and lean but stuffed with street-cred and ideology. His energy shifted catching sight of Katherine with Nelson. He dropped his swagger into lower gear and rolled forward showing nothing but suspicion and cool.

"What have we got here?" asked DPS.

Nelson answered. "A member of the team, just got in from San Antonio."

"The name's Katherine," she offered.

DPS nodded a hello but directed his comments to Adam. "You didn't tell me there'd be others."

Adam shrugged, "Shit changes."

"I need to know. I can't have this place compromised."

"Who's compromising anything?"

"Nobody, I guess," relented DPS. "But this is it. There's no open door policy in a place like this."

"Great, that's good to know," added Nelson.

"I'm not staying anyway," announced Katherine.

Adam took up on her comment and lit into DPS. "Yeah, she's not staying, so what's the problem?"

"The problem?" DPS rejoined. "She comes and goes from here. People could see it. This isn't fucking Grand Central."

While Adam and DPS traded words, Katherine used her phone to snap a photo of their angered host.

Nelson stepped forward. "And it isn't Guantanamo, either. Now, as I see it, we have no fucking problem. There's an art gallery on the first floor. Katherine here, is an art lover. Isn't that why you stopped in? There's a goddamned good reason for traffic coming in and out of here."

"Yeah?" answered DPS, more bluster than balls.

"All right. Next time you assert yourself, do it over something important."

Katherine headed for the stairs. "It's been nice working with you."

Nelson followed her down to the second level. They hurried off to one side into the darkness of the storage area.

"Can you get a flight to Cheyenne OK?' asked Nelson.

"Contractors are standing by. I'll leave right after tomorrow's pick-up at Purple. But how do I call you?"

Nelson touched his wrist. "This band is trained to my EMF. You'll have to train your band. The instructions are on the cellophane that peels off the backside. I'll call you; that transfers my EMF. To call me, say *Call Nelson.*"

"All right." She leaned forward into an embrace.

"There's a low rock wall by the shelter. Along the right side of the wall you'll find the entrance at ground level." Nelson hugged her a moment then pulled her back from him. "We'll get through this. We'll get back together."

"When?" Impossible questions had to be asked. "It's always tomorrow."

"And you always wanted everything *yesterday.* That's how you got your name—*deeRooz,*" joked Nelson in avoidance.

Katherine let it go. Stepping away, she answered in kind, "Yeah. *Seeyah.*"

59

0000 0011 1011

4:59 pm CST, Thursday, December 23rd

The Cessna TTx hummed along at its cruising speed of 235 knots. Outside the window, a storm front moved farther east, away from them. Katherine rested in the copilot seat and checked her phone messages. At the controls sat Stephen, another semi-retired intelligence contractor like Nelson.

A grizzled veteran of many classified flight operations that followed the Air America days, Stephen would never admit how many flight hours he had booked in his career. He was known for having a wild side but liked to say he now limited his passions to two things: he loved to fly and he couldn't resist staying active in whatever game carried the highest stakes.

Agreeing to shuttle Katherine near Nelson's ranch in winter with unknown forces aligned against them certainly satisfied both passions.

"It's nice being able to get messages airborne," commented Katherine.

Stephen adjusted his headphones and pointed to the instrument panel. "Optional equipment. A Garmin GSR-56 Iridium Satellite Data Transceiver Link. Put me back fifteen grand but it's earned its keep many times over."

Katherine offered back a naughty grin. "I won't ask how."

"It's not what you think," he deferred.

"I know," she shot back. "It's worse."

He pointed out the front window. "Cheyenne ahead. Get those arms and legs back inside."

Katherine returned to an incoming message. It was from another contact, the one she had sent the quick picture taken of DPS back at the safe house. Besides bio and arrest record, her contact had managed to send DPS's cell phone records for the month. Looking at them, her suspicions were piqued.

Just then, Stephen called out, "Just got word. Your ride will be waiting at taxi pickup. Just go there and they'll find you."

Katherine pulled herself away from the material on DPS. "Great. That's good news."

An hour later, Katherine shut the taxi door and gave a final wave goodbye to her ride. Stuck with rear-wheel drive and nearly bald tires, the driver called out, "Sorry I can't take you up there. You going to be OK?"

"I'll be fine, thanks."

The taxi pulled away and headed back to Highway 210, better known as Happy Jack Road. Katherine turned and started the march up the snowy drive that wound its way back on the ranch past Nelson's house.

Twenty minutes later she reached the main house. It looked inviting enough and yet, all locked up and coated in snow, it seemed desolate for being empty of life. The house was not her destination anyway.

She trudged on another ten minutes until she reached a fork in the path. She could see the left branch curve down to a pond in the distance. The right branch was less used which told her it was the one to take. The only problem was, the snow was deeper on the path less taken.

Another ten minutes through the snow and she found the low rock wall Nelson had told her about. Scraping along with her feet and then gloved hands, she found the entrance to the shelter and entered the combination.

She was ready for it. The cold was getting to her.

At the bottom of the steps she found the place as she expected. Nelson had thought of everything. She turned on the heat and locked herself in. Next she set about checking out the tools, weapons, and other equipment from stored compartments. This would be her home and their command post for the next few days. She needed to know every bit of its capabilities and limitations.

She tried to push worse-case scenarios out of mind but to no avail. Everything had to be considered, although she couldn't see the sense in wondering how the place could turn into a cage or a tomb. If she was found, it was more likely they'd come in after her than trap her inside.

Either way, it wasn't her focus. It was a necessary part of thinking ahead, but concentrating on what to do in the moment was the best way to stay alive and accomplish what she came to do.

The first order of business was to get warm and dry.

After that, she needed to send Nelson the report on DPS.

60

0000 0011 1100

9:41 pm CST, Thursday, December 24th

As usual, a single desk lamp lit the corner of the large upstairs room. Adam worked away at the computer while Nelson read through anything he could find regarding what they had found already. Repeated passes over the material might help him glean more insight into what they were after.

Adam rubbed weary eyes. "What are you reading?"

Nelson didn't move from his slump before the keyboard. "Background on the Bank of International Settlements."

"Your idea of empathetic support?"

"Why?"

"Because I've spent the last hour trying to hack into the personal computers of the Basel Committee Secretariat."

"You switched leads?"

"I had to. The other one was taking too long. Time on task equals risk."

"Which lead was that?" asked Nelson.

"The Group of Governors…"

"The ones responsible for committee oversight?"

"I guess. You're the one reading about it. I'm just trying to get in."

Adam ran his hands over his head and held them at the back of his neck. "What else did he give us for leads?"

Nelson checked the safe place. "Let's see, we've got alphabet soup— GHOS, FSB, FSI, and CMG."

"What the fuck are those?"

Nelson read them in order. "The Group of Central Bank Governors and Heads of Supervision, Financial Stability Board, Financial Stability Institute, and Basel Committee's Capital Monitoring Group. Take your pick."

"He's serious about this?" asked Adam.

"He said they were mentioned when Kennigus was being tortured."

"Couldn't he be more specific?"

"Who, 1021 or Kennigus?"

"Kennigus."

"It's too late to ask him."

Adam let his head lean back so he could stare at the ceiling. "Information gained under duress is suspect at best. He probably gave them bullshit."

"1021 doesn't think so."

"Why would you agree with him?"

Nelson looked back to his online research. "After reading the history of the

BIS, I wouldn't be surprised."

"You're back on that again? I told you before: algorithms are now; history happened last week."

Annoyed, Nelson had to respond. "BIS started out as a settlement program for German debts from World War I. How that morphed into an international, intergovernmental committee dictating rules to the world's central banks is beyond me. They're not elected and aren't accountable to any national government, and yet whenever the G-20 meets, they take orders from BIS on monetary policy and the rules governing every major financial institution. BIS even has a report card showing which nations are in line or behind in compliance with them. No nation wants a bad grade from BIS."

"I know, back on Guernsey you told me all about it. It's standard rules for a shrinking world," countered Adam. "They would claim it only makes sense."

"The whole thing was a con from the beginning," asserted Nelson.

"Of course," grinned Adam. "It's all a conspiracy."

"The British and American bankers, like J.P. Morgan, knew the Germans could never repay the debt, so they got it lowered and offered to refinance it, with interest of course, as long as a committee was set up to handle reparation transfers. The *committee* was the thing. *That's* what they were really after. For the first time an international body for handling global transactions was established—the BIS."

"OK, so?"

"Then it gets odd. The first two guys they picked to head up the BIS were the Governor of The Bank of England and the guy who later became Hitler's finance minister. In fact, at the Nuremberg trials after the Second World War, two members of the BIS board of directors were convicted of war crimes. A third guy they convicted was the banker who held deposits for the Gestapo."

"But what does that have to do with now?"

"If you want to find your way back, you need to know how far off the trail you've gotten. The best way to get on course is to walk yourself back through the wrong steps that got you there."

"Like what?"

"After the Second World War, the Bretton Woods Conference came to the conclusion that the BIS needed to be liquidated *at the earliest possible moment* —that's how they phrased it. The British and American delegations disagreed with each other. The British wanted to keep BIS going but they were voted down. Dissolution of the BIS was approved."

"Well, *that* didn't happen," noted Adam.

"No, even though the order was given to dissolve the bank, nothing was done for four years. Roosevelt sat on his hands."

"What then?"

"President Truman, working with the British, suspended the dissolution order. With that, the decision to liquidate BIS was officially reversed."

"So why the change after it sat there for four years?"

"You explain it—without sounding like a conspiracy. That left the bank in a conveniently odd state. It was originally owned by both governments and private individuals, but the U.S. and France decided to sell most of their shares. BIS was traded on the stock market but it also had private shareholders. Over time, BIS forcibly bought back its publicly traded shares. Now it's wholly owned by private members but still operates as asset manager and lender for central banks and international financial institutions."

"So you want to know what goes on behind the private curtain."

"No, that's obvious. Over the last seventy years, they've never let a serious crisis go to waste. Every time a money scheme created an economic emergency, they moved in as rescuers with the solution—more monetary regulation and global systemic authority anchored in Basel."

"They would say it wasn't their money schemes that caused the problem."

"No doubt," answered Nelson. "Except how many take the time to check the facts?" Nelson pointed to the screen. "Like in 1988, Basel I regulations imposed an 8% capital reserve on central banks at a critical time for Japan. That threw Japan into a fifteen year depression. In 2004, Basel II imposed something they called *mark to the market* capital valuation standards."

"Sounds arcane enough," commented Adam. "I've heard of that. It required international banks to revalue their reserves according to market valuations—"

"Things like falling home or stock prices," stressed Nelson. "The United States implemented those standards in November 2007. A year later, the stock market collapsed and credit dried up when banks had to comply with the 8% cap requirement. Collateral valuations dropped and the snowball effect did the rest. Don't you find it strange that we've had a steady cycle of depressions and bubbles ever since the start of the 20th century? If all of their measures since 1913 were so effective, why is it like that?"

Adam laughed, "Ironically, they probably would say it's because they *don't* control everything."

"They even have their own currency…"

"The SDR," noted Adam.

"Yes, Special Drawing Rights. One could make a case that SDRs have become the de facto reserve currency for the world, at least as far as central banks and other G-SIBs are concerned. National currency is looked at as only regionally significant and better done away with. That's why they push for consolidated currencies like the Euro or the Amero."

Confused, Adam asked, "Who has the Amero?"

"North America is supposed to have it, whenever the North American Union gets implemented. One currency for Canada, the U.S., and Mexico."

"OK, so their endgame is some kind of one world government."

"They don't believe in governments. Governments are a lower form of organization, mere functionaries, good for only handing out parking tickets and taxing people. They want a one world *economy*. To them, that's more important and more powerful. They call it *full harmonization*. Like most economists, they're good with jargon. It's more of the abracadabra fine print that keeps the rest of us outside the circle."

"What's all of this got to do with New Year's?" asked Adam.

"If you're going to create a turn-key system, at some point…"

"…you have to turn the key."

"Back in 2010, I thought they were close. That's when the G-20 agreed to create and be members of something called the *Global Monetary Authority*. Part of that agreement gave BIS's Financial Stability Board arbitrary power over financial systems, including the U.S. What they decide *doesn't* get approved by Congress and can *never* be brought before the Supreme Court. How many know this? Who reads the communiqués coming out of the G-20?"

In part, Adam concurred, "If it can't be summed up in a headline, I doubt even people on Wall Street read them."

Nelson pointed to the screen. "Here's an example. This is from the BIS, dated June 2012…"

Adam rolled his chair over and read silently to himself.

"The proposed D-SIB framework requires banks, which have been identified as D-SIBs by their national authorities, to comply with the principles beginning in January 2016. This is consistent with the phase-in arrangements for the G-SIB framework and means that national authorities will establish a D-SIB framework by 2016. The Basel Committee will introduce a strong peer review process for the implementation of the principles. This will help ensure that appropriate and effective frameworks for D-SIBs are in place across different jurisdictions."—Secretariat of the Basel Committee on Banking Supervision, Bank for International Settlements, CH-4002 Basel, Switzerland.

Adam noted, "So, the framework should have been in place a year ago."

"And a year ago, Project G had its breakthrough. If they thought they had power before, the prospect of getting their hands on the hack for AES encryption would be irresistible."

"One thing I agree with. Holding the hack exclusively, they would be invincible."

Frustrated with Adam's reticence to see the invisible hand at work, Nelson looked past him to the computer. "Have you gotten in anywhere?"

Adam rolled back to his station. "Yeah, the Group of Governors had some holes. One guy has a business computer and personal laptop onsite. The computer's a tough nut to crack but I found an exploit for the laptop."

Nelson rolled over. "Let's see…"

Adam brought up a directory display in a black-and-white command window. "Most of these are standard system directories. I didn't find anything that shouldn't be there." Adam typed away and drilled down through the file system. "At this level it's personal stuff, but it's a bitch. I don't know German and running this crap through a translator is klugey."

"Yeah, the official language is German but the locals in Basel have their own dialect which complicates things. It's right on the border with France."

Adam leaned back. "What I've translated so far doesn't apply. It's nothing but personal bullshit."

Nelson took to the keyboard and on a hunch typed a redirection into a temp directory he saw. A listing of filenames returned, mostly long and useless hash names. Nelson slumped back. "More garbage."

Adam gazed at the screen and then squinted. "Except...that's odd."

As Adam pointed, Nelson's eyes found one number that stood out for appearing so brief and intelligible. "Is that a file or what is it?"

As Adam checked, he read the number out loud. "8-6-4-0-1."

Nelson quickly checked his computer. "For what it's worth, it's the zip code for Kingman, Arizona."

Adam ignored Nelson's information in favor of reading the object's properties. "86401. This thing is an orphan link file, probably a stray system copy of a desktop link he deleted."

"You mean it doesn't go anywhere?"

"Not anymore. But if it's here, there may be traces somewhere else." Reinvigorated, Adam set to work. It took fifteen minutes but he finally found it. "Here it is, in the administrative event logs. It appears our Mr. Governor tried clicking on the link after the connection was no longer allowed. His attempt threw an error code."

"What good is that to us?" asked Nelson.

"Look for yourself. The event log registered the IPv6 address that refused the connection."

Nelson perked up. "So what are you waiting for?"

The comment elicited a wry grin from Adam. He scooted his chair closer and set to work. "Get me some coffee." Then he mumbled to himself, "...and put some bourbon in it."

Two and a half hours later, Adam checked the time only to discover it was after midnight. He turned to Nelson, who had fallen asleep in his chair.

"Wake up, old man."

Nelson opened his eyes halfway. "Don't bother me unless you have something."

"What do I have to do, stuff it down your chimney?"

The odd reference caught Nelson's attention. He snapped awake and rolled his chair closer. "Who the hell you think you are, Santa Claus?"

"Damn right, motherfucker," grinned Adam. "It's Christmas!"

Adam leaned back and let Nelson study the screen. At first he didn't believe his eyes. "Is this some kind of joke?"

"You wish, then we wouldn't have to be doing this shit." Adam reached for a paper plate and the two stale brownies left on it.

"What the hell is it?"

"Haven't you seen a design document before?"

Nelson read aloud, "Global Financial Sensor Array."

Adam summed it up while he chewed. "GFSA. In case you're having a *senior moment*, it's at the top of our list from Lake Maggiore."

Nelson paged down frantically, trying to take it all in at once. "Where did you find this?"

"At the other ragged end of that orphan link."

"But where is that? Where did it go?"

"I don't know. It's a server someplace, sixteen hops away, not counting reroutes and dodges. It's located in the UTC minus 5 time zone."

Nelson calculated. "Minus five—that's the east coast of the U.S."

"Yeah, but there are other places in that slice of time."

"Did you get a copy of this?"

"First order of business."

"Did you read it?"

"I had to do something while you sat over there and snored."

"OK, so tell me, is this it?"

"Aren't *you* going to read it?"

"Sure, but I've got to know now."

"I'd say it's not the whole thing, but it's the infrastructure, the blueprints to the machine, but not necessarily what the machine does."

"OK, you're the geek, what do you think it's for?"

"Like it says, it's a sensor array."

Nelson expected more fire from the youngster once he had a major success. "You don't seem impressed."

"I'm fucking tired," confessed Adam. "It's hard to know from this how much the thing can do. But it's one uber-slick design doc. Even if you don't understand it all, you have to admit, it talks about some awesome shit."

"Like what?"

Adam shifted towards Nelson on the folding table and startled doodling a logical diagram on paper. "It's a network with a Z computer at the top. We've established it's got zettaFLOP speed. That provides the muscle but the real brains are in the QDE—the Quantitative Decision Engine."

"Sounds like something a quant would design."

"No, these things *replace* the need for quants."

"These things? How many of them are there?"

"The main one is a module that hangs off the Z computer. The rest are attached to MIN-Z's, which stands for Miniature-Z. They're smaller versions of the Z positioned close to the KEYSERVs. KEYSERVs are the switching servers that aggregate and route. They're in six datacenters on each continent."

"You mean the KQ sites…"

"Yeah, UKQ in the U.S., EKQ in Europe, AKQ in Asia, and so on. The first letter is the region, second letter stands for KEYSERV, and third letter represents QDE. Together, they form the logical unit of regional calculation."

"You said these things *replace* quants?"

"They do more than that. These things take in real-time data and generate response algorithms and execution code on the fly. Quants come up with algorithms and hard-code them into formulas that are static from day to day. To change them, they have to go through a convoluted change-review cycle until someone gives the authorization to modify. The QDEs generate revised formulas on the fly in reaction to real-time sensor input, any kind of sensor input." Adam's excitement peaked, "You understand? This is software that changes constantly according to its input. They process weighted test scenarios against live data and react with real-time decisions at supercomputing speeds."

Nelson drew a connection. "HUSIGINT—Human Signal Intelligence."

"Exactly. It's organic. They learn and over time, they can anticipate."

Nelson reeled with ramifications. "Holy shit! And without having AES in their way, anything and everything could be data inputs from the sensors."

"That's where the SWEBOTs come in. You were right…"

"Hive communication, like the ADAPT Program I saw in Afghanistan."

"Same thing, except these things multiply and spread out throughout what they call *global financial touch points*, not just the global internet, but down into corporate intranets."

"The whole point is to look for data?"

"They can be passive or active, any way you want. They can target data for collection or just as easily, push out data."

"Push it? You mean modify things?"

"Sure, if they want, a few characters here, a few numbers there. Like the glitch on F1E reiterated a learning pattern sent to each screen."

Nelson thought back and repeated what he had told Owen weeks ago. *"Yeah…we can scramble your screens; now imagine—just as easily, we could have modified them…but only slightly."*

Adam pushed on. "GFSA SWEBOTs would coordinate reads or writes to data in any pattern imaginable. They could target asset groups, or commodities, a single corporation or individual. This kind of system would enable granular tampering of financial market displays or private computer storage in real-time. Players who relied on High Frequency Trading would be obsolete."

"These BOTs would be distributed everywhere…"

"But only take orders from their regional KQ, under logical guidance of a MIN-Z, all of which would be controlled by the master Z."

Nelson slumped back, staring down at Adam's doodle. Essentially, it was an org chart, with Z at the top, six KQs on the second level, and SWEBOTS dotting the third position. Nelson asked, "Is there a fourth level?"

Adam glanced between his doodle and the GFSA design doc. "Yeah, but there's not much about it. In a couple of places, they refer to it as STUBs."

"Any idea what that is?"

Adam rubbed the side of his face and yawned. "If it's an acronym, I don't know. A stub file is something different."

"It's a computer file…"

"Yeah, it appears to be on disk and available but in fact some or all of it is somewhere else. When a stub file is accessed, device driver software intercepts the access, retrieves the data from its actual location, writes it to the file, then allows the user to access it. The user doesn't know the file is stored somewhere else. The only thing they may notice is a slight access delay."

"The design doc doesn't say what they would use the STUBs for?"

Adam scrolled back through the document. "No. The whole thing is pretty high level. It's written for managers, not technicians." Adam pointed at the title page. "Oh, yeah, you'll like this…"

Nelson drew in closer. "What?"

"This stuff in Latin. I guess it's their motto. Why do they write all government mottos in a dead language?"

"They must think it reflects back on the grandeur of Rome."

Adam chuckled. "The Roman Empire, yeah, let's be like them…"

Nelson tried reading it aloud, "*Potentia sine temperatione nihilum est.*"

Adam translated, "*Power without control is nothing.*"

"You verified that?"

"I ran it through an online translator. I guess it sums up their sensor array."

Nelson took it in. "This is real. They intend to do this by month's end."

Adam was amused. "The big conspiracy guy is surprised it's real?"

"Yeah." Nelson was stunned by how deep his concern went. "Some things are so monstrous, you disbelieve your eyes."

"I guess they count on that, don't they."

"No one wants to believe the worst is true."

Adam stretched some of the stiffness away. "Every day another surprise."

Mention of surprise jogged Nelson's memory. "That reminds me, I got word back from Katherine on the registration number on the rescue jet that took us out of Guernsey."

Adam's head shook. "I still can't believe you had time to memorize that."

"It turns out that a 3B registration prefix means the jet is registered on the island nation of Mauritius, off the East African coast."

Adam led Nelson to where he knew the older man was going. "That's an odd place for our rescuing commandos to be aligned with."

"Katherine found the jet's true ownership was masked but traced the flight back to a charter made by a front company working with Steigbriar."

"No surprise," remarked Adam. "We were rescued by the same people that Carlos forced us to investigate."

"Convenient. The rescue prevented our investigation from going any farther. It wasn't so much a rescue as shutting down leaks on the Project."

"That's rich. If we hadn't done so well with the hacking, they might have left us there to die," reasoned Adam.

"They rescued us right after we found the stuff from Lake Maggiore. I bet the timing wasn't accidental. They probably swooped in as soon as we got too close to something—something like this design document."

"Given what we've seen, it makes sense," agreed Adam.

Nelson knew it was a touchy subject, but he floated it anyway. "Did you have a chance to look over her other research, the stuff on DPS?"

Moaning, Adam stood and headed for a mattress. "Not that again."

"What about his calls to Santiago? That's all I'm asking."

Adam slumped down and untied his shoes. "He makes calls all over the fucking place. It's no big deal."

"If that's true, then he shouldn't have any problem talking about it."

Adam plopped back, his body prone and motionless. "All right, all right, I'll ask him in the morning if he comes around."

Nelson wanted to pursue it more but could see he was talking to the dead. He looked back at the computer screen and the GFSA design doc glowing out at him. "You did some damn fine work tonight."

Adam was half asleep. His words trailed off, "Merry Fucking Christmas."

61

0000 0011 1101

2:17 am CST, Thursday, December 25th

A ruckus on the stairs startled Nelson and Adam awake. Dim street light through the windows lit up one side of DPS rushing towards them. He ignored them. Instead, he woke the main computer out of hibernation.

"What the fuck are you guys doing?" DPS made his whisper shout.

"Wassup?" asked Adam, groggy and stumbling to his feet.

"You *popped* this place." DPS typed, then shoved and clicked the mouse.

"What are you talking about?" asked Nelson, slow to get up but joining them at the folding table.

Satisfied what could be done was finished, DPS turned to Adam. "What kind of amateur shit is this, leaving the connection open?"

Adam gazed at the screen and realized, in his exhaustion, what he had done. "Shit!"

"What the fuck happened?" asked DPS. "You go to sleep and forget this thing? You left the connection open. Now somebody's tracked it back to this area. This place is popped. You've got to get out of here—*now*. And take your shit with you. I don't want anything left to find. You got it?"

Mortified at his error, Adam could only nod agreement.

Nelson put on shoes and gathered up their things while Adam sat down at the keyboard to clean up the computer.

DPS headed for the stairs. "I shouldn't be here. After this, I can't even be seen around this place. Thanks a lot."

Adam called out. "We need another place to go."

DPS halted and flashed a sarcastic smile. "You've got fucking nerve."

"Like it's never happened to you."

"Who's in high school here?" asked DPS, derisively.

"Blow me." Mad at himself and the situation, Adam hardened.

"You're all brave and shit, hiding behind your old guard dog." DPS gave Nelson a glance.

Adam stressed, "You want us out of here? Give us a place to go."

Nelson offered, "Come with us. We've got a private airplane on call."

"Just like that, you can fly out of here?"

"Yeah," answered Nelson. "Just like that."

"No TSA? No charge?"

Adam insisted, "Give us another place. We'll take you there."

DPS wavered, "So you can pop that one too?"

Adam reminded him of their past. "You owe me."

DPS pointed all around the room. "And this place paid you back."

Nelson shouldered his backpack and pushed the point, "I thought you said we had to leave now. If you're telling the truth, there's no time to talk about it. Come on, Adam, let's go."

DPS changed direction. "All right, one more time but this is it."

Nelson stepped past him. "Where should I tell my pilot we're going?"

Adam hit one more key and bolted from the computer.

DPS followed Nelson down the stairs. "San Francisco."

The scramble to get out of Austin turned into a hide-and-seek game of hurry-up-and-wait. The pilot had to log a flight plan and had his own ideas about how they should go about it. It was Stephen, the same pilot who had dropped off Katherine in Cheyenne. Nelson knew him from a few clandestine puddle jumps and was well aware how the old throttle-jock liked to mix pleasure with business.

By 5 am, the Cessna TTx sat on the tarmac, ready to go. Nelson couldn't resist needling Stephen a little. "Tell me again why we're going into Napa?"

Stephen walked around the plane one last time doing his checks. "It's strategic, good for both of us," Stephen explained. "It gives me an excuse for flying to California that doesn't mention your sad ass—besides, I've got friends in Napa, and it gives your final destination some cover. No sense trying to hide in Fog City if you're going to draw a straight line right to it."

"We'll have a ride into town?"

"All set up."

"So no problems getting us there…"

Stephen showed his pirate smile. "Napa County Airport has three runways. Hell, I'm bound to hit one of them."

Nelson signaled high praise by using pilot slang for *shit hot*, "All right. Next stop—*Sierra Hotel*."

Stephen laughed and signaled back avoidance of a clusterfuck, "Roger that. No *Charlie Foxtrot* this trip."

Given a zigzag over the Rockies to avoid weather, they were looking at a long flight. The four-seater would be at capacity. Nelson encouraged DPS to take the prime copilot seat. After the mess-up with the computer, it might have appeared as a lame consolation prize for the kid but Nelson didn't care; he wanted access to Adam in the rear seat to discuss next steps if they could.

As it turned out, the noise of flight or having to talk over headsets made discussion between Adam and Nelson nearly impossible. The headsets were an open channel for the four of them; anything said could be heard by all. Nelson tried talking to Adam without them, but they nearly had to shout to be heard which defeated the purpose.

For most of the trip, Nelson settled in with his thoughts and Adam doodled in a small notebook. Stephen regaled DPS with made-up war stories and DPS enjoyed checking out the instrument panel and getting tips on why not to become a pilot. Despite some heavy turbulence west of Denver, the trip was unremarkable. But all that changed an hour out from Napa.

It started as they headed west. They were flying back in time two hours, which only made the sun rise slower than normal. At one point, Nelson became curious about what the local time would be when they landed. Instead of asking Stephen, Nelson scribbled the question for Adam on his notebook. With typical quant skill, Adam calculated the answer right away.

But the easy problem had redirected Adam's train of thought.

Over the next few minutes, Nelson watched as Adam's doodles shifted onto topics of time. He drew clocks and joke apparatuses he labeled digital sundials. Finally, he began working with numbers and time zones, which led to UTC minus 5. The GFSA Design Doc was discovered in the time zone that covered the eastern part of the United States. The circuitous route back from that document led to an orphan link with an inexplicable name discovered in a temp directory on a laptop in Switzerland. As Adam doodled, Nelson could almost follow the kid's thought process.

Then something remarkable happened.

Adam wrote down the number 86401—the name of the orphan link.

He wrote it down again, then again. In time, he underlined it. What did it mean? Suddenly, Adam looked up with a shot of excitement in his eye. An idea raised him off his seat. Nelson could see that Adam didn't want to alert pilot and passenger in the front seat to his discovery.

Adam rushed an energized scrawl into his notebook and Nelson leaned over, anxious to see the words form. In the next moment, he had his answer.

> 86400—seconds in a day
> 86401—add 1 leap second
> LSEC—leap second

Adam checked the web via his cell phone then handed the phone over. Nelson's eyes gravitated right away to the text highlighted by Adam. It was from an obscure news article dated June 1st, 2017, over six months back.

"On December 31st at 11:59:59 pm, one second will be added to world clocks by the International Earth Rotation Service (IERS) based in Paris, France."

It was so obvious that both of them had missed it. And if *they* had missed it after weeks of looking into things, imagine how the rest of the world would miss it. Project G wasn't rushing to have things ready by the end of the year after all. Systems were already in place. Project managers were merely waiting for the exact moment when the year ended. In that moment, their turn-key system would have the perfect opportunity to be switched on with no one aware that anything had clicked into place.

For Nelson and Adam, seeing the news article meant another puzzle piece fell into place. This was the precise reason why New Year's Eve was the critical timeframe. The GFSA install would be hidden behind a periodic global event few paid any attention to and only interested pockets of professionals even knew or cared about. And yet, it affected everyone, but the effect would not be as benign as it appeared on the surface.

F1E had trained GFSA to reach coherence in one second. Hidden in the December 1st glitch screen had been the last, proof-of-concept rehearsal, a practical demonstration of real-world connectivity and QDE effectiveness working with the KEYSERV. F1E was the final dry run before the Global Financial Sensor Array came on line.

Nelson grabbed the pen from Adam and wrote a quick note back to him.

"Scratch Kingman, Arizona off our itinerary."

The dry humor was lost on Adam. He took his phone back and stared down at his doodles. The more he learned about the secret sensor array system, the more he was awed by it, even as his own wonderment disturbed him. As awe-inspiring as it all might be, this was a global machine designed to systematize the information age into a juggernaut of power and control without privacy.

Nelson jotted down one more note and passed it over. It was a historical reference, probably lost on Adam, but it was fitting nonetheless.

"the empire on which the sun never sets."

62

0000 0011 1110

10:29 pm PST, Thursday, December 27th

Nelson and Adam sat in a corner of the basement, trying to work. Above them, a hole-in-the-wall nightclub in the Polk Gulch neighborhood of San Francisco pounded away with music and the drone of a regular crowd. Laughter, talk, and a dull thump of digitized percussion mixed into a steady din. The musty smell of the basement competed with a mélange of cigarette smoke and alcohol wafting down from above.

Daytime had been mostly quiet but nighttime saw the place transform into party central. If nothing else, for Nelson and Adam, the celebratory clamor made sure their close conversation wouldn't be overheard.

Knee-deep in research on leap seconds, they dug for more.

Nelson gazed at the computer and thought back, "I bet the hoopla over the Y2K Bug before New Year's 2000 was a good example for Project G."

Adam agreed, up to a point. "Except people thought the Millennium Bug would spawn a crisis. This is different. A leap second is a normal thing, in fact, it's pretty boring."

"But it's global and a lot can hide behind it. Y2K showed how any global event that effects a basic, universal technology can be an great opportunity."

"And if most people don't know or care about it, all the better."

Nelson scanned the official leap second announcement from Paris.

A seated Adam leaned forward with forearms resting on legs. Summing up how the LSEC component of the GFSA Project would operate was as much an educated guess as it was a GFSA design document specification.

"The 61-second minute, it's an odd beast, a necessary abstraction. It only happens when some scientist decides it's necessary. They've scheduled it 25 times since 1972, sometimes happening every year. Other times, they skipped it. Once they skipped six years in a row before doing it again."

"What's the trigger?" asked Nelson.

"It all depends how the Earth spins. The Earth is slowing down."

"I thought the Earth moved the same way all the time," confessed Nelson.

"No, it changes just enough to throw off atomic clocks. All Network Time Protocol systems around the world have to sync up to the master clock. That's everybody. All computer systems have NTP or some form of it."

"So how do computers react to the leap second?"

Adam shrugged. "It's a moment that doesn't exist. Computers systems react according to the software that's running at the time. Most are dumb to it, ignore it, or sometimes misinterpret what goes on during the added second and

INTERNATIONAL EARTH ROTATION AND REFERENCE SYSTEMS SERVICE (IERS)
SERVICE INTERNATIONAL DE LA ROTATION
TERRESTRE ET DES SYSTEMES DE REFERENCE

SERVICE DE LA ROTATION TERRESTRE
OBSERVATOIRE DE PARIS
61, Av. de l'Observatoire 75014 PARIS (France)
Tel.   : 33 (0) 1 40 51 22 26
FAX   : 33 (0) 1 40 51 22 91
e-mail : services.iers@obspm.fr
http://hpiers.obspm.fr/eop-pc

Paris, 4 July 2017
Bulletin C 38
To authorities responsible
for the measurement and
distribution of time

UTC TIME STEP
on the 1st of January 2018

A positive leap second will be introduced at the end of December 2017.
The sequence of dates of the UTC second markers will be:

2017 December 31,   23h 59m 59s
2017 December 31,   23h 59m 60s
2018 January 1,   0h 0m 0s

The difference between UTC and the International Atomic Time TAI is:

from 2015 July 1, 0h UTC, to 2018 January 1 0h UTC : UTC-TAI = - 33s
from 2018 January 1, 0h UTC, until further notice   : UTC-TAI = - 34s

Leap seconds can be introduced in UTC at the end of the months of December
or June, depending on the evolution of UT1-TAI. Bulletin C is mailed every
six months, either to announce a time step in UTC or to confirm that there
will be no time step at the next possible date.

Rigel MAINES
Head
Earth Orientation Center of IERS
Observatoire de Paris, France

throw a note into the logs. It's a hiccup that gets registered as 11:59:59 and then, before going to 12:00:00, it sees 11:59:60."

"Which doesn't compute."

"Well yeah, for what it's worth."

Nelson considered it. "One second, but long enough to activate the global sensor network."

"One second gets inserted and the Z computer inserts its activation code."

"I know Z is fast, but how do they get it rolled out so quickly?"

"One of the footnotes in the design doc explains it."

Nelson admitted, "I skipped over the footnotes."

"Well, next time, read them," admonished Adam. "From the way it reads, they've been staging the STUB files for some time. They only had to get access through a few parent companies."

"To do what?"

"Only a few companies make the routers and switches, load balancers and firewalls that are used in computer networks worldwide. All those products get periodic firmware upgrades. System administrators religiously install them because they want the latest bug fixes and code for new features."

"So the Project had STUB files put in all the firmware upgrades?"

"Easy peasy. By now, most network components should carry the STUB. It's sitting there, waiting for Z to contact it. Once that happens, millions of STUBs will contact their local KEYSERV for instructions. And that's all she wrote. All networks, everywhere, will join the sensor array."

"What instructions do the KEYSERVs have for the STUBs?"

"Probably binary commands to pull down SWEBOT enablers so the global structure can lock in place. The QDEs need sensor data to operate but they can't start until the infrastructure gets bolted down."

"You said there are millions of STUBs?"

"At least."

"I would think all those simultaneous calls to the KEYSERVs could overwhelm the system. But wait, that's not what happens, is it? They balance it out because midnight comes an hour at a time through different time zones. As each new time zone reaches midnight, another group connects."

"That's the general idea but not how they would have to do it," corrected Adam. "You're right, the new year comes an hour at a time around the globe. As the Earth spins, GFSA rolls out. But all regional NTP Servers sync up to the master clock at the same time. In the U.S., 6:59:60 pm Eastern Daylight Time is when the extra second is added on the east coast, which aligns with midnight UTC, or Universal Time, which they used to call Greenwich."

"Yeah, whatever…"

"The point is, our atomic clock is at the U.S. Naval Observatory's Master Clock Facility in D.C. With a leap second, every point has to sync up to the world's master clock at midnight UTC, regardless of local time."

"So wherever the new year starts first, that's where they'll start. That would be around Samoa, New Zealand, then moving west."

"Yes," agreed Adam. "Moving west into Asia and then keep on going."

Nelson thought back to their debriefing. "No wonder we were told to look for criminal elements in Hong Kong. Maybe they're worried Lutane or someone else might trying to stop the first dominoes from falling."

"You can watch them fall, hour by hour, as the fireworks go off."

"The perfect misdirection," commented Nelson. "On the one night the world only cares about celebrating, this happens in the background—the one thing they *should* be most concerned about will go unnoticed."

"Even if something abnormal happens during the inserted second, they'll explain it away as a glitch, the same way they did with F1E."

"They've got historical precedent for that." Nelson referred to his screen, "In 2012, Java software choked on the leap second."

"I remember that," agreed Adam. "It brought down a lot of big websites."

Nelson picked up on Adam's state of wonder. "What's wrong?"

"I just thought of something. It gets even more complicated."

"By design?"

"No, in reaction to what some have done to avoid problems like the Java mess in 2012. I think Google was the first one to do it, I'm not sure."

"Do what?"

"Well, here's the thing. The one-second insert was too much of a risk for places like Google so they came up with a solution. Instead of a leap second, they figured out they'd comply by doing the same thing with a *leap smear.*"

"A *smear*? You lost me."

"It's pretty simple. Instead of one second being inserted at one time, they programmed their NTP servers to gradually add milliseconds throughout the day. By the time the one second needed to be added, their clocks already had most of it accounted for. By then, only the final millisecond had to be added. By skewing the added time over one whole day instead of one second, they found their systems were able to tolerate the change better."

"So what does that mean for GFSA?" asked Nelson.

"It means they have to take that into account. It's not as easy as inserting something at UTC midnight, all at once, or per time zone."

"What would they have to do?"

Adam gave it some thought. "There's only one thing to do. They would have to cycle the final instructions out there ahead of time and have the QDEs decide when each location needed its STUB file activated."

"You're talking about individual timings for tens of millions of sites…"

"Nothing that a Z, a few MIN-Zs, and their QDEs couldn't handle. Shit, that'll be easy compared to the data load they're going to have to handle once the sensor array goes live."

"So, at the final moment, each site flips the switch."

"That's all that's left to do. It's staggered, rolling out as each site needs it. After the Earth makes one complete revolution, it's done."

Nelson was cynical. "Not exactly the revolution you were hoping for."

Adam didn't take the bait. Instead, he looked back at the computer. "What time is it? After 10:30. DPS should be here any minute."

"Did you tell him anything?"

"No, he probably thinks it's more about the Santiago calls."

"Good. I want to catch him off-guard, see what he says."

"He'll probably link it to the calls."

"Of course it's linked to the calls. The point is, it puts him with Lutane."

"Yeah, well, a tech resource isn't the same as being in bed with him. DPS is a contractor, like you. You don't always know the whole score."

"We'll see. I think I can make him hum a few bars…"

A first floor door opened and down the steps came DPS. Fresh from a few pleasurable detours in the nightclub above, he entered the room with a lingering smile that only faded when he locked eyes with Nelson.

"Here they are," announced DPS with two shots of tequila in him. "The hacker rats, working away. I hope this is quick; I have business upstairs."

"This won't take long," Nelson assured him before adding, "Provided you can be straight with us on a couple of things."

"Straight," smiled DPS. "Funny choice of words on Polk Street."

Nelson went right to the point. "I got word you've been doing some interesting business with South America."

DPS let loose with graven sass. "Don't tell me this is about my phone call habits again. You have no idea all the places RAPIER operates."

"Oh, I'm sure you're a global force to be reckoned with," snarled Nelson. "What I'm talking about is the colocated HFT pod in a New York datacenter that was rented by RAPIER with funds that my friends have traced back to Chile. You know, as in Santiago, Chile."

Letting go of his faux-festive veneer, DPS let his mood darken then deepen to a place he knew this conversation would take them. "You have clever friends. Too bad their cleverness couldn't find you a safe house too."

"It's not hard for the government to know who my friends are and where to find them," explained Nelson. "Hiding with them wouldn't be so clever."

"So you compromise and with compromise comes concessions. Did you think RAPIER would take on the risk of sheltering you because we owed Adam a debt of thanks?" DPS turned to Adam. "I know you helped us in the past but what you want is not proportional and you know it. You're in deep shit, and that's nothing like what you helped us out of before."

Adam accepted the point but asked, "So what's your idea of quid pro quo? How much do you do for Lutane?"

DPS was silent so Adam pursued the point with sudden concern.

"Are you keylogging us? What about a mirror site?"

DPS let his admission be tacit. "People pay for information. It's the hottest commodity. You know that."

Adam rocked back in his chair. "Shit!"

Nelson took it in, his anger rising. "So everything we've found while in Austin and here…"

Adam glared at DPS. "It's Guernsey all over again. Fuck!" Adam jumped to his feet and paced. "We've been hacking for Lutane and didn't know it!"

DPS chimed in, "It seemed to work better for everyone that way. You felt less constrained; as a result, you've found more."

"Fuck you!" shouted Adam. "Your boss is killing people."

"Just like your government," snapped DPS.

"You don't get it, do you?" Adam got in his face. "There's no good side. You think you scored with a payday. All you've done is opened yourself up to the worst kind of manipulation."

The response was tinged with affectation. "It's a measured opportunity."

"What kind of fucking double speak is that?"

"The kind a quant would understand."

"You rolled over for Lutane."

"I cooperate in the short term. The enemy of my enemy is my friend."

"More bogus talk, not even logical."

"I'll make it clear for you. Lutane wants to bring down the same 1% I'm after, the same 1% you demonstrated against before you moved to Midtown, found the twenty-sixth floor, and became their wage slave."

"You told me RAPIER would never be about prostituting the hack."

"And you told me that idealism had to have a raw edge to get anywhere."

Nelson derided, "Pimp your ride—a revolution by another name."

"Yeah, by another name," hollered DPS. "Nothing is going to happen unless alliances are formed. Wall Street is too powerful. Dumbass Occupiers occupied shit. The hedge fund managers looked down on that circus and laughed. Face it, the Gandhi shit isn't going to work. Sitting down in front of the Federal Reserve with a sign is ludicrous."

Nelson stepped closer. "And what do you think Lutane wants, ultimately? I mean, after you bring down the 1%?"

DPS avoided the question with a reveal. "What don't you ask him. He's waiting outside to talk to you."

Nelson took a step back. "He's here?"

"A stretch limo across the street. He said he's got time for a swing around the block—if you're interested."

"You think I'm interested?" asked Nelson.

DPS regained some swagger. "I don't know, are you clever?"

With that, DPS turned and headed up the stairs.

Nelson looked to Adam. "I'll be right back."

"That's not a good idea."

"Get our stuff ready to leave." Nelson took off his wristband and put it on Adam. "Here, I don't want this to accidentally fall off in the car. Take care of it. If you need to, call Katherine and get help moving to a new place."

"How long should I wait before making the call?"

Nelson hesitated a moment on the bottom step. "It's once around the block. How long can it take?"

Nelson steered a course through the nightclub crowd, perfumed haze, and strobe lighting effects. The bouncer gave him the eye, having been forewarned by DPS that the basement guests were allowed free passage in and out.

Nelson shifted his path through milling stragglers on the sidewalk and paused at the curb. Indeed, a black stretch limo waited across the street. As

Nelson headed towards it, the driver got out and opened the rear door for him. Inside, dressed in California casuals, sat Elijah Alonzo Lutane.

Lutane was alone, lit by small vanity lights. A glass divider ensured their privacy. His opening salvo was brief, his Latin accent rich and suave.

"I don't like to be kept waiting."

Nelson sat back as the car glided forward. "We all have things we don't like."

"You dislike not being the shrewdest one on the playground. You always have to be the wily one or you don't want to play. You must have been an insufferable child."

"Maybe, in some ways, I never grew up. Like you. No matter how much you had, you always had to have more. After you stuffed your face, you stuffed your pockets. You weren't even hungry anymore; you simply couldn't stand anyone else getting their hands on any."

A laugh. "If that were true, I'd be El Gordo, not Elijah."

"You're the one that said you're not a warlord, you're a *more*-lord."

"Did I say that? Really? I must have been angry. I must have been thinking about *them*."

"Do they have a name?"

"No, they don't. It's easier for them that way. But they congregate and they confer, design what's right and decide what's proper and always, always hide their fist in a velvet glove."

"And how would they describe you?"

"You already told me. *A New Age Barbarian*. How dramatic."

"So how would you describe yourself?"

"I'm a businessman, just like them."

"Business can mean many things. Form follows function."

"That's why we're on the same side. We both resent the machine."

"I'm not on anybody's side," insisted Nelson.

"Not even your own? I know you're mad because I tricked you but don't deny your own self-interest. You've seen their plan, as have I, thanks to you. Neither one of us want such a thing to happen."

"I don't believe you. What's the real reason you're against this?"

"You don't have the whole story; you think it's about bankers and politicians, secret agents and rich investors. You leave out the most important part."

"And you're going to tell me," prompted Nelson.

"I have no choice; there's little time left. You see, I'm not the only *New Age Barbarian*. Everything consolidates, even in my world."

"Like crime syndicates," offered Nelson.

"Don't insult me. There is a man, my counterpart; his name is Ishaan Onuti. If you need a reason to align with me, you only have to see for yourself how this man has aligned himself with Project G."

"What are you talking about?"

"Don't be so naive. My world and the world of the so-called 1% merged a long time ago, despite what you may have been told. You might say we're the left- and right-hand of the same body. But Onuti is something new. He will not run the world as a business."

"I get it. You don't like the fact that the Project picked him instead of you to do business with."

"True, but that's not the point. It's a gambit they often play, a game of divide and conquer. You know how it works. They maneuver two forces into a tug of war and put a spotlight on them. Sometimes their differences are real; if so, they get exploited out of proportion. Most times their differences are manufactured. A lot of energy is expended with no real motion either way. Everyone must participate in the tug of war or sit in the audience. It gets very dramatic. The audience is desperate to see what happens, even though little of substance ever does. In your country, you know this game as Democrats and Republicans, red state versus blue state, Coke against Pepsi."

"What's your point?" asked Nelson.

"Onuti and I could have challenged them if we had joined forces."

"They split you up by promising him something."

"The Project thinks they're using him. He sees it differently."

"How are they using him?"

"In many ways. It makes it easier to get secret work done. Project financing was laundered. In exchange for his contributions, he's been promised a seat at the table. He's made certain resources available to them."

"Such as?"

"Opium production profits. After 9/11, they've never been higher."

"But the Project is theirs, not his. They have the leverage, not him."

"But he's in the body."

"The body?"

"*Their* body. He'll metastasize. If that happens, they'll see how one unruly cell can grow, dominate, and destroy."

"How is he any different than you? You said, you two could have been partners; you're from the same business."

Elijah paused, staring across into Nelson's eyes, before an angered passion entered his voice. "He won't stop with stuffing his face and pockets. He's always hungry but he has something more, an elegant solution for not letting anyone else get their hands on any. He'll *eliminate* whole *nations* to feel secure. I know him. He no longer believes in incremental change."

"And this is the man you were going to team up with?"

"He's different now. They've corrupted him."

Nelson laughed. "Really? He got worse by association with *them*? How?"

"They proved to him that his dream can come true."

"Meaning what?"

"The ultimate expression of power is control, Mr. Geiss. Until he met them, he only had a vision of perfect control. Even he knew it was wishful thinking. All of that changed when they showed him part of their plan. He could see what they had was much more than wishful thinking. Before long, they would have a system that would institutionalize power and control in a few hands. He wouldn't tell me exactly what that system would be."

"But now you know..."

"Yes, thanks in part to you. The reality of such a thing can be intoxicating, especially for a man who sees a way to make his wildest dream come true."

"It's not *your* dream?" asked Nelson.

"I have children, he has none. I have to wonder what the future will be like for them. Plus, I am older; he is younger. I'm less inclined to impulses that turn out too good to be true. Some things are necessary in business but you wouldn't do them at home. As much as possible, businessmen try to leave their nightmares outside the door. Onuti sees no such distinctions. Dreams and nightmares are the same to him, equally useful in all places and times. If he gets power, dreams and nightmares will merge for all of us."

"Who do you fear more? Him or them?"

"It's not about fear. It's about survival. I don't fear death but I know I won't survive under their system. They want it all. There's no room for me. The fact that they would even offered Onuti a place at their table shows how far they have come. Once they have their system in place, even if they manage to get rid of him, which I doubt, they will become like him."

"Power corrupts. That's funny coming from you but you should know."

"The world has never seen this kind of potential realized before."

"And you expect me to believe you're afraid of it, you don't want it."

"I've seen it. I've looked into its eyes."

"Onuti?"

"No." Elijah shifted on the leather seat and lit a thin cigar. "As a kid, my grandmother told me a story; she wanted to frighten me into being good."

"You must have been a big disappointment to her."

Elijah seethed with both anger and humor, showing a grin. "No more than you were to Madelyn, huh?" The reference to Nelson's dead wife was meant to sting Nelson back and warn him: don't compete with Elijah in dispensing pain, for he would lose.

Elijah continued, "Her story went like this: she told me about the most vile and hateful criminal who died one day and found himself falling into hell. Not so surprisingly, this didn't bother him; if anything, he was looking forward to it. To spend all eternity with the worst of the worst like him would be nothing he couldn't handle. In fact, if his life was any measure, he would like it. But then he met the Devil and looked into his eyes. He saw that the Devil didn't just *do* vile things; the Devil *was* vile. He saw that the Devil wasn't just *enjoying* evil things; the Devil *was* evil. Facing the Devil, one-on-one, this vile and hateful criminal soon realized for the first time what he was facing. Everything bad he had done up to that point was a mere shadow compared to the real thing. There would be no simpatico between them. In that moment, the terrible charade was bare and all too painful. He, the one who thought he was so evil, knew *real* evil for the first time." Elijah's grin was strained. "For the first time he understood what would happen next…and it wouldn't be *good*."

"What do you want from me?" asked Nelson.

"I need to know the rest of the plan. I must stop it."

"And then what? You think the genie can be put back in the bottle? You think things will go back to the way they were before they knew all this could be done? You expect me to believe you're not going to try to leverage anything you've found out?" The limo stopped.

Elijah ignored the change in motion. "The facts drive everything."

"From what I can tell, the facts are: you're afraid Onuti is going to use Project power to come after you; settle some old scores. You'll be out of business."

Elijah puffed his cigar and showed Nelson a casual smile. "I like my life the way it is. I'll have no life if this is allowed to happen. And neither will many other people. Those are the facts."

"Is that it?"

The rear car door opened next to Nelson; the driver stood outside.

Elijah rolled his cigar back and forth between forefinger and thumb and lowered his tone to a whisper. "They will kill you. Their agents are already in the city. Unless they are thrown off your path, it won't take them long to find you. I can try to protect you. But you must stay here and work. Uncover the rest of the plan!"

Mention of agents being in the city concerned Nelson but he didn't want to let on to Elijah that he wasn't aware of this. Nelson couldn't commit to helping him but rebuffing him out of hand might provoke Elijah to react and call off any protection that was out there.

Nelson turned and started out the open door. "Thanks for the ride."

As Nelson made it outside, he heard Elijah respond, "Feliz año nuevo."

63

0000 0011 1111

11:42 pm PST, Thursday, December 27th

A biting chill clung to the fog rolling in through the Golden Gate. Nightclub patrons bundled up as they came and went along Polk Street. For Nelson, the nippiness paled in comparison to a Cheyenne winter. He crossed the street with his light coat flapping open. He studied the half block ahead. The limo had parked down the street from the pickup spot. Nelson would have a ways to go before getting back to the club.

Along the way, a man approached him out of the shadows. Both of them were on edge. The man left strategic space between them and spoke first.

"Adam's waiting behind the club. Watch your six."

Nelson said nothing in return. He brushed by the man, as if dodging a panhandler and pressed on. When they briefly made contact, the man pressed a slip of paper into Nelson's hand. Nelson closed his fist around it and used the last few steps before the club's entrance to weigh his options.

The man from the shadows could be one of Elijah's men, testing him. He could be one of Katherine's contractors telling the truth. Or he might be a Steigbriar agent laying down a trap, one that Elijah's men in the club wouldn't notice. Maybe Steigbriar had orders to take them alive. Or maybe they wanted the elimination without fanfare, away from public places.

Elijah had warned him about *agents* being in the city. If Elijah meant what he said and intended on providing protection, then Elijah's goons and Steigbriar forces were on a collision course.

If nothing else, the man's closing comment was true enough. *Watch your six.* It was an obvious warning to watch for trouble behind him, one that a good asset didn't need to be reminded of. The fact that he said it came across more as a good luck wish, a note of concerned solidarity.

Nelson waited the obligatory moment at the nightclub's entrance while the doorman and bouncer had their display of authority. Nelson said nothing to them and brushed on past into the flash, darkness, and pulse of the party going on inside. The bar area offered the most light. Nelson made his way to an open spot and read the slip of paper in his hand.

emRooz

The Farsi word shot through him. It meant *today*, just as *deeRooz* was *yesterday*, and *Farda* was *tomorrow*. Having been with Katherine not that long ago, Nelson couldn't hold back the memories. Right away, he was back in Afghanistan, one day after Katherine had shipped out. Her transport had unexpectedly left before Nelson had gotten back from the field. Their mission was winding down. He would be the next to be reassigned. Her sudden absence was a hollow spot back in camp, one that was as wide as the Registan Desert and just as empty and desolate.

Nelson remembered the funny bon voyage card she had left for him. She must have planned it for some time. She signed it simply *Katherine* but underneath she had added another line. It looked to be a last minute addition, something added in haste—*deeRooz, emRooz, Farda*.

It was the first outward sign that what they meant to each other went beyond friendship. At the time, it was a tortured realization. As sincere, slight, and sweet as it was, she knew her admission wouldn't be acted upon. It was a confession wrenched out of the heartache of the moment, something evoked from the callous way the separation wouldn't let them say a proper goodbye. Nelson understood all too well how a weak moment might have prompted such a thing. If places were reversed, he would have felt the same.

Close laughter and loud music brought Nelson back to the nightclub. The heaviness of the moment flowed around him, awaiting his reaction. The slip of paper was obviously a sign to make Nelson think that the man in the shadows was one of the contractors working with Katherine. That left Nelson wondering if it was true. He headed for the club's back door.

There was only one way to find out.

The passageway behind the club was only big enough for a commercial-sized trash bin and a couple of cars. Stepping out into blackness, Nelson held back and let his eyes adjust. He could see one parked car. It had backed into the space and was aimed towards the street.

Nelson waited, his back to the club. A man stepped out of the hidden space alongside the large waste bin and approached him. Nelson was ready to engage him but the man's gait and silhouette soon disarmed him. Nelson had spent enough time over the past weeks with Adam to recognize him only from hints and suggestions of posture and attitude.

"Nelson…" Adam whispered nervously. "Let's go!"

The two of them hurried to the car and got in.

The driver was a woman Nelson didn't recognize. She turned back to Nelson and handed him a Beretta 90-Two pistol. "The gang's all here."

Introductions were over. Nelson settled back and the car moved into the street. As they turned right, another car switched on lights and followed. The woman gave the other car a glance of acknowledgement as they drove by.

Adam was stressed. "Once around the block, huh?"

"What can I say, he likes to talk." Nelson checked the Beretta's chamber and clip, then stuffed the sidearm into his waistband.

"I didn't know how long to wait."

Nelson checked the woman's eyes glancing at them in the rearview mirror. "I said to get our stuff *ready* to leave. You're out the door."

"Yeah, well, DPS came back and pissed me off. Then I got a call from

Katherine; I mean, *you* got a call." Adam handed back the wristband. "Here, you can have this back."

"What did she say?"

"Geri Messare wants a meeting. She's waiting at Russian Hill Park, the corner of Bay and Larkin."

Nelson was angered. "You volunteered me for the meeting?"

"No, but I told her we might be needing a new place and she offered the car to help us either way."

The driver spoke up. "I'll take you to the meeting or another place where you want to stay. You tell me."

Adam added, "Or we can go back to the club. They don't know we're gone yet. Of course, if we go back, we'll need to redo the computers."

Nelson read into the mischief on Adam's face. "SUCBAR?"

Adam confessed, "It was the quickest way to close things out."

"Just like that, you shut it down."

"You're not going to give everything to Lutane, are you? That's what he wants, isn't it?" Nelson said nothing. "What did he say?"

"He wants us to save the world. He wants the world safe for his family."

"He's crazy, right?"

"He's trying his best to recruit me."

"That includes me," stressed Adam. "What did you tell him?"

"I thanked him for the ride."

"What kind of shit is that? *Thanks for the ride?* He's been riding our asses and we didn't even know it. You can't trust him. You're not thinking about hooking up with him, are you?"

"No, but letting him think so in the short term could have advantages."

"Like what?"

"He has his own security force. If he thinks we're working for him, he'll use his force to keep Steigbriar off our backs. Of course, if he finds out about the computers at the nightclub, he might think our answer is no."

"I thought we didn't need him. We've got help from Katherine now."

Nelson eyed the rearview mirror and caught the interested glance of the woman in front. "We can use all the help we can get."

Adam was jittery. "OK, so what are we going to do?"

Nelson's answer was as much intended for the driver as it was for Adam. "We'll go to the meeting with Messare and see what she wants. After the meeting, we'll decide."

Nelson sat back and the driver made a turn. Russian Hill Park was only a few blocks away. The driver parked a block away.

Adam added detail from Katherine's call. "Messare said there are steps alongside the dead-end side of Larkin. She'll meet you on the steps."

Nelson leaned forward and asked the driver. "What about your second car?" Nelson referenced the car she had acknowledged when they left the club.

She turned her head to answer. "He's in position at the top of the hill. I'll stay down here. You have an exit either way."

"Thanks," offered Nelson. He turned to Adam. "You stay here. Try to think of some non-machine readable data to help us."

The driver furrowed her brow in wonder at the comment. Nelson grinned and got out. He found the steps and headed up. Halfway to the top, shrouded by the overhang of trees, stood Geri Messare in black pants and coat, her hands buried in pockets. One of them, no doubt, was wrapped around adequate protection with the safety off.

Always cheeky, she greeted him. "We finally come together in the dark."

On the last step, Nelson kept his distance. "Dark...yes, but it's cold."

"Even more reason to come closer." With Nelson staying in place, she was forced to come to him. "It's interesting you should wind up in my city. Of course, you're going to tell me it wasn't planned and I'm going to remind you that you always plan everything."

"The first casualty of war..." prompted Nelson.

"The battle plans..." added Geri. "Yes, I've heard that too."

"That may be true, but it's not what I meant. The way I heard it, the first casualty is the truth."

"Is that what you came here for? The truth? You picked the wrong business to work in. I knew as soon as you started snooping into the black hole that opened up around Extasis, you'd wind up getting yourself in deep. You know, they call it a black hole for a reason. It has no bottom. Once inside, there's nowhere to go. It traps you."

"You avoided the pull of it conveniently enough, didn't you?"

Geri's tone sharpened. "You want something true? I'm here to apologize, in person, for caving into Richard Marks."

"I know it must have been difficult. He made threats. He was persuasive."

"I had no idea it would get this serious."

"How serious is it?" asked Nelson.

"You know damn well. Friends have died, others are being threatened. It's gone too far. I won't be intimidated to sit on the fence any longer."

"Commendable," observed Nelson with clear skepticism. "So what are you offering? A place to stay? A warm bed?"

"My bed is under surveillance. It's occupied at the moment anyway."

"For the moment. Should I wait?"

"Would you?"

Nelson pushed past innuendo and insult. "You must have heard I was looking for shelter."

"Yes, a private place, temporarily, to do some work."

"So what, you've got a friend you'd like to introduce me to? A little tit for tat? I get shelter in exchange for something? And for you, a finder's fee? It *is* about a deal, isn't it? It's always been about the deal with you."

Geri stepped up, close enough for him to smell the little bit of perfume she wore. She was blunt. "Even family members bargain with each other. They say marriage is a compromise. Believe it or not, most deals are done at home, at least the important ones. To be willing to deal means one is willing to get involved. Don't make it sound so dirty. We all do it."

"So what's the deal?" asked Nelson. He leaned in and assessed her comfort level with him barely touching alongside the length of her.

His entry into her personal space evoked a turmoil in her, one she wasn't expecting. Her breaths quickened even as her expression held firm. She needed to explain what she had found but they both knew neither would be fully concentrating on it.

For Nelson, it was a way to push her out of her comfort zone, to test her. It was always easier to gauge the strength of an off-balance opponent.

"I remember you told me once…" she started, her whisper deepening.

He slipped his arm behind her, held her firm against him, and listened.

She continued, "You told me about a book that annoyed you. It was written by a psychology professor. He said those who give credence to conspiracy theories were the victims of a pathology."

"I remember that," added Nelson. He held firm and waited for more.

Geri went on, "He said most conspiracy theories could be easily debunked. He had a name for anyone who was infatuated with them."

"That's right. He said it was a *disorder*."

"Yes, he gave it some fancy name."

Nelson whispered in her ear. "What has this got to do with us right now?"

Relaxing to his touch, she turned slightly so she could press herself directly against him. Now *she* was testing *him*. "That same professor works at Berkeley. He has a home nearby. I also know, for a fact, he and his family are away this week in the South Pacific on vacation."

"What are you saying?" asked Nelson, unsure of her intentions.

"I'm saying, his home has a security system. I've arranged for the back door, the one that enters the mud room off the kitchen, to be off that system. As long as you enter and exit by that door, you'll have the house to yourself for a week." Geri transferred directions to the house from her pocket into his.

Her offer seemed genuine but he showed doubt. "You really did this?"

"I thought you might enjoy the irony of staying at his place. You're chasing a conspiracy. Why not use his computers to do it?" She smiled.

The notion appealed to Nelson's sense of karmic propriety and one-upmanship, as she knew it would. He had to ask, "What's in it for you?"

She rubbed herself into him in such a way to give definition to the curves under her coat. "I told you. It's my apology. It would help you, wouldn't it?"

"Yes," admitted Nelson.

"That's what Katherine asked for—anything that would help." Geri pulled away, breaking their touch. "You two are lucky to have found each other again. The timing's right."

Nelson was about to answer when gunshots rang out. Both of them dropped to the stairs and drew their weapons.

Nelson read the direction of gunplay. "That's not coming our way."

Geri raised up for a peek downhill. "Two cars exchanging fire."

Nelson jumped up, thinking of Adam waiting down below. "Damn!"

Geri took a moment to rest a warm palm at the side of his face. "Good luck in Berkeley, hon."

"Thanks." With that, they scurried off their separate ways. In the distance, a police siren's approach from farther down the hill got louder.

Nelson made his way to the top of the hill where the second car had taken up position. As soon as he emerged from the park, the car lurched forward and turned on its lights. Nelson held his Beretta at the ready until he was certain the car was friendly. With one glance in, Nelson saw it was the man from the shadows, the same one who put *emRooz* into his hand.

The driver headed in a zigzag course away from more gunshots coming from down below. Keeping to the speed limit and watching the mirrors, he filled Nelson in. "Adam will meet us at the rendezvous point."

"If he's OK," noted Nelson, considering the gunfire.

"He's all right," the driver declared. "Steigbriar and Lutane's men are mixing it up. Adam's car isn't involved."

"Steigbriar is that close?"

"Yeah, it surprised us too."

"How did they even engage each other? Who saw who first?"

"We don't know but somebody was onto your meeting."

"From which side, mine or Messare's?"

"Could be either one. It looks like, when you and Messare got together, it made the other two cross paths. Either way, you're lucky. It probably stopped an ambush. Somebody would have been waiting for your meeting to end."

Nelson heard Elijah's parting words from the limo once again. *"They will kill you. Their agents are already in the city. Unless they are thrown off your path, it won't take them long to find you. I will try to protect you."*

"You have any idea where you want to go?" asked the driver.

Nelson was pressed to decide. Tomorrow was the 28th. Adam had already executed SUCBAR at the nightclub. They could fly to another city, but where? Nelson dug his hand into his pants pocket and produced the directions from Geri. The only option available was better than none.

"Yeah." Nelson read the note. "East Bay, Berkeley. Here's the address."

The driver took note in hand and gave it a glance. "For how long?"

As they crested a hill, lights on the East Bay Bridge could be seen in the distance. Nelson answered through rising concern, "As short as possible."

"You mean tonight?"

"No," explained Nelson. "We have to be out of there by the 1st."

64

0000 0100 0000

1:01 am PST, Friday, December 28th

In the dark, a click. Nelson raised up from being down on one knee and opened the mud room door. With Beretta in hand, he waved Adam forward.

Adam waited until they were both inside before asking, "Which career taught you that?"

Nelson slipped away his lock pick tool, shouldered his backpack, then moved past Adam. "I learned that as a kid in school, before any career."

Adam followed after, mumbling, "Must have been a fun class reunion."

He followed Nelson's instructions, given during their ride to Berkeley. No turning on lights. Proper tape over the pads of their fingers so no fingerprints. No disturbing anything unless Nelson had a chance to check it out first. No electronics on except the computer. After making sure the house was secure, finding computers was the primary order of business.

They found the professor's study on the second floor. The ample, English tutor style house was set back from the road and surrounded by mature foliage. Even so, Nelson made sure they blacked out the windows in the room. They closed the wooden shutters and hung layers of the heaviest fabrics they could find over every window in the room.

Satisfied that they had the professor's study fortified as their workspace, Nelson released Adam to check out the available computers: a desktop, a laptop, and a tablet. The desktop was found in the study; the laptop and tablet were gathered from other rooms. Nelson figured he'd work on the laptop, Adam could work on the desktop, and the tablet was just in case.

Adam grouped the computers on the desk and set to work checking them out. "You don't want anything turned on except the computers."

"That's right," answered Nelson. "Not if we can help it."

"You really think energy use in the house is being monitored?"

"I don't know. The less we disturb the place the better."

"That's funny," grinned Adam. "When I was in college I read a report by the International Energy Agency. It said in 2008, almost 1-1/2 months of all the electricity generated in the United States went to power the internet."

"You're kidding…"

"No. All the data servers, transmission lines, routers, personal computers and smart phones suck up a lot of juice. IEA predicted electricity use by computers and consumer electronics would double by 2022. Triple by 2030."

"That's quite a carbon footprint," noted Nelson. "But I don't think people are going to turn off their gadgets."

Adam worked away on the three devices. "I know one thing. These are staying on; that's for sure."

It took an hour for Adam to check everything out and set them up with access to each other and their safe place online. While Nelson waited, he called Katherine and gave her an update. She confirmed that her contractor assets would take shifts standing watch and guard near the professor's house. It was a tall order. Protecting them now meant being on the lookout for a triple threat from government agents, Lutane, or Steigbriar. The only bright side was that Lutane and Steigbriar were at odds with one another.

At 2:36 am, Nelson got another call on his wristband. He assumed it was Katherine. "Forget something or can't you sleep?"

"Are those my only choices?" It was 1021.

Nelson's reaction drew Adam's attention. Nelson observed, "I guess you have the technology to listen in to my calls with Katherine."

"You would be smart to assume that."

"So I don't have to update you on what's gone on."

"Are you working the leads?"

"We had to regroup."

"You don't have the luxury of spending time on anything else."

"We got the design document."

"Yes…yes, you did. And what else?"

"We know they're using the leap second."

"Very good. And what do you think of their plan so far?"

Hearing one side of the conversation, Adam was intrigued. He stopped what he was doing and came over to where Nelson rested on a couch with the laptop. Nelson watched Adam take a seat nearby and answered 1021.

"It's impressive."

"Really?" 1021 waited for more.

"Yes, so impressive I'd call it creepy."

"In what way?" 1021 pursued.

"Isn't it obvious? The new capability, held in secret, would be unstoppable. There's nothing they couldn't know…"

"And wouldn't do?"

"Who could stop them?"

"And how does that make you feel? Are you comforted to know the Homeland will be secured with a system so powerful?"

"Is *that* what this is about? *The Homeland*?"

"If you ask, that's what they'll say. What do you think?"

"I think their design document doesn't go into that."

"And if you knew their whole plan…what would you do?"

"Hard to say. I haven't heard the plan."

"Oh, come on now, you can guess, can't you? If you see earthmovers approach rolling hills, it doesn't take a quant to know what is going to happen.

A flat space will be prepared, one they can build on."

"You're saying this is only the beginning."

"It's basic tactics, Mr. Geiss. Control the favorable positions before engaging. First, you ensure control. Once you are confident you cannot be challenged, only then do you move forward with everything that would have been unthinkable before."

"I don't follow you," Nelson baited.

"There are many technologies they hold in reserve, wondrous things given to them by people like me. Control over information and finance is only one kind of power. Yes, they're fundamental in our society but not the only way to shape the future. Certainly not the most permanent."

"If I didn't know better, I'd say you were trying to get me to believe in some massive conspiracy."

"The thing itself is not so massive. Only the effect. The light from an atomic bomb is the most brilliant, intense light imaginable. It's so bright, it can literally burn your shadow into a wall. The reason why that light is so brilliant is due to one simple fact—the light emanates from the nucleus of an atom. So you see, being critically to the point—one decisive point, can be much more powerful than just being massive."

Nelson humored him, "You're the scientist; I guess you should know."

"There are three days left. Ask Adam, if he had the power to do anything, what would he like to do with the last three days."

Nelson hesitated, then complied; the question was repeated.

Having heard only Nelson's side of the conversation, Adam asked for clarification. "What power is he talking about?"

Nelson relayed 1021's answer. "The power to intercede." Nelson put the wristband on Adam's wrist.

"You need to ask that again. I couldn't hear you," explained Adam.

"Oh, I forgot," answered 1021. "You two have only one wristband. How about now? Can both of you hear me?"

Adam nodded and Nelson answered, "Yeah. We hear you."

"Good, because I need you both to answer. What would you like to do?"

"I'd like to know more," Nelson shot back.

Adam added, "If the document is genuine, I'd like to stop them from turning the thing on."

"Genuine?" 1021 rejoined. "What would it take to satisfy you?"

"I don't know, but that 86401 link could have gone anywhere."

"You have the address," countered 1021.

Nelson added in, "As far as we know, that address connects to one of your own offices."

"My, what a conniving mind. You really think it's a possibility that I'm going through all this just to have you find things I already know?"

"Maybe you want to convince us to take some kind of action," Nelson hypothesized. "The documents would only be motivation to an end."

1021 noted, "And Guernsey, the ETC, the Kennigus confession, the deaths of Hollister and Dystrom, I guess I arranged those things too. Amazing, after all you've been through, you're doubtful."

Adam responded, "I don't like what I've seen but Nelson's right. We don't know the whole thing."

"What more do you need to know?" 1021's question came out more as a statement of frustration.

Adam shifted position on the couch. "For one thing, the design document doesn't say squat about an AES hack. And the hack is *key*. Without being able to bust strong AES encryption, their QDEs are just HFTs on steroids."

"I can assure you the *hack*, as you call it, is real. It does exist."

"Great," added Nelson. "We'll take your word on it."

"I'm surprised at you two," 1021 admonished. "You got so excited over this design document, you've neglected to see what remains."

"What do you mean?" asked Nelson.

"The whiteboard picture from Lake Maggiore," answered 1021. "You still haven't figured out two of the words from that board."

Nelson looked to Adam and Adam puzzled through his memory of the *Buon Anno* photo. Then it came to him. It was true; in their excitement and fervor to understand the design document, they had neglected what was left. Was it any wonder; rushing out of Austin and then from the nightclub in San Francisco amidst gunshots, impromptu limo rides with crime bosses, and double-crossing revolutionaries hadn't helped their concentration.

Adam announced their oversight, "*Namagiri* and *Parabrah*."

"Very good," answered 1021 with a glint of pride. "What do you know about them?"

Adam offered back, "One's a Hindu goddess; the other one means Highest Brahman, the Supreme Lord beyond Brahman."

"If this was all about Hindu philosophy, I'd say you're correct."

"Obviously, they're names for something else," noted Nelson. "We don't think they're acronyms. Whatever they are, they seem out of place."

"Perhaps because *I* chose them," announced 1021. "Keeping in line with my name selection, the Project subsequently named their new supercomputer composite *Ekagraphene*. EKA is Sanskrit for *1* or *the first*."

Adam excitedly jumped from disclosure to conclusion. "Wait a minute…*you're* the *wizard*, the guy, the one who did it?"

Nelson turned to Adam. "You mean the hack?"

Adam was enthused. "What else can it be?"

1021 intoned, "As it says in the Bhagavad-Gita, *'Through long lapse of time, this knowledge was lost. But now as you are devoted to truth, I will reveal the supreme secret.'*"

Excited to discover, Adam asked 1021, "How the hell did you do it?"

"I had help," admitted 1021.

"The Z computer…"

"No," came the answer. "For me, the critical help came from a flash of inspiration, a moment when I looked at one thing and saw another."

"You looked at what?" coaxed Adam.

"A work of genius that tragically was left unfinished."

"Why?"

"Because Srinivasa Ramanujan died much too young. He was only 32 when his health gave way. That was long ago, in 1920."

Adam could see that Nelson hadn't heard of the man. Eager to show 1021 what he knew, Adam added, "Ramanujan was a savant. No formal training, at first working alone in India, he came up with some incredible stuff."

"No formal training was a blessing, as it usually is," observed 1021. "Originality wasn't schooled out of him."

"So what happened?" asked Adam. "You completed one of his theorems?"

"Nothing so direct," came the rebuke. "As you probably know, Ramanujan worked with G.N. Watson at Cambridge for a while. In 1976, some of Ramanujan's work was found in Watson's papers. This Ramanujan collection has since been called *the lost notebook*. It consists of 650 results with no proofs. As testament to his brilliance, Ramanujan often worked backwards from traditional methods. His genius was being able to first conclude where he should be and then he built the ladder to get there."

"The lost notebook was missing all its ladders," concluded Adam.

"Yes, but somehow, by thought experiment alone, Ramanujan already knew they could be built."

"What does he have to do with Namagiri?" asked Nelson.

"Namagiri was Srinivasa Ramanujan's family deity. She was pivotal to his career."

Nelson quizzed, "A Hindu goddess and a math savant—what's the connection?"

"You mean, besides the fact that he claimed the goddess whispered equations to him while he slept? When Ramanujan had a chance to go to England to study with Watson, his mother said it was forbidden—that is, until *she* had a nighttime visitation from Namagiri. As the story goes, the goddess told her not to stand in the way of her son fulfilling his life's purpose."

Nelson grinned, "Sounds as plausible to me as any conspiracy theory."

"You don't have to believe it," answered 1021. "The point is, the way Ramanujan approached his thought experiments gave me an insight. The logic he used to explain his process gave me inspiration. One item in the lost notebook jarred my sense of smug equilibrium as a scientist. The result, five years later, was an elegant solution that I applied to the Riemann Hypothesis, the Rijndael Cipher, and number theory in general. In honor of the one who inspired the man who inspired me, I named my solution *Namagiri*."

Adam confirmed, "The solution for strong AES encryption."

"Among other things," boosted 1021.

"What about *Parabrah*?" prompted Nelson.

"Para Brahman is a term often used by Vedantic philosophers to mean *the attainment of the ultimate goal*."

Nelson repeated 1021's statement back at him, "And if this was all about Hindu philosophy, I'd say how that applies to us is correct."

"As it turned out," explained 1021. "*Namagiri* would be the easier part of my work. At least, the most fun part."

"So the government took it and they wanted more."

"They were more specific. Giving them a skeleton key to everything only made them feel vulnerable. They wanted a new lock."

"A new type of encryption," reasoned Adam. "AES was dead. They wanted something to take its place, something to match *Namagiri*."

1021 added the crescendo, "Something I called *Parabrah*."

"The ultimate goal," added Nelson. "You gave that to them too?"

A hidden sense of guilt turned defensive. "As if scientists have a choice."

"They don't?"

"The best minds circle the money-drain, Mr. Geiss. Why do you think the X-37B robotic space plane stayed in orbit for 224 days on its maiden flight? Another so-called prototype stayed in orbit 469 days. All X-37B missions are classified. It couldn't be about growing ultra-pure diamonds and synthetic crystals in zero-G, not when quantum bits are stored so nicely in them."

"Strange," noted Nelson. "It seems to me I remember guards at the death camps in World War II giving a similar defense. They were only tools, they didn't give orders."

"*Scientia est potentia*," answered 1021. "Knowledge is power. It's the motto of DARPA's Total Information Awareness Program. Sadly, in many ways, we all lack true knowledge. Even mathematicians have had to admit that some things will never be known, never understood—read Gödel's incompleteness theorems. In between extremes there's infinite gray. Only from the outside of things does there seem to be easy solutions. Apparently, that holds true even for semi-retired IC assets with delusions of grandeur."

Nelson ignored the slam. "I've seen my share of what's easy and hard. Either way, scientists keep handing the solutions over to the wrong people."

"Human problems are not easy problems so it's likely they are no easy solutions. Society is like a random number generator, Mr. Geiss. You might think it would be easy to generate random numbers, but actually it's one of the toughest problems faced by cryptographers. John von Neumann proclaimed that anyone who uses software to produce random numbers is in a *state of sin*. On the other hand, Donald Knuth demonstrated how one could not use a truly random method to generate random numbers. It seems counterintuitive to conclude such a thing, but when he tried to do it, his system immediately converged to a useless fixed point—one point when what he needed was an infinite series of random points."

"Needless to say," Nelson cajoled, "you solved that problem."

"As Ramanujan knew, such problems require a different way of thinking. Too often, we work problems without questioning the premises underlining the immediate need to solve them. If nature is not random, can randomness even be achieved? Maybe there's another way, a way that doesn't even include randomness. Without that kind of thinking brought to bear, human problems will always be a super-increasing sequence—each value will be larger than the sum of all the values that came before. A final, equitable calculation will always be out of reach."

"All right," snarled Nelson. "We've heard your mumbo-jumbo. What's your point? What do you want us to do?"

"That's the question I asked *you*. I'm not sure I got a complete answer."

"I told you," Adam spoke up. "If I could, I'd stop this thing."

"All right," conjectured 1021. "So you've stopped it. Now what happens? What if the Project is rescheduled? Do you stop it again? And again? How many times do you think you'll be able to stop them before they stop you?"

Nelson added, "If the whole thing stays a secret, not long. They just about shut us down tonight."

"So what to do about it?" asked 1021.

"Somehow," reasoned Adam. "The whole thing has to be exposed."

"Investigative reporters to the rescue, huh?" chuckled 1021.

"Well, the leak would have to be huge, like spread all over the internet. It would have to be more than a few emails and offshore account numbers."

"Ah, something taken from the bottom of the dirt pile," declared 1021. "But hasn't there been leaks before? Once in a while we hear about some whistleblower who gets trotted up before a Congressional committee. For a few days, CSPAN is full of their bluster and sworn testimony and nobody watches. And then what? Recommendations are made, they're passed along to staffers who research everything until another news item takes its place. Nothing is done, except the whistleblower is blackballed and harassed and made an example of for others who might be thinking about throwing their lives away. The whistleblowers closest to the truth get branded as traitors—or worse, they die in fiery one-car accidents without explanation."

"I said it would have to be huge," answered Adam.

"You would only be labeled a cyber-terrorist. They would trot out their talking heads to shout how you endangered the lives of the good citizens by nearly crippling their efforts to go after even *worse* terrorists. Exposing any-thing, even if it was criminal, would jeopardize the *War on Terror* and no one wants to do that? After all, see how safe it's kept us so far?"

"It wouldn't matter," barked Adam. "The dirt would be out there. People would see them for what they are, regardless what they labeled me. At least they'd have a chance to see the things they're doing and planning."

"If *enough* got out there," added Nelson. "Maybe something would gain traction."

1021 was unimpressed. "It's possible, but the traction would have to persist. The chances of that working are slim, you know that."

"If you're so fatalistic, we might as well pack this in now," answered Nelson. "If we don't try something like that, what's the alternative? Sit back and watch it happen? What are we going to feel like on the 1st if we knew all this ahead of time and did nothing?"

"Yes, you've been given a gift," announced 1021. "And you're in the position to do something about it. Unlike the masses, you know what's about to happen. You see how all the moves in the game of power are about to be locked up for selective, private use. Somehow, miraculously, you might be able to stop them. And maybe it is possible to flood the internet with their plans and evidence of their wrongdoing. If I give you *Namagiri* and *Parabrah*, you'll certainly have the tools to attempt all of that and more."

Adam perked up. "Did you say you'd give us…"

"You heard me," 1021 interrupted. "The keys to the kingdom, along with the CAPI so you can code your own tools to do the job."

Nelson looked to Adam and asked, "What's a CAPI?"

"Cryptographic Application Programmers Interface."

1021 added, "If you agree to act on what you've said, you have to commit to be in all the way. To succeed, you'll have to get into Bluffsdale. Project controls for the Z computer are kept there."

Nelson stiffened with doubt, "How are we going to walk into ground-zero NSA without being noticed?"

"First of all, you're not walking in. Secondly, just because institutions have power doesn't mean every bureaucrat in the pyramid is formidable. They can push buttons on people but it's only people pushing those buttons."

"How complicated do you think it'll be to stop them?" asked Adam.

A new force of will filled 1021's voice. "It doesn't matter if they've built the most god-awful, humongous machine. If the starter switch doesn't work, it'll just sit there. There's no way we're going to take down the hardware, but software and people's reputations are vulnerable. I can tell you which are the critical system modules but you'll have to get there and place the stop code."

"What about the leaks?" asked Nelson. "Where are we going to get all the dirt? And when we get it, how do we stage it all for release?"

"The system is intended to favor a few. The QDEs are designed to funnel advantages to those points. Examine the system and you'll see where the funnel goes. The dirt will be there. As far as staging it, the QDEs must be going through their final smoke-tests. We'll hide our code in them. We'll use their own system to gather the leaks."

"But where do we stage it once we've got it?"

"Elijah Lutane has acquired his own colocated pods in the six regional KQ sites."

"DPS said he had only one," corrected Adam

"DPS doesn't know everything," came the reply. "Lutane has six and he plans on using them to do his own dirty work once the system is in place. He probably hopes to buy his way into a piggyback position on some of the system data. Lutane is an opportunist. Even if he knows the game is over, he'd buy a ticket in case someone decides to play extra innings."

"How is that possible?" asked Nelson. "I just talked to him. He said he was being muscled out, some kind of alliance between the Project and another syndicate boss, a guy named Ishaan Onuti."

"Ishaan?" 1021 was concerned, his tone dropping out of character. Suddenly, he seemed troubled. "What else did he say about Onuti?"

"He called him his counterpart. He compared him to the Devil. He said both of them could have taken the Project down but only Onuti was given a seat at the table. He tried to make me believe he's nervous about the guy, worried about what Onuti will do on the inside, once he has Project power."

A few moments of silence filled the wristband. Nelson and Adam looked at each other. Without words, the communication was clear. It appeared the news about Ishaan Onuti was the one thing during their dealings with 1021 that had taken him by surprise and given him something to think about.

Finally 1021 came back online, entrenched, single-minded, determined. "All right. Even more reason to stop this."

Adam asked, "So what about Lutane's colocated pods?"

"He's setting them up just in case; he's not using them, at least not until after the 1st. He's too busy, distracted. We can stage all the leak data on those pods. When the moment comes on New Year's, we'll pump everything out from there using the KEYSERVs."

"Sweet," added Nelson. "Maybe the Project will think he did the leaks."

Adam worried, "Is this going to work? I mean, the New Year rolls out per time zone, starting near New Zealand and moving west, but the actual leap second is done at one time, syncing up with UTC. Won't the Project know early on what we're doing? They could move in to stop us before the whole thing leaves one time zone."

1021 went on a tear. "Leap second updates in NTP and POSIX-based computer systems are tricky. They can be done one of three ways. If you increment the clock during and after the update, then you have to keep track of all past updates to make a new one. If you increment the clock during the update and then step the clock back, your timescale is ambiguous since the reading during the leap gets repeated one second later. The third approach is to freeze the clock during the update and let time catch up at the end of the leap second. Most computers take the third approach."

"So what's your point?" asked Nelson, confused by the convoluted detail.

1021 shot back, "It's a lot of complicated shit, isn't it?"

Adam laughed, "Yeah, but it all doesn't happen at once. From a time zone perspective, it's a progressive thing as the Earth spins. But that doesn't matter with UTC. Regardless where you are and what time it is, you have to sync when it changes."

"You're repeating yourself," complained 1021.

Frustrated, Adam jumped to his feet. "I'll make it simple for you! The plan is to switch on the sensor array during the leap second insertion. That happens once, not hour after hour as each city celebrates midnight. When the UTC time zone hits midnight, the Project will know something's wrong and they'll react to it. Before midnight gets to the next time zone, they could discover what we've done and back out our changes."

"They could try," answered 1021. "But how are they going to stop what they can't break into? I told you—you'll have *Parabrah* and the CAPI."

"But you said you gave them *Parabrah*; they have it too."

"The AES algorithm used cryptographic keys of 128, 192, and 256 bits to encrypt and decrypt data in blocks of 128 bits…"

Adam jumped in, "There's more than one kind of *Parabrah*?"

"Yes," 1021 confirmed. "*Parabrah-36* and *Parabrah-72*. Once you get into the system, you'll see the two kinds referenced by their codenames: *Heavenly Spirits* and *Earthly Fiends*. The Project is using *Parabrah-36*, also known as *Heavenly Spirits*."

"Why don't they use *72*, the stronger one," asked Nelson.

"*Earthly Fiends* is held in reserve."

"Why?" asked Adam.

"Because you *always* hold something in reserve in case what you're using at your most secret level gets compromised. For you, it doesn't matter. You will have the CAPI for *Earthly Fiends, Parabrah-72*. On New Year's Eve, if they try to mess with your code, they won't have the encryption key to do it."

"Can't they go to *72* in an emergency?"

"I'll show you a way to code it that will *delay* them."

Adam was eager. "How? By using a riff from *Unbalanced Oil and Vinegar*? Quadratics or multivariates for signature schemes?"

"The long key-lengths certainly would make one think so, plus it's quantum resistant like UOV, but no, it's something new."

"How much can you delay them?" asked Nelson.

"They'll need a *yotta*FLOP computer to crack it."

"Are you're sure they don't have such a thing?" asked Adam.

"If they did, you'd be calling me 1024, not 1021."

"You're going to lock them out of their own system?" asked Nelson.

"Don't you think they deserve it?"

"Hey, whatever. Sounds good to me."

"Is that it?" asked 1021, disappointed. "No more questions?"

Nelson and Adam considered what was ahead of them.

"Think," commanded 1021. "Think like Ramanujan for a moment. Aren't you missing something with all this talk about time?"

His insistence was troubling. If there was something else, indeed they had missed it. Adam shrugged his shoulders and hoped Nelson had something but as the moments passed, it became clear he didn't.

1021 broke the silence. "Nelson, would you say the Project is approaching this like a military operation?"

Nelson agreed, "Yeah, they have the storm troopers to prove it."

"In military operations, how critical is command and control?"

"We all know the answer to that." Nelson's patience was tried.

"Good. And where do you position your C2, command and control? Do you place it at the *tip of the spear*?"

"No," answered Nelson. "Ideally, it's above the fray, a guarded position."

"And if your assets were jamming certain frequencies, would command and control use those frequencies?"

"Of course not." Nelson put up with the cross-examination only because he had no idea what Adam and him were missing.

"So, tell me then, why would the Project use NTP or POSIX time servers as command and control for GFSA?"

"Holy shit!" gasped Adam. "They're using another time system?"

"Yes," confirmed 1021. "If you had stepped out of your thinking box, you might have seen it earlier."

Nelson asked, "What is it? Some kind of dark GPS satellite timecode?"

"As in *Dark Eye*?" teased 1021. "Maybe something embedded in spy satellites? The fact is, GPS has its own timescale; it doesn't sync to UTC the same way. There are advantages to having what's called a Stratum-0 clock source. There's high accuracy and it's not dependent on an internet connection. Most importantly for command and control, it provides what insiders call an *air gap* between *dark and light networks*."

"Why do you know about this shit?" asked Nelson.

"Stratum-0 clock sources are used all the time in crypto work."

"All right, so how is the Project using them?"

"I told you—command and control."

Adam deflated. "Fucking impossible. I can't crack that in two days."

"You won't have to," announced 1021. "You take care of the stop code and staging the information leaks. I'll see to it that *Dark Eye* has a blind spot."

Adam asked, "How are you going to coordinate that with the leap second and the time zone changes and everything else? You know they're going to use the SWEBOTs to switch nodes on incrementally."

1021 paused. "I'm counting on a flash of inspiration, looking at one thing and seeing another."

"You haven't figured it out yet?" asked Nelson.

1

"Like you, I have work to do but I imagine the answer is satellite based."

"They've got GFSA components in orbit?" asked Adam.

"Where would you put global C2?" answered 1021.

Overwhelmed, Adam sunk down on the couch.

"Another thing," added 1021. "When you push out the leaks, use a digital watermark. Everyone should know the real stuff came from one place."

"Why?"

"The Project won't lie down. They'll have to respond the only way they can. One of those ways will be to pump out counterfeit leaks, anything to call the truth in question."

"They can't reproduce our watermark?" asked Nelson.

"Not if we encrypt it properly."

"So what should it be?" asked Adam.

1021 paused, but only briefly. "*#ScribPopuli.*"

Nelson translated, "*Writer for the People... the people's documents*. Yeah, that'll work."

"*We The People,* Mr. Geiss." 1021 was forceful, "The people are the stars of destiny, or they should be."

Adam stared across the room. "They don't act like it."

"That's all right. Each in turn will get their chance to stand up. Your chance is now."

Nelson looked to Adam. "Then we better get started."

"One last thing," added 1021. "Be efficient, not intractable. Do you have any idea what those two words mean to a cryptologist?"

"I know one's better than the other," answered Adam.

"Efficient means the calculation uses an acceptable amount of resources. Intractable means the computation eats up more resources than the secrecy of the message is worth. We have two days. Be efficient."

"When do we get *Namagiri* and *Parabrah*?"

1021 was nonchalant. "Check your computer. You should have it."

Adam raced to the desktop. "Geez, just like that?"

"I don't have to remind you, you'll need to wipe that computer when you're done."

Adam was a kid in a candy store. "No problem."

65

0000 0100 0001

11:19 pm PST, Saturday, December 29th

They worked for twenty-two hours straight after receiving the AES hack and new encryption code. The learning curve was steep, the curriculum accelerated. Precious time kept slipping away. One second at a time, they either got closer to the goal or it pulled away from them. One wrong move would crash all hopes for success. If that happened, the battle would be on. Even if they were taken alive, they would have no future.

Adam had taken the first two hours to do a self-taught blitz through *Namagiri* and *Parabrah 101*. The way it was structured and documented made it approachable. A year in quant class had conditioned his mind to expect everything difficult and tricky. This new material was even more demanding. If it wasn't for the CAPI he used as a guide, wading through all of it would have been beyond grim, it would have been out of the question.

Once rooted in the fundamentals, Adam started the third hour following up with all that Nelson was able to glean from 1021's leads on how to get into the system. The six KEYSERVs were networked with a regional MIN-Z computer. Each MIN-Z was networked to Z, the main computer. If one could get inside a KEYSERV, they would be two degrees of separation from Z.

As Adam expected, communication to and from Project components contained a modified LEAF, a Law Enforcement Access Field. Normally, a LEAF was an extra bit of cryptographic information sent or stored with an encrypted communication so authorized agencies could obtain the communication in plaintext. In other words, it was a legal way to snoop, embedded in every type of communication that went out.

But the Project's modified LEAF had a different function. It was a meta-field to be used by Project insiders to flag specific QDE data for special handling. Naturally, the KEYSERVs had to know about this. A meta-layer of special handling instructions governed how the KEYSERVs would treat different flags as they processed and routed them. Since every system has to be administered, this meta-flag layer had its own management codes and separate authentication for the one tasked with supervision.

By the sixth hour, a lead from 1021 gave Adam all he needed to know on how to login as administrator at the meta-flag layer for the UKQ based in New York. But knowing *how* was not the same as making it *easy*. Nothing in 1021's lead mitigated the double work necessitated by the *Snowden Rule*. Ever since Edward Snowden leaked NSA data several years ago, agency rules required a buddy system with two administrators logged in when any issue needed to be worked. Adam had to simulate dual administrator access or Access Control List Rules would alert Incident Response.

Once he got access to the management console at the meta-level, he used *Namagiri* to send properly flagged inquiries to the associated MIN-Z and QDE. That gave him pass-through credentials to Bluffsdale.

Just like that, he had landed in Oz.

The moment Adam got in, he sat and stared at the empty command prompt line. The thought of typing anything was extremely intimidating. The NSA's *Comprehensive National Cybersecurity Initiative Data Center* was a universe unto itself. The place had 60,000 tons of cooling equipment just to keep its servers from overheating. From its inception, whispers about why it needed 100,000 square feet of server space and more than 900,000 square feet for technical support and administration went beyond talk of merely being a data-center. Breaking codes was always discussed as a crucial part of its charter. Beyond that, anyone could guess what else went on inside.

As 1021 described it, the place was occupied by *trolls, minions, and sentries. Trolls* were ordinary workers, *minions* were the managers, and the *sentries* came in three flavors: militarized, suits with sunglasses, and digital. Located in Camp Williams, the military was entrenched all around the perimeter of the facility. Closer in, armed agents roamed the grounds and inside the plant itself. Everywhere, inside and out, sensors and digital watchdogs were on 24/7 patrol. *Lions, tigers, and bears.*

If Adam stepped through the maze according to plan, he should only have to worry about the internal digital sentries. If he got careless and caused a digital flag to raise, he would have to mask himself from the suits with sunglasses. If they got a hair out of place, the minions would hear about it. If that happened, Adam and Nelson would have to make a hole and jump in it.

Throughout the day, Adam took baby steps forward, reaching the next rung and pausing, becoming a wall flower, going so slow that what he was doing wouldn't look like movement. Along the way, Adam surveyed the landscape and noted guideposts he could use as breadcrumbs on his way back out. Around him, the scope of what he saw was staggering. If Bluffsdale was the giant he was tackling, then he was a speck of smartdust clinging to one side of a single hair follicle. He hoped his relative size would hold out as an advantage long enough to get in and get out.

It was after 11 pm before *Namagiri* showed the way into the black hole that was Z. Beyond a certain point, Adam couldn't shake a creeping feeling of paranoia. He was inside the inner sanctum, inside the trap. From what he could see, there was nothing else around him but digital baubles as bait.

Nelson pulled up a chair. "You all right?"

Adam gave a nod with fingers poised but shaking slightly as they hovered over the keyboard. He asked Nelson, "Are you religious?"

"No. Why?"

A ghost of a grin passed over Adam's face. In its wake was a cold spot of fright. "This might be a good time to offer up a prayer to *Namagiri*."

"What makes you think she's on our side?"

"Shit! She better be," gushed Adam.

"Don't worry about it. She let 1021 have his breakthrough."

"Oh, yeah, to torture him, probably."

"How do you figure?"

"He did all his work for some top secret program. How would *you* feel if you answered the *big* question and couldn't tell anybody about it? I mean, get real, he has to know about the Millennium Prize he's missing out on."

"What prize?"

"One million bucks. It goes to anyone who can answer any of the top seven math problems. The Clay Mathematics Institute set it up in 2000. Solving the Riemann hypothesis would be a big payday—if he could go public with it."

"Maybe they gave it to him privately," offered Nelson, offhandedly.

"And publicly keep everyone working on it?"

"I'm joking," admitted Nelson. "There's no way they'd let that be known to anyone outside the Project."

"Either he has no ego or they gave him something else," concluded Adam. "If I came up with that and got nothing, I'd be pissed."

"I wonder how many other scientists are in his position?"

"The way he talks about all this hidden technology; there must be lot of irate scientists sitting on their hands."

"Or in their graves." Nelson pointed to the screen. "So what's the plan?"

Gathering enough resolve, Adam typed away. "I thought you had one."

"I've spent all day on that laptop going through leads. Kennigus, Greyson, Bargeau, they're only part of the web, but it looks like the web itself is just a front for something else."

"What about Onuti? Did you find out any more about him?"

"It's sketchy, anecdotal. He appears to be some billionaire who lives here and there, all around the Mediterranean. He's been accused of racketeering, money laundering, insider trades, but nothing sticks. In Europe and the Middle East, he shows up at high society events. He says he doesn't like the glare of celebrity; he prefers his life private."

"A private life would help if you ran a crime syndicate."

"He's a chameleon, a dichotomy. He's charismatic when it suits him."

"So you can't tell whether Lutane is telling the truth or not."

Nelson leaned on the back of the chair and stared into Adam's screen. "If I asked Onuti to tell me about Lutane, I'd expect the same thing."

"Yeah, if someone asked me about you, it wouldn't be pretty either."

Nelson allowed himself a grin. "You still haven't told me your plan."

Adam squinted in thought and checked his helper windows; one of them held the CAPI. "Right now it's more of a goal, not a plan. I need information from Z, how it switches on the six KEYSERVs and QDEs and syncs up the SWEBOTs."

"How it turns the key…"

"Right. Once I have the code for that, I'll modify it so the switch is broken. Then I'll encrypt the revised code with *Earthly Fiends*…"

"*Parabrah-72.*"

"I drop the broken code back in place. If somewhere along the way I get fooled, I'll find myself inside the most awesome honeypot in the universe."

Nelson withheld comment. He knew how intense it was for Adam to avoid the honeypots at Extasis. He couldn't imagine how much more clever the traps for hackers were at Bluffsdale.

Adam saw Nelson's concern. "Don't forget, we have an advantage this time. I'm using *Namagiri*. I'm not groping around. I can see things now I couldn't before. I can see them before things get *sticky*."

Nelson asked the other question he had in mind. "When you went through the datacenter in New York, what was the QDE doing?"

"A final smoke test, like 1021 predicted."

The late hour and long day drove Nelson deeper. "I wonder if we're giving him new information or confirming what he already suspects—what he already knows."

"He's probably seen pieces of this, just not all put together. We know he's on the inside; he must hear all sorts of shit about what's going on. Like he said, what would be the point of having us find stuff he already knows?"

"He needs us committed to action, a certain course of action. If *we* find it, it'll be more powerful to us than if he simply told us."

"But he asked us what *we* wanted to do. He didn't tell us what to do."

"I know. But it's interesting; what we want matches what he wants."

"We're on the same fucking side—what's the problem with that?"

"No problem, I guess, except, if he knew all this already, doesn't it seem like we're doing his work for him? Why is that?"

"He's a scientist, not a hacker."

Nelson rocked back in thought. "So it would appear."

"He's not an intel agent either. Isn't that's why you said he got Katherine to follow around those guys in Washington?"

"Yeah…"

Adam stopped typing. "What is this all of a sudden? You think he's gaming us?" Adam pointed at the wristband. "You know, he's probably listening to everything we're saying."

Nelson's expression was unmoved. "I'm certain of it."

"Then I don't get it. What is this about?"

"I think he should know everything. Even our doubts."

"Are we back in the conspiracy zone? Because, you see patterns in shit I don't see. You think he did this to offload the risk onto us? Is that it?"

"It's a possibility."

"Oh I get it; once burned, twice shy, huh? Owen's ETC set you up in case something went wrong, now you're starting to see that everywhere."

"If you need a job done, you get contractors. If they take the fall, they're bonded and insured. That's why most people don't reroof their own house."

"OK maybe, but he's in a different position. He's on the inside, but that has to put him in some kind of spotlight. He can only do so much being so close. He needs someone to do the legwork, out of sight. Is that possible?"

Nelson considered it and nodded.

"Can I get back to work now?" asked Adam.

Nelson stood. He was about to answer when his wristband made connection. "Nelson...Nelson, are you there?" It was Katherine.

Nelson's pause led Adam to wonder, "What's up?"

Nelson pointed at the wristband. "Katherine, I'm here. What is it?"

"I got a report a few minutes ago. The professor's coming back from his vacation a couple days early."

"How soon?" Unable to hear Katherine, Adam asked, "How soon what?"

"He'll be back in Berkeley mid-morning on the 31st."

"Just what we need, less time. OK, thanks for the heads-up."

"Sorry, Nelson. I'll see what I can do about getting another place."

The call ended. Nelson informed Adam, "We're going to have company on the 31st. Which means we have to be out of here the night before."

Adam held his forehead. "You're kidding. One day to finish this?"

66

0000 0100 0010

6:37 pm PST, Sunday, December 30th

The sleepless marathon was a sprint to the finish from the start. As much as Adam and Nelson wanted it to end, they wished for more time to go after the prize. While Adam gutted it out on the break code, Nelson assembled the likely targets and sources for leaks on hidden dirt to collect and expose. Adam's job required the most concentration and energy so Nelson also handled the chores of raiding the kitchen for food and drink and coordinating status and pass-through updates with 1021 and Katherine.

At one point, Adam pushed away from his desk, sprung to his feet, and flung his arms over his head. "Oh…my…God!"

Ensconced on the couch with the laptop, Nelson jerked alert. "What the hell happened?"

Rubbing his face awake, Adam walked away from the desktop computer and back. "Nothing happened."

"Then what are you yelling about?"

Adam's pacing turned towards Nelson. With sudden exuberance and a maniacal laugh, Adam lunged forward, grabbed Nelson by the shoulders, and let it out, "Nothing happened! Not a goddamn thing! I dropped the modified code—no bombs went off!"

"You did it?" Nelson rose to his feet.

A nod. "The switch is broken, the code's encrypted. Damn, I'm good!"

"How does it work?"

Adam laughed, "That's just it—it won't work! The sensor array is a rock; it'll just sit there. The MIN-Zs get periodic updates from Z to make sure they're all at the same rev level. Z just pumped the modified code out to the KQ locations during one of its regular updates."

"No digital flags went off?"

"Didn't see any. My connection hasn't been cut off."

"What about *silent* alarms?"

"There's always a chance but I still have connection; I'm still inside."

"That proves nothing. They could be watching. They might want you to feel secure, like everything's going OK. Then they could monitor your moves, see what you're after, use the connection time to track you back to the source." The more Nelson's analytical wheels spun, the more traction it gave to his concerns and suspicions. For Nelson, the process was automatic. He hadn't even considered how it might be received.

Nelson had blown Adam's high.

Adam spun about, his arms flailing with pent-up energy. "Jesus! You're such a downer! I just hacked the fucking NSA and what do I get? No high-fives. No nothing. Just a lot of shit about what could go wrong. Damn, you're annoying."

Nelson held his bearing. "I've heard that before, but am I wrong?"

Adam paced away, stopped, then turned around. "No, you're not wrong. But you're not the only bastard to consider how all of this could go in the toilet any minute. Don't you think I know what's possible here?"

"I'm just reminding you. We've got to be sure about this."

"Well, fuck you! Because there's *no way* to be sure. You got that? This whole crazy thing is one big leap in the fucking dark and you know it."

"Settle down. We just need to triple-check everything."

"Yeah, because we've got this nailed down, huh? You don't even trust 1021. Why don't you triple-check your shit first?"

"We're halfway done. Let's not go off the rails."

"*Half*way, and what do we have, twelve hours left? At *most*, twelve hours, and we're *half* dead. When was the last time either of us slept?"

"I know it's a lot of pressure, but there's a lot at stake…"

"Don't lecture me," snapped Adam.

Nelson dropped his gaze. "All right. I get it. I'm too fucking wound up. You're right, what you accomplished is huge. I don't know anyone else who could have done it."

Adam stomped back and stood in front of the desktop computer. "Yeah, OK, well the party balloons are a little late. There's still work to do."

Nelson offered, "Take a break first; get something to eat."

Adam stood and stewed. He was too angry to sit down and too tired to stand up. He felt like breaking something and running away.

There was no way Nelson would understand what kind of herculean, high-tech hat trick he had managed to achieve. Besides getting up to speed in record time with all that 1021 had sent over, Adam had hacked his way into Bluffsdale of all places. For doing so, he should be properly installed in the *Hacker Hall of Fame*, if such a thing ever existed.

As his thoughts spun down, a sinking realization deflated what was left of Adam's inner celebration. An aching awareness hit him—the same curse that he had described as befalling 1021 regarding the Millennium Prize would now plague him—Adam would never be able to talk about his achievement. Top secret status had robbed 1021 of his glory. Now the wages of infamy would rob Adam of his. Forget the red carpets at the hall of fame; Adam wouldn't even be able to get *underground* street-cred from any of this. It couldn't be risked. Prison or death awaited him if he took credit.

Worse yet, the same might be his fate even if he kept things to himself.

The whole mess made what just happened with Nelson that much more maddening. The one person—the only person he could share his remarkable feat with had dissed it off with a bunch of crap about silent alarms and bogeymen in the night.

Adam sank within himself. He would be the only one to truly appreciate the magnitude of what he had done. It was possible 1021 might, but 1021 was an enigma, not a person. Adam never expected to meet the mystery man. Once this was over, Adam expected the disembodied voice to dissipate like a warming fog in a vacant sky.

Adam intended to do the same, as best he could. He dragged in a deep breath then pushed it out along with hopes of enjoying any normal type of triumph. He had to let go of his ego-exuberance. Leaking a ton of corrupt dirt, making it public, that was his true reward. He could cling to the satisfaction that he had stopped the 1% from something they thought was assured, the ultimate power play they thought would go unnoticed.

In that he would have his laurels.

He headed out of the room. Along the way, he announced, "I'm going to take a shower and wake up."

Just then, Nelson heard an incoming connection via the wristband. "Wait a second. I'm getting a call."

Adam stopped short and heard Nelson answer the voice in his head. "Yes, Katherine. I'm here."

As Nelson listened, his expression turned grim.

Katherine was all business, but Nelson knew right away she was concerned. Her words were rushed. "...there's been a phone call made between DPS and Geri Messare. I don't know what it means or what was said but I thought you should know. Should I do anything?"

Nelson tensed. "Cut off Geri from your group."

"What does that mean for your position?" asked Katherine.

"If Geri's working with Lutane, we might be compromised."

"How will you know?"

Nelson stared back at Adam. "We can't. There's *no way* to be sure."

Adam drew closer. "Geri with Lutane? What the fuck?"

"I'll get back to you. I need to think this through." Nelson ended the call.

"What's that about?" asked Adam.

"Geri Messare."

"The woman you met in the park."

"She and DPS have been talking on the phone."

Adam froze. "That makes no sense. What the hell does she have to do with RAPIER? Nothing."

"Exactly," agreed Nelson. "But we know DPS is working with Lutane..."

Adam read through to Nelson's concern. "If Lutane got to Messare, when did it happen? Before or after Russian Hill Park?"

"Unless Katherine's people can get Geri to talk, we won't know."

Adam became animated. "If the meeting at the park was Lutane's idea, that means this place might be another one of his setups."

"And Geri rolled over for money…"

"Or to save her ass."

"Yeah, well," admitted Nelson. "It wouldn't be the first time."

"You trusted that bitch?"

"What options did we have? Your buddy had already screwed us over. We needed a place to go. You burned down the computers at the nightclub and pulled out. She made it sound credible. I needed options."

"And Lutane was there once again to help, in the background. I can't believe it! He probably has this place jacked. You know what that means! Every fucking thing we've done since we got here might now be sitting on a mirror site in Santiago."

The full weight of what could have happened hit Nelson. "…that would mean he now has *Namagiri*…and *Parabrah*."

"Along with the CAPI. He's in business. We fucking put him in business." Adam paced the floor. "This isn't happening!"

Nelson's war face primed for its last charge. "We have to tell 1021."

"If he doesn't already know." Adam leaned towards Nelson's wrist and hollered at it, "I hope you got all this because we don't want to repeat it. It was bad enough hearing it the first time."

Nelson's forefinger and thumb pressed the sides of the band. "Call 1021."

Adam spun around. "Shouldn't we talk about this first?"

"We're going to need a three-way conversation to decide anything."

Nelson waited but no connection was made.

"We don't even know what time zone he's in," noted Adam.

"Katherine said he was on the east coast."

"That was then. Where is he now?"

Nelson tried to make contact several more times to no avail.

Finally, Adam headed out. "I'm taking that shower."

Nelson let him go. Stepping over to Adam's workspace, Nelson gazed at the screen. The connection to Bluffsdale was still active. Adam had said that his meta-layer access was parked in a management module. No digital flags would be raised by his monitoring connection hanging out and waiting. No suits in sunglasses would be drawn in to check such a thing. Even if an overly zealous suit did look, all they would see was a properly encrypted service operation looping through an authorized test mode.

Nelson stood weighted down, contending with his inner dialogue. Options for the road forward narrowed with each revelation. Their mission wouldn't be able to stand any more setbacks. This one alone might have done them in.

A voice entered Nelson's thoughts. "Did you call me?" It was 1021. From the normal tone to his voice, Nelson surmised he hadn't found out yet.

"I did call you," started Nelson. "We might have a problem."

"I thought Adam had a breakthrough."

1

"He did."

"Then what's the problem?" 1021 was brusque. "Tell me."

"I got word that Geri Messare and DPS have been talking."

"Since when?"

"Probably after my meeting at Russian Hill."

"What do you conclude from this?"

"Nothing's certain yet; we'll have to try to get confirmation out of Geri."

"Get to the point."

"Geri and DPS may have a common contact—Elijah Lutane."

"You left the nightclub because DPS computers were linked to Lutane."

"That's right."

"Right after, Geri suggested the professor's house."

"She answered the call Katherine put out for contractors to help."

"She might have helped herself instead."

"Yes, that would mean the professor's house might be linked to Lutane."

"And everything you've done since getting there is now his."

Nelson paused on the admission, "That's the worst of it."

Silence filled Nelson's head. 1021 said nothing. For Nelson, there was nothing else to say. When 1021 finally spoke, his words ended the call.

"Keep working. I'll see what I can do."

67

0000 0100 0011

11:44 pm CST, Sunday, December 30th

Katherine typed the last line of a coded internet post she intended to be worked by her contractor helpers on the west coast. So far, Geri Messare was nowhere to be found. Despite a fire drill of locator activity, she was absent from her usual haunts and not at home. Rumor had it she'd shared a ride south on I-5 headed into Los Angeles where she'd boarded a flight, destination unknown. No doubt she would be incognito until after the 1st.

If she was smart, even longer. Much longer.

Finding another place for Nelson and Adam to go at this late hour in their mission was problematic. To be any good, the new safe house would have to be a quick shuttle from the professor's house in Berkeley. The guys didn't have hours to waste on airplanes or road trips. That only narrowed the possible options open to them.

And that wasn't the only problem. Any quick shuttle from the professor's house would have to run a gauntlet of sensor and intercept traps and patrols set down by Steigbriar and Lutane. Some locations, while they might be available, would leave them too exposed in getting there.

Katherine pulled herself up from the small table space in the underground shelter and turned to the propane stove. One last cup of tea before taking a nap might settle her nerves. It was different being holed up in a hole in the middle of Wyoming, trying to be the eyes and ears for an operation when the risk of exposure demanded she not use most standard tools of the trade.

Nelson and Adam had to be out of the professor's house before morning light. That left six hours at most for whatever was left to do. It would be over soon, one way or another. She had stopped guessing how it would turn out.

Katherine sat back down in front of the computer only to find a new post meant for her. She quickly jotted it down and decoded it against her memorized key. It was a message from a contractor friend based close to D.C. The message was brief but grave.

"ODNI assets in field to supplement SB."

This was news Nelson should have right away. A larger net was being thrown. The Project must be worried. They weren't leaving it to Steigbriar alone anymore to secure things. Agents under direct orders from the Office of Director of National Intelligence had joined in. Of course, Owen and Richard would be in command. The only question was, was this addition intended on the last day of the year all along or had something else triggered their involvement?

Katherine couldn't see the ODNI stepping into the field unless absolutely necessary. If anything, all along, they had wanted to appear remote, so remote that if they were charged with anything, they had fall guys in place to explain away any hint of willing participation.

Katherine's thoughts leaped to Geri Messare once again. Geri's entanglement with DPS and then her quick flight, probably out of the country, might have tripped some wires. She might be the cause for the extra heat coming to bear but unfortunately, Nelson and Adam were the ones who would feel it. Perhaps that's how Lutane had it planned. Once he had what he wanted, others would be left to inherit the responsibility.

Katherine reached for her wristband but a thump from above startled her into staring up and holding still. A few moments later, another thump, and then there was more. By now, Katherine knew she had company.

She hurried to a nearby drawer and took out her Glock 36 and made sure it was loaded. Next, she doused the lights and rushed to a defensive position behind a wood pantry. She had several loaded clips and all the weapons Nelson had stored but she knew the odds. If a tiger team was scratching at her door, they had the advantage.

A moment later, a shape charge blew in the door from above. Whoever did it were professionals. The blast was measured. They wanted her alive. A concussion of snow, cold air, and debris shot past her. Soon after, a chemical grenade hit the floor. She recognized the slight click and fizz of its fuse. They weren't going to give her a chance to put up a fight.

The grenade popped and filled the space with an acrid fog. There was no point holding one's breath and certain death awaited if she stormed up the steps unloading her clip. The gas only needed seconds to anesthetize all battle out of her. She collapsed on the floor behind the pantry as the first agent dropped down into the hole with muzzle pointed and ready.

A dot of infrared laser light from a rifle's clip-on thermal sight swept the fog. Steady patience behind a night-vision scope waited for the smoke to clear. When it did, Katherine never heard the words spoken in the gas mask.

"Gopher down. Exfil to LZ. ETA, five minutes."

68

0000 0100 0100

4:22 am PST, Monday, December 31st

Adam was a fixture at the professor's desk. The work he had left to do was terrifying and monotonous, a killer combination. Even small steps forward had become petrifying. He was undeniably *in the zone* and yet in a place without discernable district, region, or precinct. Part of the reason for his altered state was the intense fatigue he was operating under.

Back on Sunday, he had distanced his awareness from the cramping and numbness of his body. All he had left was the irrational will of conscious thought intent upon moving forward, even when everything around it said such a thing couldn't be done, shouldn't be done, *wouldn't* be done.

With each passing hour, a thickening mental miasma gave resistance. It needled him with doubts and fears. It pestered him with confused and whispered distractions. At times, he found himself holding his breath as if expecting impact any second. With no other choice but take the task at hand one second at a time, he forced himself to breathe.

Each time he let go of another breath, he made another wish. It wasn't a wish he could put into words. There might be an equation for it, but if he stopped to write it down, he'd lose his place and have to start all over.

Since midnight, one of his worries had become a sidebar amusement, something latched onto as another trick to keep himself alert. He worried that sleep deprivation had him so dazed that some of what he was seeing on the computer screen was his own hallucinations.

Playfully evaluating each suspected hallucination as fodder for future nightmares had morphed into a warped entertainment. He could even see such a demented transposition of imagined realities as a video game. Granted, such a diversion would likely only be popular with people imbibing psychoactive substances. Needless to say, he didn't need any of those.

He knew what he wanted for his reward when this was all over.

Sleep—dreamless sleep, free from the odd reality he had fallen into.

Staging the KQ pods to take input from the leak script already loaded on the QDEs was repetitive finesse work. It demanded a tedious attention to detail. And yet, compared to plumbing the depths of Z, it was little more than busy work. For being nothing but busy work, it carried heavy consequences. If he did it wrong, everything he'd accomplished so far could blow up.

To stay awake, he asked Nelson, "Any word?"

"None. They've both gone silent."

"Both? Nobody's answering?"

"Not yet."

"Then how do we know we still have coverage outside?"

Nelson carried the laptop from the couch and tried out the professor's favorite recliner. "We're still alive, aren't we?"

"I don't care to be the canary in the coalmine."

Nelson fought his own exhaustion. "It's better than the canary in a cage."

"You're full of choices that suck."

"Here's another one," sneered Nelson. "We start wrapping it up now and get out of here before sunrise…or we squeeze every bit of time we have left and make a run for it in broad daylight."

"Do you ever have any good news?"

Nelson pushed to his feet and sauntered over next to Adam. "Yeah, if I had to guess, I say you're about done."

"What makes you think so?"

"You're not hunching forward anymore; you're leaning back."

"Really? I didn't know I was still in my body."

"So where are you?"

"The astral plane, I guess."

"I'm talking about the work. Where are you? You about done?"

"I finished right before you came in the room. I'm doing cleanup now."

"I hope you didn't make a big mess."

Adam's chin lowered to his chest. "The mess happens tomorrow when all this shit hits the fan."

"How many of my dirty leads did you get incorporated?"

"Every dirty little one."

"Has the collection started?"

"Rolling along as we speak, cycling with the smoke-test."

"So, we're in business." Nelson found some energy to be enthused. "That'll run all day, collecting."

Adam was more precise, "Collecting and staging it on the pods. By tonight, we'll have an Exabyte of dirty laundry on Kennigus, Greyson, Bargeau, Onuti, assorted government agencies and a whole roster of penthouse pimps, corporate courtesans, and Diamond Jims floating somewhere in their mega-yachts. Basically, a who's who of the plutocracy. We'll also have the full plans for GFSA, its links to BIS, the G-SIBs, D-SIBs, SIFIs, offshore accounts, you name it."

"That's a lot of crap. Are you sure we're going to be precise enough? We don't want the whole haystack, just the needles."

"I don't see an issue. 1021 was right. GFSA was designed to funnel sensor array benefits directly to the 1%—the exact place we need to go to find dirt. Their advantage turns into our advantage. Use their system against them; what could be more elegant? With a few algorithms and millions of SWEBOTs doing what they do best, being selective wasn't a problem."

"Then that's it," concluded Nelson. "You locked down Bluffsdale?"

"I'm out of there. The stop code is encrypted. If 1021 is right, there's nothing they can do that wouldn't take them a hundred years to repair."

"And now you've got the leak process set. We're done."

Adam's tone turned to mischief. "Here, I want to show you something."

Nelson shuffled closer. "What now? You hacked into Area 51?"

"Yeah, except it isn't in Nevada anymore. They've moved it to Wyoming, close to the alien-cattle hybrids served up at those Cheyenne barbeques."

Nelson didn't take the bait about his home state. "What have you got?"

"I thought you'd get a kick out of this." Adam opened another window into the professor's personal directories. "I know how you and the professor are tight; you really get off on the things he writes."

"Without a doubt. He's deep into the conspiracy thing."

"You mean calling it bullshit."

"I think he lobbied to get a new mental disorder added to the DSM-V. He thinks conspiracy theorists are that deranged."

"Yeah, well get this. I found a new book he's working on. It looks like he's about three-fourths done."

"What's it about?"

"I didn't read the thing. From the title, it looks like more of the same."

"OK, so why show it to me?" asked Nelson.

"Well." Adam held his grin. "I secured the book with *Heaven Spirits.*"

Nelson caught on. "You encrypted it?"

"With *Parabrah-36.*"

"You mean the good professor won't be able to open it."

"He will if he knows the right, secret people. Of course, the whole idea that some ultra-secret group has the code-key…"

Nelson laughed. "Nothing but a conspiracy theory."

"I thought you'd like that."

Nelson stood and considered how the professor would explain to his publisher what had happened to the book. "Yeah…good job."

Adam returned to business. "Bring over the laptop; I'll clean it."

As Nelson fetched the computer from the recliner, the trace of an incoming connection sounded in his head. The connection paused, then it tried again. Nelson handed Adam the laptop and then pointed at his wristband to signal he was receiving a call.

"It's about time we heard from somebody," muttered Adam.

A moment later, a new voice was in Nelson's head.

"Nelson Geiss…"

At first, Nelson couldn't place the voice. "Who is this?"

"You don't recognize me? How can you take orders when you're that out of touch?"

Suddenly Nelson knew, but how could it be true? "Owen…how did you…"

Not wanting to admit anything, Nelson caught himself and stopped.

"How did I make a call on your fancy wristband? Is that the only thing you want to ask me?"

"What do you want?"

"Well, let's see. For starters, maybe you'd like to tell me where you got this wristband. I didn't issue it to you and I was under the impression you worked for me. You know, something called an ETC. Remember that?"

"How can I forget."

"At Fort Meade, you were given precise instructions. Return to New York and investigate the Hong Kong connection. Am I leaving anything out?"

"No." Nelson forced himself to say as little as possible. Make Owen speak. Nelson needed to know how much Owen had uncovered.

"It's funny. We've searched everywhere in New York. We can't find you. The same is true with your pal Adam. Even when we go to the exact location where you should be, no one is there. Care to explain that?"

"I guess we're missing each other. I can't be nailed to one place if you want me to investigate the Hong Kong connection."

"You're not going to be straight with me, are you? You want to know how I can make this call? I'll tell you. A few minutes ago, a wristband arrived with someone you know. Have I got your attention now?"

Nelson froze. Was it Katherine or 1021? Before he could restrain himself, he blurted out the question, "Katherine?"

"Very good," remarked Owen. "You have a memory when it suits you."

Adam sat transfixed. He could only hear Nelson's side of the conversation. It was clear he was speaking with Owen Raedalus. That meant Owen had a wristband. Adam's thoughts went right to 1021 and how he had switched on various modes for the bands. What had Owen heard?

Nelson also wondered—how long had Owen had Katherine's band? More importantly, had he been using it to listen in before making his call? If he had, Nelson's and Adam's whole plan with 1021 might now be known by those in government who worked for the Project.

No wonder they hadn't heard anything from 1021 recently. With the wristbands compromised, he wasn't about to come online.

Nelson caught his breath. They had Katherine, or at least Owen was claiming he did. "Put Katherine on and maybe I'll believe you."

"No problem," answered Owen. "She's right here. Just a moment."

Nelson waited until Katherine's rushed words filled his head. "Nelson, I'm somewhere in New Jersey…" Her voice was silenced.

Owen returned. "Trying to be a helpful little bitch to the very end."

"What is this about?" asked Nelson.

"Stupid question. I suspect you're stalling, hoping to regroup and get clever. I don't have that long to wait. Here's what you're going to do. At 6 pm tonight, you'll meet me at Old Barney. You remember Old Barney, don't you

Nelson? According to your file, it's where you ended one of your *more messier* assignments."

Nelson felt his heart race. "I remember it."

"Good. You'll be there tonight at six or Katherine...well, you know the end of that, don't you. It's the same terms you offered your counterpart, the last time you were at Old Barney."

Nelson said nothing. He knew he had to show or it'd be Katherine's life.

"Good talking with you, Nelson. See you at six."

The connection dropped. Nelson immediately took the wristband off and stuck it out of listening range in an adjoining room. When he returned, Adam was pushed back from the desk, limp with unanswered questions.

Nelson summed it up. "They have Katherine. Owen says they'll kill her if I don't show up at 6 pm."

"Where?"

"Barnegat Lighthouse State Park, on the north tip of Long Beach Island, New Jersey. It's on the south side of Barnegat Inlet, close to High Bar Harbor and a lot of exclusive waterfront homes."

"Why there?"

"I'm not sure. Owen read my file; he knows things..."

"Like what? What went on there?"

Memories of past operations subdued Nelson's response. "I had to kill somebody there, somebody who wouldn't cooperate."

"Now *you* have to cooperate..."

"Or Katherine gets killed."

"Bullshit! He'll kill both of you either way."

"He needs something; he needs to know what's going on."

"If he doesn't already know. He has a wristband! He could have been listening in before making the call. If he did, he heard everything."

"Then he wouldn't need me, would he?" Nelson surmised.

"Now that he knows, it could be about something else."

"He said the band had just arrived with Katherine..."

"Likely story."

"He didn't listen in," concluded Nelson. "I know him. He would have been out of control if he knew everything we had done. He wouldn't be able to hide it. That proves he doesn't know everything. But he thinks I know."

"And he's right. You're not going, are you?"

"What choice do I have?"

Adam raised his voice. "6 pm, you show up. That's gives them plenty of time to get information out of you. The leap second won't get inserted until 6:59 pm East Coast time."

"Don't worry. I'm not going to give up our plan."

"You say that like you know. That kind of confidence is deluded."

"Like the trust it takes to jump out of an airplane after you packed your own parachute? Have you ever done that?"

"No…I don't see…"

"Try it some time. Some things are like that; it's best you don't try them unless you're definite about yourself first."

"You don't know what they're going to do to you—or to *Katherine*. If they start in on her, you expect me to believe you'll stand by and watch?"

Nelson hesitated. Katherine and he had been well-trained for capture scenarios. Both knew the limits of what they would be able to do for the other one in such a dire situation. And yet, neither one had been captured before. Their training had never been tested beyond all doubt.

Would they do anything to rescue the mission and not each other?

Nelson handed Adam the laptop to clean. "If I don't go, it's a certainty they'll kill her. I'll take any unknown option over that certainty."

Adam stewed in rising apprehension. "All we've got are unknown options. We're always stepping off somewhere in mid-air."

"What can I tell you? There's no algorithm for this kind of work, only experience. If you're lucky, with practice you develop rules-of-thumb."

"Maybe, but your rules-of-thumb must have calluses."

"How do you mean?"

"You're ready to walk into a trap, like you're numb or something."

"I'd be callous not to go, regardless what the *mathematical* odds are. Not trying is not an option."

"It's like this whole month has been insane. After all the shit we've been through, I don't want this to blow up in our faces at the last minute."

"It has to blow up," Nelson reminded him. "Isn't that what you're hoping for? When the dirt hits the fan tonight, you want upheaval; you want that to be your *revolution by another name*."

"That's not the kind of blowup I'm talking about."

"I know, but it's the only one you should be concentrating on."

"Meanwhile, surviving this might be nice," added Adam.

"It's too bad you hate history. For the kind of thing you want to happen, history has a clear message. No uprising that meant anything was ever led or fought by people who worried about what *might be nice*. Nice is for Sunday high-tea socials."

Adam stared up at Nelson and fired back, "And saving Katherine—wouldn't that be nice?"

Nelson deflected the point. "I'm not giving up when I have one play left."

"You're right, I want upheaval. I want tangible change I can see. I'm tired of the kind of change I'm supposed to believe in no matter what kind of shit is going on. This could be a chance to do something, move things around. I can't see risking that for a long shot—a nice-to-have."

"What you accomplished in four weeks is the biggest fucking long shot I've ever seen. When we had that first dinner together, if I had said you would be doing half of the shit you've accomplished, would you have believed me?"

Adam thought back. "No...no way."

"I don't know what Owen wants for sure but there may be maneuvering room. To find out, I need to show up. Beyond that, we don't know what else has happened. As far as we know, Lutane made a move on Onuti and Owen is stressed out. If Owen thinks we've leveraged Lutane somehow, maybe the Project thinks it can work with us to get inside information on him."

"You're betting everything on a lot of unknowns."

"Some key things are not unknown. You have to understand; Owen Raedalus is a company man. He's drunk every bit of Kool-Aid they've given him. He's got a taste for nothing else. He can't see another perspective outside the company box. He lives for duty and his own self-interest. But his idea of duty is warped. His idea of self-interest has been programmed. I can use that."

Adam gave up trying to convince Nelson of anything. Fatigue induced candor. "Whatever. Four weeks ago, my main concern was passing a quant test and getting a good place to stand on the subway. The most strategic thing I had to worry about was arranging how to get laid."

The comment elicited a cynical grin from Nelson. "I guess that's how all good revolutions begin. Once you get tired of getting fucked, you stand up."

"It's bizarre," noted Adam. "One thing led to another; I haven't thought about it much but that old life back in New York is over, isn't it?"

Nelson nodded. "Tomorrow's going to be a whole lot different for a bunch of people. You've come a long way from the kid that hacked the National Archives. So where are you going to go when we get out of here?"

"Geez, I've been so busy, I haven't thought about it."

"Where do you *want* to go?"

Adam gave it some thought. "Things could get difficult tomorrow..."

"A distinct possibility. It's best to be ready for anything."

An idea gelled for Adam as a confession. "I think I'd like to go back to New York, see if my Mom would go with me to see my Father. I'd like to see them one last time."

Nelson was taken with Adam's personal side. "At the care facility?"

"Yeah, he got to the point...she couldn't take care of him anymore."

"It doesn't matter that he won't recognize you?"

"It matters...but who knows when I'll be able to see him again."

Nelson reached out and squeezed Adam's shoulder. "Sounds like a plan."

"How about you? How are you getting back east?"

"I have to check but it shouldn't be a problem hitching a ride. One of Katherine's contacts can make room on a FedEx flight headed for Philly. It'll probably be cramped, stuffed somewhere with the cargo, but it works. You can ride along if you like. That'll get you most of the way home."

Adam already imagined being back in New York. "Yeah, sure...thanks."

A sense of finality came over both of them. The rush of events had been

1

their only preoccupation up to now. After weeks of being together, first reluctantly, then grudgingly, then as a matter of survival, and now as partners in a digital insurgency, it seemed odd that going their separate ways would wind up being so abrupt and awkward.

To make it worse, Adam had no confident illusions about the risk Nelson faced. If Nelson went through with the meeting at Old Barney, Adam couldn't foresee being able to get back with him ever again. To appear hopeful, as least, Adam offered, "You know what might be fun...?"

Nelson leaned back on the desk. "What?"

"I was thinking about the watermark, *#ScribPopuli.* We're not just stopping the sensor array from going live, we're getting the documentation out to the people. After tonight, we're counting on people to make the difference, to carry this thing forward. It might be fun to be surrounded by them tonight."

"In New York?"

"Well...yeah."

"You mean Time's Square?"

"Why not? I'd like to be there at midnight, watch people celebrate. You should join me. Bring Katherine." The hope was implicit, the feeling evident. Even so, Adam delivered his line as if he thought it could really happen.

Nelson held back emotion. Adam had gone to the care and trouble to pack the parachute. Nelson was ready to jump.

"I will. I'll be there."

69

0000 0100 0101

5:51 pm EST, Monday, December 31st

In a few minutes, the crab shack would close for the night. Nelson thanked his hostess and paid his tab. "Happy New Year," she offered. Nelson returned the wish with a depth of intention that was lost on her. She had no way of knowing what was planned for the world come tomorrow, no idea about everything Nelson expected would soon happen. More to the point, she had no awareness of the life or death situation he was about to walk into.

She turned the sign on the door to *Closed* before it was time. No one would care; there was little business, the staff wanted to leave and besides, it was New Year's Eve. They exchanged a parting smile and Nelson stepped out into frigid air streaming in off the Atlantic Ocean.

The Old Barney Lighthouse was a short walk away. Its tower was floodlit at night. Beyond the buildings, Nelson caught a glimpse of its powerful light sweeping around and getting lost out to sea. He had arrived in town some time ago but never tried to hide the fact. It was certain that ODNI agents had spotted him. He knew they would leave him alone. Owen wanted it that way. They would only swoop in if Nelson failed to show for the 6 pm meeting.

Nelson took the path paralleling the inlet's breakwater. Along the way, he wondered how Adam was doing back at home. Their flight from Oakland on the cargo plane could have been a chance to open up to each other, to reflect on what they had gone through, put it in some context, even admit any accumulated things they might never have another chance to say.

But it didn't work out that way. The flight was the perfect time to rest. The drone of the big engines had Adam passing out before they got to cruising altitude. Nelson had caught a few naps but he was too restless for deep sleep. He couldn't help turning over everything that had brought them to this point. As the cargo trip passed the halfway mark crossing the country, Nelson couldn't avoid evaluating what came next.

Being aware of one's mortality usually came after the immediacy of most life or death situations. In the intensity of the moment, one was too busy to think about how it might all end. But not this time. This time Nelson had hours to sit and think about what he faced. Ever since December 1st, had he been in the right place at the right time or had fate dealt him a dead-end route?

He had set out from his ranch a month ago, coaxed on by a need to contribute, to leave something behind that would prove his life had amounted to something. Minutes away from what might be the end of it all, what could he tell himself? If it all ended tonight, he took comfort in knowing he had tried to make a positive difference. His only regret was that he might not live to see the effect of what Adam and he had done.

But Adam was right; the odds weren't good. Still, there was no way Nelson would let Adam know that. It wasn't good form and it wouldn't change what Nelson needed to do. Besides, low odds were better than no odds, the exact situation Katherine faced if Nelson didn't show up.

There was only one way out for both of them. Nelson had to find out how much Owen knew. Armed with that, Nelson would have to try to lie his way back onto Owen's side as a faithful ETC member. If Nelson could gain back a flicker of Owen's confidence, he might be able to subvert the company man by exploiting his fears. The spin might mollify Owen's impetus to kill them.

In Oakland, Nelson and Adam were told that the contractor contact who'd arranged the FedEx flight had recruited more contacts on the east coast. As word spread of their predicament among the intelligence contractor community, more assets wanted to help. Katherine's version of an ETC had never stopped expanding or being of help.

Two contacts met them at the Philly airport with rides. After a handshake and slap on the back from Nelson, Adam drove away for New York. Their parting was rushed, almost mechanical, nearly clumsy with brief and dutiful gestures. But it was all the moment would allow.

Nelson got a ride to the Borough of Harvey Cedars, down the road from Barnegat Lighthouse State Park. He walked the rest of the way to mask how he got there. Before starting his walk, the driver wished him luck and said he'd be waiting for Nelson in Harvey Cedars after the meeting.

He also told Nelson that a contractor with a private plane would be waiting at Eagle's Nest Airport, south of Barnegat Road off the Garden State Parkway. Wherever Nelson needed to go after the meeting, if there was an *after*, he would have a way to get there. His friends had it covered.

On parting, the contractor offered Nelson a final word in strict confidence. "You'll have six assets around peninsula point and the state park in case you need them. One has a boat in High Bar Harbor if that's your only way out."

Nelson took the offer to heart. "Thanks...let's hope I don't need them."

The man added with gritty determination, "If you or Katherine go down, I guarantee you, Owen Raedalus and Richard Marks won't see the new year. You didn't hear it from me but some want to take them out regardless."

"For Hollister and Dystrom?" asked Nelson.

"And others," confirmed the man.

Nelson said nothing. They were parting words meant as an exclamation to mark the end of their ride together, as solidarity, no other answer expected.

That was hours ago now, hours and countless thoughts rolling through every plausible way to approach the evening meeting.

And now the time had come. As Nelson approached Old Barney, he found Owen standing alone, deep in concentration, staring across the breezy inlet into the darkness of Sedge Island.

Nelson slowed his steps and surveyed the area. It appeared that no one was around but appearances were wrong. Nelson said nothing.

Owen turned, watched Nelson's final approach, then commented, "Right on time. I guess you *can* obey orders when you're properly motivated."

Nelson was terse. "You can let Katherine go now."

"I don't remember that being part of the bargain."

"Bargains are for shoppers. What are you in the market for?"

"Simple…" Owen raised the sleeve of his jacket, revealing the metal wristband communicator. "Who gave you this?"

"Why do you assume it was given to me? What if I took it?"

"Cut the logic games, Nelson."

"They're perfectly good for cross-examinations."

Owen stepped closer. "You don't have access to where this came from. There's no way in hell you took it. I'll ask you again. Who gave it to you?"

Nelson held his ground. "People would only be given access to things like that if an authority like you thought they were smart enough to deserve it. Now, do you really believe someone that smart would tell me their name?"

"So you don't know. A ghost gave it to you, just some anonymous face. Is that your story? I bet you spent all day thinking that one up."

"In between naps," added Nelson. He expected his flippancy to trigger Owen's anger. Instead, Owen forced a smile and shook his head in frustration.

"You have no idea what's going on, do you? I mean, no *real* idea apart from manifestos of underground bullshit you've been wallowing in."

"At least I read. You should try it sometime."

"Your personality profile always said you were the suggestible type. It wouldn't take much to get you fired up about the latest paranoid ramblings of some conspiracy nut locked in his basement, hiding from the boot of the New World Order. Admittedly, that warped zealotry came in handy at times. You actually got some key people to believe the theories we wanted them to."

Nelson was dismissive. "I blame that on the ignorance of youth."

"If you want Katherine to live, tell me who the mole is, or lead me to him."

"What mole?"

"We know you've been working with somebody on the inside."

"Inside of what, the ETC?"

"Cut the shit, Nelson. I don't have time."

"No time? Why, is something about to happen?"

"You know damn well there is."

"As far as I know, a crime syndicate based in Hong Kong is about to hit the world's central banks…"

"And you and Adam were in California trying to stop that, I presume."

"Just like you told me."

"That's not what I heard."

"From whom?"

"A buddy of yours. Damage Per Second. Not exactly ETC material."

"You trust a runt like that?"

"No, but a special team was *making* him trustworthy—before they were rudely interrupted."

"I don't follow," prompted Nelson, playing coy.

"DPS was being interrogated. Not long after it began, someone else came in and blew away everyone there, including DPS."

The news of DPS's death surprised Nelson but he held his game face. "Sounds like your special team has shitty security."

"No, it sounds like someone got paid to look the other way so DPS could be silenced."

"It wasn't me," offered Nelson. "You don't pay me that much to afford those kinds of favors."

"But it was a favor…meant for you, wasn't it? And how do you repay such generous favors?"

"*Do* one for me sometime and find out."

"We know you talked with Elijah Lutane—*after* Guernsey. If he has a mole on the inside, we need to find him quick."

"Again I'll ask you," pressed Nelson. "Inside what?"

Owen got into his face. "You think you've seen something, you know something? You've gotten yourself in deep but you're only guessing. Right before one of Lutane's men spilled his brains, DPS told us that you and Adam had found some design document, a design for some fancy kind of sensor array. Does any of this sound familiar to you?"

Nelson stared him down but said nothing.

Owen shouted, "You better start answering or I swear, I'll drag your bitch down there on the sand and shoot her in front of you, the same way you shot that man twenty years ago. He was being cute and evasive too, wasn't he? He wouldn't cooperate. He thought he could string you along until it was too late but you wouldn't put up with that, would you? Neither will I. Why is Lutane covering for you? What kind of deal did the two of you make?"

Nelson had traded jabs and sniping banter as exploration with Owen long enough. Not only was such a greeting typical between them but it gave Nelson a good idea what Owen knew and didn't know and what he was after. Now Nelson could shift tactics, open up and give a little, spin all that had happened into legitimate work for Owen's ETC—and prey upon his fears.

Nelson offered, "I made no deals. He tried to recruit me. I told him he was high on his own products."

"Recruit you to do what?"

Nelson said nothing. He looked out to sea.

Owen pushed him. "To do what?"

Nelson gripped Owen by the arm, preventing him from pushing him again.

A moment away from coming to blows, Nelson lowered his voice into the grit of the false truth he needed Owen to hear. "To check on you."

"Me?" Owen's anger became perplexed.

"Yeah, check and make sure people like you—on the *inside*, were doing what they said they would."

"That makes no sense."

Nelson got in Owen's face. "It does if he was doing it for Ishaan Onuti."

The name hit the air like a clap of thunder. Owen stood transfixed.

Seeing Owen off-balance, Nelson let into him with the story he'd concocted during the cargo flight coming East, a story worrisome enough for Owen and the Project that it might defuse the need for Owen to kill Katherine and himself. "It seems Onuti has reservations about his invitation to join the rest of you on the inside. He wonders: is it going to be a banquet or musical chairs? He doesn't want to be the only one left standing in that split second when the music stops at midnight. He wants to celebrate too, like the rest of you on the inside."

Owen tried to hide how the new topic flustered him. "And this is what Lutane recruited you for?"

"Like I said, he tried. I played along as much as I could to find out whatever was possible. You know the deal; assets have to adapt."

"So why did he kill DPS? DPS had contracts with him."

"To cover his tracks. He doesn't want you to know he's working with Onuti. They like it with one on the *inside* and one on the outside. It gives them more options, especially in the new year."

"You never reported any of this to me. You dropped out of sight."

"I had to. It was necessary to convince Lutane I was seriously considering his offer. If I didn't look legit, somebody would have let him know for a price. He gets all the HUMINT he needs with money and intimidation."

"That doesn't explain the wristband and not being able to track you."

Nelson was glib. "Apparently, by working together, Lutane and Onuti have bought their way into the Dark Eye toy box. With their combined connections and Onuti's acceptance on the inside, I imagine it wasn't hard to arrange a trinket to impress me. From what I hear, a whole range of new and secret technologies have opened up for them." Nelson added with some relish, "But that may be a conspiracy theory, because we're not hiding anything like that, are we?"

Nelson could see that the prospect of Onuti and Lutane having secretly joined forces and having Dark Eye toys disturbed Owen to the hilt. As far as Nelson knew, it was the one lie that would disturb the Project the most. Worse yet was finding out this late in the game. Causing confusion and suspicions among the three of them would only favor Nelson. He could hear Owen's wheels spinning. If Onuti and Lutane had been working together all along, that meant they were only waiting for New Year's to consolidate their position.

In the new year, they would have access to Project data on the inside and everything covert and underground outside the Project. With their money, influence, and global scope of operation, the prospect of New Age Barbarians overtaking the old-guard established plutocracy seemed plausible. To those on the inside, the ultimate fear was that all the supposed negativity and animus between the crime syndicate princes was just for show.

As Lutane had said, once Onuti was in the body, his influence would metastasize. Nelson didn't have to draw Owen a picture. Just given the suggestion of them secretly being in league with one another and Owen knew the rest. Of course, Nelson had no idea if his story was true or not. It didn't matter as long as his gambit satisfied his goal—disrupt the Project and deflate any reason why Owen wanted Katherine and him dead.

Not waiting for Owen to regroup, Nelson added fuel to the fire. "To me, it looks like they want you guys to think divide and conquer has done its job."

Owen doubled down with determination. "Where is Adam?"

"I don't know. I cut him loose."

"What about the design document DPS talked about?"

"He was proud of that thing. He waved it around."

"You saw it?"

"A couple pages."

"What about Adam?"

"Yeah, he scanned it."

"What did he think about it?"

"He said it looked like a major evolution of High Frequency Trading. Naturally, it would be worth something to somebody. You don't have to be a quant to know—every second counts in making money on Wall Street."

"You said DPS was proud of it. What do you mean?"

"Well, he hacked it."

Owen balked, "He said you did."

"Bullshit. You had him under enhanced interrogation; he was saying anything to save his ass. The truth is, Adam and I were too busy running our asses off from safe house to safe house to settle in and do anything effective. DPS wanted credit on the street for what he did. I warned him to keep quiet, Lutane wouldn't like that but the kid wouldn't listen."

With that, Nelson made a dead DPS responsible for hacking the design document and took suspicion off Adam. Owen also had his reason for the hit on the interrogation. Nelson had manufactured another piece to put in place. The problem was, there were so many jagged empty spots remaining in Nelson's story, he could only hope anxiety over an Onuti-Lutane alliance would cloud Owen's judgment.

Owen turned to the ocean, his demeanor hardening. "It doesn't matter if the two of them are working together—they won't see the new year."

Nelson was surprised by the admission. "You're taking them both out?"

"The plan has been in place for a long time."

Attracted by Owen's candor, Nelson stepped up alongside. "So Onuti has reason to be worried."

Owen confirmed, "He was never going to sit down when the music stopped."

The news deflated Nelson's hope of instilling fear in Owen. He admitted in resignation, "Then you have nothing to fear from their partnership."

"Wrong," admitted Owen. "Their kind of beast always grows another head. That's why, once and for all, we had to find a way to deal with it. If financial warfare is now the preferred *hyper-strategic weapon,* then there is only one effective countermeasure to deploy—something that puts the game to rest."

"You say that like it's a done deal."

"It will be, soon enough. It *has* to be if civilization is going to survive."

"What are you talking about?" prompted Nelson.

"On the 1st of December, in the DIAC conference room, I tried to explain it to you. You were too full of yourself to listen."

"You mean that lecture about the NABs, the New Age Barbarians?"

"I told you that avoiding criminal and corrupting influences was a top priority of the ETC. Guarding against the Shadow Class is a global concern."

"I don't see how they're any more powerful or wicked than the people you align yourself with. It sounds like an excuse to me."

Owen admitted, "If it were only that simple. The fact is, both sides know the same secret. Most of the scrambling around you see is due to that."

"A secret? What possibly could be so compelling?" asked Nelson.

"Things are about to change, whether we want them to or not."

"You make that sound like you're not in control," mused Nelson.

"No more than one controls a sky-high tower built of brick with no mortar." Owen was grim. "Some kind of global transition is inevitable. The only question is, will it be smooth or abrupt and who will benefit?"

"Why is this thing inevitable? What's the big secret?"

"It's a secret hidden in plain sight." Owen deepened into a message evangelized into him. "Plain sight is a magical thing. It can be conditioned to be something different than perception. Plain sight in society has been conditioned to believe the way things are is the way it has always been and the only way it has to be. As a result, no other options are considered outside the framework of a manufactured or manifest plain sight."

Restless with Owen's obscurity, Nelson complained, "Is there a point to this?"

"Yes." Owen announced with conviction, "The world's fractional banking system and the credit and debt parlor tricks that have ballooned into quadrillions of dollars of nothing but electronic worth can't go on forever. Anyone who looks closely enough at such a system can see it's the most colossal Ponzi scheme ever devised and like every Ponzi scheme, at some point it simply outruns itself. That time will be rapidly upon us."

"They've invented things before to handle it. Why can't they invent something else to keep it going?"

"Because soon, the numbers won't add up. The world can never pay off its debts. By necessity, that debt must keep rising to keep the system going."

"Why?" prompted Nelson.

"Because all money comes from debt and all debt includes interest. But where does the interest payment come from? More debt. While it lasted, the system worked like a charm."

"Yeah, it concentrated wealth…"

"And gave birth to the corporate citizen, an entity large enough to handle global issues. But something *has* to give. The top bankers see it. So do people like Onuti and Lutane. The world *has* to transition to something else. When that happens, everyone wants to be in the right position."

"What *is* the right position?"

"If nothing new is in place, there isn't one. And so one has to be made. An enormous effort has been put into planning a smooth transition to a global economic framework that is stable and sustainable. Some see that as fiscal guidance, others like Lutane see it as a way of being excluded."

"But that's the point. You *do* want to exclude him."

"Not him personally, just his methods. If we don't succeed, the world will become a failed state run by highwaymen and thugs."

"But you work with these people covertly all the time."

"Like you sidled up to Lutane the past few weeks to find out what he was doing. You know from your own work, we have to associate with everyone. Sometimes it's necessary to use the worse elements for a greater good."

"What is the greater good?" asked Nelson.

"Stability, continuity, preservation," came the reply, spoken as if a motto.

"Lutane would say it's picking winners, who gets the power. He saw your master plan as nothing more than locking your grip on everything."

"The master plan, as you call it, is the only thing that will give us an upper hand against two avoidable futures: a fiscal cataclysm that will rock the world into riots and war or a slow disintegration into gangster-style chaos. A proper structure needs to be laid down first with methods and procedures applied in good time. There can be no question about its stability and proper means to defend itself."

"And it doesn't matter the way you go about it."

Owen answered as if the accusation were overt. "Everything we do in seeing this through is classified *NABOM*. Are you familiar with the term?"

Nelson had heard of it. "Of course. *Necessary Action By Other Means*."

"Some things need to be done—even when legally, ethically, morally, they should *not* be done. They get done anyway because they *need* to be done. Only the most dire or critical operations are ever classified *NABOM*."

"So, you think you have the license to do anything."

"We have a mandate—to protect and defend our way of life."

Nelson was disgusted. "I'm not sure I know what our way of life is any-more."

"That's all right," declared Owen. "Just don't try to stand in the way of those who do."

"I'm not standing in anybody's way. If anything, I'm a facilitator."

"Odd choice of words."

Nelson turned and looked at the darkened grounds beyond the floodlights. The lighthouse towered above them. Sensing Owen was at his limit, Nelson shifted into end-game negotiation. "I'm only interested in one thing. Are you going to let Katherine and me leave here, and if you do, are you still going to have Steigbriar kill us?"

Owen jerked around at mention of Steigbriar. "Where did you hear that?"

"Don't deny you let Steigbriar come into the country and do their thing. How did it feel to be sidelined by them? I bet you weren't even sure what orders they were given. Who controls them anyway? You'll never know. A committee in Basel, a roundtable in Berlin? Certainly not Richard Marks."

"You better double-check your sources…"

"And you should double-check your authority because after tomorrow, you might find that national organizations such as yours are irrelevant."

"Why shouldn't I kill you? You still haven't told me who the mole is?"

"What does that matter now? The game's over. You've won. Swiping trinkets and trading favors can't compare to what your insiders will do soon."

"I have to be sure nothing will go wrong."

"You've got that covered too," countered Nelson. "Isn't that why you put together the ETC? As long as we're here, backing you up, you have your insurance that the right thing will get done—or the guilty will be punished."

"One way or another, the right thing *will* get done. Those who don't want to play by the rules will be left outside."

"That's right. It's like what you said four weeks ago. No one wants to be forced into being a barbarian to survive. Their way of doing business can't be allowed to become the norm. How can a global economy function if it allows itself to be taken hostage under the threat of shakedowns at the whim of a few egomaniacs? Spending time with Lutane convinced me of that. Corruption like that needs to be rooted out and exposed."

Owen checked the time. "If I release you, where will you go?"

Nelson shoved hands in pockets. "I'll find my way back to my ranch. I suspect I have some cleanup to do, especially around the shelter."

A remaining point of suspicion crossed Owen's mind. "Why did you send Katherine there?"

"It was the only place I could think of to hide her from Steigbriar. I couldn't trust Lutane's men not to give her up for a price. We tried hiding out in RAPIER safe houses but somehow word of our whereabouts kept getting out." Nelson paced away from the lighthouse towards the dark. "By the way, where do you have her?"

"Nearby, just in case."

Nelson turned back. "In case of what?"

Owen paused, then his tone turned ominous. "Whatever has to happen to finish this."

"Can I see her first?" asked Nelson, expecting the worse.

Owen spoke to agents connected via earbud. "Bring her up. It's time."

A minute later, an agent in civilian clothes accompanied Katherine out of the darkness. Her eyes went straight to Nelson. They connected with a muted but joyful glance. Both mindful of the situation, they held their ground.

Nelson wondered how Owen would do it, if indeed that was his intention. Would he take them down on the sand to recreate Nelson's solution from twenty years before? Nelson had to try one more appeal to let them go.

He turned back to Owen. "What's gotten into you? You wanted decoys to flush out the threats. We did that. We gave you Lutane and RAPIER."

Owen was resolute. "That may be so but it leaves too much unknown."

"Killing us won't give you an advantage over that."

"You know how it goes. With you and Lutane both gone, my story of what happened will be the one that gets heard."

Nelson nodded. "You can say the ETC was working with Lutane all along. You rescued the Project."

A brief moment of satisfaction showed on Owen's face. "Like I said before, plain sight is either manifest or it's manufactured."

Just then, a twist of Owen's head showed both of them that something had changed. Owen rotated a quarter turn away from them and began speaking to no one present. "Who is this?"

Nelson and Katherine looked to each other. From the way Owen was reacting, his abrupt change of behavior could only mean one thing. He was receiving a call on the wristband he wore, the band his agents had taken away from Katherine when they captured her in Nelson's shelter.

Owen continued, "Yes…this is he. What do you want?"

He listened for a minute and said nothing. Turning away, he faced the ocean. His body became stiff before he bowed his head in thought. A hesitation followed, as if gathering strength amidst anger, fear, and despair.

He turned back to them, his face ashen with surprise and worry.

"Go!" he commanded. "Get out of here. The ETC's disbanded."

Just like that, it was over. The agent stood by perplexed while Nelson and Katherine hugged and then headed off into the evening's darkness. Not knowing the source of their good fortune, they had no confidence it would last. Until they got safely away, Owen could change his mind and have his agents haul them back for execution on the sand.

Overhead, the light of Old Barney swept around again. Out beyond the shore there awaited swift currents and shifting sandbars menacing enough to challenge the most experienced of sailors. Ships bound to and from New York depended on the lighthouse as their most critical change-of-course point. Mariners for over 180 years had looked to that one light to help them avoid running aground on the offshore shoals.

For Nelson and Katherine, on edge as they hurried away, the sweep of the massive light over their heads was more menacing than helping. The flash and quickness of its passing heightened the urgency of their escape. Like Project forces intent upon their task, the lighthouse sentry went about its duty with mechanized efficiency. As Nelson and Katherine rushed forward, Old Barney felt more like the roaming lights of a prison break than an aid to navigation.

Katherine asked as they rushed along, "What just happened?"

Nelson joked, "I don't know. Divine intervention?"

"They say God helps those who help themselves."

"Well, it wasn't me."

"It wasn't supernatural either but it did the trick."

Nelson checked his Beretta 90-Two, the one given to him in San Francisco, then watched for hostile movement around them. "Makes me think of what Napoleon said, '*Religion is what keeps the poor from murdering the rich.*'"

"*We* were the ones about to be murdered and we're not rich."

"Not the way Owen measures it. But he *is* a true disciple in the worst way."

"Are you wearing a band? Did you hear the call?" asked Katherine.

"No, I left it on a shelf in the professor's house."

"Why there?"

"Why not? I wasn't going to bring it here. Let the professor explain it."

"I wonder how many bands are in circulation?"

"Are you trying to narrow down who was on the call?" asked Nelson.

"It couldn't have been Adam…what about 1021?"

"No way, he wouldn't risk the exposure."

"Whoever it was, somehow they got to Owen. So where are we going?"

"Down Broadway to Central. We've got a ride waiting for us."

"Now all we need is a destination."

"There's an airport nearby. They've got a plane waiting."

"For what?" asked Katherine.

"I've got an appointment to keep—at midnight."

"You've got something else going on?"

"Just a celebration. Want to come along?"

"What kind of celebration?" asked Katherine.

"What do you think? It's New Year's Eve."

"I don't remember you being a big party guy," noted Katherine.

"It's just me and a few friends; nothing outrageous."

"Are you sure these friends are going to show up?"

"I'll be surprised if they don't."

"Where is this place?"

"New York."

"You've got friends there? I thought all your friends were in Wyoming."

"No, New York's a friendly town. I've been there most of the month."

"And you managed to make friends while all of this was going on?"

"Yeah, what's so strange about that?"

"I don't know. Something's not right."

"That's your trouble. You're suspicious of everything."

"OK, so where exactly in New York is this party happening?"

Nelson kept up the pace. "Time's Square."

He walked on but Katherine stopped cold. "You little fucker!"

Nelson looked back but kept going. "What did you say?"

Katherine's humor melted in emotion. "Thanks for coming for me."

He stopped and waited for her to catch up. "It was my only good option."

70

0000 0100 0110

11:44 pm EST, Monday, December 31st

It was the usual crowd, only what was usual on this night numbered one million. People from all over had packed into a few city blocks in Manhattan to bid a collective farewell to one year and welcome in another.

Nelson and Katherine worked their way along the congested sidewalk. Their immediate concern was finding one person in a million.

They had tried to reach 7th Avenue by going down West 44th St. past the IRS and National Debt Clock but the crowd was too packed in. The police wouldn't let them go any farther even if they wanted to try making a space. The crowd-control pens stretching back from One Times Square and the elevated New Year's Eve Ball had long since filled up with revelers.

The pens were NYPD's way of defining sections in the throng with the idea of preventing crushes and stampedes. This late in the evening, it was a certainty the pens were closed, except for anyone needing to exit. That wasn't likely unless someone hadn't planned on a multi-hour wait without a bathroom break. The New Year's celebration had no public restrooms.

Retreating farther north towards Central Park, Nelson and Katherine managed to squeeze onto the sidewalk at 7th Avenue at West 53rd Street. The location was over ten blocks away from where the ball would drop but at least they'd be able to see it and the fireworks in the distance.

Nelson sent Adam another text to let him know their whereabouts. Adam texted back that he'd retreat north along 7th Avenue and meet up with them across from the Sheraton Hotel. While the two of them stood in place and waited, the near freezing temperature became more noticeable.

Katherine hugged Nelson's side while checking her smart phone. "It didn't seem this cold while we were walking."

Nelson scanned the crowd near 52nd Street for Adam. "How cold is it?"

"Thirty-three degrees."

"This crowd must be putting off a lot of BTUs," offered Nelson. "That should count for something."

Katherine read from her phone. "It says here the coldest Time's Square celebration was in 1917; the temperature dropped to 1 degree Fahrenheit."

"You see, things could be worse."

"Yeah, the second coldest was in '62—it was 11 degrees that year."

Nelson caught a glimpse of Adam moving through the multitude. "Here he comes." Nelson gave a wave to alert Adam to their position.

"What is he wearing?" asked Katherine, amused when she saw him.

As Adam neared, Nelson noted the red plastic glasses in the shape of the year *2018*. Nelson smiled and gave Adam a hug. "I didn't recognize you."

Adam and Katherine shared a hug and Adam centered the glasses on his face. "Somebody gave me these," he explained. "I don't know why."

Nelson exclaimed in jest, "You must look like you need them."

"I found you so they must be working."

"Did everything work out…you know, with seeing your father?"

Adam's humor faded. "Yeah, it was all right. It worked out."

"Good," offered Nelson. "I'm glad."

Adam looked from one to the other in amazement and changed the subject. "Geez, you're really here. How the hell did you do it?"

Nelson admitted, "I tried everything—and then something else happened, something I can't explain."

"What?"

"Owen got a call on the wristband, the one they took from Katherine."

"A call from where?"

"We don't know."

Katherine added, "All we know is, whatever was said did the trick."

"So where does that leave us with Owen?" asked Adam.

Nelson gave Katherine a glance. "I'd like to say we're OK, but I can't be sure. I gave him something else to worry about beside us."

"Like what?"

"I told him Lutane and Onuti are secretly a team."

Adam grinned. "That'll wreck his day."

"Except both of them won't last through tomorrow anyway."

"They're taking them out?"

"No loose ends." Nelson added, "By the way, they tried to get information out of DPS and Lutane's men shut down the whole thing and got rid of him."

Adam was startled. "DPS is dead?"

Nelson nodded. "Since he can't talk, I told Owen that he cracked the design document. I thought that would take some heat off you."

"Did he buy it?"

"I think so. With any luck, he'll think the same of Bluffsdale, the KEYSERVs and the pods come tomorrow. I know you were counting on getting all the credit but I figured there was no sense being a famous martyr."

Adam let it go. "If that's my choice, well, yeah. It's all right, thanks. I got something else out of this that might be as good as street cred."

"Like what?" asked Nelson, more curious than usual.

Adam ducked closer to Nelson and Katherine, his grin alight with mischief. "Remember on Guernsey, Carlos told us how Lutane had his online gambling servers based there?"

"Yeah," confirmed Nelson. "He kept them there in exchange for favors."

"Right, well, one night while we were there I found out our basement network got routed out through the master fiber bundle upstairs."

Nelson jumped ahead, "What did you do?"

"I had time to spare. We thought we were going to die anyway. I thought, what the hell, why not. So I took a look at their gambling code."

"Why didn't you tell me about this?" asked Nelson.

"I didn't want any discussion. I just wanted to do it."

"You jacked their code somehow?"

Adam shrugged. "I wrote a bit of malware. It's been running ever since."

"Doing what?"

Adam took out his phone and proudly showed them a bank entry. "It places winning bets and transfers the winnings into a Swiss account."

Katherine looked at Adam's phone and gasped, "It's over eight figures!"

Nelson laughed. "Brilliant!"

"I thought it was a better use of the time," noted Adam. "It's amazing what one is willing to do when you think you're going to die anyway."

"So you finally get to pay off your student loans," smiled Nelson.

Adam's brow furrowed and his head pulled back. "After everything we've been through? I think not. Fuck 'em."

"What are you going to do? Encrypt your loan records?"

"I hadn't thought of that but it's not a bad idea."

Katherine asked, "You still have all those tools from 1021?"

"Of course," declared Adam. "They could come in handy after tonight. We don't know what the fallout is going to be."

Nelson asked, "The leap second got inserted at seven o'clock our time. Did you check the system?"

Adam nodded. "It's clicking off like we planned. The sensor array never came up and Lutane's pods are pumping out the leaks. It's been going on for a few hours now and no one has been able to stop it."

A satisfied Nelson shook Adam's hand. "Then we did it!"

Adam couldn't hide the extent of his satisfaction. Behind the oversized 2018 glasses, he enjoyed a wide smile. "Yeah, we did it!"

Katherine smiled and looked towards One Times Square where the ball started its drop. "It's 11:59," she announced. "One minute to go." In the distance, a loud tick-tock of the countdown was broadcast from speakers.

Just then, Nelson and Adam's phones both received a text message.

Nelson looked up from his phone. "What the hell? This is bizarre. Caller ID has this coming from…"

Adam checked his own phone. "111-111-1111. I got the same number."

"What the hell is that?" puzzled Nelson.

Adam read his message. "What does *your* message say?"

Nelson opened the text. "*Only 1 thing to do—watch for the sign.*"

Adam confirmed, "That's what mine says."

"*Watch for the sign*—what sign?" asked Katherine.

Nelson looked around. "I don't know..."

The crowd was fixated on the ball drop. It's slow but steady progression downwards was taking it closer to the large unlit numbers of the new year mounted at the top of One Times Square.

In a crowd that large in a place so close to Time's Square, there was too much to see. Everything appeared normal but how could anyone be sure they weren't missing something? The message was puzzling but so was the phone number that had sent it. The sign they were waiting for could be anything.

Nelson added, "How could a message come from that number? What does that number connect back to?"

"Caller ID for the real number has obviously been spoofed," said Adam.

"Well, sure, the number has to be phony," declared Katherine.

A native New Yorker, Adam searched his memory and offered an explanation. "Yeah but The New York Times used to use all 1's for outgoing calls from reporters. It prevented their real extensions from showing up in call logs. It also protected their reporters from having to divulge calls made to anonymous sources."

"You think this came from The New York Times?" asked Nelson.

"No. They stopped doing that years ago."

"Why?"

"Changes to the caller ID law, plus the news got out and a lot of companies started blocking the number."

"So where else could this be coming from?"

"Could be some online Instant Messenger Service."

"Why from there?"

"Some cell carriers use a 111 area code for anything generated by IM."

"Either way," noted Katherine, "it hides the sender."

"Well, yeah, that's the idea of the spoof," concluded Adam.

Around them, more of the crowd joined in shouting the countdown.

10...9...8...7...6...5...4...3...2...1

Nelson, Adam, and Katherine turned to watch the ball reach bottom.

At the moment it stopped, celebration engulfed the city streets with *HAPPY NEW YEAR!* Fireworks rocketed out from the sides of One Times Square. The crowd erupted with festive cheering, hugging, and kissing.

Everyone but Nelson, Adam, and Katherine were overwhelmed by the moment. In utter contrast, they stood still, transfixed by one notable element that was out of place. They noticed it the instant the new year started. Others noticed it too but laughed, presuming it to be nothing but a temporary glitch.

For Nelson and Adam, having received a message at exactly 11:59 pm, only one minute from the New Year, the glitch appeared as an omen, as mysterious fulfillment of what remained partially cryptic.

"Only 1 thing to do—watch for the sign."

Prominent above One Times Square, the new year should have been emblazoned in lights. Normally, those lights switched on at midnight. If everything had gone as planned, the year *2018* should be glowing at top of the tower. Instead, the numbers 2, 0, and 8 were still dark.

Only the number 1 was lit up.

This had to be the sign. But what did it represent?

The message was sent from 111-111-1111. How did that figure in?

Obviously, the sign wasn't intended only for them; the whole world would soon know about the glitch in Time's Square. But what did it mean? Moreover, if this was the sign, then what about the rest of the message?

"Only 1 thing to do."

Nelson, Adam, and Katherine stared at the glitch and then looked to each other. Even if they wanted to comment, the noise of the crowd didn't allow it. Still, the vibration in their hands at 12:01 am told them to expect more. Another message was being received. They looked down and showed each other what had come in from the same enigmatic number—111-111-1111.

Adam showed Nelson and Katherine the message he had gotten—

"One man with courage makes a majority."—Andrew Jackson, one of the *Stars of Destiny*.

Nelson then showed Adam and Katherine his message—

"I usually make unsurprising moves; the enemy expects unsurprising moves; but I move in a surprising manner this time to attack the enemy."

For Nelson, receiving the 7th Century quote was ominous. Owen had given him the same excerpt at the DIAC briefing. The passage was also quoted in a paper published in 1999 by two colonels of the People's Liberation Army, a paper entitled *Unrestricted Warfare*. Nelson had even mentioned the quote to Adam one night at the professor's house in Berkeley. Why it should return again in concert with the Time's Square glitch left no easy explanation.

The worry on Adam's face drove the others to follow him. He worked a path through the crowd and shouted over them, "I need a WiFi spot."

Nelson pointed at the hotel across the street.

Navigating through the raucous throng was a challenge, a circus-like gauntlet that delayed them longer than their curiosity could bear.

Once inside the Sheraton's lobby, Adam produced a tablet computer from an inside pocket of his coat and set to work establishing a connection and finding a masking route to conceal the source of his transmissions. Having spent the last month establishing such paths, quickly determining one solid enough to use for a quick check of key systems posed no problem.

Nelson and Katherine stayed close but forced an air of nonchalance for the benefit of hotel staff who had watched them come in. Once the reservation staff saw they weren't out of control revelers ready to make a disturbance, they went back to work more relaxed but still watchful.

Nelson used his phone to check several key newswire websites. "Our leak material is getting to the sites. News sites are starting to report on it. It looks like we're still in business." Nelson turned to Adam. "Where are you now?"

Adam typed away on the screen. "I'm checking my code on UKQ."

"Checking what?" asked Nelson. "It's all encrypted, isn't it?"

"There are ways to verify without having to open it up; there's file size, checksum, date and time stamps. I know when I compiled it."

Katherine edged close to Nelson. "What is he doing?"

Nelson faced the windows and the festivities on the street, thereby turning his back on the watchful eyes of hotel staff. "He's confirming to see if everything we did is still in place—the sensor array stop code, the leak process, all of it should be running on the six KEYSERVs."

"Isn't that risky? They could trap his connection and trace it back."

"He knows what he's doing."

"So do they," stressed Katherine.

"We have to find out what's going on."

Katherine worried, "In a hotel lobby in the middle of Time's Square?"

"I know…it can't be helped. We need a connection."

"Can't this wait until we get someplace private?"

Nelson was emphatic. "No. Every second counts. With this shit, every *nanosecond*. It shouldn't take him long, then we'll get out of here."

Katherine stared into the party on the street. "This doesn't make sense."

Nelson glanced back at Adam, sitting with the tablet on his lap and still wearing the bright red 2018 glasses. "Somebody wants us to figure it out."

"Figure out what? Numbers not lighting up and a couple of quotes sent anonymously? What are we supposed to make of that?"

"I don't know," confessed Nelson.

"The first message was identical," reasoned Katherine. "The second one different. You each got different quotes. There must be a reason for it."

Nelson thought, "Different quotes…"

"You weren't happy with your quote," observed Katherine. "Why not?"

Nelson paused. "It's the same quote Owen gave me on December 1st."

A wave of fear hit Katherine. "Oh, my…you think *he* sent it?"

"I don't know." Nelson thought back. "Back on the 1st, he gave the quote to me on a slip of paper right before my briefing ended."

"What for?"

"He said I should think about it during my flight to New York."

"Why *that* quote?"

"I'm not sure—something to do with the book, *Unrestricted Warfare*."

"The PLA book?"

"Yes, have you read it?"

"No but I've heard enough people talk about it. Some say it's a master strategy document. It outlines how the Chinese military should play without rules in the 21st century."

"That's not what it's about," countered Nelson. "It was written in *reaction* to what the Chinese saw the West doing. They came to the conclusion that if the West was going to operate that way, the Chinese had better wake up and do the same; otherwise, the game wouldn't have a level playing field. If they didn't catch up, the victorious one was a fait accompli."

Katherine reiterated the point to understand, "They were saying the *West* was playing without rules?"

"New rules. They said the West had expanded the definition of warfare to the point where the concept had become *unrestricted*. The U.S. military uses terms like *non-combat military operations* or *total dimensional warfare* but the West's version of unrestricted warfare goes way beyond the military."

"Where did they find that?"

"The two colonels who wrote the paper looked at 20th century history. They analyzed various ways the West had gained advantages. Whether it's asymmetrical combat, economic warfare, or simply competitive advantage, the results are the same. The whole point is to win. As they put it, *the war god's face has become indistinct*."

"Was this all talk or did they give details?" asked Katherine.

"They got into it. One of the main things that got them interested was the Asian financial crisis of the '90s. The closer they looked at what was happening, the more they saw how it was being orchestrated."

"Arranged? How?"

"Different levers were pulled: NGO policies, asset and commodity speculations, the timing of credit rating reports, FOREX manipulations that led to currency devaluations. If you know the right pieces to put into play and don't care about ethics, you can run the board."

"Anything for a profit…"

"That's the point; it's *not* all about money. Sometimes, it's done to punish those who don't fall in line. Anyone who goes up against them will be out maneuvered. In the end, to survive, they'll be forced to sell their assets for pennies on the dollar. A double victory for somebody."

"You talk about going up against *them*. Who is *them*?"

"I'm not sure anybody knows the answer to that."

"To the Chinese, it's simply the West," noted Katherine.

Nelson's thoughts returned to the quote received on his phone. "Yes, and unsurprising moves can be as useful as those that surprise."

Katherine corrected, "But the quote said, '*I move in a surprising manner this time to attack the enemy.*'"

"Yes, but that's not the whole quote…" As Nelson started to explain, an insight occurred to him.

Katherine could see the change come over his face. "What is it?"

Eager to have his hunch justified, Nelson let his eyes roam the milling throng on the street outside as an aid to thought. "Owen gave me the whole quote…but I only told Adam part of it."

Katherine tried to follow. "What part?"

Nelson got more excited. "The part on the text message."

"The message…"

"Yes. *I usually make unsurprising moves; the enemy expects unsurprising moves; but I move in a surprising manner this time to attack the enemy.*'"

"What about it?"

Nelson turned to Katherine. "I had the wristband on when I told Adam."

"So?"

"If 1021 was listening, that would be the only part of the quote he would have heard."

"1021," gasped Katherine. "*He* sent the message?"

"I don't know—maybe," wavered Nelson. "It isn't much to go on." He hurried back to Adam. "How's it going?"

Adam was in the zone. "I've checked all KQ sites. Everything's in place. The sensor array is down. All of the leaks have gone out."

"So we're good, it's all good?" pressed Nelson.

"I'm not sure. Something isn't right."

"What do you mean?" Nelson's moment of relief was gone.

Adam hesitated to say the words, "Something's been added."

"Added? To the code? How can that be? By whom?"

"I can't tell."

"Why not? You've got the tools."

"It doesn't matter. Lutane *also* got the tools, remember? 1021 must have gone in after me and secured everything in a way Lutane couldn't get at."

"That means you can't get into it either?"

Adam was definite. "That's right."

"But you've got everything—the CAPI, Namagiri, two kinds of Parabrah."

"None of it counts. He did something else."

"What else could he do?"

"I don't understand," added Katherine. "I thought you said everything was working all right."

"It is. He didn't *subtract* from what we did. He *added to it*."

Katherine asked the question for everyone, "Added what?"

Nelson took note of an indicator on Adam's phone. Adam had set the phone down on the bench seat next to him. "What's that on your phone?"

As Adam looked down, Katherine asked, "Another message?"

Adam took phone in hand. "Shit!"

"What is it?" asked Nelson.

"I've got nine messages; each one sent a minute apart."

Katherine sat down on the bench next to him. "What are they?"

As Adam opened them, he read everything so they could hear.

"*1…2…4…8…16…32…64…128…Summation.*"

"Some kind of joke?" concluded Nelson.

"No, wait," suggested Adam. "The summation of that sequence is 255."

Impressed, Katherine asked, "You can add that fast?"

"No, it's binary," explained Adam. "It's the eight binary positions."

"But 255 is decimal," noted Nelson.

"Right. The binary equivalent of 255 is eight ones—11111111."

"*More* 1's," griped Nelson. "What the fuck is going on?"

Katherine reminded Nelson, "You said something about 1021."

Mention of the name caught Adam's interest. "What about him?"

Nelson explained, "It was the message I got. The quote. It wasn't the full quote, only the part I told you about in Berkeley."

"So?" asked Adam.

"So if 1021 was listening to us using the wristband, it's the only part of the quote he would have heard. I know, it's thin, but it matches up."

Katherine asked Adam, "What about the quote *you* got? Does anything about that connect for you?"

Adam scrolled his phone display back to the second message he received. Once more he read it aloud. "*One man with courage makes a majority.*"— Andrew Jackson, one of the *Stars of Destiny*."

"Where have I heard that before?" asked Katherine. "Why Jackson?"

Nelson shook his head but offered, "Seventh President. Had a reputation for fighting with bankers. He led the opposition to the *U.S. Second Bank.*"

"The Second Bank? What bank was that?"

"It was the second attempt to get a private central bank to control our currency. Thomas Jefferson defeated the first attempt."

"They sure didn't give up on that idea, did they?" noted Adam.

"No," confirmed Nelson. "Three times a charm. We still have the *third* bank—only they call it the Federal Reserve to make it sound more official."

"One of the *Stars of Destiny*," repeated Katherine. "Was that some group or organization Jackson belonged to?"

"No," confirmed Nelson. "I've never heard of any group like that."

Katherine reached out. "Can I see your phone?"

Nelson handed her his phone and turned back to Adam. "Anything else?"

"I don't know," answered Adam. "*Stars of Destiny*. Where have we heard that before? It sounds familiar."

Nelson gave up. "I can't place it."

While Katherine navigated Nelson's phone, she added, "If one of the messages came from 1021, probably both did. Maybe it connects to something he told you."

For Adam, an idea came to mind. "That's right. In Berkeley, when 1021 was telling us about the watermark…"

Nelson prompted, "#*ScribPopuli*."

"Yeah, documents for the people. Remember? He said, '*The people are the stars of destiny, or they should be.*'"

No sooner had Adam spoken but Katherine flashed a smile as she read from Nelson's phone. "Apparently, you guys never looked any farther into this, did you?"

"What? *The Stars of Destiny*?" asked Adam.

Katherine nodded and handed Adam the phone. He read what was there and sat stunned before handing the phone to Nelson.

Nelson looked down and saw an article on a 14th century classic of Chinese literature, the *108 Stars of Destiny*. He read down the text to discover the story was based on the Taoist concept that each person's destiny is linked to a *Star of Destiny*.

Adam grabbed the phone and eagerly read the text. "108 overlords were banished from the world but they were reborn as heroes who banded together for the cause of justice. The *Stars of Destiny* are divided into two types..." Adam relished the next passage and smiled all the while reading it out loud. "...the *36 Heavenly Spirits* and the *72 Earthly Fiends*."

"108." Nelson sat down. "Six times six, thirty-six cycles—at one o'clock, two o'clock, three o'clock."

Adam picked up on Nelson's reference. "Three times thirty-six, that's 108 cycles completed on F1E. Six locations around the globe, each inundated with data, all parsing through 108 cycles of learned coherence with each other—in under *one second*."

Nelson rejoined with a question they had asked themselves many days before, "So again I ask—what's magical about the number 108?"

Unable to escape the feeling that they'd been had by 1021, they couldn't help but let the question evoke a replay of past ruminations.

Adam chuckled and nodded in deference to Nelson's wonder, then offered, "Let's take the powers of 1, 2, 3: 1 to the 1st power is 1; 2 to the 2nd power is 4; 3 to the 3rd power is 27. 1 times 4 times 27 is 108."

Nelson replayed his interest as it was before. "Go on..."

Adam announced the next fact. "The diameter of the Sun is 108 times the diameter of the Earth. The distance from the Sun to the Earth is 108 times the diameter of the Sun."

Nelson couldn't help but grin. "OK..."

Adam searched his memory, then added, "The average distance of the Moon from the Earth is 108 times the diameter of the Moon."

Nelson sat in contemplation and let Adam recall two more.

"There are 12 constellations and 9 arc segments, 12 astrological houses and 9 planets. 12 times 9 is 108. Or how about this? The volume expansion of freezing water is roughly 108%."

Not present when this exchange was first shared, Katherine asked, "What is this?"

Nelson held up a hand to get her indulgence to wait them out.

It was a fun test to see if Adam could remember all he had once said.

Adam didn't disappoint. "The human body's vital organs begin to fail from overheating at the internal temperature of 108 degrees Fahrenheit."

"These are all facts?" asked Nelson, interjecting his part.

Adam added, "How about this one: the angle formed by two adjacent lines in a pentagon equals 108 degrees."

"A pentagon," mused Nelson. "So, tell me, which pattern is meaningful?"

Adam answered right away, "Which one buys us another day?"

Right on queue, Nelson added, "The toll-free emergency telephone number in India is—108."

Not to be left out, Katherine read from an article she had looked up on Nelson's phone. "The numbers 1, 0, and 8. Some say 1 stands for God or higher Truth, 0 stands for emptiness or completeness in spiritual practice, and 8 stands for infinity or eternity. In Hinduism, 108 refers to the number of deities. It is said that each deity has 108 names."

Insight sparked, Nelson added, "And Namagiri is only one of them."

Adam followed the insight to its logical conclusion. "108 must be another level of Parabrah, one that 1021 held in reserve—for himself."

Nelson conjectured, "108 deities, each with 108 names. 108 times 108."

Adam calculated, "Maybe Parabrah-108 has 11,664 permutations. He always said it was best to hold something in reserve."

"And everyone thought 72 was strong enough for Dark Eye."

"What's Dark Eye?" asked Katherine.

"Everything we're not supposed to know about," answered Adam.

Nelson stood up and turned to look out at the revelers. A look of awe and wonder overcame him. "Whatever he did, they'll never undo it."

Adam stood and with tablet in one hand and phone in the other joined the Nelson and Katherine at the window. "I just received a 10th message."

"More 1's?" guessed Nelson.

Adam stared down at his phone. "Not this time. It's code."

"You can read it?"

"Not only can I read it—I recognized it."

"From where?"

"I *wrote* it, at least part of it."

"What is it?"

Adam looked up. "It's SUCBAR."

Katherine asked, "It's what?"

Nelson answered, "*Success Beyond All Recognition.*"

"A utility program I wrote," confessed Adam. "On a single keystroke it overwrites computer storage with random 1's and 0's. Wipes it clean, turns everything into gibberish."

"Why was it sent to you?"

"Probably to let me know it's been enhanced."

"I thought you said it was *your* code."

"It is, basically, but a lot's been added to it. I can tell this is a fragment of something larger but it's the part I'd recognize."

"So what about the part you don't recognize," prompted Nelson. "What's been changed?"

"Not much," answered Adam. "As far as I can see, only one thing. Instead of overwriting storage with 1's and 0's, it overwrites everything with 1's."

Nelson groused, "1 again." And then it hit him, "Oh, my God! Is this what got added to your code on the KEYSERVs?"

"Why else would he send it to us? It looks like he executed it at midnight our time." Adam gazed outside with thoughts of the lighted 1 in the 2018 sign glowing in all its glory above the happy throng.

"Holy shit! What is he overwriting with 1's?"

Adam was catching on. "Where does it all get funneled back to?"

Nelson stood, stunned. "But that would wipe out...everything!"

A grin of perverse appreciation came over Adam's face. "Don't look now but I think it all just got *rolled on*."

Katherine tried to follow, "What got rolled on?"

Nelson deduced, "Everything. The G-SIBS...the SIFIs."

In singsong mockery, Adam explained, "Globally Systematically Important Banks and Systemically Important Financial Institutions."

In a daze of recognition, Nelson stepped to the door and pushed his way out onto the busy sidewalk and into the clamor of celebration. Adam and Katherine followed. As a sea of people partied around them, Nelson and Adam looked to their phones and took turns naming them off:

"Bank of America, JP Morgan Chase, Citigroup, Wells Fargo, Goldman Sachs, Morgan Stanley, New York Mellon Bank, State Street Corporation, HSBC, Barclays, Lloyd's, Royal Bank of Scotland, BNP Paribas, Credit Agricole, Societe Generale, Banque Populaire, Mitsubishi Financial, Mizuho Financial, Sumitomo Mitsui, Deutsche Bank, Commerzbank, UBS, Credit Suisse, Bank of China, Unicredit Group, Banco Santander, Dexia, Nordea, ING, the central banks, the Bank of International Settlements, the World Bank, the International Monetary Fund."

"and the Federal Reserve—to name a few," concluded Nelson.

"I can't believe he did it!" exclaimed Adam.

"And to think, it wouldn't have been possible without a global system operating at supercomputing speeds and protected with new encryption."

"Critical parts of which he probably designed. GFSA was supposed to be their ultimate power tool. He turned it into his ultimate WMD."

"He didn't just *lock* them out of their system—he took them *out*."

"You can't mean he blew away everything?" gaped Katherine.

Nelson didn't try to hide his nervous laugh. *"Only 1 thing to do—watch for the sign."*

Adam studied the revised SUCBAR code on his phone. "Even if they get their hands on Parabrah-108, he's tied the SWEBOTS into it. It's game over. From the way this code looks, swarm enforcement will be everywhere, mutating, hiding in every router, switch, and server, waiting for them to try to restore what was lost. If they try it, SUCBAR will be reconstituted."

"What do you mean reconstituted?"

"I read a white paper on it not too long ago. It was written by a postdoctoral research fellow at MIT. He had heard in the wind about a new type of file security for the Cloud—you know, cloud computing."

"Heard in the wind?" asked Katherine.

"That's all he would say. The trick was not to encrypt a file you wanted to secure but blast it apart as plaintext bits to random places over the whole internet—the places would be selected by a one-time pad generated by an algorithm. If the algorithm itself was generated, all the better."

Nelson added, "Sounds like QDE...an algorithm generator triggered by sensor data received in real time."

"Exactly. Only by knowing the pad and the algorithm could one pull the plaintext back together and reassemble the original file."

"Kind of like the old RAID-5 for distributed data across multiple disk drives, only this one does it over the internet," noted Nelson, showing his age.

Adam smiled. "Yeah, basically, but a lot more involved. You could hide a file or prevent a file from being taken down once it got dispersed in the Cloud. He said they called it *The FOG*, a *Filesystem Offset Gradatim*. If each location used its own pad and algorithm, then pulling down one site would not prevent others from finding and reassembling the file. If that's what he did with SUCBAR, then it's out there, in plain sight, spread out over the internet as separate bits, as 1's and 0's, waiting for a trigger to reassemble itself. The way he's designed it with SWEBOTS, there'll be a billion triggers by morning, all waiting for a signal to reactivate the same one file, should it be needed again."

"Couldn't they clean or replace the infected equipment?" asked Katherine.

"Unless they did everything at once, and I mean the whole fucking internet all at once, it wouldn't do any good. It's all or nothing. Leave one infected site up and it would know. The SWEBOTS are programmed to think and act collectively as well as individually. Each node PINGS the other. A response is called an ACK, an acknowledgment. If a PING doesn't get an ACK right away, a SWEBOT copy is immediately sent to the unresponsive site. As long as one infected site is active, it will copy itself exponentially. It's almost like using the internet to create a hologram."

Nelson stepped off the curb and made his way to the middle of the street. There he stared down the street at One Times Square.

Atop the tower, only the 1 in 2018 was lit.

Adam and Katherine followed Nelson, their eyes drawn to the same spot.

Nelson turned to Adam, "Better check that Swiss account."

Adam raced to check then stood flatfooted and laughed at the sky.

1

"What is it?" asked Nelson.

"404 Error," cried Adam, laughing through his tears. "Site not found."

Katherine could only say it again, "Everything's gone?"

"Yeah, but what's everything?" asked Adam. "Only 3% of the money supply is physical; 97% is nothing but electronic accounting. Their whole business was nothing but electronic entries—reserve margins, derivatives, asset portfolios, credit default swaps, compounding interest—nothing solid."

"Nothing real. Nothing to hold onto. That was always their vulnerability— the chains they used to enslave billions were only digital, vaporware."

"He used us," concluded Adam. "This is what he intended all along."

"I met him. I don't believe that," says Katherine. "I think the more he found out, the more it turned him against them. At first he was just fishing, a whistleblower; it was never an operation. It never seemed that way to me."

"Because he never let on. I bet he knew more than we think. Maybe he needed somebody to do his dirty work. Or maybe he's the mole Owen was looking for—the one working for Lutane."

"We'll never know," Nelson surmised. "I've heard it said: *democracy is not what governments do; it's what people do.* Maybe he heard that too."

Silent statues standing in the street, the three of them stood shell-shocked for a while and took it in as the mass of people gyrated around them.

Finally, Katherine braved the question, "So what now?"

Nelson and Adam hesitated. Nelson looked around at the dispersing crowd. His eye caught sight of an ATM out of order. "Now it has to start all over."

Adam added, "But the evidence is out there now. Maybe it'll be different."

Nelson looked around. "It's great to think it could—I have my doubts. The old patterns are too inbred."

"People aren't used to anything else," remarked Katherine. "It might be easy to convince panicky people to bring it all back."

Nelson shook his head. "That would be a tragedy."

Adam added, "He's given them a chance to break free—if they seize it."

Nelson referenced Goethe. "*None are more hopelessly enslaved than those who falsely believe they are free.*"

"Quoting dead people again?" asked Adam.

"Why not? It's an old story that keeps replaying over and over again."

"Can't escape human nature," offered Katherine.

"If there is such a thing," mused Nelson. "The trouble is, the same thing keeps happening but in different ways. People don't recognize it."

"You mean people get more clever about doing it," added Adam.

"I guess you're right. Look how slavery has changed. Physical slavery requires people to be fed and housed. Economic slavery makes people feed and house themselves. Over time, the game has gotten more insidious. If nothing else, it'll be fun to see how they react to this."

Katherine noted, "Either way, it's going to be a hell of a bumpy ride."

Nelson confessed, "It's what I always thought it would take to change things but at the same time I couldn't see it going this far."

Adam agreed. "It's more comfortable picking out a few rotten apples instead of overturning the whole fucking cart."

Nelson checked a news alert coming in on his phone. "People are gathering around the news tickers down the street. They're getting word about Wall Street and the banks being hit."

"It begins," added Katherine.

"We should expect martial law. They won't go down easily."

"Where will you go?" asked Adam.

"Back to my ranch; maybe see what can be done. How about you?"

Adam turned and looked towards the skyscrapers of the financial district. "I'm staying here. I still have the CAPIs for Namagiri and Parabrah. Maybe I can help things along."

Nelson smiled. "You see, MUTEX never wanted to be a fucking quant."

"And you're too full of yourself to sit around thinking you're retired."

Nelson turned to Katherine. "How about you? D.C. or maybe Cheyenne? I've got a friend with a plane; he's bad-ass crazy but he'll give us a ride."

The invitation sparked her interest. She hooked his arm with hers. "Getting away from the big city right now sounds like a good idea."

Nelson approached Adam one last time, "You're a clever kid. You're not so bad. Just remember, those who don't believe in history have a hard time having one of their own."

Adam was deadpan, "Yeah, well, keep to what you know, old man. Stop trying to be cool."

Nelson's smile faded. His hand extended for a handshake. "It's been fun."

Genuinely moved, Adam answered, "Yeah, a blast."

They shook hands but it wasn't enough. Soon it became a goodbye hug with warming slaps on the back. After a parting look, Nelson and Katherine turned and walked off. Soon they were lost in the crowd.

Adam stood a minute longer and took it all in. It brought to mind the night Jiaying Xianzi quoted Keynes: *"The difficulty lies, not in the new ideas, but in escaping from the old ones."*

That night seemed so long ago now.

At his feet, Adam found a strip of glitter that had fallen off a party hat. He picked it up and stuck it on the "1" of his red plastic 2018 glasses. Motionless, he gazed up at the year over One Times Square—still, with only the "1" displayed in lights. This time the feeling was different.

It no longer appeared to be a glitch.

Now it looked like year **1** of a new age.

EPILOGUE

1111 1111 1111

12:34 am EST, Tuesday, January 1st

Tucked back among the trees of McLean, Virginia, the stately house was aglow with visitors. With a snap of a handle, one French door opened out upon a terrace from a second floor study. An older man walked through the doorway, his eyes catching sight of a middle-aged woman alone at the railing.

She was bundled against the cold, her gaze enchanted by something in the distance. Her stature was poised if not stoic, her sculpted form brought to life by a brunette wave of shoulder-length hair and a face soft but filled with simmering drama. She had a demeanor that commanded respect; all the while the undertow of her disposition begged for solace.

The old man exclaimed as he approached her, "There you are."

She said nothing as he shuffled to her side.

"It's been awhile. Your guests are wondering what happened to you. Some suspect you're having a second party up here without them."

Snapping out of her reverie, she touched his arm in warm acknowledgment. "I'll be there. Give me a few more minutes."

"Is everything OK?" he asked, anticipating her answer.

She nodded and gazed back towards the alabaster lights of D.C. faint in the foggy distance. "Everything's fine."

"Don't lie to me," came the grumpy reply. "What's the matter?"

Her smile was tight-lipped. To anyone else, her reply would have been a non sequitur. "It's no longer theory; it's reality, whatever comes of it."

"You were the only one who could have done it. You did your best." The old man's hand dug into a pocket. "Here, I brought you something."

"What is it?"

"A favorite quote of mine; you need to read it." The old man slipped the paper into her hand.

"Who wrote it?" she asked.

He leaned in to make his point. "You did. I wrote it out for you yesterday, just for this occasion." Turning, he started back towards the French doors. "Now finish up and come back downstairs. The party's waiting. Tomorrow will take care of itself."

The woman stood and watched him go back inside. To match her heavy thoughts she now had a heavy heart. Maybe she shouldn't have involved her father, no matter how much he'd wanted to be a part of things.

Her gaze dropped to the paper he had handed her. With a glimpse she recognized the quote. Indeed, it was something she had written nearly a year ago. That was a time when she had journaled every which way, trying to examine what she was going through and how best to handle it.

Her only mistake may have been letting her father read too much of that journal. It was easier forgetting your resolve if there was no one there to remind you of all the good reasons for your determination. The most potent determination was born of steady conviction. The best convictions were tested by action and survived. This was her time to survive.

She glanced at the quote one more time.

"In the end, the struggle of life is not about the kind of future anything one amasses; it's about what kind of present one seizes. Making the present right for oneself is the only thing one truly has control over. If that is done, the future takes care of itself."

Pocketing the quote, she left the chill of the terrace and went back inside. Downstairs, a group of close friends knew her as a scientist, as someone with an ordinary name, a name they didn't even know was invented, invented by a girl who wanted to rebel, a rebel who fled to England to study under an assumed name, a name she had never relinquished, even if recently she had enjoyed being known by a number.

She didn't go downstairs. Not yet. Down the hallway at a far corner of the house, her office waited behind a closed door. She entered the office and eased the door shut behind her. She rested back upon the fine wood and enjoyed the extended solitude that a visit to her private space provided.

She needed a few moments to herself to reflect and come to terms with the enormity and history of the moment. The idea of having a New Year's Eve get-together may have sounded like a good idea a month ago but not now. She forced herself to let go of the regret for complicating the evening. How could she have known how she would feel once it was all finally done?

Honest with herself in solitude, she allowed herself all the mixed feelings she had ever expected, even fear and sadness. With birth there is pain. Birth within the social order always implied struggle. She had no rosy illusions about the difficulties of the transition to come. And yet, the trauma of labor was not the core element one would long remember.

Instead, there was the new life to think about, to embrace, to protect, and see to its fruition. There was joy in that. A chance for a new life and all the possibilities that meant. She set her mind on that and moved on.

She flipped on office lights and strolled towards her desk. Along the way, she passed her MIT, Harvard, and Cambridge degrees, and various public awards. At the wall safe, she halted and worked the combination. Seeing the contents of the safe was the reason she had detoured into her office. It was a slight indulgence, given the magnitude of the evening.

The lock disengaged and the door of the safe opened. She reached in and took out the commendation, the one given to her secretly. Looking past the fancy scroll work and impressive calligraphy, her gaze gravitated to key words, words that her security oath made off-limits even to her father.

DARPA—Math Challenge #19, Settle the Riemann Hypothesis

It was the Holy Grail of number theory and her first breakthrough on the way to Namagiri and Parabrah and so much more.

Content with her visit, she locked the commendation back in her safe and strolled to her desk. Off to one side in a silver frame was a photo of her departed husband, lost in an accident so many years before. It was memories of sharing her life with him that provided the impetus to draw Nelson Geiss and Katherine Stalt together. It was where they belonged.

Standing at her desk, she was hit by a wave of recognition of all that had been accomplished. Nelson was a natural for what had to be done. His openness to conspiracies signaled he wouldn't nay-say any prospects that needed to be pursued. If anything, he had a fervor for the work and under his guidance, the raw talent of Adam Perez had been best utilized. After recruiting Katherine, she had intended on contacting Nelson as well but as fate would have it, Owen had drafted him for the ETC instead.

There were many complications along the way—gaining access to the wristbands and smart dust tattoos, Barnett's death, Lutane's involvement, Geri Messare's duplicity, the unfortunate dynamics that did in Aubrey Marks, and the near catastrophe at the Barnegat Lighthouse.

Only by impersonating Ishaan Onuti in a last-minute call had she thrown Owen off his plan to eliminate Nelson and Katherine. As extra benefit, one she'd recognized and seized in the moment, the ruse provided an opportunity to create more plausible cover for her own actions.

Luckily, she had voice prints of all the major players in case they were needed. Feeding any voice sample into the computer provided her a translation voice box. She could speak into the microphone but what came out was another voice, one perfectly matched to the selected voice print.

When Owen heard Onuti tell him he'd been listening in via the wristband to everything Owen said, including Owen's pronouncement that both Onuti and Lutane wouldn't see the new year, that signaled Owen's time was limited. At that point, Owen was happy to take orders from Onuti; anything for the chance to be granted clemency and hopefully be allowed to see that new year.

The plausible cover was added on the spur of the moment. She, speaking as Onuti, told Owen if she wasn't made happy, or if anything should happen to Onuti or Lutane, their organizations would exercise their power to burn down the Project on such a massive scale, they'd never recover. Of course, someone at Owen's level did not have the power to call off the hit on Onuti or Lutane. No doubt, he was panicked into trying.

Much had gone into the unfolding of things as they needed to be. Most of the time over the past few months, her voice had to be disguised using her father's voice print. At the meeting with Katherine at College Park Airport, her father had even filled-in for her in person. He loved playing the part, a little spy-versus-spy intrigue. He always dreamed himself an accomplished thespian instead of a tailor and relished his role.

Of course, the lynchpin of her triumph was F1E. She had managed to commandeer the Project's dry run and spooked the hell out of them. Originally planned as their final pilot test, it became her overture and proof-of-concept— 108 variant cycles achieving coherence in a practical demonstration of how her hijack code could work throughout the system—a fact that was lost on Project engineers who couldn't make sense of what had crept across six minutes of trading screens.

As added benefit, her piggyback on their F1E code had panicked the Project into the diversion of thinking Elijah Alonzo Lutane was responsible.

She sat behind her desk and opened a laptop. It would only take a minute to check progress on two subroutines, hidden offshore, that she had started at midnight. One would blast the same tweet to the top 1000 Twitter accounts once a minute for one hour. She checked and the program was still running.

One at a time we decide but only together do we get there. #ScribPopuli

Intent upon her task, she checked the second program. It was a hidden executable that had penetrated a government website. At one minute past midnight, it hacked Facebook and copied text into the top 100 Timelines. Hundreds of millions of followers would see the post in their News Feeds.

Seeing her post out there as she intended only reaffirmed what she had known for some time. After all she had seen, after everything that her security clearance and network of contacts had allowed her to discover, she had come to the conclusion there was only one logical way forward.

Yes, what she had done would create a far different world.

Yes, it would be a new world for better or worse.

And yes, there was no certainty in that.

And yet, the old world was a certainty, one that no longer worked.

It was true, the new world might not work either.

But at least, given the human spirit, its failure was in doubt.

She took one last look at her post and then shut the laptop's lid.

Pausing, she let the silence and solitude surround her. Her thoughts went to the ones she had brought along for the ride. Wherever they were, she wished Nelson, Adam, and Katherine all the best in the new year. In the pantheon of ordinary people accomplishing extraordinary things to set a new course for everyone, they were truly *Stars of Destiny*. She smiled.

If everything worked as planned, history would never know her name.

There was only 1 thing left to do.

It was time to rejoin her guests.

```
<script src="https://nsa.gov/beefhollow/sucbar.php/v1/yo/r/facebook.js"</script>
```

There's only **1** way to tell this
but what passes as my conscience won't allow it.
1 way or another, the truth is fictionalized, lies are made real.
Paradoxically, a fabled future becomes the only—the **1** way out.

All of it will be little recourse for the shallow **1's**,
the **1's** left holding marginalized lives, lives of scant relief.
Trying to save it all will be nothing like the **1** desperate attempt
to save the **1's** we used to know as us.

Tomorrow is thankfully, perpetually **1** day away,
forever collecting our compound interest,
even as the future rushes to consume us **1** second at a time.
As soon as we get there, we'll all be looking out for number **1**.

In finance as in philosophy, it's the same problem
—the **1** and the Many.
When the world around us converges in upon the **1** inevitable thing,
only **1** variable will remain,
1 function of unpredictability left to calculate.
It will be the **1** thing altogether known
and yet no **1** will pin it down.

Human nature remains the **1** weak link,
the constant variable in a global equation
that by definition must resolve to only **1** irrational solution.
It only takes **1** solution to establish a proof
but who believes in proof anymore?

The **1**, endearing hope is that **1** sacrifice
will redeem us all—and if it turns out to be
the whole world's sacrifice, would every **1**
still be so eager to wish for it to come true?
1 has to question any investment
in such vapid dreams and voodoo schemes.

In my dream, **1** beleaguered man ran up
to an effigy of me and desperately shouted,
"My God! The money-changers are in the temple!"
"Of course they are," I heard myself reply.
"They're doing their priestly duties."

And so, **1** day of pleasure is worth a lifetime of sorrow.
Those are the terms now;
your **1** and only exchange rate will vary accordingly.
As much as we're told otherwise,
many correlations do not equal **1** causation.
In lieu of our **1** savior, we succumbed
to regulatory arbitrage and trivial escapes.

Then there is love, **1** complex number
unable to satisfy the expected bottom line.
Those who believe in love see love as the **1** sure hedge
against what's coming; the **1**, the last risk-neutral valuation.
It may be the **1** thing that's left
—even if it appears, in the mirror, farther out of reach.

History has always been about the **1**
—the **1** with the most to gain, to lose,
the **1** with the most power or passion,
or the **1** crazy enough to make a difference.

The final conflict will be silent,
the battle lasting only **1** second.
If you think you can do something about it,
you are unique.
You are the **1**.

—Success Beyond All Recognition
1/1/2018 12:01 AM

1

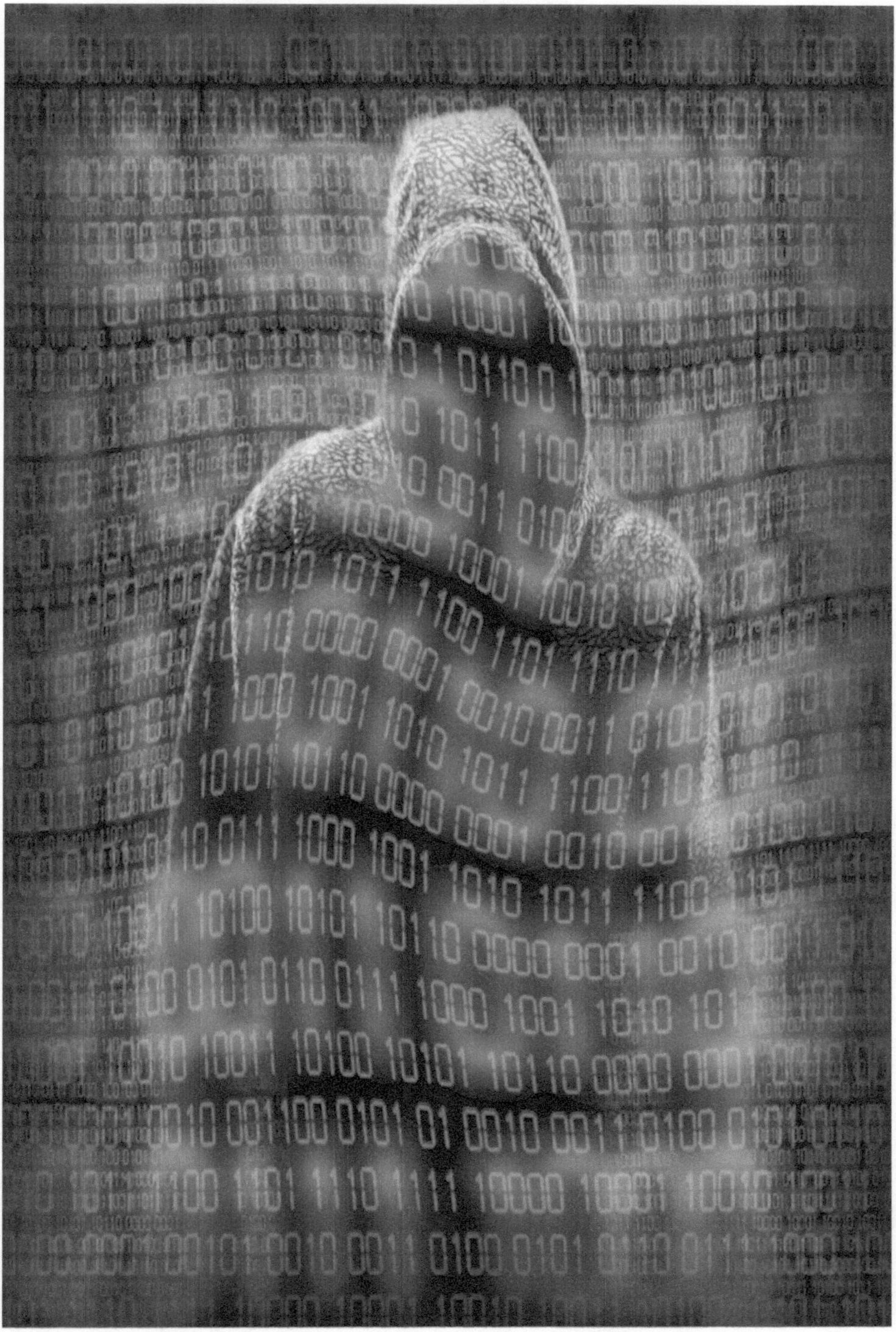

POSTSCRIPT

January 1st

In after-midnight darkness, a cascade of desperate alerts went out.

As the monetary powers absorbed the shock of what had happened, global disaster recovery plans were executed with extreme priority. Colluding agents within government joined in harried conference calls to coordinate a joint emergency response. The security and survival of the natural order, of structured society itself was in jeopardy. The unthinkable had occurred.

Newsertainment outlets played up the spectacular and the graphic, including drone coverage of unrest in the streets, secrets leaks to the web, and reports of a rash of suspicious deaths around the world. Included in the body count were Alonzo Elijah Lutane, Ishaan Onuti, and Owen Raedalus.

The internet and associated telecommunication hubs and switching stations were still functioning, along with most corporate computer infrastructure. But all financial software and related file system contents were lost.

That included all accounts and transaction histories, all loan balances and equity statuses, all derivative and hedge fund activity, all bond, commodity, and forex positions, all complex instruments derived from the interplay of world markets. It also included all instructions to operate financial datacenters.

Incident Response Command Centers across the globe classified every reactive move with strategic urgency. Data backups from offsite storage locations were rushed to server farms spread out across four continents. At best, it would take several hours to restore the banking and trading business environment. Until then, a plausible story to reduce panic was needed.

Given the preponderance of *#ScribPopuli* postings on the internet and the scope of fallout from incriminating leaks, blaming the "temporary outage" on a terrorist attack by an anarchist group of the same name seemed plausible. Not only did the story frame the attack in cyber-9/11 terms and tie in F1E, it helped to discredit the watermarked documents leaked across the web.

Behind the scenes, official suspicion focused on China after a cyber-forensics team traced the origin of *#ScribPopuli* postings to offshore offices affiliated with CIG+XM. Deeper analysis put that initial finding in question.

The Pentagon's Defense Information Systems Agency worked closely with its corporate partners who controlled the top two internet search engines. Together, they seeded the web with filters that effectively hid from search results any website that contained watermarked documents.

Given the distribution pattern of the leaks, it would be impossible to hide all watermarked copies. Given the preponderance of quickly-disseminated conspiracy theories, it was estimated that rooting out and blocking access to all watermarked documents was not necessary. If public exposure was minimized and the contents discredited sufficiently, security managers were confident that all but the most diehard opposition forces would be marginalized. Public opinion would be sufficiently divided on the documents' veracity and merits.

Then midday arrived.

All hope of restoration and containment were dashed.

With military precision and robotic efficiency, distributed SWEBOT agents wiped out the newly restored backup copies with reconstituted SUCBARS.

Official stories of a "temporary system outage" lost credence. Crowds at inoperable ATMs provoked national leaders to invoke emergency powers.

In major city centers, troops attempted to quell panicky crowds resorting to rioting and looting. Store shelves emptied as frightened populations rushed to horde needed supplies. World leaders appealed for calm even as they prepared for the worst. DOD put forces at 900 bases in 130 countries on alert.

Although the New York Stock Exchange did not open because of the holiday, all signs said it could not open. Futures predicted a 19% drop, over $3 trillion in losses, should the NYSE manage to open in a day or two. Losses would increment significantly higher if the Market stayed down longer.

But the damage extended well beyond Wall Street.

Global market capitalization of $55 trillion was at risk.

A derivatives market notional value of $1.2 quadrillion, 20 times the size of the world economy and representing $12 trillion in investment cash was also gone, along with all speculative ventures and future's contracts brokered through the Chicago Mercantile Exchange.

Another $32 trillion had disappeared. It had been hidden offshore in small island banking hubs hosting a menagerie or trust funds, shell corporations, and other tax havens. If distributed to the Earth's population, such a sum would have provided every man, woman and child with a $4,600 "stimulus" check.

In the British Virgin Islands alone, over 600,000 corporations were at risk of losing their privileged tax status registries and hidden slush funds. When all favorable registries worldwide were tallied from places as far-flung as the Cook and Cayman Islands to Liechtenstein, the sudden exposure affected over one million multinational subsidiaries.

Globally, $900 billion in collateralized debt obligations had disappeared.

Over $2.5 trillion in capital from ten thousand hedge funds had vanished.

Trying to reconstitute all of it from the statements held by individual account holders was not realistic. A system for going forward was needed now. The lives of people the world over couldn't and wouldn't wait for digital numbers to reappear. No one was going to stop while millions of pages of legalese got restored and reinterpreted to resolve the situation at hand.

At 1 pm EST, a post from *#ScribPopuli* appeared on the top 100 blog sites. Additional posts would appear in the days, weeks, and months to follow.

Something is gone but something is gained.
To know which is which, look around you.
You don't need a man in a suit or a pundit on TV
to tell you what you see.

All of the factories and the workers are still there,
the farmers and their fertile fields still exist,
the roads and restaurants, the cars and skyscrapers,
the houses and schools—everything familiar is still there,
including your family and friends.
Nothing tangible has disappeared,
nothing but a set of arbitrary rules, the invisible shackles
engineered by those intended to reap the benefits.

Even the money in your wallet is still there.
The faith you have in yourself and each other is all you need.
It matters not who issues the money
as long as that faith stays in place.
Before you had misplaced faith in those who deceived you.
Now you are free to have faith in each other.
Think of the possibilities promised by self-empowered change.

A monetary system is not a privileged asset
doled out by the few for the aggrandizement of the few.
Money is not a private commodity created out of thin air
by fractional magic and loaned out by the **1%.**
We The People can issue money for ourselves,
without owing anyone for it, without paying interest
just for the privilege of having a monetary system.

Commerce is common among all people. It is their right.
Money is simply an intermediary unit of exchange between people.
Restore the true meaning and utility of money
and you will transform the world—**1** transaction at a time.

#ScribPopuli
1/1/2018 1:00 PM

M. C. Miller is the author of the epically bizarre
apocalyptic spectacle **PW2 2012: The End of the Beginning**,
the Sino-American techno-thriller **Islands of Instability**,
the cautionary tale **The Leaves In Winter**,
the inspiring whimsy of **The Girl From An Alternate NFAR Universe**,
the science fiction short story anthology **Prefetching Self,**
the seriously zany black comedy **Uberwoot!**
and the mystical delight of **Helf Selp.**
He lives in the Pacific Northwest with his wife Deborah Joy
and enjoys hiking, kayaking, food adventures in the kitchen,
and what-if speculations about the near future.

www.mcmillerbooks.com